SHAKE DOWN THE STARS

SHAKE down the STARS

Frances Donnelly

BANTAM PRESS

LONDON · NEW YORK · TORONTO · SYDNEY · AUCKLAND

TRANSWORLD PUBLISHERS LTD
61-63 Uxbridge Road, London W5 5SA
TRANSWORLD PUBLISHERS (AUSTRALIA) PTY LTD
15-23 Helles Avenue, Moorebank NSW 2170
TRANSWORLD PUBLISHERS (NZ) LTD
Cnr Moselle and Waipareira Aves,
Henderson, Auckland

Published 1988 by Bantam Press,
a division of Transworld Publishers Ltd
Copyright © Frances Donnelly 1988

British Library Cataloguing in Publication Data

Donnelly, Frances
Shake down the stars.
I. Title
823'.914[F]   PR6054.05/
ISBN 0-593-01051-5

Printed in Great Britain by
Mackays of Chatham, Chatham, Kent

To my mother and father, with love

Shake down the stars, pull down the clouds
Turn out the moon, do it soon,
I can't enjoy this night without you,
Shake down the stars.

Dry up the streams, stop all my dreams,
Cut off the breeze, do it please,
I never thought I'd cry about you,
Shake down the stars.

Crush every rose, hush every prayer,
Break every vow, do it now,
I know I cannot live without you
Shake down the stars.

PROLOGUE

23 August 1939

VIRGINIA SAYS: 'I simply can't *believe* it.'

Unwilling to confront her furious blue-eyed stare, Lucy shifts defensively on the window-seat, gazing resolutely at the party preparations on the lawn below.

'Well, she has. Invited her, that is,' says Lucy. 'It's Beatrice Blythe, isn't it? She's won a scholarship to Mother's old training college, Hillsleigh. So Mother thought it would be a nice gesture—'

'Who cares what she's *done*? What's important is who she is. She's the daughter of the head gardener and has no *right* to be at the Manor garden-party with her betters.'

Virginia smooths her skirts so violently that she nearly rips the pleats from the bodice.

'And it's not fair on her, don't you see, Lucy? It simply goes to servants' heads when they're singled out. Besides' – Virginia abandons compassion and reverts, with relief, to malice – 'she'll turn up looking an absolute fright. You'll see. Sunday best and all the jewellery she can muster. With half her "dad's" herbaceous border on her hat, I shouldn't wonder.'

Even Lucy, good-natured to the point of apathy, is shocked by this.

'Vir, you're being absolutely beastly. You hardly know the girl —'

'Don't I?' says Virginia savagely. 'I've had to put up with the sight of her smirking face at every Christmas party at the Manor since I was *three. And* had to listen to Mrs Blythe banging on about how clever her daughter is. What's the point of educating her? She'd have done far better being put into service here with her appalling cousins. She'll still end up marrying a labourer or another servant.'

Her malice temporarily exhausted, Virginia sinks back against the window-seat. Lucy, studying her with a practised eye, decides to remain silent in the hope that Virginia's bad humour has spent itself. If only Vir could get over her bate, it could be a rather marvellous day. Not just because it's her parents' first big garden-party as tenants of the Manor. But there is just the faintest, slenderest chance that Hugh will turn up. At the very thought Lucy colours and stares even more intently at preparations below.

Lucy's suite of rooms is at the back of the Manor, overlooking the terrace and stone steps leading down to the lawns. Two long trestle-tables have been set up in the deep shade of the cedar trees, and even now are being laid for the tea. Lucy can hear soft metallic clinking as teaspoons are placed in saucers, while below her window her father confers with Verge, the butler, as to the correct positioning of the tea-urns.

From the library comes the clatter of her mother's typewriter. Not even on this day of days can Mrs Hallett neglect her muse. Which is appropriate as it is this obliging muse that has paid for the Halletts' present luxurious style of life, Lucy's recent ten months in Paris at finishing school, not to mention her impending season and presentation at Court. At the thought of all *that* Lucy suddenly feels rather ill and turns her thoughts hurriedly back to the pleasures of the day ahead. It is a hot tranquil August morning, the lake beyond the rose gardens still misty with the promise of a scorching afternoon. The stable clock strikes twelve, the strokes dying away into a hot reverberating silence.

Then Virginia says moodily: 'If *we* were still living here, Mother wouldn't have dreamt of letting a servant attend the garden-party.'

The arrival of the catering vans in the stable yard fortunately distracts Virginia's attention, leaving Lucy suddenly irritated, pondering how to respond. It seems she has three options:
(a) She could cravenly placate Virginia by agreeing with everything she said. This, alas, is Lucy's usual position.
(b) She could stand up to Virginia, telling her to put a sock in it and stop being so spiteful and unfair.
(c) She could squash Virginia flat by simply reminding her that no one gave a damn *what* Virginia's mother would have done – for, although Virginia's family own the Manor, and indeed have given their name to the village of Musgrave, there's so little money they haven't been able to live in their own house for some years. Instead they occupy – spasmodically – the Dower House, and Virginia clearly feels their declining fortunes keenly. Especially on a morning like this when the Manor is alive with flying footsteps, excited voices and a general sense of anticipation from which Virginia feels painfully excluded.

Staring vacantly at two men in brown holland overalls who have started to unpack wooden chairs, Lucy broods, for the first time in her life, on what would be the correct response to Virginia's bad humour. She is interested to discover that, though she is not yet ready for (b), she has no intention of moving automatically to her usual position of (a). But the invoking of (c) – precisely because it is the one effective weapon that will make Virginia collapse completely – is in some way beyond her.

Though not given to complex analysis of herself or of others, she instinctively knows that Virginia relies on the fact that Lucy rarely attacks and, more important, always forgives. At an early stage in their friendship she had divined that much of Virginia's ferocious bad temper concealed a kind of despair, the cause of which is never clear. Today this instinctive knowledge, coupled with a more prosaic observation that Virginia has swollen eyelids and has clearly been crying, is enough to make Lucy reject (c) as gratuitously unkind. So she says nothing.

Virtue is rarely its own reward. Clearly disappointed by Lucy's refusal to be provoked, Virginia begins to move restlessly around the room. Resigned,

Lucy watches her. Her clothes have already been laid out for the afternoon, and it is one of Virginia's nastier games simply to pick up any garment of Lucy's and hold it up against her own exquisite slenderness. It's all meant to be a terrific joke that Virginia can fold Lucy's dresses twice round her. But easier perhaps to laugh if you're slim and beautiful like Virginia, thinks Lucy.

But something's changed. Lucy actually sees Virginia eye the dress, saunter forward, then stop. Today even her malice is only half-hearted.

'Who's coming with you this afternoon?' Lucy asks.

'Ma. Oh, and Sir Fred's bringing down Ferdinand, did I tell you?'

'Really? How super. I'd have thought he'd gone back to France by now.'

'He's back the day after tomorrow.'

Ferdinand Aumont is the nephew of Madame Valbonne, at whose finishing school they have assiduously been polished and made ready for Society for the last ten months. A yellow-faced and lugubrious youth of twenty-five, he is so completely lacking in obvious physical attractions that Madame judged it safe to have him meet the mademoiselles from time to time to improve their French. Mysteriously he had taken a fancy to both of them, Virginia because she was so pretty and so cross, and Lucy because he thinks she is a typical Englishwoman. They had enjoyed many tranquil walks *à trois* in the Luxembourg Gardens. Ferdinand has a cousin in London whom he regularly comes to visit. Mrs Musgrave, hearing this, had decided to ask him down to stay at the Dower House.

'What's the state of play on old Sir Fred?' Lucy asks.

'Coming to the boil, I think.'

'What'll you do if your ma remarries?'

'Send Sir Fred a wreath,' says Virginia, scowling at herself in the mirror. 'I won't live with them anyway. He's got a house in Chesham Square. I suppose Ma would move in there.'

'But what about you?'

'I'll be married by then,' says Virginia superbly. 'And to a rather better catch than a tired old knight in publishing.'

'Is Brooke expected?'

Brooke is Virginia's god-like elder brother, recently of Oxford and now commissioned in the Royal Air Force. He is a youth of such ruthless good-looks and physical presence that Lucy, realist to the last, has never even bothered to have fantasies about him.

'How should I know?' snaps Virginia pettishly, pushing the heavy mass of fair curls back from her face. 'I don't keep his engagement-diary.'

There is a discreet cough from the doorway. Violet Kedge, cousin to the unfortunate Beattie Blythe, smiles at Lucy.

'If you please, Miss Lucy, Mr Hallett would like a word with you, and the car is here for Miss Virginia.'

*   *   *

9

Halfway down the main staircase Virginia belatedly regrets her bad humour.

'Any news from old Hugh?'

Lucy tries in vain to control her blushes and to speak in a normal voice. 'He said he'd really try to get here.'

Virginia is about to make some agreeable comment when through the open front door she sees the car sent to fetch her and her brows snap together in one long golden line of fury. She had *specifically* asked for the Daimler. Instead her mother has sent the Morris Oxford. She will look absurd being driven home in *that*. Abruptly all her attempts at good humour vanish.

'Well, who cares? He's not that much of an asset,' she drawls rudely and walks out on to the sunlit gravel without bothering to say goodbye.

Crouched in the front seat beside the taciturn Carver, Virginia again regrets her bad temper and vows she will be especially nice to Lucy this afternoon. Then as the car makes its way down the drive her good impulse is forgotten under a tidal wave of depression. There is something about the Manor – about the village itself – which fills her with gloom. Perhaps it is simply because, having spent so little time here, she always feels a stranger, out of place, unwanted. As a younger son her father only finally inherited the estate eight years ago. By that time the Manor was mortgaged to the hilt – there has been no question of ever living there. Instead the Musgraves have continued to divide their time between Cadogan Square and the Dower House. They belong, concludes Virginia, who enjoys over-dramatizing her life, to nowhere at all. The car slows down at the lodge, and Carver gets out to undo the massive iron gates. Virginia watches him, waits for him to come back, drive the car through, then get out again and shut the gates, then finally drive the car on into the village. She does not feel it is her place to help him. Outside the gate the car turns right past the handsome Norman church and the rectory and they are in the village street. Virginia looks without love at the familiar scene.

Which is to miss some of the village's attractions; for, though Musgrave St Peter is not one of Suffolk's picture-postcard villages, if it can be said to have a best month, then August is probably it. Lying in a shallow clay valley, the main street follows the bank of a tributary of the River Deben. At this time of year the creek is full of brilliant emerald-green weed floating on water which reflects the spectacular blue of the summer sky. The cottage gardens brim with roses, hollyhocks, lilies, the occasional dark spear of delphinium. The old cottages, themselves plastered pink and white, front directly on to the street, the upper storey tilting ominously over the unmade road. In the summer sun their attendant evils of rising damp and three types of rot are concealed and they look mellowed, softened, picturesque. Further along the road there is an unattractive yellow-and-grey brick building set back from the road. This is the strict Baptist chapel. There are two public houses: The Keys and the Goat and Boots. On the other side of the creek there is a village school with 'Boys' and 'Girls' carved over the two entrances. There is a small triangular village green with a war memorial and a duck-pond. Most important of all, there is a general store cum post office.

It is now one o'clock. Normally the shop is shut and bolted, the flypaper hanging in the window beside a sign which says 'Closed until 1.30'. Today the door is open, and three or four people stand inside while three more lean against the Virol sign on the wall outside.

'What's going on?'

'They've got a wireless, miss. Mr Baines brought it back from Ipswich on Saturday. They're waiting to hear the news. See if there's any talk of the war.'

'There isn't going to be a war,' retorts Virginia, alarmed to discover she is actually repeating Scarlett O'Hara's very words. And look how wrong *she* was. 'We went through all that last year and nothing happened. Sir Frederick is a friend of Mr Chamberlain, and he said he's sure he'll get us round the corner again—'

'I hope you're right, miss.'

As the car turns into the Dower House drive Virginia discovers that her stomach muscles are taut with anxiety. *There must not be a war.* Any thought of hostilities must instantly cease because next year Virginia Musgrave must be presented at Court. Officially she is 'out' now, but it will take a proper season for her to fulfil her hopes. She has pinned everything on a glamorous early marriage which will free her from her mother's company for ever. There is only one certain way which will make Virginia relax her cramped limbs at night and sleep. It is an incantation starting 'Wimbledon, Henley, Ascot, nightclubs, drinks-parties, cocktail-parties, bottle-parties, champagne, strawberries, fast cars, Monte Carlo . . .'. There cannot and will not be a war, simply because Virginia needs peace so badly.

There are no other cars parked in the drive outside the front door: clearly neither Sir Fred nor Brooke has yet arrived. The front hall seems pitch dark after the dazzling sunshine outside. Through the open door of the dining-room Virginia sees the table is heavy with silver, glass and roses for lunch. On the Jacobean hall-table is an immense bowl of scarlet peonies. Virginia pauses beside them, alert, wary, interpreting the sounds of different parts of the house: two maids talking at the top of the stairs, the ticking of the grandfather clock in the drawing-room, birdsong drifting through the open french windows in the library. There is no sign of her mother. Thank goodness for the new *Tatler* that arrived this morning, which presumably—

'Virginia! Where on *earth* have you been?'

Mrs Musgrave erupts from the drawing-room, rage and self-pity apparent in every line of her face.

'You know where I've been,' says Virginia coldly, wilfully misunderstanding her.

'I mean what on earth do you think you're doing coming back at this time. I *told* you to be here to meet our guests. For goodness' sake, I've only asked this Frenchman for your benefit.'

'Have they arrived?'

'No, but—'

'Well, I'm not too late, am I?' drawls Virginia, beginning to walk towards the gracefully curved main staircase.

'Stand still while I speak to you. You certainly are late. Do you think you can sit down for luncheon looking like that? You look like a tramp. If your father was here, you wouldn't dare speak to me like this. You're going to

11

have to buck up your ideas, my girl, if you think you can go on behaving like this once your season's started. Who on earth do you think you are . . .?'

During this tirade Virginia eyes her mother coldly, dispassionately. Mrs Musgrave has two personas: a brittle, extrovert, highly strung public face and a hysterical, self-pitying, intermittently malicious private one. Outbursts like this are nothing new. Even so, this is the third time she's flown off the handle in one morning. So there must be more at stake here than simply the question of having guests to stay. Perhaps Sir Fred is, after all, going to declare himself. If so, thinks Virginia, more fool him.

As is her wont, Mrs Musgrave has long since left the original issue (real or imaginary) and is now ranging far and wide to find something that will provoke Virginia into some kind of response.

'. . . and don't think anybody's going to pay any compliments this afternoon. With a scowl like that you ruined any looks you might have had years ago. Nobody likes you; even the Halletts just put up with you. I told you to stand still when I'm talking to you.'

Quietly Virginia turns back to face her mother, and waits while her mother gets up steam to give vent to a catalogue of Virginia's faults: her rudeness (true), her indifference to her mother (perfectly true), her terminal untidiness and general slovenly ways (quite untrue), her behaviour at her eighth birthday party which had so accurately foreshadowed exactly what a pill Virginia would turn out to be in adolescence.

It was quite funny if you managed to make yourself detached about it, but Virginia is none the less grateful when Dawson, the butler, appears at the doorway of the dining-room with a query about the seating arrangements.

Seizing her advantage, Virginia melts away to her bedroom, throwing herself down on to the fat cretonne-covered armchair next to her bed. Though her face is calm, her whole body is rigid with tension, and she discovers she has been grinding her teeth. The strain of not letting her mother hurt her, of preserving that impenetrable façade, is considerable. Will there never be any end to this particular hell? Another year under the same roof with her mother is all she could stand. After that she would take an axe to her.

Virginia's dress, gloves, hat and stockings are laid out neatly on the bed. Granger, the between maid, knocks on the door to say that Mrs Musgrave is expecting Virginia in the drawing-room as soon as possible. Virginia's response is to tell Granger to run a bath for her. No, she does not need any help with her undressing. Who cares if it is one o'clock? Virginia wants a bath.

Have things always been this terrible? enquires Virginia rhetorically of her steamed-up image in the bathroom mirror as she pulls off her camisole and undoes her suspenders. Had her father's death last autumn made things worse? In all honesty, not really. There has never been a time in Virginia's memory when her mother hasn't needed a punching-bag, someone on whom she can work off all her anger and disappointment about her marriage. Her mother and father had quarrelled all the time, bickering, sniping, occasionally shouting, but never letting up for an instant, inhibited only by the presence of servants, never by their silent son and daughter. Life was one long row which never seemed to have anything approaching a real issue, let alone a beginning or an end, or a corresponding sense of having cleared the air afterwards. Just a wearing low-key hostility which occasionally erupted into something far worse. Sometimes it had been about money. Sometimes about how much Virginia's father drank. Sometimes (briefly) her parents would be united in dislike and envy of Virginia's uncle, her father's elder brother, who had inherited everything and was running through the family fortune to satisfy his capricious young wife. And there had been a real cause for anger when he had finally died leaving the estate so encumbered with debt that there was no possibility that Virginia's parents would ever be able to move up from the Dower House to the splendours of Musgrave Manor. Whatever the causes of the rows, real or imaginary, the atmosphere of tension and ill will they had created had been real enough. But, because her father was the more brutal, it always appeared – to Mrs Musgrave, at least – that she lost every battle. There had to be someone on whom she could vent her own anger. And that someone had always been Virginia. She wouldn't have dared to try it with Brooke. Partly because Brooke had inherited quite a lot of his father's character and was perfectly capable, even at eight, of telling his mother to stow it. But mainly because, quite simply, she wanted Brooke to like her. It had been clear to Virginia from an early age that her mother did not care sufficiently for Virginia to worry if she liked her or not.

An agitated Granger knocks apologetically at the bathroom door and repeats the earlier message with even more urgency. Virginia announces that she will be down in fifteen minutes and proceeds to spend another twenty-five dressing, buffing her nails, and arranging her hair, her coldly beautiful face drooping pensively. As she dips a swan's-down powder-puff into a box of loose powder and carefully removes the shine from her nose she ruminates on the fact that Sir Fred will be here shortly and may provide the means for a really first-class mother-tease. As she gets up to go there is the sound of wheels on the gravel of the drive. Suddenly Virginia's heart leaps. Good heavens! In her fury at her mother she has completely forgotten that Sir Fred is bringing Ferdinand with him. Abruptly her spirits start to rise. Ferdinand is not at all the kind of beau that an ambitious girl would want to own, but he is a man and in the absence of any other candidates he is an extremely welcome guest. Besides – and Virginia begins to smile in spite of herself – besides, and most important, Ferdinand likes her. This is hard to resist when you are as unpopular as Virginia. Car doors slam, then abruptly the sounds of the guests are drowned by the sounds of another car engine and the sound of wheels which roar up the drive scattering gravel. That sounded like Brooke's Morgan. Virginia begins to feel better. Brooke's presence always puts her mother in a good temper. For the first time that day Virginia remembers that she is young, healthy and exceptionally pretty, with all her life before her. With a light heart she goes down the stairs to greet the guests. As always the very thought of Ferdinand has the inexplicable power to cheer her up. He is one of the few people who has the exact measure of her character yet still seeks her company, laughs at her bad humour and actually listens to what she has to say. With her first genuine smile of the day Virginia goes forward to

13

meet her guests, Lucy, her mother and all her disagreeable memories of the morning completely forgotten.

Virginia would be horrified to know the true effects of her unkindness on Lucy. Horrified, that is, to find out that they had absolutely no effect at all. As the Morris pulls away Lucy performs an unconscious gesture, a kind of straightening-up and quick movement of the shoulders. It is something to do with water off a duck's back. Whistling cheerfully in a way that every teacher she has ever known has expressly told her not to, she makes her way through the house to find her father.

Lucy likes her father. She has inherited his own easygoing phlegmatic temperament. 'In five years' time' is her father's favourite prelude to almost any statement. In five years' time none of this will matter, Lucy tells herself, pausing irresolutely outside the library door. A sudden burst of typing shows that Mother is still in full flow, so Father clearly won't be there. In five years' time, Lucy tells herself, the horror of her season, her coming-out party, the round of débutante dances will be dim memories. Lucy does not believe there will be a war, or anything else to cancel that season, in spite of the trenches in Hyde Park. But this is because she rates her own wishes rather low on the scale of divine providence.

Lucy steps through the dark and silent drawing-room, the blinds firmly looped down to keep the sunlight off the Persian carpet. Stepping out on to the terrace, the heat falls on her like a blow. Dazzled, she sees her father still under the cedar tree, still debating the correct position of the tea-urns. During his working life – before he abandoned his career to manage his wife's – Mr Hallett has been a prep-school teacher and even now carries something of that persona with him. He exudes a kind of friendly ineffectualness. Here is a man who believes stoutly that sport forms character and is not afraid of saying he's proud to be British and a member of an empire that had brought sport – and therefore the rudiments of fair play and decency – to a number of people who manifestly needed them. 'Stinks' had been his subject, but sport had been his real love. He felt he was forming character as he urged muddy-faced little boys to get the ball in and break clean. From an early age Lucy had been exhorted to wield a straight bat, take it like a man and learn to roll with the punches.

'Ah, Lucy old girl,' her father greets her happily, slipping a blazered arm affectionately through her own. 'We've called you in to be twelfth man, to give the casting vote. Just where do you think this tea-urn ought to be?'

'Definitely in the shade, Daddy,' says Lucy briskly. 'It's going to be a scorcher this afternoon, and people aren't going to want to stand around in the hot sun waiting to be served.'

'There you are, Verge. All settled and correct.'

'Very well, sir. Luncheon will be served in ten minutes.'

'Has Virginia gone?' he asks Lucy.

'Yes, they've got friends arriving. Sir Frederick Grebe and Madame's nephew Ferdinand. *You* know.'

14

'Ah ha! The curious frog. Is he a suave, charming, debonair seducer with a boater and camellia in his button-hole?'

'Really, Daddy,' Lucy starts to giggle in spite of herself. 'He's not a charmer at all. He's sort of yellow-coloured and he looks about fifty. And he wears pebble glasses.'

'Sounds irresistible. Which of you girls is he in love with?' asks her father gallantly.

Lucy squeezes his arm gratefully. He must know that, where men are concerned, in Virginia's company she simply becomes invisible. With the exception of dear Hugh of course.

'I think he just likes us. He's terribly funny. Though I'm not sure he always means to be.'

'Hope his English is up to scratch. M'French isn't what it was.'

'Oh, he's fluent. He comes over to stay with his cousin in Chelsea almost every year.'

'Chelsea, eh?' muses Mr Hallett, determined to make a figure of romance of the absent Ferdinand. 'Bit of an artist, is he? The bohemian type perhaps?'

'Dad-*dee*,' says Lucy in exasperation. 'Honestly, he's the most conventional man in the world. He works in a firm of lawyers. He goes on all the time about "the done thing". He keeps asking what is "comme il faut" in England for a single gentleman. Why, if you'd told him to wear tweeds to the garden-party, he'd probably do so.'

'What about that other young man, the one you made your mother invite, eh?'

'Oh, he's just a friend,' says Lucy, colouring red to her ears. 'We met him in Paris. His bank had sent him over for a year to work in their overseas division. He's back in England now, and he's got some holiday, so I thought—'

'Coo-ee!' Mrs Hallett, released from the tyranny of the typewriter, is waving to them from the library steps.

'Didn't you hear the luncheon gong, you slackards?' she cries gaily. 'Come on, I'm famished!'

Mr Hallett sets off with alacrity; Lucy follows more slowly. The stable clock is striking half-past one. 'O God, please let Hugh manage to get here,' Lucy prays as she follows her parents into the house.

'Who *are* all these people, Lucy?'

It is a quarter to four. The shadows of the cedar trees are beginning to lengthen. Lucy's white gloves are grey from shaking strange hands.

'Oh, the tenant farmers. People from the other village. The Master of Fox Hounds. People like that.'

'No sign of the Musgraves?'

'Not yet, no.'

'Do you think things are going all right?'

'It's all top-hole, Dad.'

'Had any tea?'

'No, I thought I'd wait until Virginia arrived. I think Major Jones is look-

15

ing for you, Daddy; he seems to have some contingency plan in case there are any evacuees.'

'Oh lor', does he really? Where is he? He's such an old warmonger.'

'He was with the vicar – no, he's getting some more tea. He's over by the urn.'

Left to her own devices, Lucy debates as to whether a conscientious daughter would really go off and enjoy herself whilst other members of the party are sitting on their own. The problem is that Lucy knows almost nobody here. Owing to her prolonged stay in Paris, she has lived for only a few weeks at the Manor. What she would *really* like to do is skulk round the front drive to see if Hugh has arrived. But that would never do. Lucy has a strong sense of duty and, recognizing at least one familiar face, goes off to be sociable. The vicar is standing, cup and saucer in hand, admiring an enormous massed clump of blue and mauve delphiniums. He is deep in conversation with a girl with her back to Lucy. Like Lucy, she is dressed in white with a broad-rimmed straw hat. The girl turns, and Lucy recognizes without envy that here the resemblance ends. The other girl is about her own age but tall, dark-haired, slender, with a startlingly good figure, and – there is no other word for it – she is beautiful.

'Ah, Lucy, hello,' says the vicar, who is bent and elderly but still possessed of a good deal of robust cheerfulness. 'A splendid day, and what a marvellous occasion your parents have made of it.' He gestures with his free hand at the two hundred or so people eating egg and cress sandwiches and examining their neighbours. 'I was just telling Beatrice that I couldn't remember a garden-party like this since – goodness me – the early twenties. Must have been in the late Mrs Musgrave's day. And that's a good few years ago. Have you met Beattie? She's currently the toast of the village.'

Lucy and Beattie shake hands.

'Beattie's off to your mother's training college shortly, and I doubt if we'll be seeing much more of you once you've qualified, eh, Beattie? Tell me, why did you choose a London training college?'

As Beattie shyly explains, Lucy covertly studies Beattie's looks, which are exceptional. There is a faint resemblance to the Kedge girls, but in Beattie the high colouring of her cousins is refined, toned down, made harmonious. Thick shining dark waves frame an oval face of a clear, almost china-like pallor. Her eyes, blue-grey and enormous, confront the world seriously beneath glossy well-shaped brows. Her full unmade-up mouth with its deeply indented upper lip has the softness and vulnerability of some kind of half-opened flower, a Christmas rose or a peony. It is a face with beauty and repose but character as well. And her clothes, notes Lucy, interested, cannot be faulted. Presumably Virginia has forgotten that Mrs Blythe is the village dress-maker – her daughter's outfit is a triumph of restrained good taste. The two girls examine each other cautiously. It occurs to Lucy that Beattie probably knows all about her from her cousins, one of whom is actually Lucy's personal maid. The safest thing, thinks Lucy, is quietly to melt away. But instead she offers her own congratulations and as Beattie smiles her thanks, an enchanting smile, Lucy knows that, Virginia or no Virginia, she likes this girl.

'Mother adored Hillsleigh.'

16

'Yes, she's been telling me about her time there. I'm sure I'll like it, too, Miss Lucy.'

'Will you mind living in London?'

'Mind? I'm longing to,' says Beattie, unguarded for a moment, then colours as she sees Lucy's surprise. 'It's—it's what I've always wanted.'

'But don't you like the village?' Fearful of sounding patronizing, Lucy adds feebly: 'I mean, it all seems very nice here.'

'Sometimes I like it. But I've always longed to live in London. Mother comes from there, you see. She came down here to be the late Mrs Musgrave's maid. That's Miss Virginia's aunt. I'd never been to London till this Easter. Then I went up for my interview and stayed with my aunt in Putney and I had a gra—a marvellous time. But perhaps if you've always lived in London it doesn't seem so special to you.'

Beattie has an attractive low-pitched voice with surprisingly few of her native Suffolk vowels. She has been coached in this, as in many other matters, by her mother.

'Do many people leave the village?' asks Lucy.

Beattie looks at Lucy, amused.

'Usually only the men. And then only to fight the Great War. Mostly girls just stay here and get married. My cousin Lily Kedge wanted to work in Ipswich, as an usherette in the Regal. She had the job and everything. But my uncle wouldn't let her go. It meant living in lodgings in Ipswich, and he wouldn't hear of it. She was that disappointed,' adds Beattie reflectively.

'I'm sure,' says Lucy, amused and intrigued. 'So what do most of the girls do round here? When they leave school, that is.'

'There isn't much choice. Mostly girls go into service.'

There is a sudden emotion in Beattie's voice, and Lucy has a sudden blinding sense of the colossal struggle that Beattie has gone through in order to stay on at school and try for higher education. For every person who has encouraged her there must have been ten who have told her that she was wasting her time, that she'd get married anyway and then what would be the use of all those certificates? And yet another ten who are quite willing to tell her she was getting above herself and putting on airs. Lucy knows that if she had had the desire or the ability for college or university it would have been arranged for her, simply by her expressing the wish. She compares her own life with the steely efforts that Beattie has had to make – and envies her.

'What did you do in London? Did you get to see any shows?'

Beattie smiles again, her whole face lighting up at the memory. 'I went to the pictures three times! It was *wonderful*. If you go in Ipswich, the last bus goes at half-past seven and you always miss the end. And we were taken to a free dance in Hyde Park. And to an art gallery.' She speaks with a hunger that holds Lucy spellbound. Where does a girl of this mettle spring from, reared amongst the stolid little village girls who go in the door marked 'Girls' until they are twelve, then leave, their dreams going no further than the boundaries of their own village? As Beattie talks, Lucy listens with alacrity. She would like to make her a friend. Yet even as the thought passes through her mind she is conscious that Beattie is speaking carefully to her because of who Lucy is. For the first time in her life she is properly aware of

17

the gap between classes, the gap that allows her to address Beattie by her Christian name yet automatically assumes that she will be addressed as 'Miss Lucy.' She longs to bridge that gap but cannot find the words. Her whole training and upbringing have been formulated precisely towards its maintenance. In the awkward silence that follows she is conscious the moment of intimacy has passed and is sorry. Then mercifully there is a sudden flurry around them, a sense of people turning round and craning their necks.

'Please excuse me,' says Lucy, relieved. 'I expect that's the Musgraves arriving.'

The torpor of the summer afternoon suddenly evaporates; there is a feeling of expectancy, a sense of straightening ties and putting shoulders back. For a moment it does not matter that the Manor, so impressive in the late-August sunshine, is in an appalling state of repair, that the general condition of the Manor farms is deplorable, the fencing inadequate, the hedges untrimmed, and the land actually 'gone back' in some exceptional cases. The Musgraves are still the owners of the land on which everyone present either works or lives and have been the owners for well over two hundred years. The Halletts may rent the Manor, but it is the Musgrave name that still resonates in people's minds.

Lucy makes her way to the terrace where her parents are greeting Mrs Musgrave.

'Awfully glad you could make it,' says Mr Hallett gruffly, pumping Mrs Musgrave's hand.

'But how sweet of you to invite us!' Mrs Musgrave ('Just call me Dah-dree') bends forward to offer a cool powdered cheek to Lucy.

'Darling Lucy, what a poppet you look in that funny little hat. Now, let me introduce our party. Sir Frederick Grebe.'

The stout red-faced man bows.

'And this is – er – Ferdinand Aumont.'

Mrs Musgrave gives Ferdinand an appalled and disbelieving look and quickly turns back to Mr Hallett.

'Isn't it wonderful that darling Brooke was able to get back from Hendon today? Is that tea? How super. It's just too faint-making, this weather, isn't it?'

Most of Mrs Musgrave's observations neither demand nor merit a reply, and with Sir Fred at one elbow and Mr Hallett hanging doggedly on to the other she makes her way down the stone steps to greet the tenants. The rest of the party follow, and Virginia and Brooke are promptly cornered by the vicar while Mrs Hallett tries to engage Ferdinand in vivacious French chatter. Lucy, having furtively ascertained that there is no hint of Hugh either on the terrace or on the lawn, stands morosely in the shade of the cedar tree and observes the lives of others.

Virginia and Brooke, seen side by side, resemble nothing so much as a pair of (at that moment) good-natured leopards. Their appearance is startlingly similar. Both share their mother's creamy-blonde hair, her long heavy-lidded eyes, the same aristocratic good-looks, the same faint aura of boredom. Brooke is the only man wearing uniform at the garden-party; for this reason alone he would stand out but, as it is, every eye is drawn to him

18

because he wears his RAF uniform like a god. Its tailoring and colour might have been designed simply to show off the breadth of his muscular shoulders and the bright blue of his watchful eyes. Virginia, as ever, is perfectly groomed, and stands teacup in hand, her long lashes demurely casting shadows on her cheeks. Virginia has some scheme afoot, thinks Lucy as she observes her friend with a practised eye and hopes with a sinking heart that the scheme doesn't involve Hugh. If he comes.

At that moment Verge appears at Lucy's elbow and positively orders Lucy to have a cup of tea. Lucy accepts gratefully and when she turns back Virginia has gone, leaving Brooke standing undecided for a moment, nodding to acquaintances, lazily scanning the crowd. Then abruptly Lucy sees his eyes focus and narrow as if he's seen something that interests him very much indeed. The lazy irresolution of his pose is suddenly gone. Lucy moves a pace to see what it is that has so transfixed Brooke's attention, and following the line of his gaze sees it is the charming Beattie Blythe innocently engaged in conversation with the verger.

The moment narrows, intensifies and concentrates on three points of the triangle. Lucy observing, Brooke assessing and Beattie oblivious of the interest she has aroused. Then Beattie raises her eyes; with a kind of shock is aware of the impertinence of Brooke's disconcertingly direct stare. Unbidden, the thought flashes through Lucy's mind: He wouldn't look like that at a girl of his own class. Beattie appears to have had a similar thought. As Brooke lazily raises his eyes from her figure to her face he smiles, confident of her response. Perhaps he expects her to colour, bridle, simper or simply look flattered. As it is, his caressing smile abruptly dies, killed stone dead by the angry look on Beattie's face. She is clearly incensed at being eyed like that. There is an instant of intense hostility. Then, most surprisingly, Brooke backs down. Charmingly, contritely he sketches a small apologetic bow. Then the considerable bulk of the wife of the local Master of Fox Hounds intervenes between the pair and Brooke is left looking extremely thoughtful. Mrs Hallett appears and asks Lucy to be a duck and see if Verge has hidden any more cream horns inside. Lucy goes on her way, glad for Beattie's sake that at this particular moment Virginia's attention is engaged elsewhere.

Beattie turns away confused, not entirely understanding what has happened. It is all part of the strangeness which can be summed up in the fact that she is actually a guest at the Manor. Not as a servant, but here on her own, taking tea on the lawn. It is as if Beattie has finally stepped through the looking-glass and come into her own inheritance. From an early age Beattie's mother has hinted that Beattie will have a special destiny if she holds her knife and fork correctly and doesn't speak like her cousins. And Beattie has listened to her mother because, courtesy of the Musgrave family, Mrs Blythe has seen a wider world. And now it seems highly likely that that wider world can be Beattie's.

By now the edges of the remaining sandwiches are beginning to curl. The tea is stewed.

Hugh hasn't come. Lucy has abandoned hope.

19

Beattie gracefully thanks Mr and Mrs Hallett, looks in vain for Lucy and decides to go. There is already plenty to tell her mother about. Daringly she decides she will walk through the rose garden past the pond and let herself out through the side-gate into the park. She wanders slowly along the boxwood-edged path, swinging her hat, memorizing which roses look particularly fine, because she knows it will please her father. Finally she stops and sits for a minute on the stone rim of the enormous goldfish-pond.

The dark water is almost entirely covered by flat kidney-shaped leaves of bright shiny oil-cloth green. Beneath they are pinkish, veined with red, curling up to form protective rings round creamy bursting buds. Fat golden carp move sluggishly through the warm water beneath the flowers. Beattie leans over and stares, entranced.

There is a light step on the gravel behind her. Beattie stands up quickly, ready to defend her presence, then to her consternation sees Brooke.

For a moment they eye one another warily. Beattie is aware that her heart is beating faster and, annoyed by this sign of weakness, puts a correspondingly stern look on her face.

'Don't let me disturb you,' Brooke says politely, and gestures Beattie back to the place where she was sitting. Beattie slowly reseats herself, while Brooke perches on the rim a few yards away. 'I wanted to see this pond again,' he says quite unexpectedly. 'When my uncle was alive he used to bring me down here to feed the fish in the evenings. I wonder who does it now.'

'My dad does. In the winter he brings a torch and they all come up to the surface when they see the light.'

Beattie falls silent, racked by indecision as to the correct way to address Brooke. Is he 'Mr Musgrave' now? Or 'Mr Brooke'? He's certainly no longer 'Master Brooke'.

Brooke stares down to the depths below the lily leaves, looks up suddenly and catches Beattie's eye and unerringly reads her mind.

'Call me "Brooke". Do people call you "Beatrice"?'

'Not nearly enough,' says Beattie without thinking, and blushes. 'Most people don't get past "Beattie".'

Brooke pulls out a gold cigarette-case, gravely offers Beattie an untipped Passing Cloud, indulges in a good deal of tapping of the cigarette on the case-lid before lighting it from a narrow golden lighter. Inhaling deeply, he turns to stare at the Manor. Beattie follows his gaze.

'Would you like to have lived here? she asks, then wishes she hadn't.

To her surprise Brooke takes her question perfectly seriously.

'I did when I was younger.' Brooke's voice is languid, husky, clipped, in intonation and tone so different from the boys in the village.

'When Uncle died and Father inherited I thought—' Something tightens in Brooke's face, and he has to struggle to keep his tone disinterested.

'Then Father explained about the finances and I realized we'd never be able to afford to live here. In the old style, that is. So there it is.' He goes on more to himself than to her: 'I saw a film once on the way back to school. It was a cartoon, in one of those news theatres in Tottenham Court Road. It was dashed amusing. There were these mice and they were drunk, only they didn't realize it, and they were dancing away like mad on a silver floor. Then somebody whisked the floor away and at first they didn't seem to notice; they just went on dancing. Then one by one they all went down the hole. That's rather like my uncle. He went on dancing long after the floor had gone.'

With an abrupt change of subject Brooke says: 'I gather from Ma you're off to college.'

Beattie nods.

'So you're brainy as well.'

Beattie meets Brooke's gaze levelly and does not give him the satisfaction of demanding clarification of the 'as well'.

'Are you enjoying the RAF?' she enquires politely.

Brooke looks at her for a moment, then starts laughing. The corners of Beattie's mouth twitch, and then she, too, reluctantly smiles.

'Yes,' he says with mock politeness. 'I'm enjoying the RAF very much, thank you.'

'Are you really a pilot?'

'Really and truly.'

In spite of herself Beattie is impressed.

'What's your college? Where is it?'

'It's called Hillsleigh and it's in London. In a place called Hampstead.'

'I know a place called Hampstead,' says Brooke, and now she knows he is mocking her gently and suddenly she doesn't mind. 'It's very near a place called Hendon where I'm stationed. Coincidence, isn't it?' Someone is calling Brooke from the terrace. He stubs out his cigarette and stands up.

'That must be our car. Look after yourself, Miss Blythe. Perhaps you'll have tea with me some time in London – if you're not too busy, that is?'

With a smile and a handshake he is gone.

Cheeks flushed and heart thumping erratically, Beattie walks sedately through the park gates, replacing her hat with some care so that anyone she meets will know she's been to the garden-party. Sadly the street is empty, save for the blacksmith's three-legged dog hopping philosophically home to the forge. Beattie knows she should go straight home where her mother will be hungrily waiting for every detail. But she feels an impulse to prolong the special day, so she pushes open the lych-gate into the churchyard, where she makes herself comfortable on a stone seat to muse about the afternoon.

To the left of the church, half-hidden by towering elms, is the square Georgian elegance of Musgrave Manor. From this distance its severe yet harmonious lines and white-pillared portico make it the classic gentleman's residence of an engraving. Closer inspection would reveal unmistakable signs of neglect and disrepair. But to Beattie's eyes the whole estate is bathed in grandeur. Across the other side of the churchyard, where the lane dips down into a hollow, is Beattie's own home.

Brooke's attentions, flattering – and faintly mystifying to the innocent Beattie – as they have been, form only part of the glorious wonder of the day. *She has taken tea on the Manor lawn as a guest.* Not as a maid like her cousin Vi, in cap and apron, winking as she handed round plates of cream horns. She has been there as a guest, an equal. It seems like a climax for a year of triumph. She has been head girl of the school, passed her Higher Certificate with spectacular grades, and on top of that has won an open scholarship to a highly sought after training college. But with the arrival of the invitation to the garden-party it was as if all Beattie's mother's predictions for her daughter had come true. From an early age she had had instilled into her the idea that a special destiny awaited those who had good table manners or, at the very least, refrained, unlike Uncle Sid Kedge, from stirring their cocoa with a knife. An only child, and fortunately a pretty one, Beattie has borne the full weight of her mother's brooding preoccupation with good manners and pretty ways. From the very beginning Mrs Blythe had been perpetually at war with the other great influence on Beattie's life – her Kedge cousins, all ten of them, led by the redoubtable Lily who was Beattie's special friend. When Beattie had come in for tea, cheeks flushed, plaits undone, ribbons long since trampled underfoot and pinafore in a pitiable state of muddied disrepair, Mrs Blythe had learnt to bite her tongue, not even bothering to enquire with whom she'd been playing. Cis Kedge – 'poor Cis' as she was universally known – was Mrs Blythe's husband's sister and there was no point in making trouble within families. But, undeterred, she had continued to work quietly away at Beattie, and her reward had been this poised and graceful girl in spite of the (as she saw it) constant undermining of the unwholesome Kedge influence. But, though Mrs Blythe might have saved her daughter from the indignity of ever unwittingly drinking the contents of her finger-bowl, the Kedges at least had saved her from being a prig. Beattie has never had any problem in reconciling these two warring influences on her life, and on the contrary looks back on her childhood as an exceptionally happy time.

But today it is as if she has left childhood behind her for ever. Her eyes fix absently on the house, her perceptions heightened by the strangeness of the afternoon's events – Beattie suddenly conscious, almost for the first time in her life, of how completely the Manor and its inhabitants dominate the lives of almost everybody in the village. Beattie's father is head gardener at the Manor as his father and grandfather had been in their turn. Beattie's mother came from London to work in the household as the late Mrs Musgrave's personal maid, a position she gave up with the utmost reluctance on Beattie's birth. The estate's history is as familiar as Beattie's own. Mr Brooke's father had inherited it eight years ago, but as a younger son he had never been able to afford to live in the Big House. Instead, Mr and Mrs Musgrave, Master Brooke and Miss Virginia had occupied the Dower House while the Manor had been let to a succession of tenants. The latest were Mr and Mrs Hallett, family friends of the Musgraves, whose daughter Lucy was to be presented with Miss Virginia. But, even if they could no longer afford to live in the grand style, for Mrs Blythe at least – and for Beattie too, it must be said – the doings of the family and whichever tenant currently occupied the Manor had far more glamour than the royal family, a glamour that even rubbed off on those in service to them. But as Beattie ponders these things, her face cooled by a breeze bringing with it the fragrance of wild roses and cow-parsley, it occurs to her that there is a contradiction in her mother's attitude: if she thought life in service was so wonderful, why has there never been any question of Beattie going into service in her turn? Whereas the Kedge girls, as soon as they turned fourteen, found themselves firmly indentured to one or other of the big families in the neighbourhood. Beattie wonders what destiny her mother has envisioned for her. Whatever it is, it is now high time she was home. The church clock is striking half-past five as she runs down the lane leading to Church Cottage, which presents an agreeable and orderly sight in the late-afternoon sunlight. It had been built for Beattie's great-grandfather in proper red brick with a pantiled roof. Therefore it is not picturesque, but on the other hand it does have a damp course and laid-on cold water and an outside flush lavatory connected to the cesspit. Downstairs there is a large kitchen where most of the life of the house takes place, and a small parlour which is used only on Sunday or when Mrs Blythe has one of her clients in for a fitting. Upstairs there is one big and one small bedroom, and above that, under the eaves, an attic room which Beattie has appropriated for herself. As she opens the front gate Beattie sees the curtain in the parlour window twitch. Her mother must be looking out for her.

If Beattie had not been so habitually wrapped up in her own private dramas, it might have occurred to her that her mother seems to spend a good deal of her life standing at the parlour window waiting for Beattie to return. As it is, it seems perfectly natural to Beattie that she should be the centre of her parents' life. None the less the fiction is always preserved that Mrs Blythe has been so busy with her own concerns that she has barely noticed Beattie's absence. Beattie goes round the side of the house to the kitchen door, to discover Mrs Blythe apparently engrossed in setting the table for high tea. Calm greetings are exchanged, Mrs Blythe advancing the view that the pattern had taken that material very well for Beattie's dress, and perhaps Beattie might like to change before they have tea. Mrs Blythe herself has changed her dress at four o'clock as is her wont. She has replaced her print morning dress with something softer with flowers, and a prettier apron. The kitchen is full of the smell of baking scones, and the warm afternoon sunlight lies in bars across the red-tiled floor. Where her mother is, there is peace and order, Beattie unconsciously concludes, as she takes in the shining china, the neatly and attractively set table. At the same time Beattie is aware of a strange new and faintly treacherous thought. This kitchen is her mother's world. Here her word is absolute. But Beattie has had experience now of another world, one to which her mother's purely domestic influence cannot extend.

'Your father will be in soon. Leave your things upstairs, and I'll have your tea ready when you come down.'

Beattie makes her way slowly up the narrow wooden stairs to the white-painted attic. By her cousins' standards Beattie's bedroom is the epitome of glamour. There is a matching counterpane and curtains in rose-pattern chintz. Beattie's clothes are hung carefully behind a curtain in the corner made of the same material. There is a white-painted chair and, under the window, the bookcase her father had made.

Changed, and with her best dress carefully hung up and her hair brushed, Beattie goes over to the window to look out into the garden. In the past year, when not actually studying, Beattie has spent a good deal of her time kneeling here, staring out across the Manor grounds. Eight miles beyond lies Dereham Market, and beyond that Ipswich, and beyond that again, bathed in a kind of lurid glow, London, a magnet towards which Beattie is irresistibly drawn. And after London why not the world?

Beattie's elbows rest comfortably on shelves crammed with the books she's bought from her earnings from apple-picking. Jane Austen, Charles Dickens, the Brontës, George Eliot are all copiously represented. But below them, hidden out of sight, are penny tales of romance that Beattie borrows from Lily Kedge. She is ashamed but cannot stop reading them, those stories of grave-faced governesses who set off from poor but respectable homes to care for golden-haired children in widowers' houses in Paris or St Petersburg. Inevitably they end up comforting (and marrying) the anguished handsome wealthy widower. Mrs Blythe is under the impression that when Beattie is qualified she will come back to teach at Dereham Girls' Grammar. Beattie knows that once she is qualified she will never return to the village. The world is beating on her windows with frantic wings, and sometimes Beattie feels her heart will burst with longing to get away, to rise out of these narrow village bounds, to see other faces, other cities, other worlds.

'Beattie! Are you coming? The tea will be stewed.'

At six o'clock Mr Blythe's boots are heard in the scullery, and Beattie goes forward with alacrity to kiss him. She loves her father. Which is not to say she doesn't love her mother, but there is something about Mrs Blythe's habitual reserve and control that discourages physical contact. Whereas Mr Blythe has all the tranquil good nature of a happy man. As head gardener of the estate his standing in the village is immense, called upon to judge flower- and produce-shows as far away as Ipswich. He is a tall spare weather-beaten man with a mild and peaceful countenance.

'Well, then, am I too late? Have you told your mother everything?'

'She's only just come in,' Mrs Blythe informs him.

'Did you have a good time? I saw you, twice, you know. Once when I came to the door of the kitchen garden and once when I was walking through to the tomato-house. You were talking to the vicar the first time, and to Miss Lucy the next.'

'I hope you had a good tea,' says Mrs Blythe. 'There were cars arriving all afternoon. Must have been close on a hundred there.'

'Lawn's taken a beating,' Mr Blythe laments. 'I can see I'll be nursing it most of this winter.'

'But who did you talk to?' asks Mrs Blythe.

'Oh, all kinds of people,' says Beattie easily. 'Mrs Hallett told me all about Hillsleigh. She loved it there.'

'What about Mrs Musgrave? What did she wear?'

'Yellow silk, with a lovely hat of yellow silk roses.'

'Ah,' says Mrs Blythe with satisfaction. 'She wore that for Ascot. Pass your father the pickled eggs, Beattie. What about Miss Virginia? And Miss Lucy? It can't be easy to dress *her*. Her being so tall.'

Dutifully Beattie recounts what both girls had worn, recalls as many of the guests as she has seen and spoken to, and describes the tea. She is saving up until the very end the most astonishing fact of all: that Brooke Musgrave

24

had actually singled her out and then said he might see her in London! But as the meal progresses she begins to feel a strange reluctance actually to tell her mother. It is her secret, her triumph. Normally she tells her mother everything. Today she is grateful that her father takes an unprecedented part in the conversation.

'Did you see my roses? And I don't think the delphiniums have ever looked better.'

'Oh goodness, yes, Dad. And I listened to what people said. They were full of praise about the garden. I went to have a look specially at the roses.'

'Don't often get a summer this good. The Halletts were lucky with the weather. They certainly got a turnout. Guests were still arriving when I left.'

'There won't be much tea left for them. More lettuce, Beattie?' asks Mrs Blythe.

Six o'clock. Lucy waves goodbye to the final guests, kicks the scraper by the front door and goes into the merciful cool of the house. She is hot, tired, and nearly in tears. Everyone else has had a wonderful day. Sounds of muted cheers even float through from behind the green baize door. Mother and Father are having a congratulatory sherry with one of Mother's many publishers. Whereas Lucy has hardly had a cup of tea, had no chance to speak to Ferdinand, barely eaten a cream horn or even had the opportunity to find out why Virginia was being so painstakingly charming to Sir Frederick Grebe, who was reacting like a rabbit in the grip of a particularly fascinating stoat, to the evident fury of Mrs Musgrave. It has been a rotten day, concludes Lucy morosely, and regardless of her white dress sits down on the bottom step of the curving main stairs and pulls off her hat and gloves to lean her aching brow against the banister. There is the sound of someone running up the gravel path, and a man appears irresolutely in the open doorway. The dying sun is shining behind him, and Lucy is only able to make out that he is wearing khaki.

'Lucy! Am I completely too late?'

In a trice Lucy is on her feet, fatigue forgotten, happiness restored. 'Hugh – how wonderful to see you – but you've joined up. You never told me – I thought you weren't coming.'

'You silly goose, I told you I'd come.' There is a new confidence, a resolution about Hugh which was not there before. It is as if in assuming the uniform he has somehow gained the full status of a grown-up. But his curly hair, boyish smile and innocent blue eyes are just as she remembers them.

'I'm so glad you're here. Can you stay the night? Would you like some tea? Or a sherry? Mother and Father are in the library—'

'No,' says Hugh authoritatively, 'I want to talk.' Suddenly masterful, he takes her by the hand and leads her purposefully through the house and on to the terrace. 'Where can we be alone?'

'There's a bench in the rose garden,' says Lucy, bemused, only aware that Hugh's hot hand is pressing her own.

'We'll go there, then,' says Hugh firmly and leads the way.

25

The rose garden achieved, he sits Lucy down and fixes her with a stern look.

'I must speak properly to you. You've heard the news, I suppose.'

'What news?'

'Stalin's signed a pact with Hitler. A non-aggression pact. That means those beastly Huns can walk into Poland any time they want and Russia will let them. It means war, Lucy.' Hugh's boyish features have assumed an expression of some gravity, and Lucy in spite of herself has to fight off a nervous desire to giggle.

'Hugh, are your *sure*? Father says Chamberlain—'

'Forget Chamberlain. It's chaos in London today. It's all talk of evacuation and clearing the coastal towns. I joined up yesterday, Lucy. I have to report for duty tomorrow evening.'

Lucy is so full of what he has just said that she hardly hears his next remark.

'Would you wait for me, Lucy?'

'Why, where are you going?' she asks innocently. Then her eyes widen as his words sink in. 'Hugh, you can't mean—'

'Oh, Lucy, I do.' Hugh sits down beside her, takes her hand firmly in his. 'Lucy, I want to marry you.'

'But, Hugh, we . . . I . . .' Lucy's voice trails away in disbelief as she searches his features for some kind of explanation.

'If I go away, Lucy, it would mean so much to me to know there was someone waiting at home. We don't have to get married at once. We could have a long engagement while we got to know each other. I do admire you so much, Lucy. I think you're a topping girl and I know I could make you happy. Say you'll marry me, Lucy.'

Hugh's eyes are moist with emotion. As Lucy stares at him, in that split second a number of quite irrelevant and unrelated thoughts go through her head. First, she remembers that Hugh is an orphan. Second, she is overwhelmingly conscious that he is now a soldier and thus deserves all the support she can give him. Third, and most incredibly of all, this good-looking young man wants her to be his wife.

'Yes, Hugh,' she says with a firmness that surprises herself.'Yes, I'll marry you. Let's go and tell Father, shall we?'

Part One

September 1939–June 1940

CHAPTER
ONE

*B*EATTIE IS LAYING OUT cups and saucers on the schoolroom table.

'You mustn't let it get you down,' says Mrs Harman, the village schoolmistress, who with the Women's Institute has undertaken to refresh the evacuees on their arrival. 'There's many like you whose plans have gone awry. Are they still outside?'

Beattie looks through the schoolroom window. 'Yes,' she says glumly.

It is four o'clock, and the smell of Sunday lunch still hangs heavily on the air. The board of the Goat and Boots creaks in the heat. Mr Hallett, Lucy and Virginia, officially designated the welcoming party for the village, are sitting in a stupor on the bottom step of the war memorial.

'We are now at war,' says Beattie to herself, trying to make the phrase mean something. In Poland people are being bombed. But it all seems unreal. The only fact she can grasp is that Hillsleigh has closed down. A telegram arrived last night to tell her so. No more information, nothing. She remembers the exultation of a garden-party, just one short week ago, and wants to weep. She will never get away now.

Outside in the grilling afternoon sun Virginia is locked in a private misery so acute she can hardly speak. In the space of a single week not only has her whole future collapsed but *Lucy* of *all* people not only has a boyfriend but a fiancé and is to be married at Christmas. She has striven hard to be nice about it all, but the effort is beyond her. As Mr Hallett gets up to stretch his legs Virginia murmurs *sotto voce*: 'It's going to look jolly funny, you not taking in any evacuees at the Manor.'

Lucy wriggles. 'I know,' she says, worried. 'But Mother says that her job will be to keep up the Nation's morale, and that means having absolute peace and quiet to write in.'

'Try explaining that to Major Jones,' says Virginia snidely.

'I say,' says Mr Hallett suddenly, 'I think I can hear a bus. In fact I can hear several buses . . .'

His words are drowned in a throbbing roar of diesel as not one, not two but seven double-decker red London buses lumber round the bend into the village. Major Jones's Morris Oxford brings up the rear. He draws alongside Mr Hallett, steps out and wrings him warmly by the hand.

'Here's your lot, Hallett,' he says confidently. 'All safe and sound.'

There is a very long silence during which the onlookers juggle figures in their heads, and even Virginia's arithmetic tells her that something has gone badly wrong.

'There must be some mistake, old man,' says Mr Hallett confidently. 'You said ten children and fifteen adults. And it's not been easy to place them.'

'Have to make do, old boy. I'll be back later on this evening to check how you've done.'

With that he gets back into the car and drives off, leaving the visitors and their reception committee to stare at each other in disbelief. Lucy and Virginia are wearing cotton frocks, while Mrs Harman, as befits her mature years and the day's temperature of nearly 90°, is wearing her second-best girdle and light-weight tweeds. In contrast the ladies from London look like a flock of tropical birds. Dressed in brightly coloured rayons with small ornate hats, all are wearing shoes with limited use in the country. Beattie, coming to the door of the school, is enraptured by them. Virginia immediately concludes that they are all tarts. Lucy is chiefly impressed by their size.

'I say, Father,' she murmurs, 'they're all awfully . . .' Her voice trails away.

'My God,' says Mr Hallett numbly. 'They're all pregnant.'

From the last three buses stumble groups of young children holding carrier-bags and cardboard suitcases. They have labels on their collars and look tired and tear-stained, travel-stained and worse. Beattie's heart goes out to them.

'Why have they all got so little luggage?' wonders Lucy out loud.

A girl of about twenty with a baby in her arms, toddler hanging on to her legs and a third child clearly only weeks away laughs uproariously. She is a striking figure in green and purple shot silk, a black shiny straw hat crowned with pansies perched rakishly over one eye.

'Haven't got none,' she splutters, hardly able to speak for mirth. 'This morning soon as the siren went we was all packed into buses. What a pickle, eh?'

'Why are some of the women getting back into the buses?'

'They don't like the look of the place – no offence, you understand. There's no chip-shop here and no films.'

'We have a post office,' says Virginia stiffly.

'Ah, but it's not the same. Driver said he'd take us on to Something St Paul if we wanted to go.'

'You won't get much joy there,' says Lucy faintly. 'There isn't even a post office.'

The green slowly fills up with householders offering accommodation. There is an unpleasant aura of the slave-market as the strongest boys are immediately claimed by farmers and the weakest ones are left. By six o'clock most of the children have found some kind of temporary accommodation. Virginia and Mr Hallett have disappeared. The square is empty save for three of the homeless mothers who sit on the steps and massage their swollen ankles. Beattie's own problems have been temporarily forgotten in her attempt to comfort the bewildered and tear-stricken children. She is sitting with one of them on her knee, while another hangs on to her leg, when she hears somebody calling her. It is Mrs Leary from the post office.

'I'm over here,' says Beattie wearily, trying to disengage herself from imploring little hands. 'What is it?'

It is another telegram. Beattie snatches it from the postmistress with trembling fingers; then, as she reads it, her face falls and she crumples the form angrily.

'Oh, it's too bad!' she says in vexation.

'Is it your college? Has it been evacuated?'

'Yes, and to Norfolk of all places. Norfolk. *Norfolk*. I've *been* to Norfolk. It's only thirty miles away.'

'When do you go?'

'First thing tomorrow. I'll have to tell my mother.'

As she turns to go, two of the youngest evacuees each grab a leg imploringly.

'Don't go, miss. Please don't go. Little Ern here will cry if you go, I know he will. He's taken a real fancy to you, miss, and he doesn't like many people, little Ern doesn't.'

This moving plea comes from big Toby, little Ern's brother. Beattie looks down at their tear-stained and woebegone faces, and her heart softens.

'Look, I have to go home now, but I'll ask my mum if you can come and stay the night – at least until we find you a proper home. Yes, really, I promise. I'll be back. I'll see you later, Miss Lucy,' she promises and, waving to them, runs up the village street in the gathering dusk. She is about to turn down the lane by the church when she hears the powerful roar of a car behind her. It must be Major Jones, thinks Beattie, and turns to wave. But the car which screeches to a halt beside her is a shiny black two-seater and at the wheel, wearing his RAF cap tipped rakishly back, is Brooke Musgrave.

'Hello, Beattie. I thought it was you. What on earth is happening? There are three pregnant women sitting by the war memorial. Is it the sins of the harvest festival come home to roost?'

'It's the evacuees; they arrived this afternoon.'

'Ah, London people. That explains it. But what are you doing here? I'd have thought you'd have gone to college by now.'

In the half-light of the lane Brooke sees Beattie's face fall.

'What's wrong?' he says, pulling off his driving-gloves and leaning over to open the door for her. 'Sit down for a minute and tell me why you're looking so blue.'

It is an invitation that Beattie finds impossible to refuse, especially since it's the first time she's been in a car. Even if it isn't moving. Gingerly she sits down on the leather upholstery, hardly daring to breathe.

'I got this telegram last night saying the college was closed. But I've just got another one saying it's to be evacuated and I've got to go to the new place tomorrow.'

'Let's see.'

Brooke smooths out the telegram and reads it.

'What an extraordinary coincidence,' he says slowly. 'Chillington Park. I know the place. I've been there to shoot. Don't look so downcast, Beattie.

31

You're much safer up there with the partridges. They'll start bombing London soon.'

'Bombing *us*?' says Beattie horrified.

'Of course. What do you think everyone's been cleared out of the city areas for? Why do you think I'm being trained to defend our shores?'

Beattie is silent for a moment and bites her lip.

'I must go,' she says at last. 'My mum and dad don't know about this yet.'

'Cheer up,' he says as he leans over to open the door. 'Every cloud has a silver lining.'

He is laughing at her now, but Beattie glares at him.

'Says you,' she retorts and slams the car door.

Brooke leans over and unexpectedly grabs her hand and pulls her back round to face him.

'You haven't asked me what *I'm* doing here today. I'll save you the trouble,' he says, grinning as she tries to pull her hand away. 'I've just had my first posting.'

'Oh,' says Beattie stiffly. 'How nice for you. Where to?'

'Place called Gatton. There's a civil aerodrome, and our chaps have taken it over. It's in Norfolk, about ten miles from Norwich. And about five miles from Chillington Park.'

There is a long silence as Brooke's words sink in.

'Oh.'

'It's not quite London, but I expect they do tea up there, too. I'll be in touch. Take care of yourself, Beattie.'

Brooke revs the engine and disappears into the dusk with a wave. Beattie runs the final stretch to the cottage on feet that have suddenly gained wings.

Brooke drives swiftly back to the Dower House, anxious to get home before the blackout. He's feeling rather pleased with himself. The car is going like a bomb, and Beattie is a nice little thing – well, that isn't true, she's a stunner though a little serious. As Brooke parks his car his father comes unexpectedly to mind. They had communicated very little or not at all, and the only piece of advice Musgrave *pére* had thought fit to pass on to his only son was the admonition that sinning was to be done outside one's class. To which he had added, after pouring another whisky and soda: 'But never sin too near to home.' It was worth bearing in mind where Beattie was concerned, thinks Brooke as he walks into the house. Besides which there are several other things currently on the go, including one little thing, who is really not very nice but extremely available, with whom he has spent the afternoon. In her flatlet, to be precise. Her name, or so she claims, is Kitten and she lives off Percy Street. Still whistling, Brooke goes into the drawing-room to pour himself a whisky and soda, where he finds a vastly relieved Virginia, already resigned to dining alone again.

After dinner they take their coffee in the drawing-room. Virginia continues to get prettier every day but, thinks her brother, clearly no better-tempered.

32

'Brooke, whatever is going to happen to me?' she bursts out suddenly. 'Why couldn't I go to London with Ma? What's she doing there anyway?'

'She's trying to arrange a passage to America but she's left it too late. She hung on too long hoping Sir Fred would propose.'

'And won't he?'

Brooke leans over and gives his sister's blonde curls a tug that makes her yelp.

'You are a *naughty* girl, Virginia. You know perfectly well he won't propose now. Not after that row that he and Ma had the evening of the garden-party. A row, incidentally, of which you were the direct cause.'

Virginia rubs her head crossly. 'I still don't see why she couldn't have taken me to London with her.'

'Well, she didn't and that's that. Anyway, where would you live? She's let the flat, and all our relations are either on their way to Gervase in Devon or gone to Canada. Why don't you go and stay with Uncle Donald and Aunt Leonie in Argyll?'

'Because I don't propose to spend my youth in a freezing castle surrounded by smelly snoring Scotties,' says Virginia passionately and bursts into tears.

'Now, now, there's no need for that. Have a whisky and cheer up. Something will turn up. It always does. Anyway, Grebe says that Beaverbrook is sure the war will be over by Christmas.'

Mr and Mrs Blythe come down to the green the following morning to see their only daughter off into the wider world. This is a scene with much potential for emotion and drama, but such is the confusion brought about by the billeting arrangements that Beattie has to fight her way on to the bus and the last thing she sees, waving hopelessly to her parents, is Major Jones caught in the crossfire between annoyed evacuees and householders. It is not at all the way that Beattie has visualized the scene as she leaves her village. In fact the whole journey lacks style and bears no resemblance to any novel she's ever read. She had hoped to travel alone in the railway carriage penning a few pensive thoughts in her diary, occasionally wiping away a tear. As it is, once she's on the platform at Ipswich and the train for Chillington Halt finally comes in, she has serious doubts that she will ever get on, let alone find a seat. The train is jammed to the very windows with people in khaki, kitbags, suitcases and harassed civilians.

Unmoved, the guard blows his whistle, and Beattie gives a wail of despair. She is only saved when a soldier takes pity on her, picks up her trunk, hurls it bodily into the guard's van and then does the same thing to Beattie. The door clangs shut and the train puffs slowly out. Beattie finds herself seated on a pile of crates, hat jammed over her eyes and a piteous wailing coming from beneath her.

'You're sitting on my cat's basket' says an acid voice beside her, and Beattie sees an old lady sitting primly on a sack of fertilizer. Pushing back her hat, Beattie tries to make out her surroundings. Bicycles are stacked all around, and at the other end of the van is a teetering pile of crates containing cheeping day-old chicks.

Beattie sits and contemplates her destiny.

It takes them two hours to travel the thirty miles to Chillington Halt, and once out on the platform Beattie discovers that Norfolk looks distressingly like Suffolk only flatter. As she drags her trunk to the barrier, a chattering noise, not unlike the day-old chicks, makes her turn round. Behind her is a crocodile of little boys perspiring in the September sunshine in their grey flannel winter uniform. A harassed-looking woman in a pork-pie hat is walking in the rear, and her face lights up at the sight of Beattie.

'I say, are you from Chillington Park? Thank goodness. I thought they'd sent someone to meet us. This is Greyshott House. I think we may have left some boys at Ipswich. I'll have to wait until the next train comes. Now, come on, everybody, in twos, please, ark fashion. I want to see *quiet* boys ready for the coach. This lady – what did you say your name was, dear?'

'Beatrice Blythe.'

'Miss Blythe will escort you to your new school. Two-by-two and no shoving.'

Somewhat bemused, Beattie leads the way smartly out of the station with thirty pairs of little boys bringing up the rear. A chocolate-coloured coach is waiting, with 'Chillington Park' clearly marked on the front. Can they all possibly be going to the same destination?

The journey takes about twenty minutes before they turn in through a vast pair of wrought-iron gates.

'I say,' says one little boy. 'Look, deer. Lots of them. Under the trees.'

'I can see the house now . . . it's like Buckingham Palace.'

'Do you think they'll let us swim in the lake?'

Beattie stares across the other side of the park to where she can see the white Palladian façade of Chillington Park. Six immense white pillars rise above a white curved double staircase leading up from the drive. The house stretches endlessly on either side, the sun touching mirrored windows and turning the lake in front of the house into a pool of gold. Beattie is silent, astonished. She had feared her luck had changed. That that first step through the looking-glass was all that she would be permitted to take. Now, looking at the vast splendours of Chillington, she understands that she has indeed come into her inheritance. She has never seen anything so beautiful or grand in her life.

The more immediate prosaic problem, however, is to try to find a home for these sixty little boys. As the coach draws up at the foot of the steps a brisk old lady with a lorgnette on a black satin ribbon comes breathlessly down the steps holding a board with a sheet of paper pinned to it.

'You must be Greyshott Prep.'

'They are. I'm not. My name is Beatrice Blythe and I'm to join Hillsleigh College.'

'In that case, how do you do? I'm Miss Frobisher, and I'm your principal. Welcome to Hillsleigh, Beatrice. These are difficult times especially since the M.O.E. seems to have made rather a mess of the arrangements. I'm sure things will sort themselves out. We're in the west wing, Greyshott is in the east wing, and there's a school of chiropody in the staff bungalows, but I'm assured they'll only be here till Thursday.'

A little hand clutches Beattie's.

'Please, miss, I feel—' But it is too late.

'Bad luck, little man,' says Miss Frobisher bracingly. 'Still, better out than in, I always say. Now, Beatrice, I'll have your trunk delivered and perhaps you'll be good enough to escort the boys to their new quarters.' Beattie sighs, then lines up her charges. On the count of three they troop up the marble staircase into the house. It was not quite the entrance she had envisaged for herself on entering her new college.

CHAPTER TWO

'DEAR MOTHER AND FATHER,' writes Beattie. 'Thank you for your letters and the gloves, which I am wearing as I write to you. Chillington is very cold, especially the bedrooms. I am still sleeping in Queen Charlotte's room, but it is not my turn for the four-poster this week.'

Beattie pauses and blows gently on her woollen fingers. Outside a fox barks once, twice in the frosty woods. Automatically Beattie wonders if she ought to check the hen-house door, then abruptly she remembers where she is and turns back to her letter. 'Work is going well and is very interesting. I've had good marks for my essays so far, but it's still strange living here. Nearly all the staff have gone except for one of the cooks and the old butler. Yesterday he helped us mark out a hockey pitch on one of the croquet lawns.'

Beattie's fountain pen slows again. All her parents really want to hear is that she is well and happy. What she actually feels but cannot bring herself to put into words is that she is homesick, frightened and confused. For someone who has allegedly longed to travel, Beattie feels she is making a pretty poor showing on her first time away from home. Perhaps it is simply that the bad news on the wireless makes her feel doubly that she is far away from the roots of her own security. It is November now, and Mr Hallett and the *Daily Express* are still saying that the war will be over by Christmas. But deep in her heart Beattie knows that they are wrong, that such a profound dislocation of everyday life presages deeper and more lasting change. Her inner confusion seems mirrored in the endless upheaval that is everyday life at Chillington. Greyshott prep school appears to be there for the duration, while the school of chiropody has moved on to Bury St Edmunds. In its place an orphanage from Cromer arrived and stayed for five days before moving to Yorkshire. Currently half a theological college is living in the east wing with Greyshott while the other half of the college is in Halifax with their tutors ineffectually commuting between the two places. Hillsleigh's daily classes are held in a series of wildly inappropriate settings: they eat in the ballroom, study in the red drawing-room, do their biology practice in the gun room, while the large billiards room has been converted for arts and crafts. There would be little free time on the course in the normal run of things, but now with gas-mask drill for the children every morning, air-raid practice, washing-up rotas and a new rota for fire-watching the girls fall exhausted into their beds at nine-thirty with a strict lights-out at ten. But it is a relief to find that Beattie is not the only one to be homesick and that many of the other girls come down to breakfast with suspiciously swollen eyes. She takes consolation from the fact that at least she is missed in equal measure. In front of her is a letter from Lily Kedge, who, in the grip of powerful emotions about life and missing Beattie, has actually overcome her basic suspicion of pen and ink and, without benefit of punctuation, has committed her thoughts to paper. Life in the village is apparently completely altered, or as Lily more picturesquely puts it:

'You would not know the village now Beattie it is so changed and full of strangers and none of them men I don't know how we girls are to marry. Our Violet and Rose have joined the Women's Army and they are in a rare old pickle at the Manor, Verge having joined the navy and no one left to wait at table. Mother took on terrible when the twins gave in their notice she said if there was no war after Christmas they would have given up a good position for nothing. We are in trouble with the black-out it keeps falling down. I should like to go away myself but will have to wait as mother is due in three weeks now and I must stay she and Iris between them having no more sense than a goat. I think it will be mother's last as there is no more room even with the girls gone. Your father came round last night and made me and Iris dig over the garden because he says we will need more vegetables for next year. Our dad has not been home since market day – good riddance say I. I have made a friend called Gloria who is at the Manor she comes from London and has two babies. She says Mrs Hallett is that annoyed and will not talk to them, stuck up I call it, but she says Miss Lucy is a good sort. I am cleaning now for Miss Piggott she has a lot of fiddly things but so far no breakages, touch wood. Your two have been down playing with our Ivy who sends you her love and the boys too. Little Ivy says a prayer for you every night. Your little Ern still dirties himself, your mother says it will drive her to her grave, but she likes having them I am sure as it stops her missing you very much as we all do dear Beat. With love from your cousin Lily Kedge.'

The library door opens cautiously and a small girl with riotous brown curly hair dances into the room, her vivid features lit up with excitement.

'I went and complained! I did!'

'Louie, you *didn't*!'

'I did, too. I said our room was too cold to sleep in. Old Frobisher started to talk about sacrifices, but I was dignified and firm and told her there might be a war on but some things weren't good enough.'

Louie Brown thought many things in life weren't good enough and where she could she intervened. The intense cold of Chillington had taken even Louie, inured to the dampness of Liverpool, by surprise. After last night, when five of them had ended up in the double bed trying to keep warm, she'd determined to do something about it.

'Gosh, you are brave. What happened?'

'Well, not a lot,' admits Louie. 'At first she said we could move downstairs and share with Helen's lot. But they're awfully noisy. But she did say that if another of the estate cottages comes free we can have that. It'd be grand, wouldn't it? We'd be over here during the day, but apparently you can have a wood-fire at night providing you get the wood. Hey! I forgot what

I came in for. Marigold's looking for you. It's your night for blackout patrol. Had you forgotten?'

'Lord,' says Beattie hastily and packs up her writing-paper. 'I'll see you for supper.' As she bolts the long heavy shutters of the library windows, the door reopens and Marigold appears.

'Are you ready, Beattie?'

'I'll just get my coat.'

It is pitch dark outside, although it is barely five o'clock. Beattie and Marigold switch on their torches (regulation size and with a beam pointing correctly to the ground) and commence their tour of the perimeter of the house. The village's air-raid warden will be along later to check anyway but, as Marigold said at prayers that morning, it is a matter of pride that Hillsleigh should show a patriotic spirit even if they couldn't take a more active part in the war. It is a long and very chilly walk. Twice they stop to tap at windows where there is a chink of light showing.

'Do you really think that planes can see cracks of light so far below them?' Beattie had asked Marigold the previous time they'd done duty together.

'If the Government tell us so, it must be for a reason,' Marigold had serenely replied.

'Ruddy daft, that Marigold is,' Louie had roundly said when Beattie had repeated the conversation to her. 'I saw a film once about a pilot. You're miles up in a plane. Stands to reason you couldn't see anything. Still, if it's the law, I suppose we have to do it.'

As they make their way cautiously across the lawn, Marigold says: 'Have you done fire duty yet? A stirrup pump should be arriving tomorrow, and I'm putting you in my team. I'll go and check the stables; you wait on the terrace.'

Beattie leans her back against the stone balustrade and stares up at the great mass of Chillington, its white luminous bulk glimmering faintly like a great liner against the night sky. Far above her, invisible in the darkness, a single plane drones its way across the sky. Beattie sighs and thrusts her gloved hands deeply into her pockets. When would Brooke get in touch? *Would* Brooke get in touch? Last night Miss Frobisher had announced the date of the end-of-term dance. Already six weeks of term had passed, and he hadn't contacted her. Perhaps he was flying night and day, perhaps he'd just been polite that day in the car. Perhaps. The subdued beam of Marigold's torch heralds her return across the paving stones.

'All's well there,' she says in her reverberant contralto, making Beattie wonder for some reason if she had ever been a Girl Guide. 'If you've got five minutes, Beattie, I said we'd wait in the front and see in the Greyshott boys after choir practice. You'd better take my arm.'

The darkness is now as dense as a black blanket, turning familiar objects into threatening obstacles. They wait at the bottom of the terrace steps stamping their feet, and after a minute or two hear a distant breathless reedy rendering of 'Run, Rabbit, Run', and up the drive comes the shuffle of marching feet. The boys greet Beattie gratefully, claiming all kinds of near-accidents in their return from the village.

'They certainly seem to like you,' says Marigold approvingly. 'Perhaps you'll do your teaching practice with them. I'll go in, and you bring up the rear.'

It is bitterly cold. Even the unheated bulk of Chillington suddenly seems inviting.

'Come on, hurry up,' calls Beattie to the small figure who appears to be loitering at the end of the queue. As the little boy draws level he stops, and in the dim light of her torch Beattie sees he is holding out an envelope. 'A man in the village asked me if I'd give you this. He had this wonderful car, it was a Morgan, and there were two men in uniform and they asked me where I was at school. I told them we were at Chillington. One of them, the tall one, said did I know you; I said of course because you brought us here on the first day, didn't you, Miss Blythe? And he said, "Hang on a jiffy," and wrote something and said could I give it to you. He gave me sixpence.'

'Cousins, where on earth are you?' bellows someone from the top of the steps.

'Oh, crikey, I'd better go. Anyway, here it is.'

Beattie follows him up the stairs into the house. She closes the glass-panelled door behind her, locks it, then puts the blackout curtain securely in position. Only then does she open the envelope. 'Dear Beattie,' runs the letter. 'Are you allowed out or do they make you toil from dawn to dusk? I tried to phone but was told I couldn't speak to you unless I was a relative. Are you free tomorrow (Sunday)? If you are, I'll be outside the post office in Chillington at two o'clock. If you can't make it, another time perhaps? Best wishes, Brooke Musgrave.' Beattie puts the letter into her pocket and goes in to supper.

Brooke lights yet another cigarette and drums his fingers on the dashboard of his car. It is five to two, and as usual he is possessed of a fearful restlessness. The only visible inhabitant of Chillington is a dozing black and white cat. Brooke gets out of the car and leans against the bonnet, smoking, thinking so far it has been a bitterly disappointing war. Having no real plans for his career, Brooke had leapt at the chance of becoming a pilot. Beneath the well-bred face and disinterested manner is a passionate longing for danger, adventure, recognition and worldly success. The reality is that the family money is rapidly running out, and Brooke is under no illusions about his future. It is up to him to make his own mark either by marriage or by some other unspecified coup. How flying is to encompass all these ends is at present a mystery. His instincts tell him that there is a future in flying, and his heart tells him that it is the only thing he really wants to do. It has become a drug he cannot do without, and he longs passionately for enemy action.

When he had been posted to Gatton his spirits had soared. But so far life there is not really that different from his final year at Oxford. A little flying in the mornings – weather or reconnaissance work at best, and at worst endlessly hanging round the hangars waiting for orders that never came. In the afternoon at college he'd probably have done some work; here they played squash or went shooting game round the airfield. Evenings are spent dining in the mess or in the Bell at Thetford. It is a pleasant enough way to pass the time, but it is not the life Brooke has envisaged for himself – no, not at all. The only real excitement has been in the competition as to who can invite the prettiest girl down for the monthly mess dance. And here Brooke, bored and careless, had made a fatal blunder. He had invited Kitten, and the whole thing had been a fiasco from start to finish. She'd certainly caused a sensation, but not the one intended. She'd proceeded to match Brooke drink for drink and ended up on top of the piano at one o'clock in the morning doing the Lambeth Walk. Two o'clock had found them having a flaming row in the centre of a blacked-out Norwich, and under the influence of alcohol Kitten had proceeded to lose not only her inhibitions but also the last traces of her Mayfair accent and reverted to the vocabulary and accent of her native Hoxton. She had told Brooke exactly what she thought of him, and in the midst of his anger Brooke had been quite surprised by the perceptive nature of some of her comments. The next morning she'd gone back to London leaving Brooke to pay the hotel bill, feeling distinctly out-manoeuvred. What he needed now was a little uncritical admiration, and promptly on the dot of two o'clock along it came.

'Hello, Beattie. You got my note. I thought it would be better if I didn't come up to the house.'

They look at one another. Brooke is in uniform, his greatcoat unbuttoned carelessly over his tunic, his cap thrown on the front seat. As always his straw-blond hair is immaculate. Beattie is wearing the new red coat and hat that her mother made for her birthday. She has borrowed Louie's compact and lipstick and looks older, more sophisticated and to Brooke's eyes instantly more available. He had forgotten how very pretty she is. Suddenly he's extremely glad of the impulse that made him write to her.

'Well, dear lady,' he says, settling her in and climbing over the door on to his own side, 'I suppose we'd better get away from here as soon as possible. What would you like to do? I thought we might go for a stroll through the woods near Gatton, then drop down to Norwich for a spot of tea. Suit you?' Beattie's reply is drowned in the powerful roar of the engine.

It is a beautiful day, crisp, sunny and exhilarating. On Friday, Beattie had taken the Greyshott boys on a nature ramble, and the November country-side had seemed uniformly grey and brown. Today the thin brilliant sunshine reveals ditches full of golden and purple bramble leaves. Scarlet hips and haws glow in the hedges, and the water in the slow-moving streams reflects the cold cloudless blue of the sky above. Beattie pulls off her hat and lets the wind tug at her hair. Brooke smiles at her, touched by her obvious enjoyment. Eventually he pulls the car off the main road and they follow the track until they come to a five-barred gate leading into the woods.

'We'll leave the old bus here. Let me give you a hand over the gate.'

The woods are carpeted with fallen leaves. Gradually the trees thin out, and they find themselves looking across the fields to the flat area that is the aerodrome. It is a peaceful enough scene that Sunday afternoon.

'Those are hangars,' says Brooke pointing to the six huge buildings covered in camouflage-nets. The runways in front are empty save for three twin-engine planes with men crawling on the wings. Beattie is impressed.

'Do you fly those planes?'

'Yes, they're Wellingtons. The men you see are ground crew – the man on top is a rigger, he's checking the frame. The wind-sock over there tells you which way the wind's going for take-off. You probably can't see it from here, but the edge of the landing-ground is marked with red lights. When we fly off at night we have a yellow flare-path to guide us back.'

'Is your plane out there?'

Brooke screws up his eyes. 'I don't think so; they had her out this morning. The white building there is the old aerodrome. The huts you can see at the back are our quarters, and the building to the left of it is our mess. It's really quite good – the food, that is. Of course we don't dress for dinner now the war's started. The other building, the hut on the other side of the field, is for the WAAF. They haven't arrived yet.'

They stand in silence for a minute, and Beattie discovers she has a very cold feeling in her stomach. In imagination she sees the propellers whirring and young men like Brooke scrambling eagerly into their cockpits. For the first time she realizes that death and mutilation can happen to people she knows. Brooke is also silent, seeing the familiar scene through Beattie's eyes, and suddenly exhilaration floods through every vein. He is suddenly intensely glad that he's asked her out.

'Come on,' he says. 'Time for our tea, I think.'

The streets of Norwich are full of uniformed men and women waiting for the pubs to open. Brooke parks the car and leads Beattie to the Willow Rooms in the High Street which is crammed to the doors with service personnel and evacuees. With some difficulty they edge across the room to where two elderly women are arguing about a tip. Brooke, secure in the knowledge of the nation's goodwill towards his uniform and his youthful good-looks, gives them a dazzling smile which causes them instantly to vacate their table, blushing. A harassed elderly woman with grey hair uncoiling from untidy earphones takes their orders and disappears. Beattie straightens her hair with her fingers, hopes she hasn't got lipstick on her teeth, and searches for a topic of conversation to interest Brooke.

'These planes you fly,' she says in her low-pitched attractive voice. 'Is it just you, or do you have a big crew?'

Beattie has said the right thing, for immediately Brooke becomes expansive, fishes an envelope out of his pocket and proceeds to draw her a sketch. 'Oh, there's a coachload of us in there sometimes,' he says, sketching happily. 'Here's the plane and here's the second pilot. He's a Welshman called Gareth Hughes and he's quite a character. Cambridge man but very sound. Then you've got a rear gunner *here* – that's Brian Parker; and in the middle here there's the wireless operator, Eddie; and there's our navigator here, who's called Neil. The old girl cruises at about a hundred and sixty-five miles an hour but she'll do more. They're nice planes, sort of big and solid – bit like flying a wardrobe.'

The aged crone returns breathlessly and with a low despairing cry of 'Tea!' proceeds to rain willow-pattern china on the table. A plate of smoking scones follows. Beattie automatically reaches out to pour the tea and asks,

41

aware of the absurdity of the question: 'Do you – er – carry many bombs?'
But Brooke's reply is sobering enough.

'I don't know how many, but it's about four thousand five hundred
pounds if you can imagine that. Of course it depends on how far you're going
and how much petrol you'll need. We haven't actually done many raids yet,'
he adds reluctantly. 'When we do, I expect it'll be naval targets, that sort of
thing. We aren't allowed to bomb land targets, you see.'

'I should think not,' says Beattie horrified. 'You could kill ordinary
people.'

Brooke piles raspberry jam on to his scone. 'That didn't bother the Nazis
much back in Warsaw,' he reminds her. 'War is war. You can't play by
Queensberry rules.'

Beattie is silent for a moment. 'Well, I hope it never happens,' she says
firmly. 'It must be hard enough in the first place to know where to drop the
bombs for fear of hitting the wrong people. How do you do it? Can you see
where you are?'

Brooke is amused, and Beattie blushes.

'My dear, you just hope for the best. If you go down too close, you may
not be able to bring the old kite up again and, anyway, you get mixed up in
their flak.' Brooke is anxious to conceal the fact that so far the only offensive
weapons he's dropped on Germany are propaganda leaflets. 'When we go
bombing we use a thing called the ETA method, which means the estimated
time of arrival. You time your journey out from base and at a certain
moment you let your bombs go and hope for the best,' he explains, grinning
at her obvious disbelief.

To Beattie, who imagined absolute precision bombing, it sounds as random as throwing a handful of stones in the air.

'You must like flying,' she says finally.

'I don't like it,' says the normally undemonstrative Brooke. 'I love it.
The first time I went up at Abingdon I wanted to snatch the controls away
from the tutor and have a go myself. I suppose that's what gets you over the
boring bits like waiting around on the ground and feeling frozen when you're
actually up in a plane. When you're flying it's just you and the clouds and the
feeling of freedom.'

'Romancing about the job again, are you, boyo?' says a voice behind
Beattie, and a stocky smiling young man with a shock of untidy dark hair
pulls out the third chair and, turning it round, sits down, resting his chin on
the back, frankly staring at Beattie. 'What's he been telling you, then, lovely
girl? All about the romance of the boys in blue? I hope he told you that none
of us has been on a raid yet. We spend all our time dressed up with nowhere
to go, Cinderellas drooping at the fireplace of life. Another cup if you please,
miss. If the war is over by Christmas, we'll never have dropped a bomb in
anger at this rate. Or perhaps the very threat of Brooke here and me across
the North Sea is enough. My name's—'

'Beattie, this is Gareth Hughes, my second pilot. Gareth, this is Beatrice
Blythe. She's a well brought up girl, so moderate your language, please.'

'Ah, you must be the lady he sent the note to. Brooke is well known for
finding the most . . . unusual girls,' says Gareth slyly, then adds: 'But this

one's the best so far. Where are you from, lovely girl?'

Beattie shyly explains about her training college while Brooke smokes and Gareth crams his mouth with scones, his eyes flatteringly never leaving her face. Beattie omits the fact that her family are employees on Brooke's estate. Instinctively she knows that Brooke does not want this information made public.

'So you're brilliant as well as desirable – rather like me in fact. Is there something wrong?'

Beattie has turned a little pale.

'It's just that Mrs Nailor, one of my tutors, has come in.'

'Aren't you allowed out with young men?'

'I don't know. There's only the theological students at Chillington and so far no one has wanted to,' says Beattie, mystified, as both men start to smile.

'Tell you what,' says Gareth, 'let's brazen it out and say hello. I can claim to be your brother or your father, or I could write a signed testimony about Brooke's habits. He's clean and house-trained but he does snore.'

Brooke punches him amicably on the shoulder. Beattie is laughing. 'I'll try to creep past her. I must go, Brooke; I have to be in at five for choir practice.'

Unfortunately, as they make their way out of the tearoom, Mrs Nailor looks up and catches Beattie's eye, and they both smile uncertainly.

'I hope they don't punish you,' says Gareth.

'Oh, it'll be all right,' says Beattie with more confidence than she feels. Brooke is clearly completely uninterested in the problem.

'Hey, Brooke, are you bringing Beatrice to the next mess dance? I warn you, if you don't, then I shall. For one enchanted evening I shall be Dante to your Beatrice.' He grabs her arms and whirls her energetically round the darkening street.

'Of course I'm asking her,' says Brooke brusquely, 'so hands off, you perfidious Welsh leek. I hope you've got your own wheels home,' he adds pointedly. 'I'll see you at Gatton.'

'You certainly seem to have made a conquest there,' says Brooke. 'In you get. You'd better put this rug round you.'

The journey back to Chillington takes considerably longer owing to the extensively blacked-out nature of Brooke's headlights. It is gone five when the car draws up a few yards from the park gates and Brooke turns off the engine, debating as to whether he should try to kiss Beattie. But Beattie in her innocence has stepped out of the car before he has even had time to turn towards her in a meaningful sort of way.

'Thank you so much, Brooke,' she says breathlessly, half-hidden in the darkness under the trees.

'Hey! When am I going to see you again? Next Saturday?'

'Sunday's the only day we have free at present, and next week I'm playing hockey.'

'Well, how about the following week?' says Brooke rather nonplussed. 'Same time, same place?'

'All right, that'll be lovely.'

He drives off quickly into the dark, leaving Beattie to open the side-gate and sprint the mile up to the house. She lets herself in through one of the garden doors, then without pause leaps up five flights of stairs to the top landing that eventually leads to Queen Charlotte's bedroom. It is a vast bleak apartment currently housing five camp-beds and a splendid four-poster with its hanging removed. It is ineffectually lit by one unshaded bulb in the centre of the room. In the corner Louie, sitting on her bed in overcoat, scarf and woolly hat, is packing clothes into a cheap cardboard suitcase.

'Get you!' she says, looking at Beattie's flushed cheeks and sparkling eyes. 'I suppose I don't need to ask you if you had a good time, but come on, tell us about it. Are you seeing him again? Is he as handsome as you remembered? Better-looking than Leslie Howard?'

'Oh, much,' says Beattie fervently, and blushes and laughs at herself. Then she notices Louie's case. 'Louie, we aren't moving, are we?'

'We certainly are,' carols Louie, getting up and executing a few tap-dance steps. 'That is, if you still want to. Oh, come on, you must come. It's even better than we thought. One of the guest-cottages is free. It's over the other side of the park, but it's a great little place. There's a bathroom and a little modern kitchen; it's just like heaven.'

'A bathroom,' marvels Beattie. 'Just think of that.' Without any more ado she begins to pack her clothes.

'Go on, tell us, where did you go with your young man?'

'Well, first we went to look at his plane, then we went and had tea in Norwich.' Abruptly, dismay floods through Beattie. 'Oh lor', I forgot. While we were in the teashop I saw Mrs Nailor and she saw me. Do you think I'll get into trouble?'

'I'll be that furious if you do,' says Louie robustly. 'Honestly, if I'd known we'd be treated like thirteen-year-olds I'd have thought twice about coming. It's natural that girls of our age should be walking out with fellas.'

At this moment there is a light tap on the door, and Marigold stands pensively in the doorway looking serious.

'Beattie,' she says, 'Miss Frobisher would like to see you in her study before choir.' Beattie follows her out of the room, her heart thumping. Bad news certainly travels fast. She is gratified to see that, for all her talk of standing up for her rights, Louie is looking as scared as she is.

Miss Frobisher had made her study in one of the morning rooms over-looking the woods at the back of the park. She is seated by a coal-fire wearing her black velvet Sunday dress with a white jabot of lace. She is fiddling with her lorgnette as Beattie comes in, and at that instant Beattie knows that she is as nervous as she is. Making her voice as unconcernedly cheerful as possible, Beattie asks: 'You wanted to see me, Miss Frobisher?'

'Shut the door please, Marigold. Now, Beatrice, I gather you were out this afternoon having tea with a serviceman.' Miss Frobisher pronounces the words as distinctly as if she were handling them individually with tongs. 'We don't encourage particular friendships for the Hillsleigh girls because – it – we . . . think it distracts you from your work. That is of course the main reason for your being here,' she goes on, gathering confidence. 'That and to bring credit to your parents who have made sacrifices for your career.'

It is clearly not the moment to mention Beattie's scholarship. 'And of course to reflect credit on your college wherever you go in the world as a Hillsleigh girl. Where was I? Oh, yes.' A lifetime of end-of-term speeches has left an indelible mark on Miss Frobisher's style of rhetoric. 'Beatrice, we are here as if we were your parents, and I *feel* that your parents might not be happy at the thought of their daughter meeting unknown servicemen and taking tea with them in public.'

During that monologue Beattie has swiftly made up her mind.

'Oh, but they do know him,' she says innocently. 'We come from the same village, you see, Miss Frobisher. My family have known him for, ah – well, all our lives. He's been posted out here with RAF Bomber Command. And he simply got in touch as an old friend to ask if he could meet for tea some day. That's all,' she adds disingenuously.

Miss Frobisher visibly relaxes. The bit about Bomber Command has gone down very well.

'I see. Well, under the circumstances we'll say no more, Beattie' – this in itself was a better sign – 'but I'm sure you'll appreciate that in these troubled times certain standards have to be maintained. We all have our job to do, be it never so humble. Just as your friend's job is to defend our shores, so your job is to study with all your heart to teach the youth of the nation. This is a time for duty and self-sacrifice,' she goes on, polishing her glass on her black velvet bosom. 'And, providing you don't take advantage of the situation and there is no obvious decline in the standard of your work, I suppose there will be no harm in old friends seeing each other from time to time. But romantic friendships are not something I encourage for my girls, war or no war. You may go now, Beattie.'

Beattie closes the heavy oaken door and follows the tide of girls clattering into the ballroom for choir practice. Normally a thinly veiled ticking-off like that with its barely concealed appeals to heart and conscience would have had the desired effect of making her feel thoroughly wretched. Today, as she takes her place beside Louie in the contraltos, she is surprised to hear no voice of guilt or reproach inside her but simply a very cool little voice that quietly murmurs that the next time she will have to be a jolly sight more careful.

'If you've got to be back by ten-thirty, then I don't see the point in going, I don't really. And that's assuming you're *allowed* to go. Why, Jean Hicks wanted to go to a concert at the cathedral last week and she couldn't because it didn't end till eleven. One weekend away from college and one ten-thirty pass and that's it. I've had more freedom at Guide camp in the Wirral.'

Beattie is silent, staring at her botany notebook. She is sitting with Louie in the junior common room, formerly the trophy room, and various villainous shaggy and fanged heads glower down at them. Another group from their year are knitting by the fire and looking over the day's lecture notes. Louie is reading yesterday's paper in a desultory way for her current-affairs class. From the hall below comes the sound of the Greyshott boys practising

Christmas carols. Beattie sighs. Since that first radiant afternoon she's seen Brooke twice. They'd driven to Bury St Edmunds and walked round the abbey gardens. The second time he'd driven her straight to Norwich to the afternoon performance of *Shipyard Sally*. Louie had been pea-green with envy for days afterwards and kept complaining because Beattie didn't seem to remember any of the plot. Beattie had found the utmost difficulty in evading Louie's questions, for she was almost unable to bring herself to think back to that extraordinary afternoon. For the fact was that, once settled in the hot anonymity of the back row, Brooke had turned to Beattie and gently run a finger down the side of her face. The finger had then, equally gently, traced the soft outline of her lips and in a single mutual movement of need they had kissed with an intensity, the memory of which even now had the power to make Beattie's bowels turn to water. In vain did Beattie later demand of herself how she could possibly have let herself go, in the space of a few hours, from being a girl who had never been kissed to a girl who had had her brassière unclipped by a man who wasn't even her fiancé. Lying sleepless in her chilly bed that night Beattie had told herself fiercely that she must be mad. Nice girls, girls like Miss Virginia and Miss Lucy, the kind of girls that Brooke normally mixes with, would surely never behave in that way. It was well known that girls who gave themselves lightly never got married – unless they went to the colonies, where women were known to be in short supply and standards lower. And yet. And yet. Then she remembered the intensity of pleasures she had never known existed, how she had gasped with shock as Brooke had parted her lips and caressed her tongue with his own, the feeling of his hands moving lightly, suggestively over the georgette of her blouse; then later, much later, the drugged enjoyment she had felt when his hands were teasing the velvet of her hard erect nipples out of her brassière. She had timidly touched his face, his neck, felt the hard muscle of his chest against her hand and within felt the hard frantic hammering of a heart racing with a desire that matched her own.

Coming out of the cinema they had leant against each other like a couple of sleepwalkers in a trance. Now, too late, Beattie recognizes the true nature of that first intense glance from Brooke on that sunlit day last August.

It was at the end of that evening, after a prolonged, cold but entirely satisfactory kiss in the darkened lane, that Brooke had reminded her that it was his mess dance on Saturday and said he hoped she would be able to come. If she wasn't able to, he told her to ring the airfield and leave a message with the girl on the switchboard. Already Beattie is tempted to do just this. The problems of getting out that night and getting back at a reasonable hour seem almost insuperable, and she is beginning to doubt whether she was wise in confiding in Louie to start with. Beattie looks across the table at her friend with both affection and irritation. They had become friends because they were both scholarship girls. As Beattie had unpacked on that very first day the door had opened and what appeared to be a cheerful little girl had romped in. Her too-large coat with its square buttons hung awkwardly on her childish frame, while pulled over one eye she wore a black velvet beret with a diamanté Scottie dog pinned firmly on the front. Beattie had stared, the thought crossing her mind that perhaps unbeknown even to

46

Miss Frobisher a girls' school had been evacuated here as well. Then the little girl spoke.

'Hey,' she said, 'I'm Louie Brown, and I'm your room mate. I'm from Liverpool.' They had become partners for going on walks and doing handicrafts partly because it was convenient and partly (though neither would have admitted it) because they needed each other's support. The rest of their year were middle-class girls who spoke confidently of tennis clubs and amateur dramatic societies and whose fathers were doctors or accountants. Louie kept her background rather hazy, but Beattie knew her father had been a docker, and in her album Louie carried innumerable snapshots taken on something called the Birkenhead Ferry of a vivid-faced crowd of tiny people who looked like her. Beattie envies Louie her large warm quarrelsome family. Louie envies Beattie because Beattie has always had the luxury of a bedroom of her own. The Brown family, however warm, noisy and companionable, live in two rooms without a bathroom. Louie feels that their acquaintanceship is not yet sufficiently advanced to enlighten Beattie of these facts.

Both girls, deeply conscious of their luck and aware of their responsibilities, tend to keep themselves to themselves and work hard. But in the privacy of their chilly cottage they talk endlessly, even though their views of the world could not be more different. Beattie is impressed by almost everything, while Louie seems determined to be surprised by nothing. If Beattie sees the world through rose-tinted glasses, Louie appears to view everything through the cold grey light of dawn. Nowhere is this more apparent than in her attitude towards the Musgrave family. Try as she will, Beattie cannot seem to convey to Louie the absolute wonderfulness of the Musgrave family.

'They're your old man's employer's, aren't they?' Louie asks, perplexed by the amount of emotion with which Beattie invests the whole family.

'Well, yes. But it's much more than that; they own the whole village and they've been there for two hundred years and they're a very old family—'

'But what do they actually do?' Louie is unable to deduce anything from this that can inspire such admiration. 'I mean, is Mrs Musgrave the lady of the manor like in books? You know, taking soup to the poor and educating people and running the village school? And having cricket matches and visiting the sick?'

'Not really,' says Beattie, unwilling to face the fact that the Musgraves' sole contribution to village life is to inspire a sense of envy about the way they live.

'Then, I don't understand. All they've got is money, isn't it? They were just lucky, weren't they? What's so special about that? They don't seem to *do* anything.'

But it isn't what they do, thinks Beattie silently, by no means ready to prune the luxuriant growth of her fantasy. It is what they are. Surely people only have more money because they deserve it on the grounds of superior intellect, finer feelings? All of which she generously ascribes to Brooke. Which is yet another reason why she cannot resist the chance of appearing at his mess dance as his partner.

'You're miles away,' says Louie, looking at Beattie with her inquisitive bird-like stare.

47

'I was thinking I really can't go,' says Beattie despondently. 'The only way would be to lie and say I was going to bed early, then just go out through the woods and meet Brooke in the road at the end of the lane. . . .' As Beattie realizes what she has just said her voice dies away in disbelief.

'You might get away with it,' says Louie quietly, giving a warning glance towards the girls round the fire. 'But it would be a really daft thing to do, Beattie. You know what they're like here. They'd send you packing if they found out. And, anyway, what's Brooke doing encouraging you to take all the risks? It's no skin off his nose, is it, if you get caught?' She is silent for a moment. 'I just wonder what he's up to, that's all.'

'Up to? What do you mean?'

'My mum says there are only two things men want from women. Mothering, and a bit of the other. If he's got a mother, what does that leave?'

'Louie!'

'Lower your voice, do.'

'I think that's a horrid thing to say,' says Beattie vehemently. 'It just doesn't seem to cross your mind that he might just like me.'

'I'm sure he likes you. Why, anybody would. You're a pretty girl and nice; he'd be daft not to. But if his family's so grand and swanky what's he doing going out with you and not with someone of his own class? My mother says that money goes where money is and, though you see dukes marrying shop-girls on the films, how often do you hear about it in real life? Don't be angry with me, Beattie; it's grand seeing you so happy, but perhaps you should just see it as a bit of fun and not lose your heart to him. Men like that . . . and girls like us . . . the men have got all the cards. I just hope he's not leading you on, that's all.'

There is a long silence during which both girls ostentatiously get on with their work. In the end Louie says timidly: 'Oh, Beattie, don't be cross with me. I didn't mean to be nasty; truly I didn't. You're like one of my own sisters, that's all, and I wouldn't want one of them to come to harm.'

'That's all right, Louie. But I don't think Brooke is like you say he is, really.'

'If you're determined to go, there's only one way you'll manage it and that's by not telling anybody. Now, if you get Brooke to pick you up further down the lane . . .' she begins *sotto voce*, and the two heads are bent together for the rest of the period.

On the night of the dance Beattie goes back to the cottage early, claiming a quite genuine headache, and leaves Louie to hold the fort and pray that Miss Frobisher won't suddenly take it into her head to have a fire-practice at midnight. At quarter-past seven she climbs out of the window with her overnight bag, thanking her lucky stars that the small cottage that she and Louie now share faces directly on to the perimeter wood surrounding the park. There is no moon, and it's fortunately dry underfoot though bitterly cold. With the aid of her torch Beattie finds her way into the wood, wrinkling up her nose at the strong smell of deer, hoping that the herd aren't on that side of the park that evening. The track in the woods leads down the hill until it joins a cattle-track which will lead eventually into the lane. Beattie stands in the shadows at the foot of the hill and waits irresolutely. There is no sign of a car yet, and she tries to get her breath back while slowing down the thunder of her heart. All around she can hear woodland sounds, rustles, creaks and faint cries. It is like being at home walking through the woods at night with her father, and suddenly Beattie is smitten by the pangs of purest conscience. What would they think of her now, her mother and father, if they knew what she was up to or, worse, if they knew what she had been up to? All her life Beattie has been encouraged to think well of herself. Beattie is a good girl, is the general opinion round the village. If anybody is likely to get into trouble, it is those Kedge girls, used to running wild with a mother always pregnant and too tired to teach them right from wrong. Whereas Beattie, who had taught Sunday school since she was fourteen – why, even the village boys were always respectful to her. And yet she is standing in a darkened wood off to see a young man, whose intentions, whatever she confidently asserts to Louie, she is by no means certain of. It is not too late even now to change her mind, she thinks miserably, knowing perfectly well that, whatever her head says, she really has no intention of doing other than what her heart wants. It is a novel but not pleasant sensation to discover that all she has been taught can be quietly set on one side when the first real temptation comes along. Part of her longs to go on being the Beattie her parents approve of, but the other part, the stronger part, longs and longs to dance with Brooke.

Abruptly, far away, she hears the faint roar of a powerful engine and in spite of herself she smiles. She remains in the trees until the car stops a few hundred yards away. Behind the subdued glow of the headlights she can see the light of Brooke's cigarette, and with a light heart she goes down to join him.

'Glad you could make it,' he says, stowing her case in the back and turning around to kiss her lightly on the lips. Beattie is aware immediately that he has been drinking.

'Wouldn't have missed this for anything,' she tells him equally coolly as they roar down the darkened lanes towards the airfield.

As they turn in through the gate and Brooke salutes the sentry on guard, he says: 'Dinner is at eight; we have drinks first in the mess.'

One of the rooms has been set aside as a powder room, and it's full of girls putting on eye-black and adjusting their seams. No one takes any notice of Beattie as she takes off her coat and glances covertly to see what other girls are wearing. She brushes her hair until it shines, adds a little more of Louie's lipstick, and is ready. The clothes-list for Hillsleigh had specified one dress for evenings, and she and her mother had toiled over this particular dress for days. The material was very good. A farmer's wife had bought it for the harvest festival then taken against it and sold it at half-price to Mrs Blythe. The rich dark red taffeta has a full skirt and a modest 'V' neck and makes a satisfactory swishing noise. Brooke is standing outside talking to one of his brother officers.

'There you are,' he says. 'Let's go and have a drink.' Once settled into two leather armchairs, a white-coated mess attendant takes their order. 'What'll it be, Beattie, gin and tonic?'

Beattie hesitates. 'Oh, yes, fine,' she says.

'Whisky and water for me.' Brooke says nothing about her dress, and she prays it looks all right. Gareth is suddenly at their elbow.

'I thought it was you, lovely girl,' he says. 'You look a stunner. Drive all the lads here wild with desire, I shouldn't wonder. Eh, Brooke, I hope you don't intend to keep her to yourself all this evening. I haven't got a girl, you know. A man with my charm! It seems impossible, doesn't it?'

'Don't believe a word he says. He's got a perfectly good girlfriend in London whom he didn't invite because he thinks she's getting too keen.'

'Are all these men here officers?' asks Beattie.

'Of course,' Gareth says. 'You don't think we'd let in the non-commissioned riff-raff here, do you? But we're not proud. They'll be joining us afterwards for the dance.'

'What's the difference, then? Can't the non-commissioned people fly?'

'Sure they can fly, but not too often in case they get to like it. They haven't come in as officers, you see, like us pilots. They're only ground crew who've been selected to fly for a period. Decent chaps, most of them,' says Gareth vaguely. 'By the way, Brooke, the Adjutant just told me I'm being transferred over to Dancey's crew for a few days. You'll have a new chap. He only arrived today. Name of Charles Hammond. Do you know him? I gather he's an Oxford man.'

Beattie sees Brooke's face darken. For a moment he says nothing, making something of a play of lighting a cigarette. 'Yes, I know him,' he says finally.

'A chum, is he?'

'He certainly is not a chum,' retorts Brooke. He then mutters something of which only the words 'bloody pansy' are entirely audible.

'That only means he didn't believe in throwing chaps with suede shoes into fountains,' purrs Gareth maliciously, thereby greatly increasing Beattie's confusion.

'I don't know him that well. He was a year or two ahead of me. I was on his staircase for my first year. I never liked him.'

'Oh, I thought he seemed decent enough,' says Gareth innocently. 'I was talking to him earlier. I think you should be nice to him, Brooke. His girl-friend hasn't turned up.'

'Really.' Brooke stubs out his recently lit cigarette, drains his whisky and gestures to the mess attendant for more of the same. 'If it's that skinny intense dark haired girl – what was her name? – Elspeth – Enid – Eleanor, that's right – then she's no loss. She was always dashing round and asking you to sign petitions and join things. Something wrong with your drink, Beattie?'

'No, no.' Beattie hastily downs her first gin, perplexed that it's rather like drinking eau-de-Cologne and obediently accepting a second. She is about to ask Brooke about what he has been doing that day when Gareth glances over her shoulder and grins.

'Here he is now. Hello there, Charles! I gather Brooke's an old friend of yours?'

Brooke stands up, and Beattie turns to get a good look at the man who may or may not be a pansy. Oscar Wilde, so Louie had told her, had been a pansy, but she had neglected to say what this actually involved. It clearly has nothing to do with seed catalogues. Confused as to what to expect, Beattie finds herself staring at a man who's actually taller than Brooke. And there is nothing particularly flowery about him. Charles Hammond has almost matiné-idol good looks, thick dark curly hair brushed into sleekness above quirky dark brows, and a quick, assessing, confident glance.

Brooke stands up, and in the split second before the men shake hands Beattie sees both faces and with perceptions heightened by her second glass of eau-de-Cologne is aware of the hostility between them. They are perfectly polite. Perhaps this is what is wrong, in the face of all the joshing jocularity and banter going on around them. It occurs to Beattie that this is the first person she has ever met who not only does not adore Brooke – he doesn't even like him very much. And she sees that in some curious way Brooke's confidence is affected by this.

The three men make ritualistic remarks about planes, flying conditions and the mess. Charles Hammond looks enquiringly at Beattie, and belatedly Brooke remembers his manners. 'This is Beatrice Blythe. Beattie, this is Charles Hammond.' Charles smiles, holds out a hand and says he is pleased to meet her. Dinner is announced, and they all walk in together.

'Are you all right?' asks Brooke.

'Me? I'm fine,' says Beattie firmly and makes something of a business of arranging her napkin gracefully on her knee. But inwardly she is confused and angry. She saw the fleeting expression on Charles Hammond's face as his gaze had travelled from Brooke to herself. She recognized the look. It was contempt. And the contempt was aimed at her.

The volume of noise is considerable, and soon bread rolls are flying around the room. Beattie, smiling uneasily, concentrates on drinking her soup, which is excellent. Once her school had been taken to the theatre in Ipswich and a group of public-school boys had sat in the row behind. It had been jokes and shouts and whoops throughout the entire performance, like primary-school children at a picnic. Beattie wonders what the servants think about it all. It is an extraordinary sensation, being waited on. Brooke, of course, can take it so much for granted that he is soon complaining sharply that his wine-glass, which appears to Beattie to be sparkling clean, has a thumbprint on it. As they wait for the next course Brooke points out some of his friends. The hero of the day is apparently Dancey, the tall red-haired boy sitting almost opposite Beattie. That afternoon he had brought his plane in so low over the field where the squadron were playing rugby that they had all actually run for cover. It is seen as a terrific joke, even by the squadron's commanding officer, a man with sleek dark hair and small moustache.

'That's old Jimmy Shannon over there; he's Canadian, one of the short-term people. Barratt over there used to be a hairdresser. Seymour flunked his entrance to Cambridge and joined the RAF instead. Ah, good – venison.'

By the end of the meal the gin, the wine and the rich food are producing the most peculiar sensations in Beattie's head and stomach, and as she stares at herself in the powder-room mirror she hopes devoutly that the flush on her cheeks doesn't betoken drunkenness or a prelude to falling flat on her face on the dance-floor. The girl of the evening is clearly the tall girl who's come with Jimmy Shannon. Word has quickly got round that she's in the chorus

51

line of *Black Velvet*. She wears a small black satin cocktail-hat tipped over one eye, while her dress is black and skin-tight with a diamanté belt. Mrs Blythe would say she looked common, but Beattie, staring at herself in the mirror, feels she looks very dull in comparison. But what does it matter? Tonight is the first proper dance she's ever been to besides the harvest home in the village hall, and she is determined to enjoy it. Inside the mess-hall the tables have been pushed on one side and a trio of musicians have appeared and are tuning up. Brooke gives her his arm, and the evening suddenly takes wings. The first hour she dances virtually every dance, for there is a shortage of girls and if she and Brooke choose to sit out a number one of the other men will come over and request the pleasure. Beattie is aware that Charles Hammond has looked their way once or twice and has made no move to join them. She is glad. Tonight there must be no tension, no atmosphere. There is a light-hearted gaiety about the dance. Beattie knows, looking round at the well-scrubbed and unmarked young faces, that the memory of it will stay with her for the rest of her life. There is a feeling of danger acknowledged but held at bay by the music and the high spirits of the few hours.

Beattie does a rather flashy foxtrot with Gareth, then notices that Brooke's cheeks are red and that he is becoming very drunk. It is now nearly eleven o'clock.

'Lord, is that the time?' says Brooke thickly. 'In that case I think we ought to take some action, don't you?' He gets to his feet rather unsteadily, puts an arm round Beattie, and they make their way slowly out of the mess-hall. Thank goodness, thinks Beattie, overcome with relief, he realizes I've got to get home. With any luck I should be back at midnight. She's doubly relieved because the combined effect of rich food and all the dancing have made her feel very ill indeed. Outside Beattie is about to go into the powder room and get her coat when Brooke catches her arm.

'Where are you off to, then?' he enquires, staring at her indignantly.

'I thought I'd get my coat.'

'You won't need your coat. It's warm enough in here.' With that Brooke takes her arm and leads her protestingly along the corridor, opens another door and pushes her inside. They are in some small anteroom filled with piled chairs and discarded furniture. Suddenly Beattie feels very frightened.

'Brooke, I really must go home now. . . .'

For an answer Brooke pulls her clumsily to him and begins to nuzzle her neck.

'Don't you think it would be nice if we sat down and had a cuddle first? Or perhaps you'd like to invite me back to that cottage of yours and we could be on our own?'

Beattie has a sudden mental picture of the immaculate Brooke climbing through the undergrowth and scrambling over the window-sill with her. She begins to laugh, and Brooke's face darkens.

'What's so funny?'

'Brooke, I share a cottage with another girl and, anyway, I'd— you'd . . .' She begins to giggle again. It is a fatal move. Brooke does not like being laughed at.

'Well,' he says unpleasantly, 'if we're not going anywhere, I suppose we'll just have to get on with things here.' With that he pulls Beattie roughly down on to a hard little sofa and begins to kiss her in a way that has nothing to do with either liking or tenderness. Jerking her head round to his, he suddenly slides a completely unambiguous hand down the V-neck of her dress. Beattie is so taken aback that for a second she lies there unresisting in his arms, then abruptly sits up and pulls out Brooke's hand from where it is painfully and unerotically trying to tweak her nipple.

'How dare you do that,' she says furiously, angry not at what he had done but at the contemptuous way in which he had done it. 'How dare you think you can just grab hold of me like that—'

'Oh, come on, Beattie, it's a bit late for maidenly modesty now. I'm clearly not the first man to have a hand down your bra.'

For a second Beattie is so taken aback she cannot speak. Then with all her strength she shoves Brooke away and gets to her feet, and stumbles to the door almost in tears. The room is going round and round; there is an ominous feeling in her stomach. Fumbling for the door, Beattie staggers out and runs down the corridor. For a moment she does not know which need is most pressing – to get her coat, to run home, to be sick or simply to have a good cry. Nature makes the decision for her. She finds a door and stumbles out, the frosty air hitting her like a blow. Leaning against the hut wall, she is violently and humiliatingly sick. Tears pour down her cheek, and as she straightens up weakly and leans against the creosoted wall she's never felt worse in her life. Shuddering with cold and shock, she stands there wondering what to do and is sick again. Panic begins to set in. Where is Brooke? Leaning carefully on the wall, she finds the doorknob and totters back into the mess corridor. She knows she must look a sight. Of Brooke there is absolutely no sign at all. How will she get home? Can she walk? Is there a taxi? Would Gareth help? With considerably more confidence than she feels Beattie sets off in the general direction of the powder room. But it is no good. That treacherous swimming sensation in her stomach is still there and—

'Are you all right?' Somebody has grabbed her arm.

'No. I think I'm going to be . . .' A door beside her is thrown quickly open, and Beattie finds herself yet again out in the below-freezing November night vomiting on to the frosty grass.

The same person takes her arm again and says: 'You'd better come inside. Where's Brooke?'

'I don't know,' whispers Beattie dully and looks up. It is Charles Hammond, assessing her with that same dispassionate and unfriendly detachment.

'Do you want me to go and find him for you?' he asks shortly.

'No,' says Beattie violently. Then: 'Yes, I suppose I'll have to.' To her consternation her voice dissolves into tears. 'I've got to get home. I'm late already.'

'Come back inside and I'll find him. Do you know where he is?'

'He's—' Notwithstanding the paralysing cold that is turning her whole body into gooseflesh Beattie finds herself blushing. 'There's a sort of room at the end of the corridor,' she mutters. 'I think he's probably there.' She then adds aggressively: 'Can we go back inside, please? I'm freezing.' And silently Charles Hammond opens the door and leads her back into the dim blue light of the blacked-out corridor. From the direction of the mess comes the faint sound of music.

'You'd better get your coat. I'll see if I can find him.' With that Charles Hammond is gone. Beattie goes to the powder room, which is mercifully empty, and repeatedly rinses out her mouth and splashes her face. She looks like a ghost. Shuddering, she pulls on her coat, finds her case and goes outside. Charles Hammond is waiting, but of Brooke there is no sign. 'Brooke's out for the count,' he tells her without preamble. 'Do you know anybody else here?'

'Only Gareth.'

'He's gone to the pub apparently. I'm afraid I don't know which one.'

'Well, that's that,' says Beattie faintly and turns to go.

'Hey, what are you doing?'

'I'm going home,' she says bleakly. 'There doesn't look as though there's going to be a lift.'

'Don't be ridiculous. You can't walk home on a night like this. You'll die of frostbite. I'll take you.'

'You don't know where I live.'

'No, I don't know where you live,' he says nastily, 'but, then, you haven't told me, have you?'

They look at one another. Beattie is aware that she dislikes this man intensely. 'I've got to get back to Chillington. That's about seven miles away.'

'Then, we'd better get going, hadn't we?'

'You mean – you'll . . .?'

Charles Hammond sighs, takes Beattie firmly by the arm and marches her out of the mess into the pitch-dark frozen night. A few dry flakes of snow whirl around them as he walks purposefully to a row of cars and opens the door of one of them. Meekly Beattie gets in, her relief at not having to walk home so intense that she can hardly speak. 'Now, which way?' Mercifully the engine fires first time. Beattie give directions in a rather faint voice, then adds: 'This is awfully kind of you.'

'It is, isn't it?' observes her companion without any particular politeness, intent on keeping the car on the narrow dark country lane. 'I'll never get used to driving in the country,' he adds more to himself than to her.

'Where are you from, then?' asks Beattie with absolutely no interest.

'Manchester,' he says briefly. 'Do you know it?'

'No,' says Beattie. They drive the rest of the way in silence.

It takes Beattie some time to recognize the lane where she will begin her perilous walk back through the woods to the cottage. Charles switches off the engine and peers disbelievingly into the total blackness surrounding them. 'Is this it?'

'Yes. I think so. I can make my own way from here.'

'Why can't I just drop you at the main gates?'

'No!' says Beattie, horrified.

Charles turns round to stare at her. 'Does that mean you haven't got a late pass from this place?' Beattie is silent. 'Then, you're an even bigger fool than I took you for.' Beattie is speechless with anger, and about to shout something rude, childish and unforgivable when Charles interrupts: 'Can you get through these woods on your own or do you want some help?'

Reluctantly Beattie closes her mouth. She would love to be able to tell Charles Hammond exactly where he gets off. Even though he'd given her a lift it didn't give him the right to patronize and insult her. Then her stomach gives an ominous rumble and she remembers how frightening the woods had been on the way down. Instead she mutters sulkily: 'I'd like some help, if you don't mind.'

Actually it's not as bad as she fears, or is it just the comfort of another presence firmly grasping her gloved hand and steering her along over hidden ruts that are even now filling up with powdery snow? They walk in silence until they reach the outer edge of the wood. Never has a cottage seemed more welcoming. Beattie feels as if she could fall asleep now for ever if she could only get inside.

'How do you get in?' whispers Charles. For an answer Beattie leads him round to the back and indicates her bedroom window. Charles obligingly makes a step for her with his hands and she half climbs, half falls over the bedroom sill.

'Are you all right?'

Beattie's teeth are chattering so much that she can hardly speak. 'I'm fine,' she whispers hurriedly. 'Thank you for your help.' But he has already gone.

Louie has put a hot-water bottle in her bed and – oh, joy! – it's still warm. Beattie pulls off her dress with shaking fingers and falls, poleaxed, into sleep.

CHAPTER
THREE

ALL LOUIE'S POWERS of threat and persuasion are needed to get Beattie awake, out of bed and ready for a double period of country dancing. Beattie staggers through the day and retires early to bed pleading another headache. It is several days before she feels herself again, and a week before she can bring herself to tell Louie what actually happened. Louie hears her out quietly, nobly refraining to imply by a look that she had told her so. She merely comments that that Charles Handbag – or whatever he calls himself – seems like a decent chap.

Needless to say Brooke makes no effort either to get in touch or to apologize.

On the first Saturday of December they go into Norwich for their Christmas shopping. At the bus station they part company to perform separate errands, arranging to meet for tea at the Silver Café at four o'clock.

As most of Beattie's presents are either already bought or made, her footsteps take her to the nearest large bookshop. The very presence of books in their shiny covers, redolent of fresh paper and printer's ink, is enough to calm the spirit and cheer the heart. Beattie hesitates, torn between the sensual delights of the stationery department and the fiction section. As she does, she notices that for once the children's-book room is full to overflowing. Small girls with pigtails and scarlet faces are trying to worm their way through a phalanx of determined older women with rapt faces and autograph-books.

'What *is* happening?'

A female assistant totters by, weighed down by two or three dozen brightly wrapped new books.

'Don't you know?' she asks, faintly scandalized. 'It's Eve Baldwin! She's actually here doing a signing!' The assistant indicates the pile of books in her arms. 'We've got through six dozen of these already. I just don't know if our stocks are going to meet demand.' With that she cries, 'Gangway, please,' and throws her weight into the pushing throng.

Beattie is electrified. Rushing to the back of the crowd, she stands on tiptoe and impatiently scans the narrow room. There is a raised dais at one end where a woman is sitting at a desk bent over a pile of books. As she raises her head, Beattie's heart leaps. It *is* Mrs Hallett! Fancy her being here today!

Mrs Hallett sits composedly, busily penning inscriptions into her latest

œuvre, The High School Girls Rally Round. For many years she has made a
considerable income from writing stories about girls in boarding schools,
scoring a notable success with her very first book. The now legendary
Hello, Leafy Tree Girls! had introduced a delighted public to Trixie, Mimsie
and Neddy, the chums of the Lower Fourth, not to mention those irrepress-
ible madcaps Josie and Tonks. It was soon possible to turn out a minimum of
three of these titles a year, especially as her audience seemed to rely on the
absolute sameness of the stories. *Hello, Leafy Tree Girls*! was followed by
Leafy Tree Girls Here Again, then *Three Cheers for Leafy Trees*! and then
Leafy Tree Fights Back. At this point her publishers had tactfully intervened
and suggested Mrs Hallett spread her net wider. As a result *The Girls of
St Asphalt's* and then *The Girls of the Castle School* and *The Chums at Ivy
Towers* had sprung fully plotted from Mrs Hallett's fertile brow. And her
readership had grown rapturously. There seemed to be no limit to the nation's
appetite for snobbery, weak plotting and formula writing.

The money had rolled in. Schoolgirls of every shade and colour in the
farthest points of the Empire had pored over the adventures of those
pigtailed panama-hatted girls trapped permanently in the Lower Fourth,
caught like flies in amber in the lurid glow of a summer term on which the sun
never set. Mr and Mrs Hallett had continued teaching until it became clear
that Eve could support them both writing full-time while George managed
her affairs. There had been a series of moves to bigger and bigger houses
culminating, when Lucy was twelve, in the acquisition of a very smart house
in Kensington Palace Gardens. Lucy was summarily removed from the suburban grammar school where she'd been perfectly happy and installed
instead at Miss McFarquerson's in Queen's Gate Terrace, where she had
been intensely miserable until Virginia, largely to annoy the rest of the form,
had made a friend of her.

Eve Hallett is still extremely vague about her own unbringing but
remarkably focused when it comes to her husband's. George's family are
County people with no money but plenty of breeding. Adept at sloughing off
her own lower-middle-class origins, Eve Hallett had adopted her husband's
background and now has a country house and a daughter who will be
presented at Court. All these miracles Mrs Hallett has wrought herself out of
her own writing. No wonder she autographs *The High School Girls in Exile*
with such a light heart.

Or so thinks her daughter. Lucy is leaning against the wall, hot and
uncomfortable in her best tweed suit, listlessly handing up volumes. Mother
always does a lot of signings around Christmas. It helps to move stock,
according to her publishers. Lucy has attended these occasions before but
never as Mother's secretary. The day seems endless. And there is still tea to
come with the 'Leafy Tree Girls' of Norwich. If this is anything like the other
branches of the Eve Baldwin Fan Club, it will be crammed with moist-eyed
middle-aged women all wanting to tell Mrs Hallett about the character they
most identify with. Lucy, the obedient daughter, is suddenly possessed of a
most unusual sensation: she wants to give three piercing screams. Instead she
fiddles with her engagement ring and gloomily surveys the crowd. It is at this
point that she catches Beattie's eye.

Her response could not have been more gratifying: Lucy immediately abandons her mother and fights her way through the crowd barracking the shop's manager to keep the convoy of books for autographs flowing along.

'*I say!*' says Lucy, emerging hat askew but undeterred from the throng. 'What a bit of *luck* seeing you! How are you, Beattie? I've thought about you a lot. Are you enjoying your course?'

'Oh, yes, *very* much.' Beattie is warmed by Lucy's obvious pleasure at seeing her. 'Are you just up for the day?'

'Yes, Mother's doing two weeks of signing. This is the beginning of the second week. Roll on the end, say I.' Lucy pulls a mock-funny face. 'Mother says she has to do it to pay for my wedding. Have you got your invitation by the way?' Beattie is speechless. 'Well, perhaps your mother decided to hang on to it instead of sending it on, the post being as it is. They were sent out a week ago anyway. I do hope you can come.'

'I'd *love* to.' Beattie can hardly believe her ears.

'What are you doing in Norwich?'

'Just ambling around really.'

'You wouldn't fancy a cup of tea, would you? Mother's due to go on to the fan club in ten minutes, and I don't think I could sit through another tea like that again. Tell you what, I'll tell the publishing rep I'm skedaddling off and I'll meet Mother later on.'

Which is how twenty minutes later Beattie finds herself in the Silver Café with Lucy Hallett. It is still only quarter-past three. Beattie hopes and hopes that Louie will turn up in time to meet Lucy, who's insisted she drops the 'Miss' and is as friendly as can be imagined. Despite the earliness of the hour Lucy manages three toasted teacakes, then suddenly says: 'Gosh, I do envy you. Having something to do. I'm Mother's secretary now. It's what I thought I'd probably do eventually; I just didn't think it'd happen so quickly. I learnt to type when I was in Paris, you see. But' – loyalty to her mother struggles in her face with honesty – 'I don't suppose I'd mind it so much if it were peacetime. But I feel I ought to be doing more.'

'What about when you're married?'

'Oh, I expect things will go on the same way. You probably don't know – we're all moving to a safe house in Yorkshire after Christmas. The Manor has been requisitioned for a Doctor Barnardo's home.' Beattie listens hungrily as Lucy launches into a long account of what has happened in the village since the autumn. It is clear that Lucy has enjoyed her time there very much indeed and is already slightly wistful at the prospect of leaving.

'One feels so useful,' she says suddenly, absently stirring her tea. 'Major Jones calls me his right-hand man! I helped the Gatleys pickle their apples. Then I volunteered to help the schoolchildren pick rosehips.'

'Perhaps you can find some other work in Yorkshire.'

'I doubt it really. Mother's getting rheumatism in her fingers and she's finding it pretty hard to type. She needs a full-time secretary. So I suppose it'll have to be me.'

'How is – er – Miss Virginia?'

'Oh, goodness, she's far worse off than I am,' says Lucy unguardedly. Then loyalty to her friend makes her add: 'She really is having a frightful time. You know Mrs Musgrave refused point-blank to have any evacuees. Well, she's rather been hoist with her own petard because she's absolutely infested with relations. Three of Virginia's great-aunts arrived in September and an old cousin who's completely dulali plus Brooke's old nanny who's simply moved in and taken control of the house. Old Vir's going mad.' Lucy smiles in spite of herself.

'How is . . . your fiancé?'

'Oh, fine. Full of beans. He's at Aldershot now.' Lucy's face, which up to now has been animated and cheerful, takes on a more sober look. Beattie pours them a further cup of tea.

'What date are you getting married?'

'The twenty-seventh. First thing in the morning, then there'll be a reception at lunchtime and we'll spend the night at the Savoy. Hugh is expecting a posting abroad almost at once. We're not sure where to yet.'

'So you'll be saying goodbye almost straight away?'

'Yes,' says Lucy sternly. There is a silence for a moment as she debates something within herself. The Silver Café is filling up, but their own table faces into a corner and they are still alone. 'I suppose I just didn't think I'd be married this early,' says Lucy suddenly, raising a troubled face to Beattie.

'Are you – are you having second thoughts?' asks Beattie delicately.

There is another pause while Lucy studies her nails.

'It's not really that,' she says at last. 'It's more.' In a rush she says: 'Do you know, I've only met Hugh four times. It'll probably only be a dozen times by the time we get married. It isn't much, is it?'

'In peacetime I suppose it wouldn't be . . . but now—'

'Yes, I know. *Everybody's* getting married. Every time I open *The Times* there's another girl from school either engaged or married. It's strange, isn't it? If things had gone as we thought, Virginia and I would have been preparing for our season. And I suppose you'd have been in London. As it is . . .' She shrugs. Then suddenly her face lights up and she stares over Beattie's shoulder. 'I don't believe it! I really don't believe it!'

'What's the matter?'

'It's Brooke! I say! Oh, he's seen us! Of course, he must be stationed near here.'

Beattie is on her feet determined to leave. A voice speaks behind her.

'Hello, Lucy, how nice to—Oh, hello, Beattie.'

'What a coincidence,' says Lucy happily. 'First I meet Beattie, then I meet you. Virginia'll be mad when I tell her. Are you joining us?'

'Yes, if we may. This is Gareth my co-pilot and this is Jimmy Shannon.' There is a considerable movement of chairs as Brooke sits down next to Beattie and Gareth, Lucy and Jimmy Shannon fall into animated conversation. Beattie desperately wants to go and is about to do so when she sees Louie peering short-sightedly through the window of the teashop. Frantically she tries to telegraph that she does not want her to come in and is going to leave. But Louie has already disappeared and shortly reappears inside ploughing her way through the crowded tables then stopping short with perplexity.

'Hello there! Another friend?' says Lucy cheerily and pulls out a chair.

'This is Louie Brown, my room-mate at college,' says Beattie, conceding

59

defeat. She makes the rest of the introductions quietly, aware that Louie is giving Brooke, whom she has not previously met, a narrow look. Then Louie is caught up in conversation with Jimmy Shannon and Lucy talks to Brooke about the requisitioning of the Manor and life at the Dower House. Beattie listens and says nothing, painfully aware of Brooke's tense body beside her.

At four-thirty Lucy looks at her watch, gives a muffled shriek and says she must go and collect her mother as they're driving back to the village tonight.

'It's been topping meeting you, Beattie,' she says warmly. 'Have a good end-of-term. I'll see you at Christmas.'

'It's time for us to move,' says Louie wistfully; she has clearly been having the time of her life with Gareth and Jim.

'Come on, we'll walk you to the bus-stop,' says Gareth gaily. The five of them stroll out into the now pitch-dark streets of Norwich. The efficient nature of the blackout is such that in order to avoid actually breaking an ankle it is imperative to link arms, hold hands or in some way defend yourself. Gareth and Jim each take one of Louie's tiny arms, and the trio rolls off in the darkness, leaving Brooke and Beattie walking silently behind. Tentatively Brooke takes Beattie's arm and eventually speaks. 'Look, Beattie, I behaved extremely badly at the dance and I know it. I'm dashed sorry. We'd – I'd had too much to drink and I said some stupid things. I really am sorry. Is there any chance of seeing you on Sunday before you go home?'

'I'm afraid not,' says Beattie frostily.

'Oh.' They walk on in silence. Brooke looks quite crestfallen. 'Then, I suppose the invitation to your end-of-term do has been withdrawn as well, has it?' he says, trying to make light of it.

Beattie struggles. It would have suited her wounded pride to say no to Brooke, but another part of her is sorry for him and wavers. Yet another part longs to see the sensation he will cause at the school dance.

'It's not been withdrawn,' she says flatly. 'You can come if you want to.'

The dimly lit bus lumbers round the corner. The queue surges forward.

'Beattie.'

'What?'

'Hammond – he didn't try anything, did he?'

'No, Brooke. He was a perfect gentleman,' says Beattie with gentle irony, bids him good night and follows Louie up the stairs of the bus.

'Ee, he's nice, Jim is,' says Louie, her face glowing. 'Brooke's that handsome, isn't he? Did you make it up?'

'I suppose so.'

'That's just as well. You've had a face on you that would've tripped a duck the past three weeks. I wish I hadn't asked that Malcolm from the theological college to the dance,' she adds, vexed. 'I could have asked Jim! My word, that was the best afternoon this term!'

The day before the end of term the Greyshott boys go home at midday, leaving the girls to get the ballroom ready for the dance. At six o'clock Beattie and Louie return to the cottage to get changed and curl their hair. The snow has hardly settled, and it has been a clear sunny day. Beattie wonders if

Brooke has been out flying, as she takes the Kirby gribs out of her hair and rolls the front lock back in a heavy wave. 'You do look nice Beattie,' says Louie a trifle enviously. Beattie assures her that she does as well and, pulling on their wellingtons and carrying their best shoes, they make their way through the darkness to the darkened house. Inside the blackout is firmly in place and the ballroom is lit as for a ball. Beattie gazes round bright-eyed with anticipation.

By seven-thirty Brooke is late; by eight o'clock Beattie is furious. Is this his way of paying her back for being offhand when they'd met? Beattie lingers in the front hall as long as she dares, but there is no reassuring roar of Brooke's car, no ring at the door. Inside all is laughter and good cheer. The wind-up gramophone is blaring out 'Down Mexico Way'; everybody, even Miss Frobisher, is dancing. Beattie eats a mince pie, declines to dance, drinks some of the cider cup, then rebellion surges within her. Clearly the evening hadn't been smart enough for Brooke, but he might have had the decency to let her know instead of letting her waste a good hour and a half of dancing-time. With a sore heart she accepts the next partner and dances every dance until the last waltz at ten o'clock. Then they sing 'Auld Lang Syne', do the hokey-cokey and Beattie's first term is over.

Louie joins her in the cloakroom, her cheeks flushed. 'Malcolm is walking me back to the cottage. Do you mind?'

'Of course not. I'm helping with the clearing-up anyway. I'll be over later.'

By eleven o'clock the ballroom is stripped and tidied and Beattie walks home through the frozen park. Malcolm and Louie must have had a good hour in front of the fire, and she discreetly calls good night. Her bedroom wall is still warm from the fire next door. Beattie folds up her dress and puts it carefully away, blanking out thoughts about anything to do with Brooke, then goes to sleep wondering if her father will come to Ipswich to meet her. As usual she dreams she is at home – this time mysteriously she has left the pantry window open. She can hear the latch clattering against the sill, then suddenly wakes with a jerk to find that the noise is real and there is someone at the window. A hoarse voice outside is calling her name. 'Beattie! Beattie! Let me in, *please*.' Terrified, she pulls back the curtain and sees the pale blur of Brooke's face. 'What on earth,' she begins, then undoes the window as a blast of freezing air blows in.

'Beattie, thank God it's you,' he says, grabbing her hand with his own frozen one, and she finds he is shaking violently. 'Let me in, for God's sake let me in, something terrible has happened.'

She stares at him for a second. 'All right,' she whispers, 'but only for a little while. Hang on while I open the back door.'

Completely mystified, she pulls on her dressing-gown, goes into the sitting-room, puts a couple of pieces of wood on the fire, then goes through to open the back door. Brooke falls rather than walks into the cottage, leaning heavily against Beattie. Through the weight of his greatcoat she can feel his whole body shuddering. But it is not until they are safely in her own room that she can switch on the light and see his face. The sight makes her recoil. His eyes are staring, and his face is chalk-white.

'Brooke, what *is* it? What's happened?'

Brooke sinks on to the sofa and doubles up. At first Beattie thinks he's coughing in a hoarse and painful way. Then she realizes he is sobbing, and as she sits down beside him and puts her arms around him tears pour down his face unchecked. He clings to her for five minutes before he will explain what is wrong. His hair is sticking up and his mouth is square from weeping, his face gone from white to red.

'Brooke, tell me, what is it?'

Brooke looks at her as if he doesn't recognize her, then says 'Beattie' with difficulty and begins to feel in his pocket for a handkerchief to wipe his face. He lets her take him in her arms again, and she can still feel the tremors of shock in his body. 'Tell me,' she begs, gently pushing the hair back from his face. He begins to talk in a fast jerky voice, his face working uncontrollably as he speaks.

'Yesterday,' he starts abruptly. 'We were playing rugby yesterday when a message came through to stand by for orders for this morning. We'd been waiting for something big to happen and we were briefed last night. We were told we were going to mount an attack on the German navy at Wilhelmshaven. We were to supply nine crews. They told us we were going up at nine-thirty and would meet the other crews over King's Lynn.'

Abruptly Beattie begins to feel very cold.

'It all went well at first. We were in such good spirits because this was our very first operation. . .' Brooke's face contorts, and he begins to weep again. 'Oh God. It took us about three and a half hours to get there. It was all right at first because we had cloud cover, then the cloud broke up and left us like sitting ducks on a pond. And sure enough as soon as we hit their coast we ran into enemy flak. It was the first time any of us had seen proper anti-aircraft fire, and it was pretty bloody terrifying. We'd got to the target by then and lost our formation; then we saw what we were looking for – this bloody great battleship lying in the harbour. We'd actually opened our bomb-doors when the formation leaders suddenly led us round again, then told us over the bloody intercom that we were going home without dropping a single bally bomb. I couldn't understand what was going on, then suddenly the whole world went mad. Gareth shouted to me that Batty Parker was saying he could see Messerschmitts coming up behind us very fast, and the next thing we were attacked on all sides. I saw three planes go down in front of me.' Tears began to roll down his face again. 'Jimmy Shannon was flying next to me, and they got one of his fuel-tanks. The whole plane went up in flames, and I saw it spiralling down into the sea. We were ten thousand feet up, Beattie, and the planes were just dropping like flies being swatted. We were in the front, so we fought things off as best we could. God help those poor devils in the rear. They must have been shot to pieces. Then Gareth shouted that our fuel-tank had been hit, and I looked out of the turret and saw fuel dropping away and I thought: Christ, this is it; we'll go the same way as Jimmy Shannon. I began to pump the fuel from the fractured tank into one of the remaining ones,' explains Brooke dully, wiping his eyes again. 'I couldn't see anybody, and there was nothing to do except go on home and wait to be picked off one by one. Then quite suddenly at about ninety miles off Wilhelmshaven they sheared off and we lumbered home any old how.

Dancey suddenly appeared out of the clouds below us, and his fuel-tanks must have been hit because about ten minutes later I saw them beginning to go down and I saw the plane hit the water. God help them in the sea, the North Sea in December.' Brooke sniffs horribly. 'We kept on going as low as we dared to save petrol. Somehow we lasted out till we got to the English coast. We lost everybody else. We got to Gatton at about half-past three, and I fired a light to show the plane was damaged. They had everything lined up on the runway waiting for us – ambulances, fire engines, the lot. I got the old crate down somehow. And when we stopped we just fell out of the plane on to the grass. Even Gareth couldn't speak. Poor old bus was full of holes, and I swear we didn't have another teaspoonful of petrol left. I told the CO what I'd seen and said, "Where's everybody else?" and he said: "You're the first one home, Musgrave." ' Brooke begins to sob wildly again. 'And we sat in the mess – Gareth and the CO and me and the other fellows that hadn't flown – and nobody came back. Beattie, do you understand? Nobody came back except us. All the people you saw at the dance – Jim Shannon, Ed Dancey, Tony Barratt, Charles Hammond, Seymour, Hartwell, Johnny Wing-Stewart – they're all dead.'

Beattie stares at him, her face frozen in a horror that matches his own.

'And for what? We didn't hit any targets, we didn't do any damage. We weren't allowed to drop our bombs because the CO decided the boat was lying too near the bloody shore. To protect bloody Hun civilians. All those trained lives gone for . . . what? And why me? Why was I lucky when they weren't?'

'How many planes were lost?'

'I don't know,' says Brooke dully. 'Fourteen perhaps. I sat around but I couldn't sleep. I had to talk to you, Beattie. I had to come and see you.' They sit for a long time in silence; the fire is nearly out. 'Can I sleep here tonight? On the sofa I mean. I can't face going back to all those empty. . .' His voice begins to shake and he clings to her.

Beattie hesitates for a moment. 'You wouldn't get much sleep on this sofa,' she says at last. 'There's an extra bed in my room. Come on, you can sleep in there. I'll have to get you up early before anyone's around.'

It is nearly three o'clock. Beattie's room is still warm, but rather than put on the light she uses the candle by her bed. When she turns back to Brooke he has taken off his tunic. Beattie catches her breath. Without the authority of uniform there is something both touching and poignant about the hard muscled torso revealed in the dim candlelight. Brooke comes forward awkwardly, his face still tear-stained and anxious.

'Oh Beattie thank you . . . you've been so kind. . .'

He reaches out to show that he is grateful beyond words that at this his moment of greatest need she has not denied him understanding and comfort. Sensing this Beattie goes automatically to take him in her arms. But the collision of their bodies is like an electric shock. The embrace of consolation turns into a long dissolving kiss of hunger and desire.

Dimly Beattie is aware that Brooke has undone the belt of her dressing-gown and is undoing the buttons on her nightdress. Then suddenly every-thing comes sharply into focus and Beattie is filled with a wave of the purest panic. This isn't what she intended to happen. Or is it? Does she really want. . .

Then Brooke pulls off the rest of his own clothes and the shock of his naked body pressed full length against her own drives all coherent thought from her mind. Desire flows through every nerve in her body, hardening her nipples, making every part of her open, moist, willing.

Unresisting, Beattie is drawn to her own bed.

Once before they had seized each other like this, but then it had been simple desire that had fired their desperate need. But now in the cold grey light of the December dawn as they cling fiercely to each other, all the time they are unconsciously searching each other's face for proof that they are alive when so many close to them are dead.

CHAPTER FOUR

'*D*ON'T YOU LOOK a stunner, then? How did it go?'

'How did Miss Lucy look?'

'Did you bring us any cake?'

'Give the girl a chance. Is it still snowing?'

Beattie pulls off her mother's moleskin cape and sits down by the range. Little Ern climbs confidently on to her knee. The Blythe's kitchen, after the whirling snowstorm, presents a warm and comforting scene. Lily Kedge has brought the baby round and is sprawled in the rocking chair. A radically transformed Little Ern and Big Toby are in their pyjamas prior to bed. Mr Blythe is poring over a sadly depleted seed catalogue. Mrs Blythe is ironing, and the smell of hot linen hangs pleasantly on the air.

'The church was absolutely packed with people. Everybody turned up. The flowers looked a treat, Dad – everybody said so – and especially the ones in the library. Miss Lucy looked lovely. She had a cream silk dress with lots of pin-tucks. Mrs Hallet told me Norman Hartnell designed it. Miss Virginia was wearing pink with a long skirt and a bunch of pink roses. Miss Lucy was carrying lilies.'

'What about Mrs Musgrave?' The ironing goes unheeded as Mrs Blythe hungrily drinks in the details.

'Oh, a fur coat over a tweed suit and a little dark brown velvet hat with a veil. They gave me a whole wedge of cake. It's in my bag, Toby. Go on, have a bit now and you can have the rest tomorrow for your tea.'

'Did you have a glass of champagne?'

'I certainly did. There was a whole table covered in bottles.'

'You wouldn't think there was a war on,' observes Lily, less impressed. 'Are you coming to the New Year do at the village hall, Beat?'

'I expect so. I can't believe Christmas is really over. Hey, you two. Shall I take you upstairs?'

Taking a hand of each little boy, she guides them up the steep stairs, Toby holding the candle. They sleep in the little bedroom over the kitchen, which is the warmest room in the house. Once they are in bed she says their prayers with them and kisses them good night. In her own attic bedroom, shivering in the piercing cold, Beattie changes out of her best costume and comes back down to the kitchen, which has emptied in her absence. Her father is locking up the hens, Lily has taken the baby home but is coming back for supper. Beattie begins to lay the table as her mother puts away the ironing-board.

'Sit down and rest your legs a bit,' says Mrs Blythe, and Beattie sinks down gratefully in front of the range and rocks herself, staring at the red bars of the fire. Her thoughts are in turmoil. She had longed and longed to come home and now equally she is longing to be away again. It was only on Christmas Day when her period had started that she'd realized for the first time the risk she'd taken. Memories of that night, the violence of Brooke's news inextricably mixed with the physical shock of what had happened afterwards seemed to have put an immense distance between herself and her family. She simply cannot relax. Or is it just in this short period she has come to see her home and family differently? Beattie is appalled to find that within a few hours of being home she is longing for the palatial spaces of Chillington – or even the comparative luxury of the estate cottage. Compared to both, her own home seems shabby and cramped – why, even the Manor, in comparison to Chillington, is suddenly just a large family house! And she has never been aware before of the pungent odours of her home: the rank smell of the oil-lamps, the fusty interior of the kitchen, her father's hair oil – all offend her. Though this is as nothing compared with the atmosphere at the Kedges' cottage. Crammed as it is with animals, children, ferrets and wood-smoke, a dense wall of fug slaps you in the face when you open the door. Almost from the first moment she'd arrived Beattie has felt a frantic need to keep washing her clothes and herself. In the space of a few months her horizons have been radically widened and an appetite created for things she hadn't even been aware of. The need for space, the need for clean clothes, to be able to have a bath every day, the need to be with people like Brooke, who smelt pleasantly, anonymously of Pears Soap and his own Cologne. These things are not important, Beattie tells herself fiercely, doubly miserable in the knowledge that she is judging her own home and the parents who love her and finding them wanting. But it is like Pandora's Box. Once raised it requires more strength of character than she possesses to lower the lid firmly again.

Mrs Blythe irons on in silence, her cheeks flushed by the heat. Beattie examines her mother covertly. It is only in the light of Louie's emotional and frequently stormy postal exchanges with her mother that Beattie has become aware of how little she and her mother actually communicate. She had written home to tell Mrs Blythe about tea with Brooke and she knew her mother would be as impressed as she was about the invitation. But nothing further was said. Conversation in the Blythe household always related to practical things. Would Beattie be wanting a pudding? Would Mr Blythe be late for supper? Did the peaches have leafcurl this year? That sort of thing. A statement of her feelings would have embarrassed her mother and been greeted by silence. But she could not but be curious, surely, of what was going on. Mrs Blythe was the late Mrs Musgrave's personal maid, and specifically from her Beattie has inherited her notions of the glamour and the uniqueness of the Musgrave family. For her mother those ideas of respect and uncritical admiration have remained unchanged for twenty years. Beattie is horrified to find herself thinking cynically that, though her mother would be appalled beyond measure to find her only daughter was no longer a virgin, when she found out who the seducer was, though she would be equally angry, a part of her would be impressed beyond words that it was Brooke Musgrave and not Harry Tonks from the forge. None the less she is afraid to be in her mother's presence for too long in case the truth is visible in her face.

'Mother,' Beattie says suddenly, 'I think I might go back early to college. I've got that much work to do this holiday and it would be simpler. . .'

Disappointment struggles in her mother's face, but she says coolly: 'Just as you like, Beattie. We'll be sorry to see you go, the boys especially.'

Beattie is silent.

'There's nothing wrong, is there?'

'No,' says Beattie quickly and looks at her mother. 'Why?'

'You seem so absent. There's nothing on your mind, is there? If you're unhappy at college, you don't have to stay there. We're very proud of you and we wouldn't like you to be unhappy.'

'No,' says Beattie hastily. 'I love it there.'

There was silence again, then her mother said: 'You don't mind us having the kiddies, do you?'

'Oh, Mother, of course not.'

From being overnight visitors Big Toby and Little Ern look like becoming fixtures in the Blythe household for the time being. In November a stout, harassed-looking woman had appeared on the doorstep with a baby, and said she was the children's mother and she'd been billeted there as well, much to Mrs Blythe's consternation. She had stayed three days in Beattie's room, tried cooking for the boys, burnt all the saucepans black, then told Mrs Blythe she liked them all but was afraid that 'His Mother', by which she apparently meant her mother-in-law back in Stepney, would set Him against her if she stayed away much longer and the children needed a father, and with that she'd walked the two weeping boys to the village, and persuaded one of the WVS women to drive her to Ipswich for the London train. Mr and Mrs Blythe were still recovering from the shock of this when a week later there was another knock at the door and another WVS worker turned up with Little Ern and Big Toby all over again, with a note from their mother saying that she'd decided they were better off where they were. In the intervening week Little Ern had started to wet himself again. Since then there has been nothing beyond a letter and a pound note to buy the children a toy for Christmas.

'No, I love having them here. There's nothing wrong, Mother, really. Don't fret.'

The back door opens again, and the rosy face of Lily Kedge appears. 'Our dad says it's the coldest winter ever,' she says, taking off her coat, gloves and muffler. 'The road's filling up nicely with snow. Lots of cars going up to the Dower House. They've got a big dinner-party with the Halletts tonight to celebrate Miss Lucy's wedding.'

'Who's up there?' says Beattie quickly, and is aware from the quick movement of the mother's head that she is watching her.

'Oh, just all the usuals plus some members of the Rotary Club because of

Mr and Mrs Hallett going. Mrs Musgrave was going on yesterday in the post office about how Brooke hadn't been able to come. She was that disappointed. Still, I expect they missed him. Miss Virginia goes around with a scowl on her face that'd turn the milk. I bet she'll miss Miss Lucy.'

There is a discreet tap at Virginia's door.

'Mrs Musgrave's compliments and would you come down to the library, please, and help with the drinks?'

'I'll be down in ten minutes,' says Virginia crossly, and stays exactly as she is, still wearing her dressing-gown, sitting chin-in-hand gazing listlessly into her dressing-table mirror.

Tonight, the night of Lucy's wedding, life has never seemed so unutterably terrible. The war, so far as Virginia is concerned, has simply been a loss of comforts plus a severe curtailment of freedom. Since September she has been closeted with her mother and a series of elderly relatives and 'guests'. Indisputably the most unwelcome is the loathsome Nanny Holwill, who had nannied Brooke but not Virginia and is currently resident at the Dower House in some vague housekeeping role. Unfortunately, she is capable of nannying and nothing else, and in the absence of real children has taken to trailing Virginia ruthlessly round the house, quizzing her as to the tidiness of her drawers, demanding visible proof that Virginia has a clean hankie and generally behaving as if she is a five-year-old under suspicion of a particularly dirty habit.

The climax had come last night when Nanny had attempted to tuck her up in bed, whereupon Virginia had found herself screaming: 'For God's sake, I'm eighteen. Leave me alone!' Whereupon Nanny, pausing only to fold up Virginia's clothes, had simply commented that she must be constipated.

But all this is as nothing compared to the fact that Lucy is now a married woman and about the leave the village. It is the final blow, the final twist of the kaleidoscope that has turned the whole of normal life upside down and back to front. It was not simply that she would miss Lucy as a friend. Much more than that, it is only at the moment of Lucy's going that she has realized how useful her friend's social uncertainty has been in bolstering up Virginia's own frail ego. The Halletts have come to their money, if not by trade, then certainly not by the time-honoured methods of land and inheritance. In the eyes of the Musgraves the Halletts are 'charming people' but 'not quite'. As long as Lucy had been there to demonstrate the 'not quite' Virginia had been very sure of who she was herself. Now she can no longer be so sure.

Virginia goes to brush her hair, inadvertently dealing herself a painful blow on the temple with the wrong side of the brush, and sits there with tears of despair in her eyes. It had all seemed so simple last summer. She and Lucy would be presented together, but it was Virginia who was going to make the match of the season, the match that would make people say what a clever little girl that Musgrave girl must be. And so pretty! Lucy was perfectly welcome to be the chief of the twelve bridesmaids at the very large society wedding, the sole purpose of which would be to silence for ever any rumours, however truthful, about the Musgraves' finances. In reality, far from achieving this marital grand slam, the unthinkable has happened. Lucy is already married and she is not. Married, and she, Virginia, has never even had a serious admirer! Admittedly Hugh would never have done for her – just another public-school boy with a dull job in the City – but the difference between knowing you're beautiful and actually having a man to tell you so is profound. And with Lucy about to disappear altogether Virginia finds herself brooding more and more about her own position.

What had gone wrong in the Musgrave family? It wasn't just the lack of money, though that was certainly part of it. The estate had been bankrupt by the time Virginia's father had inherited – partly through mismanagement, partly through the consequences of the previous Mr Musgrave having married a young and extravagant wife. Fortunately, she had been too modern to want children. The money had gone out and nothing had come in. But plenty of families had had financial problems since the Great War, thinks Virginia restlessly. There had to be other factors to make her parents so out of favour with the rest of the family. Perhaps their marriage, so long publicly deteriorating, had made them socially unreliable. As it was, Mrs Musgrave was invited to some houses but not to others. Mrs Musgrave's uncle, the Earl of Stoughton, had not invited her to the castle for some years. And Virginia is keenly aware that her aunt Lady Edridge had had to have her arm twisted to take on the job lot of presenting herself and Lucy at Court. But the final straw had been when Virginia had received a card just before Christmas from one of Mrs Musgrave's cousins. The titled and elderly old lady had retired to a safe house in north Devon until hostilities ceased. She had written not to ask Virginia to stay but to state that since Virginia was clearly not now going to be presented would she be interested in becoming her companion. Nothing clarified more clearly to Virginia the position in which she was now regarded by her richer relations. Nobody, *nobody*, thinks Virginia savagely, is going to patronize *me*.

In the drive below her window she hears the sound of tyres inching slowly up the snowy drive, and the slamming of car doors, muted laughter and cheery greetings. Virginia takes off her dressing-gown and pulls a dreary blue crêpe dress over her head, changes her shoes and sits down to brush her hair energetically.

Something has got to be done, and it is clear that only Virginia can do it. Quite simply, no one else cares. 'I *will* get away from here,' vows Virginia. 'If it means being nice to people, I'll manage it somehow.'

A sprinkling of lavender water on her handkerchief and Virginia is ready for the fray. She checks her appearance coldly in the mirror, straightens her shoulders, goes down to the library her chin held high.

Lucy travels back to Ipswich by train. To get a seat at all is a miracle. The blacked-out overhead light makes it impossible to read, but Lucy is perfectly happy with her own thoughts. She thoroughly enjoyed her wedding and the reception in spite of the piercing cold. A friend of Hugh's had driven them to London and settled them very snugly into the Savoy. Then there'd been a dinner-dance, and Lucy had been able to wear her going-away corsage. Hugh had been lit up with excitement. It was all part of the strangeness of the day to get into bed with him later on. In spite of herself Lucy colours at the memory and wonders if she's pregnant. Somehow she's sure she isn't. They'd been up early this morning in the best of spirits and in plenty of time for Hugh's train to Southampton from Waterloo.

'Take care of yourself, old girl,' Hugh had said tenderly to her. In the excitement of being a married man on the verge of a journey he had been filled with a dim exultation. But none of it seemed real somehow; if it hadn't been for the ring on her finger, Lucy felt she might simply be seeing the events happening to someone else in a film. Abruptly she had pulled herself together. 'You take care of *yourself*,' she had told him fondly, sorry that her acquaintance with Hugh was so fragmentary that she was unable to add specific wifely injunctions about remembering to keep his chest dry and to make sure his socks were aired.

Hugh had leant out of the window and kissed Lucy without embarrassment. The whole platform was a sea of service men and women embracing. Then the guard had blown his whistle and the doors had slammed. The engine shuddered and the train moved forward. Lucy had stood waving until the curve of the track carried Hugh's train from view, leaving a huge vacuum behind it. Then eyes were dried, handkerchiefs resolutely put back into handbags, and with the other wives and girlfriends Lucy had trailed back to the barrier to hand in her platform ticket and get on with her single life.

The journey from Liverpool Street seems to last for ever, with constant mysterious stops and starts owing to signal failure and snow on the line. For most of the journey Lucy stares across the carriage at a painting of Windsor Castle. She's promised to write to Hugh every day, even though it may be some weeks before his first letter reaches her from whichever unknown destination he has been posted to. Hugh suspects it is Egypt, and Lucy tries to imagine him in khaki shorts beside a camel.

Time passes. Lucy examines the faces of the people crammed into the seat opposite. On Lucy's side they are mainly service people, while facing her are a vicar, an old lady who looks like Queen Victoria and smells of mothballs, a housewife with a little boy dozing on her knee, and a girl with red cheeks and a brown felt hat who's intently studying a pamphlet on dairy farming notwithstanding the half-light. Unaccountably Lucy suddenly feels her high spirits beginning to leak away. She doesn't have to search too far for the source of her depression. It's the going to Yorkshire or, rather, not so much the going as being Mother's secretary. And in a *town*. Lucy had consoled herself with mental pictures of life on a windswept moor not too far from Haworth Parsonage, only to find that her parents have rented a Georgian house almost in the heart of York. Lucy sighs deeply and tries to sleep.

At 8 p.m. they pull into Ipswich station. Baines, the Halletts' elderly chauffeur, is there to meet her. He's been waiting for three hours but does not seem to hold Lucy – whom he likes – responsible for the present vagaries of the train timetable. Lucy climbs into the front seat in express contradiction of what her mother has told her and is soon engrossed in an account of her twelve-hour honeymoon.

The snow has been falling heavily all day, and the Daimler inches its way along the impacted roads. All is well until they turn off the Ipswich road and start descending through the lanes that lead to the village. The roads between the high hedges are thick with drifts. The old car slips and skids its way down the hill, until they round the corner that will lead them into the village street. The wheels spin frantically, fail to gain purchase on a bend like a sheet of ice and the back of the car slides gracefully into the hedge, loosening a perfect avalanche of snow.

'Oh, drat,' says Lucy, resigned, and goes to get out.

'Don't you go stepping out in those good shoes,' admonishes Baines. Lucy is still wearing her going-away costume and the fur coat that is her parents' wedding present to her.

'Well, one of us will have to go. I say, Father's wellies are usually in the boot. If you get them out for me, I can give you a hand putting the sacks under the wheel.'

In spite of Baines's protests Lucy changes her shoes and determinedly starts to jack up the back wheel. After three false starts the car surges forward on to the road.

'You'd best get in, Miss Lucy. Your parents will be that worried—'

'I tell you what, Baines, why don't you drive on and take my luggage in and I'll walk the last mile and get some fresh air.'

Baines is affronted.

'Miss Lucy, I couldn't do that; your mother'll go mad—'

'Well, tell her it was my idea. I just feel like the exercise. I'll be home in twenty minutes.'

Baines takes some convincing, but Lucy is firm, and finally the Daimler disappears off down the lane and Lucy is alone. For a moment she stands irresolutely, listening to the immense reverberating emptiness of the country-side. A fox is barking somewhere down in the woods, the wind blows softly through the hedges on either side of the road loosening showers of powdery snow which fall like castor sugar on to the dead dry leaves of last autumn. The sky is a huge empty glittering bowl, not a cloud obscuring the brilliant cold clusters of stars. In the intense frosty darkness the only illumination is the faint glow of starlight on the glimmering snow.

Lucy breathes deeply, her hands in her pockets, oblivious of her smart hat and costume, her fur coat and wellington boots. An immense feeling of peace flows through her. Her lungs ache from taking huge gulps of frosted air. This is the right place to be. In London fleetingly she had recalled the old Lucy. There is something about towns and smart clothes that will always make her feel awkward and clumsy. But against this background she is suddenly in proportion. Here her height and strength are assets, not social liabilities. Whistling, Lucy marches briskly down the road towards the village. It will not be easy explaining to Mother why she doesn't want to be her secretary, but she will manage somehow. And tomorrow she will find out exactly how to join the Women's Land Army.

CHAPTER
FIVE

'*W*HO EXACTLY is this dance for?'

'Don't ask me. Some refugees, I expect. *Don't* squash my dress. Move over to your side of the car.'

'You've got all the rug.'

'I need it more than you. My God, this weather.'

Mrs Musgrave peers dismally through the Daimler window to the blacked-out below-freezing landscape of Suffolk.

'The Towers will be like a tomb. Why Piers bought it if he wasn't prepared to heat it properly is beyond me. And Grace will be banging on about shortages. Why does one ever leave one's own hearth?'

Virginia could tell her but refrains from doing so.

'And, for God's sake,' goes on Mrs Musgrave, giving the plaid travelling-rug a savage yank, 'try to *look* as if you're enjoying yourself. Out of respect for my brother if nothing else. Not that I suppose anyone will be paying us any attention anyway.'

With the sigh of a generous-hearted woman tried beyond her strength by the insensitivities of the world, Mrs Musgrave leans drearily back against the leather upholstery.

Virginia is silent. She has no intention of putting on the usual act of boredom with Uncle Piers and Aunt Grace, whom she likes very much, notwithstanding the frugal nature of their heating. Uncle Piers is mother's brother, but fortunately not a bit like her. And with (Virginia suspects) a rather low opinion of his only sister.

The roads are still deeply potholed after the snow, and it takes Virginia and her mother over an hour to travel the fifteen miles to Uncle Piers's home. When finally glimpsed beyond a double avenue of elms it presents a curiously inappropriate scene for revelry, a pitch-black cube set against watery clouds without a single sign of life. Inside there is light but very little else.

Having being greeted by their Aunt Grace, Virginia and her mother are directed to the Chinese bedroom designated the powder room for the evening. There is a tiny ineffectual fire in the grate, notwithstanding the acres of timber outside, and the February wind, roaring round the house, ensures a cold of paralysing proportions. Mrs Musgrave reluctantly removes her mink, dabs some more Arpège on her pulse-points, and disappears as fast as possible, desperate for a whisky and warmth, anxious not to saddle herself with Virginia for her entry.

On her own, Virginia fiddles with her hair and looks round the room in a proprietorial sort of way, for with Brooke she had stayed in this house quite often during her parents' many holidays abroad. She is almost sure that behind that picture is a record of their heights at various ages. As she is on the point of climbing on to a chair to investigate, the door opens to reveal a timid-looking girl wearing steel-rimmed glasses and a magnificent fur wrap. Brow furrowed, she contemplates Virginia, then her face lights up.

'I say! Virginia, how lovely to see you.'

'How lovely to see *you*,' says Virginia, surprised but touched by the warmth with which the other girl is regarding her.

It is Lady Cecily Easte, Virginia's second cousin and Uncle Piers's god-daughter. Virginia's mother and Cecily's father, the fierce and legendary Earl of Stoughton – the one who no longer invites them to his castle – are cousins. Virginia has met Cecily many times at the Towers, regarding her with a mixture of envy and disdain. Her family is so indisputably correct that blood of an almost navy hue must circulate through Cecily's rather attenuated frame. However, Cecily's deep sportiness, her tendency to involve herself in good works, and the habit of quite unconsciously employing the vocabulary of the 'Leafy Tree Girls' would all have made her a figure of fun were it not for the fact there is something basically decent and deeply likeable about her. Plus the fact that, as even Virginia is aware, it cannot be very cheering being the only plain girl in a family celebrated for its beautiful daughters. There is the additional fact which Virginia will never acknowledge: Cecily has always liked Virginia, and Virginia is not so flush with friends that she can afford to discourage those who find her agreeable.

'What a lovely surprise. What are you doing down here?'

'Oh, just visiting Uncle Piers and Aunty Grace,' frowns Cecily, looking round at the room in some surprise. 'I don't think this can be my bedroom, can it? I must have taken a wrong turn after the loo. Still, I don't suppose it matters if I leave my wrap here. Uncle Piers tells me I won't need it. I say, I do like your dress. And what pretty shoes.'

'You look . . . lovely yourself,' says Virginia, aghast. Cecily idly peels off her sable stole to reveal a truly horrible pale blue satin décolletage. Her exposed shoulderblades jut out like coat-hangers designed for some heavy outdoor garment. In the absence of any bosom to support it the low-cut bodice of her frock falls dispiritingly forward into a peak. Why doesn't she pad her bra? Virginia finds herself thinking whilst gazing nervously at her own reflection in the mirror to make sure the same thing has not happened to her own dress. But it is all right. Her own crisp grey tulle reveals a splendid curve of white bosom. However, where jewellery is concerned Cecily is clearly the winner – assuming, that is, that those diamonds are real, and there is no reason to think they aren't. Virginia fingers her own measly string of pearls. What jewellery she possesses is in trust for her, and her mother resolutely refuses to lend her any of her own ('Terribly unlucky, darling!').

Normally, having acknowledged Cecily, Virginia would have speedily unloaded her. But today, determined to take advantage of any opportunity that comes her way that might change her luck, Virginia makes an effort to be friendly.

'It's simply years since I've seen you. It must have been two or three summers ago at Oxford.'

Cecily flushes with pleasure. 'That's right. I was having tea at Christchurch. What a lovely day it was. Oh, golly,' adds Cecily, suddenly clasping her ears. 'I've still got my glasses on. I quite forgot. Mummy made me promise I'd take them off for the evening.'

She folds them up and pushes them into a dusty black satin evening bag that had clearly done duty at Queen Victoria's funeral. Her eyes, now revealed, appear to have no colour at all. She also appears to have no eyelashes. Virginia wonders if it is worth telling her that the glasses have left a prominent red ridge across her nose, then decides that Cecily is probably too short-sighted to know or care. She watches as Cecily appears to screw powder into her nose with quick sharp jabs like somebody killing ants. Cecily completes her *toilette* by rubbing herself vigorously behind the ears where the spectacles have presumably pinched and in doing so dislodges a magnificent diamond earclip which crashes noisily into the hairpin-bowl.

'Goodness, it is a bore wearing glasses and earrings at the same time,' she remarks crossly. 'I suppose it's just such a long time since I had them on, you see.'

'Spectacles?' says Virginia helpfully.

'No, earrings,' says Cecily, backing short-sightedly away from the dressing-table mirror to get the full effect of her dress. In doing so she trips over a stool and somehow manages to bring down an occasional table and a lamp-stand as she hits the floor. Somewhat abashed, she scrambles to her feet and with Virginia's help rights the furniture. Virginia firmly steers as they negotiate the bedroom door and make their way down the double staircase to the hall.

'You see, I've just been too busy to socialize,' goes on Cecily apparently at random before Virginia realizes she is still enlarging on the earring situation. 'We've been so busy at the castle with my WVS work *and* I had to run the castle Cub pack. Their chap was called up, and I've hardly had a free moment since last August.'

Virginia is somewhat nonplussed. 'Did you have a good Christmas?'

'Christmas! It was the most extraordinary time ever! You know we had twenty evacuees at the castle?'

'No,' says Virginia faintly.

'Well, there was the Christmas party to organize for the children and one for the Cubs of course, and then a carol concert for the troops. . . Did I tell you we've had a battalion in the long meadows since November? It's made hunting frightfully tricky, I can tell you. It's been non-stop, so as a result I haven't had to dress up for simply ages. This is one of the dresses Mummy had cut down for my season. A bit of a laugh, isn't it? Mummy was frightfully worried I'd get bored but, my word, I wouldn't have missed it all for anything.'

Downstairs in the black-and-white-flagged hall the temperature is about half a degree warmer owing to oil-stoves judiciously placed where they can blow their heat through the open front door. Uncle Piers does not believe in raising the blood temperature too much – he'd seen what a hot climate had done to his soldiers in India.

Thirty people sit down to dinner, most of whom Virginia has known almost all her life. The parents have houses in and around Belgravia, and their country places are within a twenty-mile radius of Ipswich. With their children, Virginia and Brooke had played croquet, gone to dancing classes accompanied by their nannies, spent summers at Cromer and started Cubbing. It is something of a revelation for Virginia to realize that she couldn't care less if she never saw any of them again.

'I say, you look awfully . . . fit,' says the young man on Virginia's right. It is Giles Rickinstall; he has had a crush on her since she was twelve. Then he'd been a plump dull thirteen-year-old with inexplicably bad breath. Time has not succeeded in varying his infinite sameness. He is however, apparently accustomed to people conducting conversation with him with averted faces. Nannie Holwell would have loved him, thinks Virginia meanly. She would have made it her life's work to eradicate his halitosis.

'Why, thank you, Giles,' Virginia says sweetly with a faint sideways smile that has nothing to do with flirtation. 'You look rather impressive yourself. I didn't know you were in the Army. Are you on leave?'

'Two-day pass,' he informs her importantly. 'Battalion's been moved.'

'Where to?' asks Virginia idly.

'Can't tell you,' he says, rolling his eyes and pursing his lips importantly, then ruins it all by leaning forward and whispering piercingly in Virginia's face: 'Banbury actually. Why, Virginia, you look quite pale. Would you like another drink?'

'No, just a little fresh air,' says Virginia faintly.

After the meal he hangs around making the hole in the carpet bigger with the toe of his dancing-pump, then finally gulps: 'Do you think you might want a . . . er . . . dance, later . . . with anyone? Not now of course. Later? Soon? Quite soon? Now? Oh, I say!' He jumps to his feet, nearly overturning the chair in his eagerness, and offers Virginia his arm as he leads her into the first dance of the evening.

Tonight, out of sheer perversity, Virginia has decided she will be the girl of the evening and sparkles accordingly. She's somewhat taken aback at how easy it is. A few smiles, a few weak jokes, and the men are queuing up to dance with her. She flings back her pretty head and frankly roars at their feeble sallies, and when conversation flags makes spirited remarks about men in uniform and how awful the weather is. For once the evening seems to be flying by. Even the music is better than usual. The five-piece band seem determined to play every one of Virginia's favourite songs. In the interval, when they are standing near the musicians, Virginia notices to her amusement that the piano-player is giving her what Nanny Holwell would call 'hot looks'. He's a thin pale-faced black-haired youth who plays with a faint smile of amusement as he watches the dancers.

'A Jew,' says Virginia's partner as he follows her gaze. 'But quite talented, don't you think?' Virginia murmurs something and turns away, but not before she has seen the young man's face and the ironic gaze he bends on her partner before shrugging and turning back to his drink.

Cecily is nowhere to be seen. Virginia wonders briefly if she has danced herself out of the french windows by mistake and fallen into the ornamental lake. But it seems unlikely. Presumably they would have heard shouts. But where is she? With an injunction to Giles 'not to flirt with anybody else' Virginia goes out into the hall, but still no Cecily. As she pauses uncertainly the sharp-eyed piano-player appears at her elbow and smiles at her.

'I hope you're enjoying the music,' he says in a respectful voice which does not conceal its cockney vowels or its impudence.

'I think you're frightfully good.'

'Do you hear that, lads? She thinks we're frightfully good.' He is teasing her and she knows it, but it is a novel experience and it amuses her.

'What's your name? Perhaps we could play a song with your name in it?'

'I don't think so. It's Virginia.'

'Oh, there's a shame. If you'd been called Daisy, there's several I could have played. You're awfully pretty,' he adds suddenly.

'I know,' she says.

He looks at her with new interest and laughs. 'No flies on you, are there? Are you ever in London?'

'Sometimes,' says Virginia guardedly.

'We play at the Pot of Gold. Come down and see us and I'll buy you a drink. And your discerning young man.'

'He's not my young man,' says Virginia, flushing.

'All the better. Come down on your own, then.'

His eyes meet Virginia's, half-ironically, half-seriously. She raises her chin to him.

'I'll think about it,' she says coolly.

She can hear the rest of the band laughing as she makes her way, humming, up the stairs to the powder room to discover Cecily sitting with three girls that Virginia has particularly disliked since dancing school. They give Virginia frigid hellows. Clearly she is having far too good a time and not spreading the men around fairly. Virginia ignores them and straightens her hair. Her normal pose of boredom had originated entirely as a mother-tease, and it is intriguing to discover that she can irritate far greater numbers of people simply by appearing to be enjoying herself. It is rather cheering. When she emerges from the lavatory Cecily is alone. Her glasses are back on and she is reading *Dombey and Son*.

'Oh, Cecily! What are you doing that for? Come down and dance.'

'I don't go for that stuff much,' says Cecily gruffly.

Virginia sees that her eyes are red behind her glasses. 'Is there something wrong?'

'No, nothing,' lies Cecily gallantly, and two tears detach themselves from her lashes and trickle down her powdered cheeks leaving tracks like snow-ploughs. 'It's just that Father insisted I come here for three months and I'm so bored. And a bit depressed.' She sniffs horribly, and Virginia proffers Nanny Holwell's clean hankie.

'I don't understand. Why have they sent you here?'

'I met this soldier,' says Cecily, so surprisingly that Virginia sinks down on to the brocade sofa beside her in a fury. For goodness' sake, is everybody in the world involved in a love-affair except herself?

'They didn't like him?'

'He wasn't an officer,' says Cecily painfully as if conceding that the man was also a habitual wife-beater and child-molester. 'But we had such jolly times together! I've never had a boyfriend. I'm sure you've had hundreds. Terry was the first person who really seemed to like me. We both enjoy reading, you see; that gave us an interest immediately.'

'What did he do before he joined up?'

'He was a window-dresser in Selfridges – you know, in Oxford Street.'

Goodness, thinks Virginia, the Earl must have loved *that*.

'He was training to be a buyer,' Cecily goes on eagerly, 'and the head of his department believed he had real flair. But Daddy found out and was absolutely furious.'

This is not quite as dramatic as it sounds. Winter or summer, morning, noon or night, wet weather or dry, the Earl was invariably furious about *something*.

'Anyway, that's why I'm here, to forget Terry. . . . Aunt Grace wants me to help her look after the Jack Russells, but I'm not going to waste my war effort on *that*,' she goes on most surprisingly. 'I say, Virginia. Guess what? I've got a Plan. Aunt and Uncle will be livid when they find out, but I'm jolly well going to stick to it. You can't expect grown women to sit around at a time like this and do nothing. Can you, Virginia? I bet you get really bored at home with nothing to do but voluntary work.'

Virginia goes very red.

'Do you remember Charlotte Neaps?' goes on Cecily. 'She was always sick at parties. I saw her just before Christmas, and she said she was off to London to work. She hasn't got any people there at present, so her mother has found her a very superior girls' hostel in Bayswater – it's sponsored by Lady Grangemouth. I was brooding last week and remembered this and wrote off to the hostel to see if they had any spare rooms, and I got a letter this morning.' She fumbles in her evening bag and produces the envelope that she has clearly been carrying around with her all evening like a talisman. 'They say they've got rooms and I can move in any time I like.'

Virginia stares at her with undisguised admiration. 'I say, Cecily, that's really sporting of you. What will you do?'

Cecily flushes with pleasure at Virginia's approval. 'Well, once I've settled in I'll go down to the WVS headquarters and work for them full-time. Charley says she's going to drive ambulances, so I don't see why I shouldn't. I've driven tractors on the farm, and they must be practically the same,' says Cecily serenely. 'I've got to tell Uncle Piers tomorrow. I'm not looking forward to *that*, I can tell you.'

A sudden thought strikes her, and she leans forward excitedly.

'I say, Virginia! Why don't you come with me? Just for a bit anyway? It'll be the greatest fun. We could have some topping larks together and, besides,' she adds practically, 'if we both go, they really can't object. Now, can they?'

77

Virginia stares at her, and her spirits soar like that fleet gazelle that the vicar is always going on about in Psalms. A whole motherless Nanny-free vista suddenly opens up entrancingly before her eyes. And to live in London again!

'You're right, Cecily,' agrees Virginia, her face pink. 'If we both go, they really can't object – now, can they?'

CHAPTER
SIX

UNCLE PIERS DRIVES his aged Rolls down Park Lane at breakneck speed, the set of his shoulders revealing his rigid disapproval of the whole scheme. They have already been to lunch at his club, where over lamb cutlets and jam roly-poly Virginia and Cecily have been lectured about the danger of late nights and what they do to the system – unless spent in the service of some useful farming occupation such as lambing – the dangers to be expected from men in uniform, women in uniform, foreign food and most of all foreigners themselves. Cecily listens intently whilst Virginia fixes her eyes on her uncle's face and relives her triumphant escape. It was entirely to be predicted that Mrs Musgrave, having complained almost non-stop about having Virginia under her roof, should then have had hysterics at the very idea of Virginia leaving home. Even harsher words than usual had been exchanged last night, at the end of which Virginia, trembling but resolute, had simply gone up to her room and told Granger to pack. Mother had appeared halfway through the operation, had more hysterics and told Virginia it was quite likely that she would cause her early death. Undeterred, Virginia had ordered the Morris to be brought round to the front door and, thanking providence that Brooke had taught her to drive two summers ago, had actually loaded her own suitcases and used up all their petrol allowance getting back to the Towers. Cecily, waiting for her in the front hall, had clasped her unashamedly with relief. Swallowing nervously, and desperate to provide a united front, they had gone to talk to Uncle Piers.

Virginia shifts uncomfortably in her seat at the memory. At first Uncle Piers simply issued a flat no. But most surprisingly Aunt Grace had talked him round. 'Let them have a try,' she had said most surprisingly. 'They can always come home if they don't like it. It'll be a change.'

Never had Virginia liked her aunt more. Eventually Uncle Piers had conceded without any particular good grace that they should be allowed to try it for a month, and had even taken on the task of talking Mrs Musgrave into some sort of sulky agreement. By the end of that evening it had been settled. Virginia had gone to bed hardly able to believe that, in the space of a week, her entire life had altered owing entirely to her own efforts. Musgrave, the Dower House, her mother, all could now be completely forgotten. The priority was London, men, nightclubs and (of course) clothes.

What to wear, how to get new clothes, how to make the best of what she's got, broods Virginia as Uncle Piers drones on. In a final burst of malice her mother has declined to give her any allowance whilst she is in London. It is clearly down to Virginia to become what *Vogue* is currently calling 'being clever with your clothes'. There is clearly no question of borrowing from Cecily. For her triumphant entry into London, Cecily is wearing an old tweed suit, the skirt of which, like all Cecily's clothes, has a curious bouclé effect brought about by the claws of over-enthusiastic farm-dogs. With it, she wears a little beige jersey crocheted by her nanny, and a broad-rimmed deep-crowned felt hat which has apparently proved jolly useful on more than one occasion for carrying pheasants' eggs. But, then, Cecily's parents – sensible country people, as Uncle Piers always refers to them – have no use for clothes other than that they keep the rain out. Cecily's father will spend hundreds on a pedigree cow, thousands on his horseflesh, and invest heavily in diamonds and furs against the future. Thus Cecily has a choice of three different tiaras should she be called on to visit the Palace, but does not actually have a single new dress. All the frocks intended for her season had been carefully cut down from her sister's evening clothes, and the value of her entire coming-out wardrobe would probably have approximated to the value of a new pair of custom-made hunting-boots.

At Marble Arch they take a left down the Bayswater Road.

'Rum sort of area, this,' mutters Uncle Piers, who hates London anyway. They reach Queensway and turn into a cul-de-sac full of tall narrow stucco houses. Uncle Piers stops in front of number twelve. 'The Grange' as it is known by its inmates is composed of three houses side by side. There is a small discreet engraved plate on the first house, and Uncle Piers rings the bell. The door is opened by a wizened old man bent nearly double, it appears, from the weight of his green baize apron. Clearly stone deaf, he ignores Uncle Piers's shouted questions and points down the hall to where the administrator, Miss Groundsell, is emerging from her office. As she comes forward meekly arching her neck and blushing, Virginia sees Uncle Piers begin to look more mollified.

Miss Groundsell's study is permeated by an overwhelming sensation of beeswax, silence and the smell of a thousand bygone lunches. The floor is patterned in blue and brown tiles, and a clock ticks leadenly on the mantelpiece. The walls are covered with quasi-religious pictures, and there are many small tables covered with photographs in silver frames. Tea is served by a woman of such extraordinary antiquity that she can only be the life partner of the man in the green baize apron.

Whilst Uncle Piers and Miss Groundsell discuss the tragic fate of Norway, Virginia studies Miss Groundsell. She is probably in her forties but appears much younger owing to the almost preternaturally innocent look in her enormous moist-dark eyes which somehow makes her resemble a Jersey cow. Virginia can see the phrase 'a fine figure of a woman' going through Uncle Piers's head as he admires her splendid bust, mysteriously worn at waist level. Briefly Virginia speculates on Miss Groundsell's sex life and wonders how effective her control is over the twenty-five girls between eighteen and thirty-five under her care. Miss Groundsell is the niece of the Lady

Grangemouth who founded the hostel. The original purpose of the hostel, the girls are told, was to provide accommodation for single girls returning from the colonies. They still offer such girls a home, but in a time of international crisis the trustees have decided to open the doors to any girl temporarily requiring accommodation. A high standard of behaviour is demanded from the inmates of the Grangemouth, Virginia is dismayed to learn. A long speech follows full of words like 'duty', 'responsibility' and 'respect'. Virginia has already had several sermons today and again falls into a reverie as to how she can get hold of more clothes. But she comes smartly to attention when Miss Groundsell announces that, as part of the confidence they are prepared to show their girls, all inmates are issued with a key.

There is no signing-in procedure; girls are expected to be in in good time and show consideration for others by not having baths after eight-thirty.

Uncle Piers's jaw drops. 'What's this? They can come in when they like?'

'The girls are asked to be in by ten-thirty, Mr Barrington-Smythe, but we leave it to their own good sense.'

'In *that* case,' thunders Uncle Piers – curious that it is only in London that you notice how loud his voice is – 'I want no larking around from you two, is that understood?'

'Yes, Uncle,' they chorus nervously.

'I'll show you their rooms now, and the rest of the hostel.'

The first house contains the kitchens and the dining-room. Here they can eat breakfast and supper, but lunch only on request. Guests can be invited for Sunday lunch at the cost of seven and sixpence each. This room is painted dark green and is indescribably dreary. Above is another equally gloomy chamber with a shelf half-full of paperback books.

'This is the library,' announces Miss Groundsell with some pride. 'We have first-aid lectures in here and coffee evenings for charity.'

A couple of ragged sparrows cheep at them from the balcony outside the window, and from the Bayswater Road comes the low drone of traffic. Beyond are the treetops of Hyde Park.

The second house has been divided for study bedrooms, but it is to the third house that they finally go for their own rooms. Their quarters are on the top floor under the eaves and are as spartan as anything Uncle Piers could have desired. There is what seems to be a hospital bed, a rug, a chest of drawers and a wardrobe plus a small wooden chair. The rooms are painted a uniform eau-de-Nil. The only concession to vanity is a small wall-mirror placed in the darkest corner of the room at elbow height. Both rooms have windows looking out over acres of chimneypots towards Paddington Station.

Eventually Uncle Piers, having satisfied himself that there are no foreigners in the room by actually putting his head into both wardrobes, announces that he will have to be on his way as no doubt the girls need an early night after their long drive. It is half-past five.

'Now, remember. No hanky-panky. Plenty of early nights and try to stay regular. And at the very first sign of bombing you must ring home and I'll send Benson up to collect you.'

With that he kisses them, mumbles that he's paid for their first month of lodging, gives them five pounds apiece, and after a few minutes they hear the sound of the Rolls roaring back towards the Bayswater Road.

Cecily and Virginia sit down on Virginia's extremely hard bed and suddenly feel rather lost.

'I suppose we'd better unpack. What are you going to do this evening, Virginia?'

'I don't know. I thought I might ring up a few people about jobs. What about you?'

'I'm going round to headquarters to see Kitty and find out if there's anything I can be getting on with tomorrow. Are you sure you don't want me to ask about some work for you?'

'Not at present,' says Virginia morosely. 'I'm going to have to get a job. Mother's made things as difficult as she possibly can. I've got a little money in my Post Office account, but it won't be enough to keep me going for that long.'

As they unpack they hear the sound of returning feet clattering up the lino-clad stairs as doors open and baths begin to be run. Virginia wanders out on to the landing and looks at the two names on the doors facing them. One has a card with the name Rachel Stearn written on it whilst the other simply has a gold star stuck on the door. There is a letter pushed underneath, and inquisitively Virginia pulls it out to see the name. 'This room belongs to someone called Devora Templecomb. What an odd name.'

'Oh, *no*,' says Cecily, quite disagreeably for her. 'Not Devora. Her grandmother lives near us and she hunts with us from time to time – shocking seat, elbows all over the place.'

'Templecomb . . . Templecomb . . . I wonder if she's related to Bunty? She was Deb of the year, wasn't she?'

'Bunty's her older sister. My goodness, she was a wrong 'un if ever there was one. She came for the weekend once at the castle, but Mother never asked her back.'

'Why ever not?'

'Oh, I never knew the details of it,' says Cecily with maddening vagueness. 'It was something to do with our chauffeur. She was a silly sort of girl always out to shock people. She married a racing driver shortly afterwards, then she ran off with that jockey. And I know she's been married at least once since then. Her family finally packed her off to East Africa.'

'Cecily, how on earth do you know all this?'

'Our nannies were best friends,' says Cecily casually, 'so we got to hear everything.'

'I wonder what Devora's like.' There is a sudden footstep on the stair.

'Simply wonderful, darling,' says a voice from the door, and a bold-faced dark-haired girl swings into the room. 'More to the point, who the hell are you? Oh, Cecily, I didn't see you there. Are you going to be my new neighbour? Who's *this*?'

Virginia is not discomposed by her rudeness. 'I'm Virginia Musgrave.'

'Are you, indeed? Any relation to Brooke Musgrave? Yes, you must be; you look just like him. I adored him for a whole year while he and my brother were at Christchurch together. He was always sadly immune to my charms. What's he doing now?'

'RAF.'

'He must look wonderful in the uniform. He has the body for it. Goodness, am I tired, or am I tired!'

Without waiting for an invitation she collapses heavily on Virginia's bed, pulls out a mother-of-pearl cigarette-case and lighter and lights a cigarette with much dramatic inhaling and narrowing of her eyes. Virginia looks at her with interest. She has never seen anybody quite like her before. Perhaps it is simply that unlike most nicely brought up girls of Virginia's acquaintance she makes no effort to subdue her natural assets but actually flaunts them. She wears the same clothes as Virginia and Cecily, but in her case the surge of her bosom and the powerful curve of her hip make one disconcertingly aware of the body beneath the fabric. She has a broad cat-like face with high cheekbones and heavy-lidded, slightly slanted eyes. Her wide mouth, which forms a perfect Cupid's bow, is outlined in red so dark that her lips are almost purple. She looks knowing, available and slightly grubby.

'I must get changed and be on my way,' says Cecily as Devora's description of life at the Ministry of Food grinds to a halt. 'I'm not sure how to get to headquarters, but there must be a bus-stop on the Bayswater Road because I saw a line of women waiting there.'

Devora throws back her head, revealing a not very clean neck, in a throaty cackle of mirth. 'Those are tarts, darling. Remember to walk home on the other side of the road,' she goes on maliciously, 'because they simply hate competition, Cecily. And remember to keep out of Hyde Park at night. You simply can't move for the writhing bodies.'

Cecily disappears, scarlet-faced. 'Poor old Cecil,' says Devora lightly, narrowing her faintly slanted eyes against the cigarette smoke and taking another drag of her scarlet-stained cigarette. 'What about you? Are you one of the idle rich who can afford to work for the WVS?'

'No, I need to get a job.'

'Are you a good girl like Cecily?' asks Devora suddenly.

'What do you mean?'

'If you have to ask, then you clearly are.'

Devora gets reluctantly to her feet, stretches, takes an apparently approving sniff at either armpit and says casually: 'Are you doing anything this evening? A couple of officers I met last night are picking me up at seven and we're going dancing. Of course they're both crazy for me, but I'm sure they wouldn't mind if you came along, too.'

Virginia is taken somewhat aback at the gracious nature of this invitation. 'Not tonight, I'm afraid,' she says coolly. 'I'm far too busy.'

'Suit yourself,' drawls Devora and goes out humming. Cecily reappears in the smart new uniform of the WVS. In its well-cut bottle-green suit she suddenly looks alert, purposeful, defined.

'I'm off now, Vir. Perhaps I'll see you at supper.'

Virginia goes out on to the landing and calls to Devora: 'Is there a phone anywhere?'

'In the hall,' says Devora, walking out on to the landing in her dressing-gown. 'The bath is on the next floor.'

'Who lives in this room?'

'Oh, that's Rachel Stearn. Between you and me and the bedpost, she's a bit of a mystery. My dear, she keeps the oddest hours and won't tell anyone what she does, and when she comes in she always goes to sleep immediately. Maureen saw her once in Soho, apparently just standing there doing nothing. I mean, in *Soho*. I think she's . . .' Footsteps sound suddenly on the narrow stairway, and a tall thin sallow-faced girl dressed in a white mackintosh appears, her face oily with exhaustion. 'Hello, Devora.' She smiles briefly at Virginia, opens the remaining door and shuts it firmly behind her. There is a shuffling noise as she takes off her mackintosh and opens a drawer. Then a creak of bedsprings from the bed. After that, utter silence.

'See what I mean?' whispers Devora and goes down to the next floor where Virginia can hear her retelling Cecily's *faux pas* amidst howls of delighted laughter.

Had there ever been a spring as beautiful as 1940? wonders Virginia as she walks home each day through Hyde Park. The bitter winter has suddenly given way to skies so achingly blue it is like high mid-summer. As the news from Europe slowly worsens, the feeling of expectancy, of charged intensity, slowly grows in the capital, but to Virginia that tension seems like an extension of her sense, for the first time, of being fully alive. Away from the restrictions of the Dower House, and the trickling waterfall of her mother's criticism, Virginia's spirits rise like champagne too long confined in the bottle. It is enough to wake each morning and to look round at her tiny and austere room to feel completely happy.

After a leisurely breakfast in the almost deserted dining-room – the other girls having long since departed for work – Virginia saunters out to enjoy simply being on her own. It is an extraordinary fact that, though nearly nineteen, she has never walked alone in London before. There was always a car to take her to and from school, and every shopping expedition had to be attended by one of Mother's dreary housekeeper-companions. Virginia can hardly believe the extent of her freedom.

She walks endlessly in the parks admiring the spring flowers, stopping occasionally to sit on a bench and read. She takes afternoon tea at Lyons in Coventry Street. She goes to the pictures almost every afternoon and usually sees the main feature twice. One lunchtime there is a trip to a recital at the National Gallery and to inspect the handful of pictures left on show. But mostly she walks from one end of London to the other, seeing her native city properly for the first time, unaware as she saunters through those narrow courtyards and cobbled alleys that in a few short months what she's seeing will have disappeared for ever.

Much to her own surprise, Virginia finds that many of her evenings are spent with Cecily, though there is no lack of diversion if she wants it. Devora continues to offer offhand invitations amidst rhino-like yawns and tales of the previous night's activities. But Virginia is not anxious to make her London début under the patronage of Devora Templecomb and continues to bide her time.

Cecily has immediately gone to work within a few hours of arriving in London. She is currently sorting out the problems of a group of refugees from Gibraltar who have been installed, much against their will, in a hotel off Sussex Gardens. But Cecily's sense of duty clearly does not end at 5.30. Two days after her arrival at the Grangemouth she proceeds to check the shelter arrangements for the hostel, and within the hour is sternly admonishing a startled Miss Groundsell about the inadequacy of the provision she's discovered. In theory the coal-cellars and the boiler-room are to be pressed into service in the event of a Nazi blitzkrieg. But, apart from moving the coal and providing buckets of sand to douse incendiary devices, the cellar is still the same dank uninviting hole it has always been. By dint of making herself almost homicidally unpopular with everybody Cecily has the coal removed from the cellar, press-gangs groups of girls into colour-washing the walls, and gets Cripps the aged porter to install electric light, a fire, a camping-stove, a number of rugs and deck-chairs and a portable toilet behind a screen. This takes about a week, and Miss Groundsell is just starting to breathe more easily when there is another knock at the door and Cecily, white-knuckled with embarrassment but determined to carry through her duty, announces that it is unpatriotic to let all that garden go to waste and can she form a rota to have it dug up for allotments. Miss Groundsell tells her to go right ahead, secure in the belief that Cecily would find almost no volunteers to help her. But she is wrong. It is one thing to have to move coal in a damp subterranean hole but quite another to work in the garden in the expectation of being able to hoe your own lettuces later in the year. Even Virginia, initially almost speechless at the prospect of heavy digging, has to admit that working outside at eight o'clock when it is still light and a blackbird is singing in the almond tree has a certain unexpected charm. Yet perhaps the most unexpected discovery of all is how much she finds she enjoys Cecily's company. She has used her ruthlessly as a means of escape and had envisaged quietly dropping her once she reached London. Even now she is hard-pressed to understand why she spends so much time in Cecily's company. Perhaps it is simply that Cecily likes her. But there is also the fact that Virginia has unwillingly begun to admire her friend. Cecily may be a joke, but it is undeniable that she gets things done, that she has boundless energy and the good-humoured knack of cajoling other people, in spite of their grumbles, into doing their bit as well. It is evident that to Cecily ideas like devotion to duty, self-sacrifice and loyalty to your country are not mere jingoistic catchphrases, but meaningful concepts which could and should shape a life. Beneath that mild and inoffensive exterior, Virginia comes to realize, there is a core of solid steel.

'Of course, I'd love to have joined one of the women's services,' Cecily wistfully remarks one night to Virginia after a lecture (organized by Cecily naturally) by a smartly dressed Wren who is looking for recruits. 'If it hadn't been for a stupid bout of rheumatic fever when I was ten, I'm sure I'd have been A-OK. As it is, the doctor wouldn't hear of me joining up. Miserable, isn't it?'

Virginia looks sympathetic and waits rather tensely for Cecily to ask her why she has apparently volunteered for nothing. But as usual the question simply doesn't seem to occur. Cecily is the least-judging person Virginia has ever met. She has no expectations about other people's behaviour at all. But because Virginia has come to admire her and wants Cecily's approval she finds herself throwing her weight behind every one of her schemes and is astonished to find that she likes doing things like digging in the garden and learning to bandage broken limbs and douse incendiary bombs, pastimes which she would formerly have regarded with a certain bleak distance.

This quiet interim abruptly ends when the wireless in the library announces that Holland and then Belgium have fallen to the Germans. A flood of new refugees arrives in London, and Cecily's job changes overnight from a pastime to a grim, totally absorbing commitment. The newsreels are full of Nazi tanks advancing steadily across Europe.

Virginia pulls herself together as she realizes that unless she gets herself a job she will have absolutely no excuse if Uncle Piers takes it into his head to try to drag her back to the Dower House. Abruptly Virginia decides playtime is over and gets out her mother's address-book, which she has thoughtfully purloined from her bureau. There are a number of friends of the family who can be relied on to take her out to dinner, but right now what she needs is a job and the first person to ring is Sir Frederick Grebe.

Virginia rings him at his home and in her meekest little-girl voice confides that her mother had suggested she get in touch with him about a job. Sir Fred asks her out to dinner. The beginning of the evening is not a success. Sir Fred avoids her eye, keeps well away from her, and remarks fairly early on that he will have to leave early.

Puzzled, Virginia wonders what she can be doing to cause Sir Fred such embarrassment. Perhaps she is wrongly dressed. No, her dress is exceptionally smart, and Devora has actually been prevailed upon to lend her one of her less extravagant evening hats. But notwithstanding her prettiness and general air of docile good-humour Sir Fred seems hardly able to look at her and makes conversation only in monosyllables. It is only halfway through the dessert that the penny finally drops. Sir Fred is frightened she's going to make a pass at him; the memory of that August day at the Manor is still clearly fresh in his mind. Assessing the situation, Virginia deftly alters tack and, muting her seductive smiles, briskly starts to address him equally flatteringly and in quite a different tone as a father and mentor. Only Sir Fred with his knowledge of the world and his many contacts can truly help Virginia, she tells him without a trace of a blush. She hints at the conspiracy currently trying to stop her doing her bit for her country. Surely there must be some job in publishing for an able-bodied girl who can type and answer the phone?

Sir Fred steps into his new role with alacrity and some relief. Immediately he becomes expansive over the savouries. (Virginia has worked her way down the extensive menu with a will. Improving the food at the Grangemouth is Cecily's next project, and Virginia has promised to lend her her full support.) 'You'll have to understand that getting a job in publishing isn't easy at the best of times,' he informs her importantly, adding more practically:

'Especially now. It isn't a reserved occupation, you see. Unless you're working for those companies publishing stuff for the Government. . . . That's a thought. I'll look into it.'

It turns out to be an entirely satisfactory encounter. The following day a bunch of roses arrives at the Grangemouth with a little note. Two days later, over lunch at the Savoy Grill, Sir Fred confides that he's found her a suitable opening. A friend of his at Marwicks happened to mention that the fiction editor was looking for a temporary secretary. Marwicks's main source of revenue is its production of official pamphlets for the government. But two years ago they'd started a small fiction department. Sir Fred knows the fella concerned: Theo Beavers, one of the new young men and a decent chap to work for. He hadn't been called up, continued Sir Fred helpfully, because of his asthma. It will be excellent experience for Virginia, Sir Fred adds, and suggests she present herself in Bedford Square the following day.

Virginia's funds are running alarmingly low, and she is determined to get the job. At 8.45 the following morning she is standing outside the tall Georgian house in Bedford Square, its white stucco façade dappled by the early May sunshine. It has a large delicate fanlight over the door and a brass plate announcing that this is the home of Marwick & Marwick, Publishers. There is no bell. Virginia bravely pushes open the front door. Inside a cleaning woman is swabbing the tiles in the hall. Apparently, if Virginia wants Mr Beavers, she'll find him on the top floor, but nobody comes in before 9.30 and Mr Beavers is never in before ten.

Virginia creeps upstairs and eventually finds herself at the top of the house under the eaves. She halts irresolutely by the window on the topmost landing. There is a breathtaking view across the rooftops of London, and more immediately a pair of pigeons who tap encouragingly on the glass at her. Virginia, who only likes pigeons served under pastry with a rich gravy, ignores them and turns round to inspect the doors facing her. One says: 'Theo Beavers. Fiction Editor.' The next one says: 'Eleanor Carr.' A third door proves merely to be a stationery cupboard with a gas-ring, a caddy of tea, a sink and a tin of powdered milk. Feeling rather like Goldilocks, Virginia tries the largest door, the one marked 'Fiction Editor', and goes in and stops short. The room is in a state of indescribable disarray. It is hardly possible to advance even a small way because of the manuscripts lying two and three deep on the floor. Every surface contains teetering piles of paper. The dust of age lies thickly over all, interspersed with cups of tea and coffee, the dregs of which have long since solidified in the bottom of the cup. Virginia likes it all immediately.

Taking off her coat and hat, she makes herself a cup of tea and begins to try to tidy up the room. Having removed all the dirty coffee-cups, apple cores and decayed flowers, she begins to stack the manuscripts, thus revealing a rather nice old Turkish carpet. A single glance at Mr Beavers's desk decides her that any work here is pointless, so she sits down, picks up a manuscript at random and reads the title-page. The authoress's name is Lilian C. Hedge and her novel is entitled 'Too Soon the Heart.'

Intrigued, Virginia begins to read. It is a heart-stopping, heart-stirring tale of a mother's courage in Tunbridge Wells at the outbreak of war. The text is full of kindly nannies, twinkling gardeners who say, 'Why, bless you, mum,' before every speech, while the heroes are clearly the narrator's sons, Johnny and Guy, brown-haired, grey-eyed, decent young Englishmen who volunteer almost before the words have left Mr Chamberlain's mouth, pausing only to make moving speeches lasting several pages citing their mother as the fountainhead of all that is pure, decent and good about English life. The book is rivetingly bad, but unputdownable, and as Virginia ploughs on towards the boys' first leave she is dimly aware that downstairs typewriters are beginning to clatter and phones are ringing. Eventually the phone rings for Mr Beavers. First it is his tailor enquiring if he still wants that second vent in his sports-jacket; then the printers ring twice to say that they're having considerable trouble setting up the preface to *Love's Archery* and could Mr Beavers come down and sort it out himself. Virginia is about to return to Tunbridge Wells when a sack appears through the open door and proceeds to disgorge another thirty brown packages. A cheeky-faced teenage boy of stunted appearance appears to help kick them into the room. He stops short when he sees Virginia.

' 'Ere,' he says, 'I didn't see you. Did you tidy this up? Mr Beavers will be livid. Who are you? His new secretary?'

'I hope so,' says Virginia with dignity and considerably more confidence than she feels. 'Where is he?'

'Well, it's only ten to ten, and he's never in much before ten-thirty these days. It's since the twins. His wife only had 'em last month. I'm Reggie by the way. I do the post. Give me the ones to send back and I'll take them to the post office at half-past four. Are you doing anything Saturday?'

'Not with the likes of you,' says Virginia with spirit.

'Heart-breaker,' he says sadly and disappears.

At five past eleven a gaunt-faced young man appears on the stairs. He is wearing an unironed shirt and a spotted bow-tie and has circles of weariness under his eyes. He stops short at the sight of Virginia quietly reading 'Too Soon the Heart' and drops his briefcase on the desk.

'Can I help you?' he says courteously enough. 'If it's about an unreturned manuscript, I'm afraid I can't guarantee to find it. My assistant was called up after Christmas, and my secretary has been off for some time now, so we're absolutely snowed under.'

At this moment he notices that someone has been tidying up, and a deep frown appears under the lank lock on his forehead.

'That was me,' says Virginia helpfully. 'Tidying up, that is. I'm Virginia Musgrave, and Sir Frederick Grebe told me you needed someone to stand in until you got a permanent secretary.'

'Good Lord,' says the man abruptly. 'Is it Thursday already? One night seems to merge into another when you're up with babies. Make us some tea, will you, and I'll fill you in on your duties.'

When Virginia comes back with a horribly tannin-stained cup and saucer Theo is on the phone to the printers and ends up slamming down the receiver in a fury. 'Dratted people,' he says, lighting a cigarette and feeling in his pocket for something that turns out to be sugar lumps. 'Do you type? And answer the phone? Good, then you've the job. It's two pounds ten a week – not much but a living wage, so they tell me. The most immediate problem is this huge backlog of unsolicited manuscripts. Call me ''Theo'', by the way, and I'll dispense with the ''Miss Musgrave''. When you aren't typing letters you can be doing the first sort through the slush pile.' He gestures vaguely at the table by the door. 'Ones you think are no-hopers you give to Reggie. I suspect he burns them. Anything you think is halfway good put on the table here and they'll go out to a reader.'

'Are you sure I won't overlook a masterpiece?' says Virginia nervously.

Theo gives her a satirical look. 'I would say that is extremely unlikely, Virginia. War is a terrible thing, you know,' he goes on sombrely. 'It gives people who wouldn't normally have the time both the opportunity and the motive to write fiction. So far as you're concerned there are only one or two simple rules you need to know about first novels and unpublished writers. You must reject all those in handwriting and those that have no punctuation. You must also reject anything that starts with the words ''Gentle Reader''. Also anything that looks as though it might turn into a stream-of-consciousness novel. Do you know what that is?' Virginia shakes her head.

'Well, don't let it worry you. Let's just say that what I'm looking for right now are stories with a strong narrative line, a beginning, a middle and an end, and preferably in that order. And cheerfulness is all. Tremulous first-person accounts of a mother's anguish on saying goodbye to her sons is not currently what the public wants to read.' Silently Virginia places 'Too Soon the Heart' on the 'rejected' pile. 'And, for God's sake,' he adds moodily, 'look out for period drama. There's an awful lot of it about. Now, these letters.'

'I don't take shorthand,' says Virginia, flustered.

Theo wheels round sharply, his eyes narrowed, gangster-fashion. 'That's OK, lady,' he says in a passable impersonation of James Cagney. 'I don't give it.'

Virginia decides much to her own surprise that she is going to like this job.

'Now, take this down in longhand and stop me if I'm going too fast. Blah, blah, blah – that's our address. Then: Dear Mr Agnew, Though your projected trilogy on the life of Attila the Hun certainly would have a topical relevance, we have to ask ourselves whether the extant sources for this character really justify three volumes, or indeed whether this is the kind of book Marwick and Marwick can offer a home to. After considerable debate with my colleagues, reluctantly we are returning your manuscript and outline with many thanks. . . .'

CHAPTER
SEVEN

SIX WEEKS AFTER starting work at Marwicks, Virginia loses her maidenhead. It happens through sheer carelessness: she is livid with herself for days afterwards. She does not mind being thought promiscuous but she minds very much being thought stupid. Which is clearly what she's been.

The day in question is a Friday, and it has begun normally enough. She deals first with Theo's correspondence, then over elevenses writes a letter of her own.

'My Dear Lucy', she types, 'I was delighted to receive your long letter. I was beginning to fear you had drowned on the Essex marshes. Bad luck about your wellingtons! I hope the goat was sick afterwards. I haven't written for a while because as you can see I have actually got a job! And I am still living at the Grangemouth with Cecily. There are ominous rumblings from the Dower House, but so far no one has actually been sent up to haul me back. Today I'm having a quiet time because Mr Beavers (that's my boss) has gone down to the printers for the day to avoid a poet. We had the sirens on for the first time yesterday, then we rushed down to the cellars here which are full of remaindered books. I was really terrified. It's quite different from that day we had sirens in the village last summer. . . . What a long time ago that seems, doesn't it? I'm glad your parents like Yorkshire, and you're lucky to hear so often from Hugh; he must have a wonderful tan by now. Does he like being there? Pity it's not so good from the point of leave, isn't it? Here everybody talks about bombs the whole time; it's really quite unnerving. Yesterday we were given our invasion leaflets and told to look out for nuns wearing army boots. It's a joke but it doesn't seem very funny. I haven't seen Cecily for days now, not since the BEF troops started to arrive back from Dunkirk. She's running a reception centre for them at Waterloo. I gather there's a lot of Frenchmen, too. I keep wondering what's happened to Ferdinand Aumont. The last letter I got from him was before Christmas, and Ma seems to have stopped sending on letters now.'

Virginia gets up from her typewriter and wanders restlessly over to the window. Far below in the sunny square she sees a school boy in uniform go by, swinging the handle of his gas-mask case. Then two soldiers, then a girl in some sort of uniform. Overhead the sky is still the same cloudless blue, but the very quality of the air now somehow feels different. Virginia can feel

90

her own heart thudding unnaturally fast. It is almost impossible to imagine that Nazi tanks are now rolling through those quiet Parisian streets where she and Lucy had wandered this time last year. Almost as impossible as realizing that only a stretch of some twenty miles of water separates the coast of England from the Nazi horde. She read an article that morning in Reggie's *Daily Mirror* which stated firmly that this was the moment for standing together, for being with your family. Abruptly Virginia goes back to her typewriter, adds a few more lines to Lucy's letter, addresses the envelope and puts it in the out-tray. Then, her lips twisted into an odd grimace, she pulls open the middle drawer and takes out a pile of letters all written in the same wildly erratic hand on green stationery, and begins to deal with her other correspondence problem of the morning.

The Musgrave family are not avid proponents of the letter-writing art. Virginia has written four times to Brooke and finally received one postcard of Norwich Cathedral saying he is well and hopes she is behaving herself as he is too busy to fight duels on her behalf. But her mother has more than made up for his omissions. Virginia's mother's letters are now a joke at the hostel. Not one single day has gone past in the last fortnight without there being at least one green envelope in Virginia's pigeonhole: on bad days there are two.

'It keeps her occupied,' Virginia says serenely, at pains to conceal the fact that the very sight of her mother's handwriting still has the power to undo her peace of mind for whole days at a stretch. There is no logical explanation for this sudden demented outpouring. Last October, Nanny Holwell had taken Virginia on one side and started to mutter inexplicable things about her 'mother's time of life' and 'a difficult time for all of us' but it had still done nothing to explain the almost daily spectacle of Mother wrenching open Virginia's bedroom door at 8.30 in the morning, her hair anyhow, screaming at the top of her lungs, the veins standing out of her neck, her eyes bloodshot, while she abused Virginia for a whole series of real and imagined offences. Her rages were always worst in the early morning; it was as if the moment she opened her eyes she immediately plugged into a hot thick corroding current of anger and, roughly pushing aside her breakfast-tray, had to find Virginia to pass on her anger to her. It had become a point of honour with Virginia not to react, and to present a hard polished surface, to perfect what Lucy had long ago privately nicknamed Virginia's poker-faced sleep-walking act. But the cost of preserving that façade, of suppressing her own anger was terrible. Often she could not sleep until the small hours as the waves of anger jerked her limbs into wakefulness.

Reluctantly Virginia opens the latest letter and takes out the seven folded sheets. As usual, the letter starts without address, date or greeting. It is as if every time her mother picks up her pen she gets straight back into the same groove and all the paper in the world will not be enough to express her anger and frustration. Today the letter starts straightforwardly enough with the statement that does Virginia know that she, Virginia, wrecked her parents' marriage and destroyed the family? That the very second Virginia appeared she ruined a hitherto happy unit of Mr and Mrs Musgrave and little Brooke? They had never wanted another child and certainly not a girl. Nobody wanted girls, Mrs Musgrave rapidly informs her in her wild flourishing writing, almost illegible in places and heavily underlined in others. As a result of Virginia's birth and then her turning out to be an unlovable and difficult child, Mr Musgrave had been driven out of his own home and forced to stay in his club. In fact his drinking could be dated precisely from that moment. It would all have been laughable were it not for the fact that it was her own mother that was writing it.

The letter then jumps fifteen years without a check as Mrs Musgrave ranges to and fro across the years in an attempt to find fresh grievances to stoke the fire of her anger. Did Virginia realize that the cost of keeping her at Queen's Gate Terrace with her extra dancing and music lessons had made the family almost penniless? she demands, conveniently overlooking Brooke's six years at Eton and three at Oxford at the end of which Mr Musgrave had to go to his college to settle his debts. The letter rages on like this for several pages before reaching a crescendo of fury and insanity on the final page. Virginia is not to think she can take her mother's place in society. She is to stay away from her dressmaker and her hairdresser and also not go to certain theatres and restaurants. Virginia has clearly gone to London to be a tart, and people are already talking about her. This follows straight on from the remark that nobody is in the slightest bit interested in what Virginia does. She then adds that Virginia is to come home immediately but, then, she is not to come home and think she can use the place like a hotel.

With a savage gesture Virginia screws up the letter, tears up the other thirteen and drops them all into the wastepaper-basket. Having rummaged in Theo's drawer, she finds and lights a match and sets fire to them.

It turns out to be a rather rash move. The flames lick up the letters splendidly, but the room rapidly fills with fumes.

Virginia is still trying to pull up the sash of the window when she hears an apologetic cough from the door. 'I say, is Theo Beavers available? My goodness! Is there a fire?' Virginia triumphantly pulls up the window and lets the fresh air in. Turning, she sees a plump young man with a round face and very red cheeks and an expression of permanent surprise. His thick hair is parted in the middle and falls in heavy waves on either side of his large pale brow. He is wearing a dark blue shirt and yellow tie.

'Can I help you?' says Virginia, deftly seizing the remains of her elevenses and pouring them into the wastepaper-basket where they are greeted with a sizzle and then a very unpleasant smell. The young man is completely nonplussed.

'I thought I'd drop in for a word with Theo.'

'He's at the printers today avoiding a poet,' says Virginia briefly.

'Oh,' says the young man dispiritedly. 'That's probably me.'

'I'm sorry, I shouldn't have said that,' says Virginia, contrite. 'It might not be you at all.'

'I'm Stephen Seaton.'

'Oh, I'm afraid it *is* you.'

The young man does not appear to be unduly depressed and is looking with interest at the puddle of lukewarm tea that is slowly seeping out of the wastepaper-basket.

'Do you do that with all the manuscripts you don't like?'

'That wasn't a manuscript. Some boring person keeps writing to me, and I was disposing of the letters.'

He looks at her with admiration. 'I say, that's awfully strong of you. I let things drag on in the most disgraceful way because I'm weak-willed, you see,' he says sadly. 'You're frightfully pretty, you know. Are you new here? What's your name?'

'I'm Virginia Musgrave and, yes, I'm new here.'

'Not related to Brooke, are you?' breathes the young man, lighting up.

Virginia is becoming rather tired of this label.

'Sister,' she says briefly.

'Brooke,' murmurs the young man, enraptured by some private fantasy. 'Oh, he's an angel, a god. I was in love with him for a whole year. He was so cruel. I used to go and see him row . . . those legs . . . that chest! Oh, I do go on,' he says with a sudden return to practicality. 'It's nearly twelve o'clock. Do you have a lunch-hour? Would you like to come and have a drink with me?'

They go to a pub in Rathbone Place.

'Any nearer Oxford Circus and I run into my colleagues. Now, what will you have? I'm having half a pint of mild – that suit you? Oh, come on, I can afford it. I'm not a full-time writer. I work at the BBC.'

'Goodness,' says Virginia, impressed. 'Do you know Frank Phillips?'

'In a manner of speaking. That is, I see him in the canteen.'

Stephen pulls out a Woodbine, offers her one, then lights his own. 'I've always had this problem in that people don't take me seriously. For instance, at work I'm sure they see me as a rather frivolous person. Which is why I thought if I'd got something published it might change the way people thought about me. Instead of saying, "Oh, that's old Stephen; he's a bit of a clown," they might say, "That's old Stephen; he writes poetry, you know". It does sound better, doesn't it?'

'I'm really sorry that Theo . . . er . . .'

'Oh, that's all right; it really wasn't very good. I sometimes think the stage or the novel form is really more my thing. I started an outline just before Christmas about the break-up of a middle-class family as the sons go off to war, and how their mother strives to hold the family together. I showed it to my mother and she simply loved it. Is there a market for that kind of thing?'

'Er . . . that has proved to be quite a popular theme,' says Virginia cautiously.

'Then, perhaps I'll have another go at my play,' frowns Stephen. 'I did have one put on once at a Sunday-evening club. I've got an idea about seven people in a bus-shelter waiting for a bus that never comes. It's basically about the human response to fear and the condition of the world at present, and it would be jolly cheap to mount. What do you think?'

Virginia replies with perfect truth that it sounds most original. Stephen then begins an interminable story as to why he hasn't been called up, and Virginia sits there quietly enjoying her first visit to a pub. With the exception of the beer, which is quite horrible and tastes like woody water, she decides she likes it all very much – the noise, the bustle, the smell of alcohol and cigarettes, the close proximity of people, the feeling of energy and, above all, the presence of men who eye her as if they are impressed by what they see. Abruptly her spirits rise and she manages to muster a few rude phrases for her mother before dismissing the matter from her mind. Looking round with bright eyes, she decides she's been spending too much time with her own sex. She still wants to meet Lord Right, but she also wants to have some fun.

'How do you come to be working at Marwicks? Did you know Eleanor?'

'No, I just heard there was a job going there.' Eleanor is Virginia's predecessor. She has left nothing of herself in the office save a heavily annotated volume of the poems of W. H. Auden and a box of sticking plaster. 'What happened exactly? She seems to have left at rather short notice.'

'Oh, Eleanor – well, she's a rather emotional person. I think she went through all kinds of crisis. We were at Oxford together. Not that one saw that much of her. She was always wrapped up in her boyfriend and political causes. I forget what she read. Anyway, afterwards she had a job on *New Directions* – did you ever see it?' Stephen's tone is full of hope.

'I'm afraid not.'

'It doesn't matter. It only ran to three editions, but I was the arts reviewer and they published three of my poems. After that I think Eleanor taught for a bit, then she became Theo's secretary. I hadn't seen her for a while, then I happened to run into her before Christmas in Bedford Square and she seemed very down. She didn't seem able to decide whether to get married or join the ATS. The next thing I heard, she'd gone home to live and seemed to be in some kind of decline. I think she takes life too hard. She's a wonderful girl but a bit intense – always moving from one crisis to the next. Not very restful. You're awfully restful, do you know that, Virginia? One feels that one can tell you almost anything.'

As an illustration of this Stephen now begins to tell her about his own life since Oxford. People often confide in Virginia, mistaking the habitual immobility of her features for interest. Stephen tells her he is currently rather low-spirited as his mother has moved to Cheltenham and he is living in a house off Sloane Street, subletting a couple of rooms to friends. He tells her all this in a faint, rather exhausted sing-song, at the same time managing to greet a continuous stream of people who saunter by. In the end, interrupting his own views on the future of the novel, he suddenly says, 'I suppose you'll want to meet Monty . . . girls always do,' and with that he waves to someone who has just come through the door and immediately joins them. Monty is a tall and self-assured young man in army uniform with immensely black sleek hair and a small Clark Gable-ish moustache. He slides into the seat next to Virginia's and gives her a look that even she recognizes as one intended to make her knickers burst into flames.

'This is Monty Scott-Davidson; he's a sort of friend of mine,' says Stephen fussily. 'This is Virginia Musgrave; she's working for Theo Beavers.'

Monty takes a long time shaking her hand. 'Are you coming to Stephen's party this evening?'

'What party?' says Stephen irritably. 'I'm never ever going to give another party. Not after last weekend.'

'You are,' says Monty, whose conversation is by no means as dynamic as his appearance. 'Poppy and Zoe are in the George inviting everybody. They said nine o'clock at your place and bring a bottle.'

'Those girls!' complains Stephen, his cheeks twin tomatoes in his indignation. 'I let two rooms and end up living in a bawdy-house. Last Sunday I got home from seeing Mother and opened my bedroom door and found two naked people in my bed drinking my brandy. When I told them to get out they had the cheek to say they were friends of Poppy and to suggest I get in and join them.'

'You didn't?'

'Certainly not!' snapped Stephen crossly. '*He* was all right, but she was that stupid redhead who claims she was in *Black Velvet*. Anyway,' he concludes gloomily, 'we seem to be having a party tonight. Do come, Virginia.'

'Why not?' says Virginia, recklessly warmed by the memory of her incendiary activities, the beer and the hot look in Monty's eye.

By six o'clock Virginia is having second, third and fourth thoughts. She is by no means sure of the social correctness of going to a party in an unknown house given by a young man who she hardly knows whose family are completely unknown both to her own parents and to herself. While she is still failing to make a decision someone calls up from the floor below. There is a phone call for her.

Virginia leaps down to the entrance-hall with alacrity. With any luck it is Sir Fred proffering dinner somewhere expensive in Soho, thus solving Virginia's problem. But to her surprise the caller is Brooke.

'Hello there, stranger. Thought I'd give you a ring to see how you're getting on.'

Virginia is not deceived for an instant.

'Ma asked you to ring me?'

There is a long pause. Brooke is too lazy to lie.

'Sort of.'

'I'm *not coming home*, and that's *final*.'

'Steady on, old girl. It's me, remember?'

'I'm sorry. I'm just so fed up with Mother's letters—'

'She's concerned about you.'

'No, she isn't,' says her daughter calmly. 'She's jealous that I'm up here and she's down there. But there's absolutely nothing for me in the village, and don't you dare tell me to do voluntary work.'

Brooke, used to the vehemence of Virginia's speech, is undeterred.

'OK. Have it your own way. I've done my duty. What if they start bombing you?'

'We've got a perfectly good shelter,' says Virginia tersely.

'OK, OK. Pax. Tell me about yourself. Have you got a job?'

'Yes, in a publisher's. It's great fun. What about you? Are you flying all the time?'

95

'Pretty well. I'm just finishing the first tour of duty, so I'm being stood down for a few days. I'm off to see the Alberrys next weekend in Newmarket.'

'Oh, give them my regards. I saw Daphne last week at the Savoy Grill.'

They chat on easily, pleasantly until Brooke's money runs out. Virginia returns to her room, seething. How dare her mother try to get Brooke to put pressure on her! It is now a matter of the utmost importance that Virginia goes out tonight and has a good time. Especially since she is now almost sure that her mother is miserably bored in Suffolk.

Stephen's mother's house is in a smart little mews off Draycott Avenue and, in spite of her brave words, as Virginia stands outside the front door later that evening she realizes she is extremely nervous. Obscurely she feels she should not be going to this party – any party – on her own. But for once there is simply no one free. Cecily is still out doing good to the soldiers and, it being Friday night, Devora is out doing the same thing, though in a rather different way. It is a matter of staying at home or going on her own. Though honesty compels her to admit that Cecily wouldn't have dreamt of going to a party like this in the first place.

'What sort of people are they, Virginia?' she would have demanded sternly, and Virginia would have been forced to admit that she did not know.

In spite of the closed windows and blackout curtains Virginia can hear the party long before the door is opened. Inside there is a dense crush of bodies and a general sense of voices shouting and doors slamming. Upstairs in the drawing-room the wind-up gramophone is blaring to a largely indifferent crowd. Virginia gazes round in perplexity, her limited social experiences of hunt balls and refugee benefits having in no way prepared her for what she feels sure Uncle Piers would have classified as the 'Bohemian' behaviour of Stephen's friends. For a start *none* of the men wears a suit, and the girls, heavily made-up, wear clothes that Virginia is at once able to categorize as both arty and tarty. Taking her courage in her hands, Virginia enquires until she finds Stephen talking to a poet.

'You look like a good deed in a naughty world,' he bellows in her ear, adding much to her mystification: 'And what a witty hat.' He then kisses her drunkenly on the cheek and takes her arm. 'The food went hours ago, but come and get a drink.'

In the kitchen there are a number of bottles of wine from little-known parts of the Mediterranean. Stephen pours her what appears to be a small vase full of sherry. 'Monty's been looking for you. He's been talking about you all the afternoon.'

Well, he can jolly well go on waiting, thinks Virginia as she sits down and quietly sips her drink. She is just starting on her second glass when a strong arm grabs her and she finds herself locked in close eye-contact with the smouldering Monty.

'I've been looking for you everywhere,' he breathes, implying that no stone in the universe has been left undisturbed in his relentless search. 'Let's go and dance.'

Displaying considerably more intelligence than Virginia had given him credit for, Monty has hidden various bottles at strategic points throughout the house, and by midnight they are both completely plastered. The rooms are jammed to capacity now, and the blackout curtains make the atmosphere even denser.

Virginia is beginning to feel she ought to go home, and tries to unpeel her cheek from Monty's where it appears to be welded like a flypaper. She has the curious sensation that she is flying at an immense height and down below she can see everybody else looking up like ants. Even her mother would look like an ant from up here, she thinks, and the idea actually makes her laugh out loud.

'What's wrong?' says Monty with one of his burning glances.

'Oh, nothing. I'm just enjoying myself,' says Virginia.

'Good,' says Monty carefully. 'I want you to enjoy yourself.'

With that he grinds his moustache into her upper lip and shoves what appears at first to be a small pickled cucumber into her mouth. Virginia is very drunk and it takes her a moment or two to identify this as Monty's tongue. Courteously she does not object, but she does wish he'd cleaned his teeth. They have the same slippery sensation as the rocks at Cromer at low tide.

After this has gone on for some time Virginia begins to feel rather unwell and says so with difficulty.

'Tell you what,' says Monty quickly. 'Grand idea. Let's sit in Poppy's room.'

At Poppy's dressing-table two girls are repinning their bra-straps but they melt away in the face of Monty, who promptly locks the door.

'You must be terribly hot in that jacket,' he says. 'Slip it off, and I'll get you a glass of water.'

Virginia is really beginning to feel rather terrible and sits down on Poppy's filthy and crumpled counterpane. The room is beginning to tilt sideways in the most alarming way.

'Supposing we just lie down a bit until you feel better,' suggests Monty. 'And then I'll take you home.'

Virginia makes room for him on the bed beside her and closes her eyes. Outside on the stairs they are doing the Conga. She hopes they will not try to come in here.

'Oh, Virginia,' says Monty, suddenly propping himself up on one elbow then collapsing heavily on top of her. 'I love you. I adore you. You're the most beautiful girl I've ever met. I want to be with you for ever and ever and never let this moment end. . . .'

What is he going on about? thinks Virginia crossly, squashed under his considerable weight and dimly aware that someone is struggling with her suspenders. Monty continues his solitary litany in praise of womanhood, and Virginia feels a sharp pain between her legs. The room roars round and round as Virginia passes out with Monty still on top of her.

Where Poppy slept that night is never clear. Virginia wakes up at half-past six to find herself lying in a sordid bedroom on a wholly repulsive bed. For a moment she can hardly open her eyes, and when she does she almost screams with pain, for someone appears to be boring a stake through the back of her skull. Her clothes are scattered all over the floor, and she is aware that she is sore between her legs. Furthermore someone is snoring in her ear. As she cautiously edges out of bed she turns and looks at her sleeping companion. Monty is lying on his back with his mouth open. There is an oily patch on the pillow from his hair. He is still wearing his trousers and lies there legs akimbo, unbuttoned and unlovely. Virginia silently dresses, unlocks the door and makes her way down the stairs and out of the house. Outside in the mews the sun is shining brightly and there are geraniums and petunias in the window-boxes. There are no buses, and Virginia decides to walk home across Hyde Park. It is nine o'clock when she reaches the hostel and lets herself quietly in. In her room she redoes her hair, washes her face and goes down to breakfast. Cecily has clearly gone out early, and Rachel and Devora always sleep in late on a Saturday. Virginia feels light-headed and hung-over. As she goes back to her room she sees a familiar green letter in her pigeonhole. She takes it out and tears it up, then stuffs the pieces in the fire-bucket and covers them with sand. There is another envelope in her pigeonhole, and Virginia opens it without curiosity. It is from the family solicitors. Virginia had occasion to contact them on her arrival in London and now, as Mrs Musgrave is apparently neither receiving nor answering letters, in the event of any family business they contact Virginia. The letter is short and to the point, informing her that the tenants of the Musgraves' flat have decided to surrender the lease early and have actually moved out. As a result the porter now has the key. Can Virginia please apprise her mother of these facts?

Virginia refolds the letter thoughtfully. Her first thought is that it might be worth going round some time to see if any of her old clothes could be made over or refurbished. Then she has a second thought which leaves her breathless with excitement, her hangover forgotten. She remembers that prolonged and mysterious trip Mrs Musgrave made to London straight after Mr Chamberlain's broadcast. She had come back to the Dower House with a distinctly smug look on her face, but no new clothes. Virginia knew that look on her mother's face. It meant she'd been on a spree. With any luck the stuff would still be in the flat, thinks Virginia, and within ten minutes is on her way back across Hyde Park to Knightsbridge. It is the work of a few minutes to collect the keys before Virginia is letting herself into the flat in Cadogan Square. Her heart is beating so fast and so loudly that for a moment she has to lean against the door. It is quiet and very dark after the sunshine outside. Because of her extended time in Paris this is the first time in two years that Virginia had been here and she finds it strange to think she never thought of it as home. Most of the best stuff has gone into store, but even so it does not explain the desolate feeling in the flat. Can places absorb memories? thinks Virginia, and suddenly finds she can hardly breathe in this atmosphere. Abruptly she runs down the hall to her mother's room. A quick glance through the wardrobes reveals that there is nothing here. Impatiently she goes back to the hall and glances around. Of course! That fifth bedroom that's now used for the storeroom. Virginia fumbles with the bunch of keys and at last finds the right one. She turns on the light and surveys the room. Clearly her mother's maid has been here before her. Mother would never have left things so tidy. There are two chests of drawers and a large wardrobe which seems worth investigating.

To her unspeakable delight Virginia's suspicions prove to be well founded. The bottom three drawers of the first chest are entirely filled with dresses packed in the tissue paper in which they left the shop. Virginia sits back on her heels and is staggered. Even she is taken aback at the riches displayed. There must be a thousand pounds' worth of clothes here. Day dresses, sumptuous evening gowns, a couple of very smart little two-pieces, shoes, handbags. . . . Virginia really admires the taste which her mother has displayed in arraying herself to meet Armageddon and begins to pack them into a convenient suitcase. It is criminal to think of them mouldering here. In the top drawer are a number of shallow boxes from the Cerisette in Bond Street. They yield cami-knicks, petticoats, some enchanting camisoles and two new nightdresses. Not to mention the half-dozen pairs of silk stockings that she finds underneath. Goodness, she's filled the suitcase already! There is nothing for it but to take the other one, and she hasn't even started on the other chest of drawers yet.

At first it is disappointing, yielding nothing but Brooke's old school uniform. But when Virginia pulls out the bottom drawer she is assailed by the most gorgeous smells and knows she has struck lucky again. There are two whole unopened bottles of 'My Sin' and one of Chanel No. 5, not to mention creams, foundations, lotions, bath essences and talcs. There are two dozen large cakes alone of geranium soap and another six boxes of Yardley's Lavender. Devora must never be allowed to get her hand on *this* lot, thinks Virginia briskly, and carefully packs the other suitcase. After she has appropriated several charming little embroidered blouses from a shop in South Molton Street, Virginia turns her attention to the wardrobe. This proves a little disappointing. Her mother's best furs are either at Musgrave or in store at Harrods; still, that silver fox, though long in the tooth, is very chic for the evening, and a poor-quality mink is better than none at all with another cold winter forecast. At the bottom of the wardrobe Virginia finds fresh treasures. Two new evening bags and four pairs of evening shoes. Virginia tries the shoes on and finds they fit perfectly. At last she and her mother are the same size. This thought gives her an obscure satisfaction. Now she is nearly ready. There are just one or two things to do. There is a pile of hat-boxes in the wardrobe, and Virginia goes through them quickly in a desultory way, removing three of the smarter creations. Briskly she goes through the pockets of her mother's coats, and the results are quite gratifying – thirty bob in cash, a whole packet of cigarettes and a pair of very pretty earrings that Mrs Musgrave must have pulled off at the end of the evening and forgotten about. Virginia shuts the cases, locks them and puts them in the hall. Then she searches around until she finds what she wants – a really sharp pair of nail-scissors. It is a matter of seconds to tip out a dozen of her mother's hats on to the bed and briskly and efficiently cut them to pieces with the nail-scissors. Only when the carpet is strewn with tulle, velvet and straw does Virginia replace the scissors, lock the door and return the keys to the porter.

Flush with her ready cash, she hails a taxi. She feels not a single pang of guilt. Possession being nine-tenths of the law, she has the stuff and she's going to keep it.

(As chance will have it, Virginia is never called to account. In November a shaken porter brings the news that the Musgrave flat has had a direct hit and been completely destroyed. 'Good,' says Virginia and puts the phone down.)

Virginia totters upstairs with her two laden suitcases. She has to pause and get her breath back on every landing but finally makes the safety of her own room where she carefully unpacks her treasures, gloating. The last cake of soap is safely stowed away and she puts the cases in the boxroom at the end of the corridor, and is suddenly aware of a tremendous lassitude. Running a bath, she notices with a detached, almost scientific, interest that she has blood on the inside of her thigh.

After her bath she goes back upstairs, passing an exhausted-looking Rachel on her way out. From Devora's room comes the sound of a gramophone and the smell of pear-drops. Devora is lying on her bed waving her fingers in an attempt to dry her nail varnish and reading the copy of *Vogue* which the girls are expressly forbidden to remove from the library downstairs.

'Turn the record over, will you, darling?' she murmurs, her eyes still on the article. 'It says here that the Suivi is the only place to start the evening. Perhaps I'll get Eric to take me there tonight. My word,' she says slyly looking up, 'you had quite a night of it by the look of things. Something on your mind?'

'Yes,' says Virginia, sitting down unasked on the bed. 'Tell me where you go for one of those things that stops you having babies.'

Devora looks at her from half-lowered heavy lids, a curious expression on her face. It is amusement, contempt . . . . and recognition. Virginia is clearly one of them now.

'Well, my dear,' she says with a throaty purr, 'how the mighty are fallen. I hope Cecily doesn't know,' she adds maliciously. 'Don't go, silly. Here's the address. He's in Welbeck Street. If you give him a ring on Monday, he'll fix you up. He's a very sympathetic man. By the way . . . why don't you join Eric and me tonight? I'm sure he's got a friend. He's on leave and he's really rather a hoot. Money to burn as well.'

'Thanks,' says Virginia, getting up, 'Perhaps I will.' She goes back to her own room, locks the door and lies down, her eyes hot and prickly from lack of sleep. After all, what did it matter? What did anything matter, come to that?

CHAPTER
EIGHT

'CLOTHES! Why does everything always come down to clothes?' No answer is forthcoming to this (in any case) purely rhetorical question. Beattie is in one of the subterranean laundry-rooms in the Great House preparing her limited wardrobe for a weekend in the country. She whistles quietly to herself as she conscientiously folds and presses. It will be the longest time she's ever spent with Brooke, and surely asking her away with him to meet his friends must indicate some sort of statement of commitment?

Beattie's iron slows. She had come back to college hoping that their night together had proved to be the start of a real intimacy between them. But as the days have lengthened into spring and then into summer she has realized that she and Brooke approach a love-affair from entirely different positions. The only certainty she has is that her own feelings seem to grow stronger, regardless of his treatment of her. She craves his presence. He is like a drug to which she has become instantly and obsessively addicted. At the same time Beattie feels she is struggling in quicksands desperate for firmer ground. Since she has met Brooke she seems to have become two different people: the old vigorous sensible Beattie, and a timid obstinate sort of person who wants Brooke so desperately that she can drown out any interior voice which tries to tell her that Brooke is not at all the person she pretends he is, nor does he remotely feel for her what she feels for him.

And now Beattie is properly involved with Brooke he begins to reveal a volatile and unpredictable temper that terrifies her. Anything can trigger him off: an imagined slight from a waiter, too slow service from shop assistants. Brooke can fly into a fury that will create tension for the whole afternoon afterwards. Sometimes he will pick her up in a bad mood and then nag at her about something small and unimportant such as her hair or her dress. Or he'll say her lipstick is smudged, and go on and on at her until Beattie is actually in tears. Then he'll tell her she's a silly little thing, kiss her and drive on again whistling, his good humour apparently restored. On other occasions he will simply not talk to her at all, and sit in silence.

They continue to make love, usually in Brooke's car, always with the maximum inconvenience. In a country area like Chillington it is inconceivable that they can book into a hotel for the afternoon as man and wife, and as it is Beattie knows perfectly well that she puts her own career in jeopardy

101

each time she makes love to Brooke. Why on earth does she do it? She is usually so tense that there is little pleasure in the act. And she has no clue as to Brooke's feelings – if any – for her. She longs to know that she is at least special for him, but she is now too beaten, too discouraged and finally too frightened to ask. Though Beattie may have a limited idea of what a relationship and marriage are really like, she does at least have a very clear idea about courtship, and try as she may to bend the evidence she knows perfectly well that Brooke is not behaving like a man who's planning for them to share a life together. In the village, if you are courting, certain public rituals have to be gone through to announce the seriousness of your intent. After a certain number of walks on Sunday afternoons or perhaps trips into Ipswich you would visit his family and have tea with them, and the following week he would come to yours. You would meet his friends. You are seen publicly as a couple. Eventually you would become engaged and the girl would begin to prepare a bottom drawer. The banns were called, you married at the village church and either moved in with his parents or your own until such time as you could afford your own home.

The situation with Brooke, stripped of all its glamour, is that she's having sex with a man who has never made any mention of a shared future with her, with the added irritant, so far as Beattie is concerned, that she has lost any position of strength she might have had, by sleeping with him. Everything seems to have happened either back to front or in the wrong order, and out of this mess is meant to come love, security, marriage, happiness – all the things that Beattie has been brought up to believe are the primary goals of a woman's life. From January onwards Louie is in despair with her and, seeing her come home yet again with red eyes, has a row with her of such monumental proportions that neither of them dares broach the subject again.

'Look, Beattie,' Louie finally shouts. 'Just don't ask me for my opinion again. You keep asking me what I think. I tell you, and you get furious with me. You don't want my opinion; you want me to say what you want to hear. Well, I can't do that. I was brought up to speak my mind, and I don't know what your Brooke is up to but I do know he shouldn't be sending you home in tears like this, breaking your heart and interfering with your work and not caring twopence whether or not you get caught for what you're up to. So just don't let's talk about it again. You must live your own life.'

But none the less it had been Louie who had insisted that Beattie got herself 'fixed up' as she so horribly put it. And it had been a horrible business. They had gone to Norwich for the afternoon. In one of the backstreets Beattie had given a false address to a family doctor, claiming to be evacuated down there. The doctor's surgery was squalid, the housekeeper suspicious, and the doctor old and seedy.

'But at least you're all right now,' said Louie afterwards as they enjoyed a congratulatory teacake in a teashop opposite the cathedral. 'Men! They never think of it until it's too late. That's how my sister got caught, you know. I like children. But I don't want to have eight like my mum and all in two rooms. If you had a baby now, they'd send you off home before you could say "gripe water".'

102

So why does she keep going out with Brooke? Beattie finds herself asking this question with increasing frequency as winter turns into spring and spring gives way to early summer. Well, she loves him. But what does that mean? It means she loves being with him, and when he is being nice to her she is the happiest person in the world. But there are other reasons so inextricably mixed up with her feelings that she hardly knows herself what it is that binds her so tightly to Brooke. There are a whole series of unworthy reasons for not giving him up, like his car, the pleasure of being seen out in it with him. There is the fact that Brooke is who he is and that she is who she is and that they are having an affair. That his newly formed squadron believe him to be some sort of superman and that he has a potent effect on other girls at Chillington. There is also the matter of his promise to take her to London to see *Gone with the Wind*, currently the ambition of every girl in the college, and to stay in a hotel and to go dancing. In other words there are always a million reasons in her mind, both profound and superficial, why she cannot give him up when it comes home to her, as it soberly does from time to time, that she is living a schizophrenic existence and taking terrible risks – risks, incidentally, which *he* seems totally unaware of, and on the whole not very interested in.

And anyway.

(These bouts of introspection always ended with an 'and anyway'.)

Since Brooke is flying almost every night now, how can she expect him to be normal when he is in a constant state of tension and anxiety? This partial truth has its usual tranquillizing effect on Beattie. And, besides, hasn't he asked her away to spend the weekend in Newmarket with him? This is surely the mark of a man who is beginning to feel committed.

Beattie folds her clothes carefully and bears them gingerly back to the cottage where she spends the whole evening curling her hair, buffing her nails, plucking her eyebrows and polishing her shoes. Louie looks on and says nothing.

Brooke is late picking her up, and when he does appear he is in a terrible mood. The car leaps forward, and Beattie turns to him in concern. 'Brooke! Your face! What's happened?'

'I was in the Bell yesterday lunchtime and two Hooray-Henrys back from Dunkirk duffed me up in the gents'.'

'But why?'

'Oh, apparently the RAF has a new role. I thought we were there to fly planes. Apparently it's our real job to protect the infantry when they cock things up. They wanted to know where the RAF was during the evacuation. Jesus,' says Brooke furiously, 'we don't exist to provide cover for the Army. And a fat lot of good it would have been; we'd have thrown our planes in and lost them as well as the ones they'd already lost over France. But I'm late because the bloody car wouldn't start. I knew there was something wrong with the distributor leads and I asked that ass Simpson to have a look. He said he'd done it, and listen to the engine.' He lapses into silence, his driving clearly indicating the depths of his irritation and bad temper. As they approach Newmarket, Beattie asks him tentatively who will be there this weekend.

'Lord, didn't I tell you? We've known the Alberrys for years. Lord A was one of Father's best friends. Daphne's a sweetie; you'll love her. Gerrard's home for two days' leave and he's brought a couple of friends from the regiment. I was at school with them – Peter Guyler and Michael Hope-Bravington. Michael's unofficially engaged to Daphne, though as it's still not been in *The Times* I'm not sure if it's on. Peter's girlfriend, Popsy Gleadell, is coming as well. Oh, and old Gareth is due for lunch tomorrow. They fixed up for Jossie Eidenow to come over for supper to even up the numbers.'

Beattie is hoping that Brooke will have some word of reassurance to offer for her first foray into the old upper-class tradition of weekending, but after narrowly missing a man and his dog and expressing himself violently on the subject of pedestrians Brooke puts his foot down hard on the accelerator and drives on in silence.

The Alberrys live in a large red-brick Gothic pile that bears a disturbing resemblance to St Pancras Station. A maid whose aged and lined face looks incongruous beneath her crisp white cap and streamers answers the door and lets them into a wide, dimly lit hall which manages, even on a hot June day, to smell of wet dogs. As the maid struggles in with their bags an elderly querulous voice from the back of the hall hails them.

'Ah, Brooke old man, there you are.' A crabbed, bent, elderly person shuffles forward. This must surely be Alberry *père*, thinks Beattie, putting on a kindly welcoming smile only to find when the full light falls on him that this elderly person is apparently about Brooke's age.

'Hello, Gerro old man.'

The two men punch each other ritually on the shoulder.

'I say, that's a shiner. Lamp-post?'

'Bloody Army.'

'Ours or theirs?'

'Yours, I'm afraid. Beattie, this is Gerrard. Gerrard, this is Beatrice Blythe.'

'Thrilled,' says Gerrard, offering her his hand. 'Adams,' he roars without taking his eyes from Beattie's face. The aged maid appears enquiringly at the doorway. 'Is their stuff out of the car?'

'Yes, Mr Gerrard.'

'Then, take Miss Blythe to her room. She needs to powder her nose.'

It is a command, not a suggestion. Beattie meekly trails upstairs behind Adams to the third floor. She is about to unpack her case when the maid's voice reproves her from the doorway. 'There's no need for you to do that, miss,' she says, eyeing Beattie frostily. 'I'll unpack for you while you have your tea. Her Ladyship is on the lawn.'

With that she withdraws, leaving Beattie feeling thoroughly rattled. She takes off her jacket, brushes her hair and powders her nose. From the back of the house she can hear the sound of female laughter. Retracing her footsteps back to the hall, she finds her way out through the french windows on to the terrace. A group of young people are either lying on the grass or sitting in deck-chairs. In the centre is an elderly woman with a vague expression and a grey silk dress. She is sitting in front of a tray on a low table which is entirely covered by a vast silver tea-service. Beattie waits hesitantly for a moment, then Brooke notices her, offers her his deck-chair and introduces her off-handedly to the group. Curious faces smile, assess her dress, then return to their own conversations. Beattie is handed a cup of tea by Lady Alberry, who murmurs something inconsequential about gnats.

The overwhelming impression given by Brooke's friends is, first, how much noise they make, and, second, how different is that noise from, say, the voices of the girls at Chillington, or those of the Kedges at play. Here, everybody talks all the time at the top of their voice, as if the content of what they're saying is so original and so amusing that it really needs a megaphone to do it justice. Then, again, there is the accent in which it is spoken. If anyone at college had said, 'Oh, frightfully well said, Brooke,' in that exaggerated banshee screech of lengthened vowel sounds, they would never have lived it down throughout their college career. At Chillington it would be described as getting above yourself; here it is simply the patois of the natives.

Daphne Alberry is sitting a few yards from Beattie almost at Brooke's feet. She is a small restless girl with a neat-featured face and curling yellow hair. She reminds Beattie instantly of Miss Frobisher's canary with her endless restless fidgeting, her incessant high chatter and her way of saying 'Oh! Oh! Oh!' whenever anybody bravely contradicts her. She also clearly cannot keep her eyes off Brooke. Beattie begins to feel like an actor who has turned up for a performance and found the play has been changed, yet is still somehow fully committed to taking part. At first her silence bothers her, but gradually she realizes she need not worry. With the exception of Lady Alberry, who turns to her after about five minutes and clearly cannot remember her name, and wants to know if she needs more tea, no one says a word to her.

Popsy Gleadell, ginger-haired, buck-toothed and freckled, is sitting on Beattie's right in conversation with Peter Guyler, a shy sallow youth with a boil on his neck. Beattie listens astonished to the conversation or, rather, the lack of it. In the space of nearly an hour the only words she hears Popsy utter – frequently, it is true – are the comment 'Oh, no!' But somehow she has made it into an entire vocabulary. For example, if she is being playful she can say 'Oh, nooooo!' punctuated with an affected laugh. If the conversation gets really exciting, as when Peter is describing a particularly nasty bit of traffic outside Headingley, then she can say 'Oh, no!' in a clipped concerned sort of way at short intervals. If the conversation simply becomes too exciting, as when Peter tells them the story about the set-to he has had with the man at the garage about his crankshaft, Popsy will simply let the occasional 'Oh, no!' trickle from her lips as she stares at him with rounded eyes. It is a virtuoso performance in dullness. Gerrard comes out on the lawn to join them, the only man in uniform. Now wearing a panama hat with a black ribbon and with a walking-stick at his side, he looks exactly like the famous portrait of Bismarck at eighty. He then proceeds to excite Popsy almost to the point of hysteria with his account of the difficulties of getting a good bridge four together in the mess.

Daphne's intended, or not intended – only *The Times* can clear up this dreadful area of uncertainty – is talking to Brooke and Daphne. He is tall and dark and rather saturnine with well-oiled hair. Beattie dislikes him at first sight but would be hard-pressed to give a rational reason for it. Perhaps it is simply that he looks cold.

The shadows lengthen on the lawn, Beattie enjoys her tea and cucumber sandwiches, and presently they go into the house for drinks. At this point Peter Guyler turns to her, dragging his gaze reluctantly from Brooke, and says: 'I'm awfully sorry, I've forgotten your name.'

'That's all right,' smiles Beattie, 'I've forgotten yours as well. My name is Beatrice. What's yours?'

'Peter,' he says reluctantly. 'I say, what pack do you hunt with?'

'I don't ride,' says Beattie cheerfully.

'Don't ride, eh? My word! Oh, I say, Brooke, I can't let you get away with *that*.' And he turns happily back to Brooke again.

Lord Alberry joins them for drinks or, rather, lets them join him. During the entire weekend Beattie is never to see him without a drink in his hand. He gives her a surly nod and sits down beside his son on the sofa. Beattie has heard of women growing up to resemble their mothers, but this is something quite new. Sitting side by side, it is extremely hard to know if the child is the father of the man or vice versa. With his jutting jaw, putty-coloured face and hunched shoulders Gerrard has the air of a man getting in training for the label of 'crusty old bachelor' by the time he is twenty-eight. He notices Beattie looking at him and fixes her with his cold contemptuous stare.

'I suppose you don't play bridge.'

'Why do you suppose that?' asks Beattie, deciding once and for all that they are simply the nastiest set of people she has ever met.

Gerrard looks at her for a long moment, then simply turns away.

'I saw you talking to old Gerro,' says Brooke as they go up to change for dinner. 'He's a scream, isn't he? I'll give you a tap when I'm ready.'

Left alone in her over-chintzy room, Beattie goes immediately to the mirror to confirm *(a)* that she's not become invisible and *(b)* that she's not contracted some disfiguring affliction since she arrived. But, yes, she is still there. The simple fact is that these people don't know her and apparently don't want to.

The Alberrys dress for dinner, and half an hour later she and Brooke descend the stairs in their evening best. There are more drinks, then into the dining-room after some muted bongs on the gong in the hall struck by the withered arm of Adams. Beattie discovers she has Lady Alberry on her right and Peter Guyler on her left. Brooke is at the other end of the table next to Daphne. Peter Guyler's head is permanently drawn in Brooke's direction like a plant racked by some mysterious tropism. Faced with his back and Lady Alberry's profile, Beattie tries to draw a few syllables from her Ladyship's pinched lips. It is almost hopeless. Beattie is currently reading *Mansfield Park*, and two minutes' conversation with Lady Alberry makes her speculate as to whether her Ladyship herself is reading the book with a view to modelling herself on Lady Bertram. If one of her children directly addresses her, she manages to arouse herself to some reply, usually taking

106

the form of an endorsement of what the child has just said. 'Too amazing,' she murmurs when Daphne is going on about the evacuated children in the village, and 'Too shocking!' is her reflection when her son starts complaining about the state of first-class carriages. Out of the blue she leans forward and asks Beattie what she does. Beattie replies that she is training to be a teacher, whereupon Lady Alberry looks at her with an expression almost of interest and says apparently in reply: 'Worms are rife you know. I simply can't understand it. We had poor Benjy done a month ago and it's all back again. My husband,' she says, leaning forward with quiet emphasis, 'is livid.' With that she turns to endorse a remark from Daphne, after which she turns back to Beattie and asks her again what she does.

Beattie is obscurely pleased to find that the food isn't very good Chez Alberry, even though the drink continues to arrive at the table as if from an underground stream. They're all slightly tiddly as they return to the drawing-room for more drinks and coffee. It is only ten to nine, and Beattie's spirits sink at the thought of another three hours of this. Several games are suggested, but in the end Lord and Lady Alberry retire to bed leaving them simply to sit and chat. As Daphne said, 'With old friends, the nicest thing in the world is just to sit around and chew the rag.'

Such rag-chewing as is done is conducted entirely by the men with Daphne and Popsy repeating their duet of the afternoon, until Popsy, worn out with loquacity and whisky, falls asleep next to Benjy and his worms. It is the men who actually talk, and within a few minutes Beattie is mystified by the superficiality of what they say. Opinions are offered about service life. The other three men are all stationed at Boston but so far have seen no active service. They're all clearly enjoying the Army as a holiday from their normal mundane lives in the City, but beyond that they have little to say about the war. Beattie, listening to the idle ebb and flow of their conversation, wonders if they are aware of how often they contradict themselves, sometimes within the space of a few minutes. The common man is simultaneously the salt of the earth and a disgrace to the education system. Class simply doesn't matter any more, and it is absolutely essential to plan your war so you can spend it with the right people. No one cares a hang these days which school you go to, they all loudly agree, yet Beattie has never met a group of people who literally cannot make conversation without making it clear every five minutes or so that they had all been to Eton. Perhaps I'm just jealous, thinks Beattie wryly, wondering if this is the moment to burst into reminiscences about dear old Dereham Market Girls' Grammar School. The thought makes her smile briefly.

Brooke's friends behave like a group of people who've been assembled purely to reassure each other. They speak endlessly of the memories that unite them: their first hunt ball, the dancing classes in Knightsbridge, their first wall games, that extraordinary house-party at the Steepletons'. Whatever had happened to Charlie Steepleton? Was it true that his long-suffering family had finally sent him to Rhodesia? At this point Beattie begins to nod and she tells Brooke that she thinks she will go to bed. There are a chorus of goodnights, a pause, then Peter asks Gerro what on earth happened to that stuffed tiger he brought to Oxford with him.

At a quarter to one Brooke slips into Beattie's room, then into her bed, finally into her. It is the first time that congress has actually taken place in a double bed, but Beattie is too tired to appreciate it. Afterwards Brooke has a cigarette before returning to his own room.

'You were very quiet tonight,' he remarks. 'They're a jokey crowd, aren't they? Lord, the times I used to have with old Gerro and Daphne. She was my first real girlfriend. All during her season I spent a fortune coming down from Oxford to see her. It never came to anything; she's got nothing coming to her, old Alberry's mortgaged to the hilt and it wouldn't have done. Michael's old man is loaded; she'll be far better off with him. She's a great girl. First-class shot as well.'

'What time is Gareth arriving?'

'Lunchtime. Jossie Eidenow will be over, too. She's an absolute poppet.'

'Don't tell me,' says Beattie, stifling a huge yawn, 'I'll simply love her. Good night, Brooke.'

At breakfast the next day Daphne actually speaks to Beattie. She suggests they have a game of tennis. Apprised by Brooke in advance, Beattie has brought her tennis things with her, and trimly clad in aertex shirt and shorts she proceeds to pulverize Daphne in three straight sets. The luncheon gong is going when they finally call it a day, with six-two to Beattie in the final set.

'I say, you do play well. Do you belong to a club?'

'No, I just play at school,' says Beattie, aware that Daphne is noticing her properly for the first time and rapidly exchanging indifference for dislike.

They change and join the others for lunch. Gareth has arrived by this time and immediately springs to his feet and kisses her, warming Beattie's rather chilled heart.

'How are you, then, lovely girl?' he asks fondly.

'Wonderful,' says Beattie, bravely noticing Daphne has sat down next to her brother and in answer to his question has made a face and said something under her breath.

Gareth introduces her to Jossie, a tiny, intense, breathless sort of girl with the slowest voice Beattie has ever heard outside the classrooms for the educationally subnormal. She favours a Popsy style of conversation, with subtle variants of injecting a very long pause between the 'oh' and the 'no', thereby gaining a reputation for desperate sincerity. She has two topics of conversation: her Scottie dog and her hay fever. Fortunately for her, she is extremely pretty.

After lunch a scratch tennis tournament has been arranged. Four couples are to take part with Gerro acting as umpire: he has given up tennis years ago apparently. It is a very warm afternoon indeed, but Beattie is aware of an atmosphere of tension that goes far beyond the weather. Beattie and Brooke thrash Gareth and Jossie, then stop for lemonade, while Daphne and Michael defeat Popsy and Peter. At four o'clock there is to be a final followed by tea. Daphne comes and joins Brooke and Beattie on the ground where they are enjoying a rather jokey conversation about tactics. Brooke has been gratified but somewhat taken aback to discover that Beattie is a rather better player than himself.

'I'll be ready in a couple of jiffs,' he says to the girls and goes off in the direction of the house. Beattie feels Daphne eyeing her carefully. But when she speaks it is in the friendliest possible way. To start with, it is simply a long string of compliments. Where had Beattie learnt to play so well, and did she have to practise that amazing overhead smash of hers? Beattie answers her courteously enough and wonders in her new-found cynicism where it is all leading. It soon becomes apparent that what Daphne actually wants is information about Beattie – where she comes from, who her people are, where she'd been to school, that sort of thing. It is Beattie's experience that people rarely want information for good reason: knowledge is, after all, power and clearly the result of her tennis prowess has simply been to upgrade Beattie in Daphne's eyes to the category of threat. In much the same way she has stonewalled Daphne's returns with her excellent overhead smash, Beattie evades her with vague answers or no answers at all. Brooke finally returns and tells them both to stop lolling around and start playing. Daphne is clearly in a very bad temper and plays her worst game of the day. Beattie and Brooke win easily, and Beattie sits down to tea feeling extremely cheerful.

Gareth brings his cup and saucer over and sits at her feet next to Lady Alberry. By dint of sheer perseverance he actually manages to have something approaching a conversation with Lady Alberry and reproves Beattie when her Ladyship eventually goes in to dress.

'You're far too diffident,' he says. 'People like that, you just have to keep banging on their head to keep their attention. I've got an Aunty Gwen just like her.'

Beattie giggles, aware that she is being disloyal to Brooke, but what does it matter? She is unlikely ever to see these people again unless – and that 'unless' seems to be growing fainter and fainter as the months pass. For the first time she faces the fact that there is no place for her in Brooke's life and stares at the daisy heads below her chair, completely defeated.

In any other company it could be reasonably assumed somebody pretty, intelligent and well mannered would at least be noticed. Here she counts for nothing because she hasn't been to the right schools, and could not produce the appropriate coded past. But does she really want to be included? Not really. But there is something deeply galling in being rejected by people that she herself despises.

At six o'clock they go in for the inevitable drinks, and Beattie is aware that there are new tensions and undercurrents of hostility that she does not understand. Brooke is very much the focal point of the group, with Daphne acting as his consort. Gerro and Peter seem physically drawn towards Brooke and can hear no voice except his. Popsy is sulking at Peter's lack of attention, while Michael clearly likes less and less the spectacle of his soi-disant fiancée hanging on to the arm of an old boyfriend. Added to this, Beattie is becoming uncomfortably aware that Gareth is really paying her an absurd amount of attention and that Brooke has noticed.

Lord and Lady Alberry come in towards the end of the drinks, sepulchral and creaking in greenish black, looking like Death and his consort on their way to the final judgement. Actually they are on their way to a Rotary dinner and dance. Left to themselves there is a sudden rush of adrenalin, and a good deal is drunk in a very short time.

Beattie goes up to change and finds that her red evening dress has been laid out for her on the bed. There is a faint musty indefinable smell in the air that makes her wrinkle her nose. It is impossible to open the windows because of the blackout screens, so she goes and runs a bath, dumping into it everything she finds on the bathroom shelf. Fragrant and dressed, she is putting on her face when Brooke knocks at the door and comes in, his colour high as the result of the sun and the whisky he's been drinking. Beattie realizes belatedly that Brooke is on the way to becoming very drunk indeed.

'Ready, my pretty? as Gareth would say. He seems to be finding you awfully attractive tonight.'

'Your friends seem to find you awfully attractive all the time,' retorts Beattie, subduing the heavy line of her brow with a smear of Vaseline.

'That's understandable. I'm awfully attractive. Men, women, horses, they simply can't resist me.'

'Why does Peter think you're so wonderful?'

'He's bound to me by chains of vice. I used to beat him regularly. I had to stop it eventually because he was getting to like it too much. No, I'm only joking. He was my fag, that's all. I think he hero-worships me a bit even now. Perhaps I should tell Popsy; she'd have a lot more success if she stopped sulking and used a riding-crop on him.'

Brooke laughs and bends forward to admire his own reflection in the mirror above Beattie's head.

It occurs to Beattie for the first time that all the eddies and small whirl-pools of tension and dissatisfaction involve Brooke in some way or another and that he is actively enjoying setting people at each other, then observing the consequences. It is with a feeling of foreboding that she follows him downstairs. Gareth is waiting for her and immediately pounces on her, seating himself beside her and telling her at some length and in some consider-able detail how pretty and how lovely she looks. Grateful as she is for some crumbs of interest in this bread pudding of indifference, Beattie is at first puzzled and then frankly irritated by Gareth's behaviour. It is one thing to tell someone you like their dress, quite another to be still going on about it at the top of your voice thirty minutes later. He continues to talk to her with a kind of feverish intensity, desperately trying to hold her eyes while his own gaze flicks constantly over her shoulder to where Brooke is holding court with Daphne. Then quite suddenly Beattie knows what it is all about, all his desperate desire to hold her attention. It has nothing to do with her, Beattie, at all. It is simply that Gareth wants to compete with Brooke and she is the pawn in the struggle. As she realizes this she looks at Gareth with some contempt and abruptly turns to Jossie, who is sitting beside her composedly talking to Michael. She is not going to be used like that by anyone. Beattie tells Jossie she likes her dress, which is actually delightful, being silver faille over taffeta. It supplies sufficient conversation, at Jossie's speed at least, to keep them going until dinner is announced.

Beattie takes care not to sit next to Gareth, much to his evident annoy-ance, and finds herself between Jossie and Michael. The meal is a repeat of the previous one so far as conversation goes, only tonight Gerro and Peter throw bread rolls at each other. Jossie regales Beattie with the latest developments in hay-fever cures and autosuggestion. Beattie listens with half an ear, and with the other half monitors the conversation around her, wondering if nothing has happened to these people since they've left school and they feel compelled to go on about their school days in such an obsessive way.

In the drawing-room afterwards, Daphne winds up the gramophone and, by dint of not actually letting go of Brooke's sleeve, persuades him to dance with her. Eventually he tears himself away and steers Beattie around the room a few times, but Daphne isn't deterred for a moment and simply dances with all her partners parallel to them and talks to Brooke over their shoulders.

Eventually Gerro gets tired of watching them dance – he'd given all that up years ago, he said – and suggests since it's a warm evening outdoors that they go out and play a game. But what? Daphne favours sardines. Jossie rather touchingly says she loves hide-and-seek.

'Let's take a vote,' says Brooke, acting as master of the revels.

'Oh, do, let's,' drawls Gareth, his pupils alarmingly dilated by drink. 'Do let's take a vote. Let's play up and play the game, shall we, Brooke? Must do things ship-shape and Bristol fashion. Let's be democratic at all costs, shall we? Brooke's frightfully keen on democracy, you know. I mean, there's nothing of the snob about our Brooke. Why, nowadays he even takes his gardener's daughter away to his posh friends for the weekend, eh, Beattie?' There is a sudden hush. Brooke merely looks bored. Gareth is grinning maliciously at Beattie, while Daphne is open-mouthed with delight. It is clearly far better than she dared hope.

'Shut up, Gareth, you drunken Welsh pig,' says Brooke finally.

'Hands up all those who want sardines? And all those who want hide-and-seek? OK, hide-and-seek has it. Who's going to be it?'

'Oh me,' cries Peter. 'Baggy me. I'll give you all fifty from *now*. One, two, three, four. . . .'

Beattie walks out into the warm June night and follows the path past the tennis court. She does not know or care where she's going and eventually finds herself in some kind of orchard on the edge of the vegetable garden. A full moon is coming and going behind a bank of cloud. She sits down and leans her back against an apple tree, regardless of her dress.

'What does it matter anyway?' she tells herself angrily. She doesn't like or respect these people. But obscurely, deep down, something is hurt. In humiliating her, somehow Gareth has humiliated her father as well, a man she loves and respects. She will not forgive Gareth for that. There is a light footfall on the grass, and Brooke appears swinging a whisky-bottle.

'Why aren't you hiding, you old spoilsport? Come on. We'll sit here in the shadow.' Brooke is obviously extremely drunk, and unwillingly Beattie joins him in the long grass.

'Cheer up, for Christ's sake. Gareth has just had too much to drink. I was a fool to bring him. We'll just have to pretend it didn't happen.'

'Oh, really?' says Beattie with irony. 'Gareth brings up my background in a deliberate attempt to humiliate me, and I'm supposed to ignore it, am I?'

111

'That's about the size of it,' says Brooke, taking a swig from his bottle. 'Come here. Peter couldn't find one of his own feet; he'll be hours yet.' With that he pulls her down beside him and tries to take one of her breasts out of the neck of her dress.

'Brooke, will you keep your hands to yourself?' says Beattie through her teeth. She has never felt less like making love. She tries to push him away, but he lies on top of her and tries to pull up her skirt.

'Come on, damn you,' he whispers fiercely. And just as fiercely Beattie fights back.

The moon comes out from behind a cloud and suddenly the orchard is flooded with cold silver light. Over Brooke's shoulder Beattie sees something that makes her sit up with a shriek. A man is standing in the shadow of the poplars, his face white and grey in the moonlight, his shoulders bowed like an old man. His small mouth is pouting in sensual concentration as with his hand pumping rhythmically in his mercifully darkened crotch he attempts a solo performance of what Brooke is seeking to achieve with Beattie. Beattie scrambles to her feet, her heart pounding, but Gerro has gone. Brooke sits up livid.

'What the *hell* has got into you tonight?'

'Your hateful bloody friends, that's what's got into me,' hisses Beattie. 'Didn't you see Gerro standing there watching us?'

'You're imagining things,' says Brooke.

Beattie picks up her skirts and runs. The place is a madhouse. Faintly from the direction of the house she can hear Peter calling 'I'm coming, I'm coming'. Chance would be a fine thing, thinks Beattie grimly as she bypasses the shrubbery and almost screams as someone catches her arm and draws her into the shadow of the summerhouse.

'Where are you off to in such a hurry, lovely? Is the bogyman after you? Why don't you hide here with your Uncle Gareth?'

'You, Gareth, can go to hell.'

'Oh, hoity toity, aren't we, all of a sudden? It was only a joke, Beattie, what I said. Come one, give us a nice smile.'

'Will you *please* let go of my arm?'

'No, Beattie, not until you give me a nice smile. One of those smiles you normally save for Brooke. He's a lucky man, Brooke, isn't he? But I doubt if he appreciates it. One day you'll know I did you a service here tonight. It's good to be reminded of reality once in a while. Because he won't marry you, Beattie. There now, don't struggle. And that's what you want, isn't it? It's what all nice girls want.'

His fingers bite cruelly into her bare arm. 'Brooke won't marry anyone like you, any more than he'd marry that amateur tart Daphne. Brooke never thinks beyond one day at a time, but there's one thing that Brooke thinks about the whole time and that's the main chance, and believe me, Beattie, you can't compete. You're a pretty girl, but when Brooke decides to get married he'll marry money. Somebody rich enough to enable Brooke to live the way he thinks he deserves. And you'll be left high and dry, lovely girl – and, do you know, you'll be much better off. Do you know why?'

Gareth is pressed against Beattie now, his obsessive whisky-sodden voice droning in her ear.

'Because he's not a very nice person, your Brooke. You don't know what I mean? Perhaps that's because you're a nice girl, and he's not a nice man. No one actually likes Brooke, you know. Oh, weak people flock round him because they want to *be* like him, but they don't *like* him. They want to know that secret of his strength. Well, I'll tell you what the secret is: he doesn't care about anybody in the world except himself. Of course they worship him at Gatton. If you fly with Brooke, you know you'll be safe because he cares terribly about himself and that's all. So why don't you abandon the sinking ship, Beattie, before the rat starts abandoning you? You and I could get along. I've been crazy about you ever since – Aaaaagghhhh!'

Beattie has regained her balance and, grabbing Gareth by the lapels of his evening suit, knees him hard in the groin with all the pent-up anger of the evening. Then she pushes him over backwards and makes her way to the house.

'Seen you, Beattie,' calls Peter.

'Go to hell,' says Beattie brusquely and strides on into the house.

'No one seems to be playing properly,' she hears him complain as she lets herself into the side of the house into what seems to be a study. She kicks off her shoes and collapses on the sofa, her head throbbing. Then, worn out with anger and the amount she's had to drink, she simply falls asleep.

When she wakes she wonders first where she is. Then it all comes back. The house is quiet and she is very, very cold. Clearly everybody was asleep hours ago. She catches sight of the luminous clock on the desk. It is nearly two o'clock. She goes out into the hall and listens, then silently begins to climb the stairs. The house is a pool of darkness. Nobody stirs. Beattie opens her bedroom door and finds no accusing Brooke asking where the hell she's been. The room is mercifully empty save for that faint musty odour. She goes to the bathroom, takes off her dress, washes and makes her way thankfully to bed. As she closes her eyes pictures of the events of the evening flash wearily in front of her like shorts at the cinema. Resolutely she tries to push them away and is just about to fall asleep when unmistakably she hears a sound in the wardrobe at the side of her bed. Instantly she stiffens into sitting position, her heart thudding. But there it is again, unmistakably a faint clattering among the coathangers. Trembling, Beattie puts on the light, puts on her dressing gown, then taking her confidence in both hands wrenches open the wardrobe door.

Sitting on the floor of the wardrobe, his knees jammed under his chin and the folds of Beattie's coat piled up on his head like a judge's cap, is Gerro. He regards her drunkenly for a moment in surprise, hiccups, then begins to crawl out of the wardrobe on all fours. He pulls himself up by hanging on to the handles of the chest of drawers and looks at Beattie owlishly.

'Spoilsport,' is all he says. 'Daphne always lets me watch.'

With that he lurches out of the room taking with him the smell of old man and decay. Beattie sits on the bed wondering if everybody in the house is crazy except herself. She can't sleep now. She decides she will find Brooke. His room is on the floor below hers, and she tiptoes lightly down the stairs and taps on his door.

'Brooke. It's me. Beattie. Can I come in?'

There is a quick exclamation and a girl's voice, hastily smothered by Brooke. Then a long, long silence. Beattie leans against the door, then turns round and goes back to her bedroom. She doesn't know how long she sits on her bed with her wrap clutched round her, but when she looks at the clock again it is half-past three. She is quite calm now. They are due to stay until Monday morning, but Beattie will not stay another night in this house, not another day, not another hour. She repacks her suitcase and gets dressed. It is gone four o'clock now; the darkness is already beginning to thin out and lighten. As she'll clearly be spending most of the day travelling, she goes into the silent kitchen – the trays have been laid for breakfast – and makes herself marmalade sandwiches. There is no one around to see her let herself out through the front door. It is a wonderful morning, clear, fresh, cool, the birds noisy in their appreciation of the coming day. Swinging her case briskly, Beattie sets out for the station. It is five o'clock when she reaches the platform for Norwich, and she sits quite contentedly and waits. At six o'clock a porter appears and says that a train that has been due since nine o'clock the previous evening will be arriving within the hour. Beattie thanks him and, enjoying her marmalade sandwiches and copy of *Mansfield Park*, reflects that, as mornings go, sitting in comfort on an empty sunny platform away from the horrors of the Alberry household takes quite a lot of beating.

When the train finally arrives Beattie wonders if she will ever get on. Both seats and corridors are full, and there is a wall of kitbags, duffel-bags and gas-masks, and leaning against them in khaki are their owners. There is a second row of people behind this, and rows of exhausted faces stare at Beattie as she pleads and pushes and finally succeeds in squeezing her way to a space between two stout ATS girls. Hardly has she recovered from the shock of getting on when she is disconcerted by a sudden cry of 'Coming over', and the two ATS girls duck and tell Beattie to do the same thing. A pair of stout brown lace-ups suddenly swing over their heads, shortly followed by a red-faced little boy who is handed on like a parcel, until he reaches the toilet and is taken inside by another girl, then is passed back up the corridor in the same way. Beattie stares out over the flat morning countryside. Her elation is beginning to seep away and she is left with the usual feeling of confusion, doubt and uncertainty. Had she imagined it all, the rudeness and the snubs? Even if she had, she concludes bitterly, she certainly had not imagined the presence of Gerro in her wardrobe, nor had she imagined what Brooke. . . . The thought of that makes her too angry. Should she have stayed and tried to make the best of it? But since Brooke's friends had made it so clear that they didn't like her surely she was under no obligation to act politely. This conclusion seems to be a just one and, propped up handily on either side she falls asleep where she stands. The train crawls on, moving slowly between anonymous stations. All the place-names and platform-boards had been removed the previous week because of invasion fears. It takes them another two hours to reach Norwich station where Beattie stumbles out into the mid-morning sunshine. There are no buses or trains on Sunday between Chillington and Norwich, so clearly it is a matter of either walking or hitching a lift. She is standing there feeling tired and a little forlorn when across the street she sees a group of RAF officers and quickly turns away lest they are friends of Brooke's. She is about to walk briskly past with her face well averted when, most surprisingly, someone crosses the road and says her name. Beattie turns, irresolute, and to her astonishment recognizes Charles Hammond. 'It is Beattie, isn't it? I thought it was,' says Charles with a friendly but somehow guarded smile. Perhaps he suspected the imminent arrival of Brooke from some quarter.

'Yes, hello – er – Charles. Are you better now?'

Through Gareth, Beattie had learnt that two of those missing planes from that ill-fated raid on Wilhelmshaven had in fact turned up. Peter Dancey's crew had baled out over Germany and been picked up to become prisoners for the duration of the war. The plane in which Charles Hammond had been second pilot had limped back later across the Channel and crash-landed somewhere in Essex. Charles, badly injured, though from flak, not from the crash-landing, had never returned to Gatton. Brooke declined ever to discuss that night again, so she had never known the exact nature of Charles's injuries. He looks well enough now, she thinks, fit and sunburnt, and to her annoyance she discovers all over again how absurdly handsome he is. Though, to give him his grudging due, he doesn't seem overly conscious of his looks.

'OK-ish. I'm still having a bit of treatment. I've been working at HQ at High Wycombe until I can fly again. I'm just up for the weekend to see a few friends. How's Brooke?'

'He's fine. Busy of course.'

'Of course,' says Charles politely, though a gleam of irony in his eye annoys Beattie immensely. She is aware yet again of a faint *frisson* between them which has nothing to do with liking. Though on the surface Charles's manners are perfect.

'Been away for the weekend?' He indicates her case.

'That's right,' says Beattie brazenly, belatedly aware that she is tired and that both her dress and her spirits could do with refreshing.

'How are you getting back to – where is it? Chillington, isn't it?' The mention of that name is enough to recall that whole ghastly incident, not to mention another more recent ghastly incident, which Charles can know nothing about. Beattie blushes, is furious with herself for finding herself doing so, and remarks rather tersely she hasn't yet decided how she's getting home.

At that Charles looks directly at her, and in that single assessing look Beattie knows that he has guessed that things stand in exactly the same impasse as they did before.

'I must go now,' she says firmly, irrationally furious with Charles, who has turned her moment of elation at leaving Brooke into a moment of humiliation at the reminder that she has allowed herself to be put in the same position all over again.

'Do you have to?' says Charles, most surprisingly. 'Only I'm getting a lift to Gatton at two p.m. We could drop you off if you don't mind waiting till then. The pubs are almost open. We could have some lunch if you want.'

She is so taken aback, for a moment she can find nothing to say. Dislike of Charles struggles feebly with lack of sleep and a general feeling of exhaustion which is beginning to make her legs go weak. Finally she says: 'Thank you. That's very kind of you, Charles.' Which for some reason makes him laugh out loud as he picks up her suitcase.

'What's so funny?' she snaps.

'You are,' he assures her, grinning, and declines to elucidate further.

He takes her to a public house in Fore Street which has a garden adjoining. They sit side by side on a rustic bench, Beattie with her lemonade and Charles with his half of bitter. A chattering group of girls in ATS uniform appear at the gate of the garden and make themselves comfortable at another rustic table. Beattie follows Charles's gaze.

'Don't you approve of girls in uniform?' she asks tartly.

'I was thinking about a girl I know who's just joined up and wondering how she's getting on. I've got no objection at all to girls in uniform. Though I won't deny it's a distinct pleasure to see a pretty girl in a summer dress covered in poppies.'

Beattie takes in his words and is suddenly tense.

'Beattie. Do relax.' He speaks directly to her for the first time. 'Look at me.' Unwittingly Beattie looks up at him through her lashes. 'That was a purely disinterested compliment, if there is such a thing. I wasn't making a pass. I expect you find that hard to believe. I should think you're pretty used to men making passes, aren't you?'

'What a stupid remark,' says Beattie surprising even herself, and wondering whether it is the lack of sleep or her sheer dislike of Charles that seems to have so effectively removed the guard from her tongue. 'If I say I am used to passes, you'll think I'm conceited. If I say I'm not, you'll think I'm just too stupid to notice.'

Charles starts to laugh again, revealing extremely white teeth, and a network of laughter-lines around his eyes. Belatedly, Beattie acknowledges Charles is a very attractive man indeed, and the knowledge does not make her like him any more. 'What is it about me that you seem to find so amusing?' hisses Beattie, furious.

'I don't quite know what it is,' he says honestly. 'Perhaps I've just never seen simple dislike struggling so hard with the need to be civil. You must be really desperate for this lift. So what went wrong last night? Brooke being his usual charming self, was he?'

Abruptly Beattie gets to her feet and moves to go.

'Hey, come on, don't go.' Charles stands up, considerably taller than herself, and effectively blocks the way. 'I'm sorry,' he says contritely. 'That was a cheap remark. Do stay.'

Silently Beattie sits down again. 'You don't like Brooke very much, do you?'

'I don't like Brooke very much; I don't like him at all,' says Charles briefly.

'Why?'

Charles shrugs. 'Does it matter?' he says apparently bored.

'It matters to me,' says Beattie carefully. 'Since the dislike you seem to feel for him is washing off over me as well.'

Charles sits back in his chair, his hands in his pockets, and studies Beattie dispassionately. 'I don't dislike you, Beattie. I think you're naïve, credulous and misguided – Oh, are you off again?' Charles's hand closes on her own and keeps her on the bench beside him. 'But I don't dislike you.' Charles is perfectly aware of how furious he has made her and is grinning at her.

'*Let go of my hand.*'

'Of course, I could also add that I think you're beautiful – far too beautiful for that ass Brooke. Intelligent and loyal, and you have a sense of humour – a quality much lacking, in my experience, in really beautiful women. But the trouble is if I did say all those things you'd probably think I was soft-soaping you, wouldn't you? So it's impossible to win, isn't it?'

They look at each other for a tense moment, then Beattie grudgingly starts to smile.

'That's better,' says Charles imperturbably. 'Do you think if I go and get us another round and some sandwiches there's a reasonable chance you'll still be here when I come back?'

When he returns, Beattie is sitting composedly, having straightened her hair, determined not to let Charles get under her guard again. 'So tell me about yourself.'

'I'm studying to be a teacher.'

'Primary or secondary?'

'Primary.'

'Enjoying it?'

'Oh, very, very much,' says Beattie, enthusiastic. 'What about you? What are you doing now?'

Charles's manner is equally friendly, but Beattie has a sudden sensation that he has withdrawn part of himself from her.

'Oh, still recovering,' he says pleasantly enough. 'I got rather a lot of stuff in the legs on the way back from Wilhelmshaven. They got most of it out, but I'm still not a hundred per cent. They'll have me back here any time I want. The trouble is at present they don't seem to want to let me fly.'

Beattie is astonished. 'Do you still want to?'

'Of course. There's nothing else.' Charles speaks more sharply than he intends. He adds: 'I'm sorry. That was pretty rude. I desperately want to fly again. I dream I'm at the controls of the plane night after night.'

'Even after—'

'Even after that.'

'What do you do at High Wycombe?'

'Oh, various quasi-intelligence things – analyse aerial photographs, that sort of thing.'

There is another pause. The clock on a neighbouring church strikes the quarter-hour. It is nearly time to go. Beattie is secretly relieved. She has serious doubts as to how long she will be able to sustain conversation with the odd, abrupt young man.

As they walk back towards the station, Beattie racks her brains for something to say. On a sudden inspiration she asks: 'How is your girlfriend – was it Eleanor?'

The effect on Charles is extraordinary. He wheels round, his face suddenly tense and suspicious. 'Who told you about her?'

'Brooke – or perhaps it was Gareth,' stammers Beattie. 'I do beg your pardon, I didn't mean to pry. It was just that the night you arrived at Gatton Gareth, I think it was, happened to mention that your girlfriend wasn't going to be able to attend the dance that night.'

Charles walks on in silence, biting his lip. Beattie feels she could have

117

bitten off her tongue. Clearly there has been a row at the very least, if not a separation.

'Eleanor is fine,' he says quietly without any particular emotion. 'She went back to live with her parents after Christmas. She's the one who's having a try at the ATS.'

'Oh,' says Beattie, anxious to avoid inadvertently detonating another land-mine. They walk in silence to the station yard, where they find Charles's friend already waiting. In twenty minutes she is back at Chillington, this time being dropped at the main gate.

'Goodbye, Beattie. It's been nice seeing you again. I don't expect our paths are likely to cross again in the future, so take care of yourself.'

'Thank you for the lift. I hope things go well for you in the future.'

By the time Beattie has walked through the side-gate into the park and has spontaneously broken into a run, up the broad drive, all thoughts of Charles Hammond have gone from her mind. As she runs over the rise she can see Louie and a group of her year playing croquet on the lawn in front of the house, and the clack of mallets on balls echoes across the lake where a few Greyshott boys are paddling in the shallows. Abruptly Beattie's spirits soar, and energetically she whirls her case round and round her head. In an instant she casts off a whole year of anxieties, doubts and tensions. Never has she felt so free, so relieved. Finally, it is all over with Brooke. It is as if chains and weights have been lifted from her back.

Part Two

July 1940–May 1941

CHAPTER
NINE

*D*EVORA IS LATE AGAIN. Normally it doesn't worry Virginia. But Leicester Square on a hot July evening isn't the best place for a single girl to be just standing around. The arrangement was that Devora would meet her here with Clive and Tony at half-past six. They were due to have drinks, then dinner, and there was a party later in Mount Street. But it is now ten to seven, and there is still no sign of anyone. Bother the girl, thinks Virginia crossly, beginning to feel distinctly uncomfortable. Why can she never be on time? Even as she stands there, eyes resolutely fixed on nothing, a bold-faced woman with a large hat, heavily made-up face and a low-neck moiré dress stops beside her and suggests in a polite neutral tone that Virginia should move along if she doesn't want a heel in her face. Tight-lipped, Virginia abruptly makes her way further into the square where she can sit down and keep an eye out for Devora.

It is a hot and languid evening, people enjoying that spacious moment before decisions about the evening and entertainment have to be made. On the other side of the square the over-made-up woman has joined a gang of sailors and is sauntering up in the direction of Piccadilly with one of them. Is there always this number of prostitutes in London? thinks Virginia, her eyes moving from doorway to doorway where groups of women are smoking and leaning negligently against the brickwork, their eyes always scanning the crowd. The square is slowly filling up with uniformed men and women strolling arm-in-arm. A man is playing a saxophone at the entrance to the Tube; the strains of 'Shake Down the Stars' linger on the air with the summer smells of green leaves, fried onions, cigarette fumes and cheap perfume. Outside the Odeon, a vast orderly column is beginning to shuffle forward for the evening performance of *Gone with the Wind*. Above everything is the continuous high thin cheeping of starlings.

Virginia pulls out her compact and is aghast to find she has a smut on her nose. She has had her hair done at lunchtime and looks, she knows, stunning. As if to endorse this fact, three different men stop and ask quite courteously if she fancies a drink. Feeling increasingly annoyed at the absent Devora, Virginia declines. Clearly, the best thing to do is look occupied, and she rummages in her shoulder-bag for one of the ubiquitous unsolicited manuscripts. Unfortunately, the one she is reading at present inspires no enthusiasm in either the head or the heart. It is the story of a passionate young titled

121

schoolboy who is tired of civilization's false conventions and tends to say so every page or so, especially when he's in bed with his girlfriend, Elsie, a long-suffering munitions-factory worker. Boredom seems a heavy price to pay for fornication with a lord, but so far Elsie has not felt the need to utter a single word of protest in fifty pages. Come to that, she's not said anything at all except 'I don't mind if I do' since he picked her up at the Kardomah. Thanks to Virginia's exceptional industry, they've got through almost the entire backlog of manuscripts, though a fresh wave is building up in the next room. Nothing more has been said about finding Theo a permanent secretary, and Virginia has discovered to her astonishment that she actually likes working, bar the getting up early in the morning.

Still no sign of Devora. It is nearly quarter-past seven. Virginia decides she will give her ten more minutes, then walk down to the Savoy and wait for William Burmeister III. He has been in Kent for the day, filing some copy on Fighter Command. Virginia selects a cigarette from her case and lights it with a matching lighter. Both are presents from Willy, as are the cigarettes, her perfume and her nylon stockings. Brooding on the aforesaid Willy, she blows out a thoughtful cloud of smoke.

'Excuse me,' says a voice beside her. 'Are these seats taken?'

An exhausted-looking woman in a straw hat with cherries, three children under five clinging to various parts of her person, is standing by the seat.

'No, sit down,' says Virginia, picking up her bag.

'Ta ever so,' says the woman tiredly. 'Now, Terry, don't wander off on your own. You're to stay here quietly till Uncle Thomas comes.' She stows a cheap cardboard suitcase under the seat and feels about in her holdall. 'There now,' she says vexedly, 'I must have left them on the kitchen table. You couldn't spare me a cigarette, dear, could you?' Virginia offers her one, then lights it for her.

'That's heaven,' says the woman gratefully. 'Taken us two hours to get here, you know. From Battersea, that is. First we couldn't get a bus, then the man told us the wrong stop to get out. I couldn't have walked another step.' She shoves a dummy into the mouth of the youngest baby, and shifts the toddler on to her other knee. 'Been ever so good really,' she says, 'but I shan't be sorry to be on our way tonight.'

'Are you going on a holiday?'

'Holiday? I should think not,' says the lady with fine scorn. 'No, we're off to Halstead. We was evacuated out there last August because I've got a brother there. But when the bleeding bombs didn't fall we came back to London. Didn't want my old man coming home on leave and not finding us there. He's been in Redcar since September. I don't want to go now,' she adds with candour, 'but my brother reckons the bombs is getting nearer to London, and it'll be our turn next. So I get packed up this afternoon, leave the key with a neighbour and put our address on the door, for my old man. And here we are.'

They smoke for a minute or two in silence.

'Is you thinking of staying on, then?'

'Well, I hadn't thought about moving,' says Virginia, surprised.

'It's the children, you see,' says the other woman obliquely. 'It's different

122

when you're on your own. Where's that Terry got to? I told him to stay here.'

Terry appears of his own accord, clutching the hand of a tall weather-beaten man who has the look about him of Mr Blythe.

'There he is,' says the woman with undisguised relief, and gets to her feet. Her brother picks up Terry and puts him on his shoulders, takes the middle child in his arm, and with his other hand takes up the suitcase.

'Just you take care of yourself now, dear,' says the woman in a friendly way, relieved at finding her brother, wiping some of the lines from her face.

She can't be more than a year or two older than me, thinks Virginia, but she looks twice my age.

It is now half-past seven. Damn Devora. Virginia pauses, irresolute. The square is suddenly full of people of every nationality. A group of Polish airmen accost her and try to persuade her to go dancing. Virginia suddenly begins to feel rather oppressed, and decides that she will after all go home. As she walks into Charing Cross Road she sees a man coming towards her wearing the uniform of the Free French Army, chatting volubly to a tall young man in a cord jacket. For a second Virginia's heart leaps. There is something in the way the Frenchman is gesturing that reminds her of Ferdinand Aumont, but it can't be him. It is only when the Frenchman and his companion draw abreast that Virginia realizes it *is* Ferdinand.

Being Virginia, she immediately grasps his arm in a highly unwise way, considering the area they are in. But he turns round, courteously enough, with an enquiring look on his face, then his expression slowly changes from astonishment to admiration, and from admiration to joy, and they fall into each other's arms without self-consciousness. Ferdinand's friend moves them firmly to the side of the pavement.

'Ferdinand, it's so lovely to see you,' says Virginia, her face radiant. 'But why didn't you let me know you were here?'

'I've been here two weeks and already written twice to the Dower House,' says Ferdinand, holding on to her hands in an unaffectedly pleased way. 'And each time I have asked your mother to send you a letter to say I am in London.'

'The old bat,' says Virginia angrily. 'She never writes at all now.'

'But what wonderful luck to meet you here of all places. What are you doing? You look *ravissante*, so *soignée*, so distinguished, so beautiful.'

The other man with him coughs.

'Forgive me, Alexis, I should have introduced you. This wonderful lady is Virginia Musgrave. This is my English cousin Alexis Seligman. Come and eat with us and tell us all your news. I promise I will not say a word about Dunkirk, because everybody talks of nothing else and it is all too sad. Besides, it's a crime to bore a beautiful woman. You look very different from the Virginia I knew last year.'

As they stroll along arm-in-arm, chatting animatedly, Virginia is suddenly aware of how glad she is to see Ferdinand. It is good to be with someone you actually like as opposed to someone you can't get out of going to bed with. In many ways Ferdinand is an unlikely candidate for a friend of the bosom. Yet she likes him, his pessimism, his mixture of *savoir-faire* and *petit*

123

bourgeois practicality, and perhaps most of all the fact that he so obviously likes her. Certainly in his time he has seen her in some pretty frightful moods and still, undeterred, had sought out her company afterwards. He was probably the only person in the world who could lecture and scold her without her taking violent offence. Ferdinand and his silent companion take her to Greek Street to Antoine's where Ferdinand says the food is still magnificent, as indeed it is. But Virginia is so busy recounting details of her triumphant escape from the Dower House that she hardly notices what she eats. By the time Ferdinand has told her what has happened to his family and what he is doing in London, they have reached the coffee stage and Virginia is belatedly aware that Ferdinand's companion has hardly been offered the opportunity for a line of conversation throughout the whole meal. At this point Ferdinand disappears to make a phone call and Virginia, full of goodwill, turns graciously to include him in the evening's festivities.

'I'm sorry,' she says, with her most seductive smile, 'we're being frightfully rude.'

'You are, aren't you?' says the young man directly, this causing Virginia in sheer surprise to turn off her seductive smile like a light. For the first time she looks at him properly, and he stares back at her unabashed. Ferdinand's cousin is a very tall, thin, powerfully built young man with thick dark ungreased hair flopping forward in a long lock into his eyes. Virginia has noticed of late that after a few sentences of conversation with almost any man the effect of her beauty is such as to make him abandon any critical faculties he might have. But it is clear that her looks are far from having this effect on Alexis. Completely immune to her charm, he does not even respond to her smiles. Virginia is suddenly and infuriatingly aware that she feels threatened by him. Even the way he dresses, carelessly, casually, is somehow an attack on her own careful appearance, as if he doesn't care what impression he makes on other people. He has an air of knowing who he is and not minding what other people think about him.

'What are you doing in London? Do you have a job?' he asks in a bored sort of way. 'I bet you drive officers around.'

'Of course I have a job,' she snaps, wondering why on earth she's let this conceited young man get under her collar. 'I work in a publisher's office if you must know. Tell me, is it your asthma that keeps you out of uniform?'

'Men in uniform excite you, do they?'

'Believe me, that's not the reason I find you unattractive,' says Virginia witheringly and goes off to powder her nose.

When she returns Ferdinand is pouring her out an Armagnac, his eyes beaming owlishly behind their thick lenses. 'The *patron* sent it over, he wants to drink to your health,' he explains. Virginia blushes prettily, raising her glass to thank him. She catches sight of Alexis' expression and resists a strong temptation to stick out her tongue at him.

'We meant to go and see *Gone with the Wind* tonight, but we set out too late,' says Ferdinand. 'Do you go to the cinema much, Virginia?'

'Oh, yes,' says Virginia enthusiastically. 'All the time.'

'What sort of films do you like?' asks Alexis in all innocence.

'Hollywood musicals,' she smiles, having placed him instantly as a

124

would-be intellectual who probably only likes Continental films shot in a darkened room with no subtitles. 'I adore the "Golddigger" series, and Fred Astaire of course. I suppose I just love singing and dancing, that sort of thing.'

'Alexis makes films,' says Ferdinand, amused by the hostility between them.

'Oh, really! What kind?' yawns Virginia.

'Not Hollywood musicals, I'm afraid,' says Alexis nastily, his gaze contemptuous. 'I suppose I'd find the material too intellectually taxing. I make documentary films now, about real people and their lives.'

'My God,' says Virginia elegantly, by now very angry indeed. 'You mean those boring shorts they show off in the Movietone news, before the big feature? The ones where everybody gets up to get their ice-cream? I saw one last night about lifeboatmen; I nearly fell asleep,' she adds quite untruthfully, since it had been enthralling and the whole cinema had clapped at the end.

'I was first director on that,' says Alexis, his face suddenly dark red with anger. 'And it was a bloody fine film. Good night, Ferdinand. Thanks for the dinner. Give me a call tomorrow.' With that he gets up and walks out, leaving a rather awkward silence.

'Oh, Virginia, now what are you doing? You've hurt his feelings. It was a good film, you know it was. He is very talented, that one. His films win prizes.'

'He was so rude,' says Virginia crossly.

'Well, we neglected him. Shall we go after him and talk him round?'

'Must we? I'd much rather talk to you. I can't believe he's your cousin. You aren't a bit alike.'

'Certainly he's my cousin. Our mothers are sisters.'

'How did his mother come to live over here?'

'She came on holiday and met Daniel Seligman. He was a Jew of course.'

'Did her family mind?'

'They minded more that he was twenty years older than her. None the less, it was a very, very happy marriage. Each year either I came to England or Alexis came to Paris or our château.' Ferdinand gloomily contemplates the current fate of the château.

'I'm sorry I was rude about his films,' says Virginia belatedly. 'But I felt he was getting at me.'

'He's a bit moody these days.'

'Why?'

Ferdinand shrugs and gestures for the bill.

'Oh, I don't think he's sure what he wants any more. Before the war he worked in ordinary films. You know, the kind of films you like. And the next thing I know Alexis wants to make documentary films about ordinary people. It's not really his style – or perhaps it's just not what I thought was his style. I still haven't got to the bottom of it all yet.'

'Is he married?'

'He has a rich girlfriend.' Ferdinand purses his lips.

'What does that mean?' says Virginia amused.

'She wants to marry, but he doesn't,' says Ferdinand succinctly.

'Poor girl,' says Virginia serenely. 'She must be desperate.'

'Not so,' scolds Ferdinand severely, somewhat belatedly coming to the defence of his cousin. 'He is much sought after.'

'Now you're getting cross with me,' says Virginia disarmingly, as they leave the restaurant and make their way through the long unlit twilight canyon that is Oxford Street. 'But I'd much rather hear about you. How long were you in France for? Did you actually get shot at?'

Virginia never finds out what it is that Ferdinand is actually doing in London but, whatever his duties, they leave long stretches of the day free and he takes to turning up regularly at lunchtime at Marwicks. He says it is a shame to monopolize her evenings when she is doing so much for the morale of fighting men. Over a pub lunch Virginia tells him about the night before, whom she has met. She hopes he will stay for ever. The very pleasure she takes in his company makes her conscious that, though she is extensively courted – nay, run after – she is often lonely. Brooke rarely answers her letters. Cecily has had some kind of promotion and is now completely absorbed in distributing clothes that have arrived from America for the evacuees. Lucy is an excellent correspondent but is currently working with a harvesting gang in Essex and is too pulverized with tiredness to be able to manage more than the occasional postcard. Devora has two subjects of conversation, both boring, neither repeatable. The sight of Ferdinand's pebble glasses and earnest expression in reception each day never fails to cheer her up. About a week after his unexpected arrival in London, they meet the unpleasant cousin again in the Pillars of Hercules. The encounter is unplanned: Alexis is sitting at the bar with a truly astonishing-looking girl and is distinctly embarrassed to see them. His companion has no such inhibitions and advances eagerly forward to say hello, her many platinum curls bobbing as she asks with some excitement if they, too, are in films.

'I'm trying to break in myself,' she confides, accepting a gin from Alexis with a simper. 'Just down in London for the week. I was Miss Morecambe Sands last year, and my dancing teacher says I should go professional.'

So even Alexis has his casting-couch, thinks Virginia amused. Alexis clearly reads her thoughts, and she could swear he blushes.

'Mr Seligman's taking me to the studios at Pinewood this afternoon,' goes on Miss Morecambe Sands confidentially. 'I just hope it's all leading somewhere.'

Virginia and Ferdinand carefully avoid each other's eyes, and after another drink Alexis insists it is time they are on their way.

'Poor Alexis,' says Ferdinand when they are on their own again. 'He has too kind a heart.'

'Oh, come on, Ferdinand, you don't think he's doing it for her benefit, do you?'

'Those girls, they see his name on the credits of a film and turn up at the production office asking for him. He has no interest in girls like that. Besides, he has a girlfriend of his own.'

Virginia looks unconvinced and starts to tell Ferdinand about a very nice dress she has seen that morning in John Lewis's.

But she is aware that it cannot be long before Ferdinand is called upon to take some more definitive part in the war. About three weeks later he turns up unexpectedly at the hostel one night and actually finds Virginia at home spending a rare night in and taking advantage of the fact to plant out some cabbages for Cecily. She is dragging two buckets of water up a cinder path, when she sees Ferdinand advancing gingerly towards her.

'You English and your gardens,' he grumbles. 'It's like Marie-Antoinette playing in the cowshed.'

'In the dairy, I think. I'm not *playing* at it. I'm planting cabbages for the autumn. What do you think of that?'

'Makes me feel a little ill. This love of cabbage is all part of the English obsession with their bowels. I did not think I'd be so lucky as to find you in,' he says, brushing the wheelbarrow handles gingerly before making himself comfortable on them.

'No, I decided I couldn't be bothered to go out tonight, so I rang and cancelled.'

'Who was it? The lucky Sir Fred? Or good William? Is Andrew still in favour? Don't tell me Le Vice Anglais is back in London?'

'I wish you wouldn't call Simon that,' says Virginia annoyed.

'Ah, it is my joke. His is so much the Continental idea of the English public schoolboy, that's all.'

'Actually it was Willy. He's got a press conference at seven, and I couldn't face sitting round all evening waiting for him to finish so I thought I might as well stay at home and be useful. If you've come to take me out for a drink, I won't refuse.'

'I came round to ask you for dinner.'

'In that case,' says Virginia, putting down her trowel with alacrity, 'I'll slip up and change and be with you in the front hall in ten minutes.'

Ferdinand takes her to the Milles Fleurs, currently Virginia's favourite restaurant. 'A new frock?' he enquires, as Virginia shakes out her silk napkin.

'From Willy. You wouldn't believe the trouble I had trying to persuade him to buy it. He's so generous sometimes, and at other times so stingy. It's heaven, isn't it? Everybody at the Grange will want to borrow it. Fortunately, it's a size eight, so it won't fit anybody but me.'

The nice thing about Ferdinand is you can tell him anything and he is never shocked. In his company Virginia completely relaxes, secure in the knowledge that, like Cecily, Ferdinand listens but never appears to judge. With him she never feels she has to play the part, to be Virginia the aloof, the mysterious or the punishing, depending on whatever role her escorts seem to expect of her. Ferdinand seems quite happy with her as herself. She often wonders what it is between them that makes them so completely relaxed. Perhaps it is as simple as the *fact* that there is no sexual tug between herself and Ferdinand. To be with Ferdinand is to be soothed and calmed.

Ferdinand reads the menu with the close attention of a man studying the stock market, then orders dinner with the seriousness of a man dictating his will. Then and only then does he sit back and relax. The band begin to play a muted version of 'Careless', and he leans over and takes her hand.

'Bad news, I'm afraid. I heard today I'll be leaving England the day after tomorrow.' Virginia does not try to hide her disappointment.

'Oh, Ferdinand. How rotten. Where are you going?'

'My lips must be sealed. For the sake of argument I shall say Africa.'

'Then, you'll be gone months. I shall really miss you,' she says, trying to smile.

'You,' scoffs Ferdinand lightly. 'You with all your friends and admirers.'

The waiter brings the wine. Ferdinand tastes and approves. 'But why do you go on living at the Grange now? You could have a flat of your own and live in style. Hasn't Willy offered to set you up yet?'

'Well, sort of. We always stay at a flat in Davies Street that belong to some friends of his in America. It's very ritzy, and I suppose I could live there if I wanted to. But it's things like ration-books. I couldn't bear having to queue up for food, so I suppose ultimately it's the convenience. Anyway, if I left the hostel it might be the last straw so far as home is concerned.'

'What are the other girls like?'

Virginia reflects for a moment.

'There's only one real division,' she says at last. 'There are the ones who get flowers and the ones who don't. The ones who don't have committee meetings and knitting circles, and belong to the Christian fellowship and have cocoa in each other's rooms. The other girls are out most of the time.'

'And what kind of girl are you?' enquires Ferdinand teasingly.

'Well, naturally I'm the girl who gets the most flowers,' says Virginia, entirely without conceit. 'But it's not to say I don't have spasms of staying in and sewing with *les girls*. The trouble is my life always seems to go in extremes. At the very moment I think I'm never in or alternatively that I haven't been out for three nights, it usually means that that period is over and I'm going to start doing completely the opposite thing again. I seem to move from one end of the spectrum to the other for no good reason. I just get restless. When I first came to London, I had this obsession about going out to nightclubs and restaurants. I just had to be out every single night of the week. I love things like starched tablecloths, and the smell of perfume and cigar smoke, and silver and good glass, and dancing for hours on end. It was just the being there. It never mattered who I was with; I just wanted to see myself reflected in the mirrors around the walls.' She stops, embarrassed.

'And now?'

'Oh, now I want those things more than ever. Though sometimes I like staying at home with *les girls*. Then I get restless and I have to be out again having a good time. And if I don't like the nightclub or the restaurant, or it isn't good enough, I simply refuse to stay.'

'And they accept this, your young men?' says Ferdinand clearly mystified.

'Of course. The nastier you are to men the more they seem to like it. I don't understand it. Particularly Willy.'

Ferdinand is silent for a moment. 'Well,' he says in a neutral tone, 'at least I know I need not imagine that you are pining when I am gone. You will be able to amuse yourself with your new conquest, Andrew. Is he fun, this young man?'

'I don't know what you mean by "fun",' says Virginia shortly, 'but he can do it three times whereas Willy can only manage it once after which he has to tell me what a wonderful wife and mother Adelaide is back home in New York. After that he falls asleep on top of me. Don't look so shocked,' says Virginia gaily. 'You did ask.'

'Virginia, I'm worried about you,' begins Ferdinand.

'There is no need to be. From what I've heard about Brooke's exploits since I've been in London, I'm simply following in the family tradition. I'm a great believer in having fun and taking my pleasures like a man.'

'I would not mind,' says Ferdinand clearly, 'if I did not see that you were so obviously unhappy.'

There is a long silence, then Virginia raises brilliant blue eyes to his. 'I prefer this life to the one I led at the Dower House.'

'That is your stupid theory of extremes again. There is a middle course between living with your mother in the village and your present life.'

'Ferdinand, I do believe you disapprove of me.'

'No,' he says quietly. 'But I would be much happier if you had someone you cared for. I would be happier knowing that there was a man in your life for whom you felt more than contempt.'

This silences Virginia for a moment. Then she says: 'You want me to be serious about somebody. That's not what I want. Not yet. Being serious leads to marriage, and I know what that means. Oh, Ferdinand, don't be cross with me. It may be the last evening we have together, so let's get drunk. Don't let's talk about my silly old sex life. You've simply no idea how much I'll miss you,' she adds with unintentional irony.

With Ferdinand gone it is as if some brake has been removed finally from Virginia's behaviour. And as June lengthens into July then into August the pace and tempo of her life increase until whole weeks pass without her being able to remember where she has been or whom she was with. She rushes home to be changed and ready by six for drinks which invariably lead to dinner. After that, if it is Stephen's friends, there is a whip-round for a bottle, and somebody somewhere is always having a party. If Virginia is dining grandly – as she quite often is these days – then it is nightclubbing and dancing to 2 a.m. It is not possible to smuggle men into the Grangemouth – ineffectual and worthless as Miss Groundsell is, Virginia rightly concludes that this could be the final straw – so if congress is to take place it is a matter of finding an empty room at a party or the back of someone's car. There are a few men for whom Virginia will take the risk of staying out all night, but this relates entirely to what they can offer her in return. For example, it is very well worth taking any risk with Willy since they either stay in Davies Street or else he will take a room for her at the Savoy. Either way, the breakfast next morning is well worth the boredom of his sexual performance. Andrew is another who can claim special privileges, his parents having gone to Shropshire leaving him sole possessor of a large and extremely grand flat in St James's. Andrew is attached to the War Office in some extremely loose capacity. When she asks him what he does, he merely looks mysterious and says it is decision-making work. In the light of the mental contortions Andrew has to go through, even to decide whether they should eat before or after the theatre, Virginia finds this mystifying. Still, he is extremely rich and distinguished and dances like an angel.

But already, in the short time she has been in London, she is beginning to hear of former lovers who are now dead. Halfway through lunch one day, Stephen announces that he has heard that very morning that Monty is no more. Virginia is enchanted, but asks in suitably muted tones if he has died in action.

'Not really,' broods Stephen. 'He was still training, and he was a bit slow off the mark with his hand grenade. Poor Monty. He was never any good at maths at school.'

Virginia feels a sudden hysterical desire to bray with laughter. But there are other servicemen that she thinks about more gently when she hears from their friends that in their own slang they 'copped it'. Curly Totten up from his RAF station in Kent, with whom she had spent a happy drunken week in July, is shot down and burnt to death within three days of his return. There was a very nice Northern Ireland boy called Mark who had picked her up at a war correspondence meeting under the very nose of Willy. He'd been staying with friends in Hampstead, and he and Virginia had spent the day and most of the night on the heath. He was off to the Mediterranean at the end of his leave, and Virginia received one letter from him and then silence. Later she hears that his ship has been torpedoed. Beaky Johnson, Davy Seth, Harry Bright, all pilots up from Kent or Sussex during that hot headlong summer, with whom she has danced and laughed and made love, all end up as names on a casualty-list. It is as if life is composed of two different rooms. In one room people like herself are dancing and singing and behaving as if nothing is wrong. In the other there are screams, torture, death, burnt flesh, anguish, disfigurement and broken hearts. Sometimes in the early morning when she cannot sleep, her senses over-stimulated by whisky, nicotine and the wail of the saxophone, Virginia wonders if she can go on cheating fate like this for ever, or if one day she will be called upon to enter that other room and acknowledge its existence. For the time being at least, she will put that moment off with dancing and drinking and relentless late nights. Devora is her companion and guide in their racketing passage through the blackout of W1. Though Virginia is already beginning to realize that she has overtaken Devora and no longer needs her. But she will put up with her patronage and occasional spite, not to mention her eternal borrowing of clothes, because Devora still has her uses. She is lazy, dishonest, self-centred, and smells at all times like a damp face-flannel. She is irritating when sober and embarrassing when drunk, which is usually after two sweet sherries, but she still has one thing going for her: she knows everybody, is invited everywhere, and her voracious appetite for pleasure is equalled only by Virginia's.

At the beginning of September the pace becomes too much, even for Devora. Virginia goes into her room one day after work to find her packing for the weekend.

'Has Eddy got leave, then?' asks Virginia, watching in fascinated horror as Devora sorts out her garments by the simple process of sniffing them.

'No,' says Devora crossly. 'I'm off Eddy. I've decided I need a bit of taking care of so I'm going to Henley for the weekend.'

'I thought you hated your aunt.'

'I do, but at least I'll get breakfast in bed and catch up on my sleep.'

Devora is in a decidedly bad mood. She has been in for an abortion earlier that week, her third, and she is still grumbling about it. 'Honestly,' she sighs, consigning a pair of cami-knicks mercifully to the wastepaper-basket, 'I really do have the most frightful luck. I don't understand it, because I'm always so careful.'

Virginia forbears to point out that by eight o'clock Devora is usually so drunk she has no way of knowing whether her Dutch cap is safely installed or on her head.

'You're bloody lucky,' she goes on sourly to Virginia. 'I don't know how you manage to do it. You lead the life of Riley and still manage to look as though you'd arrived from the country yesterday. You're like that chap in the book that that pansy fellow wrote. You know, the one who committed all those sins that never showed on his face till he died. With any luck you'll end up as a horrible corpse.'

'Even if I do,' retorts Virginia stung, 'I rather doubt if you'll be restored to innocence on your deathbed.'

Virginia is furious at Devora's jibes about her own conduct because, although she behaves exactly in the same way as Devora does, she in no way associates her own conduct with hers, and works on the curious assumption that somehow, deep down, none of the things she does touches her. But the conversation has the effect of making her realize that a period of restraint and sobriety may be the answer – if only by way of a change. She will be a good girl, at least for this weekend. So, later on that night, by dint of twisting the unfortunate Cecily's arm almost out of its socket, she persuades her to take an evening off. They are to go dancing on Saturday evening with two outstandingly dull and well-born men from the Ministry of Food, whom Virginia has long had in the back of her mind for just such an outing. On Saturday afternoon she sits out in the garden taking up the hem of a dress of her own for Cecily to wear. It is a marvellously hot and tranquil September day, and Virginia feels a kind of peace. Even the news on the wireless that morning is good: apparently Britain is holding her own in the skies.

'There's a bottle-party tonight in Beaufort Street,' says the girl sunbathing next to Virginia in halter top and shorts. Gloria has a room on the corridor below and had been Devora's chosen companion until she had fallen in love with a Guards officer, and now stays in to knit him mammoth sweaters.

'Thanks, but Ces and I are already booked,' says Virginia languidly. 'We're going dancing at Quags.'

The wind is gently moving the rustling leaves overhead when suddenly all sounds are drowned by the long crescent wail of the sirens.

Gloria is suddenly white-faced. 'Do you think it's another practice?' she says uneasily.

Then Virginia remembers the woman in Leicester Square. 'I think we'd better go in all the same,' she says uncertainly. 'Just to be on the safe side.'

131

Then as they turn to go they hear it for the first time: the even throbbing wave of sound as aeroplanes come in from the east. Paralysed, Virginia stands riveted, her eyes straining in the direction of Oxford Street, beyond which is the City and the docks, and at that moment she understands that wave upon wave of planes, piloted by young men like her brother, are following the blue line of the Thames into the very heart of dockland and beyond. 'Come *on*!' screams Gloria, suddenly hysterical. 'Don't stand there, come *on*.' Finally she grabs Virginia's unresisting arm and drags her towards the garden door. In the hall the air-raid siren warning has been taken very seriously indeed. There is a confusion of girls clattering down the lino-covered stairs, clutching gas-masks and buckets of sand. Virginia takes the stairs up to her room in threes, crashes through the door, and in a single mechanical movement picks up her identity-card, torch and a bar of chocolate and puts them into her handbag. By this time the warbling of the sirens has stopped, and Virginia is suddenly petrified that a bomb will fall on her before she reaches the cellar. She cannot breathe easily until she is safely installed in the boiler-room. Someone hands her a deck-chair and she makes herself comfortable and prepares to be terrified. Then of course nothing happens. After half an hour terror is slowly being replaced by mild annoyance. Virginia begins to wonder if the all-clear may yet sound soon enough for herself and Cecily to make their date.

At first it seems as if her wish will be granted. By 5.30 nothing has happened, and by six o'clock people are becoming restless and talking about making cups of tea. Then at five past six a tremor like a shiver of premonition passes through the whole building and in a split second the whole world goes mad. Sounds, momentarily unfamiliar, which years later will still have the power to make Virginia wake sweating in terror, rend the air around them.

Now the planes are overhead, wave after wave of throbbing roar. There is the hushed staccato rattle of the anti-aircraft guns in the placements in Hyde Park. There are whistling, ripping, tearing noises of high explosives which end in thunderous crashes that shake the house to its very foundation. From the Bayswater Road the tinny bells of fire engines constantly racing by. There is the shriek of shells and the dull thud of walls collapsing. Inside the Grangemouth walls shake and brick dust pours through the distemper. The light swings madly round and round. Almost out of their minds with terror, the girls cling to each other shrieking, whilst whistling thunderous crashes seem to be happening only a few yards away. Virginia wants desperately to pray, but not a single line of prayer will come into her mind.

It is impossible to estimate how long the fury continues outside. It is hours before Virginia thinks to look at her watch, then stares at the dial in complete disbelief. Can it really be two o'clock in the morning? How on earth can time have gone so fast? And still the planes drone overhead and the crashes and the screams of the girls go on. Eventually, preposterously worn out by fear, Virginia falls into an uneasy doze, and when she wakes the other girls are packing up their deck-chairs and brushing brick dust from their hair. 'Has the all-clear gone?'

'Yes, five minutes ago. Miss Groundsell thinks it's all right to go back up to our rooms now.'

132

Stiff in every limb, gritty, dirty, but still alive, Virginia follows Gloria slowly up the cellar steps. The other girls go immediately to their rooms; but Virginia, drawn by an impulse she does not understand, opens the front door and walks out into the street, down to the Bayswater Road.

It is like waking up in a different world. Fire engines still roar by, their bells clanging madly. Across London from the direction of the City and the Surrey Docks she can see a continuous thick column of black smoke, drawn up into the serene early-morning sky. Around her the very quality of the air is different, choked with dust and ashes and clouds of mauvish-brown smoke. The house opposite the Grangemouth has had a direct hit, and fire is still burning intermittently on the remains of the ground floor. The shoemender's on the corner has simply disappeared, and in its place is a crater. There is a curious smell. A raw, new, completely different smell which over the next eight months will become so familiar she will hardly notice it. It is the acrid odour from the high explosive of the bombs which will linger round demolished buildings for hours. It is the smell of the torn, dismembered, wounded houses, the smell of smashed bricks, torn timbers, shattered stone. Virginia draws that smell deeply into her lungs. She recognizes immediately what it is. It is the smell of violent death.

CHAPTER
TEN

'*I*T SEEM STRANGE TO ME, him being a Methodist and getting engaged to a publican's daughter,' says Beattie.

'Perhaps he's hoping to convert her. We weren't engaged but we had. . . . an understanding. He told me it was off in the food-hall in Lewis's. I felt a right fool.'

'Well, cheer up. Now that we're allowed to go to servicemen's dances, you'll soon meet someone else.'

'Maybe. Where's her Highness tonight?'

'Doing fire-drill practice, I think.'

Louie sniffs. 'I thought things seemed quiet.'

'Come on, Louie, she's not that bad.'

'She just gets on my wick with her stories about the Bradford Gilbert and Sullivan Society, and how she's got her own bathroom, and what she wore at her birthday party—'

'But she's jolly generous about the food-parcels she gets from home.'

'She can afford to be,' grumbles Louie, who is clearly beyond any simple cheering-up, and Beattie lets her be. The presence of Barbara Ann in the cottage, or 'Barbr'ann' as she pronounces it, or you-can-call-me-Ba, acts as a continuing irritant to Louie's already low spirits. Ba is one of the two new second-year girls sent to Hillsleigh to complete their teaching diploma, and Beattie has never met a more unlikely prospect of a student teacher. Ba's appearance is much influenced by movie magazines, and temperamentally she swings hourly from despair to ecstasy and back again. Beattie and Louie are still taken aback by the sight of Barbr'ann's shoulder-length red curls tossing in passion, appearing at the cottage door to announce that yet again her life is ruined.

But even Beattie sometimes has to fight off feelings of envy. Barbr'ann's father is an ice-cream manufacturer in Bradford and, as the youngest of five children, on her own admission she's been spoilt all her life. In the company of the girls at the cottage she's like an heiress up for the weekend. She has her very own portable wireless, something that Beattie and Louie still can't get over, and has the Light Programme blaring cheerful music all day and all night. She has a pale blue dressing-gown with quilted satin lapels like those worn by Ginger Rogers, a crocodile vanity-case with her initial on it, and her very own bicycle, a tourer with dropped handlebars. Her clothes are expensive and numerous, and though Mrs Blythe might have raised her eyes at some of the colours she could not have faulted the quality. Privately, Beattie rather likes her, for there is something about Ba's brazen good humour that reminds her of Lily Kedge. But Louie and Ba are at odds from the moment they meet.

'Does she never stop talking about herself?' Louie is enquiring, after twenty-four hours of Barbr'ann's company.

'Why does Louie wash all her clothes in TCP?' Ba is quite reasonably demanding after two days, and takes to spraying ashes of roses liberally round the sitting-room. Beattie, suspecting that Louie has experienced the same moment of truth about her own home that she felt at Christmas, makes vague conciliatory noises, and hopes they will learn to co-exist. Especially since Beattie is determined to work to make up for all those weeks of inattention in her first year. Teaching practice has started, and Beattie has her own form of the Greyshott boys. She is elated to discover she loves teaching and that she has a natural talent for it. What with that and being captain of the hockey team with a tricky fixture-list to arrange she hopes they will speedily learn to settle their differences without involving her.

Fortunately, Louie's luck is about to change. She does her own teaching practice in a village called Wearam. Whilst waiting for her lift home, a group of young men in uniform stop to chat. Pretty soon one of them is hanging around the school gates every day to walk her to the point where the milk-lorry picks her up. The young man's name is Vince, but he is too shy to ask Louie out, contenting himself with dropping heavy hints about a dance in Wearam village to be held the following Saturday. He and some of his mates are going. Why doesn't she bring along a few friends as well? Louie bounces back to the cottage in high spirits. Beattie, preparing the following day's lessons, gives her half her attention and agrees to go to the dance to search for the elusive Vince. In the end several of them are to set off the following Saturday, but they very nearly don't go at all because, an hour before, Beattie discovers exactly what this young man Vince does and in what service. She is furious to discover that he is a rigger from Gatton. 'You should have told me before, Louie,' she says angrily. 'You know jolly well I'd never have agreed to go if I'd known.'

'That's precisely why I didn't tell you. Honestly, Beattie, you can't spend the rest of your life planning your lessons and writing fixture-lists. It's not as if Brooke's likely to be there. He's not going to bother himself with a village social, is he? He's far too grand for that kind of thing. You don't have to come if you don't want to.'

There is a silence, during which Louie continues painstakingly to unroll her best stockings up her thin, child-like legs and anchor them firmly in suspenders. Barbr'ann, who has just wriggled into Her Black, is outlining her mouth in Holly Red by the light of a candle. The electricity is off, and there is no oil for the lamps at present. Louie goes into her own room to change.

'You've hurt her feelings now,' Barbr'ann observes. 'She didn't mean to pull a fast one. She just got a bit carried away. She wants to go that badly. It's on account of that fellow who threw her over. She was quite cut up about that, you know.'

Which all makes Beattie feel much worse. She goes on taking the metal curlers out of her hair and wonders why it seems to occur to no one that she might still be quite cut up about Brooke. It is four months since she has seen him, and it is not easy to erase the image of the first person to whom you have given your heart and considerably more besides. She still dreams incessantly of him. The summer holidays seemed endless, in spite of the hours she spent helping out at the Manor with the Dr Barnardo's children. Lily Kedge has taken over as postmistress to the village, and as an unabashed reader of other people's postcards is able to tell Beattie that Brooke has been home twice to the Dower House during the summer. But neither time did he come and see her. Couldn't he at least have shown they were still friends? she thought bitterly. But perhaps they never had been friends. She'd never really known Brooke, and Brooke had no interest in really knowing her. And just when she was congratulating herself on having got over him there was that article in September in one of the papers. An American journalist had spoken to him after the first heavy bombing raid on Berlin in August. It was a glowing article, dwelling much on Brooke's good looks, personal skill and courage, and the admiration he aroused in his crew. Furtively, Beattie had cut the article out of the *Daily Mail* and hidden it in her Bible.

She thinks of all this as she stares at the curlers in her lap. Perhaps she is being selfish. And perhaps Louie is right; it's hard to imagine Brooke putting on his Brylcreem and setting off for an evening's entertainment in Wearam village hall.

Which is how she comes to find herself there later that evening with Louie, who is lit up with an internal glow that has nothing to do with the long frosty cycle ride through the October lanes. But as Beattie inhales the familiar village-social smells of sweat, feet, cheap perfume and hair oil all her earlier misgivings about the dance flood back, and she tries to make herself as inconspicuous as possible. The walls of the hall are hung with red, white and blue crêpe paper and banners urging support for the Norwich Spitfire Fund. The rest of the girls from Chillington crowd in behind her, clearly cheered by the solid throng of men and women foxtrotting around the room.

'I jolly well hope he turns up, Louie.'

'So do I,' says Louie, anxiously redoing her lipstick.

Beattie stares casually around the room, annoyed to find that her heart is beating so fast. Louie's cup overflows as Vince appears at her elbow with gratifying promptness, introduces Beattie and Ba to his friends, and they are soon all slow-waltzing around the room with the rest of the crowd.

'He hasn't come,' thinks Beattie in relief, and begins cautiously to enjoy herself. It is like every other village social she has been to in the last year. There are spot waltzes, a Paul Jones and a Gay Gordons. Louie bobs up beside her, her eyes bright with happiness.

'Come and have some wicked orange squash with me,' she says and leads Beattie over to the trestle-table against the wall. 'You're not still cross with me, are you?'

'No, of course not,' says Beattie. 'He looks smashing, your Vince, and he's a terrific dancer.'

'He says you look like Hedy Lamarr. By the way – you'll *never guess* – he's borrowed a van, and he said he'll take me home with the bike. Good, isn't it? I'm sure he can manage a couple of other bikes, so we needn't leave till later.'

At ten o'clock there is a roll on the drums to announce the result of the raffle. The curious nature of the prizes tells its own story of current shortages. For example, the star prize for the evening isn't a bottle of sherry or even a box of chocolates, but three torch batteries. Louie wins a packet of Kirby grips and Beattie silently longs for the sherry for her parents, but to her astonishment she hears her name being called out for the box of chocolates. What riches! It's only half a pound but it seems like gold dust to the sweet-toothed girls at the cottage. Feeling the evening has really paid for itself, Beattie gets ready to dance the last dance before they will have to go. It is an 'excuse me', and Louie and Vince are already causing universal annoyance by refusing to be parted. Beattie dances first with a tall NCO, then with a cheerful-faced boy with the stripes of a rear gunner on his tunic. As they laugh over something, Beattie sees his eyes glance over her shoulder and his face grow rueful.

'Oh, you aren't going to cut in on me, are you, old man? Us chaps don't stand a chance with the pretty girls against you pilots.'

Beattie stiffens from head to foot as her partner steps back into the crowd and Brooke quickly puts an arm around her waist and dances her away. In the shock of his physical presence, his body so close to hers, Beattie is speechless. She is also rigid with anger, furious with Louie and furious with herself. She'd show Brooke just how little their parting had meant to her.

'Jolly good luck you winning the raffle, and for me, too. I'd never have known you were here in this crowd.'

Beattie doesn't reply. After a minute or two, he says: 'Are you going to dance the entire dance in silence?' It appears they are. 'Well, in that case there isn't much point in carrying on, is there?' says Brooke angrily, stopping short and causing two couples to crash into them.

'If you remember,' says Beattie distinctly, 'I didn't ask you to dance.'

With that she walks off the dance-floor to the powder room, pulls on her coat and scarf, then steps out of the side-entrance to the hall. She finds her way to the bicycle shed and with difficulty manages to disentangle her own. It has belonged to one of the gardeners at Chillington and has a cast-iron frame and a cross-bar on which you could have conveniently roasted an ox. Despite her long skirt, she manages to scramble aboard, and is soon pedalling briskly away in the direction of Chillington. The moon has gone in now, and clouds obscure the few stars in the sky. There is not enough light to see her home, and she gives a cry of dismay when the front light on the bicycle flickers and then abruptly goes out. She is faced with the prospect of either cycling on in the dark and hoping for the best or walking and waiting for the others. She's dithering and trying to decide what to do, when a car suddenly shoots over the brow of the hill behind her. Even the dimmed-out headlights still have the power to startle. Beattie wobbles fatally, then slowly and ingloriously topples into the ditch. She is thrown clear on to the overgrown opposite bank and lies there winded, the bicycle wheels whirring madly in the ditch beside her.

The car stops abruptly. Brooke jumps out and reaches down into the ditch for her. 'Oh Christ! I'm sorry. Did I startle you? Are you hurt? Here, give me your hand.' He pulls her to her feet. 'I was waiting for you outside to ask if you wanted a lift home, and somebody said you'd gone already. . . . I was going to drive you back. . . .'

'If I'd wanted a lift, I'd have asked,' hisses Beattie, nearly in tears. 'I've got a tongue in my head, you know. You've ruined my only good pair of stockings. I'll never be able to get them repaired. Now, if you'd have the decency to get my bike out of the ditch, I'll be on my way again.'

Brooke pulls the heavy machine out of the ditch, while Beattie checks in the dim glow of his headlights that she still has everything in her handbag. She gives a cry of dismay.

'My chocolates! I must have dropped them.'

Brooke steps cautiously into the ditch and feels around a bit. 'Here you are. I've got them. That's the good news. Do you want the bad news?'

'What do you mean?'

'Your front wheel is buckled. You'll never be able to cycle home on that.'

'Then, I'll walk,' she says, grabbing the handlebars from him.

'Don't be daft, Beattie. You've got no lights and it's a good few miles to Chillington. I'll put it over the back and—'

'I don't want a lift from you,' suddenly shouts Beattie, losing all self-control. 'Can't you get that into your thick head? I don't want anything to do with you ever again. Just leave me alone.'

There is a long moment of silence, then Brooke sighs and says, apparently at random: 'I'm sorry, you know. About that weekend. I wanted to write, but I didn't know what to say. Did you get back all right?'

'No,' says Beattie rudely. 'I was murdered on the train.' She feels in her bag for a hankie.

'I never meant it to be . . . like that.'

'What *exactly* are you sorry about?' hisses Beattie. 'The fact that friends insulted me or the fact that you asked me away for the weekend then proceeded to go to bed with someone else?' Even in the dim light Beattie sees Brooke redden.

'We—I behaved rather stupidly. I was very sorry about it afterwards. Gareth is dead, you know. He came with us on that raid to Berlin and we lost him over the sea coming back.'

'I'm sorry,' says Beattie more quietly.

'Look, stop shouting at me and let me help. You really can't manage that thing on your own, not now it's out of action. Let me put it over the back and take you home. Then I'll leave you at the gates and never darken your door again. OK?'

In some obscure way Beattie feels defeated, but none the less meekly goes round to the side of the car, while Brooke easily picks up the heavy old bike and lays it across the boot. He goes to open the door for Beattie.

'No fast cornering with that on the back,' he remarks, and they look at each other properly for the first time. It is that look that undoes Beattie: when he pulls her into his arms and kisses her, instead of struggling she finds herself responding hungrily to the intensity of his kiss. In the space of a few seconds it is as if her whole body has opened up to him. He holds her in his arms, pressed against the car, and when the long kiss ends he simply holds her, gripped tightly to him, his hand stroking her hair, her cheek against his. She can feel the tension leaving his body, and he sighs deeply. After a while he says: 'I did miss you, you know. I wanted to write but I didn't know what to say. Pride, I suppose. I wanted to come and see you when I was in the village but I didn't meet you anywhere, so I thought you must be avoiding me. I only went to that awful dance because the men said there were some girls coming from Chillington.'

'I'm on the phone,' she says stiffly.

'So am I,' he reminds her gently and pushes a wave of her heavy hair back from her face. 'Are you seeing somebody else?'

Beattie hesitates. She would dearly love to be able to say she's unavailable. But 'No,' she says uncertainly. 'I'm not seeing anybody else.'

He pulls her to him again, then tips up her chin so that he can look at her before he kisses her.

'Come on, I'll do the decent thing and take you home.' They drive back at a very sedate pace indeed. Outside the Chillington gates he says: 'I'm sorry about your stockings. I'll get you some more.'

'But I'm not seeing you again.'

'So you aren't. I forgot.'

He reaches up and takes the bicycle off the back of the car. 'I was hoping I could tempt you to another of our mess dances. With your friend Louie since she seems to find the company of my rigger so irresistible.'

Beattie feels the familiar sensation of the net closing in on her.

'And I *really* feel bad about those stockings,' goes on Brooke. 'I'll tell you what – at least have tea with me on Sunday so that I can give you some new ones, or I'll feel really terrible about them for ever.'

'I'll think about it,' says Beattie, and begins to wheel her bike through the gate.

'Sunday, then? Same time, same place?'

'Perhaps.' Beattie hears Brooke laughing as he starts up the car. She parks her bike and walks on to the cottage where she builds up the fire and eats one of her chocolates. With monumental self-control she puts away the rest to share with the other two when they come in.

Pretty soon she is singing 'Down Mexico Way' and wondering what she will wear on Sunday.

139

CHAPTER
ELEVEN

*W*ITHIN A FORTNIGHT Beattie is seeing Brooke regularly, and within a month he is sleeping over at least one night a week at the cottage. No one mentions his occasional presence, but obscurely Beattie feels Louie's unspoken disapproval, while she herself is uneasily aware that if she were ever to change her mind about being Brooke's girl Barbr'ann has shown herself more than willing to volunteer for the post. Fortunately, Barbr'ann had met a serviceman in Morecambe that summer and most of her attention is occupied with writing to him. So Beattie is left to argue alone with her own conscience as to the wisdom of what she's done.

But, whatever sane and sensible arguments Beattie can come up with, something inside her screams with anguish at the idea of not being able to see him again, however great the humiliation of knowing the best course and yet failing to pursue it. Resolutely, Beattie tries to push it all out of her mind. Quite apart from fears about his commitment there is now the constant anxiety about his safety. Night after night she lies tense in her bed listening to the faint sounds of anti-aircraft fire from Norwich, then the planes that have got through passing over in receding pulsing waves, heading for Birmingham and Coventry. Sometimes Brooke wakes up and identifies the planes by their engines. But mostly he lies dead to the world in her arms, worn out with the seemingly endless invasion practices and his present tour of duty. Yet Brooke at this time is a different creature, and it is this that makes Beattie most fearful of all. He has a kind of sheen about him, a sense of exultation and recklessness that can only mean he has at last found the danger he craves. In September he had changed planes again, and now pilots a long black twin-engine Whitley. Seeing it for the first time, Beattie had gasped. It was quite simply a machine for killing. They had gone for another autumn walk through the woods at Gatton, and Brooke had pointed out his own plane outside the hangar. He had singled it out with all the pride of a mother identifying her own child in the playground, while Beattie had looked on it with something approaching horror. The same horror she feels when she finds that because of the danger of invasion Brooke now carries a revolver with him at all times. He even brings it to the cottage. It brings the war, not only to your doorstep, but actually into your bed.

'She's a grand-looking plane. Don't you think?'

'She looks . . . very powerful. Is that something painted on the front?'

Brooke smiles. 'Oh, that's Musgrave the mouse. Haven't you seen it? It's in that strip cartoon in the London *Star*. Old Garson – he's my navigator now, a grand chap – painted him on as our mascot. And the ground crew put a bomb on for every completed mission. There's eight on the Whitley already.' There is no disguising the pride in his voice. They stand for a moment in silence. There is a smell of wood-smoke in the calm autumn air, and the stubble in the fields on the other side of the valley is washed a delicate gold.

'We mostly fly to Holland now,' goes on Brooke absently. 'Looking for oil-refineries or steelworks. We go out each night to try to even out what they're doing to London.'

Brooke slides an arm through hers as she gazes up at the calm faultless profile against the turned-up collar of his greatcoat. Brooke speaks so casually, so calmly of the dangers that he and his crew face. It is impossible to imagine him out of control or sweating or crazy with fear.

Later on that afternoon, they find a discreet sunny place on the hillside and make love on the rug from Brooke's car. Afterwards the rug comes in handy against the chill of the setting sun as they lie there and listen to the sounds of the planes taxiing and taking off from the airfield below them. Brooke strokes Beattie's hair absently and narrows his eyes as he follows the flight of the planes into the mackerel sky over their heads.

'Will you go on flying after the war?' As soon as the words leave Beattie's lips, she knows she has said the wrong thing. She can actually feel Brooke go tense beside her.

'I never think of anything more than an hour ahead,' he says, 'which I think probably takes us about up to opening-time.' He looks at her more gently. 'It's best that way, you know.'

Beattie is silent. Brooke's sudden changes in mood still have the power to terrify her, and she is constantly braced against the fear of his anger. She is well aware that Brooke is on his best behaviour, consciously trying to control his temper, and that they are enjoying a tentative honeymoon period together. If only it could always be like this, thinks Beattie, fishing for her suspender-belt. Part of her still hopes and hopes that he'll always be in a mood like this, and that they'll be happy ever after. But common sense tells her that this is extremely unlikely, that people do not on the whole change – mostly they start off the way they mean to go on. But deep down she still hopes that if she loves Brooke enough he will ultimately be changed. It is a futile hope, and she fully acknowledges it as such.

'Coming for a drink? We're all meeting at the Bell.'

'I'd like that,' she says, and they look at each other. It is a rueful look of mutual appraisal. Brooke's glance says that he is aware that he is not always kind to her, but he is making an effort. Beattie's look is considerably more spirited than it would have been a year ago, and it says quite clearly: 'You may think I'm crazy about you, but don't forget I've proved I can do without you.' Reluctantly they both start to smile. Brooke pulls her to her feet, brushes the grass seed off his coat and they walk back to the car.

The Bell is already packed to capacity, and Brooke and Beattie are hailed on all sides as they go in. Beattie is privately appalled to see how few of the faces she had known from last spring are still around and, as the winter

141

months draw on, how few of the faces around the bar stay constant. Even Brooke's own crew are always changing.

'The trouble with flying with Brooke,' says Sandy Blair, Brooke's current cheerful Scots co-pilot, 'is that he trains you too well. You get promoted too fast.'

'That's true. I lose all my best crews that way,' says Brooke glumly.

A woman's place as an RAF girlfriend was, as Beattie had observed, to be seen to be pretty and on the whole not to be heard. Certainly not to be heard to make tactless remarks about where's so and so. If she asks anybody at all, it will be Brooke, and privately, and the words 'Oh, he bought it a couple of nights ago', uttered in a certain tone of voice, mean that that is the end of the conversation. Sometimes people drop into enemy territory and end up as prisoners of war. Sometimes people are picked up from the North Sea. But mostly the loss of the plane means the end of the matter. There is a whole series of chilling jokes and stories that you have to listen to and laugh at. Such as the one about 'Ten-Minute Hastings' who was killed on his first mission, ten minutes after he'd reached the German coast. Or the rear gunner who'd arrived newly trained in the afternoon and enquired where he should put his things. 'I shouldn't bother if I were you,' he is told by a hardened veteran younger than Brooke. 'You won't be coming back tonight.'

The average life-expectancy of a rear gunner after training is a week. There was the boy from Plymouth who wanted to fly with an open copy of the New Testament on his knees. Brooke had had a series of talks with him and managed to persuade him that there were other ways of serving his country. In the middle of this endless, barely controlled hysteria and seeming callousness there is Brooke whom people actually touch for luck before setting out each night.

Beattie has never felt integrated with this other side of Brooke's life; but, then, she tells herself, why should I be? She and the other girls who drink with the pilots know nothing of the real dangers that they're faced with. The daily knowledge that tonight might be the last night, the night when the very least you could suffer might be burns, broken bones or permanent disfigurement. The girls that Beattie meets hanging round the pilots are a motley crew. The wives keep themselves deliberately low-key and live their own lives. Widows are not encouraged to hang around the district; it is felt to be bad for the morale of the surviving men. But for single girls like herself it is a different matter. They at least have chosen to be there. Beattie cannot understand how it is that some girls can go resolutely from one pilot to the next. She knows that if anything happened to Brooke she would never want to see Brooke's friends or the airfield ever again. But for some girls it is like an addiction. They cannot stay away from the possibility of drama and danger, if only by proxy. They also cannot stay away from Brooke as Beattie very soon discovers. It was that newspaper article that had done it; these days to have a drink with Brooke means the automatic presence of three girls hanging on to his every word. Brooke finds it amusing, and Beattie finds it best to seem as if she does as well.

There is an all-ranks party at Gatton just before Christmas, to which so many of the Chillington girls are invited that Miss Frobisher finally concedes defeat and a coach is booked to take them. Brooke brings home Beattie in his car and stays the night afterwards at the cottage. They swap Christmas presents in bed. Beattie has knitted him a scarf, fortunately started last March before they had broken up. It is the standard twenty-foot length which has been decreed as the only possible way to keep out the cold in the freezing cockpit. It has been put together by dint of buying old woolies at jumble sales, unravelling them, then reballing the wool and knitting it up again. With this scarf goes the real jewel of the collection, a jersey she has knitted for him to fly in, in proper Air Force blue wool, which her aunt in London had made a special journey to D. H. Evans to buy. It is a fine piece of work, and Brooke is enormously impressed, insisting on trying it on there and then and wearing it in bed until it becomes impractical. For Beattie, there is a gold compact and lipstick. It is a very good night. Two days later there is the Christmas dance at Chillington, and at the last moment Brooke declines to come on the grounds that he's got a free weekend and needs to get away from everything. Beattie is not at all sure that he hasn't gone to see the Alberrys. She is completely crushed but tries not to show it.

'He wants a kick up the backside, that one,' is Louie's comment. But she makes it privately and to Ba.

Perhaps Brooke feels badly about it, too, because there is actually a Christmas card from him waiting for Beattie when she arrives home. Brooke is as careful about not committing himself to paper as an adulterous husband, and the fact that he's bothered to send her a card and signed it himself makes Beattie feel a whole lot better about the short separation. She hides the card and the compact and the lipstick at the bottom of her underwear draw, and in considerably better spirits prepares to enjoy Christmas.

Mrs Blythe has already announced quite casually that she's invited Lucy Hallett to come for Christmas lunch. Nothing so clearly marks the change in world affairs as the fact that nobody except Beattie finds this in the least remarkable. Lucy is working on Christmas morning but manages to turn up promptly at twelve o'clock laden with presents and goodwill.

'My word, it is snug in here,' she says, looking round with pleasure at the Blythes' cheerful Christmas-morning kitchen. Ern and Toby have spent the last two weeks making and hanging paper chains. There is a good deal of holly, and the smell of roast chicken hangs pleasantly on the air. Mr Blythe, in his Sunday suit, is reading a new copy of *Adam the Gardener* that Beattie has managed to buy for him. The two boys are playing in front of the range with Toby's Christmas present, a puppy, which he has already insisted he will call Beetle.

'Did you have to get up early and milk?' asks Beattie.

'I certainly did. But there isn't much else to do, and once I've done the afternoon milking, then I'm finished for the day. I've bought a bottle of sherry. Shall we be daring and have a pre-lunch drink?'

'What'll the toast be, then?' asks Mr Blythe.

'Peace 1941,' says Mrs Blythe firmly, and Beattie and her father and Lucy echo her soberly and clink their glasses.

'Don't we get any to drink?' says Toby, scandalized.

'You wouldn't like it anyway,' Beattie consoles them.

143

'I would so!' Toby tells her firmly. 'The Vicar gave us a sip after we'd been carol-singing.'

Lucy starts laughing. 'Here, come on, open your presents, then you can put away the paper in time for lunch.'

Covertly Beattie examines Lucy. It is almost exactly a year since she's seen her owing to Lucy's perambulations around East Suffolk. It is no exaggeration to say that in that short space of time her appearance has been totally transformed. Even her corduroy breeches and clean dark green jersey somehow give her an air of distinction. She has lost all her puppy fat, and her hair has grown out of its short obnoxious perm and is simply held back with a slide and waved at her shoulders. It is as if physically she now feels completely at home in her body. Her strength and height no longer embarrass her. She bears absolutely no resemblance at all to that slouching ill-at-ease girl of the garden-party. Little Ern, normally mistrustful of strangers, climbs happily on to her knees.

'It was such a stroke of luck meeting your mother last week in Ipswich. I'm only working five miles away, but I honestly haven't been in the village – goodness, for a couple of months. And I don't often go into Ipswich. I had to go in that afternoon to pick up a new fitting for the cooler. Mrs Musgrave did ask me if I wanted to go over on Christmas Day, then she decided to go to the Towers. So I was quite resigned to having Christmas on my own. This is a lovely treat.'

'What are you doing exactly?'

'Oh, still working as a relief milker. I've been doing that since the harvest ended. They haven't found me a permanent job yet. I suppose I'm more useful to them being mobile. I'm at the Charrington's farm at Five Ways; do you know it? They've got a wonderful herd of Friesians. The chap who normally looks after them has gone into hospital for five weeks, so I'm there until he comes back. How are your studies going?'

'Ah, Beattie's a proper teacher now,' puts in Toby helpfully.

'Well, almost,' says Beattie. 'I'm doing my teaching practice at a prep school that's been evacuated into Chillington with us. I'll be properly qualified next summer.'

'What will you do then? Do you think you'll come back and teach in the village school?'

Beattie is aware that her mother is listening with the keenest possible interest.

'I haven't decided yet. There'll be a job going where I am, actually teaching in a boy's prep school.'

There was a united chorus of disapproval from Toby and Ern.

'Oh, Beattie, you said you'd be coming home in the summer.'

'Well, we'll see,' says Beattie hastily. 'I haven't really made up my mind yet anyway. Do you want me to help you, Mother?'

'I think we can all move to the table now,' says Mrs Blythe. 'Have you washed your face and hands, children? Toby, get an extra chair in from the other room. And put that dog down. He's got to learn to sit and be quiet sometimes.'

After Mrs Blythe's magnificent roast chicken lunch, with a rather smaller

Christmas pudding than usual, Lucy goes off for afternoon milking session, while Beattie and the boys and Mr Blythe, having washed up, walk down to the post office to Mrs Leary's wireless, to hear the King's Christmas message. Lucy reappears later on in the afternoon and, along with Lily and the younger members of the Kedge family, they go for a long cold walk. It is a crisp, clear, exhilarating sort of afternoon, the red ball of the sun slipping down behind the bare branches of the distant woods by four o'clock. When they return there is Christmas tea, after which Beattie and Lucy wash up in the scullery.

'Do you hear – er – from Miss Virginia much?' says Beattie.

'I certainly do. She's a marvellous correspondent – much better than I am, I'm afraid. She writes almost every week. I never realized how nice it was to get letters until I left home. Virginia's always seem to arrive on a Monday and, if I hear from Hugh, for some reason that's always on a Saturday. And Mother and Father write when they can. Did I tell you Hugh had sent a picture of himself? He's in North Africa now; he looks wonderful in his desert rig. I sent him some books for Christmas; I do hope he gets them. He likes that fellow Hemingway. Ernest Hemingway. He's an American writer. I asked Virginia to get me his latest novel and some short stories, and she very decently did and sent them on to me. She's working for a publisher, did you know? She must be having quite a tough time at present. Mrs Musgrave's frightfully worried about Brooke of course. I saw her about a week ago, and she talks of nothing else. Do you know it's my first wedding anniversary next Tuesday? Me being married for a year! I still can't believe it. And it's a year since I started with the Land Army.'

'Was is difficult actually joining?'

'No, not really. You have to contact the nearest rep to you. And I already knew Mrs Caulder because I'd done some work taking rosehips with the village children. She used to collect the sacks up and take them to Ipswich. I just got in touch with her and told her I was interested, and she came and talked to me and asked me all the usual things about whether I was fit and healthy, whether I had a bicycle and things like that, and there it was. Then they had to see my parents to make sure that they didn't object, and that – um – wasn't really quite so easy.'

'I remember you saying that your mother was keen for you to stay on working as her secretary.'

'Hm,' agrees Lucy noncommittally. 'She certainly wasn't very happy about me going off and doing anything else. Of course Mother does see herself as having an important part to play in keeping up the morale of British young people, and I think she thought I'd be better employed helping her than cutting the tops off sugar beets. So I had rather a sticky period with them. In the end, Father came down on my side and I thought I'd just better press on.'

'Do they like Yorkshire?'

'Well, they do now. The house they took in York turned out not to be suitable. Mother said she couldn't concentrate there for some reason, so Father had to find somewhere else, and in the end they moved to Harrogate. And so far that seems to be working out all right. I had a nice letter from Mother for Christmas – she's just been awarded some Commonwealth gold

145

medal for her books, and that new series about "The Troublesome School-girl" seems to be going terribly well. She's a girl who's constantly in trouble and gets everybody's back up, and the sales have been awfully good, so Mother's quite buoyant at present.'

'Where did you do your training, then?'

'Well, I had a real bit of luck. I was prepared just to start tagging along learning on the job, but they managed to get me into the agricultural college at Swaffham for two weeks, which was the most enormous help. I mean, you spend your time milking replicas of cows rather than the real thing, but it does give you a bit more confidence. Then I was sent down to a farm in Essex and I spent my first two months muck-spreading and harrowing.'

'Didn't you find it awfully boring?'

'Surprisingly, no,' says Lucy reminiscently. 'Even though the tasks are the same, no two days ever seem alike. I was jolly pleased to find that I was quite good with the animals, particularly horses. The farmer there said I had a way with animals. I was very chuffed because I've never thought of myself as having a way with anything. In the summer I was a member of a threshing gang and we were sent round from farm to farm with the thresher, helping out where we were needed. That was great fun. We all lived in the same cottage and had such a laugh in the evenings. One of the girls taught me to tap-dance! I wouldn't have missed that for anything. Then we got split up again and since then I've been milking. There's some talk now about finding me a permanent farm, but I can't say where it will be. It's really up to them where they want to send you. Honestly, it could be anywhere in Suffolk.'

At eight o'clock Lucy sets off cheerily to cycle the four miles back to the farm. It is a clear and frosty night, the bright starlight making it almost unnecessary for her bicycle-lamp. Warm with good food and good feelings, Lucy pedals happily onward, reviewing the past year. In some ways, in spite of the fact that Hugh has been away, it has been the best year of her life. There is something about being married, or being Mrs, of feeling placed in society, that suits Lucy very well. Knowing that she is Hugh's wife had instantly given her the most enormous rush of confidence. And this, coupled with the extraordinary knowledge that she really is a rather useful person round the farm, has completely altered Lucy's view of herself. She has erred on the side of modesty in the description of her duties to Beattie; in reality several farms asked for her services full-time, but it is the area rep who has insisted on spreading her around as wide a range of jobs as is possible. She is now as good a milker as an experienced herdsman, and generally has a way with the stock. There is always plenty to tell Hugh about in her letters, and she is gratified that his letters are equally happy in return. He is enjoying his job, enjoying North Africa, and talks fondly of the time that they'll be together again at some unspecified date in the future.

In fact the only person who isn't as delighted by Lucy's metamorphosis is Mrs Hallett. Out of loyalty, Lucy had soft-pedalled the reality of her mother's reaction when Lucy had told her she didn't want to go to Yorkshire. Mrs Hallett had been incensed beyond anything that could be rationally explained. It was an unpleasant shock, and it had made Lucy briefly realize the extent to which she and her father tended as a matter of course to give in to her mother on every issue. Mother was the pivot and the centre of their family, not to mention the wage-earner; and normally things proceeded in the way Mrs Hallett wanted. So Lucy's announcement was seen in the light of total disloyalty. Of course Mother was getting more and more important, and perhaps she expected to be treated as the major writer she now thought she was. But if it hadn't been for Father taking her part Lucy doubted very much if she could have withstood the tidal wave of Mrs Hallett's annoyance. And for three months after they'd left the village it was Lucy's father who wrote every week and not her mother. Still, she had written a nice enough letter at Christmas. So presumably all was forgiven now.

Lucy pedals slowly up the incline to the cottage where she currently has lodgings with a doctor and his wife. She has a book to read that Virginia has sent her for Christmas, some home-made sweets that Mrs Blythe has given her as a Christmas present, and the prospect of sitting with her feet up on the fender with the doctor's wife while they have their cocoa. Lucy breathes deeply, conscious that she has probably never been happier in her life. Invasion or no invasion, her life is pretty marvellous. If it has been this good in 1940, then surely 1941 can hold only even better things.

Beattie is also feeling quietly optimistic as she puts the children to bed, then goes up to her own room to enjoy the indulgence of a final look at Brooke's card. She opens her underwear drawer, then stops short. The card and the lipstick and the compact are still where she put them, but she knows that the clothes around them have been moved. It can only be Mrs Blythe who would have been to that drawer, and with a feeling of apprehension Beattie wonders how much her mother really guesses about her life at Chillington. She sits on her bed for a minute wondering if she ought to confront her mother and mention the matter. Then suddenly Mrs Blythe is there in the doorway looking flushed and self-conscious, her hands plucking at her apron. Beattie faces her warily. She suddenly sees her mother objectively, as you might catch sight of a well-loved face unexpectedly in a crowd of people and see it as a stranger would. Mrs Blythe is a good-looking woman with thick shining hair like Beattie's own, rolled back from her face and secured in a bun at the nape of her neck. She has her daughter's heavy winged eyebrows and fine skin. But her expression is quite unlike Beattie's, for she has a guarded face with a mouth that rarely smiles, the lips held firmly together at all times in a conscious watchfulness. Beattie stands up, unconsciously bracing herself for some kind of cross-questioning, then to her relief and astonishment sees that her mother for once is actually smiling. In fact Mrs Blythe is surrounded by an aura of dim excitement that makes her almost hardly recognizable.

'I just wanted to give you something,' she says, even more surprisingly, and stepping outside the door brings in a suitcase that Beattie has never seen before, and hastily shuts the bedroom door behind her.

'It's another Christmas present,' she says hurriedly, much to Beattie's mystification as she has already received a truly wonderful scarlet knitted jumper and skirt from her mother. She puts down the suitcase, which is old

147

and leather-bound, and when she raises the lid there is an immediate faint fragrance of Chypre, a perfume that Beattie remembers somehow from a long time ago. Her mother then starts to undo swaths of tissue paper, talking in a way quite unlike herself. 'I thought you might need . . . something special for going out in the evenings,' she begins, avoiding her daughter's eyes. 'I always wanted you to have these things eventually, but I—you might as well have them now. They were my Lady's, you see,' she goes on. 'When Mrs Musgrave found out how ill she was she sent for me to choose a dress of hers to keep.'

She smooths open the tissue paper and reverentially draws out a long black evening dress in velvet. It is a full-length, classically simple dress with a low V-neck bound with black satin piping which forms the narrow shoulder-straps. It is lined with a black silk georgette, and Mrs Blythe reverentially turns the skirt back to show Beattie the workmanship inside.

'It was made by Molyneux – that's a very famous dressmaker in Paris. Mrs Musgrave bought it in 1930. I know it's ten years old, but because it's a classic it doesn't matter. You could wear it tomorrow and still be the best-dressed person—' She checks herself. 'There's a satin jacket to wear over it, see? Feel the fabric. It's beautiful, isn't it? You and the late Mrs Musgrave look pretty much of a size, I'd say. There are shoes, too, in this bag and an evening bag to go with it. No, don't thank me. As I say, I've always wanted you to have them, and I thought you might just as well have them now.'

Downstairs, the backdoor bangs.

'That's your father,' says Mrs Blythe with an odd guilty look. 'Pack them up and put them with the rest of your things. You never know when you'll need them.' With that cryptic comment she goes away, leaving Beattie staring after her in utter perplexity.

Downstairs in the kitchen, her father is pulling off his heavy boots.

'It's freezing harder tonight. And they say on the wireless that it's going to get colder and we'll have a temperature at New Year's Eve below zero. You best remind your mother to bring in her geranium cuttings, eh, Beattie?'

Mr Blythe's prophecy is correct. On New Year's evening, the temperature is well below zero, even in central London. When Virginia pushes open the door of the Grangemouth she finds that, if possible, it is even colder inside the building than it is out. Most of the girls are away until the New Year, and the heating has been off for a week. Virginia has divided time equally among her suitors, culminating in two days with Simon and his friends at the flat. Unfortunately, by midday today, she had discovered that when they were not actually drunk, dancing or in bed she and Simon have absolutely nothing to say to each other. And, as more and more people turned up at the flat, suddenly the thought of an uninterrupted night in her own bed became more and more attractive. In the end she'd simply packed her case and walked out the backdoor. And even in the cold and desolation of the empty Grangemouth she still feels glad to be on her own. Switching on the corridor lights, she makes her way up the stairs in the empty house. From the basement she can hear the faint sounds of revelry from the Cripps radio. Once in her own room, she feels around for the blackout curtains, then switches on the light. Leaning against the door, she is charmed by the tidiness and order of her attic room, almost Japanese in its austerity. Then, frowning, she runs a finger along the top of the chest of drawers and finds it thick with dust. Surely this can't all have happened in six days? There is a faint movement across the corridor in Devora's room, and she crosses the landing to investigate. As she opens the door she gives a scream, for she is staring straight out into the frosty night sky. A cloud of starlings whirl up into her face, then shoot skywards through a huge gaping hole in the roof above. From the light on the landing she can see that the room is a shambles. Someone has attempted to pile up the slates and rubble against one wall, but every surface in the room is inches deep in thick white dust, and liberally splattered with bird droppings. Then another door opens off the landing, and Cecily appears blinking short-sightedly, tying up the cord of her too-small Jaeger dressing-gown.

'Who—? Oh, it's you, Vir.'

'Cecily, has anybody reported this? Those chimneys are going to fall right into the room unless something is done quickly. When did it happen?'

'Christmas Eve apparently. I wasn't here. I've told old Cripps, but he says there's nothing can be done till Monday.'

'Cecily, what are you doing here anyway? I thought you were going to stay with your cousins.'

Cecily looks embarrassed and side-steps the question.

'It's awfully dark, isn't it? What time is it?'

'About five o'clock in the afternoon.'

'It can't be,' says Cecily in stupefaction. 'I went to bed at eleven o'clock last night.'

'Then, you've slept the clock round. What on earth have you been doing over Christmas?'

'Oh, the usual things,' says Cecily with her customary vagueness. 'I felt a bit queer yesterday and was told to go home and get some rest.'

'You don't mean you've been working all Christmas? Cecily, you must be crazy. No wonder you look pale. I don't think you're at all well. Go back to bed and keep warm, and I'll steal the Groundhog's paraffin-heater. No, go on, I insist, and give me your hot-water bottle and I'll get it refilled. I'll bring you up some tea when I've finished abusing old Cripps.'

Eventually Virginia persuades Cripps at least to cover the hole with a tarpaulin for the night, and takes the stove upstairs, lights it and returns again to charm Mrs Cripps into making them baked beans on toast. When she finally returns to the top landing, Cecily's room is pleasantly warm and Cecily is back in bed, blowing her nose energetically. Virginia suddenly feels more cheerful than she's done for days.

'I don't think I've seen you to talk to properly for about two months. Now, tell the truth. Why did you let everybody think you were going to your cousins?'

The scrupulous Cecily wriggles at this lie of omission if not of commission.

'It was a ploy to avoid going home. I knew if I went they'd never let me

149

come back here again. And I knew that if I told you that I was staying in London, you'd have felt duty bound to ask me to spend Christmas with you. And I wanted to work. It was only a white lie, Vir. Don't be cross with me.'

'I'm not cross with you. I just think you need a rest. What did you do?'

'Ordinary things,' says Cecily with a dreadful false brightness quite unlike her normal reserved manner. 'They've given me Stepney as an area to work in, so I go over every morning and every evening after the bombing with the mobile canteen, and I serve food and take the bombed-out families to the rest centre, then try to get them sorted out. You'll be amazed to learn,' she goes on with the same ghastly vivacity, 'that I've apparently got a real talent for telling people that their relations are dead. I spent hours at the incident enquiry point, telling people bad news. Yesterday morning I was on duty off the Commercial Road and this soldier came up and said he'd got a forty-eight-hour pass and he couldn't find his wife and kids. It was my happy duty to tell him he was now a single man and, furthermore, not even a father, since his wife and children had all died on Friday night.'

Cecily is talking too loudly and too emphatically, and the hand that holds her teacup is shaking so violently that the clattering almost drowns her speech.

'Do you know what he did? He stared at me, then his arm sort of swung up in a reflex and he punched me on the side of the jaw. The next thing I know, I'm flat on my back and he's picking me up and we both can't stop crying. I've never known anything like it before. Even when I take people to the mortuary they don't normally hit me afterwards. Extraordinary, isn't it? Kitty found me sitting down having a howl, so she told me to come home and go to bed. I suppose that was what I did.'

'Drink up your tea,' says Virginia briskly, privately appalled at the sight of Cecily on the verge of hysteria. 'I know what we both need.' She disappears into her own room and comes back triumphantly with a small bottle of brandy.

'Theo gave me this for Christmas, and I'd locked it away to keep it out of Devora's thieving hands. Go on, have a glass.'

'Is there anybody back yet?'

'No. Rachel's gone away for a fortnight and Devora went home in the end, I think.'

'Good riddance to her,' snaps Cecily, most uncharacteristically, and drains her two inches of brandy in one gulp and holds out the glass for some more. 'I can never understand what you see in her, Virginia,' she adds most surprisingly. 'It's her affair, if she's got the morals of a goat, but her complete selfishness really does appal me.'

'Well,' says Virginia in a curiously hard voice, 'if you condemn Devora, then you've got to condemn me, too. Our lives are remarkably similar.'

'I don't condemn,' says Cecily, flushing, her eyes on the counterpane. 'And I'd never even mention you and Devora in the same breath. I was talking to her just before Christmas, and it's as if part of her is dead some-how. Yes, thank you, I'll have another glass. I don't know what you're up to half the time, Vir. I don't mean I don't know where you are, I mean I don't understand you. What drives you on at such a furious rate? I could understand it if you enjoyed it all, but somehow I never feel you're happy. Forgive me, I'm just going on.'

'Don't worry,' says Virginia slowly. 'You're not the first person to make that particular observation. I don't understand myself most of the time. It just seems at present that all I want is some kind of oblivion. I don't know why I go to bed with so many people I despise, but I do and there it is. Sometimes I feel like Alice falling endlessly down a well and never finding the bottom. Oh God, Cecily, how on earth did we come to be talking about such a boring subject as me? Lets talk about something else, please.'

'No, don't let's,' says Cecily most astoundingly. 'I see you so rarely, the next time I won't be drunk enough to dare,' she adds cheerfully. 'You see, I've been worrying about you for such a long time.'

'Worrying about *me*?' says Virginia, amused.

'Remember when you were younger and you came to stay with us once at the Castle, we teased you and called you Poker Face because you never gave anything away?'

'Well, what about it?'

'That's the look you've got now. It went away for a bit when you first came to London. You used to smile a lot, and you looked quite jolly. Then you sort of froze up again.'

'Oh, well,' says Virginia flippantly. 'That's the way the British take their pleasure. With a look of real pain.'

But Cecily is not so easily distracted. 'You need—oh, I don't know what you need. Do you still get those letters from your mother?'

'I had a couple before Christmas.'

'I wish you'd get things sorted out with her.'

'Cecily, whatever has got into you?'

'Danger can suddenly make life seem awfully simple,' says Cecily at random, pushing her limp brown hair back from her face and tipping the last of the brandy into her glass. 'All the things I've seen through the past few months have made me realize that the only important thing is concentrating on living your own life in the best possible way, and throwing away the bits that hold you back, that stop you from really becoming yourself.'

Virginia looks at her in perplexity. 'Are you suggesting I throw away my mother?'

'No,' says Cecily, then adds most astoundingly, 'but it might be better for you to face the fact that, though she probably does love you, she'll never be able to love you in the way you want her to.'

'Cecily, that's a terrible thing to say.'

'I don't mean it to be terrible. Quite the reverse. In a funny way I think that you and I have the same problem, and I've been thinking for a while that it might be better if I said these things rather than just thinking them. You see, Pa and I don't get on. I was the fifth daughter and, as you know, there's quite a big gap between me and my sisters. Jean is the nearest, and she was already fifteen when I was born. They must have hoped and hoped they'd get a boy, and not only was I not a boy I wasn't even a beauty like Mother. One day when Pa was jawing on and on at me about not talking to guests, it just suddenly came to me that he didn't like me very much as a person – and, though I wept a bit, it was somehow a huge weight off my mind. It somehow took all the onus off me. I hadn't done anything wrong; it wasn't my fault. It was just the kind of person I was and the kind of person he was. And after that I stopped hoping for things that I knew couldn't happen. Am I making any sense at all?'

'Perfectly, but I don't know how you can live with knowledge like that,' says Virginia, who has the distinct impression that someone has just shot a cannonball through her stomach. 'I mean, if your parents aren't on your side, then what hope is there?'

'Well, it's sad, but there it is,' says Cecily vaguely. 'But the point is once you're grown up and strong enough to be on your own it doesn't really matter. The important thing is to think you're worthy of love and that you'll find it. But by endlessly standing around hoping your parents will change, you just tie yourself to the past. It's what happens now that really matters, isn't it?'

Overhead the air-raid siren suddenly pierces the silence with a warbling howl.

'Now, this once,' says Cecily, settling herself down more comfortably and giving a huge yawn, 'I'm not going anywhere; I'm staying in my nice warm bed.' (Virginia knows then that Cecily really must be drunk.)

'Well, in that case, so will I,' says Virginia, 'but I'd better take the paraffin-heater just in case. Are you going to sleep now, Cecily?'

'Believe it or not, I am,' says Cecily with another mammoth yawn. 'Sleep well, Vir darling, and ignore me if I was talking a lot of twaddle.'

Virginia slips into her own cold bed, finishes off the dregs at the bottom of the bottle, and lies there meaning to ponder deeply what Cecily has said. However, the next thing she knows is that it's still pitch dark and someone is banging on Cecily's door, saying she's wanted on the phone. There is no light, and it's very cold. When Cecily comes back upstairs, Virginia hears her begin to dress.

'Cecily, you're not going out, are you? It's only half-past five. Are you sure you're feeling all right?'

'I don't feel very good, but Kitty's just rung and said they bombed the City last night and apparently every fire engine in London was out. They need volunteers for the canteen-vans, and I just can't not go. I say,' she adds, coming to Virginia's room as she pulls her red jersey over her head, 'you couldn't come along as well, could you? It would be the most tremendous help. Kitty will be here in fifteen minutes to pick me up.'

Virginia opens her dry mouth to shriek a protest, and instead gets up and meekly begins to get dressed.

Kitty turns out to be a Kensington housewife with an immaculate Marcel wave.

'Apparently it's absolute chaos over there,' she says, jerking her head in the general direction of the City. 'You've never seen anything like it. It was all paper, you see; half the publishers' warehouses in London must have gone up. And, it being a holiday, there was no one on duty; they dropped incendiaries like rain, and instead of people chunking the bloody things out every blooming one must have started a fire. And of course the Thames would have to be at low tide, so they couldn't get the water up. What a shambles.'

She drives them to a yard in Ebury Street, full of parked vans and lorries. To Virginia's astonished eyes it seems at first that all the people loading them are grannies. Then she sees some girls in their twenties and thirties who wave to Cecily.

'We'll take one of the tea-vans. That means we can manage it on our own.'

'Shouldn't you ask somebody? Are you sure it's all right me being here?' asks Virginia uneasily.

'My dear, there's no one here to ask. There's no one in charge; you just get on with what needs doing. Unless there's something that needs doing more. I'll just ask Alma if she knows what's going on.'

Alma is staring into the engine of a lorry with a look of rage on her face.

'This is Virginia, Alma. She wants to help. I thought we'd take a tea-lorry over to the City.'

'Good idea. Diana's taking a couple of vans over in about twenty minutes. You'd best follow her.'

Inside the building that adjoins the yard, people are milling round waiting to talk to two women who sit at desks at the end of the room. Four or five elderly women are making ham sandwiches in a kind of conveyor belt. Nobody seems to be in charge, and yet a great deal is getting done. With Virginia's help, they load up their van with powdered milk, tea, sugar and cups.

'We'll just get some sandwiches in, too, and we can brew up when we get there,' says Cecily, as Diana begins to toot her horn impatiently. 'Right,' says Cecily in a businesslike way, 'in you get. What a good thing you wore your slacks.'

It is cold beyond belief. As they drive through streets full of smouldering buildings and broken glass it is hard to tell if it is dawn that is breaking in the east, or simply the red inferno that is lighting up the sky.

'This is fun, you coming along like this. Jolly sporting of you. I say, Vir, did I talk an awful lot of tommy-rot last night?'

'No,' says Virginia, holding on to the side of the seat as they roar down Fleet Street, 'I think you talked an awful lot of sense.'

153

CHAPTER
TWELVE

'HAVE YOU SEEN the list?'

'I've come straight from the station. Who's teaching where?'

'I'm at Greyshott this term,' says Louie in tones of the deepest satisfaction. 'Old Ba is at Dereham – she won't like it. You're teaching at Sedgemoor. It's not too bad. Jethro from the milk factory drives right past the door. Had a good Christmas?'

'Lovely,' says Beattie, who is already on the familiar treadmill of wondering how long it will be before she can reasonably expect to hear from Brooke. 'How about you?'

'So-so. We spent most of it in the shelter.'

'Is Ba back yet?'

'Yes, and she's delirious with passion. She came down early and spent three nights of joy with Eric in London. It's the real thing again – so, please, no jokes.'

'You seem a bit down, Louie. Is there something wrong?'

'Oh, I just hate leaving me mum. I do really. It's frightening up there, and if you could see Liverpool – it's like a battlefield. My old primary school's just a hole in the road. I feel I ought to be with them suffering, instead of being safe here. Me mum can't cope on her own. Our Debbie is turning out to be a real handful, and Mother doesn't know the half of what she gets up to. I saw Miss Davis, my old headmistress, and she said Debbie has been truanting for over a year. She's only fourteen, and she's already going to the cinema with men in uniform. The trouble is she looks old for her age, and she's as pretty as a picture. I gave her a right talking-to one night, and she told me I was jealous! I boxed her ears, I can tell you. She was going to go to college like me, but now she wants to go and work in a munitions factory. The money those girls are earning! But it seems to make them awfully bold—'

There is a crashing noise outside as Barbr'ann drops her suitcase and dances into the room. Her eyes are shining and she is wearing her hair rolled up at the sides in the new style. She looks on top of the world.

'Hello, Beat. Did old Miseryguts tell you I've been staying with Eric?'

'She did mention it.'

'It was wonderful. Do you want to hear about it?'

'Did you bring any food back with you?' asks Louie.

'I'm afraid Eric and I ate most of it.'

154

There is such a groan of dismay from the two other girls that she relents. 'I've put a few things by. Put the kettle on and we'll have a nice chin-wag.'

'There's no teapot.'

'Then, we'll make it in my hot-water bottle. And I've got a packet of coconut fancies.'

'I feel quite faint when you say that,' says Louie weakly. 'Come on, tell us the full ghastly story. It'll end in tears, as my mum would say, so enjoy it while you can.'

'You're jealous,' retorts Barbr'ann, who is pouring water into her hot-water bottle, spooning in tea, screwing on the lid, then waving it animatedly round the head.

'There. Tea up.'

'Why does everybody think I'm jealous?' enquires Louie.

'Start at the beginning. How did you get away early?' asks Beattie.

'Well,' says Barbr'ann cosily. 'It wasn't easy, I can tell you. I had a letter from Eric just after Christmas, saying that he had three days' leave, and was there any chance of coming down to London. Well, *naturally*. . . .'

The weather mercifully is much milder than the previous winter, and it does not snow until the end of February. Beattie and Louie are sitting round the fire, their feet on the fender while Louie finishes her marking in a desultory sort of way. She is teaching the top form of Greyshott that term and coaching four boys for their Common Entrance.

'It's going to be jolly cold going out tonight,' says Beattie with a yawn. 'Do you think it's worth going over for supper?'

'I don't think it's worth it, but I'll go anyway because I'm that hungry. When I look back on these two years I shall just remember feeling starved the whole time.'

'Do you want me to take up the hem of your dress for Saturday?'

'I suppose so.'

'You don't sound awfully keen. I thought you really liked Vince.'

'I do like him; it's just that whenever I get involved with a fella it comes to a point when they start talking about the future and you know they mean marriage. Len was just the same.'

'You are odd,' says Beattie. 'I thought you were cross with Len because he didn't want to marry you. Did he ask you?'

'Oh, lots of times,' says Louie most surprisingly. 'I kept on being vague about it, and in the end I suppose he lost patience. It's just that I get so churned up at the thought of getting wed. Sometimes marriage just seems a bally trap – pardon my French. You know, they lead you to the altar and you're princess for the day, and the next thing you know you're being handed their linen to wash and being asked why dinner isn't on time and there's babies everywhere.'

'Louie, that's daft, and you know it. You don't have to have babies if you don't want them.'

'That's as maybe, but what do you actually get from being married I'd like to know. I've really started to think about that lately. I mean, if it was

155

still before the war, if I wanted to get married, I'd have to give up my teaching at once. It's crazy. I'm marrying a man, he gives me his name, and he gets my employment prospects. And it's not that I don't like babies. But I feel I've already been through a lifetime of motherly feelings and come out the other side. Don't forget you were brought up in a nice house with just three people in it; we had two rooms and nine people, and we shared our toilet with fifteen others. It makes a difference, you know. You're lucky being an only child. How do you think your mother managed it?'

As usual Louie's frankness has the effect of provoking equal frankness in Beattie. 'I'm not sure that she consciously did manage it. I think she may be a bit older than my dad actually – she never tells anybody her age. She had me as soon as she got married, then there were two more after me, a girl and a boy, but they both died a few weeks after they were born. It was ever so sad. They've both got nice little graves in the churchyard, and Dad tends them every week. But there don't seem to have been any more after that.'

'Lucky her. My mum got married at sixteen and had me in the same year and started the way she meant to go on. There were three that died in our family, and if there hadn't been, and my dad dying, too, we'd probably be in double figures by now. Treble figures possibly.'

Beattie giggles.

'It all comes down to money,' goes on Louie reflectively. 'There's five in Ba's family, but they can afford to say "the more the merrier". That's the difference.'

'Where is Ba? I haven't seen her since breakfast.'

'She had a pass to go into Norwich to see the dentist but, knowing her, she's probably gone to the pictures.'

'Is she still writing to Eric? She's been very edgy lately.'

'She should be getting worried about exams. She hardly did any work in the holidays.'

Beattie begins to put away her books. 'It's ten to seven. She'd better hurry up if she wants supper.' As she speaks the front door opens. 'Is that you, Ba? Did you go to the pictures?' There is a bang as Ba shuts the door and goes straight into her bedroom. 'Oh, no doubt she'll tell us later. Have you got my *Pride and Prejudice* by the way? Helen wants to borrow it.'

'Ba's got it in her room. Ask her if she's finished with it.' Louie gets up and stretches, and goes out to beat cheerily on Ba's door. 'Are you walking down to supper with us?'

There is no reply, and Louie tentatively opens the door and goes in. Beattie hears her say 'Hey now, love, what's wrong? What are you crying for?' She can hardly see Ba, who is sitting in the darkness with her coat still on. 'There's a fire in the other room.'

Candlelight reveals Ba's face as pale and puffed with weeping.

'What *is* wrong?' asks Louie, mystified.

Ba looks at her. 'I'm pregnant; that's what's wrong.'

'You daft cow,' says Louie crossly. 'Didn't you use anything?'

'Eric said he'd take care of all that.'

'Well, that's great, that is; that explains everything. What are you going to do? Are you *sure*?'

'I went to the doctor today. I've missed two periods.'

'Will he marry you?' asks Beattie.

'He can't. I wrote and told him, and he said he's married already.'

'Look, you'd best come into the other room and keep warm. You can't sit in here in the dark.'

Barbr'ann sits docilely on the sofa, tears rolling down her cheeks.

'I don't understand. Didn't you know he was married?'

'Of course I didn't know. How can you tell when men don't wear rings like women? And if a man seems fancy-free and doesn't mention his wife how are you to know if he's married? I kept hoping I'd made a mistake and that it was the cold weather or something, because usually I'm as regular as clockwork.' Ba wipes her eyes and sniffs horribly. 'I had to buy a wedding ring to wear to the doctor's surgery, and when he examined me – I said I was on holiday here – he said: "I've got some good news for your husband." Good news, I ask you. And I said at once I didn't want it. Then he stopped smiling at once, and said "I'll pretend I didn't hear that, young lady." '

Beattie silently hands her a hankie. 'What are you going to do?'

'Do? I'm going to get rid of it; that's what I'm going to do.'

Both girls exclaim. Ba raises a blotched tear-stained face. 'What else can I do? My parents would die. They'd actually die if I had a bastard. You don't understand. I'm still the apple of their eye . . . Daddy's little girl. And I'd have to leave here before my exams—'

'Ba, you don't know that for sure—'

'I do so. Helen told me about a Welsh girl who was here a couple of years ago. She got pregnant in her final year, and the man married her at Easter, but they still made her leave before her exams. I want an abortion. Someone must know how to get one round here. If not, I'll have to go to London. Are you seeing Vince tomorrow, Louie? Can you ask him? Servicemen always seem to know about these things.'

'Can't Eric help?'

'I got my last letter back this morning, saying he'd moved camp and they had no forwarding address.' Ba's lips begin to shake again.

'Are you sure this is what you want, Barbr'ann?' asks Beattie.

'Yes, I'm sure, Beattie. Don't try to talk me out of it. What chance do you think I'll have of getting a decent man to marry me with an illegitimate child at the back of the picture?'

'Come and have some supper.'

'There'd be no point,' says Barbr'ann heavily. 'I'm that churned up today, I won't be able to keep anything down.'

She goes into the bathroom, and presently they hear her being sick. Beattie and Louie set off up the snowy drive.

'What are we going to do?' says Beattie, aghast. 'We can't let her destroy the baby. It's murder, Louie, you know it is, and it's illegal. If she gets caught. . . .'

'It strikes me she gets caught either way,' says Louie. 'She couldn't cope with the baby; she's like a child herself. You know that. Of course I know it's murder. That's what I said to me mum when I took her along to be done for the first time. Then she told me what the man did, so the second and third time we had to go I kept my mouth shut. It's a rotten business, whatever happens.'

Louie has arranged to meet Vince in Norwich on Saturday afternoon, and while she is gone Beattie and Barbr'ann go for a walk. Beattie is extremely confused. Until Louie explained the facts, she didn't even know what an abortionist did. Once Louie had told her, in fairly unvarnished language, she began to look as sick as Barbr'ann. Part of her longs and longs to persuade Barbr'ann not to do it, to take a righteous stand. But there is another part of her that says, finally, reluctantly: 'It's her life, it's her decision.'

They are doing their lesson preparation for Monday when Louie comes in. Barbr'ann looks up with a face of such open anxiety that Beattie's heart contracts with pity for her.

'Did you find out anything? Can Vince help?'

'He couldn't, but a friend of his knew someone and phoned him. He's real ace, is Vince. He says there's a chap in Norwich, near the station, who helps people. If you go in tomorrow afternoon, he'll give you an address. It'll cost you twenty pounds, though.'

Barbr'ann gives a sigh of relief.

'Ba, I know it's no help to say this,' says Beattie, unable to meet Louie's eyes, 'but must you do it, really?'

Barbr'ann looks at Beattie with more affection in her glance than she's ever shown before.

'I've got to, Beattie,' she says, trying to keep her voice firm. 'I've got no choice.'

Sunday morning means two lots of church, then lunch. At ten to two Barbr'ann comes out of her bedroom wearing her best coat and hat and carrying a handbag as if it has a bomb inside it.

'Hold on,' says Louie, 'I'm coming with you.'

'So am I,' says Beattie firmly.

'Don't be daft,' says Louie, not unkindly. 'There's no point. Stay here and have a nice fire ready for us when we come back. Have you got enough money for a taxi home, Barbr'ann?'

Beattie tries to study, but finds her mind is anywhere but on her books, and her eyes keep straying to Barbr'ann's little travelling clock on the mantelpiece. In the end she goes out to the back of the kitchen and starts to chop some wood for kindling. It is a grey, cloudy, overcast day with low clouds scudding across a grey sky. Bad flying weather, thinks Beattie automatically and at that moment hears the faint toot of a motor-horn in the lane. It must be Brooke, she thinks, her heart lightening, reflecting that for once he had hardly been in her mind for a couple of days.

Brooke is waiting by his car, smoking, the collar of his coat turned up against the cold February day.

'Hello, stranger,' he says when he sees her, and leans over to kiss her. 'Sorry I haven't been in touch for a few weeks. I went to Northern Ireland for a couple of jobs. I've got an hour or so free now. Come and have tea with me?'

Beattie puts on her coat with alacrity, reflecting that Barbr'ann and Louie can't be back much before six anyway.

'What was Northern Ireland like?'

158

'Covered in mist. We were trying to spot submarines, and half the time we couldn't even find the aerodrome.' Brooke has now nearly finished his second tour of duty, and if Beattie hadn't been so preoccupied that day with Barbr'ann's problems she would have noticed the beginnings of a subtle change in him. The shine, the dim exultation, that had come with his first successful tour has now gone. In its place is the beginning of a deep internal bone-weariness. 'You must be coming up to the end of your term again,' he says suddenly during tea. 'When are you going home?'

'Yes, it's an early Easter this year. I'm going next Tuesday. I'm going to help with the Barnardo's children again. But I've got a lot of work to do. My final exams are only three months away now. But what about you? Have you got anything special planned?'

'There's something big happening next week. We're on alert now, which is why I have to be back in half an hour.'

'Do you know what it is?'

'Sort of. I'll tell you afterwards if we manage to hit it,' he says with a grin. 'Any more tea in that pot?'

Brooke clearly has as much on his mind as Beattie, and for a long time they simply sit hand-in-hand in silence. Beattie is trying to steer her thoughts away from what is happening in Norwich and is just grateful for his company. When Brooke drops her at the gate he says: 'I won't be seeing you again before I go. If I can, I'll drop you a line to let you know how it went.'

With that he pulls her close and looks at her hard, as if memorizing her features, then he kisses her surprisingly gently. 'Goodbye, little Beatrice,' he says with his familiar mocking smile. 'Be good.'

Beattie lets herself into the cottage, puts the blackout into place, then lights the fire. But it is nearly nine o'clock before she hears the sound of a car in the lane outside. She runs out with a coat over her shoulders down the frozen path to the gate that leads out into the lane. A taxi is throbbing there, the snow swirling round and round in the light of its headlights. Then she hears Louie's voice.

'Beattie, is that you? Come and give us a hand, will you?'

Beattie opens the side-gate and sees a man and Louie supporting Barbr'ann, who has clearly just fainted. With Beattie's help they prop her up and half drag, half carry her into the cottage.

'Had one too many, has she?' jokes the taxi-driver.

'That's right,' says Louie and shuts the front door firmly.

They lay Ba down on the sofa, and Beattie brings her in some tea.

'Bring a bowl and we'll do what we can for her.'

Barbr'ann begins to moan quietly to herself. Louie gently pulls up her skirt. Beattie gives an exclamation of horror. 'Louie, she's bleeding everywhere!'

'Of course she's bleeding,' says Louie savagely. 'How else do you think you abort a baby? Get us some hot water and a flannel, will you?'

Gently Louie washes the blood off Barbr'ann's stomach, thighs and legs and replaces the sodden bloody wadding with a fresh cloth.

'Is it always like this?'

'Not if you have it done by a doctor, I suppose. But that costs money,' says Louie briefly.

159

'She's lost so much blood and she's till bleeding,' says Beattie uneasily. 'Will it stop?'

'It will later on. Least it usually does with my mother,' says Louie, gathering up the red cloths and carrying the enamel bowl full of rosy water back into the kitchen. 'Has anybody been asking for us?'

'No, I went over at supper-time and said Ba had tummy ache and had gone to bed. They didn't ask where you were. Did you stay with her . . . when. . . ?'

'Of course I did. She had to hold on to something. She'd never have stood the pain on her own,' said Louie matter-of-factly. 'My God, I'd like just one man to go through an abortion; it would be legal, free and universally available by the end of the week. They take an equal share in making babies, then bugger off at the first sign of trouble leaving the woman to cope. I tell you, Beattie, unless a woman can decide herself she wants children you might just as well forget about educating them at all. You might as well go back and live up trees. Oh, don't cry, Beattie, for God's sake. It isn't kind to bring a child into the world if it isn't wanted. This little bugger wasn't wanted by anybody. The lady who did it seemed all right – well, clean at least. So, providing Ba hasn't caught anything, she should be better by Monday. We've had nothing to eat, though, and I'm that starving.'

'I've saved you some bread and marge from supper. I'm sorry it isn't more.'

'There's no more of Ba's emergency rations, is there?'

'Only the Dundee cake in the tin.'

'Let's have a bit of that. If this isn't an emergency, I'd like to know what is. Thank God it's only two days till she goes home.'

By late Sunday night the bleeding has stopped. Beattie tells the mistress on duty that Barbr'ann is having a very painful period, and she is allowed to stay in bed for the rest of Monday. On Monday evening Beattie helps her pack. Louie and Ba are to travel to London together and then Louie will see her on to her train. She looks at Barbr'ann as she waits for the coach to arrive to take the girls for the London train. She is laughing and chattering and joking as if she hadn't a care in the world. Then she comes to say goodbye to Beattie and, though not a demonstrative girl, she suddenly puts her arms round Beattie and hugs her. Beattie is shocked to find that Barbr'ann is still trembling.

Beattie hitches a lift to Chillingon Halt and sits on a windy platform waiting for her train. She feels emotionally drained. Overhead, invisible in the clouds, there is the droning roar of the formation of planes that can only have come from Gatton. On the news that morning they said there had been more bombing the previous night in Essen and Cologne. Could that have been Brooke's special mission? A few days after her return to the village she receives two cards in the same post. The first is in Brooke's handwriting. 'All well here,' it reads. 'Have a happy Easter. Best wishes. B.' The other card is a home-made Easter greeting, much decorated with chocolate eggs and chickens. Inside it says: 'Happy Easter. All well here, thank goodness. Much love from Barbr'ann.'

160

CHAPTER THIRTEEN

'*I* STILL DON'T SEE why you won't come out,' says Devora. Her presence always irritates Virginia, but tonight it is almost unbearable. Rather like having an inquisitive child in the room with you, thinks Virginia crossly. Devora has her eyes and nose into everything.

'I say, where did you get this lipstick? Can I try it?'

'No,' says Virginia rudely. 'I might catch something. For Christ's sake, Devora, sit down and shut up, or if you're going' – her tone makes it quite clear which she'd prefer – 'if I find you've taken anything with you, I'll kill you. You've lost more of my Kirby grips in the last six months than I've lost in a lifetime.'

'You're in a bloody awful mood,' says Devora, not taking the hint and collapsing heavily on Virginia's bed.

'I'm not in a mood. You just get on my nerves with your endless fiddling around.'

'Oh, do come,' says Devora, reverting to her original plea. 'We're going to the Cotton Club. They're rather dreamy chaps; I picked them up in Kingsway. South Africans. Lots of dough.'

'Take Carole with you.'

'She's already booked. Oh, Virginia, you are becoming tedious. Don't tell me you're going do-gooding with boring old Cecily again. You've probably got nits by now. All East Enders have them. Mother says the evacuees had to be bathed in Lysol before decent people would take them in in Oxfordshire.'

'I thought your mother refused to take any.'

'She saw them on Didcot station, and that was enough. So where are you going tonight? Community singing in Hoxton?'

'We don't go community singing, as you very well know. And I don't go all the time; I just go on Saturdays and Sundays. And don't call Cecily either boring or old in my presence.'

But Devora isn't even listening.

'You wouldn't lend me your crêpe de Chine blouse, would you?'

'You're right, I wouldn't.'

'You are a cow. Did you enjoy Harriet's party? It was very unsporting of you not to come in fancy dress.'

'No, I did not enjoy Harriet's party.'

161

'How strange. I had a whale of a time. Where did those stockings come from?'

'Willy.'

'And that bottle of perfume?'

'Freddy.'

'Is he back in London? I wonder why he hasn't phoned me. Goodness, he was crazy for me last summer—'

'Devora, I've got a terrible headache. Can't you shut up?'

'I had a terrible headache yesterday,' says Devora confidentially. 'Honestly, the fuss they made about letting me off early from work.'

'It was lucky you managed to recover in time to go out with that Yank last night.'

'It was, wasn't it? But Chuck is such a sweetie. Since you're all dolled up to go somewhere you might as well tell me where.'

'Dinner at the Dorchester,' says Virginia briefly, and unlocking her wardrobe takes out her best dress, hangs it on the back of the door, relocks the wardrobe and puts the keys back in her bag.

'God, you're so bloody tight-fisted with your clothes,' complains Devora enviously as Virginia slips off her wrap to reveal camisole and knickers in champagne-coloured silk. 'Did Willy buy you those? Honestly, you have all the luck. All I ever get from Yanks is nylons and Lucky Strikes.'

'You choose the wrong ones,' says Virginia, stepping into the long soft pliant tube of gold satin and drawing it up to slip her slender arms through the narrow shoulder-straps. Mother really did have excellent taste.

'What's that?'

'Hartnell,' says Virginia, busily doing up a multitude of hooks and eyes under her arm. She examines herself critically in the mirror.

'I'd look terrific in that.'

'You couldn't begin to get one of your arms into it,' says Virginia rudely and starts to do her face.

'I saw Bobby Haskins yesterday. You know, the chap from the *Star*.'

'Of course I know him,' says Virginia witheringly. 'I introduced you to him.'

'Well, he said all the foreign correspondents will be leaving London soon. He said it would be Russia next for the Nazis. Said they'll all be off to Moscow. You won't be getting any more presents from Willy.'

'What nonsense,' says Virginia contemptuously, making a Joan Crawford mouth for her lipstick. 'Willy can't cope with the English winters. He wouldn't last ten minutes in Russia.'

'Goodness, that neck is low. Pity you haven't got any bosom.'

'I've had no complaints,' says Virginia drily and begins to unpin her hair, carefully counting the hairpins into a matchbox as she shakes out the heavy shoulder-length mass of honey-coloured waves.

'Who's taking you out tonight?'

'Adam Congleton.'

'What, is that still on?'

'I've only known him for a month.'

'That's a long time for you. He's gorgeous, isn't he? Tell me' – Devora

162

leans forward avidly – 'what's he like . . . you know . . .?'

'About six foot four, I should say,' says Virginia coldly.

'Oh, Virginia, you are funny. Who else are you dining with?'

'Brooke's in London for the day,' says Virginia, tired of evading her. 'He's been decorated, and we're going out to celebrate.'

'And you're not inviting me? Vir, you are a pig! No wonder you've been so shifty. You know how crazy I am about Brooke. I know, I'll put off those two chaps and you can lend me that black dress and I'll turn up as a surprise. He's not bringing anyone, is he?'

'Devora, I neither know nor care if he's bringing anyone –'

'Well, then.'

'– but I do know that Brooke finds his own girls and would not be amused at me fixing anything for him.'

'Don't be stupid. Just give me that dress and I'll run and change—'

'Devora, if you're not out of here in three seconds,' says Virginia serenely, 'then I'm going to hit you very hard indeed with this hairbrush.'

When Devora has flounced out, leaving the usual unappetizing echo of her presence, Virginia automatically completes her *toilette*, gets out her fox fur and douses herself liberally with 'My Sin'. What she needs is a drink, not so much a snifter as a tumbler of brandy. It is hard to see how else she's going to provide the sparkle necessary for tonight. She sits erect and stares at herself in the mirror, the ravishing immaculate blank-eyed image of herself. Then her shoulders slump as she sighs and rests her chin on her hands.

'You're just tired,' she tells her reflection in a forlorn attempt at comfort. 'Tired and a bit fed up.'

She has had thirteen continuous interrupted nights, partly owing to the bombing and partly owing to the complexities of her social life. But it went much deeper than that. The papers kept saying that when the spring came the bombing would stop. But it was now early May and the sirens still blared night after night. Nine whole months had gone by of living hand-to-mouth, of trying to keep some semblance of life going in the face of total dislocation. The exhilaration of the autumn days had long since drained away. Every morning when Virginia woke exhausted she swore that tonight she would stay in and have an early night. But by evening someone would have rung, or Stephen would have appeared, and she would be compelled by her own restlessness to go out. The streets of London were like an illustration of the palace of the Sleeping Beauty: everywhere people dozed in the buses or in the Tube, and it is nothing to walk along the streets and see firemen and air-raid wardens leaning up against the brickwork in doorways, exhausted after a night's work and asleep on their feet. Each day Virginia wakes feeling she has a heavy weight on her chest that has to be physically dislodged before she can sit up. And the coming of the milder weather has somehow simply served to emphasize her tiredness. It has also brought the unwelcome consequence that in walking across Stepney bombsites you can suddenly be assailed by the unmistakable smell of human corruption and decay far below. There's nothing to do except tell the warden that he can dig the body out, but it leaves a bad feeling. You are used, but never accustomed, to the thick pall of smoke hanging over London when you open the door each morning. The fact that everywhere you go seems to be carpeted with broken glass. It is an automaton's existence, and Virginia, like thousands of others, is beginning to wonder how long she can actually survive.

But there are other, more immediate causes for depression. On Monday it was announced that Marwicks are to leave London and set up their offices in Aberdeen. Staff who want to go are to be found accommodation, and Theo Beavers and his wife have already made plans to let their flat. They are to move at the end of the month, but Virginia has no intention of going with them. Leaving London is out of the question. But where would she find another job? And, more to the point, where could she find a job that had the necessary category of 'reserved occupation' that is her insurance against being called up? There is already a frightful rumour that by the end of 1941 all girls of her age will be liable for conscription. The awful spectre (for Virginia at least) of wearing a uniform and living in a Nissen hut abruptly raises its head again. So far the only alternative is to join Devora in the Ministry of Food. This is not a prospect to raise the spirits. Absently Virginia begins to buff her nails, and her lips tighten. Devora's casual reminder of Harriet Downing's party had jarred her.

Or, rather, not so much the party but whom she'd met there. Ferdinand's bloody cousin, Alexis Saltcellar, or whatever he called himself. What happened at Harriet's party was bad enough, but added to what had already happened just after Christmas was quite enough to make her feel that if she ever met Alexis she'd gladly strangle him.

She'd had no expectation of ever seeing him after that disastrous evening last August, then in early January he'd unexpectedly rung her at Marwicks.

'Hello,' said a voice coolly, 'this is Alexis.'

Recognizing the voice and instantly on the defensive, Virginia had countered: 'Alexis who?'

'Come off it, Virginia. How many Alexises do you know? This is Alexis Seligman.'

'Oh, Ferdinand's cousin,' Virginia had said sweetly. 'Well?'

'I was wondering if you were free for lunch. I've had a long letter from Ferdy and there's a bit in it for you.'

'Oh,' Virginia had said, her whole tone immediately altering. 'All right, where and when?'

Having named a pub and a time, Alexis had rung off.

Virginia had turned up late and found Alexis deep in conversation with two younger men hanging on to his words with an almost dog-like intensity. 'You'd better cut along now,' he had concluded briskly, noting Virginia's arrival and giving her an unsmiling but not exactly unfriendly nod. 'Tell them I'll be be back at two. Hello, Virginia. What are you drinking?'

'Gin, please.'

While Alexis had gone to the bar she had examined him covertly. That day against the cold he had been wearing an obviously American grey and white tweed overcoat. It was the kind of coat Virginia had always liked on James Stewart.

'Admiring my coat? Ferdinand got it for me last summer. He bartered something with somebody at the American embassy. Drink OK?'

'Splendid,' Virginia had said coldly. She was furious to discover she was having some difficulty meeting Alexis' eye. Why on earth should you be embarrassed by this creep? She had told herself sternly and put on her most frigid expression. 'Who were the young men?'

'Oh, my assistant directors. I got promoted.'

Alexis clearly had no problem at all about meeting Virginia's eye and was examining her in a detached and leisurely way.

'Have I got a smut on my nose?' she had demanded at last, unnerved.

Alexis had smiled, showing very white teeth. His rather stern-faced features were transformed.

'Do relax, Virginia. You must spend so much time making yourself look agreeable that you can hardly complain when people stare at you.'

This was in the nature of a distinctly two-edged compliment and left Virginia feeling distinctly out-manoeuvred.

'Ferdinand's letter,' she reminded him coldly.

'Ah, yes, Ferdinand's letter,' said Alexis teasingly, very much at his ease, his half-pint of bitter in his hand.

I shall finish this gin, Virginia had told herself quietly without altering her expression, and after that I'm going to leave, letter or no letter.

There had been a pause during which no letter was produced and Alexis had continued to stare at Virginia, who had become more and more furious.

'You don't like me very much, do you, Virginia?'

'No,' Virginia had said without a pause.

'Why?'

Virginia had stared at Alexis in disbelief. If she had said that to most of the men she knew, they'd have simply curled up and died in front of her. Alexis, on the contrary, seemed completely unperturbed, reducing her to the status of a naughty child in the face of a sensible adult. Virginia's fingers had tightened on the stem of her glass and she had debated whether it was worth wasting the rest of a perfectly good g. and t. by heaving the whole lot in his face.

'Why don't you like me?' Alexis had persisted.

Virginia swallowed hard and abandoned all pretence at civilized behaviour.

'Because you're so bloody conceited.'

'Isn't that strange? It's the quality that irritates me most about *you*. Still, you're very beautiful. You reminded me last summer of a cat we once had. A very beautiful white Persian. She was a lot like you. Ravishingly immobile features and a full complement of claws.'

Virginia had drained her glass quickly prior to leaving. Then, most surprisingly, Alexis had smiled at her again, but this time it was a wry self-deprecating smile.

'That should give you some idea of how much you annoy me by not liking my film.'

'Look,' Virginia had said in a tense furious undertone she hardly recognized as her own, 'I came here today because you'd heard from Ferdinand and I'd like to hear about that letter. If it'll make things happen any faster so I can leave, I *liked* your bloody film. It's just you I can't stand. Will that do? If it won't, then I'm leaving.'

165

By this time Alexis had been laughing so much he had to put down his beer.

'And as far as cats go,' Virginia had added suddenly, 'you're not averse to playing with people yourself, are you?'

'Not as a rule,' Alexis had admitted without rancour. 'It's just something about your granite-faced cast-iron conceit that provokes me to see if there's anything behind it. All right, all right. Here you are.'

From the depths of his overcoat pocket he produced a crumpled envelope with her name written on it in Ferdinand's flowing Gallic hand.

'How did you get to hear from him?'

'I send letters to the embassy and I assume they send them on.'

'Do you miss him?'

'Yes, very much. We're about as unlike as two people can be, but I just can't imagine the world without him. He's very fond of you, you know.'

'I hope so.'

'He loves you. Always defends you,' Alexis had added provocatively.

'So who is always attacking me?' enquired Virginia, immediately on the defensive again; then, seeing Alexis' grin, she had managed a small sour smile herself.

For the rest of the time they'd chatted in a general way about films they'd seen. As the clock behind the bar finally struck two, Alexis had pulled his coat and muffler round him and said noncommittally: 'Well, it's been very nice seeing you, Virginia—'

'I doubt if that's true, but it must make a change from people hanging on to your every word and telling you how wonderful you are.'

'It certainly was a change from that,' he had agreed gravely. 'Listen, do you want to go and see that film at the Pavilion? I was thinking I might go on Friday before I go to a party. I know I haven't been awfully friendly, so come to the cinema with me and then you can criticize my taste.'

'I thought you didn't like films like that,' Virginia couldn't resist saying.

'Come on, pax. This low-key hostility is quite exhausting to maintain as dialogue. Do you want to go or not?'

'Yes, why not?'

'OK, I'll pick you up at seven. Where exactly is this place where you live?'

With that he had gone, leaving Virginia to fret at her own lack of presence of mind. What on earth had made her say yes? She didn't even like Alexis.

Ferdinand's letter had had little news but a great deal of warmth and affection. Liking for *him* made her decide not to turn down his perfidious cousin's invitation.

Then, quite unexpectedly, on Friday morning her period had started, producing such violent cramps and dizziness that Theo himself had gone down to the street to get her a taxi to take her home.

Dosed with aspirin and with her own and Cecily's hot-water bottles on her stomach and her back, Virginia had finally conceded that she was not in a fit state to go anywhere. Shivering with cold and dizziness, she had forced herself down to the telephone-box in the hall, then remembered to her dismay that she didn't even know which company Alexis worked for. She was brooding over this when it occurred to her that he might be in the telephone directory. Fortunately he was, at a Chelsea number. A man had answered the phone.

'I need to contact Alexis,' Virginia had said in her most clipped tones. 'Do you happen to know where he is?'

'He's dubbing somewhere,' said the other person, much to Virginia's mystification.

'Are you likely to be speaking to him?'

'Yes, he's phoning here at five. Can I give him a message?'

'Yes, please. Could you tell him Virginia Musgrave phoned to say she was very sorry, but she's unwell and not able to meet him tonight?'

'He'll certainly be sorry about that,' said the other voice unexpectedly. 'I hope you feel better soon.'

'Oh,' said Virginia surprised. 'Thank you, goodbye.'

With that, she had refilled her hot-water bottles, crawled back to bed, taken some more aspirin and fallen into uneasy sleep from which she was awoken with a start at six o'clock by Devora.

'Got the curse, have we? Tough luck. I always take gin myself. Aren't you going out tonight, then?'

'Absolutely not,' says Virginia firmly.

'In that case shall I tell Jim Ashby you're too ill to come to the phone?'

'Oh God! He would be in London today of *all* days. Give me my dressing-gown, will you?'

Jimmy Ashby is a friend – more than a friend – from last July. He was a shy, rather charming young man with whom Virginia had spent several relaxed and pleasant days during his leave in London. He had been posted to the Orkneys in August, and since then he and Virginia had exchanged occasional letters.

Back again in the inhospitable telephone-box, Virginia had said feebly: 'Jim, hello, how are you?'

It was soon clear that Jim was not all right at all. Virginia listened with growing dismay. One of three brothers, the eldest, Guy, had died during the BEF retreat at Dunkirk. The youngest, Teddy, had yesterday been reported missing. He was in the merchant navy, in a convoy of tankers in the Atlantic.

'I'm just in London for a few days before I set off for – well somewhere in the Mediterranean,' Jim had said awkwardly. 'It's the most infernal cheek getting in touch like this, but I just wondered if I might possibly see you for a couple of hours. I feel so bloody. I had to ring my mother and father this morning to tell them about Teddy. It was terrible. I would have phoned you before but we were told we were going straight to Southampton so we've only got these few hours in London by mistake. I'm getting a train from Waterloo at ten-twenty. If there was any chance, just for a drink, it would be so lovely to see you.'

Virginia had sighed and ground her teeth, then remembered the fate of Guy and Teddy.

'All right, Jimmy, but do you mind awfully if we just make it a drink? I'm a bit under the weather today—'

167

'Oh, Virginia, you are an angel, you really are. Look, I'll be round at the Grange with a cab to pick you up at seven o'clock.'

Which is how Virginia had found herself, half-doped with aspirin, at Jules Bar in Jermyn Street at eight o'clock. But Jim had been so delighted to see her, so solicitous about her health, so grateful for her company that it seemed churlish even to have considered not coming. In the end they had early supper in Frith Street at the end of which Jim said: 'I say, do you mind awfully if we just drop in on a friend on our way back? It's his wife's birthday, and I said I'd just stop by and say hello. It's only in Green Street, which isn't too far away from where you live, is it? Then I'll pop you in a taxi home.'

A party was the very last thing that Virginia felt like but, as luck would have it, fate intervened. As Jim rang the doorbell of the flat the air-raid siren started to warble in the street outside. The front door opened to reveal their host rallying the guests to go down to the shelter. And almost the first person Virginia had seen was Alexis Seligman. There was no point in attempting to conceal herself; he caught sight of her as Jim put his arm protectively around her. With a shrug Alexis had turned away.

'Listen, darling,' Jim had said, blindly unconscious of the havoc he had wrought. 'I think I'll go back down to the street and take my chances grabbing a cab; I'm going to miss that train otherwise.'

'Then, I'll come down, too,' says Virginia firmly.

Outside the street had been full of hurrying figures. By some miracle an empty cab was waiting on the corner.

'You take the cab,' Jim had said with a nobility which made her remember him with affection for the rest of her life. 'Take care of yourself, dearest Virginia, and thanks a million for tonight. It meant a lot to me.'

She was destined never to hear anything from Jim again. His ship was torpedoed in the Bay of Biscay the day after Teddy was finally reported alive but in enemy hands.

Virginia had gone home, sunk in gloom, determined to ring Alexis the next day and at least apologize and explain. But after a sleepless night in the coal-cellar – the bombing had been particularly bad that night – she found the impulse had passed. Why on earth should she have to explain? It had been a perfectly genuine refusal. She hadn't stood Alexis up for Jim. But the last thing she wanted was to see him again. Which she had done, under conditions of maximum embarrassment, at Harriet's party.

She hadn't wanted to go. She had had a pulverizingly tiring day in Stepney with Cecily, and she particularly disliked home-made fancy-dress parties. In the end Adam persuaded her, but as a protest she wore her black crêpe frock and pearls. It had turned out to be a rather good do, but somehow Virginia never managed to get into the spirit of it in spite of the rivers of illicit whisky that seemed to be flowing in every room. Also she quarrelled with Adam in the car going there and again during the evening, and they were both sulking. Because it was a basement flat no one bothered to go out when the sirens went and, much to her annoyance, they had ended up staying the night there, sleeping on the sofa with an eiderdown over which she and Adam had fought all night. At six o'clock Virginia was just beginning to drop off when the door opened and people began to tiptoe in and out looking for coats and shoes and scarves. The final straw was when Virginia felt someone actually moving the sofa and sitting up indignantly to give the person a piece of her mind found herself unexpectedly face to face with Alexis Seligman. As they stared at each other in disbelief Adam chose that moment to turn over and heave the eiderdown off her, leaving her momentarily in her underwear under Alexis' surprised glance.

'What the hell are you doing here?' she'd said, furiously grabbing the eiderdown and heaving it back. 'And what the hell are you doing under this sofa?'

'I'm looking for my other glove . . . ah, here it is. So sorry to have troubled you,' he'd said with grave politeness, all things considered.

He had paused to run his eye over Adam's recumbent form. 'I suppose I don't have to ask you what you're doing?'

With that he had walked out of the room. Virginia had been so livid that she'd immediately got up, dressed and gone home without even bothering to wake Adam. It had taken chocolates, gardenias, and dinner at Claridges to get her back into anything approaching a good mood. Now Virginia grinds her teeth again at the memory. If she ever comes across Alexis again, she vows, she will get her own back. Then downstairs somebody shouts that Adam is waiting for her in the hall, and picking up her evening bag she takes one final look in the mirror and reflects that she will more than do Brooke credit. It is nearly six months since she has seen him, and she will never admit, even to him, how much she misses him. He writes sporadically and occasionally phones, and he had a bottle of champagne delivered to the hostel by one of his friends on her birthday. But his life is still a closed book to her. It is evident how well thought of he is by the RAF. After Christmas there had been a long piece about him in the *Daily Express* written by an American journalist who had spent three days at Gatton and actually flown on a mission with him. He had come back saying he would sooner face Hitler personally in a boxing-ring than go on one more mission. But Brooke never mentions his flying. He might just tell her if he had a new plane or the weather had been bad, but nothing else. But she knows from the very tone of his letters, however brief, that he has found his niche. Like her, he craves change, danger, conflict. But how long he will continue to be able to live life at this pitch remains to be seen. He had already been awarded his DSO last August and this time is to receive the DFC. Virginia has no idea what he had done to deserve either.

Adam has his own car and petrol allowance, and they make their way down the Bayswater Road through the early-evening traffic, past the newly created bath depot in Hyde Park where baths rescued from bombed houses are laid out in incongruous lines. It does not add greatly to the beauty of the park, which is already disfigured by sandbags, trenches, barrage balloons and rolls of barbed wire.

Adam is the latest of Virginia's long string of escorts. He is a friend of Simon's and like him is permanently immaculate in a uniform that is destined never to see active service. He is a tall strapping youth with the air of one born to command, though contrary to appearances is frankly terrified of

169

Virginia and her increasingly violent rages. He appears to worship the ground she walks on. It is a combination of qualities that Virginia particularly likes in a man.

Brooke is staying overnight in the Grosvenor House Hotel and he has arranged to meet them in the foyer of the Dorchester. As Adam parks his car in the forecourt Virginia sees her brother's black two-seater sliding into a parking-space further along and her heart lifts. She sees him open the car door and get out, surveying the scene with a slow impertinent stare as if he owns it. Stephen is right, thinks Virginia, he *does* look like a god, wearing his uniform as elegantly as any Savile Row suit. When you drew nearer you were aware of lines of strain around his eyes and the fact that he had lost weight: all of which made one more aware of the skull beneath the skin. But his thick blond hair was as immaculate as ever, and she can see how many glances he attracts.

Virginia is about to call out a greeting when he goes round to open the door of his car and she nearly laughs out loud. Trust Brooke! In London for only a few hours and he's already found himself a girl! Virginia can't see her very clearly, but from the back she looks an absolute stunner, a tall girl with a head of upswept dark glossy curls and a long evening dress in tight black velvet.

'Brooke,' calls Virginia and starts forward in the light to say hello. Then she stops dead as the couple turn round. The girl on Brooke's arm is Beattie Blythe, the gardener's daughter.

'I say, that's well timed,' says Brooke, unruffled, and coming forward kisses Virginia on the cheek. 'You must be Adam Congleton. I'm Virginia's brother and since she seems to be too overcome with happiness to introduce her this is Beatrice Blythe.'

Inside the foyer Brooke turns to his sister. 'Can you take Beattie down to the powder room to leave her coat? We'll be in the cocktail lounge.'

Virginia often dines at the Dorchester and leads the way in silence down to the powder room where she leaves her fur and Beattie hands the woman her evening jacket. Then both girls go to the rosy mirrors, overtly to examine their make-up but covertly to examine each other. Clearly Beattie has been to the Palace with Brooke today and, for all Virginia knows, on the previous occasion as well. It is all the worse because Virginia has had no idea, no clue, not even the faintest notion that Brooke has been seeing Beattie. For how long have they been going out? Did Mrs Musgrave know? Were they lovers? The simple way to find out the answers to at least some of these questions is to ask Beattie herself, but even to speak to her is beyond Virginia who is rigid with anger. To address even a single syllable to her would be to acknowledge her presence: if nothing else, Virginia can freeze her out of conversation this evening. She is filled with such savage hatred of Beattie that she fancies she can taste bile in her mouth. And the worst of all, the very worst of it, is – Beattie looks sensational. Like a duchess, a million dollars, a cover girl. If only she'd looked like a peasant, Virginia could have borne it all more easily. But that frock! That bag! Those shoes! The frock is clearly a Paris model, and even if not this season's look it is unmistakably *soignée*, sexy and entirely acceptable. How has Beattie had the gall to enter places that sold things like that, let alone got the money to buy them? Virginia pushes out of her mind the picture of Brooke sauntering behind Beattie into a smart dress shop in Bond Street and paying for the things in a lordly way. How on earth could that gauche blushing girl of eighteen months ago have turned into this elegant and sophisticated person? Beattie's hair and make-up are immaculate, and her nails are perfect. In the worst mood of her life, Virginia puts her compact and lipstick back into her bag and silently waits for Beattie to finish washing her hands.

Beattie guesses with complete accuracy what is going through Virginia's head. She had seen that initial unguarded expression on her face when she had first recognized Brooke's partner. Beattie feels no particular sense of triumph and had no inhibitions about admiring Virginia's own appearance. She thinks she looks the very last word in beauty and elegance. She also knows there is just one question in Virginia's mind now: where had she got that dress? Well, she'd just have to go on guessing, she thinks, as the two girls silently reascend the stairs.

For three members of the party at least, the dinner-dance is perfect. Even a reduced menu at the Dorchester is a vast improvement on everyday hostel fare, and Maurice Winnick and his orchestra are in particularly lively form. Then a few minutes after they've taken their seats for dinner a marvellous thing happens. There is a roll on the drums and a spotlight shines unexpectedly on their table and Maurice Winnick himself comes to the microphone to welcome Brooke Musgrave, one of the country's most distinguished bomber pilots, to the night's entertainment at the Dorchester. Brooke is completely up to the occasion and simply stands up and smiles when people start to clap. Virginia catches sight of Beattie's face, overflowing with love and admiration. My God, she's crazy about him, she thinks bitterly. Well, much good may it do her. During the meal Adam tries several times to draw Brooke out about the incident which has won him his latest distinction, but each time he is put off with an even more frivolous and evasive answer and in the end Adam, baffled, gives up. It isn't until Brooke disappears briefly to talk to friends on another table that Adam hits on the bright idea of asking Beattie. Does she know what events have won Brooke his DFC?

'Oh, yes,' says Beattie eagerly, and Virginia has a sudden image of her sewing the new ribbon on Brooke's uniform, 'He got the earlier decoration for exceptional keenness and devotion to duty in building up crews,' she goes on, avoiding Virginia's eyes. 'But he got this one because of an incident in February when they were trying to bomb the railway lines in Cologne. Brooke's plane got two direct hits; one blew out the perspex in the cockpit, the other one hit the petrol-tanks. Brooke stopped the plane going into a dive and managed to get her back on course. The other people in the plane put the fire out, but the wireless operator died of burns later on. A huge part of the plane was burnt away, but Brooke managed to get it all the way back to Gatton. They had everything out waiting for him, but he got the plane down successfully. I saw the plane afterwards, and you simply wouldn't believe the damage—'

'Beattie, are you spreading rumours about me again?' says Brooke, coming up behind her.

'I certainly am,' she says gaily, looking up at him with an expression that clearly shows her feelings.

'In that case I shall punish you by making you dance with me,' he says and leads her out on to the dance-floor.

Virginia watches them sourly. All that Beattie has said shows clearly how close she is to Brooke. But why her? Why, with a million pretty girls to choose from, has he chosen Beattie Blythe? And why, oh, why had he chosen to confide in her and not in his own sister? Adam follows her gaze and misinterprets it.

'Stunning-looking girl, that,' he says. 'Reminds me a bit of Hedy Lamarr. Nice, too, isn't she?'

Virginia does not reply. She is watching the relaxed and easy way that Brooke and Beattie dance together, how their bodies fit without embarrassment. Belatedly she realizes they are sleeping together.

'I think I'd like to go home now,' she says suddenly to Adam.

'Nonsense,' says Adam briskly. 'On your feet, young lady, and we'll have a canter round the floor.'

The evening wears on. Ironically, for once there is no air-raid warning to break up the revelry. One of Brooke's friends asks Beattie to dance, and Brooke languidly offers his arm to Virginia. They begin to move round the floor to the strains of 'Yours'. After a second or two Brooke says: 'I heard from Ma yesterday. She still wants you to go home, you know.'

'I know she does,' says Virginia crossly, 'but I'm not going home, so there's nothing to discuss.'

There is a silence for a moment or two, then Virginia bursts out: 'Brooke—'

'Don't even say it, my love,' says Brooke blithely, his step never faltering for an instant. 'Your face made your feelings quite clear when you saw her.'

'Does Mother know?'

'No. And she won't unless you do something silly like telling her, Virginia.'

'I think you're mad,' says Virginia violently.

'Darling Virginia, I'm a great believer in letting people do what they want to do.'

He turns his head and gives her a very direct stare. To her acute embarrassment Virginia suddenly finds she is blushing.

'If I choose to have an affair with one of our servants, that's my business. If you choose to sleep your way round London – you really should remember how service people gossip, Virginia – then that's your affair. Though why you're so jealous of Beattie I can't understand.'

'I am *not jealous*.'

'Well, just leave her be. She's a nice little thing, and this is our big night out. Now, come on, how's your job going?'

Virginia swallows. She has by no means exhausted her venom, but there is something in Brooke's voice, so mild and pleasant, that warns her that she is in danger of going too far. Brooke does not suggest a second dance.

Beattie is talking to Adam, who is clearly enormously taken with her.

'We're going home now,' says Virginia.

'Here, I say, I'm enjoying myself,' protests Adam feebly.

'Brooke, I've got a terrible headache, so if you'll excuse us we'll go. I'm so pleased about your decoration. Thank you for a lovely evening.'

She kisses him, makes no pretence of saying goodbye to Beattie and storms out of the room. Adam drives her home and at the end of the journey they quarrel so violently that she knows that this particular goodnight will be goodbye. What the hell. She could pick up something better than Adam by simply standing in the Bayswater Road and shouting. It is many hours before she finally sleeps, consoling herself with the thought of a long lie-in the following morning.

What Virginia has forgotten is that Cecily is expecting her to don her WVS armband and help out in Stepney. When she bangs on the door next morning at 6.30 Virginia wonders dully if you can eventually die from lack of sleep. Then the bitter memories of last night surge back and her limbs jerk into wakefulness. Abruptly she heaves herself out of bed and pulls on her slacks, two jerseys and a coat and ties her hair up in a scarf. It is better to have something that keeps her mind occupied if nothing else.

On the way over Cecily says there has been heavy bombing at Hoxton last night and it is there they are to drive their canteen-van to serve breakfast to the firemen.

'Dirty night last night,' says one man confidentially to Virginia. At eleven o'clock volunteers are needed to peel potatoes at a nearby hospital. Two hours and thirty pounds of potatoes later Cecily and Virginia have lunch in the canteen, then go on to the emergency ward where Cecily has news for a man who hasn't been able to trace his wife. Virginia manages to joke and chat with other patients who in spite of appalling burns, fractures and shock still remain resolutely cheerful, ready to flirt. She remembers vividly her first visit to this ward; she had been tense with embarrassment at what to do and how to behave when a wild-faced old man had suddenly touched her hand and whispered, 'Is there a jerry about, miss?' to which she had gently replied: 'Don't worry, there are no Germans here.' Cecily had overheard this exchange and drily interrupted: 'He wants a potty actually, Virginia.' Virginia reminds Cecily of this as they leave the ward and they both burst out laughing at the memory.

'What's to do now? Are you finished?'

'I've got to drive a homeless woman to a new flat,' says Cecily, looking at her watch. 'They've found something for her in Ladbroke Grove. Are you going to do some station duty? Kitty's at Liverpool Street, and I said we'd try to get along some time this afternoon. It's only looking after children while their mothers get themselves organized.'

'Okey dokey,' says Virginia resigned. Actually she quite likes station duty. You just stand there in your WVS armband and people come flocking up to you. At 4.30 Virginia sees Cecily waving to her from the end of the platform. Virginia is joggling a rather damp baby in one arm and rocking

173

a pushchair with her other hand whilst the children's mother enquires about trains to Grantham.

'How's it going?' asks Cecily.

'Was your lady all right?'

'No problem at all. Look, I've just picked up blankets for the rest centres. Are you game to take them round with me?'

'I've got to wait for this woman. She won't be a few minutes.'

'Did you have a good time last night with old Brooke?'

'Oh, super,' says Virginia, trying to inject some enthusiasm into her voice. 'What did you do?'

'My dear, I actually had an early night. Wasn't it blissful that I chose one without a siren? I'd spent the previous night in the Tilbury shelter and I don't believe I got a wink of sleep all night. You'll never believe this, but I was sharing the stall with a horse and you know how cackhanded they are about their feet if you see what I mean. Ah, here she is now.'

The mother returns gratefully with her tickets, and Virginia and Cecily steer her into the train and wave her off. Cecily's van is in the station yard.

'Are you going out tonight?'

'I might. Sir Fred's in London and he's asked me to give him a ring. I just hope he's remembered to bring me my honey.'

'Does he like Shaftesbury?'

'I think so. He says he gets a bit bored, though.'

'Are you sure you want to do the blanket run?'

'I said I'd call him about seven. We'll be done before that, won't we?'

'Jolly well hope so. There's a load of children's clothes in the school hall, and I said I'd help sort them out providing it's a quiet night. You look tired out, Vir.'

'I feel a bit stale. I tell you what, if you've got a couple of hours free tomorrow, shall we go up the Heath and look at the blossom? You'd never know it was spring, living in central London.'

By the time they have reloaded the van and started touring the rest centres, people are beginning the evening drift towards the shelters. Visiting the rest centres is not cheerful work. The children hanging round the doors are pale-faced and exhausted. Inside their parents are dully gathering up their belongings for yet another night underground. It has been a very long winter.

It takes them an hour and a half to complete their tour and they are almost at the end when Cecily turns to Virginia and says, 'Let's go back and—' but her words are drowned by the warning siren at the end of the road.

'Oh, drat,' says Virginia crossly. 'That's the bally limit. I'll be here for hours now.'

'Perhaps it's just a false alarm,' says Cecily. Then faintly but unmistakably they hear the throbbing of planes from beyond the estuary. 'There's an overground shelter at the end of the next street. I think we'd better leave the van here and go,' says Cecily anxiously. 'I jolly well hope it'll be all right. The van, that is.'

Suddenly the street is full of the sound of flying footsteps, and women clatter by on high heels, their skirts flattened against their thin white legs. An air-raid warden is yelling at them to get a move on, and reluctantly Virginia and Cecily run down the street to the shelter. Inside is jammed, for it is one of the better shelters in the area, put up just before the bombing started and stoutly reinforced. There is electric light, good ventilation and proper toilets in cubicles. It is so full it is hard to find a place even to stand. In the end the girls struggle over to the far wall and sit against it.

'Wish I had a ciggie,' says Virginia longingly.

All around people are settling down for a quiet night's entertainment. Books and knitting are produced, sandwiches are unwrapped, and everybody chats at the top of their lungs. It could have been Brighton beach. Then the bombing starts. Virginia has spent nights in Stepney before but always in an underground shelter. Never has she felt so completely exposed. The noise in an above-ground shelter is almost indescribable. Far above the throb of the planes goes on and on. All around shells whistle down accompanied by the clatter of incendiaries hitting roofs and pavements. Then there is the whistling roar – like a tearing sheet – of the high-explosive bombs, and the thuds and crashes as they find their targets and walls collapse. Far away there is the staccato clatter of anti-aircraft guns and as the evening wears on the frenzied clamour of fire engines racing by. Somewhere a dog is howling, and almost every moment there is a thud which shakes the whole foundations of the shelter.

Virginia puts her hands over her ears but not before she has heard Cecily say: 'I think we're in for a bad night tonight.'

As usual when terror takes over, Virginia loses all sense of time. Towards midnight there is a lull, people begin to relax tense limbs and talk at the top of their voice. There is a general feeling of pent-up relief as if everybody has let go at once.

'I know what'll happen now,' says Cecily, resigned, and gets up. The next thing is two teenagers begin to scrap furiously about nothing and in the corner a man and a woman almost come to blows. Cecily wades straight into the fray, separates them good-humouredly, deals with a little boy who has a nosebleed and generally exudes reassurance. Virginia has never admired her more than at this particular moment. Eventually Cecily suggests they can do with some singing, and to Virginia's astonishment the whole shelter joins in. It is an odd situation; she can see people resent Cecily making them sing and at the same time they rely on her with her posh accent and air of authority to take command and make them do it. They start off with a few hymns to keep themselves in credit with the Almighty, then move on more confidently to 'The Man Who Invented Beer' and are just beginning 'Poor Little Angeline' when the bombing begins again and Cecily urges everyone to sing louder and drown it. Anxious glances are exchanged, but the voices don't falter, and the last thing that Virginia sees before the bomb falls is Cecily smiling at her and urging her to sing up. Then the wall next to her suddenly rears up into a giant wave and Virginia feels herself being physically swept up and sideways like a swimmer in a stormy sea. She clings to the ground below as if it were a cliff-face and she must keep her foothold there at all costs. Choking dust fills her mouth, and she is aware of crashing masonry as something hits her on the head and she sinks unconscious into that stormy sea.

When she comes round she finds she is spreadeagled on her face, pinned like a starfish under an immense weight of material. It is pitch dark. Then she registers the most terrifying fact of all: that she is now outside and can actually hear the drone of the planes in the cold clouds far above her.

Thank God, she thinks dully. I must be alive. Her next thought is Cecily.

She tries to say her name but finds her throat is full of gravel and dust. Coughing and spitting feebly, she tries again.

'Cecily, where are you? Can you hear me?'

There is a terrible painful pause, then a voice says raggedly almost in Virginia's ear: 'I'm here.'

Dimly Virginia begins to distinguish the different weights on her body. Some sort of girder is lying across her legs; her left arm is numb under what feels like a weight of masonry. There is rubble pressing into every part of her body. Something begins to trickle steadily down her face, and there is no possibility of freeing an arm to wipe it away. It is still pitch dark and bitterly cold, and nearby somebody is moaning. Virginia can see only a couple of inches in front of her.

'Cecily,' she says again, 'are you hurt?'

There is another long pause, and Cecily answers even more faintly than the last time: 'A bit. Are you?'

'I can't tell; I'm covered in things. My head hurts.'

'Can you wiggle your fingers, your left ones?'

It takes Virginia some time to register that her fingers in all probability must still be on the end of her arm and then to work some feeling back into them. As her stiff fingers begin to move she feels Cecily's own hand reach out and grasp her own.

'There. We'll just have to hang on until they dig us out. They won't be long. Try to close your eyes, Vir. God, take care of us,' says Cecily so faintly that Virginia can hardly hear her.

A lot of time passes. Heavy thuds continue remorselessly all around them, then a particularly loud bang wakes Virginia from her semi-doze. She is instantly aware of the tons of rubble and wood piled above her. She had imagined herself like Alice falling down the rabbit-hole. Now it seems as if she has truly hit the bottom. Only the rabbit-hole has fallen in on top of her. She begins to cry weakly and feels Cecily wake up.

'Don't cry,' Cecily says tiredly, almost in Virginia's ear. 'It'll be light soon, and they'll find us. Just as soon as the all-clear goes. Ow!'

'What's wrong?'

'I think my leg's broken.'

More time passes. When Virginia is next fully conscious the bangs and the thuds have stopped and there is a difference in the quality of light. Surely it must be morning soon. Oh, start digging quickly, she prays. Panic begins to stir inside her, she wants to scream and struggle but she cannot move, held down as remorselessly as if by a giant's hand. Then Cecily speaks again, almost in her ear. She sounds stronger now.

'Can you hear me, Vir?'

'Cecily, I'm so frightened,' she whispers.

'There's no need to be,' says Cecily, though her words are beginning to slur. 'They'll dig us out. I'll be in hospital for a bit with this leg but we'll be all right. Do something for me, Vir?'

'Anything,' says Virginia tiredly, imagining Cecily wants her to shift her hand or something.

'Can you tell my parents what happened? And be sure to tell them that I loved them and thought about them all the time.'

Terror clutches Virginia's heart.

'Cecily, you're going to be fine. If it's just your leg, why, they'll put that in plaster and you'll be all right in no time.'

'Do it, though?'

'Yes, of course I'll do it.'

Virginia feels Cecily sigh and relax.

This time she must really have fallen asleep, because when she wakes she thinks at first that she is back at the Grangemouth. Then the memory of last night comes rushing back. Then, suddenly, very far away high above them she hears a tinny clinking clicking sort of noise. Relief floods through her, and tears run out of the sides of her eyes into the dust below her face.

'Cecily,' she says urgently. 'Wake up. I can hear them digging for us. Listen.'

She feels Cecily clutch her fingers faintly.

'I said they would,' but her voice is now so slurred that Virginia can hardly hear her. 'Remember what I said to you at Christmas, Vir, and remember . . . how dear you are to me.'

But Virginia hardly hears her and only much later remembers the words. It takes another two hours to lift the girders and the debris. There is a terrible temptation to start to wriggle and flail about. But if she does Cecily might get hurt, so she lies there and prays as the sounds get nearer.

'Soon be here, Cecily,' she keeps whispering. 'Don't worry, we'll have you in hospital in no time at all.'

The light grows steadily brighter, and a huge sob breaks from Virginia's chest. Finally she hears a voice above her.

'Is there anybody down there?'

Virginia tries to gather her strength to shout 'Yes'. Instead all that comes out is a long-drawn-out wail. But it is enough. They have heard her. There is a flurry of activity, and suddenly she can see daylight. Then a pair of wellington boots scramble down to a few inches in front of her face. Virginia can hardly see them for the tears that are flowing non-stop.

'Just a little longer, ladies,' says the voice again, then shouts up: 'There's two of them down here, and one of them looks pretty bad.'

The little longer takes another two hours. Then Virginia feels Cecily being gently lifted off her back and to her own humiliation she finds that she simply cannot move. It is as if all the pressure is still there, draining her, holding her down. Somebody asks her if her legs are OK and she says yes, and then a strong pair of arms picks her up very gently and she is lifted up to the blinding daylight and handed to another pair of arms who lift her yet again and pass her on to another man until finally they are on solid ground. Virginia stares round unable to grasp what is happening, while the man in the tin hat and boiler-suit holds her upright against him. A whole crowd of watchful silent people are staring at her in horror. Ambulance girls, salvage workers, wardens, what are they all doing here? She turns her head sideways with difficulty. And gasps in disbelief.

The whole shelter is gone, completely gone. So are all the surrounding streets. All that remains is a crater about twenty feet deep where men are digging feverishly. Beyond that is an open stretch of road, and on it Virginia can see mounds covered by canvas shrouds. There must be a hundred at least. Whatever is happening, thinks Virginia crossly, and where is Cecily? Then she sees Cecily is being lifted on to a stretcher and is filled with the most profound relief. But as they turn her over and lay her gently on her back Virginia cries out with horror and disbelief. Cecily's face is unmarked, but her chest is stiff with congealed blood. Then a very strange thing happens. The stretcher-bearer picks up one of the canvas shrouds and begins to slide it over Cecily's feet.

'What are you doing?' cries Virginia in terror. 'She must go to hospital, she's badly hurt, she's got a broken leg, can't you see?'

The stretcher man looks at her with pity in his face and goes on drawing the canvas shroud up Cecily's broken body.

'She's dead, miss,' says one of the ambulance men gently.

'She can't be,' screams Virginia, and with a strength she has never known she possesses she pulls herself free and hobbles across to Cecily. She falls on her knees beside the stretcher and tries to push down the stiff shroud, hugging Cecily to her.

'Cecily, darling Cecily, don't leave me, don't die.'

The crowd stands silent at the spectacle of Virginia, sobbing, imploring, calling hoarsely to her friend while she rocks her stiffening body in her arms. Then Kitty appears and kneels down beside her, trying to reason with her. But it is no use. In the end two of the ambulance men have to drag Virginia to her feet and forcibly lead her away, still weeping and calling as Kitty gently eases the shroud over Cecily's lifeless body.

Part Three

July 1941–May 1942

CHAPTER
FOURTEEN

'WELL, I THINK we all did pretty well considering the exciting time *some* of us had during the past two years. Of course we knew Helen would come top. But she never did anything else but work, did she?'

'What kind of report do you think she'll get?'

'So-so. She never really took part in things, did she? And Miss Frobisher's keen on that. She thinks community spirit is important. I don't think she played games at all, did she?'

'She sang in the choir, didn't she, Beattie?'

'What?' says Beattie automatically.

'Helen, Cloth-Ears. Did she sing in the choir?'

'I don't remember.'

'You've done all right for yourself – third in the whole year. Your parents will be chuffed to death, I shouldn't wonder.'

'I suppose so.'

'Have you heard from your school?'

'Not yet.'

'It'll be strange to be back in the old Pool again but Mam could do with the extra money, that's for sure. Has your aunty decided if she's going to come and live with you?'

'What?' says Beattie automatically again. 'Sorry, I was miles away. What did you say?'

Barbr'ann and Louie turn round to stare at her. They are lying in the long grass overlooking the croquet lawn, which today is being used for the Grey-shott boys to play cricket against a neighbouring prep school.

'Talking to you is like talking to a brick wall,' complains Louie. 'What's on your mind?'

'I'm still trying to decide if I want the job at my old school, or whether I'd prefer to try to get a job in Ipswich, that's all.'

'You've really decided you don't want to stay here at Greyshott?'

'Yes. I think my parents would like to have me a bit nearer home.'

'You're leaving it a bit late, aren't you?'

'It'll sort itself out.'

'I never thought I'd be sorry to leave this place, but I am now. We've got Sefton Park, but it's not the same. Still, I've got three weeks at that work-camp in north Wales.'

181

'What you doing there?'

'Picking something,' says Louie vaguely. 'What do they grow in north Wales?'

'Leeks?'

'Not in August surely?' says Louie quite seriously.

Beattie bursts out laughing.

'You can laugh, but I shall be feeding the nation. And feeding myself and all. Do you know, I worked it out yesterday that we haven't had a fresh egg here since the end of last term! It's all that disgusting dried stuff now. I don't understand. We're woken up every morning by the sound of cockerels. What on earth do they do with the eggs? Vince says the pilots have two for breakfast if they know they're flying that day. . . .' Her voice trails away. Typically Louie, having put her foot in it, decides to press on.

'Are you going to see Brooke before you go?'

'I haven't decided.'

'Well, you've only got three days left. Did I tell you Vince wants to come and see me in Liverpool? I don't know if I dare let him. It might put him off for life. Either that or he'll fall for our Debbie. Are you off again? You can't sit still for a minute.'

'I have to get my packing sorted out,' says Beattie. She walks back through the Great House for a moment and stands in the entrance-hall, enjoying the coolness and silence. She recalls the first moment she'd stood there, excited, lonely, bewildered. Through the door leading into the library Miss Frobisher can be seen arranging roses. She looks up and smiles at Beattie.

'Are you all packed up to go? I can't believe our first set of teachers here have already qualified. We'll be very sorry to see you go, Beattie. Your work has always been very satisfactory, even if I've felt that sometimes we didn't have your full attention. Still, you're only young once, and war is a difficult time for young people. I've been asked for a reference from the High School and I hope you get the job. It'll be a very good first post for you.'

Beattie slips outside again and slowly walks back to the cottage. Most of their year are in the drive going down to the village to make their goodbyes to the shopkeepers. Beattie wanders aimlessly into the kitchen and stops short. Louie is ahead of her, washing her smalls.

'I thought you were off to the village,' says Beattie.

'I've changed my mind. I want to talk to you.'

'What about?' yawns Beattie with apparent unconcern.

'Whatever it is that's wrong with you. You aren't speaking, you've lost weight, you act like there's a sheet of glass between you and everybody else. What is wrong, for goodness' sake? Is it still Brooke? If he's breaking your heart, why don't you just swallow your pride and ring him up? It's not worth making yourself so unhappy. I don't know what to do with you, Beattie. You come home hysterical from that weekend in London; you won't say anything about it, you won't tell me what's wrong. What on earth did Brooke do that can make you not want to see him again at all?'

Beattie is silent for a moment and then, to her consternation, finds tears pouring down her cheeks.

'Come on, sit down and tell me about it. What went wrong? You went off in such high spirits.'

'I don't know what went wrong, but as soon as Brooke turned up I knew things weren't going to work out all right,' says Beattie hopelessly. 'He's so tired, Louie, so tense. He doesn't know what he's saying half the time. We went up to London, and Brooke was drinking all the way. We got to the Palace and that was all right. Then in the afternoon he sent me off to have my hair and face done. We met a friend of his for a drink, and I could see Brooke was drinking non-stop the whole time. Then we went on to that dinner at the Dorchester. And that was . . . that was all right. But afterwards when we got back to our hotel Brooke suddenly went mad. He was just drunk out of his mind,' concludes Beattie miserably.

There is a long silence. Louie's brow is furrowed.

'Well, what did he say?'

'Oh, he accused me of wrecking the whole weekend, of being jealous of him, flirting with everybody just to make him look ridiculous. I mean, there wasn't a single word of truth in what he was saying. I love Brooke.' She notices the tense of the word she has used and colours. 'I care about Brooke so much, and I was so proud of all his achievements. But there was just no reasoning with him. We were staying in this wonderful bedroom, and it was a nightmare. Then the sirens went, and Brooke refused to go down to the air-raid shelter and he wouldn't let me go down, either, and in the end the manager of the hotel had to come up and Brooke hit him. Then we were left alone. I tried to calm him down, but he just wouldn't listen. We made love, but he . . . he . . . wasn't able to get there. And in the morning we tried again and it was still no good. Then he drove home and on the journey it just got worse and worse and worse. He was raving by the time we got to Chillington. I kept looking at him and I just didn't recognize his face. I don't know what's wrong with him. He threw my case out on to the road and told me I'd wrecked the whole weekend. And I told him then and there that I never wanted to see him again as long as I lived.'

Louie is speechless but, as ever, tries to be practical.

'Why on earth do you ever want to see him again? He's mad. You must realize that he's barmy.'

'He's not, Louie! I know he isn't. It's just he's been under pressure and tension for so long, he's beginning to crack—'

'Well, whether that's true or not, things aren't likely to change, are they? What's the sense of you going back and knowing you're letting yourself in for more of that?'

But Beattie won't meet her eyes.

'Beattie, are you sure you're telling me everything?'

Absurdly Beattie finds herself blushing and stares at the empty range. She is about to say she is just feeling tired. Instead she finds herself saying: 'I'm going to have a baby.'

'I thought perhaps you were,' says Louie with the calm of absolute despair. 'You and Ba, you're a right bloody pair. Didn't you have your thing in?'

'Yes. I don't understand it, because we didn't – Brooke never – but I took it out again immediately afterwards and perhaps it was too soon. I've been praying for so long that it wasn't true. As long as I kept it to myself I could pretend it wasn't happening.'

'When was that weekend in London?'

'The first week in May.'

Louie does some rapid calculations.

'That means you're ten weeks gone. You must have missed twice. You'll have to do something about it quickly if you're going to. Have you told Brooke?'

'No. I – I wrote to him yesterday and asked him if he could meet me tomorrow before I go home.'

'If he asked you, would you marry him?'

There is a long pause, and Louie sees clearly from the pain and bewilderment in Beattie's eyes just how much she loves him.

'Yes, if he wanted to.'

'It'd be one way out,' says Louie, hoping her tone doesn't convey the scepticism she feels about this ever happening. 'Well, we'll just have to see what happens. Come on, let's go down to the village and say goodbye.'

'Don't mention this to Barbr'ann, will you? I don't want to upset her.'

Upsetting Barbr'ann, thinks Louie privately as they set off down the road, is the least of Beattie's worries.

Beattie's note is noncommittal, simply telling Brooke that she is going home for good on Saturday so is he free on Friday afternoon for a couple of hours? She'd wait for him in the village and if he didn't come she'd assume it hadn't been convenient.

In actual fact, if Brooke *doesn't* come, Beattie doesn't know what she'll do. It is with fantastic relief that she hears the engine of Brooke's car shortly after half-past two. She is sitting on the seat by the war memorial trying to build up her courage by reminding herself that she is now a fully qualified teacher. It has absolutely no relevance to the moment except that Brooke will be getting a wife who can earn her own living – if he wants a wife, that is. She stands up, her heart slugging away like a dynamo in her chest. Beattie has taken a good deal of care about her appearance today and is conscious that she looks her best, if a little pale. Brooke draws the car alongside her and they look at each other for the first time in two months. In that split second Beattie's private fantasies of marriage, happiness and weddings crumble quietly in front of her and she knows before a word is said what Brooke's response will be to her dilemma. He smiles at her a little warily, then opens the car door. She is suddenly shockingly aware of how much tireder and older he looks. He has lost weight and somehow gives the impression that his face has become lined with strain, like an old person's. It hasn't of course. It is just tension, as if he is holding his features together by conscious effort.

As usual, no allusion is made to the last encounter.

'I've only got a few hours,' says Brooke. 'We're standing by for something tonight if the wind changes. I hadn't realized you were going home so soon. Vince told me you'd done rather well in your exams. Congratulations and all that.'

'Thank you,' she says lamely.

'Shall we go to Sedgemoor? That tea-place by the river will be open today.'

They'd been there a couple of times when Beattie had been doing her teaching practice in the village school. The waitress remembers them and finds them a table on the lawn. It is a hot breathless summer day, bees droning peacefully through the herbaceous border next to the table. Brooke sighs deeply and takes out his cigarette-case. Beattie wonders where and when to begin. Instead, she says: 'You look awfully tired. Are things all right?'

He shrugs and leans out to touch her wooden chair.

'I finish my second tour this month.'

'Surely you won't have to start another one straight away?'

'No, I'm off to Dishforth to do some training. A few of us have been picked to work on a new plane; it's all rather hush-hush. What about you? What are you going to do next term?'

'That depends,' says Beattie carefully.

'On what?'

'Brooke, I—'

'Scones and cakes, isn't it? I'm afraid the cakes aren't up to much this week, but the jam's home-made,' beams their waitress. 'By the way, I couldn't have your autograph for my little boy, could I? He saw the article about you in the *Daily Express*.'

Brooke obliges with very good grace, and Beattie pours out the tea. Then they both speak at the same moment.

He says: 'You'll never guess what. I've just had a letter from a publisher. They want me to—' At that moment Beattie takes a deep breath and says: 'Brooke, I'm going to have a baby.'

'What?' says Brooke, stunned. 'Christ,' he says under his breath, and all the good humour in his face vanishes. 'That's all I need at present. Are you sure? Have you seen a doctor? I thought you were going to take care of that side of things.'

'No, I haven't seen a doctor and, yes, I'm sure.'

'How far on are you?'

'Ten weeks,' she says quietly.

'Well, you'll have to get rid of it. Do you know anyone?'

So that is that. Beattie begins to feel rather ill.

'I'll give you a cheque. There's a man in London – in Welbeck Street, I think. He did a friend of mine—'

'Brooke, it's a baby, yours and mine. Its not just a tooth you have out. Doesn't it mean anything to you?'

'I hate babies. I don't like children, and the very idea of them makes me feel ill,' says Brooke in a tense undertone. 'Does that make my position clear?'

'I can't get rid of it,' says Beattie almost inaudibly.

'Then, have it.'

'You can't just switch off responsibility like that.'

'I'm not switching off responsibility for anything. I've offered to pay for an abortion.'

'In other words you'll give me help providing I do what you want.'

'Look, Beattie, I've got a million things on my mind at present, including the safety of a large number of men tonight, and I—'

'I'm sick of considering you and your bloody job,' hisses Beattie, tears

185

pouring unchecked down her cheeks by this time. 'Stop trying to hide behind it. I've got a right to be considered as well. Why can't we marry and have the baby? Are you afraid I'll disgrace you? If I'm good enough to take to Buckingham Palace and good enough to share your bed, I'm good enough to marry.'

'Look, Beattie. Get this straight. I'm not going to marry you. When and if I get married it'll be to someone who can bring me money. For God's sake, what future would we have together? Don't you realize that my mother wouldn't even receive you?'

Beattie sits and gazes unseeingly at the table. She does not see that Brooke's hands are trembling violently as he stubs out his cigarette. She gets up and walks out of the garden. Brooke throws some money on the table and catches her up.

'I'll drive you home.'

'There's no need,' says Beattie calmly. 'The walk will do me good, I'm sure.'

He goes to catch her arm, and she turns quickly and with an arm strengthened by numerous games of tennis hits him so hard across the face that he staggers and nearly loses his balance. For a moment they stare at each other, Brooke white-faced except for the scarlet mark of Beattie's hand. He is shocked into silence.

'The last time I saw you I said I hoped I'd never see you again. I still hope so,' says Beattie evenly. 'And I can add that I wish to God I'd never met you.' With that she turns for home. Brooke does not come after her.

'Are you sure this is it?'

'Of course I'm bloody sure. What I want to know is are *you* sure this is what you want?'

Beattie and Louie are standing in a backstreet of Norwich, not far from the cathedral. The houses are small and terraced, built of ugly grey and yellow brick. In the torpor of the early afternoon they have a shuttered and secretive air. Two cats lying on window-sills eye them narrowly. There is a pub on the corner and in front of them a small general store. Beattie clutches her handbag more firmly and thinks briefly about her parents. The thought sobers her considerably.

'Yes, I'm sure.'

'Come on, then,' says Louie firmly and they cross the road to the small shop. On the door is a sign saying 'No Nivea, no Kirby grips, no shoe polish, no Brylcreem'. The bell jangles loudly as they let themselves in. Louie is taken aback to find a ten-year-old girl behind the counter.

'Is your dad around?'

'He's away fighting.'

'Who's the man who's normally here?'

'That's my brother. He's taking a nap.'

'Go and tell him there's someone needs to see him.'

'He doesn't like to be disturbed,' says the little girl, eyeing them dubiously.

'Just cut along and tell him,' says Louie, who is rapidly losing her temper, and the little girl disappears out of the shop into the back room.

It is an all-purpose shop which appears to be lacking almost everything. On the till there are further lists of goods that aren't available, while most of the biscuit- and sweet-jars are empty. Beattie fixes her eyes on a cardboard cutout of a bar of chocolate, and Louie counts the number of flies on a very old fly-paper. Then there is a faint commotion in the next room and a young man appears yawning and buttoning himself up. Beattie looks at him, almost exclaims with horror, then has to fight a treacherous desire to put her hand over her stomach to protect the baby against such an evil-omened person. He is not old, probably only in his twenties, but every angle of his face, brows, cheekbones, jaw bulge in tight shiny wedges of flesh, while his mouth, cutting his bulbous face in half, is a thin line that dissects his features like a toad's. As he speaks he keeps whipping out his tongue to moisten his thin upper lip.

'What can I do for you ladies?' he says in a soft and rather insinuating voice.

'You were able to give me an address at Christmas,' says Louie boldly. 'I want it again, please.'

He looks at her and then his eyes flick sideways to Beattie. Beattie feels quite faint.

'Have you got an envelope?' he enquires innocently. 'Then I can write it down for you.'

Beattie passes over the blank envelope containing the twenty pounds which she has borrowed from Vince. The man disappears and returns after a few minutes with another envelope in his hand.

'This is the person you want,' he says and smiles at Beattie. The effect is so horrifying that she turns away.

'Your friend not feeling very well?' he says in a soft voice. 'I expect it's the heat.'

Beattie can still feel his snigger as they walk back down the mean street.

'You've got to get to the other side of town,' says Louie heavily. 'There's no bus, and I can't imagine we'll find a taxi in this area. Come on.'

The town is full of servicemen in uniform. The girls walk briskly to avoid being accosted.

'Bloody men,' says Louie morosely. 'You wonder if they're human most of the time.'

'You can't say that about Vince.'

'Vince is ace. But he's the exception that proves the rule.'

They've been walking for some time when Beattie announces that she has a stitch and she'll have to sit down and rest. By now they are in the residential part of the town and sit on a bench underneath a lime tree. Beattie puts her head between her knees.

'Are you all right?'

'Fine. Just pregnant. Are we far now?'

'No. I still don't understand why you couldn't ask Brooke for the money since he's offered to get the thing done properly.'

'I told you why. I don't want to see Brooke again and I don't want to have anything more to do with him and I didn't want to take anything from him.'

'All right, all right,' says Louie, feeling in her pocket for a peppermint. 'Here, have one of these and rest up for a minute.'

187

In the next road a clock strikes three. Beattie straightens up and begins to look for a hankie to wipe her perspiring brow.

Then she says: 'Louie, you're not going to like this, but I can't go through with it.'

Louie sighs, feels in her own pocket for a hankie and hands it to Beattie.

'I never thought you would, if you want to know the truth. But I thought I'd better go along with you anyway. It's your decision and your life. But why especially, why now?'

'There's no special reason. Its just that everything inside me says no.'

'What will your parents say?'

'I don't want to think of that yet.'

'Will you keep it?'

'I don't know. I just think it deserves a chance.' Beattie hesitates for a moment. 'I know that you think I'm daft, but last night I dreamt that it had been born and I was holding it. And this morning I could still feel the weight of it in my arms.'

'I think you're crazy, Beattie. I do really. You'll find it difficult to get a job with a fatherless child.'

'I know that.'

'You'll find it even more difficult to marry,' says Louie sombrely. 'Men don't like having a reminder around that you've been with somebody else.'

'I know all that. If the worst comes to the very worst, I can always get it adopted or fostered until I could take care of it myself. But I can't not give it its chance. I like babies. I want to have it.'

There is a very long silence.

'Well, then. We can give Vince back his twenty pounds.'

'Let's have a look at what the man says.'

Beattie opens the envelope and takes out a folded sheet containing one five-pound note. Louie snatches it from her, her face scarlet.

'What's all this about? What does the note say? Where's the rest of my money?'

' "This woman is a friend of mine. Can you take care of her?" ' reads Beattie perplexed.

'The dirty bastard,' hisses Louie. 'The filthy ruddy swine. He's making fifteen pounds off every miserable girl that comes to him.' She is choking with rage. 'Come on, Beattie.'

'Where are you going?'

'Going? I'm ruddy well going back to get the rest of Vince's money, that's where I'm going.'

Beattie runs after her. 'Louie, you can't. He'll never give it you back.'

'He will,' says Louie with grim emphasis, 'or I'll take him to the police if need be.'

It is after 5.30 when they arrive back at the general store, and the 'Closed' sign is hanging in the window. Undeterred, Louie beats on the door next to the shop and urges Beattie to keep on banging on the shop door itself.

'Go *on*, do as I say.'

The combined racket is enormous in the quiet afternoon, and people begin to come out of their houses and stand on the pavement and murmur. Finally the face of the young man, clearly frightened, appears at the shop window.

'Go away,' he shouts. 'I'm not opening this door. We're closed.'

'You let us in,' shouts Louie. 'And if you don't open this door in ten seconds I'm going to stand here and tell your friends exactly how you earn your living. And my friend will go and get the police as well. Just you open this bloody door.'

The bolts are drawn and the next thing is the door is opened a crack. Beattie throws the weight of her fury against it and pushes it open, imprisoning the young man against the wall. He slams the door shut behind him and turns with such venom that Beattie falters. But Louie is not deterred for an instant.

'You ——— ——,' she says quietly, but with such hatred in her voice that he actually takes a step backwards. Beattie stares at her friend in admiration. She's never even heard the word said before. 'You rotten cheating sodding bugger. Where's that sodding fifteen pounds you stole from me? You give it to me or I'll go to the police and get you done for procuring abortions. I've got the address and the note written on it in your handwriting, and I swear if you don't hand me over that money I'll go to the police. I don't care if I get done as well. If you don't cough up, I'll see you get seven years.'

'Right,' he sneers, 'let's see you do it.'

'Beattie, you stay here and make sure the little turd doesn't scarper,' says Louie. 'We passed a police station on the way here, didn't we?'

'That's right,' says Beattie with considerably more confidence than she is feeling. 'Two roads back, on the corner by the church.'

'Just a minute,' gabbles the young man. 'I'll give you your bloody money.' He pulls open his wallet. 'Here's the fifteen pounds. Now get out of here.'

'I want the other fifteen pounds you stole from me as well. From the other girl. That's right. Another fifteen pounds.'

'You're out of your mind.'

'Give me that money or my friend will go to the police and while she's gone I'll smash a few of these empty jars. . .'

The young man opens the till and slaps another fifteen pounds on to the counter. 'You get out of here,' he screams, 'and if I ever see you here again—'

'If I ever see *you*,' says Louie with a deadly emphasis which makes him draw back, 'I'll kill you, and that's not just a threat. Do you understand?'

She slams the door so hard the bell can be heard jingling halfway down the street. A crowd of curious people are standing on the opposite pavement, but Louie ignores them.

'Louie, you were *wonderful*.'

'It was Vince's savings. Couldn't let him get away with that.'

'What about Barbr'ann's money? Are you going to send it on to her?'

'No, I'm not,' says Louie firmly. 'She's got money to burn. Money doesn't matter to her. No, you're going to keep that.'

'Me? Why?'

'Because you're penniless, pregnant and unemployed, that's why. Come on. I can take the later train to London tonight. Let's go and have something to eat. It's the last we'll see of each other for a while.' She sighs. 'We can't call it a celebration, but I suppose you could say it's a decision.'

CHAPTER

FIFTEEN

'WHAT YOU MUST DO', says Beattie's mother, adding a smear of margarine to the loaf and cutting off another careful slice, 'is make her see it's her duty to herself to come and live with us. At least for a holiday until she's made up her mind. I've said it all to her, but I don't think she reads my letters.'

'Supposing she won't come?'

'You'll have to make her. I'd go myself, but I'm on the jam-making rota for the next three weeks. She's staying further down the road with that woman she plays bridge with.'

'I'd come with you myself,' says Big Toby, who after two years of regular meals looks a very different prospect to the grubby skinny little boy in plimsolls who had clung to Beattie's legs on that fateful first day of the war. 'But you won't believe the amount of work that Uncle Edward and I have got to get through – and there's my chickens, you see.'

Toby has put his pocket-money into chickens and increased the stock of their hen-house to eighteen fowls, all of whom promptly go off lay, in Toby's opinion, if he as much as goes out of earshot of the house.

'His family have offered her a home in Manchester,' goes on Mrs Blythe, firmly removing Toby's fingers from the breadboard, 'but I can't think she'd prefer Manchester to her own kin. Clean hands, please, boys. I can hear Uncle Edward at the gate.'

Mr Blythe comes in, takes off his boots in the scullery, washes his hands and changes his jacket; he smiles at them all, kisses Beattie and sits down, observing briefly that the birds have got into the fruit-cages again.

'Was Lily here at midday?' asks Beattie casually.

Her mother gives her a sharp glance. 'You're mighty anxious for the post these days, young lady.'

'Perhaps she's got a young man in the forces,' says her father teasingly.

Help comes from an unexpected source.

'She only wants to see Lily because they're going to that silly dance on Saturday,' says Toby disparagingly. 'I don't like dances. You don't play any games, and there's no cake.'

'Little pitchers,' declares Mrs Blythe, shaking her head.

'Have you decided to go to London, then?' asks Mr Blythe.

'Mother's decided,' says Beattie drily, 'and I don't mind trying.'

'She need only stay here until she's found another home,' repeats Mrs Blythe. 'Have some more bread, Beattie, do. I don't know what they fed you in that college, but you've come back with an appetite like a mouse.'

'Is there any pudd'n?' asks Toby.

'There is for those who've eaten their greens. More eating and a little less chat, please.'

Beattie looks amusedly at the two brown heads bent obediently over their plates. The boys divide their favours equally in the Blythe household. Big Toby is sunburnt from working with Mr Blythe in the Manor gardens, while Little Ern is pallid from long comfortable afternoons indoors spent helping Mrs Blythe make jam. It is a good thing, thinks Beattie with conscious irony, that her parents are so fond of children. Her eyes go automatically to the calendar on the wall above her father's head. The middle of August. She is well into her fourth month now, and already her brassière is too small and she needs a chain of safety-pins to keep any skirt together. Louie has written three times suggesting she come to Liverpool and get a job there until the baby is born, but Beattie is in the grip of a curious paralysis. She knows the first thing to do is to tell her parents. She has already written to the school in Ipswich and withdrawn her application, but somehow she cannot bring herself to speak. She misses Louie badly, her directness, her common sense, her unshockability. She has had one letter from Barbr'ann, who is at home in the centre of her family and out dancing every night. That could be me now, thinks Beattie, then resolutely puts the idea out of her head; it's too depressing.

'I'm glad you're going to see your aunt,' says her father later, privately that night. 'I think it'll set your mother's mind at rest.'

Beattie sincerely hopes so. She has arrived home to find her mother consumed by a mood of manic energy. In the first week of August she had decided to spring-clean the house and from daybreak to dusk she is scrubbing, ironing and polishing. As she is already a conscientious housewife the house is in any case in apple-pie order, and in vain does Beattie complain that this frenzied activity is unnecessary. It has all been done against the possible arrival of Mrs Blythe's older sister.

On the train next day Beattie has plenty of time for solitary reflection. In her bag is a map and packet of egg sandwiches made from Big Toby's precious hens' eggs. According to Toby, hens didn't lay much in the summer because they found the weather 'tirin' '. At present Beattie doesn't care much for the hot weather, either. Very soon she will have to go to the doctor and tell him about the baby and that way get her green ration-book and the right food for the baby, or so Lord Woolton says. She wonders if he will mind feeding an illegitimate child and falls into the usual fruitless speculation as the fields of Essex crawl by. If only she hadn't gone to that village dance. If only she'd been more firm about not starting up again with Brooke. Try as she may, it is impossible not to see the long chain of events that lead to the present disaster as being anything other than her own fault. Pride goes before a fall, her late nan would have said. Mrs Musgrave and Virginia would just dismiss her as 'that kind of girl'. Louie thinks she is plain daft – unlucky but daft none the less. But at least Louie always tries to help.

191

Brooke thinks. . . . Well, clearly Brooke never thinks about it at all. She has heard from Lily that he has been up to London twice to see Virginia, who is in hospital after being blitzed. But he has never come home to the village. Beattie jerks her thoughts away from him with an almost physical pain and finds the train is edging into London. Everywhere there are bombsites and doorless houses. There is a gritty dusty feeling in the air, and people move slowly as if they are exhausted. As they draw into Liverpool Street they pass a train going the other way, laden with rubble from burnt-out buildings.

'Where are they taking that?' she asks a soldier next to her.

'It's going up to East Anglia to build new airfields so we can bomb the buggers.'

London is hot and sticky, and Beattie is sweating heavily by the time she reaches Denselow Avenue. She can remember vividly how impressed she had been with Putney the first time she had been here two years ago. Coming from the country at the height of summer, with nature surging and burgeoning and thrusting at every ditch and field, she had been chiefly struck by the firmness with which nature was contained in the gardens in the red-brick villas, with their snowy white lace curtains, glossy front doors, and shiny brass knockers. The atmosphere in the road had been one of orderly calm. Today she stops at the top of the avenue in sheer disbelief. A landmine has fallen on one side of the street, and four houses are simply not there. There is evidence of another bomb further down the road in that there is not a single house there with its windows intact. All the orderly front gardens have vanished to make way for vegetables. Beattie makes her way to where her aunt is staying, wondering if Aunt Madge will be very upset. Her impression of her aunt, after her stay in London, was of a woman who defined herself largely through her home and possessions. She was the kind of woman who declared frequently that she liked to see her own things about her and that she was a 'home body'. She had married well according to the standards of her mother's family. Beattie had been distinctly in awe of her. Her own mother has never been particularly forthcoming about her family: all Beattie knows is that her mother's mother was widowed early and left with two little girls to bring up on her own in Islington. Both daughters had started in the clothing trade at fourteen, then gone into service. Aunt Madge had gone as nanny to the household of a wealthy solicitor and his wife in Manchester. She had stayed there as the mainstay of the family, or so she liked to tell people, for fifteen years. She had then secured the affections of a solicitor's clerk called Arthur Goodchild, who worked in London, in Holborn, and was exactly twice her age. Her husband was now dead and therefore could safely be described as a saint. There had been no children. Beattie knew her uncle only as a black-bordered photo on the piano.

There is no reply at the front door, and Beattie's about to knock again when she hears voices from the garden and pushes open the side-gate. Her aunt and a neighbour are sitting under the apple tree, knitting. Aunt Madge stands up with a welcoming smile, and Beattie kisses her.

'I'll give your mother ten out of ten for determination,' says Aunt Madge, laughing hugely. Beattie stares at her in perplexity. Can this really be the homeless bereft elderly widow, as Mrs Blythe likes to refer to her?

'I've had a letter from your mum every morning since the bomb fell and I had another this morning telling me that you were on the way. I'll concede defeat. Have you had any lunch? Oh, you've got sandwiches. Egg! I say! You don't see a lot of those out here. Well, if you insist. Just one. My word, these do taste good. Not that you shouldn't be eating them yourself, Beattie. You're that pale. What's your mother thinking about? It's all that studying; it drains the life out of a woman. You drink up your tea and tell us how you are. Mrs Ellis and I are sitting here having a nice old chin-wag about our adventures. We went up West yesterday and had a lovely tea at Lyons at Marble Arch.'

She goes on to describe what they'd bought and how they had to walk up Oxford Street (both sides) before they could find a pair of shoes to fit her bunions. Beattie listens with increasing confusion. Aunt Madge is transformed. There is no other word for it. She even looks different. For a woman who needs her things round her and can't abide borrowing she has clearly adapted with no problem at all to the spirit of the times. She is wearing a peculiar maroon skirt, a cardigan whose buttons clearly won't meet and a rather odd yellow blouse. She catches Beattie's curious glance and nudges Mrs Ellis.

'She's wondering what on earth I've got on, aren't you?' she says laughing. Beattie shakes her head and blushes.

'I got this lot from the WVS and a lot more besides. Just my luck to lose everything before clothing starts being rationed, but at least I'd taken my fur coat to the shelter with me.'

'Do you mean you've lost everything?'

'Every little old thing,' says Aunt Madge gaily as if it was the most amusing thing in the world. 'I came up the shelter steps that morning, looked at where the house should have been and I thought: That's it Madge; you've had your chips there. I was just glad Arthur wasn't alive to see it.'

'I'm awfully sorry,' murmurs Beattie, confused.

'There's no need to be. The insurance people will pay up and that's that. Besides, I've seen far worse than me.'

Beattie is increasingly puzzled. She expected her aunt to be hysterical with grief and anger and she is quite sure that that is her mother's expectation as well.

'You can tell your mother I'll come to Suffolk, but it can't be before tomorrow. I've got the insurance men coming first thing and I must see them. And I promised I'd see the vicar before I went. What'll you do, young Beattie? There's an extra mattress in the vicarage if you want to stay overnight and travel with me tomorrow.'

'I think I'm probably needed more at home,' says Beattie, not altogether untruthfully, but aware that she is feeling increasingly ill and, most unusually for her, longing to get out of London.

'Well, you sit here in the garden and have a bit of a rest before you travel back. I've got to nip up the road and see a few people but I'll be back in an hour's time. It does seem a shame, you coming all this way to get me. I've got a visitor stopping by later, so you can have a bite of tea with us before you go.'

193

Beattie leans back in her armchair, marvelling at her aunt's nonchalance in the face of disaster. How pleased Mother will be, she reflects and falls asleep wondering if she will get a seat for the return journey. She is dreaming she is already back at the village when in her sleep she hears someone say her name tentatively. Then she opens her eyes and with a shock sees a man standing in front of her, blocking out the sun. She puts her hand up to her eyes to see who it is. It is a tall man in RAF uniform. She stares at him in total disbelief.

It is Charles Hammond.

'Beattie,' he says, his surprise equal to if not greater than her own. '*You*? Are you really Madge's niece?'

Beattie tries to struggle into a sitting position, which isn't easy in a deck-chair.

'Yes, of course I am,' she says dazed. 'But what on earth are you doing here? And how do you come to know Aunty?'

Charles hooks another deck-chair with one of his long legs and sits down beside her. Beattie is suddenly blindingly aware that she is sweating, ungroomed and pasty-faced.

'Oh, I—'

'There you are! Have you made yourself comfortable, Charles? Give us a hand with this tray, will you, Beattie? Now, have you done the introductions?'

Seeing that Beattie is completely nonplussed, Charles quickly intervenes. 'We were just saying how extraordinary it is, Madge, that Beattie and I already know each other. Yes, really. Remember I told you I was stationed in Norfolk before the accident? Well, Beattie's training college is only a couple of miles away and we had . . . mutual acquaintances.' It is a masterly pull-together of some of the more acceptable facts.

Aunt Madge lightly smites her own knee in wonderment.

'There now! Isn't that a thing! Would you believe it?'

'But how do *you* know Charles?' asks Beattie.

'Know Charles?' Her aunt stares at Beattie in comic disbelief. 'Know the boy I dandled on my knee as a baby? Come on, Beattie. You know I was in service in Manchester for fifteen years. Well, it was to Mr and Mrs Hammond, Charles's parents, God bless their souls. I was taken on to deal with young Charles here. He was only three months old when I got him,' goes on Aunt Madge dreamily in a way that clearly causes Charles acute embarrassment. 'Oh, the prettiest baby you've ever seen in your life. And no trouble! Just loved his grub, then went back to sleep. Well, well. What a small world. He drops in to see me today of all days when you're here, Beattie, and then you and he are already friends. Wait till I tell the vicar. He won't believe it.'

'Are you on leave?' asks Beattie stupidly since it is unlikely that a service-man AWOL will be sitting in the garden enjoying tea.

'Yes, I've got a few days free and I suddenly thought I'd drop in and see Madge.'

'Well, come on, Charles, tell us all your news. Are you still up at High Wycombe? Aren't they letting you fly yet?'

'Not yet,' says Charles lightly. 'I'm still hoping the squadron will take me back in the autumn.'

He and Madge chat on in a desultory way about neighbours and old friends from Manchester, while Beattie sits slumped in her deck-chair and wishes she were dead.

'So what's happened to the house?'

'Well, it was let for the first year of the war,' Charles explains, 'then the people who had it wanted to move to Wales and I haven't found a new tenant. I don't want to go back there and live on my own after the war, so I'll probably sell it.'

'Sell The Laburnums!' Aunt Madge's tone is wistful. 'What a shame. Don't you think you'd like to live there with your own family and children?'

'Well, that may be a long time off.' Charles's tone is evasive.

'And what's happened to that nice young lady of yours? What was her name – Eleanor, wasn't it? The last time I spoke to you – and, my word, that was a while ago – it must have been a year ago at least – you were just about to get engaged. Have you fixed a date for the wedding yet?'

'I'm afraid that's all off now.'

Charles has himself rigidly under control, and his tone expresses only a mild social regret. 'We're still very good friends but we decided it just wouldn't work out.'

'There now!' muses Aunt Madge. 'You never can tell, can you, with these things? I'd have thought you would have had that much in common, her being so keen on books just like you.'

'Well, it's probably all for the best,' says Charles with the air of one closing the subject. 'How did you get on in your exams, Beattie?'

This carries the conversation on safely for another twenty minutes. Then Beattie gets up ostensibly to get some more water for the pot and, as she does so, abruptly she finds herself falling backwards, and when she comes round something cold and pungent is being dabbed on her forehead.

'Eh, Beattie! You don't like this hot weather, do you? You just put your head between your legs now and keep quiet for a minute. I'll go and get some water.'

Charles has fetched her a glass of water, and Beattie drinks it thirstily, still dazed.

'It's just the heat,' she says falteringly. 'I think I really will have to make a move and get the train back to Suffolk. It's cooler out there. Perhaps I can get a taxi or a tube. . . .'

'I've got a car outside,' says Charles unexpectedly. 'I'll drive you to Liverpool Street if you want.'

Beattie stares at him with almost embarrassing gratitude in her eyes. 'Drive me? Can you really? Are you sure it isn't too much trouble?'

'It's no trouble at all. Just rest quietly for a moment.'

Beattie rests in her chair while her aunt pours out fresh cups of tea and chatters with Charles about the events on the radio. At twenty to four Charles looks at his watch and says, 'Beattie, if you want to get home tonight, I think you ought to make a move now.'

'Aunty, do you mind if I go? I can at least tell Mother that you'll arrive tomorrow. If you ring the post office and let me know the time you're leaving London, I'll wait at Ipswich for you tomorrow afternoon.'

'I'll do that,' says Aunt Madge. 'And just you take care of her, Charles. I reckon you worked too hard for those exams, Beattie. You look that strained.'

Beattie neither knows nor care what make of car Charles owns; the wonderful fact is that it goes and obviates the need for another journey on a suffocating Tube. They drive in silence until they get to Oxford Street where the traffic is heavy and they have to slow down again.

'How are you feeling? Do you want the other window open?'

'That'll be nice,' says Beattie in a far-away voice and passes out again. When she comes round she finds the car is parked in a side-street and that she is leaning forward with her head between her knees. As she straightens up Charles silently hands her a clean hanky to wipe the sweat from her face.

'Beattie, what is wrong with you?'

Under his direct blue-eyed gaze – Beattie has forgotten just how direct his gaze is – she begins to blush.

'I'm pregnant.'

'Ah,' says Charles thoughtfully, adding astoundingly: 'I thought perhaps you might be. You don't smoke. Mind if I do?'

They sit in silence for a moment. Charles lights a cigarette, then turns to look at her, concerned.

'You're in a bit of a spot, I take it. Do your parents know?'

'No.'

'How far gone are you?'

'I don't want an abortion,' she says elliptically. 'Anyway, it's nearly four months now.'

There is another long silence.

'I take it it's Brooke's. Doesn't he want to marry you?'

'I don't want to marry him.'

'So what are you going to do?'

'I may go and live with a girl I was at college with and have the baby there.'

'And have it adopted?' he asks expressionlessly.

Beattie shakes her head. 'I thought at first I might do that, but I don't think I will now.'

'Illegitimate children have a pretty rotten time. You won't find it easy yourself with a baby in tow.'

'Are you trying to help or depress me?' says Beattie with some asperity.

Charles sighs. She can see her news has distressed him.

'Have you any money?'

'A little,' says Beattie, remembering the fifteen pounds she keeps locked in her trunk along with, most incongruously, her Dutch cap.

'Whatever you decide, you've got a tough time ahead. Does it ever strike you that the only time I ever meet you is in a crisis?'

Beattie smiles, unable to meet his eyes.

'Most of my life is pretty ordinary stuff,' she says dully. 'This has just come out of the blue.'

'The problem is that I'm due to meet an air marshal in an hour, else we

196

could talk about things further. Give me your address in the village. Are you on the phone?'

'No.'

'Well, I can write at any rate. Did you tell Madge?'

'*No*,' says Beattie violently. 'No one in my family knows. And I think it would be the last straw for Mother if she knew I'd confided—'

'Well, you're going to have to confide in somebody pretty soon. I'll keep in touch, and if you want any money let me know.'

Beattie looks wearily at him.

'Why are you doing this? You don't even like Brooke.'

Charles looks at her expressionlessly, taking in the exhaustion, the anxiety and Beattie's aura of sadness.

'At present you need looking after,' he says briefly. 'Not in general, I'm sure. You seem a pretty capable sort of girl to me. But if you haven't told your parents and Brooke isn't coming across you need help from somebody. If Madge is coming down to stay with you, she might help break the news to your parents.'

Beattie simply cannot envisage any way in which she can tell her parents but nods without speaking.

'It's such a coincidence, you going to see Aunty Madge today of all days,' says Beattie.

'It is, isn't it? There was something I wanted to ask her, so I just dropped her a line on impulse and—'

'I'm sorry, did I stop you having a proper talk?'

Charles looks at her oddly for a moment and smiles.

'No. I found out what I wanted to know. Or, rather, I found out there wasn't anything to find out,' he adds somewhat obliquely. 'Come on, I'll take you to Liverpool Street. I just wish there was something I could do to help. Are you strong enough to travel?'

'Yes, I'll feel better once I get out of London. Up to now I've felt absolutely fine. It's just . . . being so fearful about the future.'

Wednesday becomes Thursday. Thursday, in the way that Thursdays will, becomes Friday, and Friday, unchecked, slides into Saturday. On Saturday morning Beattie sits outside with her mother and aunt, topping and tailing gooseberries for jam. The boys are up at Hill Farm hindering the harvest. Beetle is fast asleep under the table that they've carried out to the back garden. Toby's chickens can be faintly heard at the bottom of the garden. Aunt Madge is clearly enjoying herself, humming a dance tune and exclaiming over the size of butterflies on the Buddleia. Beattie sits quietly, aware that this is decision day. After three relatively trouble-free months of pregnancy she was violently sick last night. Fortunately it happened on the way to collect the boys from the farm, and no one knows. But Sid Kedge has been in earlier in the morning and left two rabbits, which Mrs Blythe has asked Beattie to skin and draw. Normally she'd have done it without a second thought. Today she cannot even contemplate the thought, let alone

197

the deed, without her stomach standing up and complaining in a very virulent way.

Mrs Blythe is also working on the gooseberries, but her movements are not as swift and deft as they normally are. Quite apart from her own private problems, Beattie is worried about her mother. She has never known her like this. Normally Mrs Blythe is an even-tempered and calm, if somewhat enigmatic, woman. Now for the first time Beattie is aware that she knows almost nothing of her mother's deeper feelings. She is in the grip of some mood that Beattie is completely unable to interpret. It clearly has something to do with her sister, and Beattie listens to the curious conversation they are having, a continuation of a dialogue that has gone on ever since Aunt Madge arrived. It is immediately clear that Mrs Blythe is as taken aback as Beattie by the sight of her resolutely cheerful sister. Whenever Aunt Madge is questioned about her experiences she invariably turns them all into a joke and, baffled, Mrs Blythe withdraws. But Mrs Blythe seems determined to treat her sister's apparent composure as a front and again and again returns to the subject with a 'now you can talk freely, now you needn't put a brave face on it any more', only to find that the brave face that her sister wears in public is exactly the same as she wears in private, much to her annoyance. Even Beattie is beginning to feel it is somewhat tactless to keep coming back to her sister's losses, to enquire so tenderly about the three-piece suite, the marble chiffonier, the walnut bureau, the piano, when you know perfectly well that Aunt Madge has escaped in the clothes she stands up in. Aunt Madge replies vaguely and cheerfully.

'It's a terrible prospect, to face the future without a home of your own,' Mrs Blythe muses, displaying such a shocking lack of tact that Beattie feels constrained to intervene.

'What will you do when the war's over, Aunt Madge?' she asks quickly. 'Will you live in London?'

'I may do. I may not,' says Aunt Madge with the serene indifference that is clearly a red rag to her sister. Appropriately she then breaks into 'Red Sails in the Sunset' while teaching Beetle to shake hands.

What is it Mother is trying to prompt her into saying? wonders Beattie. Surely she should be glad she's taken it so well; instead of which, she seems – there's no other word for it – cheated by her sister's resilience. She keeps feeding her sister her lines, and Aunt Madge resolutely fails to respond. Instead of being the weeping ruin sustained only by the presence of Beattie's mother, she's turned out to be the life and soul of the party. The two boys adore her and normally won't leave her alone. Yesterday she'd made them all laugh for two hours on end and she'd even made Beattie's father chuckle a couple of times over supper. Furthermore she has helped round the house, done her bit with the fruit, and seems quite interested in the prospect of scouring the neighbouring ponds with the boys for scrap metal. She is a delightful guest to everybody except the person who asked her, who is clearly getting crosser by the minute. Aunt Madge begins to talk about her husband's sister in Manchester where she is going to spend the following week and what a caution she is when Mrs Blythe interrupts, quite rudely for her, and asks Beattie if she's going to sit there all day or does she think the rabbits

198

will take their own innards out. Beattie gets up silently, goes into the scullery, looks at the rabbits and is immediately sick in the sink. She is bracing herself to go back outside and tell her mother this, and whatever else the explanation necessitates, when there is a sharp rat-a-tat at the back door and Lily appears.

'Only me. Must rush. Last delivery today. Two for you, one for your aunt and one for your dad. Ta ta.'

Beattie immediately recognizes Brooke's handwriting and is aware of a kind of roaring in her ears. She runs up the stairs and into her own room and shuts the door. Her heart is going so fast she can hardly breathe. He has changed his mind; he must have done. And suddenly a dazzling vista opens up in her mind's eye. . . She sees herself going down to tell her mother, not that she is pregnant, but that she and Brooke are engaged, and she knows instantly and prophetically that Mrs Blythe longs for this every bit as much as she longs for it herself. Her hands shake so much that she can hardly open the envelope, and in the end she tears it across – and as she does so, a small folded square falls out on to the floor.

Puzzled, she looks inside the envelope. There is nothing else. She picks up the square of paper and unfolds it. It is a cheque. There is no note. No letter saying Brooke has had a change of heart and longs to see her and marry her. Just a cheque, made out to Beatrice Blythe, for the sum of £100 and signed by Brooke G.K. Musgrave. Nothing else. Beattie sits down rather quickly on her bed and stares blankly at the faded wallpaper. She can actually feel sweat trickling between her breasts and collecting in the bodice of her dress and is aware that her whole skull is sodden. After a long while there is a tap on the door and her aunt says, 'Are you there, Beattie?' and opens the door.

'You don't want to get too upset about your mother,' she begins, clearly thinking that Beattie has retired in a huff. 'I think she's just . . .' Then in a different voice she adds: 'What in the world is wrong with you, child?'

'Well, basically,' says Beattie in a new harsh tearless voice, 'I'm going to have a baby. That's the main problem, but there's others like the father doesn't want to marry me and he's sent me a cheque and no note.'

Silently her aunt sits down on the bed beside her and takes the cheque from Beattie's fingers. For a moment the Christian name at least means nothing to her.

'Does your mother know? Or anybody? I suppose I should have guessed. How far on are you?'

'Seventeen weeks,' says Beattie tonelessly.

'What has he sent you this for? An abortion?'

'I don't know. I told him I wouldn't have one, so I imagine he's just washing his hands of the whole affair.'

Beattie finds she's beginning to shake.

'Well, there's nothing for it. Your father will have to see him and make him marry you. He's one of the Musgraves, but who is he?'

The thought of Brooke being threatened by Mr Blythe is so ridiculous that Beattie begins to smile in spite of herself.

'What's so funny? It's high time he faced up to his responsibilities like a man.'

'He won't do that,' says Beattie tiredly. 'He'd never marry me. Father couldn't persuade him and I – I wouldn't want to marry him like that.'

'Yes, young lady, that's all very well being proud, but it's not just you. What about your parents?'

'I'll go away and have it somewhere else.'

'Don't talk so daft,' snaps her aunt. 'Now, who is the father? Who is this Brooke Musgrave?'

'Oh, it doesn't matter,' says Beattie wearily, 'because he doesn't want to marry me anyway—'

'Who doesn't want to marry you anyway?' says another voice, and Mrs Blythe steps into the room. She is very pale, and Beattie is instantly aware, first, that she must have been standing outside the door listening for some time and, second, that there are cords of tension knotting her mother's neck.

'Have you got something to tell me, Beattie?' she says in a voice of dangerous calm.

Beattie stands up and faces her mother. 'I'm going to have a baby. I've been trying to tell you since I got home, but the time never seemed right.'

Her mother stares at her and then moves briskly across the room and slaps her hard across the face. Beattie screams, and her mother would have hit her again had her sister not intervened.

'For goodness' sake, Betty, that's not going to help anyone. Leave her be.'

Mrs Blythe seems suffocated with anger. She shakes off her sister's hand and grabs the weeping girl's arm.

'You'll break your father's heart, you know that, don't you? Who is the father, or don't you know?'

Downstairs they hear the sounds of the two boys returning for their lunch. Madge goes to the kitchen, and Mrs Blythe closes the door behind her. Beattie realizes that she is very frightened indeed. Her mother sees what Beattie is holding in her hand and twitches it out of her fingers. Before Beattie can stop her she has seen the signature and her face changes.

'Oh, I see,' she says bitterly. 'He pays you, does he? Well, you let yourself go very cheaply, my girl. How could you do it, Beattie? Didn't you give any thought to your father and me and our good name in the village? How do you think we'll feel, having an illegitimate child of the Musgraves? You must have known someone like that would never take you seriously? He's been stringing you along and you've been too conceited to see it. And it's your father and I who will have to put up with the consequences of your loose ways.'

Beattie is hardly able to believe her ears.

'Mother,' she says steadily. 'When you gave me that dress and those shoes and that bag, where exactly did you think I was going to wear them? For country dancing in the gym or perhaps the village hall at Chillington?'

Her mother flushes an angry mottled scarlet.

'I didn't know what you were going to do with them. I didn't know you were going to wear them for going out whoring.'

'Don't give me that,' shouts Beattie, suddenly galvanized by her own anger. 'You knew I was seeing Brooke or else you'd never have given me

200

those things. You may not have said anything but you've encouraged me in your own way because you were just as flattered as I was. If I was telling you now that I was marrying Brooke, you'd be out of your mind with excitement. It would make up for a lot, wouldn't it? You wouldn't even have to feel envious of Aunt Madge, would you? It's bad enough that she doesn't feel as depressed as you'd like her to, but if you go on long enough I'm sure you'll succeed in making her miserable.'

Her mother goes to hit her again, and Beattie pushes her so hard that her mother falls backwards over the bed.

'I'm not blaming anyone for what's happened to me,' she says in a voice she hardly recognizes as her own, 'but don't act all virtuous with me, Mother, and pretend to be shocked by my presumption. You must have had some idea of what was going on and you've never checked me by as much as a word.'

Mrs Blythe gets up, straightens her hair with trembling fingers and walks out of the room. Beattie hears her clattering down the stairs. She sits down on the bed and finds she is shaking from head to foot. Tomorrow she will leave home for ever and go to Liverpool. She will do anything rather than stay here. Then she thinks about her father, and her eyes overflow. From downstairs she can hear the cheerful sounds of the boys having lunch. She stays where she is, her back pressed against the wall, her mind a blank. As she feels around in her pocket for a hanky to wipe her eyes she remembers there had been another letter and belatedly takes it out of her pocket and smooths the envelope. The writing is unfamiliar. Drearily, without hope, she opens it. Glancing at the bottom of the page, she sees it is from Charles Hammond. For a moment she is tempted to shove it back unread into the envelope, then she glances at the first sentence and stiffens from head to foot. It is not a very long letter and has clearly been written in a hurry.

Dear Beattie,
I am writing to ask you to marry me. I would have asked you on Tuesday but I thought you would say it was just an impulse, so I decided to wait and write instead. I have just heard that I have got some leave this weekend Saturday and Sunday – we could have the service then. But I am jumping the gun, imagining that you will say yes. I know that you are not in love with me, but if you are determined to have the baby it will be better for both of you if it has a legal father. If something happens to me afterwards, then there's no harm done; and if things don't work out, then we can cut our losses later. This is not the kind of proposal a girl longs for, but it is one solution. If your answer is yes, wire me at the above address and fix the church in your village for Saturday morning. If it's no, wire me anyway. I haven't forgotten what I said about helping you financially and I can make arrangements with my bank.
This is not a rash proposal.

Best wishes from
CHARLES HAMMOND

201

Beattie stares at the single sheet in bewilderment. Then turns it over expecting to find some kind of explanation on the back. What on earth can he mean writing her a letter like this? Can he possibly be sincere? Can it be that he is really in love with her? She stares with unseeing eyes down at the garden below. If she married Charles – if – but how quickly the impossibility is becoming a possibility in her mind – it would immediately solve some problems while creating a whole set of new ones. She hardly knows him, let alone loves him. Could he really mean it? Yet when she thinks back to him, the directness of his glance, she knows that he does mean it, however rash the proposal is. That at heart he is a serious man and willing to undertake responsibility for her dilemma because she is unable to cope on her own. But if she accepts him – terrible, weak, treacherous thought to have at this moment – if she accepts him, she would slam the door on Brooke for ever. How can you even think of him now? She tells herself angrily. You can see how much his responsibilities mean to *him*.

The door opens again. It is Aunt Madge with a cup of tea.

'Here,' she says without preamble. 'Drink this. Shouldn't have made it, because we're short of tea. But I need one even if you don't. Now, cheer up and don't mind your mum too much. It's a shame but not a tragedy. You're young enough to get this over and start again. You'll have to go to the doctor tomorrow for your green ration-book and your vitamins. But he'll want to know what you're planning to do. So let's get this straight. You aren't planning to marry the father?'

'No.'

'When's it due?'

'March or February, I'm not sure.'

Her aunt sucks her teeth thoughtfully for a moment, then notices the letter in Beattie's hand.

'What's this you've got?'

Beattie takes a deep breath.

'I've – I've had a letter from Charles Hammond. When I saw him on Tuesday he guessed I was pregnant. I've – I've known him for a couple of years one way and another. And he's written and asked me to marry him.'

For the one and only time in her life Aunt Madge is completely speechless. Her eyebrows shoot straight up into her hair-net, her mouth drops open, and she breathes noisily and asthmatically, her hands automatically smoothing her borrowed skirt.

'Say that again.'

'Charles Hammond. He's written asking me to marry him.'

Aunt Madge shuts her mouth, clicks her false teeth several times and takes her spectacles out of her pocket.

'Can I have a look at the letter?'

Silently, Beattie hands it to her. Aunt Madge reads it slowly, once, her lips moving silently, then all over again.

'Well, I never did,' she says, more to herself than to Beattie. Then briskly she hands her back the letter and says with suspicious enthusiasm: 'Well, that's that, isn't it? He's a good boy, is Charles Hammond, but of course I knew his parents for fifteen years. And they were as nice a couple as you

202

could hope to meet. And you've got a lot in common, haven't you? You both like books, don't you? And he really is the top drawer, young Charles, though I say it myself. The kind of husband a girl could feel proud of. Well, that's your problem solved, isn't it? It's providence, that's what it is.'

Beattie stares at her aunt, aghast. 'Aunt Madge, you really can't think . . . . Do you mean you think I ought to accept? I still don't know what to do.'

'I'll tell you what you're going to do, young lady. You're going to come down to the post office with me and send Charles a telegram to say you'll marry him. You're going to be sensible, Beattie, and think about the future for you and your baby. Nobody wants a woman with a bastard in tow, Beattie, believe me. I've seen it happen, and there's only happy endings for girls like that on the films. You'll marry Charles. He's made you a decent proposal, and you'll be safe, safe from gossip and spite, and free to get on with your own life. Why, once you've had the baby you can go back to your teaching if you want to. If you don't marry Charles, you'll be condemning that child to a poor future. It's clear that you can't expect any help from the real father. What kind of a man is it that sends you this money with no note and no word of kindness and comfort? He just wants to buy you off and save himself trouble. He's a wrong 'un, and you'd better wash your hands of him.'

Beattie, her face now in her hands, wants to say that it isn't true, that her aunt doesn't know the strain and pressure that Brooke is constantly under. But another part of her says that even if he had said no to her, but had been kind and given her support in having the baby, it wouldn't have hurt so much. It is a fact that he cannot even bring himself to be generous for fear of being caught.

'Now, if you're sensible,' goes on her aunt, 'then you'll take the second chance the good Lord has given you, and your whole life won't be dogged by one mistake. When you're young, Beattie, you think a lot about love and that sort of thing. But marriage, I can tell you, is having a good respectable man who'll *stand by you*. You'll see. If you've finished your tea, I'll go and get my hat and we'll be off to the post office.'

Beattie looks at her incredulously.

'Yes, young lady, you heard me. And, while I remember, you can send that cheque back to the other young man who's so conspicuous by his absence and so busy he can't even write a note to say he's sorry. Wash your face and come with me. That's what we're going to do.'

'The vicar's car is at the door, Beattie. Are you nearly ready now? You look wonderful, you really do.'

Lucy Hallett, wearing a navy-blue suit, has a spray of salmon-pink roses pinned to her shoulder. She looks as radiant as the bride.

'Stand up and let's have a look at you. The dress took in beautifully. I'm so glad I kept it and it's had another chance. How do you think she looks, Mr Blythe?'

'She looks grand. Here's your flowers, Beattie. I did them myself. Best roses in the Manor garden, these are.'

'See you in church,' says Lucy and disappears.

As they go out the front door, Beattie stops and grasps her father's arm.

'Do you think I'm doing the right thing?' she asks desperately.

Her father sighs and, avoiding her eyes, tucks her hand into his arm.

'It's not the kind of wedding we had planned for you, Beattie. But your aunt says Charles is a good boy and you'll just have to hope that things sort themselves out in time. Come on now, we mustn't keep Sid Kedge waiting.'

The vicar has lent his car to enable Beattie to travel to church in style. Uncle Sid is their chauffeur, and the car has been decorated with ribbons made from strips of hemmed sheet by the younger members of the Kedge family. They travel slowly down the village street as befits the gravity of the situation, and Beattie, grasping her father's arm tightly, surrounded by the unfamiliar smell of oyster satin and the perfume of the roses, remembers odd scenes from the hectic week that has led up to today. The extraordinary thing is that no one has guessed. No one knows she is pregnant and nobody knows that Charles is not only not the father but also as much a stranger to Beattie as he is to anyone else. Her aunt being in the village adds validity to the fact that Beattie had met Charles as a friend of the family and, besides, everybody is marrying at a few days' notice nowadays. The nicest thing is how pleased everyone seems to be for her, how delighted they are to contribute food for the reception. The worst of it is her mother, who, far from coming round to the idea, has only agreed to go to the church this morning after Mr Blythe has had a word with her. Even so, she is merely wearing her Sunday best and has sneered openly at the corsages which Mr Blythe was painstakingly making for everyone.

'I'll never forgive her for the way she's behaved, never,' vows Beattie, gazing out into the familiar village street from behind a thick layer of veil.

All the planning for the reception has been done by Aunt Madge. It is she who has drawn up the list of guests, then dispatched the boys to take the invitations round by hand. Then it was she who made the trip to the local food office to find out what they are entitled to in the way of extra food for the reception. The mainstay of the meal will be bread rolls filled with rabbit in aspic, masquerading as chicken, and as much Spam as anybody can eat. Beattie has spoken once to her future husband on the phone, and he sounded distant and businesslike. He says he will get the ring, and if it is the wrong size she'll be able to change it for another later on. He adds that he is bringing a couple of chaps down with him. He's also booked a room in a hotel in London for the honeymoon night. He thought they might go to the coast, but apparently you need a special pass and he wasn't sure how long it would take to get. He adds that he is due back at High Wycombe at nine o'clock on Sunday night and off to Scotland the following day. Half-relieved that he seems to expect no emotion from her, yet feeling somehow cheated, Beattie quietly agrees to it all and says she will see him in the church at eleven.

'Have you told your parents?'

'Yes,' she says.

'How are they?'

204

'Mother's angry. Father hasn't said anything. Don't worry,' she adds, 'they'll like you when they meet you,' with rather more conviction than she is feeling.

Her mother's attitude hurts deeply, but even in the midst of that pain she is puzzled. Nobody can feel particularly cheered when a daughter comes home and announces she is pregnant, but it is hardly a unique offence. Indeed, the village is one long history of hasty marriages and near-misses, and on the whole nobody thinks any the worse of anyone because of it. But the fact is that Mrs Blythe seems more angry at the prospect of her daughter being *spared* her shame than of being exposed as an unmarried mother. And when Lucy came round and offered her the use of her own Norman Hartnell wedding dress Mrs Blythe nearly went through the roof. She wanted Beattie to get married in her winter coat and hat, without guests, and preferably with no reception. Beattie, she says fiercely, will get married in white over her dead body. When Beattie does borrow the dress she refuses point-blank to alter it for her. Beattie cannot believe that it is her mother acting in this spiteful and violent way. In the end her aunt alters the dress and has helped her prepare this morning.

They are nearly at the church now. Beattie can see a little knot of wellwishers by the lychgate. Her father suddenly clears his throat, mindful of Sid Kedge in front.

'You mustn't be upset by your mother,' he says obliquely. 'You'll understand better when you're older. Believe me, she means no harm.'

They have arrived, and Beattie is spared the trouble of replying. Lily is standing in the porch, wearing Beattie's winter coat and a beret she's made herself from a velvet cushion. Her wedding present is a precious roll of film, charmed out of an elderly chemist in Ipswich. She has also borrowed a camera and appointed herself photographer for the occasion. 'Smile, please,' she begs, clicking away for dear life. 'Just hang on for one more now a minute. I can't get the hang of this thing. Just let me wind it on. There! I've taken two of Charles and his best man and I'll save the rest for the reception.'

Charles. She has almost forgotten that it is he whom she is here to meet. As they enter the church a sea of curious faces turn towards her and the organ triumphantly breaks into 'To Be a Pilgrim'. Beattie sees the back of her fiancé, very tall and erect in his RAF dress uniform. Then as she reaches the aisle he turns and looks at her. With a stab of piercing grief she realizes that deep down she had still hoped, by some miracle, that it would be Brooke who turned and regarded her gravely as she took her place beside him. Instead it is Charles Hammond who smiles reassuringly and takes her hand.

As the vicar begins the wedding service Beattie has a sudden fleeting memory of Lucy's wedding day and remembers how she had stood at the back of the church and marvelled that the girl, wearing this very dress, could marry a man she barely knew.

'I'm afraid I didn't have time to book for a show,' Charles says apologetically. 'But I've got us a very good table at the Mille Fleurs. And I thought you'd like the hotel. Mother and Father had a little flat off Harley Street for Father's business trips to London, but it's let at present.'

Beattie smiles her thanks. 'This is lovely, Charles. Would you mind if I lie down for a bit?' She blushes horrified lest her remark could be misconstrued.

'That's probably a good idea. Make yourself comfortable. We don't have to be out until seven.'

Left alone, Beattie examines the glamorous bedroom and adjoining bathroom, then worn out by her early morning, the excitement of the wedding and the long journey to London finds herself toppling headlong into bed and falling deeply asleep. It is dusk when she wakes up. Charles is at the door.

'It's half-past six, Beattie. You'll have time for a bath if you want one.'

Notwithstanding the strangeness, the total unreality of her circumstances, Beattie still manages to enjoy the evening. The ill-fated dark red taffeta dress fortunately still fits her even though her bosom is beginning to surge rather obviously in the V-neck. Charles says how nice she looks and clearly doesn't remember the last occasion he'd seen it.

The food is excellent, and afterwards they dance almost every dance. Beattie is wearing her wedding corsage on her dress and the *patron*, scenting a honeymoon couple, sends them over a bottle of sparkling wine. It would all have been even more wonderful if Beattie had any idea at all what she and Charles were doing there together. Charles shows every sign of enjoying the evening and is responsive and friendly. But he says nothing to her until they are back at the hotel and getting ready for bed. Beattie, embarrassed beyond anything she can imagine, sits in her dressing-gown, brushing her hair, waiting for him. He reappears from the bathroom in a spotted dressing-gown, looks around and enquires courteously: 'Which of the beds do you want?' Beattie is flummoxed. She would have been startled had he suggested they slept together, but is even more taken aback that the thought doesn't seem to have crossed his mind.

'Well – I – I don't mind.'

'Do you want a final drink? I've got some brandy in my flask.'

'That'll be nice. Look, Charles, I don't know what you expect or want or—'

Charles takes his time pouring them both a brandy.

'Well, nothing really.'

Beattie stares. 'It doesn't make any sense of you offering to marry me.'

'That's easily explained.'

'Do you mind if I get into bed? I get backache if I sit up for very long.'

'Go ahead.'

Thankfully Beattie scrambles into bed aware that Charles is watching her. She wishes she had something more glamorous to wear than her best cotton nightdress.

'Did you enjoy today?' asks Charles most unexpectedly, and when Beattie says yes he looks genuinely pleased.

'I'm glad. I didn't want it to be a gloomy day. I thought Aunt Madge would burst with pride.'

206

As well she might, thought Beattie, not without irony. Must have cheered her up enormously, her niece marrying her employer's son. Whereas poor Mrs Blythe's employer's son simply made her daughter pregnant.

The hotel faces into Bayswater Square and is very quiet. So far there have been no sirens. Charles sits by the window, looking down into the gardens below.

'Why did you offer to marry me?' says Beattie tonelessly. 'And what kind of a marriage is it?'

Slowly Charles turns back from the window and comes over and sits on the chair by her bed.

'I married you to provide your baby with a name, Beattie.'

'But, Charles, nobody does that. You're not in love with me – you hardly know me and you don't even like the baby's father. And you've ditched your chances of marrying by committing yourself to me. It makes no sense. Why?'

'Well, as I said, it's really all quite simple. You see, I'm illegitimate myself. I only found out relatively recently.'

Beattie stares at him in complete disbelief.

'What? What about . . .? How do you know?'

'Oh, my parents – I suppose I should still call them that – my foster-parents really, I suppose – told me. On my twenty-first birthday. About four years ago.'

'Does Aunt Madge know?'

Charles gives her his brilliant and attractive smile.

'I don't think so. That's what I went to Putney that day to find out.'

'Charles, how *awful*. Weren't you able to because I was there?'

'Oh, no, we had a bit of a chat before I went outside and found the niece she was talking about was you. But it wasn't easy. She worshipped my parents, and she was very happy up at Manchester. It was a sort of golden time in her life, and I started probing gently as to whether she knew if there'd been anything unusual about my birth, and it was quite clear she didn't. As far as she's concerned I'm Madeleine Hammond's son.'

'But I don't understand. Why on earth didn't they tell you before and, come to that, if they'd left it that long why did they tell you at all?'

'The way it was put, it was an ultimate gesture of trust and confidence. An indication of how much they loved me. You see, I was very fortunate. They were both devoted to me, and I think – I think I pleased them. And that day – it was after my twenty-first birthday party – Father called me into the study to tell me. It was as if the knowledge was being offered as a kind of gift: we show you how much we trust and love you in that we can even reveal this.'

Beattie's own problems are completely forgotten in her perplexity at Charles's narrative.

'Did it . . . what did you feel like when they told you?'

Charles is feeling in his dressing-gown pocket for cigarettes and matches. He lights a cigarette, draws on it deeply, gets up to find an ashtray and comes back to her bed.

'Oh – well, at first just curiosity. It didn't remotely affect the person I thought I was. I was feeling pretty pleased with myself that summer. I'd just graduated, I'd got a good first, had a couple of short stories accepted and I was – well, unofficially engaged, I suppose. So I just listened to what I was told and didn't really think to ask any more questions. I don't know how interested I was at that time. They told me that when my mother – I'll call her that – when she found she couldn't have a child she and my father decided to adopt. A year later she was told there was a baby available. I was about ten days old then. I was told all this by my mother, and somehow it didn't seem important. It was as if it was history, as if it had happened to somebody else. It didn't sound like anything in my life. In a funny way I felt I was reading it all in a book. What I didn't realize was it mattered like hell to Eleanor.' He sighs deeply.

'How long had you known her?'

'The whole time I was at university. For the first year I just admired her, but she seemed out of my reach.' His face softens in spite of himself. 'She was very lively and involved in everything. One of the leaders of her year.'

He is silent again, smoking, then looks at Beattie directly. 'I loved Eleanor, you see. She's a marvellous girl. Even now I won't hear a word against her.'

From whom? Beattie wonders.

'It was just . . . . Naturally I told her – and at first she thought it was quite romantic, I think. She made up a lot of funny stories about the King of Ruritania. She's got a very lively imagination. Then – I don't know – things started to go wrong. She was very tense and edgy whenever I saw her. I went off to teach for a year, and she came to London to work as a secretary to some publisher. That summer I joined the RAF. In the autumn she broke off the engagement.'

'But why? What difference did it make? It didn't alter the person you were.'

'I think I never understood her properly. She's one of those people who appear full of confidence about everything. She's very popular and very pretty and very bright. And quite clearly, although she didn't want it to be so, the fact of my being so literally nobody bothered the hell out of her. That time I met you first at Gatton – you know, when I'd first arrived – that was when I guessed that something was wrong. She sent a telegram earlier in the day saying she couldn't make it. I went down to London the following weekend and tried to have it out with her. We sort of patched things up. Then I had . . . then Wilhelmshaven happened and I got injured and she came to see me. But I knew it wasn't going to last. Finally I had a letter from her mother saying Eleanor was ill and had gone back home. Then I got a letter from Eleanor herself saying she was sorry, but she wanted to break off the engagement.'

'She wrote to you while you were ill to tell you she was dropping you?' Beattie does not mean to be so brutally direct but she can hardly believe her ears.

'I think she was having a nervous breakdown. She simply gave up her job overnight and went home.'

Charles's tolerance has the effect of petrol on the fire of Beattie's indignation, but she contents herself with the question 'So what happened to you after that?'

'Well, I – I didn't feel terribly good. Especially when I found they wouldn't have me back in the squadron to fly.'

Charles is silent for a moment, gazing at the carpet unable to meet her eyes. Then he looks up at Beattie without seeing her, and she is horrified to see, even now, the remembrance of that pain in his face.

'It was at that point that both my parents – well, I keep calling them that because if they weren't my parents I don't know who were – died unexpectedly within a few months of each other. Father had had a bad heart for a long time and was nearly eighty. He died in his sleep, and Mother simply faded away about three months later. They were lost without each other. It was only after Mother's funeral that I began to get curious as to who my real parents were – my mother at least. I asked around, but the doctor who had arranged the adoption had died years ago and no one seemed to know anything about it. Then somebody mentioned that I'd been baptized at a certain church in West Didsbury, and I thought of going back there to check – only to find that the church had been bombed about a fortnight before. It seemed as if I was never intended to find out who I really was. So I stopped looking. But it made me very conscious of one thing. Even though I was the one who actually ended things with Eleanor I somehow felt that the fact of my illegitimacy had cost me the relationship. I heard quite casually about a month ago that she had married. I don't know the chap. Then I thought I'd go and have one more try for information, from your aunt. The extraordinary thing is that I was thinking about my mother that day and wondering what she must have felt like when she found she was pregnant with me. Wondering if she was young and terrified and alone and if anybody had tried to help her. Then I met you in Madge's garden. When I saw you asleep in the armchair with that look of sadness and anxiety on your face.'

'You married me because of that?' Beattie is stunned.

'No. I married you for the baby's sake. Don't worry, Beattie. I'm not under any illusion that you're in love with me.'

Beattie blushes.

'They've passed me fit for flying again. And I thought quite selfishly that if I was going to be killed I'd like to leave someone behind me who'd mourn me.'

Beattie is silenced. 'Are you going back to the same squadron?'

'No, thank goodness. I've been transferred to Leeming in Yorkshire. It's all right, Beattie. I've told you I'll take care of you and I will. I know we're not in love, but you need help and I can give it.'

He smiles at her again rather sadly. 'It's nice to know I can be of use to someone. You'd better get some sleep now.'

With that, he stubs out his cigarette, leans over and kisses her on the cheek in a brotherly way, pulls up and straightens the satin eiderdown, then turns off the light and gets into his own bed. For a long long time Beattie lies there staring into the darkness. Charles's revelations are a fitting conclusion to a week of strange and preposterous events.

CHAPTER
SIXTEEN

'YOU CAN TYPE, but what else? Shorthand? Filing? Can you operate a switchboard?'

The employment agency is hot and indescribably drab, a small airless grey-painted room with a desk, two chairs and a filing cabinet. At the desk sits a girl of Virginia's age with skin tones that almost exactly match the paint. When she speaks – she never smiles – it is to reveal teeth so discoloured and so randomly placed that Virginia feels obliged to address herself to the wall behind the girl's head.

The girl clearly regards Virginia as a threat to the nation's security.

'What was your last job?' she adds suddenly. 'Why did you leave?'

Patiently, Virginia explains yet again about the air raid and the months she has spent in between in a nursing home. The girl sniffs horribly and clearly does not believe her.

'Well, if anything comes in for you, Miss Musgrave' – the "if" is about the size of the Albert Memorial – 'we'll let you know.'

Virginia closes the frosted-glass door behind her and makes her way into the warm Soho evening. She has very little to do. Willy is out of London and, besides, he is not currently very pleased with her. Really, she should go back to the hostel. Instead she goes into a café on the corner of the street. The man behind the hissing tea-urn eyes her with obvious admiration and asks her in wooing tones what she wants. For her, he adds, he can rustle up toast and apricot jam.

'I'm sure I know your face,' he adds. 'You're in films, aren't you?'

'Flatterer,' says Virginia.

'No, really. Aren't you with the film people? They all come in here. Why, I've served Mavis Du Foy with beans on toast in my time.'

Virginia shakes her head, amused, then settles down at a table by the window with an evening paper. The secretarial jobs all sound indescribably dire. The man brings over toast and margarine and a curious jam that tastes something of apricots but has lumps in it that look suspiciously like marrow. Or is it turnip? Virginia sips her tea, staring unseeingly at a poster on the wall telling her there is a holiday welcome for her at Southend-on-Sea. What she needs right now is not so much a holiday as a new job and somewhere else to live. Sheer inertia has driven her back to the Grangemouth, to a room in another house. Summer is coming to an end, and her headaches are getting less. But even in spite of the fact that her mother has now belatedly decided to give her an allowance she still needs a job.

When she'd left the London Hospital, she'd been sent to nursing home in north London to convalesce. There the days had passed peacefully as she sat or read in the garden. A few friends had braved the journey out to see her, whilst others, like Theo Beavers, wrote long, cheering but admonitory letters, urging her to leave London and come and live in Scotland.

'There's no future in staying there,' he concluded. 'They can start bombing again any day. It won't take the Germans long to get to Stalingrad, judging by the speed they got through the Low Countries. Then they'll turn back to Britain and finish what they started. Don't forget your job's here. We can always find a place for you to stay.'

Lucy also had had to content herself with writing, not visiting, claiming she was in the teeth of harvesting, but still managed to find time to go to Ipswich to buy Virginia books and send them on to her. There had been a letter from her this very morning, hoping Virginia was better, and ending up with a cryptic PS: does Virginia know anything about hepatitis? Virginia is still puzzling the significance of this.

Of the visitors who had turned up at the nursing home in person, Stephen had proved to be the most constant. He invariably arrived with anthologies of poetry, and peardrops which he said he got under the counter somewhere. They always came stuck together in the bottom of a brown paper bag. In between digging them out with his Scout's penknife, he'd outline the plot for a new novel, complain about the stagnant nature of his love-life, and hint darkly that the BBC were stifling his soul. Devora turned up once, ate most of the peardrops and announced that she did not like hospitals, she was funny that way. Willy also said he could not stand hospitals and their attendant messages of death and infirmity, but he did at least write and send her flowers, fruit and candy, so she could hardly complain.

But the most unexpected visitor was Brooke, who actually drove up to see her two Saturdays running. The meetings gave her much cause for reflection, not all of it pleasant. She had been touched by the concern he had apparently displayed but was aware for the first time how little they really communicated. He did volunteer that he was about to pilot a new plane that could fly immensely long distances and said it was a cracker. Also that he'd been to see a film about Bomber Command and that it had been most frightfully good. Analysing their meetings afterwards, Virginia bleakly concluded that all her life she had hoped there would be a moment when Brooke and she would open their hearts to each other. But for the first time she had had to accept that Brooke was simply incapable of the feelings she had long ascribed to him. Furthermore, he did not want to know about her own feelings and would have been embarrassed had she mentioned anything more personal than her headaches. It was the first time she was able to see her brother in a detached way, stripped of the glamour that had always surrounded him. He was like a locked room. Loving Brooke must be like endlessly tipping water on to a sponge: he absorbed it all and gave nothing back.

Her mother had also come to London and had managed to sit for a whole

211

hour with her without saying 'I told you so'. She had wanted Virginia to come back to the Dower House to convalesce, but Virginia had politely refused. It was one thing to spend a fairly amicable hour with her mother, but quite another to live with her.

Besides, Cecily's mother had asked her to stay at the Castle. It was a relief to be there, if only because she could talk about Cecily. The curious thing was that not one of her visitors had mentioned her, presumably thinking that the subject was too painful for Virginia to dwell on. Yet Virginia had longed and longed to talk to someone about her friend, for during those first delirious days at the hospital it was as if Cecily had become almost more real to Virginia than she had been alive. Virginia thought about her obsessively and wept without restraint. It had been like the death of a beloved sister. No, it was worse than that. It had been like the death of part of herself. Gradually it came to her that she was continuing to grieve so violently because she was afraid of losing Cecily altogether. But even as she grasped this she suddenly realized with absolute certainty that she would never lose Cecily, simply because Cecily had loved her and in doing so had mysteriously passed into Virginia's own heart and become part of her. She could not lose Cecily, because Cecily had loved her. Yet it was strange that even in the relief of that recognition there was no immediate peace. The knowledge was accompanied with a kind of anger at the power you gave people if you allowed yourself to love them. It was a dangerous business loving people, was her final unconscious conclusion. You open the door a crack, and they flooded in uncontrollably and made you vulnerable in new and terrifying ways.

By now the café is beginning to fill up, but Virginia, who normally has no trouble in placing people socially, is still not clear who the people are coming through the shabby door. Most unusually, there is no one wearing uniform, and they all make a great deal of noise. Perhaps they're all theatricals, thinks Virginia uneasily, then returns to her own interior reverie.

The trouble is that her life seems to have come to a full stop in every direction. There is no one she particularly wants to be with, and no place where she feels she really belongs. Devora has almost abandoned asking her out in the evenings. There is now a tidal wave of rich good-looking young Americans living in and around Grosvenor Square, and she could be out dancing every night if she wished. But so far she has manifestly refused to take advantage of the situation. It is six o'clock now, and she will be too late for supper. She decides she will eat here and then go to the cinema afterwards.

'I say,' says a voice beside her, 'is this place taken? Good heavens! Hello, Virginia.'

It is the elusive Rachel Stearn. Virginia has not seen her since she returned to the hostel, but she is exactly as she remembered her – tired, greasy-faced and businesslike. Today she is wearing a black shirt and trousers, her hair in its usual limp bob pushed behind her ears. She pulls out the vacant chair.

'I was awfully sorry about Cecily,' she says lamely. 'You're back at the Grange now, aren't you? You've got my cousin Hetty's room. She moved out in June.'

The man at the counter comes over to their table, placing a sardine salad, rissoles and baked beans on toast in front of Rachel, who proceeds to eat them in alternative mouthfuls, as if she hasn't seen food for years. The door jangles open and a small girl with red curls tied in a turban darts over to their table.

'Have you seen Derek?' she asks without preamble. 'If he comes in, tell him I've gone on. We went to see it last night at Tottenham Court Road. They cheer like anything afterwards, you know. Especially the RAF boys.'

'It is good, isn't it?' agrees Rachel, her rather heavy features lighting up. 'Are you stopping?'

'Can't. We're off to Scotland first thing. Something to do with children in schools,' she adds vaguely. 'God knows how long we'll be up there.' She waggles her fingers. 'See you when I see you. Don't let him get too conceited.' With that she vanishes.

Virginia would like to have followed up this cryptic exchange, but the delicate matter of the unknown nature of Rachel's profession lies like a boulder across their conversational path. Rachel eats on, absorbed. She has just started on the cold apple pie when the door opens again and a freckle-faced youth in painting overalls appears.

'He's waiting, you know.'

'I said I'd be back at seven and not one minute before,' snaps Rachel. 'Tell him to go for a walk or something.'

The door slams shut again, and Rachel stares moodily at her pie. 'Your time isn't your own,' she remarks to no one in particular. Then she remembers Virginia. 'What on earth are you doing in here? Are you slumming or have you decided you want to be an actress? I thought the Savoy was your normal stamping-ground.'

Her tone is far from friendly, and Virginia stares at her.

'I'm looking for a job and I had an appointment at an employment agency on the corner. Why on earth would I be hanging around this dump if I wanted to be an actress?' she enquires coldly.

'Well, this is where most of the film production companies eat. Before they go to the pub.'

'Here?' says Virginia in tones of the purest surprise. Her own view of life behind the cameras has been formed entirely through show-business films about bitter-sweet off-stage romances that seem to take place at the Ritz. 'It's not very glamorous, is it?'

'It's not a very glamorous profession,' says Rachel, again not in a very friendly way, and finally the penny drops.

'Rachel, is that what you do for a living? Do you work for a film company?'

'Of course I do,' says Rachel matter-of-factly, clearly unaware of the rumours Devora has been circulating about her. 'Otherwise why on earth would I be in Wardour Street at this time of night?'

'Well, no one at the Grangemouth seemed to know what you did,' says Virginia, picking her words with some care. 'We just used to see you coming in at strange hours looking exhausted.'

'Oh, that was because of my cousin Hetty. My father wanted me to stay

213

in Manchester and get a job in my cousin's firm. I wanted to come to London and get a job in films, but Father wouldn't hear of me leaving home unless I came with Hetty and lived in the hostel for Jewish girls on Gower Street. I ask you. I held out for Grangemouth and took a job in a solicitor's office. Then after a few months I simply handed in my notice where I was working and didn't tell Hetty.'

'So how did you get into films?'

'Film *production*,' she corrects. 'Gosh, I'm starving. Have you any more pie, Tony? And a tea, please. I looked up all the production companies and wrote to them and I got a job as a secretary with Reel Film Productions. That's where I am now. Except that I'm training to be a film editor,' she says in a voice which barely masks her pride. 'We all do a bit of everything. Mostly I edit film, but when I went on location once I was the unit manager. There were only five of us on the shoot,' she admits, 'but I did the manager's job. Gladys was furious,' she adds with relish, smiling at the memory. 'Of course, you never get any free time, and people keep asking why you're not in the services, but it's jolly interesting. And we get a petrol allowance, which is divine. Hamish Grange trained me,' she adds, lighting up a very pungent Woodbine, then leans forward with the air of someone admitting to a guilty secret. 'You see, I want to be a director.'

'And go to Hollywood?'

'No, silly. Why on earth would I want to do that when there's a perfectly good film industry here?' says Rachel, scandalized.

Virginia feels a faint echo of a previous conversation but can't place it.

'There's so much going on here. We do mostly documentary stuff. We're funded by the Government, so we do a lot of shorts as well – you know, torch flashes, what to do with a butterfly bomb, how to use a stirrup pump, what to do on an allotment, that sort of thing. Then we do big features, usually about groups of people with a particular job in the war. *Bomber Command* was one of ours,' she adds with some pride. 'I helped to cut that.'

'How extraordinary. I was thinking of going to see that tonight. My brother's a pilot, and he saw it and thought it was frightfully good.'

'That's what Trudy was talking about. She was the girl in the turban. She did continuity on it. But do go and see it. He's—'

The door opens yet again, and a red-faced bald-headed Scotsman suddenly appears at their table.

'Rachel, have you gone into early retirement or can I expect to see you back some time this evening?' he asks in the pure fluting accents of Glasgow, his tufted sandy eyebrows jerking furiously.

'I'm just finishing supper,' says Rachel crossly.

'In that case I'll join you,' says Hamish Grange and proceeds to eat the remains of Rachel's apple pie. He fixes Virginia with a glittering grey eye. 'I suppose you're trying to get a screen test?'

'I'm trying to get a job as a secretary,' says Virginia, affronted. 'Why on earth should I want to be in films?'

'A good question. No one's ever found a satisfactory answer. Well, there's a secretarial job going in our production offices because Doris has handed in her notice again and this time she says it's for good. Apparently

214

she's been offered a job as understudy on an ENSA tour doing *No, No, Nanette*.

'She must have lost her mind,' says Rachel.

'She never had one,' says Hamish briefly. 'You employ a girl like that for the pleasure in seeing her bend over the wastepaper-basket.'

'Well, then,' Rachel tells Virginia, 'there's a job. Mr Myerberg's secretary. The trouble is you'll hate him.'

'Hate who, or is it *whom*?'

'They won't want to hear filthy grammatical talk like that in the office,' Hamish admonishes her.

'The company has two producers, Pat Blain and Ira Myerberg. Pat's the big noise. Everybody treats him like God, though he's very mild. He's all right, and I suppose Ira is really,' says Rachel doubtfully. 'It's just that he used to be an accountant and was only brought in to keep us out of the red. But he's seen too many films about the way film people behave, though he's sex mad anyway. Though it's not his fault. The girls who apply for a job in film production always think it's a quick way to a screen test. They don't even realize we're not that kind of film company. Doris, for example, was Miss Leamington Spa 1938 and she was frightfully pretty and – er – well endowed. The girl before that was Pearl – she was Miss Devon Cream Puff, I think. Anyway, they all want screen tests and they all end up leaving because their bottoms are black and blue. Poor Mr Myerberg,' says Rachel, somewhat surprisingly. 'I can see why he's confused. They come in with cleavages cleaving, all looking terribly available, then when he takes advantage they slap his face. He doesn't realize they wouldn't give their all for anything less than a one-way ticket to Hollywood.'

'He sounds appalling,' says Virginia faintly.

'He's a woolly lamb most of the time. Why don't you go in and see him?'

'What, just turn up?'

'That's right. You'd better get in quick, though, or they'll get an agency girl.'

'Are you sure Doris has gone?'

'Certain sure,' says Hamish. 'She took her lightbulb with her, the hard-hearted girl.'

'Oh, dash, that means she's taken her soap as well,' laments Rachel.

'What should I wear?' calls Virginia after their departing figures.

'Try a suit of armour,' calls Hamish, and they disappear hiccuping with laughter into the early evening.

The film about Bomber Command is at a news theatre in Tottenham Court Road. First there is a long newsreel about the German troops marching in Russia. Then a series of shorts on how to deal with fires in the home. This is followed by two excellent Tom and Jerrys, then the film itself. There is no plot; it simply follows the career of one crew at a Norfolk base from early evening when they are briefed prior to their takeoff, and there is some extraordinary footage of them dropping their bombs over their targets in the Ruhr, followed by the long journey home.

The sight of planes taking off over the flat Norfolk fields and church towers affects Virginia profoundly. For the first time, she knows the

215

anxieties that young men like Brooke are subjected to every night of their flying lives. The audience, who have been restive and permanently on the move during the earlier part of the programme, sit in silence, listening as the reverberating pulse of the propellers ebbs and flows across the darkening sky. At the end they actually clap, and Virginia finds herself wiping away tears. Then the people in front of her stand up, and she misses half the credits, but she does at least see the name of the film company: Reel Film Productions and an address off Soho Square.

I'll go tomorrow, thinks Virginia, suddenly elated by the prospect, and ponders what to wear. If she goes in her tight black dress and furs, she will clearly get the job but it will be raising quite vain hopes in Mr Myerberg's susceptible breast. Though why these hopes are now in vain Virginia has no more way of knowing than why she had said yes to so many people last year. The fact is that at present sex simply isn't what she wants. Willy isn't amused at discovering he is required to make the lightning transition from lover to best friend, and there have been a couple of rather unpleasant scenes with people still in the grip of out-of-date information about Virginia's sexual availability. The fact is that for the time being she simply doesn't want to do it.

In the end she decides on her best tweed suit and silk blouse and is ironing the latter when Devora comes sighing into the room, her face a lurid rash of red spots.

'I suppose it's useless expecting any sympathy from you.'

'You were warned about buying cosmetics from men on street-corners. Cheer up, it'll probably only last a day.'

Devora sniffs. 'Did you get a job?'

'No, but I heard of a vacancy in a film production company.'

Virginia describes her meeting with Rachel Stearn. Devora is agog.

'So that's what she's been doing. A film company. Get you. I've often thought I could make it in films.'

'You'd have to start washing your neck before you could risk anything approaching a close-up. Anyway, it's not that kind of film. They make information films and documentaries.'

'Oh, them,' says Devora dismissively. 'How boring. About real people's lives, I suppose. I mean, why bother? I went to a party once in Charlotte Street; there was a whole crowd there. Terribly scruffy. Not a suit in sight. I couldn't stand them. I suppose I'm just too lively a person. I need variety, glamour, excitement.'

'You find them, do you, in the Ministry of Food?'

'You're just jealous.'

Devora fiddles with her watch-strap then says, far too casually: 'Was that David Sinclair who took you out last night?'

'What's it to you?'

'Don't be so snappish. I thought I recognized him, that's all, when you went out to the car. We were at dancing school together.'

'And he never told me,' marvels Virginia.

'How did you meet him?'

Virginia shakes out her blouse and hangs it on a hanger. 'At Adam's drinks-party.'

'He's stinking rich,' says Devora sourly. 'And of course there's a title when his uncle pops off. Of course,' she adds, cheering up, 'he's rather dull. Are you having a thing with him?'

'Hardly.'

'Fix you up with a terrific Texan tomorrow.'

'No, thanks,' says Virginia, switching off the iron.

'You know, it doesn't grow again if you stop doing it,' observes Devora nastily and flounces out.

Reel Film Productions have their offices at the top of a tall thin house in a seedy street off Soho Square. At ten o'clock Virginia knocks at the outer door, but there is no reply. The only sign of life is the noise of someone droning faintly in one of the inner offices. Virginia follows the sound, taps on the door and goes in. A rather formidable-looking man is sitting on the desk, his arms folded, his chin sunk on to his chin as he intones something Celtic and melancholy. He is wearing a hideous old tweed jacket with leather patches on the elbows and a white Arran polo-neck jersey. Instinctively Virginia feels she has come to the right place. In the corner a girl is filing letters. She is sallow-faced and bespectacled with a head full of oily sausage curls worn in a pompadour.

'I'm looking for Mr Myerberg,' says Virginia, and the singing abruptly ceases.

The man and the girl exchange a look of amusement which annoys Virginia intensely.

'They're all down at the cutting-room. May I help? I'm Pat Blain, the other producer in the company.'

'Has Mr Myerberg promised you a test?' says the girl, running her eyes derisively over Virginia's immaculate platinum page-boy hairstyle and well-cut suit.

Virginia treats them both to her most freezing stare. 'I understand Mr Myerberg wants a secretary.'

'Can you type?' says the man.

Virginia loses her temper. 'Of course I can type,' she says witheringly. 'Why on earth would I be applying for a job as his secretary otherwise?'

This silences them both for a minute.

'Do you have any references?'

Silently Virginia produces the two letters that Theo has written for her. Pat Blain reads them, taking his time. He looks at Virginia with a disconcertingly direct stare that belies his mild manner.

'You'd better go and have a cup of tea and come back at about twelve.'

As Virginia shuts the outer door she hears the girl say: 'She won't last five minutes. All girls like that want is a screen test.'

Virginia wonders if she will faintly prejudice her chances if she goes back and punches the girl on the nose, but instead goes for a walk round Soho. When she returns the outer office is silent. The inner office is jammed with people and cigarette smoke. There is a meeting going on. Everybody turns round to stare, and finally Mr Blain comes to her rescue.

'Ira, this is . . . er. . . . She's looking for a job.'

A dark-haired, rather fleshy young man with bulging eyes and pebble glasses gets slowly to his feet, eyeing Virginia as if he can't believe his luck. He leads her into his own office and waits expectantly.

'I'm a friend of Rachel Stearn's,' says Virginia coldly. 'She told me you needed a secretary.'

'Ah, Doris,' says Mr Myerberg, somewhat elliptically. 'I've studied your references,' he goes on, his eyes firmly fixed on Virginia's breasts. 'I really like them. However,' he says, abruptly jerking his eyes away and adopting a stern manner, 'this is a demanding job, you know. Long hours, lots of pressure, plenty of fun but in its right place, mind.'

Virginia is speechless. Fortunately he interprets her silence as rapt interest.

'We do need someone in a hurry,' he admits finally. 'Supposing we take you on for a week and see how we like each other?'

Pay is finally mentioned. Apparently she will be getting ten shillings more than at Marwicks, to her quiet jubilation.

'Come back at two and I'll explain the ropes to you,' Ira promises, his eyes gleaming oddly behind his glasses.

Two o'clock turns out to be a repeat of ten o'clock except that this time not even Pat Blain is there. The girl, whose name is Millie, regards her with increased suspicion.

'Got the job, have you?' she enquires, mildly disagreeably. 'Come on, you can come clean with me. What are you really after? You'll never get a test with this lot and, if you did, frankly you'd have to do something about that accent.'

'I simply haven't got a clue what you're talking about,' drawls Virginia, turning on Millie the famous ice-blue Musgrave stare that has quelled natives and yokels for over two hundred years.

'Don't tell me, then,' says Millie, affronted. 'See if I care.'

She begins to rattle away noisily at her typewriter. Virginia is soon deeply immersed in *Vanity Fair*. At three o'clock there is a phone call from Mr Myerberg saying he has had to see a distributor and could Virginia come in first thing tomorrow and they will sort something out. Resignedly Virginia picks up her bag and spends a useful evening thinning out her carrots.

No further comment is ever made about Virginia being on trial and, after two weeks of waiting for the expected showing of ropes by Mr Myerberg, Virginia decides it is down to her to try to interpret this curious looking-glass world. It is quite unlike anything she has ever known. For a start everybody loves their job and talks of nothing else. Now, Virginia quite enjoyed working at Marwicks, but in the main she still sees work as the intervening slab that separates the morning and the evening. Here there is no such division. It is nothing to go in in the morning and find the office thick with cigarette smoke at nine o'clock, full of people with red-rimmed eyes discussing the editing they had done overnight. Exactly who all these people are and what they do will clearly take weeks to work out. Especially as Millie parts

218

with information as if it is money being docked from her pay-packet. Occasionally Pat Blain will volunteer information. For instance, in answer to her tentative enquiry 'What's the difference between a producer and a director?' he'd furrowed his brow and said: 'That's a good question. Put simply, the director is responsible for everything that happens in front of the camera, and the producer takes care of everything that happens behind it. You know, budgeting, sorting out casting, the script, keeping overall control. Mind you,' he goes on ruminatively, 'that doesn't mean that I don't myself direct when I feel like it, but in the main the definition holds good.'

'So where does the money come from for making these films?'

'The Min. of Inf., and it's my job to convince them it's money well spent.'

It is, then, apparently Mr Myerberg's job to prevent the company spending any of the money at all. There are usually three films in production, and almost every day when Virginia opens the post there is at least one set of laboriously inscribed figures from an inscrutable group of men called 'The Hourly Boys'. These men, Millie tells her with the utmost reluctance, are the cameramen, the carpenters and the soundmen, who, like the rest of the location unit, are paid by the hour.

The rest of the company receive monthly salaries paid from Mr Myerberg's coffers with the utmost reluctance. Once a week Mr Myerberg sighs and groans over the company accounts with the accountant, Mr Samson, and many pleasant jests are exchanged about the Herculean nature of their task. Every day seems to bring a new face into the office. Virginia never does discover how many people work for the company, because besides the three major features there are also numerous shorts in production.

'What happens to the film? I mean, as it's made.'

'Well, if it's location it's sent to London and developed in one of the labs round here,' says Pat Blain helpfully enough. 'Then, it's either taken down to Denham to be edited or handed over to Hamish and Rachel to be edited in the basement. They do something called a "rough cut". Then this is all put together to make something called "the rushes", which is the first put-together sequence of the unedited film. I have to see the rushes at this stage for a sort of progress report, and then Mr Myerberg has a look at them to see how his money is being spent. When the filming is finished, the director edits the final version with Hamish in the basement. Then they add the sound and the music.'

Virginia is grateful for this simple guide to making a film but still finds the personalities of Reel Film Productions hard to comprehend. From the start she feels that she simply does not fit in. The offices are always full of people making jokes in a rather ferociously funny way; she strongly suspects that most of the time they are laughing at her rather than with her. Perhaps it is her accent. Perhaps if she blurs her vowels and speaks through her nose like Millie people will stop turning round and staring every time she opens her mouth. Quite apart from that, there is a fairly long stretch at the beginning when every time she opens her mouth she somehow manages to put her foot in it.

Like the time when everybody had gone to the Highlander leaving Virginia holding the fort. The outer door burst open and a furious red-faced man with

pebble glasses and an enormous beer-gut had reeled in. He had leant threat-
eningly over Virginia's desk, breathing whisky fumes, and told her thickly to
tell Pat Blain that if he, Billy Gavin, didn't get his money by six o'clock, then
he, Billy Gavin, would be taking his services elsewhere. Later on that day
Virginia had duly relayed the message, adding helpfully that she thought he
seemed like some kind of vulgar drunken tradesperson. The tradesperson
turned out to be their star cameraman, and Virginia could see that this story
would still be circulating Reel Films long after she'd left. So, all in all, despite
the interest of the job and the better pay, Virginia has already made a mental
note that she will give the job three months' trial and move on if it is not to
her liking. There are a couple of things that definitely bother her, the chief
being Alexis Seligman. About a week after she had joined Reel Films she was
having a drink with Stephen in a pub in Old Compton Street. Raising her eyes
from her drink, she saw the back view of somebody disappearing out the
door and was almost sure it was Alexis. Without thinking, she had called his
name. From the way that he had turned round and said hello Virginia was
sure that he had already seen her and was trying to get out unnoticed. He was
fairly cool, to say the least, considering that quite a few months had passed
since she had seen him. Virginia, who had been disposed to be pleasant, was
furious at his determined attempts to be unfriendly. After a few noncommittal unpleasantries Alexis had simply nodded and said he had to go.
Virginia had been furious. 'What a boorish person he is,' she complained to
the loyal Stephen.

'Not a very warm reception,' he agreed, adding: 'It was strange really,
because he'd been staring at you for about half an hour from the other side of
the bar. You didn't see him, did you? I thought at first he was looking at me,
but no such luck.'

'Oh,' said Virginia, perplexed but not mollified. So it was with no
feeling of delighted surprise that she discovered, fairly early on, that Alexis
also worked for Reel Film Productions. As one of the directors, if not its star
turn. . . . It was he who had made *Bomber Command*, and he is currently in
Blackburn shooting some kind of epic about girls in tank factories. She
knows he does not like her and she does not like him, and furthermore he
knows rather more about her than she would like broadcast round this
particular office. He is at least out of London for a couple of months and, so
far as Virginia is concerned, is yet another good reason for avoiding a
long-term commitment to Reel Films.

But the more immediate problem turns out to be Mr Myerberg, who's
fantasy about Virginia grows steadily more obtrusive as the days and then
the weeks roll by. In Virginia's presence, Mr Myerberg's knees jig, his feet
tap, his Adam's apple jerks convulsively, and he is either losing his voice or
clearing his throat so explosively that Virginia's nerves, which have never
been the same since the bombing, are soon stretched to breaking-point. He
sits indecently near her during dictation until Virginia is forced finally to tell
him one day that he is giving her claustrophobia. He has an infuriating habit
of simply materializing out of nowhere during her lunch hour, usually when
she's trying to finish her library book. His invariable gambit at moments like
this is to leap nimbly on to the side of her desk and, cigarette in hand and in

the face of her total indifference, to try to regale her with what in American films are known as 'wisecracks'.

At the beginning he is an irritant, but only a minor one. After the third week he begins to press his suit more strongly. The trouble with Mr Myerberg is that he has seen too many 'B' movies. Having become a film producer (in the financial sense at least) has raised the totally vain hope that what he normally only experiences secondhand on the silver screen at the Gaumont, Golders Green, will now be his for the asking. He seems to have some kind of running scenario in his head entitled 'The Ladykiller and the Blonde/Redhead/Brunette Secretary', and to Virginia's extreme annoyance she discovers that she is currently filling the supporting role.

In the normal run of events she would have had no difficulty handling him, were it not for the fact that at Reel Films they all work odd hours and Mr Myerberg's courage seems to rise proportionately as the hands of the office clock move past six o'clock. For a while Virginia successfully evades him by developing a headache on the dot of 5.45 each day and coming in early to finish the work. In the end it is Pat Blain who unwittingly precipitates the crisis. There is a fortnightly meeting for all the directors and scriptwriters who are in London, and normally Millie types the agenda and notes. On this particular day Millie is needed at Denham, and Pat asks Virginia if she'd mind staying on and doing it.

Owing to the scholarly awfulness of Pat's handwriting, she is still hard at work at 8.30 when Mr Myerberg makes a highly unwelcome appearance in the outer office. Virginia gives him a perfunctory greeting and speeds up her typing. With any luck she'll be out of here in ten minutes. That is, until Mr Myerberg looms up behind her, tells her what lovely hair she has, and proceeds to try to stroke it. Virginia jerks her head away and gives him a freezing look. Unfortunately, the fact that she hasn't actually slapped his face – the usual response to Mr Myerberg's courting moves – is seen as an actual encouragement, whereupon he leaps upon the desk beside her, leans forward and says, 'May I call you Virginia? I think you could be my sort of girl, baby,' and proceeds to try to kiss her.

Virginia has never been so outraged in her life. She pulls angrily away, feels around beside her for her handbag and, grabbing it by its strap, swings it up and sideways and hits Mr Myerberg as hard as she can. He gives a gargle of disbelief; then, his long legs thrashing wildly, overbalances and disappears over the side of the desk into the wastepaper-basket.

Virginia leaps to her feet and prepares to indulge in a little ritual rage.

'How dare you!' she shouts, thinking if he can follow a script so can she. 'What sort of a girl do you think I am? What have I ever done to lead you to think that I would find your approaches acceptable?' Elizabeth Bennett herself couldn't have faulted that one, she thought with satisfaction. At this precise moment the door opens, and Millie and Pat Blain appear as Mr Myerberg rolls feebly on the floor in an attempt to free his foot from the wastepaper-basket. Ignoring them, Virginia slams her way through the remaining text at top speed and Mr Myerberg slinks away.

This incident, ludicrous as it is, proves to be something of a turning-point in her life at Reel Films. People are still equally rude and offhand, but

221

at the same time she is treated with a degree of respect. Mr Myerberg could not be more formal and more resentful, and abruptly reverts to calling her 'Miss Musgrave'.

Things suddenly start to get better. Millie extends a cautious invitation to lunch, Virginia goes drinking with several of the directors, and two of the company scriptwriters take her out to dinner complaining, in almost identical language, that the film industry is a large-scale plot to sabotage the written word. Rachel, once she has seen that Virginia has become accepted and is no longer the greenest girl in the school, unbends slightly over coffee and tells her to be wary of Millie as she is in love with Pat Blain and still suspects Virginia's motives, that Trudy the continuity girl has a wicked tongue and can't keep a secret, and Gladys is the only one really to avoid. Gladys is the unit manager of the film Alexis is making in Blackburn. Virginia absorbs all this information, making a mental note to keep her eye on the progress of Alexis' film. It is the middle of November now, and she reckons she will at least be free of his company until Christmas.

CHAPTER
SEVENTEEN

*L*UCY IS CLEARLY GOING TO BE LATE. For once Virginia doesn't mind, ensconced quietly as she is behind a gin and tonic at one of the best tables at Le Poisson d'Or. A pianist is discreetly rendering a selection from *The Desert Song*, from time to time giving Virginia a hot and melting eye. Serenely, Virginia concentrates on her drink, secure in the knowledge that she is the best-dressed and prettiest woman in the restaurant.

When Lucy had written last week to say that she would be in London for the day and could they meet for supper, Virginia had been surprised to discover how much she was looking forward to seeing her. At the same time, however delighted she was to see her friend, it was also crucial to look her very best to mark the clearest possible distinction between Virginia's life of metropolitan sophistication and Lucy's existence down on the farm.

Virginia goes to order another gin only to find a fresh drink already at her elbow with the compliments, says Ernest the head waiter, of the gentleman by the door. Virginia raises her eyes to the appropriate table, faintly smiles her thanks and lowers her eyes coolly again, examining herself with some satisfaction in the cutlery. It has taken her some time to get her style right, but now finally she knows exactly how she wants to look. The big breakthrough had come when she'd simply realized one day that if she wanted more clothes they didn't necessarily have to be new ones. She had discovered a perfectly splendid woman in the Marylebone Lane who sold a mixture of good secondhand clothes and antique bric-à-brac, and from her Virginia had bought a series of judiciously selected items guaranteed to give style and tone to her existing wardrobe.

Tonight she is wearing a small stark black tricorn hat under which her hair is swept up in a series of carefully pinned thick honey-coloured curls. The tight black fitted velvet jacket which does such startling things for Virginia's figure is actually Victorian, while the ruffled white blouse with its fine frills cascading almost to her knuckles has been made by Virginia herself. Her make-up is more discreet than it was a year ago but somewhat more accomplished. She gives her own reflection a little nod of approval. At this moment there is a flurry by the main door.

'Lucy! I say, Lucy! I'm over here, you twit!'

'Lord, I missed you in this intimate gloom. Vir, how lovely to see you.'

Smilingly, Virginia proffers her cheek.

'You look absolutely topping,' continues Lucy, seating herself comfortably beside her. 'New hairstyle? Really suits you. Yes, I'll have a sherry, please.'

Virginia, competently ordering the drinks, is aware of slightly mixed feelings, some of which are a surprise. Lucy looks completely different. As the Yanks would say, 'She looks really OK'. Not *soignée* or *svelte* or any of the words that Virginia aspires to, but definitely not *farouche*. In fact she looks very nice indeed. Her hair, grown out of that awful woolly perm, is now worn loosely in a shoulder-length bob held back from her face with a tortoiseshell clip. Her skin is tanned and clear, her lipstick and powder skilfully applied. She is wearing an extremely smart costume in a particularly pretty shade of hazy blue with a matching silk blouse.

'You look lovely yourself.'

'Do I? Gosh, that's nice to know,' says Lucy simply, making Virginia feel guilty. 'There's something about London that always makes me feel stupid. When I leave home I feel perfectly all right, then by the time I get here it feels as if I've put on all that fat again and I've mysteriously developed spots. Strange, isn't it?'

Virginia knows very well what she means, especially since, paradoxically, she has not yet risked going back home to the Dower House lest she have a similar experience. But she's not ready to be quite as honest as that, so she says: 'Don't you miss London at all?'

'Not at *all*. My feet are positively aching, and I've only walked here from Claridges. And yet I'm never tired in the country.'

Once the waiter had taken their order, Lucy stares around her with frank interest at her surroundings.

'There's nothing remotely like this in Ipswich, you know,' she observes. 'It's the only big town I ever see and then only when the pigs go to the market. Mother says my social life is getting too limited.' Lucy giggles. 'I don't think she means the pigs, though.'

'How are your parents?'

'Oh, it turns out it's only Mother down here after all. She sends you masses of love by the way. I'd really hoped Daddy had come down, but he's been suffering from gout, so Mother persuaded him to stay at home.'

'What were they coming down here for anyway?'

'Oh, several reasons, all bookish. Gosh, oysters! I can't remember the last time I had them. Mother's won some gold medal from the Children's Library Association, and that was being presented this afternoon. And she had to come down to sign some new American contract this morning. Oh! Did I tell you? A Canadian film company wants to film the first five 'Leafy Tree' stories.'

'Good heavens,' says Virginia with commendable restraint. 'How wonderful for your mother. Have her wartime school stories done well?'

'I should say so. *High School Girls in Exile* is already in its sixth printing. I didn't have a chance to find out any more, because I thought Mother and I were having lunch together, but it turned out to be a buffet lunch for fifty at the Savoy for Ma's fans. Gosh, I'd forgotten how embarrassing that can all be. I wouldn't mind, but all the fans are so old they can't have even started to read Ma's books till they were in their late twenties. Ridiculous, isn't it?'

'Arrested development,' comments Virginia knowledgeably. She has recently read a magazine article about Freud.

'Potty if you ask me,' says Lucy briskly, who clearly hasn't. 'Gosh, Vir, you look so glamorous it's quite intimidating.' Her tone is wistful. 'Have you got loads of beaux to your string?'

'Well, one or two. And one in particular is rather nice. But you look simply marvellous yourself. Your hair is so pretty now. Did you have it done in Ipswich?'

'Oh, no, Lily Kedge came up to the farm last week and permed it for me. You are an old snob, Vir. I can see exactly what you're thinking.'

'Well, she is the local poacher's daughter. I can't believe your mother would approve of you widening your social circle with *that* tribe. And I can't believe she's a very amusing companion. Unless you want to learn about mole-traps.'

'Well, I don't expect you to find her that funny but we have a lot of jokes together. She's ordinary like me,' says Lucy resignedly, aware that for all her improved appearance and confidence she has slipped straight back into her usual role of trying to placate Virginia by flattering. 'I mean, I'd never be able to live on my own in London as a bachelor girl and have a glamorous job with a film company,' she adds with a glance at Virginia's extraordinary hat, perfect maquillage and unchipped nail-varnish. 'Lord, I've got so much saved up to tell you, and now it's completely gone out of my head. But I'll be seeing you at Christmas, won't I? I saw your ma at church last week and she said you might be coming home.'

'She's written and asked me, but I simply haven't made up my mind. It's a pretty gruesome prospect except that I saw Uncle Piers last week and he told me something so extraordinary about Ma that I feel positively obliged to go home. Did you know she's got a boyfriend? Someone called Bertie. Does that mean anything to you?'

Lucy is as intrigued as herself.

'I wonder if it could be that little chap with a sandy moustache. He was at a drinks do at the Dower House about a month ago, but there were so many other people milling around I never sorted out who he was. I suppose it could have been him,' adds Lucy thoughtfully. 'I mean, he was hanging around your mother all the time and laughing too much at her jokes.'

'That must be him. Only a man in love could find my mother amusing,' says Virginia unfeelingly.

'Oh, come off it, Vir, she's a lot better than she was.'

'Will you get much time off at Christmas?'

'Not really. The cows still have to be fed and milked and watered. I had to plead, beg and cajole to get today off, I can tell you.'

'What time do you get up?'

'Oh, about five usually.'

Virginia feels quite faint and falls on her steak with some alacrity.

'It's not so bad really,' goes on Lucy. 'I found the trick is to tear yourself out of bed before you're properly awake. Then the animals are so pleased to see you it makes it all worth while. Cows can be surprisingly affectionate.

225

And we've got three heifers at present, and they're the dearest little things. Our milk yields have shot up since I've had sole charge of the herd. Oh, you mustn't let me go on like this for ever; it must be so boring for you.'

'It certainly has the charm of novelty. Do you hear much from old Hugh?'

'Since he was ill his letters have been a bit sporadic. I tend to get a long period of silence, then I get six together.'

'Do you miss him madly?'

Lucy blushes, disconcerted by the direct question.

'Well, yes, I suppose so—'

'You mean you don't,' teases Virginia. 'At heart I think you prefer the cows.'

'Virginia, you are *awful*. I didn't say that at all. It's just jolly difficult to try to keep a relationship going when you've only got letters. I try to make mine as interesting as possible. But there was more to say when I was travelling around with a threshing gang with the other girls. Now I'm on my own there's nothing that's particularly new unless we've had the ratcatchers in or something.'

'I kept on meaning to ask you – what was all that about hepatitis in your letters last summer? I was touched by your belief in my medical knowledge.'

Virginia is trying to catch the waiter's attention as she speaks and misses the sudden guarded expression on Lucy's face.

'Oh, that – it was just Hugh. He got ill in May and he – he wrote some quite odd letters afterwards. I got a bit worried in case he wasn't getting over it properly. I went to see Dr Body and he said he was probably just depressed at being away from me for so long. But I think he's better now. I feel guilty sometimes about my letters being so dull. We used to talk a lot about books, but nowadays I'm so tired I go to bed straight after supper so there isn't really much time for reading. Unless I make an effort I don't see anybody other than the McFees from one week's end to the next. Oh, and Jubal. He's the oldest farmworker and he talks quite a lot to me.'

'It was the most incredible stroke of luck, you getting a permanent job near Musgrave.'

'You don't know the half of it,' says Lucy with some feeling. 'I never ever expected it. I was quite resigned to being casual labour for the whole of the war. Then my rep pitched up one evening and said that a farmer had asked for a permanent girl near Musgrave. I ran straight upstairs and packed and I moved the same night. Do you know the McFees? It's one of your family farms.'

'Oh, vaguely. I think they were at the garden-party. There are a couple of Scottish families out that way; I think they all came down in the twenties. From Lanarkshire, wasn't it? One of their daughters was a parlourmaid at the Dower House until she got married. Don't you find them awfully dour?'

'Well, they aren't what you'd call great chatterers. But they all work incredibly hard, even Mrs McFee, and it's a wonderfully run farm. And they're very appreciative of what I do even if they don't pay much. Gosh, that was delicious. That pudding alone will give me something to talk about for weeks.'

'To whom?'

'Oh, Lily and Beattie—'

Too late Lucy realizes her mistake.

'What on earth do you want to talk to her for?'

There is a note in her voice which makes Lucy instantly defensive.

'I like Beattie. And she's having the most frightful time. Her mother had a stroke in October and she was at the cottage hospital at Dereham Market for nearly a month. Beattie's had to cope with everything. I've been in to see Mrs Blythe once or twice, but she hardly knows who her husband is, let alone anyone else.'

Virginia yawns delicately and orders coffee.

'And Mrs Blythe has been incredibly decent to me. I saw her at church last Easter and we were chatting about shortages and I happened to mention that I didn't seem to have any clothes for the summer and what a joke it was when I'd brought that great trunk of stuff home from Paris for my season. So Mrs Blythe said she'd take it all in for me. Of course I paid her for it, but she really did them beautifully. Don't you remember this suit? It's the one I got from Madame Vionnet in the rue du Bac. Don't you remember we used to meet Ferdinand in the café next door after my fittings? Goodness, that seems another age now, doesn't it? Anyway, I suddenly went from being the girl with no clothes to being a girl with a whole new wardrobe. Why, I even wore this suit to Beattie's wedding.'

Virginia's cigarette abruptly freezes in mid-trajectory to her scarlet mouth.

'Beattie's wedding? When? To whom?'

She is so clearly taken aback that Lucy stares at her in surprise.

'She got married in August. Didn't I tell you? Lord, it must have been just before the thresher broke down and I didn't get in touch with anybody for a few weeks. Trust me to miss out reporting the only big event in my social calender. It was a really lovely do. They had the reception at the Goat afterwards. It all happened very quickly because Beattie's husband had been posted to Scotland. He only had forty-eight hours, just like us. Beattie looked absolutely wonderful. Like a film star. She wore my dress,' adds Lucy matter-of-factly, stirring more sugar into her coffee.

'She what?' asked Virginia, stunned. 'She wore your what?'

'I lent it to her, I—'

'She wore your wedding dress?'

'And veil. She looked—'

'*You let her wear your Norman Hartnell wedding dress*?'

Virginia looks so faint that a solicitous passing waiter actually offers her a glass of water. Brusquely Virginia waves him away. Then in a furious undertone she says: 'Lucy, have you gone absolutely mad?'

'What do you mean?'

'I think I've heard everything now. You let Beattie Blythe, the gardener's daughter. . . .' Virginia can hardly muster sufficient contempt to spit out the words. '*You let her wear your wedding dress*?'

'Well, why not?' For Lucy, her tone is almost sharp. 'What's the point in keeping it in a box for my grandchildren?'

Virginia fixes Lucy with her most basilisk stare.

'It's a matter of *style*, Lucy,' she hisses. 'There are some things one simply never ever does. I'm going to powder my nose.'

Left to her own devices, Lucy stares miserably round at the room and suddenly has a great longing to be back on the farm in her own cold primitive

227

attic room. Her mother had told her there was a bed at Claridges for her if she wanted to stay the extra night in London. But abruptly Lucy decides she will brave the horrors of the train journey home. Providing she can find Liverpool Street in the blackout. Furtively Lucy checks in her bag for her return ticket. As she does so, she catches sight of a packet of air-mail letters neatly tied together with baler twine. There had been something she had particularly longed to discuss with Virginia tonight, but of so personal a nature that she would have found it hard to bring up the subject with a sympathetic audience, let alone a Virginia who flounces back, her brows one straight line of annoyance.

'Whom did she marry?' she demands without preamble.

Lucy stares at her startled.

'Beattie? Oh, gosh, I didn't tell you? An officer from Brooke's squadron. Isn't that a coincidence?'

'Isn't it, though?' says Virginia ominously. There is clearly a mystery, and Virginia is determined to get to the bottom of it.

'She met him while she was at her training college. I know Brooke's squadron was stationed somewhere near Beattie, because do you remember I met him that day when I was with Ma in Norwich. Anyway, Charles – that's Beattie's husband – seems awfully nice and incredibly handsome. Rather like Laurence Olivier, only a bit more friendly. He isn't flying at present because he was injured in a raid about a year ago, so he's been working on something frightfully hush-hush for the RAF in London. But he's been posted back to another squadron now, so he'll be flying again soon, I suppose.'

'Why isn't Beattie in Yorkshire with him?'

'I think they probably decided it was best for her to stay with her family until the baby was born.'

'She's expecting a baby?'

'Yes, just after Christmas. Lily thinks they've jumped the gun a bit—'

'When in the New Year?'

Virginia's manner is now so feverish that Lucy stares at her.

'February, I think. Why?'

Virginia does some rapid mental arithmetic and almost exclaims aloud in her triumph.

'Vir, you look quite strange. Are you all right?'

'I'm fine. Just thinking.'

Virginia is silent, recalling that frightful night at the Dorchester when she had to watch Beattie and Brooke together. Beattie had been in love; there could be no two opinions on that subject. And it had also been perfectly obvious (to Virginia at least) that they were sleeping together. So if there was a baby due it had to be Brooke's. It *had* to be. It was simply impossible that Beattie could have been carrying on with anyone else while she was so much in love with Brooke. Virginia feels a deep heartfelt surge of pleasure. She is delighted that Beattie has been punished for her presumption in carrying on with her betters. Then, just as abruptly, pleasure gives way to a deep corroding rage as she remembers that Beattie has found someone to marry her to cover up her shame. Beattie has got away with it. Virginia acknowledges without flinching the part of herself that longs to see Beattie alone and friendless and disgraced. On top of everything she is carrying Brooke's child.

Oblivious, Lucy is saying: 'I don't think she minds if it's a boy or a girl; in fact, what with Mrs Blythe being so ill, I don't suppose she's even thought—'

'Does the husband think the baby's his?'

'What?'

'If Beattie's pregnant, the baby certainly isn't her husband's. It can't be. I met your wonderful Beattie in London. In May. She was staying at the Grosvenor House with Brooke,' drawls Virginia disdainfully in her most contemptuous tone. 'He must have been amusing himself with the silly tart for the past two years. Ever since that stupid garden-party in your mother's, I shouldn't wonder.'

Lucy visibly shrinks back from the venom in Virginia's tone. Virginia regards her dispassionately. For a married woman, Lucy is still appallingly shockable. Virginia can also see instantly that Lucy is hurt that Beattie has not confided in her. For some reason that makes Virginia angrier than ever.

'For God's sake, don't look so wounded, Lucy. You look like one of your dratted cows. Dash it all, she'd only been a few miles from him in Norfolk. It must be his baby, and he's very sensibly decided not to marry her. What a joke she's married someone else in his squadron. I just hope he realizes he's got a pig in a poke.'

'I can't believe it,' says Lucy almost inaudibly, 'I just can't believe it.'

'Can't believe what?'

'I can't believe that Brooke would act so badly.'

Lucy's response is so completely not what Virginia is expecting that she is almost speechless.

'*Badly. Badly*?' Virginia's face is crimson with anger. 'Lucy, my dear, as I said before, you're out of your mind. The Musgraves don't marry servants.'

By now there are two corresponding spots of colour in Lucy's face.

'Honestly, Vir, you sound like some daft historical novel. That sort of thing simply doesn't matter any more now. Especially when the person concerned is pretty and intelligent and better-educated than either of us.'

'Those things may not matter to *you*,' says Virginia coldly, not at all pleased by that dig at her education, 'because your background is rather different from mine.'

'Whatever her background is, she would have made a wife any man would be proud of. And if Brooke had been a *real* gentleman he would have faced up to his responsibilities and married her. Beattie isn't the kind of girl to be light in her affections. She must have really loved him to . . . to . . . be intimate with him. And you're only saying those things because you're jealous of her. You always have been. You're glad she's in trouble. I can see it in your face.'

'Not light in her affections,' mimics Virginia. 'You'll have to stop reading Ethel M. Dell, Lucy. It's ruining your prose style. She's just a stupid common little slut with alleycat morals.'

'The man who married her is an officer and his father was a solicitor and a member of the Chamber of Commerce in Manchester, and his wife was—'

'Lucy, I don't care a damn about his blasted wife,' shrieks Virginia, but quietly as she realizes their table is beginning to draw curious glances. 'Our bill please, quickly.'

Once outside the blackout cosiness of the restaurant, the two girls stand on the darkened pavement, embarrassed.

'Where are you going?'

'Home to Musgrave. There's a train at eleven from Liverpool Street. I'll pick up a lift in one of the milk-lorries in Ipswich.'

'This is so stupid, quarrelling over someone so completely unimportant.'

Lucy swallows hard, torn between a natural inclination for peace and the memory of that hot anger she felt at Virginia's spite in the restaurant. Then she says: 'I don't like to quarrel; but I don't like to hear you speaking so unkindly of a friend of mine, any more than I'd let anyone speak badly of you.'

Virginia is so astonished that it takes her a moment or two to find words. Then, carefully adjusting her black hat to a more rakish angle, she turns to face Lucy.

'Well, if you've got her friendship, you clearly won't need mine any more, will you?' she says coldly. And without saying goodbye begins to walk towards Shaftesbury Avenue. She walks briskly, but not so fast that Lucy can't overtake to make things up.

But Lucy doesn't follow her. At the end of the street, Virginia's confidence fails and she turns to look back the way she's come. Lucy is nowhere to be seen. Anger fills Virginia's heart to the very brim.

'Well, *let* Lucy become Beattie Blythe's best friend. Much good it will do her. Trust Brooke to act sensibly. The idea, the very idea of having Beattie as a sister-in-law.' Abruptly Virginia remembers Brooke's look of desperate unhappiness when he had come to see her earlier in the summer. Firmly she pushes it out of her mind. It would be worth going home at Christmas just to witness Beattie's discomfiture. Really, if Lucy hadn't turned so crusty it would have been the most amusing evening.

The night is clear and frosty without a moon. With any luck there won't be a raid, thinks Virginia and decides to walk round to Willy's flat. Her heels ring out confidently as she cuts across Piccadilly and up Regent Street to cut across Bond Street. Taxis are drawn up outside Claridges, and in the gloom men and women in evening dress are setting out for an evening's night-clubbing. Virginia has almost passed the hotel when a familiar voice makes her jerk her head round. It can't be! But it is. There is Mrs Hallett under the canopy of the hotel wearing a very good mink and a lot of rather fussy jewellery. Virginia is about to say hello when she see Mrs Hallett turn and take the arm of a man who has just successfully hailed a taxi. Virginia watches in disbelief as the man, who is elderly but undeniably good-looking, tucks Mrs Hallett's hand protectively into his arm and gives her the kind of look that instantly convinces Virginia that this is no business associate. So engrossed are the couple that they pass within a few feet of Virginia without a glance in her direction before climbing into the taxi.

Virginia stares after them. No *wonder* Mr Hallett hadn't been encouraged to come to London. Well, well, well. What an evening this has been.

Virginia pauses for a moment. She has just remembered that this is Willy's poker night and, barring an actual airborne invasion by the Krauts, he will be engrossed in his cards until dawn. Thoughtfully Virginia directs her steps towards Bayswater instead.

Had Virginia but known it, Lucy fully intended to try to make things up but to her own absolute astonishment had found her legs simply declined to move in that direction. Instead she'd found herself wheeling smartly round and making her way up to the darkened canyon that was Oxford Street. At Tottenham Court Road Station Lucy pauses, irresolute. There had been an air-raid warning just after lunch and since then nothing. Was it worth taking the risk of trying to walk to Liverpool Street Station? A soldier bumps into Lucy in the gloom, and enquires if she fancies a drink.

'No, thank you,' says Lucy firmly and sets off briskly in what she hopes is the direction of Liverpool Street Station. Surely if she keeps walking east she must eventually hit it. Then miraculously a taxi throbs to a halt in front of her, and Lucy leaps gratefully aboard.

The station at 10.30 at night is still as crammed as if it were Bank Holiday. Babies cry or doze in their mothers' arms, small children play hide-and-seek happily around the luggage-trolleys. There are a number of service men and women dozing on their kit-bags. As usual the railway personnel are parting with information about trains to Ipswich as if it were classified information, but from a friendly porter Lucy discovers the bad news: the eleven o'clock train is running nearly three hours late. But the good news is that the eight o'clock train is still to arrive and there is every reason to believe it could appear within the next half-hour.

'Tea up!' calls a cheery voice from the end of the platform, and Lucy joins an orderly queue which quickly forms round the WVS tea-urn. Lucy gratefully accepts a cup from a woman with an immaculate Marcel wave – Kitty, if she did but know it – and gratefully sinks down on to the edge of an empty luggage-trolley. She closes her eyes and tries to doze, but the day has been too strange and the events too various to allow her to relax.

High above in the roof-struts pigeons are flying to and fro, even at this late hour. Lucy's thoughts veer in a similar series of tired zig-zags from subject to subject. Mother had seemed pleased to see her, but Lucy wishes there had been more time to talk. She had been . . . lit up in some peculiar way; perhaps it was just getting that medal. Mother liked the recognition of success.

It is strange that sitting here takes her thoughts straight back to the farm. Jubal, the McFees' oldest farmhand, and a man of such advanced and hoary age that even he was hazy about the exact date of his birth, had told her idly one day that he'd had a cousin who'd left the village to help build this station. Goodness knows when *that* had been.

'Did he make a lot of money?' Lucy had panted between hurling beets on the top of the stack. Jubal had taken his time replying.

'Don't know about that. He never came back.'

231

'Didn't he write?'

'Didn't know how to,' Jubal had said. It had been one of his chattier days. He had then added most surprisingly: 'But he told a fella who did come back that the only bit of London he ever saw was the bit of sky through the slats in the roof.'

Lucy wonders idly if that cousin had sat where she is sitting now and had longed and longed with the same passionate longing for the Suffolk country-side. In London she is nothing. But doing a job, knowing above all that she's doing the job well – Lucy already knows that these are things of inestimable value. Which reminds her of something rather less pleasant. With a sigh she opens her handbag and pulls out the packet of letters. If only Vir hadn't been in such a vile mood. If only her mother hadn't been so busy. But perhaps it was Lucy's own fault for mentioning Beattie's wedding. Perhaps everything was Lucy's own fault really. But fancy Beattie and Brooke. . . . Lucy blushes hotly and hastily tries to direct her thoughts elsewhere. She'll think about Beattie tomorrow when she has more time. Though the true extraordinary facts about Beattie's pregnancy do a great deal to explain why Beattie currently looks so unhappy. And there was Lucy thinking it was because her mother was ill.

But as for Hugh. . . . Lucy goes to open the packet of letters, then leaves them. She knows them off by heart anyway. But what does it all mean? she asks herself for the hundredth time. She'd been longing for today, simply for the opportunity to talk about it to her mother at the very least, if not to Virginia. But, as it is, she is going back to Musgrave just as perplexed as when she left this morning.

There'd been a period of two months in the summer when there hadn't been any letters from Hugh at all. Then there had been a batch of three, all apologizing for the delay occasioned by Hugh's hepatitis. He had felt truly frightful, he said, and so depressed he'd wanted to die. Now, suddenly, he was on the mend and as a result proceeded to fire off a series of rapid communications to his wife about his mental state. Page after page of introspection began to arrive at Home Farm, all of which Lucy conscientiously read with increasing perplexity. Hugh kept saying he had 'found' himself. Where had he been? thought Lucy mystified, being a fairly literal sort of person. Hugh then announced he was going through a spiritual crisis. Lucy wondered if this meant he was going to join the Roman Catholic Church and actually went to see Dr Body to see if a religious crisis often followed hepatitis. Dr Body was able to reassure her on that score but in very little else. He urged her not to brood and reminded her that hot climates did strange things to men.

Since then a desultory trickle of letters, then silence. Then three more letters had arrived together, each one informing Lucy that never had Hugh felt more vigorous or forceful! Apparently hours of lying on his back staring at the ceiling of the hospital in Cairo had enabled him to rethink his whole life. In this respect he owed a particular debt of gratitude to one Julia Heap, an American nurse. In the last of the three letters there was actually a note from *Julia* to *Lucy* written in Miss Heap's horrid loopy handwriting, sending her best wishes and urging her to keep up the good work 'somewhere in England!'

Her initial reaction was to think how good it was that Hugh was now better and how courteous of Miss Heap to write her a note. This was followed by: Hugh has certainly taken his time getting better and why on earth does Miss Heap think that Lucy wants to hear from her? Both these responses were then wiped out by a mood of such jealous frenzy that Lucy began to wonder if she was actually going mad. Pacing up and down in the lambing-shed (her attic bedroom allowed only three steps each way before she cracked her head on a beam), Lucy had searched her soul as to whether she was justified in being suspicious or simply failing in her first real test as a wife. Surely a *proper* wife would be grateful to Miss Heap for helping Hugh through a difficult illness. Surely this was the moment to display understanding and sympathy. In the end she had written Hugh a stilted note wishing him a speedy recovery and completely ignoring the message from Miss Heap. The following day she'd torn her letter up.

At this moment the Ipswich train hoves into view and what seems like the entire population of East Anglia attempts to get on. By some miracle – there is no other appropriate word for it – Lucy finds a seat and, worn out with the day's emotions, manages to fall instantly asleep against a clergyman's shoulder. When she finally wakes they are inching their way into Ipswich, it is nearly four o'clock and bitterly cold. There are still no pale streaks of light visible from the east as Lucy marches briskly out of the station to the main road, where with any luck she hopes she will see one of the milk-vans. The town is utterly silent, utterly deserted, but even in the centre of the city streets the sweetness of the country air flows along the deserted pavements. In spite of herself Lucy is calm. Perhaps she is imagining things, she decides as she hears the welcome rattle and roar of Stan's milk-van breasting the hill. Lucy's power of positive thought is such that by the time she is stepping down from the cab just outside Musgrave she has pushed the problem firmly out of her mind. The sky is beginning to lighten and it's started to drizzle. Undeterred and whistling cheerfully, she strides up the muddy track to Home Farm. There is already a light on in the kitchen; Mrs McFee is an early riser, and the kitchen range is stoked and glowing. The breakfast-table is laid with a blue and white check cloth, and the two sheepdogs jump up to give Lucy an animated welcome, as she flops down on one of the Windsor chairs and inhales the familiar smell of wood-smoke, stone floor and warm dog.

'Och now, I wasn't expecting you till lunchtime,' Mrs McFee exclaims calmly.

'Couldn't stand London a second longer,' says Lucy without preamble. 'Any chance of some breakfast? I've just got time for a mouthful and to take this lot off.' She casts a distasteful eye over her wet clothes.

'There's a clean pair of breeks for you on the line, and I washed your jersey. Pounded it with stones more like to get the mud off.'

'Oh, gosh, thanks. That's really kind of you. Sam pushed me over in the lane again.'

'Beats me why you bother with that bad-tempered horse.'

'Beats me sometimes. I just like riding.'

Lucy yawns hugely and stretches. She is glad to be back.

'I'll have your breakfast for you when you come down. Did you have a fine day in London? I saw Beattie at the post office yesterday and I told her you were away to the city.'

'Oh, all right.' Lucy had already forgotten most of it. 'But it's lovely to be back. How is Beattie?'

'Tired. She says her mother's a bit better and said a few words. It's a blessing she decided to stay on home until she had the baby instead of following her husband, isn't it?'

'Yes,' says Lucy slowly, 'I suppose it is.'

As Lucy climbs thoughtfully to her attic bedroom to change into her warm breeks, three miles away in the frozen back garden of the Blythes' cottage Beattie is letting out the hens. Or, rather, not so much letting them out as bullying them out of the nice warm fug of the henhouse into the chill drizzle of early morning. With many baleful looks the hens totter out, not even the prospect of their morning mash managing to appease their obvious disgruntlement. There is absolutely no need for them to be up and around at 6 a.m., but if Beattie can't sleep she doesn't see why anybody else should. Back inside the kitchen even Beetle is declining to do anything more active than apologetically wag his tail before falling deeply back into doggish slumber. Defeated, Beattie pushes her hair out of her eyes and wearily starts to riddle the range. There is absolutely no need for her to do this; it is Mr Blythe's first task when he comes down at half-past six. But Beattie is simultaneously possessed of a total torpor and a terrible restlessness. She cannot sit down and put her feet up for twenty minutes without becoming prey to anxieties so violent that she has to find another task to occupy her hands if not her mind. It's just not fair, says Beattie out loud to herself, and suddenly to her own consternation in the silent kitchen, bursts into loud tears.

Unfortunately even Beetle is too far gone in sleep to comfort her. Then the baby kicks suddenly, firmly, so hard that Beattie has to grab the side of the kitchen table to catch her breath. Defeated, she sits down in a rocking chair by the range to brood over her fate.

Nothing more aptly symbolizes her new state than the sight of her own trim athletic body slowly expanding into an ungainly shapeless lump, forcing her to walk with her stomach thrust forward and preventing her from lying or even sleeping in any comfort. Beattie sits slumped in the chair, knuckles in her mouth, tears sliding slowly into her unbrushed hair. Her life is over. Nothing good can ever happen again. She has always envisaged that this autumn, the autumn after she'd finally qualified, her life would start. But by some cruel trick of fate the path she has taken to lead her from home has turned out to be circular, leading straight back to where she started, with the initial horror that at twenty freedom seems to have been lost for ever. Suddenly and irrationally Beattie is haunted by the spectacle of her aunt, Lily's mother, Ciss Kedge, mother of ten, her energy and figure, not to

234

mention looks, self-respect and any shade of independence, gone for ever.

If Beattie was in slightly less of a trough of self-pity, she could quite reasonably have asked herself exactly how much energy, self-respect and independence Aunt Ciss might have demonstrated had she never borne a child in her life. As it is, in Beattie's present mood of despair, it seemed like the final proof of the trap she has fallen into. Louie was right. Chillington was the narrow path to freedom and independence. But now instead of her life beginning she is living at home as she has always done, and through her own stupidity expecting a child that she doesn't want, by a man who clearly despises her, having committed herself legally to another man she hardly knows in order to square the first mess. On top of that, unless the war continues indefinitely, it's unlikely she'll ever be able to use her teaching qualification since it's only since the war started that married women have been allowed to go on teaching. What had it all been *for*, Beattie keeps asking herself, all those endless examinations in her teens, all that study and home-work, if it's all to end boiling nappies in the copper, something the stupidest girl in the village school could do? Oh, it's all unfair, unfair, thinks Beattie angrily, her eyes fixed dully on the red glow of the range. Her only outlet is to write long angry letters to Louie, who as usual is not backward in coming forward with direct advice.

'Dear Beattie,' she had written back in her firm round teacher's hand-writing, 'there is only one thing wrong with you at present and that is that you've got too much time on your hands. Can't you get some kind of a job, if only for a month or two, until the baby shows? You might feel different if you had a little money of your own.'

Having swallowed her initial fury at the idea that anything in her present state might be her own fault, Beattie had taken her advice and actually written to a London prep school evacuated to the next village. The response had been instantaneous and gratifying. The very next day the headmaster had written back by return post urging Beattie to come for interview at her earliest convenience. Beattie had already been making plans to get a lift when Aunt Madge had come shouting to her in the kitchen, to tell her that her mother was ill, she must run and fetch the doctor. Beattie had found her mother lying rigid and sightless on her bedroom floor and knew prophet-ically that the bad times were only now beginning.

They had taken Mother to the cottage hospital at Dereham Market for a month. The only good thing was that Aunt Madge had been prevailed upon to stay and help. Otherwise Beattie didn't know what she would have done. Any ideas about teaching had been abandoned then and there. Running the Blythe household turned out to be a nightmare that never ended. She had forgotten the horrors of Monday morning, the washing and the mangling and the problem of what to do with the washing afterwards when it wouldn't dry and flapped damply around the house for the rest of the week. Not to mention the long evenings of tedium heating up the irons, then ironing the endless piles of linen and underwear. The end-result might give some sort of fleeting satisfaction but it was quickly undone by the sight of Big Toby and Little Ern returning drenched and muddy from football or collecting salvage. There were the horrors of the family ration-books and the complicated points system therein. In addition there were Christmas presents that Mrs Blythe had started to make that had to be finished, and the extra food they were entitled to for Christmas, collected and transformed into something approaching a celebration.

At first Beattie would go into the hospital every day to sit by her mother's bed as she lay unmoving and unmoved. Eventually Dr Body had to tell her that she was doing herself more harm than good sitting there weeping, and after that she only went in once a week with the children. Given time, the doctor speaks of a complete recovery. But Beattie does not believe it, and at all times has to fight off the feeling that it is punishment for her own unkindness to her mother. And as for Charles – well, in so far as Beattie was prepared to think about him at *all*, he was simply another source of annoyance and irritation in the existing mess. Even the sight of her name on his letters, Mrs Beatrice Hammond, made her want to vomit. She is not Mrs B. Hammond. She is still Beattie Blythe, the prettiest girl in the village with all the world before her. Unfortunately only she seems aware of that fact. Sometimes (not often) she tries to be fair to Charles. He is a kind man, an attractive man; in fact she sometimes thinks that if they had gone into normal married life they might have made something out of the hasty and ill-conceived relationship.

But, as it is, if it weren't for Lily's wedding photographs she would sometimes have difficulty even recalling what he looks like. But to her own disgust she finds that she is perfectly prepared to go on taking his money whilst unable to face the fact herself that she has no intention of ever committing herself to him. In actual fact – this is the part that makes her hate herself the most – she hoards most of the money in a cake-tin under her bed. She knows perfectly well she'd be far better off spending money on proper maternity clothes or a layette or even having her hair properly permed so she didn't look such a terrible fright. If Charles comes home now, he'll get a shock, she told her reflection in the mirror with vindictive satisfaction, wondering at the same time what kind of insanity was making her rage against the only person who showed any real concern for her. Everything was upside down and back to front.

Why, it was only a year ago that she was complaining to Louie that Brooke showed no interest in anything to do with her life. And now she was complaining just as vociferously to the long-suffering Louie that Charles kept asking her endless questions about the people who'd been at the wedding, about her parents and the village, how she spent her time. Come off it, Louie had robustly replied, can't you see that he's trying to court you? A bit late now, Beattie had grumblingly retorted. Often in the blessed interval of quiet after the children and her parents have gone to bed, before she herself lumbers up to the attic, Beattie sits tipped back on the rocker, her feet on the range, listlessly going through Charles's letters, trying to work up some appropriate feeling for him. There is so much about Charles which, if circumstances were different, she might have responded to. Charles is a passionate reader, quite unlike Brooke who saw literature primarily as a means of keeping women occupied if he was late for a date. Charles is also a passionate cinema- and theatre-goer, anxious to discuss what he's seen and to ask Beattie's opinions of books and films that they've both enjoyed. Moreover, from the very start of their legal life together he has made strenuous efforts to involve her in his life and to become involved in hers. The personality which emerges from his letters is a warmly attractive one. Why, then, does she resist so strongly any attempt to enter his world? In almost every letter there is a message of good wishes and congratulation to Beattie from one or other of his friends in either the squadron or the university. There is even an invitation to stay at the parents' home of Charles's best friend, Guy Berrisford. Guy is apparently in North Africa and has to confine his congratulations to a series of enthusiastic letters. Mr and Mrs Berrisford want to meet Beattie and suggest they come for the weekend when Charles next has leave. 'I'm sure you'll like them,' Charles had written optimistically. 'Guy's father paints portraits, and his mother used to be a designer at Liberty. They've got the most lovely house near Kew Gardens. What do you think of the idea?'

What Beattie actually thought about the idea was barely printable and for two days she was hardly able to speak for indignation. The last thing, the very last thing, she wanted to do was to appear in public with Charles as a couple. What she wants is to keep her marriage restricted to as small a space as possible, as if by depriving it of all light and oxygen she can kill it off altogether. After two weeks' silence she finally writes a stiff note back to Charles saying that unfortunately her mother's illness precludes the possibility of leaving Musgrave at the present moment but she thanks Mr and Mrs Berrisford for their kind offer.

But frequently guilt sets in – particularly if Beattie is due to go to the post office to collect her married woman's allowance. But try as she might to control her mood she still finds herself, almost on an hourly basis, swinging madly from a sense of gratitude to Charles to complete fury with Charles, not to mention a sense of almost cosmic outrage at the position (as she sees it) that fate has put her into. But one thing is sure: nothing that Charles says strikes the right note. If he writes she is annoyed with him, if he doesn't write she is furious. But her anger finally reaches its zenith when Charles sends her a wedding present late in October. It hadn't even crossed her mind to provide anything for him, and Aunt Madge's suggestion that she should knit him a jersey in Air Force blue provokes such a storm of tears and rage that her aunt doesn't even dare suggest it again. So yet again, as Beattie sees it, every time she switches on her smart new battery-powered wireless, she is in Charles's debt. It costs her something of a struggle to write a warm and convincing thank-you letter, and then she is furious when Charles doesn't reply for six weeks. As Big Toby frequently remarks to Little Ern and increasingly in Beattie's hearing, there is just no pleasing Aunty Bee at present.

By now it is getting lighter, and Beattie gets up with a sigh to put the kettle on for tea. At half-past six Mr Blythe appears, fully dressed with his boots on, ready for a day's work in the Manor's vegetable gardens where fresh produce has to be provided for the 150 Barnardo's children who are lodging there. He kisses Beattie affectionately and asks her if she's had a good night.

'So-so. I fall asleep quick enough but I wake up early.'

'That's like your mother. Well,' he ends uneasily, 'as your mother was. I'd often hear her creeping downstairs at four o'clock.'

Nowadays Mrs Blythe spends most of the day asleep and her waking hours to all intents and purposes in a remarkably similar condition. The subject is not dwelt upon.

'What are you doing today? Is it your check-up?'

'No, not till Friday. I've got a load of ironing.'

There is a sound on the wooden stairs, and most unexpectedly Aunt Madge appears in her wrapper and curlers in the doorway.

'Well! You've beaten me to it. I was going to bring you up a cup of tea, young Beattie.'

'It's no trouble, Aunty, you know that.'

A series of thuds on the stairs announce the arrival of Ern and Toby still in their pyjamas, rubbing the sleep out of their eyes. Beattie puts on the breakfast, bids her father goodbye, reminds him that tea will be early as she's going to the knitting circle tonight, and serves breakfast, falling hungrily on her own porridge. The days of morning sickness are long since past, and Beattie, as Big Toby recently disparagingly remarked, will eat anything that isn't actually nailed down to the table.

Quarter to eight. Beattie begins to prepare her mother's breakfast-tray aware that it's Thursday and there may very well be a letter from Louie.

'Aunty Bee, Aunty Bee, what are we having for lunch?'

'Lunch?' says Beattie outraged. 'What do you mean, lunch? I haven't washed up the porridge-plates from breakfast.'

'You're going round to Cis Kedge's for lunch,' intervenes Aunt Madge most unexpectedly. 'Yes, you are. I asked Lily to ask your mum yesterday. No, not a word, Beattie. You and I are going into Dereham. The vicar's picking us up from the memorial at half-past nine.'

'But, Aunt Madge, I've got a million things to do here and I look terrible,' moans Beattie.

'The ironing can wait. You've got plenty of time to pin up your hair. Now, boys, off to school with you. Fifteen minutes.'

The back door crashes shut with the boys.

'Aunty, I don't want to go to Dereham—'

'Well, you're going, young lady. You're seven months gone and you haven't even got as much as a pair of bootees for the baby. We're going in to get some wool and to buy Christmas presents, and I don't want to hear another word. Is that the gate? It must be Lily.'

It is Lily with a seed catalogue for Mr Blythe and a letter for Beattie with a Liverpool postmark.

'Nothing from Charles today, then,' says her aunt, clearly disappointed.

'No – I owe him,' says Beattie guiltily, unable to meet her aunt's eyes.

'Are you coming along to the knitting circle tonight?' asks Lily.

'I may be,' says Beattie evasively. In fact only wild horses or the personal intervention of Hitler himself will keep Beattie from the knitting circle tonight. Each week it meets in a diffcrent house in the village, and tonight Mrs Musgrave has graciously offered the Dower House for the circle to meet and gossip and have tea.

Promptly at 9.15 Aunt Madge reappears in the kitchen wearing a plum-coloured coat with a mock-astrakhan collar and a dark red knitted hat, its narrow brim pulled well down over her forehead against the December cold.

'Mrs Leary's coming in at eleven o'clock to give your mother her elevenses.'

'Got it all worked out, haven't you?' says Beattie nastily, trying ineffectually to loop her fuzzy hair back from her face in its former shining wave.

'Someone's got to, girl,' Aunt Madge reproves her briskly, studying the shopping list she's made on the back of an envelope. 'And while we're at it we'll get some wool for your mother—'

'My mother', says Beattie viciously, jabbing a safety-pin through the lining of her school coat to hold the two sides together, 'has already told me that she won't be knitting a stitch for my baby.'

'She'll come round. When you stop sulking. Are you taking your orange juice?'

'Yes,' says Beattie crossly.

'And your vitamin pills?'

'Yes. And I've got my green card as well.'

'Shall I shut Beetle in the scullery?'

'No, let him be. Once we're gone he'll go up and sit with Mother.'

In the hall Beattie catches a sudden unguarded sight of herself in the hall-stand mirror, and it is the final image of a nightmare. She has not bothered to buy a single pregnancy garment, and as a result, eight weeks away from her confinement has only one outfit that will fit her: her school gymslip. In the mirror the startled face in a bottle-green gymslip, the unkempt hair make her seem as if she is still at school, still the favourite daughter of the house. Except for that inexplicable lump that pulls open the pleats and makes her stand in that strange ungainly way.

Undeterred by her large glowering niece in the back seat, Aunt Madge chats cheerfully to the vicar as they bounce through the frosty rutted country lanes in the vicar's badly sprung Austin Seven. Towards Dereham even Beattie begins to cheer up at the sight of the shops with their modest Christmas decorations and stares hungrily at the pretty clothes on display.

'What we want first,' says Aunt Madge, peering short-sightedly at her list, 'is wool. Now, come on, Beattie. You can do your Christmas shopping later on.'

At one o'clock Aunt Madge finally takes pity on Beattie, who is reeling under an accumulation of shopping-bags, and takes her to the Copper Kettle.

'My treat,' she says firmly, settling them comfortably in a corner overlooking the High Street. 'What'll you have, Beattie?'

'Welsh rarebit,' says Bettie. Her cravings, such as they are, take the form of a modest obsession with cheese. As the current ration is about an ounce per person a week – just about a decent mouthful, in her opinion – she spends an absurd amount of time devising ways of getting more.

'I'll have the same,' Aunt Madge tells the waitress before settling herself comfortably. 'You're looking a bit more cheerful, I must say. I was beginning to think you'd forgotten how to smile.'

'There isn't much to smile about at present, is there?' says Beattie tartly.

'Really,' says Aunt Madge, quietly sarcastic. 'You're young, healthy, fit, going to have a baby and you've got a good husband.'

'Aunt Madge, I haven't got a husband, as you well know—'

'Shh! Keep your voice down, do. You've got a perfectly good husband if you'll just give him a word of encouragement. Have you asked him home for Christmas?'

'No, I have not.'

'Well, why ever not?'

'Because I hardly know him, that's why,' hisses Beattie, 'and anyway he hasn't said he wants to come.'

'Well, he'd have a job, wouldn't he, considering you don't even read his letters and hardly bother to answer them.'

Beattie goes very red.

'I don't think you're playing fair, Beattie.'

'Playing fair! He suggested marriage, not me. And I've never regretted any single act as much.'

This succeeds in completely silencing Aunt Madge, who bends her knitted head and ostentatiously eats her Welsh rarebit in a frigid silence.

With a terrible gulp Beattie puts her face in her hands as tears begin to cascade down her face.

'There, there,' says Aunt Madge, fumbling in her handbag. She produces a handkerchief with a violet embroidered in the corner, smelling, as does everything in her bag, of eau-de-Cologne and peardrops. 'Come on now, Beattie. Dry your eyes and have a good blow. I know you've had a bad time, what with your mother being took poorly and everything, but you're so cross at present there's no reasoning with you.'

'Everything's so awful,' says Beattie, dabbing ineffectually at the stream of scalding water which pours unchecked from her eyes.

'I know it seems like that now. But when the baby's born—'

'When the baby's born I'll be finished,' says Beattie flatly. 'My life will be completely over then.'

Aunt Madge gives her a sharp glance. 'Is it that young man who's still making you cry?'

Beattie does not answer but gazes defeated at her own untouched Welsh rarebit. How could she possibly tell anyone – even the sympathetic Louie – that she still dreams of Brooke, night after night, strong, tiring, painful dreams full of anger and pain and longing? She cannot stop thinking about him. What will happen to Brooke without Beattie to worry about his safety, willing his safe return? How can she explain to anybody that there are times that she would willingly kill Charles Hammond for having effectively blocked the way back to Brooke? In her heart of hearts Beattie knows perfectly well that whatever barriers lie between her and Brooke are solely of Brooke's own devising. But this is not a time for logic. Then Beattie catches what her aunt is saying and all thoughts of her own problems are driven straight out of her mind.

'Oh, Aunty, you can't,' she wails. 'We were counting on you to be here for Christmas. It won't be the same without you; you know Mother and I aren't even talking.'

'No, Beattie, I've made up my mind and I'm going Monday. I promised I'd go up to my sister-in-law last summer, and it's high time I went. I'll be back at the end of January. It'll give you a chance to get talking to your mother again. While you've got me here you two won't give each other as much as the time of day. And that's not kind, Beattie. It's not like you.'

Beattie's tears are forgotten in a surge of rage.

'Aunt Madge, I don't think she's spoken to me since I got married.'

'She'd have a job, wouldn't she?' said her aunt drily. 'Eat up your lunch, do. Go on, you can have half of mine as well. I only ordered it because I know you like it. She's been difficult, Beattie, but she has had a blow. She had such high hopes for you – too high, I used to think.'

'She's got no right to go on the way she's done. When Ivy Bowers of the village shop got pregnant and had no one *at all* to marry *her* Mother knitted for her *and* took care of the baby when Ivy went into Ipswich to try to find a place. It's not such a terrible crime I committed; I don't understand her. She's different. She had changed when I came home from college in the summer.'

'I reckon she's had this illness coming on for quite a while. But I think there are other things bothering her, too.' Aunt Madge looks at her niece consideringly, lips pursed. 'If I talk to you man to man, can I trust you to keep a secret? I can't bear to think of you two at each other's throat over Christmas. Whatever your future is, you're going to have to be at home for a good few months yet, so you'll have to knuckle down, young Beattie. Your mother's having a bad time, and I think I know why. Did she ever tell you much about her own family?'

Beattie shakes her head, her curiosity aroused.

'Well, you know there was just the three of us – us two girls and Mother. Father was never very strong – he had a bad chest and he died when I was six. I know that you think your home isn't too grand nowadays, Beattie' – Beattie blushes and says nothing – 'but, believe you me, you've got no idea what real poverty's like. We had one room, all three of us, and that was our room for everything. You try bringing up two little girls in somewhere like that and trying to be respectable. We shared a sink and a toilet with ten other families. Mother took in dressmaking to make a living for us. We both did well at school but we couldn't stay on because we had to be out earning. We were both apprenticed to dressmakers, but I didn't take to it and instead got a job as a nursery nurse to a very nice family in Holborn. He was a solicitor, and when their two children didn't need me any longer they put an advertisement in the paper for me and that's how I got my place at the Hammonds'. Oh, I had a happy time there, but I knew I'd have to move on eventually. When I met your uncle, and he asked me to marry him, even though he was good bit older than me, I said yes at once, because he had a house, you see, and that meant a lot in those days. All this time your mother was still in London. We were never that close. I don't know why. But she did well enough. Eventually she was apprenticed to a dressmaker in South Molton Street. I never knew how she came to meet Mrs Musgrave, but the next thing I heard was she was her personal maid and travelling here, there and everywhere with her. I don't know how she met Stanley Trace, either, but it must have been when she was still in her early twenties. The Musgraves had a house in Eaton Square then, I do remember that. Anyway, suddenly she was walking out with Stanley Trace. He was a bit of a toff. He came from Macclesfield where his father was a big draper. Stanley was in London to do his accounting exams. I never met him, although your mother was courting him for nearly seven years.'

'*Seven years*? Why on earth didn't they marry?'

'Didn't have any money. It was all dependent on his father. And he said he'd promised his father he wouldn't marry before he qualified.'

'So what happened?'

Aunt Madge hesitates, absently smoothing the creases out of her napkin.

'I never knew the rights of it,' she admits at last. 'He always seemed to have just one more exam to do. Then when he finished he went back home, and your mother was going up to meet his family. She was that excited – she had her bottom drawer all ready. Then the day before she was due to go she had a letter from him saying he'd married someone else. A friend of the family. Someone rich, your mother said, but she never spoke of it again. It broke your mother's heart. She just couldn't believe it. He'd kept her on a string, and there she was – twenty-eight and not married.'

'So how did she get to marry my father?'

'It was the time that Mrs Musgrave started to be ill. As a result they were at the Manor House more. Your father had just been made head gardener, and I think your mother simply decided then and there that she'd marry him. He had a good position and a house of his own; he was a respectable man. She must have been getting panicked about Mrs Musgrave dying, because by then they all knew she had TB. Of course, your father was six years younger than she was—'

No wonder Mother's always been so cagey about her age, thinks Beattie.

'The first I heard was when the wedding was fixed up. We came up for the day. She went up the aisle with you well on the way. My word, you did remind me of her on your wedding day. I suppose she always hoped that you'd achieve what she'd *always* wanted. You know, a good marriage and a position in life. I just don't understand why she's so discontented now. I suppose it's bad luck that the other children died, and all her ambition ended up on you. You must know she brought you up very differently from your cousins.'

'I suppose so,' says Beattie, who is desperately trying to assimilate all this astounding new information. 'I just put it down to her London ways.'

'It's only since I've been down here with her that I've understood her a bit better. You'll have to make more of an effort, Beattie; you know it's up to you and not her. Myself, I don't see why she's still so upset. Charles Hammond is as good a boy as ever lived and you're an officer's wife, which is no small thing. But I suppose it wasn't what she planned. Though I'm hard-pressed to know *what* she had planned. Perhaps if I'd been a bit more downcast about my house she'd feel better. The trouble is you can't say what you don't feel. There are thousands worse off than me. My word, that was a bit of a speech, wasn't it? Ask the lady for a spot of hot water. Now, I don't want you to let on by as much as a syllable what I've told you. Just don't forget that your mother's had her troubles, too. Go on, have a toasted tea-cake and some of that apple sponge. I've told the vicar we'll meet him at half-past two.'

Later that night, Beattie mutinously casts on her first row for a matinée jacket. About fifteen of the village women meet each week to knit together; normally it's a cheerful gossipy occasion. Tonight even the doctor's wife is subdued into silence by the famous bonus of the Dower House drawing-room.

Not that they lack entertainment. Mrs Musgrave talks on in relentless monologue for two and a half hours. It is an evening of mutual incomprehension. The women feel uncomfortable in all this alien splendour but feel it is their duty to be there and make Mrs Musgrave feel wanted. While Mrs Musgrave is under the impression that she's conferring something in the nature of a treat on the village women and would actually much rather be playing patience and sipping a g. and t. By nine o'clock most of the women are getting restive and once the refreshments have appeared begin to melt away. Beattie, however, spins out a cup of tea and nibbles her sandwiches with a daintiness that even Mrs Blythe couldn't have faulted. Avidly she hangs on to Mrs Musgrave's every word. The only aspect of the festive season that actually concerns her is whether Brooke will be coming home. Finally Mrs Leary at the post office tentatively enquires: 'Will you have a full house, then, Mrs Musgrave, for Christmas?'

'I should say so,' says Mrs Musgrave, delicate and fine-boned in the glow of the pink-shaded table-lamp beside her. 'Virginia's actually deigned to spend Christmas with her family. I gather she's doing some pretty important work for this government film company, so I suppose she finds it hard to get away. Lucy says she saw her in London, you know.'

'What about Mr Brooke?'

'Oh, Brooke!' Mrs Musgrave's face suffuses with animation, and she actually lays down her knitting to enjoy her favourite subject fully. 'Well, my dears, I gather he's flying a new plane. Very very hush-hush, or so I'm told. I can't say *any more*.' Her tone, however, is full of meaning, implying that there is very little that Brooke does not confide to his dear old mother. 'I'd love him to come home,' she goes on dreamily, 'and I know how much he longs to be with us. But he's such a boy for dedication. He's in his third term of duty – and there's talk of more promotion. If he does turn up, I suppose it'll only be a matter of hours. They seem to need him all the time at Gatton. Morale, I expect. Some people are like that, aren't they? And Brooke has friends nearby at Newmarket. In fact I'm beginning to suspect one special friend. I keep telling him it's high time he settled down. Are you all right, Beattie?'

'I'm fine, I'm fine, thank you, Mrs Musgrave,' says Beattie breathlessly, having just been severely kicked in the ribs by Mrs Musgrave's first grand-child. 'I'm afraid I'd better be making a move now, if you'll excuse me. I don't seem to be able to keep awake past nine o'clock. Good night.'

243

CHAPTER EIGHTEEN

'No, OF COURSE YOU CAN'T take Beetle to church, Ern.'

'But he could just sit in the porch and wait for us. He'd be ever so good—'

'That time you brought him to Evensong he howled the whole time. He's best left at home here looking after Mother.'

'Can I take my engine to church?'

'*Of course* you can't. For goodness' sake, Ern. Take a Dinky car. But only one.'

'But it's not fair. . . .' Little Ern, his hair newly shorn to look 'decent' for Christmas, sticks out his lower lip and looks alarmingly like a bulldog.

'One toy only, please. It doesn't look proper to be playing in church.'

When Mr Blythe intervenes, which isn't often, it is with a mild firmness which means that there are no possible grounds for discussion. Resigned, Ern slides his Dinky toy into his mackintosh pocket and pulls on his new gloves.

'Are you ready, Beattie?' her father asks.

'I think so,' says Beattie, casting a last despairing look around the kitchen. The chicken is stuffed and ready, the vegetables peeled, and the Christmas pudding has been steaming away on the range since seven o'clock this morning.

'Isn't that Aunt Madge's coat?' enquires Toby inquisitively.

'Yes, it is,' says Beattie in a voice that makes it clear she wants no further comments.

'I've never heard the church bells ring,' observes Ern, his hand in Beattie's, restored to equanimity.

Mr Blythe opens the garden gate and the little party sets off up the village street.

'You will soon enough when we win the war,' Toby tells him stoutly.

'Do you want to take my arm? You look done in,' says Mr Blythe.

Silently Beattie takes her father's arm and as she does so realizes that she is so tired that she can hardly put one foot in front of the other. At the same time she is keyed up almost to the point of hysteria. There is still a chance that Brooke has come home for Christmas and, if he has, he'll certainly come to morning service. Though if he does – oh, why had she taken so little care of how she looked? Yesterday afternoon, galvanized into panic by the sight of herself in the mirror, she had run down to the village shop to get Kirby grips to set her hair. But Mrs Leary had looked at her in pitying disbelief – it was over a year since they'd had Kirby grips, she told the despondent Beattie. Most folk now were using pipe-cleaners. Needless to say there was no proper shampoo, either, just the slimy gritted residue of boiled-down bits of soap. And the results were truly frightful. Instead of the shining shoulder-length waves that Mrs Blythe had coaxed out of Beattie's hair there was now a dry frizzy mass of exploding corkscrews, most of which were pulled firmly under her hat. She'd meant to do some work on Aunt Madge's coat, which was now the only outdoor garment that fitted her. But what with the last-minute preparations for Christmas and the abortive attempts to set her hair, she simply hadn't had the time. And maroon wasn't the most attractive shade for someone with a permanently green tinge to her complexion.

'Are you sure you feel well enough to go in?' Beattie's father asks her as they join the stream of people going in through the lychgate. It is a mild grey winter morning, quite unlike Christmas. 'You should have told me you wanted that pudding put on so early. There was no call for you to get up.'

'I'm all right, Father, really.'

As much as Beattie dreads what she will find in church she dreads even more the prospect of discovering that Brooke had been there and that she has missed him.

'Will Mother come down for lunch?'

'You'll have to ask her yourself.'

'She doesn't answer me.'

Inside the porch they can hear the church organ playing, and through the open carved doors comes the inimitable smell of the church at Christmas – cold stone, old wood, paraffin fumes, all mixed with the scent of pine and evergreens.

'Drat! Someone's got our pew!' fumes Toby *sotto voce*.

'We'll have to sit sep'rit. There's some seats near the front, Aunty Bee,' says Ern.

Grasping the two boys firmly by the hand with a confidence which she is far from feeling, Beattie marches down the aisle as the organ bursts into 'Hark, the Herald Angels Sing' and the congregation shuffles to its feet.

Inching into their pew, Beattie is scorchingly aware that she is sitting directly across the aisle from the two pews containing the party from the Dower House. Fervently trying to open her prayer-book, Beattie discovers that her hands are shaking so badly that she cannot even hold it. Silently Toby takes the book from her, finds the place and hands it back.

Biting her lip, Beattie stares at the words, then completely without her own volition finds her eyes have left the text and have fixed themselves hungrily on the pews across the aisle. So many people are crammed into the church this morning that it is impossible at first to see who is actually there. Mrs Musgrave is on the outside, her fur coat and large hat effectively masking the person next to her. Cautiously Beattie leans back and tries to see who it is standing next to her. As the congregation sits down Beattie gets her first uninterrupted view of the Dower House party. Virginia sits next to Mrs Musgrave. Beyond her is a short man with a sandy moustache who is a frequent visitor to the Dower House. Beyond that there is a couple whom Beattie does not recognize. In the pew behind there are two of the Musgrave great-aunts, an elderly man and another couple. There is no blue greatcoat, no sleek blond head bent meditatively over hymn-book. Brooke is not there. He has not come home.

In that moment of realization waves of faintness begin to pour over Beattie. Beneath her heavy coat her whole body is suddenly bathed in perspiration and the baby shifts convulsively, uneasily, as if feeling desperately for firm ground. As Beattie sits, torpid, legs apart, her gaze hopelessly transfixed on the Musgrave pew, Mrs Musgrave leans forward and reveals Virginia fully for the first time. Beattie catches her breath. Never before has she realized how alike Virginia and Brooke are: that clear-cut, almost stern profile makes them seem like twins, modelled from a single image. Both have the same thick heavy fair hair, the long heavy-lidded eyes beneath strongly marked golden brows, the same deeply indented upper lip and the same full lower lip curving tenderly up to meet it. At that moment Virginia turns and with a little shock catches Beattie's hungry gaze. Virginia surveys her coolly and at her leisure. She had already marked Beattie's entrance, noting the too-long coat, clearly internally secured by safety-pins, the fuzzy hair, the undarned ladders in Beattie's mud-spattered lisle stockings. Insolently Virginia outstares Beattie. She is wearing a grey velvet pill-box hat with a small veil and furs over a beautifully cut pale costume. Her make-up, hair and nails are immaculate. It is as if the girl from the cover of *Vogue* has mysteriously dropped in to the village church for the Christmas service. Beattie knows exactly how she must look but no longer cares. In that instant of seeing Brooke's features in Virginia's contemptuous face, something finally snaps in Beattie's heart. The great lump of grief that she has so steadfastly tried to ignore during the past eight months suddenly begins to expand itself in such an alarming way that she feels she may actually explode under the pressure. Swallowing hard, she whispers to Toby: 'I'm not feeling so good. I think I'll go home.'

'But, Aunty Bee, you'll miss the drink and the mince pie at the vicarage.'

'I don't think I could manage it anyway. You go with Dad, and tell him not to hurry back. Dinner won't be till half-past one.'

Avoiding curious eyes, Beattie makes her way out of the pew and quickly out of the church into the quiet December morning.

The kitchen is warm and empty, Beetle having philosophically gone out for a walk on his own. Still in her outdoor coat Beattie sits down at the kitchen table, puts her gloved hands to her face, and begins to sob. Her sobbing makes a hoarse ugly sound which frightens Beattie, but what frightens her more is that she can't stop.

The latch on the door to the hall suddenly clatters into life.

'Who's making all this noise—?'

Beattie looks up astonished, swollen-eyed and wild-haired. Mrs Blythe stands there, wearing her dressing-gown. She looks exactly as she did before her stroke. Why, she isn't ill at all, goes fleetingly through Beattie's mind, before another wave of misery engulfs her.

There is a dragging sound as Mrs Blythe pulls up one of the wooden chairs next to Beattie's. She knows her mother is struggling for words.

'Did you see him at church?'

Beattie is so astonished that she forgets to sob and stares at her mother. Wordlessly she shakes her head, and hot tears start to pour down her cheeks. In spite of herself she begins to sob again in a heartbroken way. Until now, until this very minute, she had not known how much she had counted on Brooke undergoing some kind of change of heart. She knows he cares for her – he can't go on acting this badly. And at Christmas, too. Surely his heart will have been softened. . . . But clearly it is not to be. Whatever Brooke feels for her, he feels more for himself. Whatever Beattie's misery, he wants to keep his own hands clean. Yet if Brooke had turned up now, this morning, and asked her to come back to him, she would have packed and been ready to go within the hour. Of Charles and her marriage, she suddenly realizes, she would think nothing at all. She could hardly recall what he looked like. All her longing, all her hopes, all her dreams are still tied up in Brooke. And he does not want her: there can be no further illusions on that score.

Beattie feels something being pushed into her hands. It is one of Mrs Blythe's best lawn handkerchiefs.

'I thought I'd see him,' says Beattie dully. 'I still can't believe he hasn't – but he wasn't there. But – his – Miss Virginia was there and she looked so like him.'

Beattie's voice breaks, and she sobs into the hankie scented with eau-de-Cologne, crying not only for the loss of the person she loved but also for the loss of all illusions, for the end of childhood. There is nobody now who can kiss her and tell her this will be all right. No one to step in and right all wrongs for her. Her own choices have brought her to this pass; there is no way back to the security of innocence.

What she wants right now is for her mother to put her arm round her and comfort her. Not to tell her that things are going to be all right when they manifestly are not, but simply to reassure her that she is not completely alone. But such an action is beyond Mrs Blythe, who may love Beattie, but who cannot touch or be touched. Instead she says roughly: 'What you done to your hair, then?'

'I curled it.'

'With what?'

'Pipe-cleaners.'

Mrs Blythe makes a *tisk-tisk* sort of noise and removes Beattie's hat, shaking her own head as she does.

'We can use this lot for cleaning out the saucepans.'

Beattie tries a watery smile and fails.

'Have I done everything right for dinner?'

It is becoming clear to Beattie that Mrs Blythe has probably been up for the past month whenever the house was empty.

'You didn't sew up the bird properly. You'd have had your stuffing all over the roof of the oven. Do you want a cup of tea?'

Beattie nods, notices her sodden gloves for the first time and pulls them off, then unpins her coat under her mother's critical gaze.

'You've let yourself go. You'll be sorry later.'

'Who'll care?'

'You'll care. Don't want to end up like Cis Kedge, do you?'

'I hadn't planned to, no.'

'Dare say she didn't, either,' says Mrs Blythe drily, twirling a strand of Beattie's hair around her finger. 'I'll make us the tea and a sandwich. You need some food inside you. You scoot up and get my grips off the dressing-table.'

Under Mrs Blythe's skilful fingers Beattie's hair is subdued and finally tamed into a recognizable hairstyle.

'What you wearing that old gymslip for?'

'Only thing that'll fit me.'

'Well, tomorrow you can let out one of the dresses your aunt left. If you must wear that today, you can at least put something pretty underneath it for Christmas. There's that pink blouse of mine with the tie-neck. It'll look nice with your hair up. There. That's better.'

Mrs Blythe sits down to her tea. Mother and daughter regard each other warily.

'That's a good watch.'

Beattie looks down at her wrist, startled.

'I'd forgotten I had it on. Charles sent it to me for Christmas.'

Though it is actually on Toby's insistence that she's put it on.

'That's thoughtful of him. Did you send him something?'

'Yes.' Beattie is uncomfortably aware that two secondhand volumes of verse – assuming that he even likes poetry – do not remotely add up to the splendour of a watch.

'Is he going to stick by you, this Charles? Haven't seen much of him since the wedding, have we?'

'That's because I haven't asked him to stay,' says Beattie, astonished that her mother is being so direct and curiously annoyed at this oblique criticism of Charles. 'He does want to stand by me.'

'You're not sure if you want him to.'

'Yes,' says Beattie slowly, facing this fact for the first time.

'Why did he marry you?'

Beattie can hardly believe that this is Christmas morning with the pudding hissing companionably beside them and that she and her mother are having a conversation about her marriage.

'He was sorry for me. He's illegitimate himself.'

'Well, I never,' breathes Mrs Blythe, more animated than she's been in years. 'Does your aunt know?'

'No. And I don't think you should tell her. Charles only told me to explain why he'd married me. He was sorry for me, remembering his mother, I suppose. And he married me instead.'

Mrs Blythe is silent.

'Adopted. Fancy that! And all this time your aunt not knowing. Does he know who his parents were?'

'No. He tried to find out, but it was no good.'

'How did you come to know him anyway?'

Haltingly Beattie explains. Mrs Blythe listens hungrily to the narrative, breathing deeply, unconsciously firming her lips.

'Well, he's done you a good turn, then, hasn't he?'

'I suppose so.'

'No "suppose" about it, gel,' says her mother surprisingly firmly. 'Did you write and invite him for Christmas?'

'Sort of,' mutters Beattie.

'Well, you'd best decide what you want to do once the baby's born. Are you going to stay married to him or what?'

'I don't know,' says Beattie, desperate.

'Does *he* want to stay married?'

Beattie is silent for a moment.

'Yes,' she says reluctantly. 'I think he does.'

Mrs Blythe picks up the tea things with some of her old briskness and glances at Beattie's watch.

'Twelve o'clock. Time that chicken was going in. Is Lucy coming over for tea?'

'Yes.'

'Then, you'd best have a lie-down after lunch. You look that peaky. The boys can help with the washing-up. They're late back, aren't they?'

'They've gone to the vicarage with Dad.'

'Oh . . . I was forgetting. The vicar's mince pie.'

There is almost a note of irony in Mrs Blythe's voice. Beattie stares at her mother in perplexity. For the very first time she wonders if Mrs Blythe, the dutiful, the conscientious, the good neighbour, actually enjoys the limitations of village life. Then Mrs Blythe gives herself almost a mental shake and fixes Beattie with a sharp look.

'Go up and put that blouse on and powder your nose and try to put a cheerful face on for your father.'

On Boxing Day, Lucy turns up for lunch at the Dower House.

'I say, hello, stranger,' says Mrs Musgrave, proferring a pale powdered cheek. 'Bertie, take her coat and get the poor girl a drink. We didn't half miss you on Christmas Eve. Bertie's punch went like wildfire – there was no saving any of it. We missed you.'

'One of the cows started to calve, out of the blue. And as it was two of them, twins, if you see what I mean, I really couldn't leave them,' says Lucy, cheerfully accepting her drink. 'In the end I had to stay up with them all night. I missed church and everything. Hello, Vir, how lovely to see you. A very happy Christmas.'

'Bertie wants to hear all about the calves, don't you, Bertie?' says Mrs Musgrave cosily to her consort, removing a speck of dust from his jacket in a proprietorial sort of way. 'I think we're going to make a countryman out of you yet, aren't we, Bertie?'

And with that Virginia sees Lucy firmly button-holed until the luncheon gong summons them to the dining-room. Not that Lucy seems to mind. She is wearing a very pretty full-skirted tartan dress, her hair is nicely done and she seems in high spirits. From being her old stammering social self she is now positively an asset to the party. It is Virginia who is the silent member of the group. She simply cannot believe it. It is as if Lucy has become the favourite daughter while she is the random visitor. All her beauty, all her poise seem to go for nothing in this household. She might never have been away at all.

If Virginia had been less preoccupied with her own feeling of injury, she would have noticed that Lucy's spirits had a slightly false quality to them. As it is, Boxing Day at the Dower House is the final straw, making her long to be back in London, long to be drunk, admired, oblivious. In London she is somebody; here, mysteriously, she appears to have become invisible.

The Bertie person turns out to be mystifyingly unattractive, and clearly in love with her mother. He is permanently glued to her side as if with treacle. Virginia, remembering the brutal good-looks of her father, is completely at a loss to know what her mother can see in him, since his dominant character-istic seems to be that he simply cannot bear to have her out of his sight. He also starts every other sentence with the words 'Dahrdree says . . .'. He is the head of a government department that has been evacuated to Yoxford. Mrs Musgrave is at all times more lit up than the Christmas tree in the hall. Apart from her mother and Bertie, permanently hand-in-hand, there are two aunts, three men in uniform, four married couples and a good many floating people who have simply dropped in for drinks and somehow never left. So far Virginia has contented herself with enjoying the food, which is excellent, war or no war, and raising her own spirits periodically in the absence of any confirmation on the subject, by telling herself that she is the most attractive woman present. But she knows perfectly well that the main reason she has come home for Christmas is to make sure that Lucy eats humble pie and apologizes. Virginia is still amazed at the way that Lucy stood up for Beattie last November – amazed but not pleased. She is of course prepared to let bygones be bygones – but on her terms of course. After all, it's a friendship that's lasted years. She's quite prepared to make things up with Lucy once Lucy has apologized and suffered a little.

The opportunity comes, or so Virginia thinks, when they go out for a walk after lunch with Mrs Musgrave's new dog. It has started to snow, but not actually settling, and the countryside has a dull heavy feeling. Much to Virginia's indignation it is neither a satisfactory walk nor conversation. They chat on in a desultory way about the films they have seen, and Bertie, and what's going on on the farm. Twice Virginia alludes lightly to the last time she saw Lucy, positively handing her on a plate the opportunity to apologize. But Lucy remains doggedly unresponsive. In the end Virginia says rather huffily that since they have clearly run out of conversation that they might as well go home for tea. Lucy says she has to be off again anyway for afternoon milking. After that they hardly speak. It is mortifying, thinks Virginia crossly. And when at half-past six a girl from the Grange rings up and asks her if she wants an early lift home the following day she accepts with alacrity.

So when Lucy turns up unexpectedly to see Virginia before lunch she finds she has already left. Courteously declining an invitation to stay and take pot luck, Lucy thrusts her hands deep into her greatcoat pockets, pulls

250

her brown felt hat more firmly on to her brow, collects Sam from the Dower House stables and rides him on down to the forge, her ostensible reason for coming to the village. If only she'd tried to talk to Virginia yesterday. Or even suggested meeting again today. But yesterday it had all seemed too much, too painful even to begin to try to give voice to her thoughts, and she'd lost the opportunity. Briefly Lucy considers talking to either Beattie or Lily, then dismisses the idea. They would be sympathetic, shocked, angry on Lucy's behalf, understanding, but some problems demand a friendship of older standing, and for once, she would welcome Virginia's toughness and lack of sentiment.

Old Mr Tonks at the forge, summoned from retirement by his son's calling-up, is a slow worker at the best of times, but never more so than when nimbly trying to avoid Sam's yellowed teeth and flailing hoofs.

'He's a bad lot, this horse of your'n,' he grumbles as the red-hot shoes hiss in the cold water.

'He's not that bad,' says Lucy automatically, her thoughts far away as she sits comfortably on the wall outside the forge. The air has a curious dryness and sudden mildness. Enormous pale grey feathery clouds are beginning to pile ominously on the horizon. Mr McFee had told her that there would be proper snow before the day was out. Lucy sighs deeply, knowing she will have to bring in the pregnant ewes before she starts milking.

Normally the prospect of a busy day exhilarates her. Today lead weights seemed to have attached themselves to her feet.

Though had it really all come as such a shock? Hadn't she suspected that there was more than just friendship between Hugh and this Julia Heap person? She'd received two letters in early December, both detailing the growth of Hugh's friendship with the fair Julia, with whom, Hugh confided, he seemed to be able to share more and more. Could Lucy very kindly send out some poems by a chap called John Pudney who's reckoned to be quite good? Julia had a real passion for poetry, and he'd loved to get her some new stuff for Christmas. In the same letter he'd enquired most tenderly about her life at Home Farm and asked her to outline a typical day for him – 'I love to imagine you at work,' he had assured her. Stiffly Lucy had written back telling Hugh that her chances of getting hold of any new books of poetry in under six months were extremely slim. Then silence until the day before Christmas, when a brief businesslike note had arrived from Hugh informing her that further to his last letter (which letter?) he had decided to go ahead with the divorce. He would of course provide the grounds. He enclosed the name of his family's solicitors in Lincoln's Inn Fields and suggested Lucy contact them to make the necessary arrangements.

The 'previous letter' never arrived. Lucy spent Christmas Eve in the cowshed with a cow deep in calf, hardly conscious of where she was or what she was doing. She was aghast to find out how upset she could be. On Christmas Day she could hardly eat or sleep and spoke only in monosyllables. Boxing Day at the Dower House had been a torture with people constantly asking her how Hugh was. But it had been impossible, completely beyond anything in her, to as much as mention it to Virginia that afternoon, even to raise the subject. Why, she could barely concentrate on what Virginia was saying, so busy was her wretched imagination with thoughts of how happy Hugh and Julia must be celebrating their first Christmas together.

Last night she'd had a frightful dream that Hugh was dying somewhere on the farm and she couldn't find him. It had been enough to convince her that she'd have to talk to someone or go mad. But she had left it too late. Virginia had already gone. Perhaps she's got a young man to go back to, thinks Lucy, quite unnaturally sentimental, then rightly reproves herself for being so wet. But oh! the difference between suspecting something awful may be happening and the pain of discovering that it actually is. As thick white flakes begin to fall Lucy rides a dispirited Sam back to the farm. Virginia must almost be in London by now, she thinks, and whistles to Towser to come and get the ewes in.

The snow catches up with Virginia as they pass through Chelmsford, making an already slow journey almost interminable. It is actually nine o'clock and freezing cold, not to mention pitch dark, by the time they reach the Grangemouth, making Virginia vow that she will never ever go to Suffolk again except in mid-summer or a heatwave. Elizabeth, who had offered her the lift, disappears almost immediately they enter the house, and Virginia is left to make her own way through the darkened and unheated rooms to the top floor. As she slowly climbs the steps to her own landing she realizes her relief at being back is slowly being replaced by inexplicable waves of fear. Abruptly she puts down her suitcase to wipe her sweating hands and to try to calm her hammering heart. Leaning against the banister, she tells herself to calm down, wondering what on earth it can be that has caused these wild symptoms of anxiety. Then it all comes flooding back. At this very time last year she had come in and met Cecily and they had had their first proper talk. It was after that that she had begun to help Cecily. Tonight Cecily's presence seems to fill the whole house. Virginia leaves her case in her new room and stands for a moment, irresolute. Then slowly she finds herself making her way down the stairs and up the back staircase into the other house. Cecily's room is still unoccupied. Virginia pushes open the door, then goes in and sits on the bed, her back against the wall. She sits like this in the frozen darkness for a couple of hours, her coat still on, listening to that appalling silence in a state of absolute despair.

Part Four

January–December 1942

CHAPTER
NINETEEN

*I*T IS MILLIE'S BIRTHDAY, and it is the end (finally) of the shooting of *Factory Girls* – both good reasons, in Millie's opinion, for having a party. Wisely she decides to hold it in the production offices, correctly concluding that few people will travel to Gidea Park for Spam rolls. That afternoon Virginia helps her to decorate the office, then goes home to change. She studies herself in her mirror, for some reason expecting to see lines of old age on her face induced by almost four weeks of being on the razzle since she's come back from the Dower House. She isn't even sure she wants to go to this party. The job is OK, but so far as men are concerned it's a dead loss. The only man she might have set her cap at was Pat Blain, but tonight as always, he'll have a ring of double steel: his wife is turning up and in the background there is always the glowering devoted Millie. As she absently buffs her nails somebody calls up from the hall to say there is a trunk call. Well, if it was someone making a better offer, she'd forget the party. In the telephone-booth in the hall it is both dark and cold, and echoes of supper – small helpings of rissoles and rice pudding – seem to have impregnated themselves in the very woodwork. As Virginia picks up the receiver, for no good reason she has a sudden premonition of disaster.

'I say, Virginia, it's—'

The line crackles madly into nothing.

'Who? You'll have to speak up.'

'It's Bertie here. Bertie Austen,' somebody shouts. 'You know, your mother's friend. She's too upset to ring you herself.'

'What is it? What's wrong?'

'I'm afraid it's Brooke. We had a telegram this morning. He didn't come back from a raid yesterday. I delayed ringing until I'd made a few enquiries.'

Virginia finds that her knees will not support her and slowly slides down the wall to the floor.

'What happened?'

'He was on a bombing raid to some oil-refineries in Rotterdam. They say his plane caught fire. Several people saw it go down, but they aren't sure if anybody managed to get out. I'm afraid that's all we know.'

There is a long silence.

'Are you still there, Virginia? I'm so sorry to be the bearer of bad news, but your mother is quite – well, she's in bed now.'

255

'Is it hopeless? Do you think there's any chance?'

'Quite a few come back. Or at the very least end up in a prisoner-of-war camp. That would be better than. . . . Just remember not to lose hope. I'll be back on the phone to you as soon as I know anything.'

Virginia sits with the purring receiver in her hands until she hears voices in the outer hall and pulls herself to her feet, replaces the receiver, then with a heavy heart goes back to her room. There is a leather-bound folder of photographs next to her bed. On one side there are pictures of Lucy and herself in the Champs-Elysées, Lucy monstrous in a flowered tussore dress. There is Lucy in her wedding dress. There is a newspaper cutting from the *Paddington Mercury* showing Cecily in her WVS uniform, loading a bath for salvage on to a lorry. On the other side is a single studio portrait of Brooke looking alert, handsome, purposeful, taken only this Christmas after he had been awarded his wing-commander stripes. Virginia looks at the picture for a long time, her heart thudding oddly.

'O God, our help in ages past,' says a voice automatically inside her. But God had revealed Himself as no help at all the last time she had really wanted anything. Abruptly she shuts the folder, takes out her gold evening dress and begins to do her face. Piling her curls on the top of her head, she pulls on her fur coat and goes down to get a taxi.

The roar in the production office is audible in the darkened street outside. Two-thirds of the people there are total strangers, but there are enough familiar friends bearing drinks to make her feel glad she's come. Dropping her fur wrap on to the pile of coats, she can see from the amused glances she's attracting that she is dramatically over-dressed – or under-dressed, depending on the way you looked at it. But what the hell, she concludes. Briskly she accepts a double gin and tonic from Billy Gavin, who has come wearing overalls that seem to contain a bottle of spirits in every pocket. She eagerly drinks off her glass in one gulp.

'Have another,' shouts Billy, eyeing her in alarm. 'That's a powerful thirst you've got on you, Duchess. Are you drinking to get drunk or to enjoy yourself?'

'To get drunk,' says Virginia, and pours herself another and drains it in the same way. Soon things are beginning to recede from her in the most reassuring way. 'Who are all these awful people?'

'Search me,' says Billy, producing yet another half-bottle of gin from somewhere in the region of his armpit. He takes a hefty swig, follows it with a mouthful from a tonic-bottle, courteously wipes both the tops and hands the two of them to Virginia.

'Millie's asked everybody in the phone-book, if you ask me. There's quite a few people from the Army Film Unit and a couple of people from the Crown lot. The rest are just workers and hangers-on. Hey, how would you fancy being my wee lassie for just one night?'

'I certainly would not,' says Virginia, whose head is whirling pleasantly. 'You couldn't afford me. Not with a wife and four children. Can I have another drink?'

The Spam rolls have long since vanished, and the volume of noise and the dense pall of cigarette smoke make it almost impossible to see or hear. Mr

Myerberg approaches her with a flashing smile but recoils when Virginia actually bares her teeth at him. There is a gramophone in one of the outer offices, and several couples are jitterbugging. Virginia makes her way across the room, greeting people she has never met with a gracious smile and a kiss.

'You're pissed, Musgrave,' says Trudy disapprovingly.

'Not yet, but I jolly well soon will be. Anyone here of interest?'

'Depends what you like. Ronnie Lemaire is over there talking to Pat. He's the one who played the captain in the submarine epic from Ealing. Trouble is, the chap with him is his boyfriend.'

'Who else?'

'Peter Barlow. He's the coming man at Ealing, whatever that means. Oh, and there's Alexis of course. You're worth making a pass at, aren't you, darling?'

'I'm the only man here who's even faintly attractive,' Alexis assures her, appearing suddenly at Virginia's elbow. 'Hello, Virginia. I heard you decided to turn an honest penny in the production office.'

It must be all of a year since Virginia has last seen Alexis. He looks remarkably the same, but there is a new confidence, a new assurance about him.

'How are you getting on?'

'Very well, thank you,' says Virginia coldly, wishing he would take his eyes off her décolletage and aware that Trudy's ears are out on stalks. 'Have you heard from Ferdinand?'

'Not since November. Have you seen the rushes of *Factory Girls*?'

'Oh, yes,' breathes Trudy. 'They're fantastic, Alexis. Your best yet, I'd say.'

'What did you think?'

Virginia shrugs elegantly. She also has seen the rushes and secretly is as impressed as anybody by them, but wild horses wouldn't have dragged the information from her. 'Everybody thinks you're wonderful; you don't need my praise as well.'

'Oh, but I do,' says Alexis, staring at her in the offensive way that she remembers had originally triggered off her dislike.

'Over here, darling,' he adds to someone standing behind Virginia, and a dark-haired gay-faced girl slides out of the crowd and puts an arm through his. 'I don't think you've met my girlfriend, Holly, have you? This is Virginia Musgrave, she's a friend of Ferdinand's.'

Virginia and Holly shake hands.

'Was it difficult – in Blackburn I mean?' gushes Trudy.

To Virginia's surprise, Holly answers for Alexis.

'Oh, pretty bad. We had incredible trouble with the interiors, didn't we, darling? And it was hell working in that factory. I really don't know how those girls stand it. Alexis, Daddy wants a word with you. Could you come and say hello? He's just over there.'

They disappear into the crowd.

'She's marvellous, isn't she? Holly I mean. She went to Oxford and she's already had a novel published.'

'Is she really Alexis' girlfriend?'

'Goodness, yes. They're virtually engaged. Or, rather, I think they were engaged and then they broke if off, but it's all on again now. She's Sir Charles Denvers's daughter, you know.'

'I don't know.'

'The boss of Imperial Lion Films, idiot. You'll never get anywhere as a crawler if you don't know who to suck up to. I didn't know you knew Alexis,' she adds abruptly.

'I don't. I know his cousin. He introduced me to Alexis once. I think Alexis is a crashing bore. End of story. And take that lemon-squeezer look off your face, Trudy. It wouldn't become anybody.'

They watch as Holly leads Alexis over to a shrewd-faced bald-headed man who is talking near the door to Pat Blain. Holly grabs her father's arm with the confidence of a much-loved child and with her other arm draws Alexis to her.

'Everybody loves Holly,' goes on Trudy suddenly. 'She's so friendly and sweet. Not a bit stuck-up considering.'

'Considering what?' says Virginia in her most freezing voice.

'Well, she's terribly clever. And she writes screenplays. But she wants to be a director. I'm sure she will be, because she's terribly brainy and so popular with the crews. Don't you think she's pretty?'

'No,' says Virginia. 'She's got scurf on her collar, the hem on her skirt has got safety-pins in it, and if she intends to go on smoking so heavily she should do something about the nicotine stains on her fingers.'

'You are a bitch, Virginia.'

'Yes,' agrees Virginia sadly. 'I'm famous for it.'

The rest of the evening has a curiously speeded-up quality. The following day Virginia can only remember strange disconnected scenes. She distinctly remembers being sick into a fire-bucket full of sand, held for her by the helpful Billy Gavin, whereupon she did the same for him. At some stage she had seen Millie doing the Charleston on the top of Pat Blain's desk. Either before or after that Billy Gavin had fallen down three flights of stairs and was found asleep in the hall below, apparently unharmed. Very much later Virginia remembers finding herself sitting in the cubbyhole under the stairs with Dennis, the messenger boy who has just started with the company. Dennis is fifteen and red-headed and wants to be a cameraman and reads magazines about the Continental cinema in his lunch hour. Why she should have told him about Brooke she simply could not say. But she did. And she remembered him sucking in his breath and unselfconsciously taking her hand in his own hot dry little paw.

'Most of them come back, you know,' he said eventually. 'I saw a film about it once, so it must be true. Tell you what,' he had added excitedly, 'I'll tell my mum to pray for him. You wait. She always gets results, does my mum.'

Virginia had thanked him, touched. All she could see at that particular moment was a sobering picture of Brooke turning over and over in the sea, his fair hair darkened by the waves, his eyes dull and unseeing. Presumably that must have prompted her to go home, for the next thing she remembered was trying to find her fur cape. To her extreme annoyance she found two people fornicating on top, and as she didn't recognize either of them had no compunction about tipping them on to the floor. Fortunately they had been too far gone to notice. Somebody had called good night to her as she went out, but she had ignored them. It might have been Alexis, but she wasn't sufficiently interested to find out. She had dreamt about Brooke all night. The next day, mercifully, is Saturday. All day, deaf to the knocks at her door, Virginia lies curled up in bed, her thumb in her mouth, her curtains tightly drawn. Finally at five o'clock she gets up, has a bath and goes down to the hall.

Home Farm shares a party line with five other farmers, so at best it's not an easy number to contact. Only tonight there is no line at all. Three times Virginia dials the number, only to be greeted with the 'unobtainable' tone. Ready to burst into tears Virginia finally rings up the post office and succeeds in raising Mrs Leary. Obligingly Mrs Leary says she will ask Lily to tell Lucy to ring Virginia when Lily takes up the post on Monday morning. It is hardly the instant communication that Virginia had hoped for, but it is better than nothing. Dispirited, Virginia joins the other girls and goes in to supper, and is just finishing her semolina and strawberry jam when Miss Groundsell herself appears in the doorway, flustered, saying there is a long-distance call for Virginia in her office. Instantly abandoning her pudding, Virginia flies down to Miss Groundsell's office and eagerly picks up the phone.

'Virginia! Hello! It's me, Lucy. I got your message!'

'Oh, Lucy. . . .' Absurdly Virginia wants to burst into tears. 'But how – I didn't think you'd get the message until much later on—'

'Oh, it was the purest luck. You probably know the party line is down at Home Farm, so I had to ride down to the village anyway to ring for an ambulance. It's just come. And Mrs Leary saw me on the green and came running out.'

'Why? What's happened? Who's the ambulance for?'

'You'll have to speak up, Vir. The noise here is absolutely deafening. I'm in the box by the war memorial.'

And, indeed, the noise *is* deafening. It is mysteriously as if Lucy is not standing in a quiet blacked-out Suffolk village but somehow has strayed on to the Great West Road. Waves of engine noise continue to roar past, rendering her almost inaudible.

'Who's hurt?' shouts Virginia.

'Mr McFee. The tractor must have turned over on top of him. Both his legs are broken and goodness knows what else. The awful thing is he must have been lying there for hours before I found him. It was quite frightful – I couldn't shift the tractor, you see. But he's on his way to Ipswich Hospital. But why did you ring? Not that it isn't lovely to hear from you,' she shouts.

Then the line miraculously clears and it is as if Lucy is standing beside her, roaring engines or no. Virginia promptly bursts into tears.

'Vir darling, what is it? What's wrong?'

'It's Brooke. There's been a telegram saying he's missing. Bertie rang and told me.'

'Oh, God. Oh, God,' says Lucy stupidly. 'I'm so sorry. Could he still—?'

'No one seems to know. But people do come back from . . . things like that, don't they?' she adds uncertainly.

At that moment Virginia actually sees Lucy in her mind's eye, sees her square her shoulders, feels her firming up her stance and consciously injecting a note of confidence in her voice. By Lucy and by Lucy only will Virginia allow herself to be comforted.

'Goodness, yes. Of course they do,' says Lucy robustly, and Virginia knows that it is for this that she has rung her. 'Why, when I was training in Essex there was a girl in my hut with two brothers in the RAF, and they both crashed and one found his way back through Spain and the other was in a prison-camp and he's still there, he's perfectly OK. The important thing is they were both safe. You mustn't ever despair. Oh, goodness, I wish I was there properly to help you; you must feel so dreadful.'

'It's so nice just to talk to you,' says Virginia, and an awkward silence falls. Then to her own utter astonishment Virginia hears herself say: 'You'd better tell Beattie. About the telegram I mean. I expect she'd want to know.'

'Oh, heavens. And she had her baby on Tuesday. It's a girl. Oh lord, Vir. I'm awfully sorry, I'm going to have to go in a minute. That was my last shilling. – No, you certainly cannot! Can't you see that this box is in use? – Honestly, you wouldn't believe it but some Yank burst in and wants to use the phone. That's what the noise is by the way. They started arriving after lunch today. There are going to be three airfields around Musgrave alone. Can you believe it? It's been lorries and more lorries all day. When I first saw all these steel-helmeted men arriving I thought the Germans had invaded us. But I suppose we're being invaded anyway. Dear Vir! Do ring me again if you want to talk to someone. They'll have mended the line by tomorrow morning. Do try to keep busy. I know it's a silly old cliché, but it does help. And I'll be thinking about you.'

CHAPTER <u> </u>
TWENTY

*T*HE Grangemouth, London W2
9 April 1942

Dear Lucy,

Thank you for your long letter. It gave me – as Mrs Epps who is currently cleaning our corridors would say – quite a turn. And I've waited a day or two while I've pondered on it all.

I quite understand you not wanting to talk about it at Christmas – my own response to awfulness is always to bury things out of sight for as long as possible. But when it's causing you all this pain I'm sure it's better talked about.

I read (and enclose) the letters Hugh wrote last year and have come to the conclusion that, as our American allies would say, poor Hugh has temporarily flipped his lid. I don't think you can deduce anything more than that, and I especially don't see why you should have to go ahead and submit to all the vileness of making divorce arrangements – unless of course you feel so angry about it that you really do want a divorce, and quickly. At the risk of sounding like Evelyn Home (does she really exist?) Hugh is away from home, he's been quite seriously ill and he's *undoubtedly* lonely. It *might* turn out that this Heap person (who could take seriously anybody called Heap? except Charles Dickens of course) is just a passing fancy. I appreciate all you say about duty, and not getting going when the going gets tough (our allies again!) but Hugh does have a duty to you as a husband. Nobody forced him to take his vows, and all he's done so far in that role is to send you a series of tactless letters. Quite apart from anything else it's just not good manners. Unless you really feel you want to take some action I'd let things ride for a bit.

I'm OK, the better for having stayed in for a few early nights in order to get to grips with my Advanced First Aid exam. Sometimes I wonder what I'm doing still staying at the Grangemouth. One of the girls on my floor has asked me if I'd like to share a flat with her in South Kensington, but even though I could afford it now Ma's coughed up an allowance for me I don't seem to have the energy to make a decision. Since Brooke disappeared I seem to live in a kind of limbo. I don't even seem able to concentrate on anything for very long. Bertie's rung twice, you probably know, simply to tell me there isn't any news but to keep smiling. He may be all sorts of an ass but he's got some nice instincts. Furthermore, if he hadn't been around, Ma would definitely have flipped her lid, too – she wrote to me at Easter and really sounded quite pathetic.

You didn't say anything about life at the wee homestead. How are you coping without the man of the farm? Do write back when you've got a chance. It's so lovely to get a long letter.

Love from
VIR

P.S. Don't even *think* of *ever* buying anything of John Pudney.

Home Farm, Musgrave, Dereham Market, Near Ipswich
27 April 1942

Dear Vir,

Thanks for the super letter. It cheered me up so much getting it off my chest. I felt so relieved that you didn't think I should act immediately, I was terrified you'd say you shouldn't let him treat you like that, you should stand up for your rights etc. etc. when at present I can barely crawl out of bed in the morning let alone think about long-term decisions. I know exactly what you mean about the lack of energy or even the ability to concentrate. I feel so stunned even now that beyond dealing with the day-to-day I'm completely useless. Fortunately I haven't heard a syllable from Hugh since December. It's got to the stage when I dread being told there's an airmail letter for me. It's funny when I think how much I used to look forward to hearing from him.

I'd much rather think that Hugh had 'flipped his lid' than that he'd really fallen in love, but some days I wonder if it was inevitable that he would find somebody else, men being what they allegedly are. But do you realize it's three years and three months since I last saw him? And before we married we'd only met eleven times. I went through my old diaries last night, and what a melancholy business *that* was. It gave me the most extraordinary feeling remembering what we were like in 1939 and how things have changed. The one for '39 is full of things about worrying about dressmakers, and buying the right shade of glove and appointments with the milliner and wondering if Mr Tony has made a mess of my hair. It seems another world now, doesn't it? I suppose the real strangeness of it all is that I never ever imagined myself working for a living – well, nothing more taxing than typing up Ma's manuscripts and keeping the library full of fresh flowers to keep her imagination stimulated. Ma really is becoming a bit of a prima donna. She now can't write unless she has fresh roses in the room with her, so she has them sent up from London every week. And she's taken a suite at Claridges because she needs to confer with her publishers so often about overseas rights – she comes down almost every month. I can't see why she can't use the telephone like anybody else, but still.

So far as I'm concerned – well, life here at present isn't easy. You might say it was dreadful, except that it's not likely to change so it hardly seems worth saying. Nevertheless I fear that I will not be able to resist complaining for a paragraph or 4. Poor Mr McFee is frightfully ill – it's a miracle he survived at all and sometimes we all wonder if it wouldn't have been better if he'd died. He's got compound fractures of both legs and one arm, a broken hip, six broken ribs and a fractured skull. It will be months and months and months before he's well enough to come home, let alone work, and in the mean time we flounder on from crisis to crisis. I remember when I came to Home Farm I was so impressed because everything ran like clockwork, everybody seemed to know what they were doing. Everything has fallen apart. For the first week Mrs M simply sat and wept and couldn't even do the chickens. I had to ring my area rep, and she very kindly sent me an extra land-girl called Stella to help out for a few weeks else I don't know *what* we'd have done. The awful thing is that I've ended up completely in charge – simply because no one else will take the responsibility. So now things are running better and everybody hates me. Old Tom and Jubal have worked here all their lives but are perfectly happy to let things *not* happen, and when I finally notice and start shrieking 'Why didn't you tell me that the plough needed attention?' or 'It's time to put the teaser in with the ewes' or 'We should have started sowing North Field first' they always say in an injured way 'Didn't ask, did you?' as if I read minds as well as everything else. At first I thought they were behaving like this because they didn't like taking orders from a woman. Now I think it's simply that they aren't used to anything except obeying orders. The result is sulks all round with Mrs M/F permanently red-eyed and the daughters dropping in day and night to try to cheer her up.

All this would be *bad enough* (you can see I'm in a real bait today!) without those blasted infernal troublesome noisy Americans building runways on two sides of the farm, disturbing the cows and really drastically affecting our milk yield. The final *straw* was when I found three of them *actually milking Daisy*! I gave them merry hell about the milk quota and they looked quite crestfallen, so then *I* started to feel *awful*. In the end I asked them back to tea at the farm on Sunday. Mrs M/F promptly had hysterics and said she was going to spend the afternoon sitting in the dairy but in the event stayed exactly where she was and seemed more cheerful since her lord and master fell off the tractor. The boys turned out to be really nice. They all come from New York, somewhere called Brooklin – Brooklyn? I'm not sure, but they told me they'd never seen a live cow before and they wanted to see how she 'worked'. I told them they were jolly lucky they'd chosen Daisy! I'd imagined all Yanks would be sophisticated seducers like Clark Gable but these boys were unbelievably young, they told me they'd barely ever left their own neighbourhood before. They've all come over here to fly, the planes start arriving in a fortnight, and after that I doubt if we'll ever know a moment's peace again. Sometimes I really can't believe how things have changed. The village shop is full of Americans and the lanes are full of jeeps. I'm sorry to say it is not bringing out the best in the village girls.

I saw Beattie last week. She asked me if there was any news of Brooke. I told her that I hadn't heard anything. She looks much better now the baby is born but a bit harassed. The baby is very sweet. She looks like Beattie but so far has no hair.

I'm sorry to rattle on about myself. When you write tell me exactly what life is like in your film company. I am writing this in the barn sitting on a bale of straw watching the rain falling into the yard outside. I've just discovered that one of my boots is leaking. In comparison, you seem to be living a life of some glamour!

Lots of love from
LUCY

172, Ferndale Road, Liverpool 8
10 May 1942

Dear Beattie,

You will have to forgive the long long silence, but as you can see from the change of address an awful lot has happened since I got your last letter. First of all, I am so glad that everything went well and that you and Annie are going on so splendidly – she sounds a grand baby. I look forward to seeing a snap of her when you have some done. As regards us all at the 'Pool – well, I don't really know where to begin. First of all our Debbie announced after Christmas that she was going to get married (at 17!) and Mother went mad until she found out that Debbie was in the family way as well and went properly barmy. The father is 19, he's called Dave, and stationed at Birkenhead. He seems nice enough but he doesn't say much. They got married at the beginning of February at the Register Office on Mount Pleasant. We had a bit of a party afterwards and some snaps were taken – I'll send you some when I get them. Two days later we had the first really bad bombing raid we'd had since Christmas. Mother didn't want to go down to that shelter – no one did – but I forced them and I'm glad I did because our building got a direct hit and there's nothing left now except rubble and bricks. I don't think I will ever, ever forget coming out of the shelter at 7 o'clock in the morning and finding bright sunshine and clouds and clouds of brown smoke and that terrible sharp smell you get after a bomb. We started walking towards home and we all stopped short and crashed into each other and Mother said 'You've taken the wrong turning, Louie,' and she actually turned round quite confidently to go the opposite way. And I said, 'Mother, Mother, this is it, it's been bombed,' and she fainted. We spent the next week at a rest centre in Upper Parliament Street. The WVS run it and they did their best – we came in with the clothes we stood up in and that was all. Thank goodness I'd taken all my books into my room at school. WVS got us more clothes and comforted Mother. If they hadn't, I don't know what we'd have done. I had to go in to school regardless. Then after a week a colleague at school told me there was a house to let near hers. At first I thought we'd never be able to afford it but we went to look anyway just to try to cheer Mother up. Oh, Beattie, you've never seen anything like it! Three bedrooms, a breakfast room, a nice snug sitting-room and a proper kitchen and a scullery. No bathroom of course but a good outside toilet and only us that use it! We worked it out that with my money and some lodgers we could afford to take it. Mother said she'll cook for them. So, we've taken a year's lease on it – I signed the forms on Monday. One of the totters lent us a cart and we bought a lot of secondhand furniture from the market and brought it home on Tuesday. So now we are settled in and as snug as you like. There is a good big shelter in the garden next door, and I make sure we all go out there every night.

I think Mother is becoming a bit more like her old self. We have let the front bedroom to 2 girls who work in the Ministry of Food office. They are Welsh and go to Chapel but are quite friendly. We have a bit of a garden and Mother loves that. Debbie will stay with us until the baby's born. I hope it will all turn out for the good, but it seems terrible to say that when ten of our neighbours died.

I seem to have written pages about myself and said nothing about you. Forgive the paper, it's all I have at present. It's 3A's spelling test and as you can see they are still struggling with the letter i before e in spite of all my efforts to fix it in their heads.

I have just pulled out your last letter and I'm blushing to discover it was written on 9 February! It must have been at the end of your stay at the nursing home. It was right decent of Charles to suggest you had Annie there – I'm sure that week afterwards of peace and quiet must have been a great boon. Beattie, there's no point in asking me what you should do about this Charles Hammond. I just don't know. It seems to me that he's acted very decently – and he's hardly forced his attentions on you. Perhaps he's waiting for you to make a move. Do you really want a divorce? You hardly know him – and, though you won't be pleased with me for saying this, you haven't given him much of a chance, have you? I wish I'd met him. I was sure I had until you sent me the wedding picture, then I knew I hadn't – I've got a good memory for handsome men.

Talking of which – at least I've now got somewhere nice to invite Vince if he comes up and stays. He's asked *me* down to Gatton in the summer – he can get me a room. I could come and see you, wouldn't that be a laugh! Anyway I must go now and do some marking. I can see the postman further down the street – I hope he's got a letter for me from Vince – I haven't heard from him in weeks. I wrote to him as soon as we were bombed out so he wouldn't send any letters to the wrong address. Keep cheerful. I'll write again soon. Mother sends you all her love and is pleased the baby is so well.

Lots of love from
LOUIE

Then below, in a quite different handwriting, a wild PS:

Beattie, I've just heard from Vince about Brooke. I'm so sorry. So sorry. Vince says they haven't given up hope at Gatton, so you mustn't, either. I'll get Mother to pray for him. I'm thinking about you, don't forget that.

Church Cottage, Back Lane, Musgrave, Near Ipswich
18 May 1942

Dear Louie,

It was so good to get your letter – I had begun to fear the very worst. The lady in the post office has a sister in Cheshire and she had told me about the heavy raids and I was afraid something terrible had happened. I'm sorry about your home but glad about your new house. It sounds grand, and just the thing to cheer up your mother. Give her my love.

Here there isn't much news, which is odd really because everything has changed, but I suppose nothing much happens to *me*. Annie is a good baby, or so I'm told; she only cries when she's hungry and she sleeps the rest of the time. Mother is properly on the mend and loves Annie. The village is awash with young men in olive green and the children come home every day with chocolate and fruit. You'd think a mother with a three-month-old baby would be immune from men getting fresh but it is not the case – I am sick of being pestered. It's difficult because the vicar wants us to be friendly. We've had several lots of young men to tea. The ones who actually come into our home are very nice and have very good manners and are delighted to talk about their homes in America.

There's still no news of Brooke. I try not to think about him too much. I wrote to Charles just before the baby was born, thanking him for all his kindness, particularly that business of booking me into the nursing home. It was *heaven*. I could move in there tomorrow and never come out again. And he sent me back such a nice letter saying that my letter had cheered him up because he'd begun to think maybe he'd done more harm than good in suggesting we marry. And he told me they'd had a terrible winter up there and that 29 members of his squadron had died. (He isn't flying apparently, I don't know why.) That made me feel awful because I'd never as much as asked him a syllable about his own life. I was feeling quite warmly towards him and thought I'd invite him down to stay as soon as the baby was born, then I heard about Brooke. Lucy came into the nursing home to tell me. She was fearfully embarrassed at having to admit that she knew about Brooke and me but she said Virginia had said I ought to know. I suppose that was nice of her. Brooke's mother is a sight. She stops almost total strangers in the street to tell them about Brooke. She's obsessed with him. As I say, there's no news except the Red Cross would have found out by now if he was in a prisoner-of-war camp. As it is, he could still be alive but in hiding.

My cousin Lily Kedge is in love with an American called Greg who comes from somewhere called Santa Monica. We haven't found it in the atlas so far but we may be looking in the wrong place; it certainly isn't near New York. As a result she's been plaguing me and Lucy to go to the base for a dance. So far we have both refused, but Lily is getting so dispirited that I can see we'll have to go once to keep her quiet. I had a nice letter from Barbara Ann when Annie was born and a whole boxful of baby products. I can't think where she got them – Mother says she hasn't seen the like of them since before the war. Thank you *very* much for the wonderful pram rug – both the boys wanted to have it on their beds, it has been a real struggle to keep it for Annie! It would be wonderful if you came down in the summer. Please do try. I'm going to write to Charles this week and ask him if he'd like to come down for a few days some time and try to straighten things out between us, at least try to sort out what his intentions are. It seems an odd thing to be enquiring of one's husband. Write again as soon as you have the time.

Much love from
BEATTIE

Reel Film Productions, Soho Square, W1
1 June 1942

Dear Lucy,
I am delighted to hear that you have become a captain of agriculture, but not a bit surprised – you clearly have the Dunkirk spirit, and Mr Churchill must be proud of you. The only bit of current news I have is really no news at all, and that is that a friend of Brooke's was in London about a fortnight ago and took me out to lunch. In the spirit of generally trying to cheer me up he told me they are still hopeful at Gatton that Brooke is alive but injured and being taken care of by Dutch partisans. It's pure supposition but it was enough to make me give a larger donation than usual to a raffle for Dutch refugees at the Savoy (a really terrible dance. Why does one go to these things?).

I wrote and told Ma what Desmond had told me and got the most heartrending letter by return – I never thought I'd find myself saying 'poor Ma', but she really is in such a state one can't but pity her. I've always known Brooke was her favourite but somehow it doesn't seem to matter any more – I just wish he'd come home. If he finally doesn't, I suppose it'll be some consolation for Mother to know he had a child but she'd make such a to-do about it that I rather dread the idea of telling her. Especially as she's never had an inkling of anything going on. It suddenly occurred to me the other day that I had a niece – it was a very strange feeling.

You ask me to tell you what it's like here. Well, I can tell you in one sentence. It's a madhouse. The people who work for Reel Films – and, I suspect, anybody who works in the film industry – all have one thing in common. They are absolutely obsessed with films and think about nothing else. You might assume since they make their films for the Ministry of Information that they are passionately interested in the war as well. But the war just happens to be the current subject-matter. I've never met a group of people so completely turned in on themselves – they only talk about the work in hand and that big row with Ealing/the Army Film Unit/the MI. (there's always at least one major crisis on the go). Before I came to London I'd never met anyone who was passionate about *anything*, let alone *work*. Theo Beavers is pretty passionate about the English novel but he keeps it to himself. (He sent me the new Evelyn Waugh by the way. *Wonderful*. I've lent it elsewhere but will send it off to you if you GUARD IT WITH YOUR LIFE.) Anyway, you get the picture of Reel Films. During the day they talk non-stop about the films they're making – and at night they go to the cinema or to the rushes of someone else's film and they talk about that all the next day. The only perk of the job is that I do get to see quite a few free screenings.

It's very strange to have ended up in the same company as Ferdinand's cousin. (No news of Ferdinand, worse luck.) Alexis Seligman is currently our golden boy, which means that half the company worship him (particularly the females) and the other half – particularly the directors – complain non-stop to Pat Blain, who is Top Brass, that Alexis is given all the best crews and the lion's share of the budget. All of which is perfectly true, but the MI currently thinks that he can do no wrong. He's had a string of real successes, so I suppose they want his golden touch to last as long as possible. The scriptwriters complain that Alexis is impossible to work with because he never tells anybody what he's doing, but just makes notes on a bus ticket which he then loses. (It sounds unlikely, somehow, given the size of your average bus ticket.) One way and another I seem to spend a lot of time listening to people complaining about Alexis but I can get on with my typing at the same time, so I don't take it all terribly seriously.

But my dear! I clean forgot! My only real piece of exciting news and I forget to lead off with it! You will never never guess! I'm doing some modelling for *News Chronicle*! This photographer just rang me up one day and said someone had suggested me for a feature they were doing called 'Best Dressed on a Budget' (!). One of their fashion editors took me out to lunch, told me I would do and came back with me to the Grangemouth to select some outfits to be photographed in. It's all going to be in next week's paper, so don't forget to look out. The extraordinary thing is the photographer has already rung again – he said someone on *Vogue* 'wants to see me'. It's rather fun. Anyway, that's all my news. Hope you are well, keep cheerful and write to me soon.

Love from
VIRGINIA

Home Farm, Musgrave, Near Ipswich
29 June 1942

My dear Vir,
Yes, of course I saw your photographs and was thrilled out of my wits and so is your ma! Bertie told me she said she could have wished they'd been in *The Times* or even at least in the *Telegraph* but that you'd certainly come out very nicely. I thought you looked *wonderful*, exactly like a model but much prettier and friendlier somehow, they always look so haughty don't they? Has the *Vogue* thing come to anything yet? I've cut out all the photographs and will start a scrapbook if this is to be a regular occurrence! I found your description of life at Reel Films quite alarming – I find it bad enough having to cope with Jubal's complaints let alone half the workforce's. But things have quietened down a lot – though I can't think why I am using that particular expression since the noise level morning and evening is unbelievable. They've started flying daytime raids from Musgrave, in the most extraordinary planes like wardrobes called B17s. (I owe all this technical information to the Blythes' Toby, who is obsessed with anything to do with the Yanks.) When I take the cows in for milking at 7 o'clock I see the planes take off, simply laden with bombs, and I stand and wait to see them coming up

over the elms at the boundary hedge of the farm. Sometimes it seems as if their sheer bulk just won't let them clamber up into the sky but somehow they always take off and you can hear the engines dying away for minutes afterwards.

They start coming home mid-afternoon and I just can't not count them back – especially since their losses have been so huge. Didn't the RAF stop daylight bombing raids because they were so dangerous? They've had some truly terrible losses, and I feel so sorry for the crews – most of the boys you see in the village are my age or even younger.

For once I, too, actually have some news! I went to Yorkshire last weekend to see Mother and Father. I hadn't planned to – the whole thing was a shambles because I only got to hear about the lift up to Harrogate on Friday morning and by then it was too late to send a telegraph, so when I arrived I discovered Mother had gone to London for the weekend to see her American agents!

Still, I have a *lovely* weekend. Lots of delicious food and plenty of hot baths. Dad was thrilled to see me – it may have been a good thing that Mother wasn't there because I could give him my full attention. I was a bit taken aback by how he looked – he's lost an awful lot of weight and he seems to be getting pains in his chest and is generally out of spirits. We talked non-stop about what I was doing and what *they* were doing, but I kept feeling he wanted to say something to me but couldn't quite bring himself to. When I finally asked him on Sunday morning if there was something wrong he went bright red and pulled his moustaches, the way he always does when he's embarrassed, and muttered something about Mother being terribly sought after these days and him not wanting to be a brake on her. That made me pretty cross, I can tell you. Considering Dad's been behind her all the way with her writing. So I tried to cheer him up about that and told him he was as invaluable now as he'd always been. I just hope it's true. Ma's got a new book out by the way called *For the Sake of St Margaret's*, and it's the first book of hers I've found completely unreadable. Needless to say it's selling like the proverbial.

I got the same lorry back on Sunday afternoon and we crept home to Musgrave arriving at 4 o'clock in the morning as the sun was coming up. I was pleased I'd seen Dad. I'm going to make an effort to see them more often.

Other than that, what's new? Lily Kedge has finally persuaded Beattie and myself to go to a dance at one of the bases. Neither of us wants to go – they send a lorry to the war memorial at 8 o'clock to pick up the girls – it's like pigs going to market. But Lily tells me her future happiness depends on us going, so put like that it seems a small sacrifice to make. I'll tell you all about it when I write next.

Lots of love from
LUCY

CHAPTER
TWENTY-ONE

'MOTHER, SHE SLEEPS LIKE A LOG. She'll never wake up before twelve, and I'll be home long before that. I wouldn't go but for Lily asking me especially.'

'You do look nice, Aunty Bee,' says Toby approvingly. 'Don't you think so, Aunt Madge?'

'You look fine, Beattie. And anyway I think it's high time Beattie had a bit of fun.'

Mrs Blythe sighs and shakes her head.

'It's the way the girls round here are behaving about the Yanks – I don't want our Beattie tarred with the same brush.'

'Which brush is that?' askes Little Ern, interested. 'Is it the one I brush Beetle with?'

Mrs Blythe smiles in spite of herself.

'Never you mind, young man. More tea, anybody? If you've finished, you two can get down and get ready for bed, please, Toby.'

'Ten minutes to rearrange my swaps.'

'Ten minutes only, then.'

'What swaps are they, Toby?' Aunt Madge enquires, interested.

'Cigarette cards,' begins Toby importantly. 'I got two off Charlie Biggs. . . .'

Beattie goes over to the Moses basket where Annie is lying, chortling to herself, momentarily content but clearly in the expectation of an imminent feed. Leaving the warm kitchen, Beattie goes to her bedroom to get her a clean terry square. She is not pushed about going out tonight; it is literally a favour to Lily, who nowadays, as Aunt Madge drily remarks, has not only stars but stripes in her eyes as well. But it is worth going out simply to remember she is not only a mother, to have the opportunity to dress up, to feel the unfamiliar smear of lipstick on her lips, to know that the old Beattie is still there – that the present motherly, breast-feeding, permanently harassed Beattie hasn't been taken over for life. Feeding Annie herself has certainly brought back her figure, and the vitamins that Lord Woolton insists his pregnant mothers need have given weight and gloss to her hair and a sheen to her skin. The youthful Beattie, the wide-eyed girl with the hollows of adolescence still in her cheeks, has gone for ever. But the character of the woman who regards her from her bedroom mirror has yet to be decided.

Back in the kitchen on the clear end of the table Toby is displaying his newly acquired cigarette cards to an interested audience. There is a sudden rat-a-tat at the back door.

'Oh, that can't be Lucy already, is it?' groans Beattie. 'I thought she said eight o'clock. It'll take me a good three-quarters of an hour to feed Annie. . . .'

She opens the back door, letting in a waft of the damp scented May night. The garden is in darkness, and in the half-light from the kitchen Beattie dimly discerns a tall man in an RAF uniform. The shock makes her gasp and clutch the door-frame. Then the man moves forward, and the beam of light from the kitchen falls on to his face.

It is Charles Hammond.

'Why, Charles,' says Beattie feebly, her heart beating so frantically that she feels she will faint. Fortunately Aunt Madge is already nimbly on her feet and moving forward with alacrity.

'Charles! Charlie Hammond! Well, I never did. And here's me only thinking of writing to you this morning. . . .'

Charles, clearly reassured by the warmth of Aunt Madge's welcome at least, steps forward into the kitchen. He and Beattie eye each other, then awkwardly Charles bends down and kisses her on the cheek.

'Well, Charles, this is a pleasant surprise,' says, most surprisingly, Beattie's father, who with great firmness and dignity comes forward, shakes Charles by the hand and consciously draws him into the family group. Mrs Blythe in her turn offers her hand in turn, and in those split seconds of greeting Beattie sees the kitchen as it must seem to Charles's eyes. Two years ago she would have fretted about the dingy walls, the lack of furniture, the primitive oil-lamps, the simplicity of the supper on the table. Tonight she sees only the people: her mother and aunt admittedly in crossover cretonne overalls but dignified, welcoming, Father in his working clothes, and the two round-eyed well-scrubbed little boys in pyjamas. Charles clearly sees nothing to complain about. The strain in his face lessens, leaving only a man who is very glad indeed to sit down amidst a circle of welcoming faces.

'I know I shouldn't have just dropped in out of the blue but I - I only learnt today that I had some leave and had to report to London later in the week. As I was going to be passing this way I thought - I do hope you don't mind. . . .' he concludes hastily, and Beattie knows perfectly well that, although his remarks are addressed out of deference to Mrs Blythe, it is to Beattie that he is really making his appeal.

'I'm really glad you've come, Charles,' says Beattie, trying to inject a note of warmth into her voice, finding herself unable not to respond to the unconscious sadness in Charles's face.

'The question is where Charles is going to stay,' muses Mrs Blythe, making it quite clear who's châtelaine of the house. 'Now, if the boys—dear me, do you know there really isn't room to swing a cat here, Charles, and the sofa in the front room is too short—'

'Charles will get a room at the Crown and have his meals with us,' says Mr Blythe, making one of his rare entries into conversation but as usual intervening to some purpose. 'There's bound to be a room at the Crown. I'll walk on up while Charles has his supper, and he can leave his traps there by and by.'

There is a thin wail from the Moses basket by the range.

'You haven't seen Annie yet,' says Toby and goes to pick the baby up before Beattie can speak. 'She's a very good baby, is Annie – aren't you, sweetheart? – hardly cries at all. She looks just like Beattie, doesn't she?'

Toby tenderly tucks Annie's shawl more securely round her and hands her over to a bemused Charles.

'She's a dear little baby, isn't she?' appeals Toby anxiously.

Charles looks at Annie, and a series of emotions struggle in his face. Finally he smiles and touches the little girl on the cheek.

'Yes, she is a dear little baby. And she's the image of you, Beattie,' he says, and his eyes meet Beattie's properly for the first time.

'Though Beattie's got more hair,' observes Ern dispassionately. 'Was Beattie born bald?'

'No, she had a mass of fine dark hair right down into her eyes.'

'We'll have to feed Annie up.'

'And Charles, too. Take Charles into the scullery to wash his hands, Toby—'

There is another brisk rat-a-tat at the back door and the sound of giggling and scuffling. Toby leaps to his feet again.

'That'll be Lily and Lucy. Hello! How are you!'

'Hello, all. Why, it's Charles Hammond, isn't it?'

Lucy and Lily, dressed up in their best, and hair curled, advance on a bemused Charles.

'This is my cousin, Lily Kedge,' says Beattie. 'And Lucy Jennings, who's a friend of ours. I think you met them both at the wedding.'

'Yes, of course I remember. You took the snaps, didn't you, Lily?'

'That's right. Fancy you remembering that! Well! This is a facer. I suppose that means you won't be coming to the dance, will you? Unless Charles wants to come too. No, I suppose he wouldn't want to. Still, you'll be staying over, won't you, Charles? So you must come and have a drink with us tomorrow. You can meet Greg.'

'It's very nice to see you again, Charles,' is Lucy's rather quieter greeting. 'You seem to have brought the good weather with you.'

'We'll have to be on our way,' says Lily with a hasty glance at her watch. 'Can't keep the boys waiting. Ta ta, Beattie. How is the little love, all right, eh? She wants her grub, doesn't she? She'd have the buttons off my shirt if I'd let her.'

With many more cheerful exhortations to have a good evening the two girls disappear off into the darkness, leaving Charles looking faintly stunned at the volume of noise and traffic passing through the kitchen. Then just as suddenly the room begins to empty. Little Ern and Toby are led firmly off to bed. Mrs Blythe disappears to shut up the chickens. Mr Blythe has already set off to enquire at the Crown. Beattie, resigned to the fact that all existing plans for the evening must be abandoned, sits down in the rocking chair, goes to open her dress, then stops, blushing.

'Do you mind if I—? I mean, I'll go into the other—'

'Of course I don't mind,' says Charles brusquely and, picking up the cup of tea that Mrs Blythe has poured him, comes and sits across from her in Mr Blythe's high-backed Windsor chair. 'Look, Beattie, if you really would rather I didn't stay, I won't. I seem to have got everything wrong. I didn't mean to stop you going out.'

'That's all right,' says Beattie hastily, telling herself firmly that there is no need for her to explain to Charles that this is the very first time she's ever been to a dance at the base, and she certainly isn't that kind of girl, whatever that kind of girl is. Oh, goodness, what a tangle. 'Lily asked me and Lucy to go along and keep her company. Lily's walking out with—'

'Someone called Greg,' finishes Charles for her with a smile that suddenly lights up his whole face. For the first time Beattie smiles properly, too.

'That's right. He comes from California, a place called Santa Monica. They grow oranges there, imagine. Anyway, we said we'd go and meet his friends – you know, to see what kind of person he is. But I can just as well see them at the pub. Perhaps you'd like to come, too.'

At this moment the teat falls out of Annie's mouth and she gives a roar of disapproval. Hastily Beattie shoves it back in and a greedy silence falls again.

'She looks – er – er – a very healthy baby,' says Charles politely, then he catches Beattie's eye and they both start smiling unwillingly. 'I'm sorry. That's a pretty meaningless sort of remark. But I haven't had a lot to do with babies. Being an only child, I don't think I've ever even nursed one. But she does look like you. Even I can see that.'

Mrs Blythe comes in from the hen-house, pours herself another cup of tea and sits down at the kitchen table. She then proceeds to question Charles in a grave and courteous way as to how he is, how his health has been, and how his job is going. It is thus that Beattie learns that Charles is to be transferred from his present squadron to intelligence work somewhere near Oxford.

'Well, that'll be nice,' says Aunt Madge, coming in on the end of the conversation. 'You'll be able to pop over here in no time at all. Won't he, Beattie? Is it a promotion, Charles?'

'Yes, I suppose so,' says Charles with hardly the outburst of spirits one would expect from such an occasion. 'As I said, I was only told this morning, and as I had a bit of leave owing they told me to take it before I started the new job.'

'Then, you must spend it here,' says Mrs Blythe with quite unexpected firmness. 'Unless of course you've made other arrangements?'

Charles is clearly taken aback.

'Well, that's very nice of you, Mrs Blythe, but I wouldn't want to impose—'

'Do stay, Charles,' says Beattie. 'At least for part of the week. It'll be a waste to be in London with all this beautiful weather.'

'I'm only sorry we couldn't put you up but, as you see, we've got a full house,' says Mrs Blythe with a look of astonishment that always crosses her face as she realizes that she now has a family of seven people. 'But you'll be comfortable enough at the Crown. And, as Mr Blythe says, you must come here for your meals.'

273

Conversation flows on in a cheerful way, leaving Beattie to concentrate on Annie, who likes to have her undivided attention at mealtimes. Even so, Beattie is able to steal odd glances at Charles. His natural courtesy makes him respond in a polite and animated way to the conversation, but Beattie can tell he is tired and it is an effort for him to speak.

Nine o'clock is striking by the time Annie has fully satiated her hunger, been changed and taken up to Beattie's room to sleep by the warm chimney-breast.

'Will you come to church with us tomorrow, Charles? We leave on the dot of half-past nine. You need to set out that early these days to get a seat at all, what with the evacuees and the visitors.'

'I'll walk up to the Crown with you,' says Beattie, pulling on her coat.

Outside the cottage she asks: 'Did you come by car?'

'Yes, it's parked by the church wall. Ow!'

In the darkness Charles almost topples over and clutches Beattie.

'I can't see a hand in front of me and something just shot through my legs.'

'I'm afraid that's Beetle. It's one of his tricks. Here, take my arm, and we'll go up the back way to the main street. Don't worry, I know where I'm going, so you won't trip over. I feel bad about not being able to offer you a bed at the cottage.'

'That's perfectly all right. It was wonderful to have such a warm welcome. It's standing room only, isn't it?'

'I remember when it used to be just the three of us. The house didn't seem big then.'

'Do Toby and Ern see their parents?'

'Not since – goodness, not since November thirty-nine. But of course we didn't know their father. We all wonder if their mother was killed in the Blitz. We've never heard of her since she sent them presents that Christmas. The boys did say once that their father was called up early and sent overseas, but we don't know if it's true or just something their mother told them. It's odd – the boys are so open in some ways, but if you ask them anything about London they clam up. . . . Here we are. This is the Crown.'

The room Mrs Gliding has to offer is clean and relatively comfortable with an armchair, a chest of drawers and a single bed with a flowered coverlet.

'And so it'll be bed and breakfast for how long?'

Charles glances questioningly at Beattie, then says: 'Well, definitely till Wednesday. Would you like a drink, Beattie? It seems the least I can do when I've messed up your evening.'

'I told you, you didn't mess up the evening. I was only going because of Lily.'

In the small brown varnished bar they are quickly joined by Mr Blythe, the infamous Sid Kedge, poacher and father of ten, and the vicar who believes that an occasional drink in the pub brings him closer to his parishioners. In fact over the next three days Beattie finds that far from being forced into a series of unwelcome tête-à-têtes with Charles she is rarely alone with him. It is as if Charles's coming has signified a general sense of holiday.

'Come on up to the airbase,' pleads Toby, who goes up every day after school to watch the planes returning.

'Well, you can go if you want, but I think it's all wrong, that standing round and watching,' says Beattie, suddenly wrathful. 'It's not just a spectacle, Toby, for us to go and admire. Those young men have got mothers and fathers and goodness knows who else at home who must be worried out of their minds. If you want to go and look at the planes, that's one thing, but don't forget it's people who drive them and they can get hurt and maimed.'

Abashed, Toby goes up on his own. The following day Charles offers to drive them all to Ipswich to go shopping, and in the end they stay and have supper and go to the cinema. It is a gala occasion. That is Monday. On Tuesday, Charles helps Mr Blythe saw up a fallen tree on the estate, helps Beattie to do the local shopping and plays cards with them all until it's time for the boys to go to bed.

On Wednesday when Charles turns up he takes Beattie on one side. 'Look, I've got to go to London tonight. Is there any chance of us spending a bit of time together today?'

'That will be nice,' says Beattie, who is by no means sure it will be. 'We could walk up to the pond and have a picnic there if you like.' Inwardly Beattie has been dreading being alone with Charles ever since he arrived. But why? she keeps asking herself crossly. She knows the answer perfectly well. She is afraid Charles will ask her what she wants. And all Beattie currently wants is not to be asked that particular question.

As they walk down the village street, Annie beaming at the sunshine in her perambulator, Beattie can see Charles breathing deeply and enjoying the air.

'It's not always like this, you know.'

'Like what?'

'The sun and things. I sometimes think spring's the best part of the year in Suffolk. But winters here last for ever – there are months and months when it starts getting dark at half-past two. But I suppose it makes you appreciate all this much more.'

'It reminds me of where I was at school,' says Charles most unexpectedly. 'We were right in the country then. I'd forgotten how much I must have liked it after Manchester.'

'Did you like school?'

'Well, yes and no. I think I'd have been perfectly content to stay at my day school in Manchester. But Dad wanted me to have a public school education, so I did. It had its good moments. And I can see now that I was very well taught. Though I'm not sure I'd send my own children to boarding school,' he adds without thinking, and an awkward silence falls.

'We can go through the park if you like. There's lots of daffodils in the woods.'

As they walk up the drive to the Manor, a crowd of young children playing rounders come running up to Beattie, begging to see Annie. Charles is introduced, then the mistress in charge firmly shoos the children back to their game.

'Is this where Brooke . . . lives?'

Charles has clearly taken some care about the tense of the verb.

'No,' Beattie tells him brusquely. 'It belongs to his family, but Brooke's father was the younger son so they never actually lived here. It's always been let. *They* live at the Dower House at the other end of the street.'

'Oh, that nice Queen Anne house with the magnolias.'

'That's right.'

Charles pauses for a second, eyes screwed up against the morning sun while he contemplates the Manor.

'Pretty little place, isn't it?' he says at last. 'It's much smaller than I'd imagined. Really it's just a big family house, isn't it?'

The Beattie of three years ago would have been outraged beyond measure by such a slighting remark, but having seen Chillington Park she's forced to agree.

'Not in very good condition, though,' goes on Charles absently, narrowing his eyes as he studies the roof and guttering. 'It would take a lot to make all this good again. How long are the Barnardo's people staying?'

'I don't know. No one seems to know. Till it's safe to go back to London, I suppose.'

'Which way now?'

'Round the shubbery and across the ridge.'

They walk on in what Beattie hopes is a companionable silence. When they reach the woods she says: 'It's not much of a place really; it's just we come here a lot with the boys. It looks a whole lot better since they pulled out the junk – it all went for salvage to Ipswich. But we get frogspawn from here in the early spring – and we've actually skated on here for two winters. Oh, and in the summer the boys always swim here if it gets that hot.'

'The boys swim in that?' Charles enquires, incredulous, staring at the thick emerald-green surface of the pond.

'Oh, yes, that's only weed,' says Beattie, amused. 'Why, up to ten years ago the families on the other side of the wood used to drink from this pond. Then they put in a well behind one of the cottages.'

Part of the charm of the pond is that it is in a sheltered hollow which holds all the available sunshine. The bank opposite is thickly starred with primroses. Beattie parks Annie in the shade then spreads a rug for Charles and herself to sit on. She has brought a book and advised Charles to do the same. Busying herself with the picnic-basket, Beattie tries to put together a suitable opening remark for a serious discussion. When she feels she has both the remark and the confidence to deliver it, she turns firmly to Charles only to find he has fallen deeply asleep on the plaid rug, his book unopened in his hands.

It is clearly no idle doze. He has fallen into the deep, almost motionless sleep of a man who is literally bone weary. So instead she prises the book out of his fingers and leaves him to enjoy his rest, planning to make use of the unexpected luxury of reading in absolute peace. Then slowly her own head begins to nod and finally all three of them sleep peacefully under the shifting green branches.

Annie is the first to wake, talking companionably to herself until Beattie opens her eyes and sees from her watch that it is nearly one o'clock. Charles is still asleep, his dark head pillowed on his arm. Without disturbing him Beattie gets up and feeds Annie, sitting on a broken log overlooking the pond. Then abruptly the sound of Charles's angry voice makes her jerk her head in astonishment. He is still lying on the plaid rug but his body has stiffened convulsively as he beats on the ground with his bare fist.

'Charles,' calls Beattie urgently, gathering Annie to her as she stands up, perplexed. 'Wake up. What is it?'

With a terrifying suddenness Charles jerks into a sitting position and total wakefulness, his face pale save for where his sleeve has made a red mark on his cheek. It is immediately apparent that he has no idea of where he is or what he's doing. Then slowly the woods, the pool, the pond, the high call of the cuckoo overhead and Beattie's anxious face come into focus.

'Charles, what is it? Did you have a bad dream?'

Wordlessly Charles passes a hand over his brow. He is trembling.

'Skip it,' he says violently, so completely out of character with his usual polite self that Beattie stares at him. But he goes on harshly: 'Just forget it. Is it lunchtime? I feel I've been asleep for hours.'

'We've all been asleep,' says Beattie quietly, putting Annie back into her pram and getting out the string bag with their picnic in it. Silently she sets out the flask and the Bakelite mugs and the sandwiches. Charles sits for a long time in silence, then looks up at Beattie with no particularly friendly expression on his face.

'You haven't told me much about yourself. I suppose there hasn't been much time to find out how you are.'

'I'm fine,' says Beattie lamely. 'And Annie's well.'

'Are you going back to teaching?'

'Teaching? With a baby in tow?'

'Well, presumably you could find someone to take care of her for a few hours a day.'

'I haven't even thought of it.'

'Don't you ever feel you want to use your training?'

'Oh, I think about it all the time,' says Beattie in a heartfelt way that surprises even her. 'But don't forget I never got to use my diploma. But I really loved my teaching practice. I felt I was quite good at it and I've always liked the children.'

'I can understand that,' says Charles unexpectedly. 'Why not get a part-time job? There must be loads of private schools evacuated round here if they can't take you on at the village primary.'

Beattie is startled by the turn of the conversation. 'I suppose I could make enquiries,' she says slowly. 'I just never thought – though I'd love the chance.'

Her tone is rapt and wistful.

'I've taught, too, you know,' says Charles most unexpectedly and with more friendliness than he's shown since he's woken up. 'In the year before I went up to Oxford. At a prep school in West Didsbury. I enjoyed it, much to my surprise. In fact—' He checks himself.

'In fact what?'

'Well, before Christmas I had to do something to take my mind off what was happening at the base. I write a bit, I've had a try at poetry and done some articles, but I thought just for fun I'd try a thriller. I've read so many I

277

thought I could make a good fist at one myself. So I set it in the prep school where I used to teach. It seemed ideal. If you can't have a country house in the snow, a prep school which is a closed community and full of eccentrics is just about the next best thing.'

Beattie is mightily impressed. 'How's it going? Have you finished it?'

'It's two-thirds finished. I find it a bit difficult to write the gory bits. In the end I made sure all the murders took place two rooms away and by the time the bodies were found the people had been dead for hours. But I did enjoy writing it. I just couldn't find the right conclusion. So I've rather left it on one side.'

'You must finish it. I'd adore to read it. I love thrillers, only it's so difficult to get them out of the library. It's what everybody wants, that and Trollope.'

'I've got shelves full of them. You must let me send you some.'

'That would be kind,' says Beattie awkwardly, and they fall silent. Then Beattie asks: 'Is your tea all right? I would have got you some beer but there was no time—'

'The tea's perfectly OK.'

'Do you think you'll be going back to Yorkshire?'

'No.' Charles is emphatic to the point of rudeness.

'I'd love to know what's happening to you but I never—'

'What would you like to know, Beattie?'

There is almost a jeering note in Charles's voice. Beattie stares at him in astonishment.

'Nothing – if you don't want to tell me.'

'I was under the impression you weren't frightfully interested anyway.'

'Then, don't answer – if you don't want to,' says Beattie, her temper suddenly rising. 'It was a civil question, and I don't see why you can't give a civil answer.'

'All right. I'll give you a civil answer to your civil question. After we crashed it was nine months before I was considered fit to fly. They had me in the intelligence work I'm going back to now. They'd have kept me there, but I was determined to get back to flying. When I got to Drifforth they still didn't think I was quite ready. So instead I became a briefing officer. On the understanding that eventually I'd be allowed to get back to flying.'

'What does the briefing officer do?'

'Oh, it's quite simple. Instead of being killed yourself, you brief other men so they can be killed, and when they don't come back you sit down and help the adjutant compose letters of condolence to the next of kin. . . .' Charles's hand is shaking violently round his Bakelite mug of tea. The source of his nightmare is now obvious.

'Charles, you should have told me this.' Beattie is aghast at the look of despair and humiliation in Charles's eyes.

'I would have done,' he says with savage suddenness, 'if you'd ever once asked me how I was and what I was doing.'

Beattie is scarlet, silent.

'Well, perhaps that isn't fair,' goes on Charles disagreeably. 'I mean, there was never any question of a real marriage between us, was there?'

'Did you want there to be?'

Startled, Charles looks directly at Beattie.

'I – I hoped there might be . . . something. But you're absolutely determined there isn't going to be, aren't you? You're still crazy about Brooke. I can almost read your mind. He's never out of your thoughts for very long. I suppose it isn't easy to forget someone when you're in a village which even has his name. But don't expect me to have sympathy with you, Beattie. You may have got into this mess by accident but it's you who's keeping yourself there. You're a fool. You want to think the best of everybody – you want to feel that everybody feels the same emotions as you. Well, let me tell you, sweetheart, Brooke doesn't. Brooke was always far too frightened to let himself feel anything. He left a trail of girls he treated badly at university. And if he'd married you you'd have led a dog's life—'

'Stop talking about him as if he's dead,' screams Beattie at the very pitch of her lungs, and the cuckoo above their heads is abruptly silenced.

'For God's sake, Beattie, come out of your dreams. Of course he's dead. He's been gone nearly three months now, and nobody's heard a word.'

'He isn't dead,' cries Beattie passionately. 'If he was dead, I'd know it, I'd feel it.'

Realizing what she has said, Beattie falls silent.

'Well, there's nothing to prevent you wasting your whole life if that's what you're bent on,' says Charles, his face suddenly as pale as Beattie's is red. 'But you're not going to waste mine as well.'

'*All right*,' snarls Beattie, beside herself with emotions that she cannot even classify let alone comprehend. 'Let's go right ahead and get a divorce and you can pursue Eleanor all over again.'

At the mention of her name the colour suddenly rushes to Charles's cheeks.

'So you haven't been entirely wasting your time in Yorkshire, then. You managed to keep in touch, did you?' taunts Beattie. 'Well, so much for your marriage vows. She's clearly giving her marriage every possible chance, isn't she? Are you sleeping with her again?'

There is a sudden aghast silence as Beattie realizes what she has just said. But Charles's response shocks her far more.

'Yes, as a matter of fact I am.'

'Then, *how dare you* tell me I'm wasting your time?' screams Beattie. By now the noisy wood around them is completely silent. 'How dare you tell me that you hope there might be something between us? How long did that hope last? It doesn't matter whether Brooke's alive or dead. If you thought there was any future for us, you wouldn't have gone with Eleanor. And if a divorce is what you want, then go right ahead and do it. You very decently provided the grounds – though we could have pleaded non-consummation anyway, couldn't we? We could have pleaded non-bloody-anything.'

With that Beattie bursts into a storm of tears.

'Beattie, I—'

'Don't you dare touch me – you – adulterous hypocrite. . . .'

'Then, I suggest we end this charade and go home.'

In tight-lipped silence they walk back to the cottage.

279

CHAPTER
TWENTY-TWO

HIGH Wycombe
14 June 1942

My dear Beattie,

I've already written to thank your mother for her kindness but I felt I must write to you – parting on such bad terms depressed me beyond measure. I'm sorry for my share of our quarrel.

Like you I feel that matters are a complete mess between us but don't know what to do for the best. I am now wondering if it might be better after all if we were to start divorce proceedings. I'd be very sorry indeed if you wanted this but, on the other hand, our arrangement was completely open-ended. I hope I'm not flattering myself in thinking that you've been better off married and supported whilst having Annie. But I've no intention of trying to commit you to things that were never included in the original bargain.

On a practical level, I think your idea of going back to teaching is excellent – I hope you'll pursue it, if only for a couple of days a week. And our conversation about my detective story has had the excellent tonic effect, making me fish it out of the tin trunk and reread it. It still lacks a conclusion, but to my surprise it wasn't nearly as bad as I'd feared. Furthermore – much more heartening! – I could see immediately what was wrong with it, so my visit to Church Cottage has had that positive result as least. I'm enclosing some books by that writer I told you about, Dorothy L. Sayers. I hope you'll enjoy them.

I was going to tell you about the new job but I seem to have run out of paper – anyway it might be censored. Perhaps I'll have an opportunity to tell you about it later. If there's no future as man and wife, I'd be sorry if there's no opportunity for us to keep in touch. Your happiness and wellbeing will always be important to me.

With best wishes,
CHARLES

Dear Charles,
I was glad to get your letter because I felt wretched after our quarrel. It was a tonic having you here, everybody said so, then suddenly it all goes wrong at the end and I'm left biting my tongue.

I feel all the time you must despise me for being such a hopeless person, not knowing my own mind. But if I said I did I'd be lying. I can say with absolute certainty that I'm more grateful to you than I can ever put into words for not having to go through my pregnancy alone and risk having the finger of scorn pointed at me – though you hear in the paper about women having babies out of wedlock today, things have not changed much in our village and they are not kind to babies with no fathers. As if it was any fault of theirs.

I thought a lot about what you said about teaching and decided to take action. I have a friend from Chillington called Louie (I don't think you ever met her) who has been saying the same thing to me since Annie was born but somehow it never seemed to get through. But when you'd gone I wrote to the headmaster of a school near us called Ormond Lodge. It was evacuated to Suffolk from a place called Dulich? or is it Dulwich? They're in the next village to us, Musgrave St Peter on the way to Dereham Market. The head-master wrote by return of post and asked me if I could start immediately! I had to tell him Annie wasn't weaned yet, nor would she be until July, so it's been arranged I'll start at the beginning of September. I can do mornings until Annie is used to me being gone and then do full days. I was that pleased when I got the letter back saying they'd followed up my references and they were delighted to have me! Mother says they must be desperate if they say that sort of thing to a girl of 21, but I was pleased and went upstairs and got out my teaching books for a refresher course. In the mean time I am practising on Little Ern, who is a slow reader.

I hope you will feel free to come again, especially since the weather is getting better. Mother says to tell you you are welcome any time, you can always ring the post office (Musgrave 132) and tell us you are on your way. The boys and Aunt Madge send you their love. I have read all the Dorothy L. Sayers and very much enjoyed them – the vicar has them now but after Lucy has read them I will keep them safe for you. You seem to be always thinking about sending me things and I haven't got anything to send back except my thanks, which, believe me, are sincere.

With best wishes,
BEATTIE

Postcard to Louie from Beattie,
15 July 1942

Dear Louie,
So glad you are able to come – we have repainted the sitting-room in your honour. Ring the post office to tell them what time you are due and we will hang out flags. Everybody is longing to meet you. The boys have made a bow

to put on Beetle's collar. Hope Vince is well. Gatton seems a million years away now.

Much love from
BEATTIE

Home Farm, Musgrave
10 August 1942

My dear Vir,
This letter will not be nearly as long as it should be considering the very long time it has taken me actually to get around to writing it. But this is the busiest time of the year – we've had the thresher here for 2 weeks now and we've had to work all day and quite a lot of the night to get the harvest in. Thank goodness for the full moon or we'd never have finished all the carting and stacking.

Still no word from Hugh (thank goodness). Mr M/F's legs are out of traction but he still doesn't seem awfully cheerful. He asks about the farm in a vague sort of way but he's quite likely to put these same questions all over again at the end of the same conversation. I had a rather gloomy letter from Father saying that his doctor wants him to have an operation – it's only a minor one, but he seems generally out of sorts. Mother is apparently very well – I haven't heard from her in months. I simply adored *Put Out More Flags*. I only managed to read it by carrying it around with me at all times wrapped up in a teacloth to keep it clean.

I'm going down to the Blythes' on Sunday – Beattie has a friend from college staying. Annie still has no hair and the two boys are in disgrace for rubbing her head with a cut onion. Apparently old Mr Tonks at the forge told them it was a way of curing baldness. I think Mrs Blythe was more cross about the waste of the onion than the fact that Annie smelt like a stew for days afterwards.

I was most impressed to hear that you were going again to the Castle – there can't be many people who still insist on dressing for dinner – you must have to take loads of clothes with you. It sounds the ideal situation to meet Lord Right – assuming he's on leave that week. I may take a few days off in the autumn and go up to Yorkshire. Right now I can't imagine the work ever ending. I think I'll go and jump in the river. I've been using the chaff-cutter for the past two days and even my ears are full of dust. Still, we can't complain about the weather at least. Have a lovely holiday and don't forget to tell me all about it.

Much love,
LUCY

Postcard from Louie to Beattie dated Liverpool 8, 28 August 1942.

Dear Beattie,
Just a very quick note to let you know that I got safely home. The train from Euston took for ever but Toby's egg sandwiches stood me in good stead. I was the envy of everyone in the carriage. I can hardly believe what a lovely time I've had, I think it was the best two weeks of my life. It was grand seeing

Vince but what a good time we had at the cottage. I told Mother I don't think we stopped laughing from the moment I arrived to the moment I took that milk-lorry into Ipswich. Give my love to everybody and thank them for making it the best holiday ever.

Lots of love from
LOUIE

Exton Castle, Near Melton Mowbray, Leicestershire
28 August 1942

My dear Lucy,
This will just be a short letter to let you know that I am having a très grand but slightly odd time here. By night we dine in a style in which Edward VII would feel perfectly at home and by day we work non-stop picking off fruit and bottling it. But it's all been the greatest fun and I've had the most relaxing time. Bottling raspberries gives one plenty of opportunity for reflection on my career. For quite a long time, just having got away from Musgrave was enough but I've decided that I really must stop drifting. I'm not quite sure what I mean by that, whether I should be contemplating A Serious Marriage, or getting a more important job, or simply leaving the Grange and taking a smart bachelor girl's flat in Onslow Square. But I don't really want to change the job. Matthew – he's the photographer from the *News Chronicle* – keeps on at me that I could make a go of modelling but, as I told him, it hardly qualifies as a reserved occupation and if I leave Reel Films without another reserved job to go to I'll be in the ATS before you can say 'mascara'. Anyway I always find it very hard to think of modelling as a proper job. So all in all I'm not quite sure where these dramatic changes are going to come from, it's just that I feel there ought to be some. Much love anyway and I'll write at more length when I get back.

VIRGINIA

PS You were quite correct about Lord Right . . .!

CHAPTER
TWENTY-THREE

*T*HERE IS SOMETHING about return-
ing to London in late summer which is peculiarly cheering to the spirit, or so
concludes Virginia as the taxi ploughs its way from King's Cross to
Bayswater. The parks are still heavy with dusty foliage, the grass covered by
lounging servicemen, and outside the cafés tables and chairs have been
spread in a pleasingly Continental fashion. All of which leads Virginia's
thoughts to Ferdinand and his mysterious trips and long silences. At the
hostel she is about to browbeat Cripps into taking her luggage to her room
when she catches sight of a whole sheaf of letters in her pigeonhole and
knows instinctively that one of them will be from Ferdinand. Which proves
to be exactly the case.

'Virginie, where are you?' it opens dolefully enough. 'I'm in London for
a few days only, and nobody can tell me where to find you. I will be at this
number until Thursday only. After that my time is not my own. Please please
call.'

Without preamble Virginia sprints for the phone-box and hastily jabs
some pennies into the slot. By some miracle it is Ferdinand who answers. His
response could not be more gratifying.

'Oh, it's you, it's you. I was beginning to despair of ever seeing you
again.'

'I've rung you the very second I got in. I've been on holiday. If only I'd
known, I would have come home earlier.'

'Not a second too soon,' sighs Ferdinand. 'I'm off again tomorrow and I
was despairing of seeing you. Why didn't you answer my letters?'

'What letters? I never received one.'

Ferdinand makes tut-tutting, shoulder-shrugging noises. 'Clearly they
have all gone astray. But I did get a letter from you about Brooke and I wrote
to your mother. Is there any news?'

'None at all,' says Virginia sadly. 'I don't know when they give up hope
officially—'

'Never,' says Ferdinand, 'never at all. I gather you are pursuing a career
in films.'

'Hardly,' says Virginia cheerfully. 'I just type up the estimates. But I like
it. You must have been in contact with Alexis.'

'Yes, we went to see his new film last night. I told you he was talented.'

'H'm,' says Virginia. 'When will I see you? Are you free this evening? If you don't ask me out to dinner, I'll come round and pester you until you do.'

'In that case I have no option but to pick you up at seven-thirty. And please please look extra beautiful. I've come from a place where all the native women wore veils and all the white women needed them.'

It is already past six and, galvanized into frantic energy, Virginia takes the stairs four at a time, pausing only to turn on the bath and put the 'engaged' sign firmly into place. Outside her door is a square Cellophane box full of gardenias with a note from Willy expressing the wish that he'd like to see her for dinner tonight so he could hear about her vacation. Which instantly necessitates another trip back down to the hall and a hurried conversation with the ever obliging Willy. Replacing the receiver, Virginia remembers her bath, gives a shriek of horror and legs it briskly upstairs, discovering that the hot water, as she had feared, is well past the approved black painted line. Still, no one appears to have noticed and, pinning up her hair, Virginia prepares to make herself beautiful. At 7.30 precisely Ferdinand is in the hall, and in the most undignified way Virginia simply falls into his arms. Ferdinand looks, if possible, a little older and yellower. Virginia hugs him unashamedly, her eyes full of tears.

'Oh, it's just such a long, long time since I've seen you,' she says unsteadily. 'It was before the bombing started, wasn't it? You came round and I was doing the allotment, do you remember?'

Ferdinand studies her intently, taking in at one glance the impact of her beauty, which is like a blow. 'Yes, I remember, I took you to the Mille Fleurs. Now, if you cry,' he says firmly, 'then your eye-black will be spoilt, and as I have never seen you look so beautiful that would be a tragedy. Come along. I have a taxi waiting. What can I say that will instantly make you smile? I have bribed the head waiter to give us the best table at Chez Antoine and I bought you some splendid presents.'

'Oh, Ferdinand, I love presents. What have you bought me? The clothes in London simply defy description. Why, I've seen grown women wearing ankle-socks. It's all rationed now and terribly, terribly ordinary. You'd hardly believe it, but I had to sell my sweet-coupons in order to buy a decent winter coat.'

'Ma foi! This is truly the end of civilization. I hope you got a good price for them.'

'I certainly did. A shilling each. And I've bought some heavenly cloth at Harrods, and a little woman in Marylebone Lane is making it up for me. Have you bought me any stockings by any chance?'

'I thought your American would supply those.'

'Well, he does sort of. He's really frightfully generous, though we're not as close as we used to be. Though, funnily enough, I think we're better friends now than we were. But I do so adore getting unsolicited presents. One gets so tired of dropping hints. Are we here? Good.'

The restaurant is everything Virginia most likes, being intimate, expensive and full of the smell of the most delicious food. Ferdinand studies the menu with the air of a man who feels that this may be the most important decision of the evening and, having ordered for both of them, casts an incredulous eye over the considerably reduced wine-list. Virginia sighs with contentment. A delicious meal is clearly on its way to them. Then with a lordly gesture Ferdinand sets aside all menus, tastes and approves the wine, then quite unselfconsciously takes Virginia's hand. It's strange that so many people who have taken her hand that year simply make her flesh crawl. But with Ferdinand it is as if his warmth and steadiness are actually flowing into her. In his company she feels grounded, safe, secure. With Ferdinand she never has to dissemble. Never has to think of what to say to him. The only problem is if there will be enough time to say it all. And it is with considerable annoyance that Virginia hears that Alexis and his fiancée are to join them for the dancing later.

'Oh, no, not really,' says Virginia in quite unashamed dismay. 'I'd hoped I'd got you all to myself just for this evening.'

'Do you know Holly?'

'Gosh, yes. I met her – when was it? – oh, at a party at the production office,' says Virginia. 'It wasn't a very glorious evening. I got drunk and was sick and she was being Daddy's radiant little girl. As you can gather, I didn't like her too much.'

'Who do you like?' teases Ferdinand, off at a tangent in an instant.

'I like you, you old flatterer. And Willy now that we aren't going to bed any more. And Lucy of course.'

'Is she still being stalwart with the cows?'

'Lucy must be one of the success stories of the war. She ought to be decorated. She's running the whole farm because the farmer has had an accident. I don't know how she'll adjust to being a wife after the war. Well, she may not have to,' adds Virginia soberly. 'Hugh's in Cairo and has fallen in love with someone else.'

Ferdinand is immediately agog.

'With who? An Arab boy? A woman in khaki? A camel? A nun?'

'Ferdinand, don't be silly,' giggles Virginia. 'He got ill and he met this American nurse at Cairo Hospital. He thinks it's the real thing; he sent Lucy the most tactless letters you can imagine and told her to fix them up a divorce. I told her to do no such thing. That was last Christmas, and I don't think she's heard a word from him since. I suppose it may just sort itself out after the war.'

'I'm gratified you can speak of after the war. Exactly how are we to win it?'

'Well, now the Americans are on our side—'

'They were never not on our side.'

'Well, you know what I mean. It's up to them now. We won the Battle of Britain, don't forget.'

'I'm not likely to forget it,' says Ferdinand with some feeling. 'You British go on about nothing else, that and Dunkirk. Well, I don't have your optimism. When I see the Americans actually on French soil and my grandfather's château liberated, then I will believe it. At present, I am told my grandfather's home has been requisitioned as a rest centre for German officers.'

'How frightful for you,' says Virginia with genuine sympathy, 'and how strange that we're both invaded in our own way. Lucy says that Musgrave has got an American airfield on either side and they're still bringing over more men. Can you imagine Musgrave full of *Americans*? Why, I remember when they used to turn out and stare at people who'd come from London. Lucy says there are even Negroes, to build the runways. Oh, I say, this looks simply wonderful.'

'Tell me about Brooke,' says Ferdinand, busy with his oysters.

'There's really nothing to tell,' says Virginia, raising her extraordinarily blue eyes to his. 'There was a telegram. You know all that. Then nothing. They were bombing some oil-refinery at Rotterdam and they'd all dropped their bombs but his plane got caught in flak as they were coming back. Or so someone's told Mother. Brooke's plane went down, and it was burning quite badly; but it was night-time, you see, so nobody knows who baled out. I keep saying my prayers and there's a woman in Stepney, she's our messenger's mother, and she's made Brooke one of her special intentions,' Virginia adds with a smile that doesn't quite reach her eyes. 'She's a papist, you see. I'm not sure Brooke would approve of being prayed for by a Holy Roman, but I expect it's all the same to God, if He's there at all. He's been awfully quiet lately.'

The waiter removes their plates, another refills Virginia's glass, while a third picks her silk napkin from the floor and replaces it with a fresh one. Ferdinand studies Virginia curiously in the flattering soft light of the table-lamp. Her face is a pure oval framed with thick heavy curls swept up on to the crown of her head. It is a beautiful but still mask-like face with a life behind it held severely in check. He wonders if anybody has got near to touching her heart. He doubts it.

'Are you quite well now? Somehow I didn't expect you to stay in London.'

'Oh, I work on the lightning-not-striking-twice principle,' says Virginia cheerfully. 'I had a spell in a nursing home, then I felt all right again. I get a few headaches now, that's all.'

'Are you still thinking about Cecily?'

'She's still very much on my mind. It's her parents that I've been to stay with these last two weeks. It was good to have the opportunity to talk about her with her mother. She's awfully nice. I've always felt a bit indignant because I didn't think they valued Cecily enough. I think now they probably did but just didn't say so. Do you like my outfit by the way?'

Virginia is wearing a stark black and white Lelong floor-length gown with Willy's white gardenias.

'I do not think I have ever seen you look better.'

'It's the purest heaven, isn't it? Cecily's mother gave it to me. It's some-thing she wore in 1931; she told me she'd have no further use for it.'

'Tell me about your love-life.'

Virginia grins. 'I still deal in quantity rather than in quality, but with the proviso that I'm celibate. Actually I see Willy and a few other people. I've had quite a few proposals over the past year, but I don't seem to find anybody I want to take that seriously. Except—'

'Except what?'

'Oh, I met this rather nice man. At the Castle. Tom Berkeley. He's just an hon. now but eventually he'll be a lord. He's thirty and really rather nice. I saw quite a lot of him in Leicestershire.'

'Ah ha!' says Ferdinand, looking almost animated. 'I am delighted. At last it seems you are being sensible.'

'Ferdinand, I don't know how you had the gall to say that. You don't know anything about the man except that he's thirty and he's got a title.'

'From that I think I can fairly deduce that he must be comfortable and landed, and respectable, too, if he's invited for dinner at the Castle. He sounds as if he could be the man who will provide you with the right framework. The right framework is very important, Virginia. Never forget that. You must not rattle around for ever.'

Virginia is suddenly unaccountably angry.

'That's only because you believe in doing the conventional thing,' says Virginia, wondering why she is so annoyed with Ferdinand. 'For all you know he could be a habitual wife-beater and embezzler.'

'Well, if that is so,' says Ferdinand briskly, 'you must proceed no further with the matter. But if he is wealthy, good-tempered, not vicious, and anxious to marry you, then it is time you thought of marriage. And doing the proper thing. How else will civilization be carried on unless people marry the right people and have children? Do you like this young man?'

Virginia toys with her fish. 'He's terribly nice. I met his parents, too, while I was there. They seemed to like me.'

'What kind of people are they?'

'Country people. Their estate marches with Cecily's father's. And they own a lot of land in Scotland, and I think there's a castle there. Tom's mother breeds Labradors. I can't quite see me doing that.'

'What would that matter? Once you're married you may do as you choose. But it is important to make first the good marriage. It is crucial in setting the tone of your subsequent career.'

Virginia listens, mildly irritated. Though still possessed of her own private dreams and fantasies, the kind of calculation that Ferdinand is expressing is beyond her. Goodness knows, this talk of the right marriage had been the most popular topic at finishing school. But that seemed another world away now. In the drama of day-to-day survival, in her current sense of making her own destiny, those old conventions now seem as antiquated as crinolines or bustles. But are they? Abruptly Virginia becomes aware that that sense of disquiet that Ferdinand's owlish comments have triggered off has nothing to do with her – well, not much. What *is* bothering her is that this talk of propriety has brought the image of Beattie Blythe to her mind. For that was why Brooke had declined to honour his obligations, wasn't it? Virginia is startled to find herself having framed the thought that Brooke had any obligations to Beattie; her stoutly maintained position had been that Beattie was a servant and, anyway, 'that kind of girl'. On either count she had no particular rights. With Lucy alone has Virginia discussed Beattie's child. Ferdinand is the last person to talk to about it, she decides. Immediately she finds herself saying: 'Brooke left a child, you know. There's a girl in the village who had Brooke's baby just before he disappeared.'

Ferdinand raises his eyebrows and purses his lips.

'He's sinning a little close to home, that one. That is, if you are really sure it is his.'

'I'm almost positive. I met the two of them in London about the time the baby must have been conceived. She was potty about him, anybody could see that.'

'And Brooke wouldn't marry her? So she's unsupported.'

'Oh, no, she found someone else to marry, p.d.q.'

'Do I know her?'

'You saw her that day at the garden-party. A dark-haired girl wearing white. The gardener's daughter.'

'I remember her well,' says Ferdinand slowly. 'As you say, a dark-haired girl wearing white. I remember, too, that Brooke was riveted by her. A beautiful girl but not a silly one, I would have said.'

'What's a silly girl, then?'

'A girl with no moral sense,' says Ferdinand freezingly.

'I fear that's probably me,' says Virginia coolly. 'Isn't it strange how things work out? I've got no moral sense and I don't get caught, and she's got lots of sense and she's left holding the baby.'

Ferdinand looks at her reproachfully but says nothing.

'Anyway, she married someone else. Actually an officer from Brooke's own squadron. So I suppose she hasn't done too badly. Presumably it must be a *mariage de convenance*. That is, if he can count up to nine.'

'Do you know why Brooke didn't . . .?'

'Ferdinand, really. Brooke's ambitious – you know that. He wouldn't let himself be caught by one mistake.'

Ferdinand is silent.

'You don't approve obviously,' says Virginia.

'I don't approve or disapprove,' says Ferdinand, 'but I do know for a girl to be poor and of respectable parents and have neither the means nor someone to take her part when she is pregnant is not an easy position. Did Brooke settle any money on her?'

'Goodness, Ferdinand, I don't know.'

'Why don't you like her?'

Virginia pulls her gaze away from her veal and grins. 'As you pointed out, I don't like many people. I don't think I dislike her, or do I? No,' she says almost in surprise, 'I don't think I do dislike her any more. When she was younger she used to be stuffed down my throat as the good girl of the village. I suppose I envied her and when she got pregnant I was really glad she'd got caught. And I was quite sorry when I found she'd got someone to marry her,' says Virginia with a terrifying honesty that Ferdinand always seems to provoke in her. 'But since Brooke disappeared – it's impossible to describe – it just changes every-thing. When you feel the pain of such a real tragedy everything else seems to pale into insignificance. I wasn't even that close to Brooke. Well, I thought I was, but I'm not sure that Brooke's really close to anybody. But I know it's terrible to love someone who just disappears and leaves that space in your life. It's as if it's a hole out of which everything good drains. She must feel terrible.'

'You should go and talk to her.'

'Ferdinand, really! What on earth could we say to one another? She'd just think I'd come to crow. I don't see what good it would do. But if – but when – I mean, if it's ever finally officially declared – I mean, if Brooke doesn't come back', says Virginia in a rush, 'I suppose our solicitors could write to her or something.'

After their meal Ferdinand orders champagne and they move briskly and happily around the dance-floor.

'Tell me, do you do this vulgar dance from America?'

'You mean the Jitterbug? Gosh, yes, but so far only with the girls in the hostel. None of us has dared try it out on the dance-floor.'

'Alexis and Holly are keen dancers. They go to some place called the Palais. Is it in Hammersmith?'

'That's right. I've been there once or twice myself. It's quite fun. There are two sessions of dancing there, and if you're in the mood you can just go on dancing all day and all night.'

'To me there is no romance to whirling your ankles past your ears,' says Ferdinand judiciously. 'But for Alexis and Holly it is different. Ah, there they are. You've dragged yourself away from your meeting, then?'

'Of course we did. Couldn't miss your last night, now, could we?'

Alexis and Ferdinand embrace formally on both cheeks in the French fashion, then Alexis turns and offers his hand to Virginia.

'Hello. Had a good holiday? I think you've met Holly, haven't you?'

'Very nice, thank you. Yes, I believe we have met.'

'Have you eaten?' asks Ferdinand.

'We had supper at Holly's before the meeting. I must say it's the first time I've had to conduct a production meeting in full evening dress. It subdued everyone nicely. I must remember that when Billy next steps out of line. Champagne? Wonderful. Let's have another bottle while we're at it.'

In the genial explosion of corks, toasts and general goodwill Virginia sits quietly, demurely, suddenly glad that she has taken so much trouble over her appearance, that she has pretty clothes, that she is attracting both covert and overt glances from other tables. Evening dress has wrought a wondrous change in Alexis – or is it simply that she is seeing him properly for the first time? The austerity of the black and white throws into sharp relief his strong dark-browed features, the deep-set eyes, the disconcertingly direct stare, the long line of cheekbone, the thick glossy ungreased hair. Discretion reluctantly intervening, Virginia drags her gaze from Alexis and studies Holly, who exudes happiness like an aura. She is pretty, concedes Virginia finally, secure in the knowledge that she, however, is beautiful. Though her whole appearance would be radically improved in Virginia's opinion if that really rather nice dress had enjoyed even the remotest proximity with an iron. But Holly's attractions clearly lie in her vitality, and in the animation of her pretty features, the sparkle in her friendly brown eyes. Ferdinand clearly likes her. So why don't I? ponders Virginia, accepting another glass of champagne. It's not as if Holly isn't positively putting herself out to be pleasant to her – but, had she known it, this is in fact a fatal thing to do. When any woman is nice, Virginia immediately suspects patronage. Still, there is absolutely no point in ruining the atmosphere of Ferdinand's leave, so Virginia listens quietly to the conversation which very quickly reverts to the topic uppermost in Alexis' and Holly's minds: Alexis' new film. Holly is as full of it as if she, and not Alexis, is directing it, thinks Virginia sourly.

'It's about this marvellous man that Alexis met called Walter Maggs,' says Holly animatedly. 'He was decorated after saving someone's life in the Blitz. We're going to film it down at the docks, just as it happened. It'll be amazing.'

'Pat Blain and I have been talking about doing a retrospective film about the Blitz now that there's so little bombing,' explains Alexis with rather more lucidity and considerably more courtesy. 'I happened to meet a journalist who'd just interviewed Walter; he's in the Auxiliary Fire Service. It struck me he'd make a first-rate subject for a short. I've spent the last two or three weeks with him down at the docks. We're going to film a day or, to be more precise, a night in the Blitz. It's the night Walter saved the man's life, starting late afternoon when people are going down to the shelters and ending when they come out at sunrise.'

Virginia feels it is about time she made her presence felt.

'So it'll be Walter Maggs acting himself?'

'*Being* himself, I hope,' corrects Alexis, amused. 'Provided I can coax a lifelike performance out of him. I spent quite a lot of time drinking with him and met his family, and I'm hoping he'll be relaxed in front of the cameras.'

'I can never quite understand why you always want real people—'

'Because it's documentary, not feature film,' Holly tells Virginia kindly.

'I know that,' says Virginia coldly. 'But in some of the documentaries I've seen, where they've made a huge point of using the actual people, the people have been so wooden they haven't seemed real at all. They would have done better to use actors. I don't understand how you expect people to be unselfconscious and themselves when you've got someone like Alexis there barking 'Action!' when you're trying to perform your normal daily duties. I would have thought people weren't themselves simply because there was a whole crowd of people standing there observing them, making them self-conscious.'

Holly is staring at Virginia in quiet disbelief. Clearly Virginia has made some unforgivable *faux pas* like shouting 'Bum' at a royal investiture.

'But, you see, you're presenting real people in real lives, not just a manufactured portrait or the Hollywood Dream Machine.'

'I don't see why it would be any less 'real' if you have actors in the parts,' retorts Virginia.

'I agree with Virginia,' says Alexis, most surprisingly. 'I started off thinking that the documentary method was the only way that you could show how people lived. I really did think I could intervene unseen in their lives and show other people what went on. But, though I think some quite good things have come out of the films, reluctantly I've come to the conclusion that if you want to record a certain kind of reality you alter it simply by being there. But it's sort of six of one and half a dozen of another. I know this film would have more poignance, more impact, more resonance, if the man on the screen in front of you is the real man. If it was an actor, though the story would be impressive, I don't think the degree of identification would be

291

there. The film will be a tribute to him. But come on, we mustn't monopolize the conversation like this. What have you been up to, old man? Any idea where you're going to next?'

Conversation moves into less contentious channels. Virginia listens, aware that her good mood is slowly evaporating and it isn't difficult to trace the cause. Holly is getting on her nerves. In fact the contentment of the pair of them is having an excluding effect on Virginia which infuriates her. She is not accustomed to being used to define other people's happiness, and the assurance of this cocky, dull, badly dressed little girl (the fact that she is actually older than Virginia is supremely irrelevant) infuriates her beyond words. Especially since in Virginia's opinion it is clearly borrowed glory.

'What exactly are you going to do on this film?' enquires Virginia innocently.

'Not much,' says Holly glumly, much to Virginia's secret glee. Then she promptly out-manoeuvres her by adding: 'You see, I've just had a script accepted about life in the woman's army. I was in it for the first year of the war myself, and they start filming in two weeks' time in Shropshire. What do you do, Virginia?'

Quietly Virginia tells her that she is Ira Myerberg's secretary.

'Oh,' says Holly, clearly casting around for something positive to say. 'Still, I suppose you won't be doing it for long.'

Patronizing cow, thinks Virginia. Out loud she drawls, 'Well, we can't all hope for a life as interesting as yours, Holly,' and turns to Ferdinand to enquire about his family. It is her turn to exclude.

Out of the corner of her eye Virginia sees Holly flush with annoyance at that entirely gratuitous jibe. Throughout the rest of the evening Holly shoots odd glances at her, wondering if, after all, she is a threat. Clearly she is not used to being disliked – unlike Virginia, who on the whole rather expects other women to be hostile to her and is always stimulated into really bad behaviour by their dislike. For the rest of the evening, consciously or unconsciously, Holly hangs on to Alexis' hand and every word. Toying with her half-empty champagne-glass, Virginia is suddenly aware that the sight of the two of them together gets on her nerves. Conversation polarizes itself, so that Alexis and Holly talk to Ferdinand and Virginia talks to Ferdinand and Alexis. It is all rather stupid. Alexis, however, notices nothing, and since he only has one real topic on his mind soon reverts to his film.

'I've been jolly lucky about the staffing. I've got Billy of course as cameraman and Bert Rhodes for sound. They're both the best, though Bert can be a pain to work with.'

'Who's doing your continuity?'

'I'm not sure. Pat's offered Sandra Jarvis, but I'm still hoping for Trudy. Have you met Sandra? She did those shorts about allotments.'

'Oh, her,' says Holly dismissively. 'You don't want her,' she says with an unconscious flick of her eyes in Virginia's direction. 'She's a real time-waster, a sort of professional glamour girl. Hold out for Trudy. She knows something about hard work.'

Virginia smiles nicely as Ferdinand tops up her glass and makes a mental note to put as large a spoke as possible in Holly's wheel at the earliest opportunity. Then Ferdinand asks Holly if she'd like to dance. Alone at their table Alexis raises his eyebrows in a questioning sort of a way to Virginia and jerks his head towards the dance-floor. It is not the kind of invitation that Virginia is accustomed to receive.

'I'm not a dog, you know,' she finds herself saying with a fury that astonishes her. 'I do actually respond to words.'

Alexis grins at her, amused at her outrage.

'Then, let me tender a formal invitation. Would you like to dance?'

'Yes,' says Virginia sulkily and follows Alexis on to the dance-floor. Rather to her annoyance, Alexis dances well for someone whose mind never seem to be more than six inches away from a can of film. Virginia relaxes a little, giving him the curve of her cheek and the shadow of her downcast lashes. Alexis clearly doesn't feel the onus is on him to speak and instead sings a snatch of the words and suddenly whirls Virginia round and round in a flurry of complicated steps, then slows down and grins at her.

'Enjoying your evening, Miss Musgrave?'

'As much as a time-wasting glamour girl ever enjoys anything.'

'Are you enjoying your job at least?'

'Yes. Of course I only see it as something to fill in the time between the daily hair appointment and the cocktail hour. I give the money to the Spitfire Fund,' she adds nastily.

At this point the band slow to a halt with a few concluding flourishes and they clap politely. Virginia, on the point of returning to her table, sees to her amusement that Holly has firmly started off the next dance with Ferdinand. Presumably she's been reading those magazine articles about letting your man have his own life, thinks Virginia maliciously as she slips back into Alexis' arms. This time the dance is a slow waltz and, though he is holding her perfectly correctly, Virginia is triumphantly conscious of a slight *frisson* between them. This is going to be easier than I thought, she concludes to herself, tucking away the information in the drawer of her heart marked *revenge*. She allows herself to relax in his arms, her hand resting lightly in his, conscious that she is looking her best and people are taking not one but two or three looks at her. They dance the last few minutes of the dance in silence, and Virginia is aware that she would very much have liked Alexis to kiss her.

'I enjoyed that,' she says quietly with her intense blue-eyed stare that says considerably more than words. Back at the table Holly hails Alexis as if he's been abroad for some months and spends the rest of the evening talking feverishly about the holiday they've planned once they finish Alexis' new film. Virginia is aware that Holly is now considerably less sure of herself than she'd been at the beginning of the evening. She studies Alexis, aware that though his face lacks the conventional good-looks of Brooke it has a personality that compels attention simply because it generates such blazing energy and good humour.

At that moment she feels Holly's eyes on her and gazes vacantly at the band. It would be rather fun to detach Alexis from the prickly Holly. Not that she has any long-term interest in Alexis. Particularly since Tom has appeared on the scene. Drat. She had completely forgotten about Tom. But once he was safely back with his battalion it would be several months before she saw him again, giving her plenty of opportunity for causing mayhem. It isn't that she doesn't want them to get married, she decides magnanimously, but she wouldn't mind ruining Holly's peace of mind for a couple of months. It would require some careful thought. Getting men had never presented any real problems, but somehow Alexis posed more of a challenge. She's always had the unpleasant feeling he could read her mind, or at least gauge her intentions without too much difficulty. Perhaps she should just wait and take advantage of circumstances. With Holly in Shropshire for three months and Alexis in London there are certainly excellent opportunities ahead for putting in the boot.

'It was a lovely evening,' she says to Ferdinand much later and with some warmth.

They are enjoying a bottle of brandy that Ferdinand has brought with him. During his short stays in London he occupies the same featureless flat in Knightsbridge overlooking the park. Virginia puts off the light in order to draw back the blackout and gazes down into Hyde Park. The moon coldly illuminates the trenches. Ferdinand puts his hand under Virginia's chin and tilts her face up to him in the half-light.

'Look at me,' he says. 'What are you up to, young lady?'

'Me? Why should I be up to anything?'

'You are up to everything,' says Ferdinand, laughing hugely at his own joke.

Virginia gives him her most Cheshire Cat smile.

'Just my usual tricks. You wouldn't like me to be bored now, would you?'

He ignores her remark and says rather obliquely: 'You don't like Holly.'

'I don't like Holly.'

'She'll be a good wife for Alexis.'

Wife. The word jars Virginia.

'She bores me to death,' she says with rather more violence than the occasion demands.

'She could perhaps stop biting her nails, but she is very bright and she is very much in love with Alexis.'

'Goodness, you should visit our production office. Everybody's in love with Alexis.'

'Except you?'

'Except me. You know me – I traded in my heart for nylons years ago. Which reminds me, Ferdinand darling. Didn't you say something about presents?'

294

CHAPTER
TWENTY-FOUR

'**M**OTHER, she's had seven months' breastfeeding,' says Beattie, trying desperately to keep her voice calm and controlled. If she doesn't, Annie will grizzle with colic and/or spleen for anything up to two hours instead of going sweetly down for her morning nap. Beattie smiles abstractedly at Annie and prays that none of her own anxiety will leak into the milk, thus apprising Annie that this is a day different from any other. Is it her imagination or is Annie narrowly eyeing the unfamiliar sight of curlers in her mother's hair?

'I've oiled your bicycle chain, Beattie. I hope that machine is safe. It's far too big for you.'

'I know, Dad, but I can't be relying on lifts from milk-lorries—'

'Or Yanks,' puts in Mrs Blythe firmly.

'—from *anyone* if I've got to get there for eight-thirty each day. I think it was nice of the vicar to offer.'

'Call me when breakfast is on the table,' says Mr Blythe *en route* to the hen-house. With that the kitchen is suddenly empty save for Mrs Blythe laying the table. Even Beetle is absent, out on the paper round with Toby and Ern. Through the open door the back garden is dimly seen, still wreathed in mist, waiting for the first fragile rays of September sun. The grasses are heavy with dew and laced over with cobwebs. Annie's eyes are beginning to droop comfortably, and in a minute Beattie prays to herself she'll be able to put her in her cot and get herself ready for school.

Catching sight of the rigid set of Mrs Blythe's shoulders, Beattie sighs and steels herself. Under pressure Mrs Blythe has agreed to give Annie her mid-morning bottle.

'What time will you be back?'

'I've *told* you, Mother. By two o'clock at the latest. She'll be asleep after her bottle till three. She won't even know I'm gone.'

Mrs Blythe rattles the kettle lid and fills the kettle noisily from the pump in the scullery.

'Whether she knows it or not isn't the point. Your place is here with her. I don't know what people in the village are going to say.'

Annie is by now firmly asleep. Almost bursting with rage and nervous irritation, Beattie carries Annie upstairs and puts her in her cot. With that she brushes her hair, puts on her costume and blouse with fingers shaking so hard she can hardly do up the buttons. Downstairs Mrs Blythe is making toast.

'Mother, I don't care – I really don't care what people in the village are saying.'

'That's been obvious for some time,' says Mrs Blythe nastily. 'Your place is with your baby. Poor little mite, she's had a hard enough start in life—'

Beattie is suddenly so incensed she can hardly breathe for rage.

'Mother, you're talking absolute rubbish—'

Delighted to have provoked her normally taciturn daughter into angry speech at last, Mrs Blythe swells like a turkey-cock.

'How dare you speak to your mother like that!'

All the accumulated resentments of the past year are suddenly out in the open as Mrs Blythe, galvanized by fury, glares at her tall daughter.

'You've got no right going out to a job with a young baby at home. You should be here looking after her. It isn't natural or right. And don't you dare tell me there's a war on.'

'Mother, Annie won't even know I'm gone.'

'And what about after half-term? Who's going to look after her when you're working at that school full-time?'

'Would you like me to pay you, Mother?' enquires Beattie nastily, aware that any moral advantage she may have had has now completely disappeared as she descends into the same vein of childish spite as her mother. 'Is that what you want?'

'That's good coming from you,' retorts her mother. 'Money seems to be the only thing that matters to you, Beattie.'

'Mother, I'll say this once more, then you can talk to yourself if you want. I'm not doing it for the money. I'm doing it because I need to get out and get a job. And the only reason you're making a fuss is because you're jealous.'

At this crucial moment Beetle skips in through the back door, accurately gauges the atmosphere, and with tail lowered goes and sits behind the coal-scuttle. Oblivious, Ern and Toby rush in exclaiming about the frost, their faces rosy from the early-morning chill, demanding porridge and clean clothes for PE today. Beattie silently checks the contents of her attaché case.

Tight-lipped, Mrs Blythe puts the porridge on as Mr Blythe reappears briefly to take a saucepan of bran mash and potato peelings out for the chicks. Toby gloatingly counts the number of eggs he's brought in and enters them in his egg-book.

The pips are announcing the news as Mr Blythe comes back and joins them at the breakfast-table.

'This is the news at eight o'clock and this is Frank Phillips reading it.'

An instant and profound silence falls over the breakfast-table. Even little Ern breathes more quietly. Beattie, trying to force porridge down, scarcely hears a word. In an hour's time she will be facing a class of her own. It is over a year since she's taught. Will she have forgotten everything? Supposing they don't like her? Supposing the other teachers realize she hasn't got a degree and despise her? They all seemed quite friendly when she visited the school at Open Day back in the summer, but still. . . .

'Don't you want your toast, Aunty Beattie? Can I have it if you don't?'

'I don't seem to have much appetite, Toby. You can have it if you want to. I'll have to be on my way shortly anyway.'

Having checked the condition of Annie's clean nappies on the drying-rail and checked to see that the others are soaking properly in the pail in the scullery, Beattie goes up to have a final look at Annie. The little girl is sleeping peacefully, her thumb drawn up to her mouth. At seven months she is still completely bald save for a faint silky colourless fluff. Beattie gazes down at her daughter with something approaching despair. Is she neglecting her? Is she evading responsibilities in being away for five crucial hours each day in her daughter's life? Will Annie grow up fatally flawed as a result of her absent mother and an ambiguous parentage? Beattie almost groans aloud, then pulls herself together. This will not do, she tells herself firmly, pulls on her hat, picks up her attaché case and goes back down to the kitchen.

'I'm off now,' she announces with more firmness than she feels.

'You look ever so smart, Aunty Bee,' says the loyal Toby.

'Good luck, Beattie.' Her father actually gets up to see her off. 'Mind you be careful with that chain on your good stockings,' he says. 'Not nervous, are you?'

'A bit,' admits Beattie, tears in her eyes.

'You'll do all right. Your mother will get used to the idea. She's proud as a peacock really, you getting a job in a posh school like that.'

Waving gratefully, Beattie climbs aboard the huge old-fashioned bicycle and pedals up the lane towards the village street.

Even though it's only a quarter past eight, the street presents a lively and animated scene. There is already a small queue at the post office, and two plough-horses are tethered outside the forge where Mr Tonks is building up the fire. As Beattie pedals slowly past a voice calls urgently: 'Oi! Our Beattie! Hang on a minute, do.'

It is Lily Kedge with the postwoman's bag slung firmly over her shoulder.

'Off to the new job, are we?'

'Yes, no thanks to Mother.'

'Still taking on, is she?'

'Yes, don't ask me why.'

'She'll get over it,' says her niece calmly. 'There's talk that Fulbrights Engineering in Dereham Market will have to run a bus round the villages soon, they're that short of women for the assembly shop. Our mother says that the day they do she'll be off like a shot. There'll be a nursery next in the village hall, you mark my words. Here, I've got a letter for you. From High Wycombe.' Lily winks knowingly. 'Good of him to write, isn't it – him knowing it's your first day at school, I expect.'

'Yes, he's thoughtful like that,' admits Beattie, wondering if she's got time to open it. 'Lord, is that quarter past eight already? I'll have to get a move on. You're late, aren't you?'

297

'I'll say. Had to take a telegram up to the Dower House. Where is that dratted letter.'

'A telegram? For whom? What about?' enquires Beattie urgently.

Busily sorting through the piles of letters, Lily misses the sudden anguish in Beattie's face.

'Oh, it was good news right enough,' she says casually. 'Morning, Mr Chew. Yes, I'll be there directly and I'll take your other letters. – I know it's good news because they told me all about it. Not half they didn't. It was an official telegram and it was all about Mr Brooke. He's alive after all. Good, isn't it? Still in Holland apparently, but they think he's alive. Mrs Musgrave's *friend*' – Lily sniffs – 'he opened it, and Mrs Musgrave read it and had hysterics. They both took on that much that he had to get us all a drink. Gave me a sherry at eight o'clock in the morning! Couldn't say no, could I? There it is. I hope he's well.'

'Who?' says Beattie stupidly.

'Charles of course. Oh, I say!' Lily's naturally rosy cheeks become even redder as with a screech of brakes an American army jeep rounds the corner and draws up noisily on the other side of the green. 'Is that Greg?'

'I think so. I'll have to fly now, Lily. Can't be late on my first day.'

Beattie pulls the heavy bike back upright, leaps aboard and sails off down the main road. She can hardly breathe for emotion. Brooke is alive. Not dead, not lying disfigured and burnt at the bottom of the North Sea or in some ignominious foreign grave. He is alive, and that means he will be coming home. Standing up on the pedals, Beattie can barely resist the temptation to shout aloud for joy. Whatever happens, Brooke is alive.

So swiftly do Beattie's feet bear down on the pedals that she finds herself at the gates of Ormond Lodge with no clear idea of how she got there. As she dismounts a stern, bent, grey-faced, elderly man who she knows to be Mr Plaistow, the chemistry master, is there before her to undo the heavy lock.

'Ah, Mrs Hammond. Good to see a new member of staff approaching her duties with such alacrity. Grand morning, isn't it?'

'Wonderful,' says Beattie with her broadest smile and pushes her bicycle up the drive. Small figures clad in winter grey flannel are perspiringly playing cricket on the front lawn and nudge each other as Beattie walks by.

'I hope you're going to like being with us,' observes Mr Plaistow. 'I never thought I'd get used to being in the country after Dulwich. We spent the first few months in Ipswich, and we were all quite sure we'd be back in London by Christmas. Then once the bombing started Dulwich had a direct hit. I gather there's just a crater where the chapel used to be. Sad, isn't it? So it looks like we're going to be here for the duration. Did you know the people who lived here before?'

'Not really,' says Beattie, unwilling to reveal the fact that it was in this house that her cousin Lily had undergone her first disastrous term of service. 'They were a retired army colonel and his wife. I think they kept themselves to themselves. They decided to move to Somerset.'

The panelling inside the entrance-hall is now completely covered with fixture-boards and house notices. Drake, Nelson, Scott and Wellington are the names of the houses. Beattie knows she has been appointed to

Wellington. There is the instantly familiar smell of school, of old lunches, chalk and the smell of new flannel winter uniforms. In the staffroom tea is brewing.

'You've met everyone, haven't you, Mrs Hammond?'

'I think so.'

'Assembly is in ten minutes. Your peg and locker are over there. Would you like a cup of tea or would you rather see your classroom?'

'The classroom, I think,' says Beattie, having conscientiously smiled at each member of staff.

The house is a mixture of the domestic and the institutional. There are still chintz curtains at some windows, but on every wall there are stern injunctions about not running in the corridors, not leaving the house without their gas-masks and at no time leaving on the electric lights. Beattie's classroom is a small drawing-room looking out on to the front lawn. The room is completely bare except for ten small desks and chairs and a desk for herself.

'You'll hear the bell for assembly shortly.'

Left to herself Beattie sits down at her desk, unpacks her pencil-case and writing-pads and surveys her first classroom. Its absolute austerity in no way deters her. It'll be easy enough to brighten up the walls with a few projects, she tells herself firmly. And all that space means there's plenty of room in the corner for a nature-table. Not to mention plenty of space for the better declaiming of poetry and acting plays. In another part of the house a hand-bell begins to clang raucously. Instantly there is the sound of many small pairs of scurrying feet. Out on the lawn the grey figures begin to form into lines. Beattie gets up, checks her seams are straight and prepares to go into assembly, her spirits resolute. Suddenly all her fears are gone. It's like taking out a familiar set of clothes that have lain unused for a year and finding, much to your gratification, that they still fit perfectly. Beattie leans for a moment against her desk, suddenly reassured. In this chalk-smelling, rather drab classroom she suddenly has a sense of herself again. Not as Charles's wife or Annie's mother or the boys' friendly older sister. Here she is a professional person.

And Brooke is still alive.

The morning passes without incident. Form IIIB show no more signs of the beast in man than can be expected from a normal set of eight-year-olds. And some show pleasing signs of wanting to co-operate.

'You'll be coming to us all the time, won't you, after half-term?' enquires the smallest member of the class hopefully.

'That's right,' says Beattie kindly. 'I'll be with you all the time then.'

At half-past twelve as the ravening hordes are hungrily lining up outside the dining-room and Beattie is packing away her new register there is a cough from the open door.

'I say, Mrs Hammond, there's a phone call for you. It's in the head's study.'

'A what? A phone call for me?'

'In the head's study,' repeats the little boy patiently. 'It's your husband.'

'My—oh—I'll come along straight away.'

It is the first phone call that Beattie has ever received. And from Charles of all people.

The headmaster has tactfully absented himself. Gingerly Beattie picks up the receiver. 'Hello?'

'You've got the receiver round the wrong way, Mrs Hammond,' says the small boy with quiet satisfaction before he vanishes.

'Hello,' says Beattie with considerably more confidence. 'Is that you, Charles?'

'Yes, it's me. Can you hear me all right? This isn't much of a line, is it? Well, how's this for a piece of detective work?'

Never had Charles sounded so relaxed and cheerful.

'It's *wonderful*. How on earth did you get the number?'

'Oh, the directory. I knew you'd be starting today and I thought I'd see if I could get a number and talk to you direct. It's the most stupendous news, isn't it?'

He knows about Brooke, thinks Beattie, mystified, and how generous he is to know how pleased I'd be.

'Yes, I was delighted,' says Beattie cautiously. 'I don't seem to be able to take it in even now. When did you hear?'

'Oh, yesterday. The funny thing is I'd simply given up hope. I suppose so much had passed I simply thought there couldn't be any good news. That's what's made it more of a shock, I suppose.'

'I was terribly pleased. I suppose it's proof that you should always be an optimist,' says Beattie with some feeling. 'I heard just as I was setting off for school.'

'How's it been today?'

Beattie looks round cautiously. 'All right so far, I think. Mother's not making things easy but she'll get used to it in time. You must have got the news awfully quickly, because Mrs Musgrave only heard early this morning. She got a telegram sent from RAF, I suppose.'

There is a very long and perplexed silence from the other end.

'Telegram?' says Charles sharply. 'What telegram? What on earth are you talking about?'

Beattie has a sudden uneasy sensation in the pit of her stomach.

'The telegram saying Brooke was still alive,' she says slowly. 'It arrived first thing this morning. I thought – I thought that's what we were talking about—'

'Didn't you get my letter?' demands Charles furiously. Beattie's hand flies to her mouth then to her suit-pocket where the unopened letter crackles accusingly.

'Oh – yes – oh, Charles, I'm so sorry, I collected it cycling when I went to school and I haven't had a chance to open it.'

'Oh.' Abruptly all the animation drains out of Charles's voice. 'So you haven't read it.'

'No – I – I assumed when you said "good news" you must mean – I'm

300

sorry, Charles, what does your letter say?' concludes Beattie lamely, blushing from head to foot.

'Well, I suppose it's very small beer in comparison with your good news,' says Charles expressionlessly. 'It's just that I've had my novel accepted. That detective story. I heard yesterday. Marwicks have decided to take it. They wrote to me a nice letter. It'll be out at Christmas.'

'Oh, Charles, that's wonderful, wonderful.'

'I thought so,' says Charles quietly. 'I'll have to run now, Beattie. I've borrowed someone else's phone and he'll be back in a minute. Is Annie all right?'

'Yes, she's—'

'You'll have to tell me the next time you write. Goodbye for now.'

Beattie listens for a long time to the metallic purring of the receiver before she realizes that Charles has put the phone down on her.

CHAPTER
TWENTY-FIVE

'WHAT'S the meeting about?'

'Oh, for Alexis to rally the troops. Tomorrow's first location day. They're doing the scenes in the fire station. Lucky them. I wish I could go filming. Bet you wish you could, too.'

It was typical of Millie to reveal a desire herself and hastily attribute it to somebody else.

'Where's Myerberg?'

'Gone to the dentist. One of his crowns is loose. He's left you a pile of letters.'

Virginia begins to type, whistling horribly the while. At 11.30 the office begins to fill up. Billy Gavin appears wearing his flat cap back to front, swinging a coil of rope and exuding whisky fumes. Where Billy manages to get whisky is a mystery to everyone except Virginia, who knows that he does favours for a friend of Willie's at the embassy. It isn't ethical of course but, then, if you did observe the letter of the law you got nothing. No nylons, no nice clothes, no cosmetics and no booze. Virginia entirely approves of rationing. It is just that it isn't conceivable that she should be denied what to her are life's absolute necessities.

Billy sits on the edge of her desk and indulges in some quietly bawdy badinage. Then Alexis appears with the ubiquitous Holly hanging on to him like a burr. Virginia studies Holly dispassionately. Today she is wearing a bright scarlet belted jersey and beret, her vivid heart-shaped face alight with vitality and happiness.

'Why is she still around?' says Virginia *sotto voce* to Trudy, who has just drawn up a chair beside her. 'I thought her own film went into production this week.'

'It does. But she's putting off Shropshire and the evil hour of separation for as long as possible,' says Trudy and coughs. 'What's it to you, Miss Curious? Fancy him, do you?'

'No, it's Holly I could go for. I've always liked girls who don't shave their armpits.'

Trudy snorts, then giggles. 'How do you know she doesn't shave?'

'She's clearly way above anything as trivial as that. Are they engaged?'

'They were, then they weren't. Then it all started up again. I think she wants to,' observes Trudy. 'And he'd be a fool if he didn't. Her father's—'

302

'Yes, I know. But does he have any real clout?'

'You bet he does. Alexis is as ambitious as hell; he won't want to stay in documentary films for ever. He's already been approached by other companies. If he ever decides he wants to sell his soul and go to Ealing, he'll be on a terrific screw. And her dad's got all kinds of connections in Hollywood. Plus the fact that they're rolling in money. Her mother is American, and they're all rich over there. I went to their house once at Denham for a party. It's like Buckingham Palace. And Holly is so sweet and absolutely potty about him. He is about her, too, I think.'

'Really,' says Virginia.

'Yes, really,' says Trudy and coughs again.

'You don't sound very well.'

'What's it to you?' says Trudy, immediately suspicious. 'After my job, are you?'

'For Christ's sake,' says Virginia quietly. 'Give me a nice fuggy office any day of the week.'

While they wait for Pat Blain to arrive Virginia covertly studies Alexis. She is aware suddenly that he has matured strikingly in the last two years and makes a mental note to get his biography out of the office file. At this point she finds Holly's eyes on her with no friendly expression on her face and abruptly goes back to her typing. It would be fatal to put the wind up Holly; she might just refuse to go off to Shropshire if she caught a whiff of Virginia's real intentions.

But what, after all, are my intentions? Virginia enquires of herself as she absently folds a letter into an envelope. Tom has been to London twice to take her out to dinner, and she thoroughly enjoyed both occasions. But none the less it will still be Christmas before she sees him again, and in the meantime Alexis is in London and Holly is in Shropshire. Part of her wants Alexis' attention. But, more than that, a part of her still hasn't forgiven him for knowing what he knows about her early days in London. It would be pleasant to have him in her power instead of vice versa.

After the meeting they all adjourn to the pub round the corner. Virginia sits with Dennis and Billy, who by now is lacing his bitter with neat whisky. To her surprise Alexis himself comes over to speak to her, and something in his manner – a faint embarrassment – bespeaks a consciousness that hadn't been there before that evening with Ferdinand.

'I had a letter from Ferdinand this morning,' he explains rather lamely. 'He asked me to pass on his address and implore you to write to him and to apologize for not contacting you before he went. He said he did ring once but you were out gadding.'

'How sweet of him,' said Virginia. 'I'll certainly drop him a line.'

Alexis tears a page out of his pad and writes down an address in South Kensington in a strong, rather beautiful italic hand.

'This is a new one. Apparently you write letters to this address and they forward them by carrier-pigeon. Ferdy told me about your brother by the way. I'm really sorry. I met him, you know, when we were doing the recce for Bomber Command at Mildenhall. Suppose there's no news, is there?'

'There certainly is,' says Virginia, her usual rather bored expression transformed by a smile of pure joy. 'He's alive at least. I only heard this morning. They didn't know if he managed to get out of his plane in time, but apparently he did, and landed in Holland but broke both legs with the fall. So he's been in hiding. But his friend got back and that's hopeful, isn't it?'

Alexis looks at her animated face properly for the first time, and unconsciously his own expression softens.

'Yes,' he says gently, 'I'll say that was very hopeful. But he had a reputation for luck, didn't he? That's why I wanted to use him. As things turned out, I'm glad I didn't.'

'Why?'

'All the boys we filmed are dead.'

Virginia has a sudden image of Brooke's body rolling over and over weightlessly in the North Sea and shudders.

'Two pints coming up with a gin for the lady. Hands off, Alexis, I saw her first. I keep offering to make her a star and put her name forward for film flashes but she says no. She's wedded to her typewriter.'

Alexis punches Billy amicably on the arm.

'Are you going to see the filming?' asks Billy.

'I knew it,' says a voice *sotto voce*. It is Millie trying to disguise herself as a beer-mat.

'I'd love to, but I shouldn't think it's very likely,' replies Virginia regretfully. 'Mr Myerberg seems to go into a decline if I'm late from lunch.'

'Weaned too early, I shouldn't wonder,' says Billy rather surprisingly. It was he who had lent Virginia that article on Freud. 'That young lady of yours is looking for you,' he adds, and as Alexis looks round Holly appears at his elbow.

'Darling, we must go. I said we'd see Daddy for a late lunch, and he's got a table at Simpson's for us. Had you forgotten?'

'Oh God, yes. Look, love, I can't possibly get away now; there's much too much to do. Can't you go on your own? I've got a whole pile of things, and I haven't even begun to talk to . . . . ' They move away into the crowd.

'True love, eh?' says Billy Gavin, gazing into the bottom of his glass for inspiration. 'Who are you going to marry, then, Virginia? Someone rich and famous?'

'And titled if I get half the chance. I'm off back to the office.'

But whatever hopes Virginia might nurse of Alexis' immediate seduction are dashed when the entire production team simply disappears for two months. It is only in the middle of November when fortune at last seems to favour her plans. At ten o'clock one Friday morning Trudy's mum rings to say that Trudy won't be in to work because she's got shingles, contracted from a nephew who has chicken-pox.

The news has a truly electrifying effect on Millie, who half-rises out of her typing-seat. It is clearly the opportunity she has been dreaming about. Without drawing breath she informs Pat Blain modestly and immediately that she is the very person for Trudy's job, and if she jumps into a taxi with her typewriter she can be at the Surrey Docks in twenty minutes. Most unexpectedly Pat Blain demurs.

'Oh, Millie, I was counting on you to come along to the Ministry of Information this afternoon,' he says plaintively. 'I've got to have someone who knows about the figures. Virginia wouldn't have a clue. It would make much more sense if she filled in for a day or so for Trudy while you hold the fort here. And Ira's got to go to Shropshire for a few days to see how they're spending his money, as he insists on calling it, so he won't need her. And when I go down to Pinewood I need you to take notes about the editing. No, the best thing would be if Virginia goes. After all, it'll only be for a day or so. And knowing Alexis there'll be hardly anything to do. He never does a proper script. It'll just be typing the call-sheets and looking alert. Gladys will be logging the shots and doing the real continuity.'

'I don't mind going,' says Virginia dubiously. 'It's just I'm terrified I'll get in the way.'

'If you are,' Millie assures her with considerable malice, 'a great many people will let you know.'

The obliging Dennis carries her typewriter down to the taxi, and Virginia finds herself driving through the ruined streets of the Surrey Docks in search of a pub called the Red Lion where the film production company has its headquarters. Inside the saloon bar a thin man is polishing glasses.

'We're closed.'

'I'm – er – looking for the film company.'

'They're at the fire station, first left, second right. You can't miss it. You can leave your typewriter here.'

In spite of the seeming simplicity of the instructions it takes Virginia some time to find the fire station, which presents a formidably buttoned-up appearance in the morning sunlight. Disconcerted, she loiters around outside, then decides to take her confidence in both hands and stride in through the side-door. Having done so, she finds that she has stepped not only into a large room but also into a blaze of light and, as luck would have it, the best take of the day. It is her misfortune that they are shooting that way and that Ginger, the second assistant whose job it is to keep a look out for marauders, has just gone round the corner for a leak. Somebody shouts at her, then Alexis shouts 'Cut' and a number of people ask her what the hell she thinks she is doing, the loudest and angriest of whom is Alexis.

'Gosh, I'm so sorry,' mutters Virginia, appalled by the tidal wave of annoyance that has crashed down on to her unprotected head, 'but I was told to come down, and there wasn't anybody outside. I didn't realize—'

'Don't you know enough about filming to know that your *never* enter the film area without finding out if they're rolling?' hisses the appalling Gladys.

'We might as well break for lunch. We'll never get that set up again before the break,' says Alexis, directing a furious glance at Virginia. 'What the hell are you doing here anyway?'

'Pat sent me here as a replacement for Trudy.'

'Christ,' says Bert, the sound recordist, whom Virginia has long suspected of disliking her. 'A bloody amateur. That's all we need.'

The room begins to empty at surprising speed. Mr Maggs and his friends are the only ones who show any sympathy.

'Shouldn't worry about it if I were you,' says one of them. 'We've only been doing that scene since six o'clock this morning. It's early days yet,' he adds and winks at her.

But Virginia is clearly in disgrace. During the lunch break no one speaks to her. Alexis is far too distraught to notice anything and keeps pushing his long dark forelock out of his eyes in a gesture of despair. He is accompanied at all times by three silent young men who keep their eyes constantly fixed on his face like dogs trying to define the mood of their master. These are his assistants. The unit manager is apparently the appalling Gladys, whose oily black curls slip out of a a grimy turban as she abuses everybody within earshot. Gladys has the trick of talking with a cigarette on her immobile lower lip. Horrible though it looks, it is in its own way a blessing, for otherwise you would have seen the colour of her teeth. As usual her lips have been outlined in crimson lake earlier in the day and now only the outline remains, seeping into the cracks and lines round her mouth. The visual effect of her mouth is horrible, but what comes out is indescribably worse. After lunch she draws Virginia to one side and tells her in a few terse sentences that if she ever catches her messing up one of Alexis' shots again she'll get her sent straight back to Soho Square. This, at least, is the gist of what she says. Virginia, ears burning, makes her way back to the fire station and sits at the back hating everyone.

During the tea-break Gladys finally condescends to tell Virginia what she ought to be doing, adding that since she is clearly too incompetent to do it anyway, she, Gladys, in addition to keeping the whole show on the road, will do Virginia's job as well. Virginia's sole task will be to type the script notes and compile the call-sheet for the rest of the unit.

When at nine o'clock the action finally grinds to a halt Virginia still cannot decide whether filming is interesting or the most boring thing she's ever experienced. On the credit side the actual atmosphere – the lights, the cameras, the fact that people do actually say things like 'Quiet, please' and 'Action' – is quite entrancing. On the debit side it takes five hours to set up to film a forty-second scene until it meets with Alexis' approval, at the end of which she feels an irresistible desire to set about Alexis' head with one of the fire-buckets. Finally, as they are packing up, thinking it is time she undertook some duties she enquires of Alexis in a rather truculent voice as to whether there is anything she has to do for him before they go home. This provokes the carpenter to chortles of rude laughter. Alexis, however, is far too preoccupied to pick up the innuendo.

'We'll stop for something to eat, then you can do the call-sheets and a few notes for me,' he says abstractedly.

The something to eat turns out to be fish and chips for twenty, and Virginia is expected to go and get them with one of the assistants. They stand round and eat while Virginia radically rethinks her ideas about glamour in the film industry. It goes without saying that it is the first time in her life that she has eaten fish and chips. Finally at 10.15 Alexis turns to her and says he'll give her what notes he has for the following day. He then begins to feel absently in his pockets and finally announces in tones of some irritation that he's lost the script for the following day.

'What's it like? Was it in a folder?'

'Don't be stupid,' he snaps. 'It's on the back of a Basildon Bond envelope.'

Other people help him search. Virginia looks at him with a dawning feeling of horror and finally announces in a very small voice that she thought she might have seen it on a crate over there and she might just have thrown it away with the chip paper. Moving with extreme rapidity towards the dustbins, she is still not quick enough to avoid hearing Gladys saying: 'Alexis, she's absolutely hopeless. Who on earth employed her in the first place?' In a blacked-out alley at the back of the fire station Virginia, with a cigarette-lighter, begins to dig around in the unsavoury depths of the dustbin. Wrapped in the chip paper and now liberally smeared with oil and vinegar is the missing envelope. Gladys gives her a look which would strip paint off a door at fifty paces and announces that they will be in the pub for the call-sheets when they are finished. Virginia and Alexis are left alone in a darkened room while he dictates the notes for the shooting script for the following day.

'Do fifteen copies of that and give them to Gladys. And tell her it's another five-thirty start.'

Savagely Virginia jams a piece of paper into her typewriter, and longs from the bottom of her heart for Mr Myerberg to return from Shropshire.

In time, of course, it gets better. Trudy's shingles continue, and as there is no one else to fill in Virginia finds the two days lengthening into a week, then into two. By the end she is almost enjoying herself. It takes a while to recover from the early starts – but, as Lucy says, in the end you get used to it. And there's the added bonus of the petrol allowance which she can use in Stephen's borrowed Morris Oxford to drive to the docks. To her annoyance Trudy finally announces she is well enough to come back to work just as they are beginning to film some of the action scenes outside. In fact, despite its occasional *longueurs*, on balance Virginia does enjoy filming, once she's accepted the fact that it's 1 per cent action and 99 per cent setting up while the technicians quarrel and declare everything to be impossible – usually before the idea is fully out of Alexis' mouth.

Finally Trudy informs Alexis via Gladys that she'll be able to struggle back to work the following day, much to Virginia's vexation. Her planned campaign of revenge and seduction is not so much at the blueprint stage as never having left the drawing-board. The problem is that Alexis is never alone. At all times his three assistants are standing mutely at his elbow, with Gladys and Billy Gavin firmly in tow. Virginia concludes that she will simply have to think of a new plan.

Her final day's filming starts inauspiciously enough. Up pulverizingly early for the last of the early-morning sequences, after lunch they set up for some shots of the river. Standing on the docks of the November Thames, the wind flaying even her gloved hands, Virginia manages to keep herself conscious solely by reminding herself that by the end of today she will be able at least to get a tepid bath and an early night. At 5.30 with the impenetrable gloom of the November night falling as thick as a curtain Gladys says casually: 'Coming to the pub, then?'

307

'No,' says Virginia firmly from between frozen lips. 'I'm off home. I'm finished now.'

'In that case,' says Gladys immediately, 'you can go back to the fire station, get the shooting script and the stuff we need for tomorrow.'

'Oh, Gladys, it's miles away. Can't one of the assistants go?'

'Certainly not. What exactly do you think you're paid for?'

'I still don't see why I've got to go. What do I do with them anyway?'

'Bring them back here of course.'

'But I wanted to get off. Look, I'm not needed tomorrow anyway. If one of the boys gets them, he can bring them with him tomorrow morning.'

Gladys fixes Virginia with a stony stare, and mutinously Virginia finds her complaints dying on her lips.

'We'll be in the Hope and Anchor in Dove Street. You can resume your social life afterwards.'

It's all very well for them, Virginia grumbles to herself inching the car forward through the blacked-out dockland streets. They simply haven't *got* another life. Why, half the time I don't think they even know there's a war on. They make films about the war; that's about as far as it impinges on them. All they care about is filming. It's not like that for me.

Inside the fire station Virginia receives a gratifyingly warm welcome from Walter Maggs and his friends, who are just brewing up prior to starting night duty.

'Been working you hard, has he?'

'Oh, a slave-driver, believe me. You think you'd be able to adjust to a life of film stardom, Mr Maggs?'

There was much guffawing and passing around of mugs of hot sweet tea. Afterwards the dense chill of the dock area seems even less inviting. Gritting her teeth and grinding the gears, Virginia finds her way back to the Hope and Anchor where, as usual, the film company have managed to take over the saloon bar.

Musing on the fact that before the war she'd never been into a pub, and under no circumstances could she ever have imagined herself entering one on her own, Virginia pushes open the saloon door expecting to be hit by the usual wave of maudlin cheer, lacklustre conversation and the smell of sawdust and warm beer. The smells are certainly there in abundance, but that is all. The saloon is crowded, but most unusually there is complete silence save for a red-faced old woman at the bar who is abusing someone at the top of her lungs.

'No uniform? No duties? Why aren't you away fighting while other decent men are getting killed? How much did your father pay to keep you at home?'

At this point the barman appears to remonstrate with the woman, and Virginia glances round in disbelief. The crew are standing by the bar, carefully studying their drinks and avoiding each other's eyes. The locals are sitting well back in their chairs, clearly enjoying the spectacle and hoping for a second bout. There are a number of servicemen present, backs ostentatiously turned to the group at the bar. As Virginia edges her way over the harangue starts up again with renewed venom. As Billy Gavin moves to one side Virginia catches sight of an old woman in a toque hat pulled well down over her forehead. Beneath it, her nose and cheeks are bright red with broken veins. As the crowd parts Virginia sees that the person being harangued is Alexis.

'Can't anybody stop her?' mutters one of the braver assistants to Gladys, who gestures angrily to him to shut up. The old lady hears the other voice and turns round to glare. As she does her eye falls on Virginia, innocently standing clutching her notes.

'And she's another of you, I suppose. Another who thinks she's too good to soil her hands for her country. You can tell the kind of woman she is by her clothes.'

Virginia is scarlet with rage and humiliation.

'There's a blush of guilt and shame. You earn clothes like that on your back. Makes you sick, Lady Muck pretending she's better than the rest of us. You make me sick, *sick*, the lot of you.'

With that the old lady throws an arm wide to demonstrate the breadth of her moral disapproval and in doing so somehow manages to up-end herself from her bar stool, disappearing suddenly from view in a welter of thrashing veined legs.

There is a moment of appalled silence. The scene is grotesquely, painfully funny. All that is visible of the woman is a pair of salmon-pink rayon bloomers and a hat jammed down firmly over her eyes. Then someone walks over, screens her from the now guffawing crowd, helps her to her feet, and brushes the sawdust off her coat.

'What the hell does Alexis want to help that gruesome old hag for?' demands Gladys rhetorically of her gin.

'Kind hearts and a desire for a quick dissolve,' announces Billy, sliding an arm around Virginia, who is still rigid with fury at the woman's unprovoked attack. 'Cheer up, duckie, I know you're no girl of easy virtue.'

'You would,' Gladys tells him acidly. 'If you've finished your mission of mercy, Alexis, Virginia's got those notes you wanted.'

'Oh, hi, Virginia. That was nice of you, but you really needn't have bothered. I could have got one of the assistants to go.'

Virginia gives Gladys a look that tragically does not seem to injure her in any way, and dumps the folder on the bar without comment.

'Virginia doesn't like being called a good-time girl.'

'Poor Virginia. When she gives up so much of her free time to keep the Yanks amused.'

'I'll bet there are nights she doesn't sleep at all. And not just the Yanks. There's no side on Virginia. She's just as nice to our boys, provided they're officers of course.'

Daily exposure to similar barbed pleasantries from her working colleagues has thickened Virginia's skin considerably. Normally she is able to give as good as she gets; but tonight, tired, cold and fed up, she is suddenly almost in tears.

'You've got your notes,' she says brusquely. 'If that's everything, then I'm off.'

'Hey, come on.'

To her annoyance Virginia finds her arm firmly grasped as Alexis pulls her round to face him. 'Stop and have a drink for goodness' sake. If I'd known Gladys had sent you off, I'd have stopped her. Come on, it's gin, isn't it?'

'Look, I don't want a drink, I just want to go *home*.'

'It's your last day, isn't it? At least let me get you a drink to thank you for your sterling efforts.'

Suspecting she is still being mocked, Virginia is about to try to think of something really squelching to say when to her own fury her eyes fill with tears.

'Come on, working for me can't have been *that* bad.' Tactfully, just as he had shielded the older woman Alexis now draws her back to face him, screening her from the rest of the company who in any case are now completely absorbed in watching Billy Gavin's version of the three-card trick.

Feeling defeated and cross, Virginia climbs on to a bar stool and leans limply against the bar. She is furious with herself for crying. Furthermore, who in all conscience could embark on an elaborate plan of revenge with their eye-black running? Only when Alexis actually sets a gin in front of her does Virginia finally look at him; and, aware of her scrutiny, Alexis simply commandeers another bar stool, resting his elbows comfortably on the bar beside her.

'What's wrong, sweetheart?'

'Nothing's wrong,' hisses Virginia, furious to note the effect that seemingly casual endearment has on her pulse. 'I mean, it's been an end to a perfect day, hasn't it? I enjoy being insulted, particularly by offensive old women. I expect you're going to tell me she's the salt of the earth, patriotic wife and the mother of a son lost in the merchant navy.'

'That's pretty good "B"-film stuff. Sadly it's not true. The barman says she got stood up at lunchtime by a soldier, so she's been drinking ever since. Now, why that should make her hostile to chaps in civvies like me, I can't imagine. In your case I'm afraid you just strayed across her line of fire.'

'Alexis, if you imagine you're going to talk me round into feeling sorry for that old vulture—'

'Of course I'm not going to, but why does it bother you so much? You don't know her, she didn't know you – it was just random nastiness.'

'Why did you just stand there?'

Alexis shrugs, feeling in his jacket pocket for cigarettes.

'I felt sorry for the old dear. It must seem pretty odd to see anyone without a uniform. As I remember, you remarked on it yourself on our very first meeting. Oh, come on, Virginia, stop leaping up and down like a jack-in-the-box. Look, drink your drink, have a fag with me, then I'll release you from this hideous nightmare to go back to brightening Ira's life.'

'I just can't see why she didn't pick on Gladys.'

'Virginia, don't let's be disingenuous, shall we? Gladys has many virtues, but sartorial loveliness isn't one of them. You stand out because you dress to attract attention.'

'I do not!'

'Yes, you do. I don't think I've ever seen you badly dressed.'

'I can't imagine how *anyone* can attack an outfit like this. These slacks are cut down from a man's pair of golfing trousers,' Virginia tells him crossly. 'I got this jacket in a secondhand shop and altered it myself. This is a man's shirt that I bought for twopence in a jumble sale, and the lace collar I actually found in a dustbin. Does that sound like the wardrobe of a kept woman?'

'Really.' Alexis is clearly interested. 'The point is it all looks marvellous. As I said, I've never seen you badly dressed. You're lucky enough to be able to put clothes together with flair.' Then he adds somewhat mockingly: 'The girl who's known to be clever with her clothes.'

Virginia stares at Alexis, eyes suddenly narrowed. Alexis smiles his blandest smile.

'Was it you who suggested me for that feature?'

'To old Matthew – yes, it was as a matter of fact.'

'How did you know he was looking for someone, and why me?'

'I've known him for years. He had a room in my house a few months ago. He has got rather keen on you – though you probably know that. He told me all about you. I know a lot of people who know you. And a very fascinating subject for study you've proved. Two more of the same, please.'

Virginia stares at Alexis. Alexis looks innocently round the bar feeling for another cigarette. There is a roar from where Billy Gavin is sitting. He is balancing beer-glasses into a pyramid, much to the barman's consternation.

'Billy's getting very drunk,' says Virginia disapprovingly. 'Shouldn't you stop him?'

'Why? We're finished for the day. Anyway,' goes on Alexis, paying for the drinks and turning back to give Virginia his undivided attention, 'he's always the same. I've seen old Billy drink himself into a coma at lunchtime and the moment I say "Back to work" he's icily sober. I've never faintly managed the trick myself. That's why I normally stick to halves. Be an angel, Virginia dear. Let me have a cigarette. I can't imagine that Willy lets you go short of them.'

The use of Willy's name is a deliberate provocation. Silently Virginia produces her cigarette-case, which is, as usual, full to capacity with Lucky Strikes. She is further aware that when she looks directly at Alexis he looks away from her but once she stops staring at him he immediately starts covertly to examine her.

'Well, aren't you going to ask me?'

'Ask you what?' says Virginia coldly.

'How I come to know so much about you.'

'It barely interests me,' Virginia tells him, aware, none the less, that she is becoming very angry. 'I can't think why you bother.'

'Oh, I told you. You're an interesting field for study. Plus the fact that Ferdinand asked me to keep a brotherly eye on you.'

'Decent of him. I must tell him not to waste his time next time I write.'

'He's very fond of you,' goes on Alexis, apparently riveted by the puddle of beer on the surface in front of him.

'I am of him.'

'That was obvious that first time I met you. Do you remember? In

311

Leicester Square. I don't think I've ever been so completely ignored in my life.' Alexis grins at her.

'Bad for the old *amour-propre*.'

'It certainly is. No one wants to be overlooked by a beautiful woman. Especially since, though I love Ferdy like a brother, in affairs of the heart I've never seen him as competition. You made a bad slip there, Virginia. That and slagging off my film. You were lucky to get out alive that night.'

'Poor Alexis. It's not enough to be the toast of the production offices and get good reviews. We've got to love you as well, have we?' jeers Virginia.

'In an ideal world, yes.'

'As I remember, you were pretty bloody rude yourself that night. About my taste in "B" films.'

'I *was* pretty nasty,' Alexis allows. 'Especially since I've directed so many "B" films myself. But I wasn't about to let you get away with anything. Another gin?'

'No, two's my limit when I'm driving.'

'You're not thinking of going, are you?'

'Will you please take your hand off my arm and stop playing the fool? People are looking at you.'

It occurs to Virginia that Alexis is a great deal drunker than she thought.

'I see. Keeping ourselves for Tom, are we?'

In spite of attempts at iron self-control that remark hits the mark as accurately as Alexis had intended.

'Tom who?' says Virginia in her most freezing tones.

'Tom Berkeley. I gather he's your number one man at present. Ferdinand will be delighted that at long last you've decided to be sensible and opt for Lord Right.'

'Tom isn't a lord.'

'But he will be, won't he? That excites you, does it?'

'Not nearly as much as it seems to excite you.'

Virginia gathers her things together preparatory to leaving. Playfully but none the less firmly Alexis takes Virginia by her slender wrist.

'You should be grateful to me. I've certainly done what I can to advance the affair.'

'What do you mean?'

'You haven't met Tom's younger brother David, have you? He was on my staircase at college and he's one of my best friends. We had supper a couple of weeks ago.'

Virginia forces her wrist to lie unresistingly in Alexis' steel grasp.

'I gather Tom's really smitten. David knew you worked for Reel Films; he wanted to know all about you.'

Momentarily Virginia feels quite dizzy at the thought of what damage Alexis' special knowledge of her past could do to her present reputation. Alexis, knowing he now has her full attention, keeps hold of her arm, his thumb lightly caressing the gilt hairs of her wrist.

'What did you tell him?'

'Alexis, what time are the rushes tomorrow?' says Gladys suddenly from behind them. 'And we're getting hungry. Are you coming to eat?'

'Alexis, you still haven't given me any notes for—' As the rest of the company surge round the bar Virginia quietly disentangles her hand, slides off her bar stool and melts into the freezing November night. The car coughes, splutters, complains deeply, then condescends to start, and Virginia drives away at a reckless speed anxious to put as much space between herself and Alexis as possible.

What on earth had got into him? After a month of almost studiously ignoring her he suddenly grabs her arm and hangs on to her. And what had he said to Tom's brother? Virginia groans aloud and slams her gloved fist on the steering-wheel. The idea was that she should have the power to put a spoke in Alexis' wheel, not vice versa. He had been out to rile her tonight but why? Whatever the reason, he had certainly succeeded. And yet. And yet . . . .

After parking the car a few yards from the Grangemouth, Virginia sits slumped in the chilly leather- and oil-smelling darkness, pondering the evening.

Next morning the office seems even dustier and quieter than usual. There is a bunch of roses on Virginia's desk, and an extremely sour look on Millie's face.

'I hear you made a right bloody fool of yourself on the first day,' is Millie's greeting. 'The roses are from Ira. *He* missed you. He's already gone to Denham. There's a file of letters a foot thick waiting to be typed.'

'Hello, Virginia, nice to see you.' Pat Blain's somewhat kindlier greeting. 'Did you enjoy continuity?'

'Don't forget to let Ira know it's Alexis' rushes tonight,' adds Millie.

By midday Virginia hasn't made up her mind whether she will see the rushes, but by 2.30 she has definitely decided that she won't. At 4.30 she congratulates herself on the wisdom of her decision and at 5.30 is furious to find herself walking briskly down Wardour Street towards the Ship with Millie prior to going on to the cinema with her.

The Ship is full, but fortunately not with red-faced women haranguing strangers. The first person she sees, pale but resolute, is Trudy, just up from her bed of pain. With her is Rachel back from Shropshire for the weekend.

'How's Shropshire going?'

'The purest hell. I don't think it's stopped raining since we arrived. And the film's a shambles. Did you know old George Handly is directing it? I didn't find out until I got off the train. If I'd known, I'd have stayed in London with the food flashes.'

'What's wrong with him?'

'He drinks and he can't make decisions. Stuart's his first assistant and he has to keep stepping in and saying, "Right, George, we'll do it this way," and George just says "Yes, yes, anything you say, dear boy". And the sheep! They make the most appalling noise.'

'Baa-ing?' asks Virginia, straight-faced, and demonstrates.

'Yes,' says Rachel, interested. 'Just like that. I played a sheep once in our school play. I'd play it quite differently now. Actually, it really is a bit of a disaster in Shropshire. I'm not superstitious, but sometimes it's as if the whole thing's jinxed. You know the girl who was playing the lead had to drop out at the last minute – and I do mean the last minute, actually the first day of filming? Her dad found out what she was doing and wouldn't let her. She's a Plymouth Brethren or something. So we had to re-audition on the first day of shooting. Can you imagine? We're terribly over budget.'

'How's Holly?' asks Trudy.

'Frantic. I really began to wonder if she and Alexis had had words before she left London, but she rings him twice a day so I suppose they must be OK. George gets furious because she's never there when he wants her. But she's got the wind up properly about something.'

'It's a pity Alexis couldn't have directed for her.'

'That's what she says. Pat's funny like that sometimes. It's his Presbyterian upbringing or something. Do you remember when we had that chap – what was his name? – Eddy – do you remember he stood in and did a few films for us and he started to take out Ira's secretary – who was it? – and the *next* thing was—'

'Drink up, girls. It's twenty-five past six. We'll be late otherwise.'

The Coronet is a small, fuggy, moderately squalid private cinema club off Wardour Street, patronized by lovers of the Russian and Japanese schools of expressionist cinema. Reel Films have almost exclusive rights to show their rushes here between performances, and as usual there are a crowd of people gathered to see Alexis' latest offering. With Rachel and Trudy, Virginia slips discreetly into the back row. Keeping her eyes fixed firmly on her handbag, she appears to fiddle for her cigarettes. Finally an exasperated Trudy shoves a battered pack of Craven 'A' under Virginia's nose.

'What are you rooting for? Have one of mine, for God's sake.'

'It's OK, I've got my own,' snaps Virginia crossly, raising her eyes for the first time and encountering Alexis' glance from across the cinema. Cursing, she gives him a frigid nod, then turns away as the lights go down.

The rushes are the usual jumbled sequence of shots interspersed with Alexis' voice at the beginning and the end of the take. Nevertheless there is something there. He seems to have been able to drag something approaching a lifelike performance from Walter and his friends. Despite Holly's shocked protestations Virginia still can't see why they don't use actors rather than people from real life. But with Walter and his friends you have the sense of eavesdropping on their conversations and actually sensing Walter's thinking.

'I think it's going to be good,' says Rachel stoutly afterwards. 'Coming for a drink, Musgrave?'

'No,' says Virginia with unaccustomed firmness. 'Choses à faire, mon brave. Incidentally, Millie, did you remember to bring my pay-packet with you?'

'Certainly not. I left it in the drawer with the carbons. Didn't I tell you?' says Millie innocently.

'No, you didn't.'

On her way to the office Virginia debates as to whether she really need go back to Reel Films or whether she could borrow from Willy. Then she remembers that Willy has in any case gone to Mildenhall, at least until tomorrow, so there is no alternative. The rest of the girls at the Grangemouth are even more broke than herself.

George the maintenance man and Mrs Epps are purifying the offices. Millie has taken care to cram her wages right at the back of the drawer, and Virginia has just located the brown envelope when there is a footstep in the doorway.

'It's all right, Mrs Epps, I've got what I came for – Oh, it's you. Do you want Pat? He said he was going to the pub.'

Alexis advances further into the room, his hands thrust deeply into his overcoat.

'It was you I wanted. I'm afraid I was rather off colour last night – not to put too fine a point on it, drunk.'

'You were absolutely vile,' retorts Virginia, who has never seen any virtue in being gracious in victory.

'Will you let me take you out to supper tonight to make amends?'

'Thank you, but I already have an engagement.'

'Oh.' Alexis appears to be almost crestfallen, but he smiles nicely anyway and says, 'Well, another time perhaps,' and turns to go.

'Alexis . . . .'

'Yes?'

For a long moment Virginia and Alexis eye each other, then without a word, Alexis grins and holds open the office door for her and they go down the steep dusty stairs together.

'Bianchi's suit you?'

'Lovely.'

Virginia is alarmed to observe that Alexis has already booked a table. Had he been so sure she'd come? Alexis catches her expression and reads it unerringly.

'Not certain. Just hopeful.'

Virginia colours, annoyed at the way that Alexis seems to wander in and out of her thoughts at his leisure, and resolves that tonight she will be the one in charge. If there was ever a moment to take her revenge on Holly, then this is it – but how exactly does one set about charming Alexis? Especially as he has revealed himself to be absolutely impervious to her charms from almost the very first moment he'd met her. And yet, and yet. Alexis is a great deal more carefully dressed than usual. Almost as carefully dressed as Virginia, who had told herself that it was necessary to look good on her first day back at the office.

Having ordered drinks, a rather tense silence falls. Normally on new dinner dates Virginia's ploy is to arrange herself as gracefully as possible, then sit back and let the man make a fool of himself. Tonight she is annoyed to discover that, far from being disconcerted by her alluring and enigmatic pose, Alexis seems not even to notice it and instead starts straight in on the subject closest to his heart.

'Well, what did you think of the rushes? *Wonderful* will do. *Sensational* even I would find over the top. But I don't think I can accept anything less

315

than *riveting*. Or, in your case, *too riveting*.'

Virginia opens her mouth to be annoyed, then catches Alexis' eye and smiles unwillingly.

'You know I don't talk like that.'

'That's true. I suppose I just always expect it. I can't understand why a posh girl like you is hanging round Fitzrovia. Anyway, what did you think of the film?'

'All right, I found it riveting. That isn't to say I understood what it's all about, and I still don't understand why you get those sudden shots of tugs on the river, but I thought it was interesting. Is that enough?'

'It errs on the side of hyperbole, but it's a great step forward from your earlier views on my films.'

'It had nothing to do with your films. I just didn't like you.'

'Do you like me now?'

'A little more,' says Virginia with a familiar sensation of being out-manoeuvred.

'How much more?'

'Enough to let you take me out to dinner,' says Virginia, exasperated. 'Why do you ask so many questions?'

'You're so buttoned-up.'

'I'm *not* buttoned-up.'

'You may think you're unbuttoned to an almost obscene degree, but you don't "trade" in conversation. You're pretty expert at dragging information out of other people but you never offer any back. It leaves people feeling uneasy.'

'Really?' asks Virginia, already bitterly regretting accepting Alexis' invitation and wondering if she will cause a sensation if she leaves before the first course arrives.

'You present yourself like a sheet of blank paper. You're never quite all there. I can never tell what's going on in your head.'

'Perhaps nothing at all.'

'That was my conclusion for a very long time. But Ferdinand assures me that I'm wrong.'

'You are *bloody rude*,' hisses Virginia *sotto voce* but none the less furious and getting to her feet. 'I don't give a damn what you think of me. And you can offer your dinner to one of the many ladies crazy for your company. *I'm not*.'

Alexis grabs her arm and pushes her back into the chair. People are staring.

'I'm sorry, I really am sorry,' says Alexis and most surprisingly leans over to take her hand.

Unwillingly Virginia raises her eyes and finds Alexis smiling at her.

'That was just my version of shock tactics. I never seem to be able to get any response from you. I thought if I shocked you into speech, then I might. But the idea was that you suddenly overflowed with girlish good humour, not that you slapped my face and walked out. I'll have to alter my script and take it back to the drawing-board. Please don't be offended. Here's our soup. What do you normally chat about when you're out with your cavaliers?'

'They talk, I listen.'

'Don't you let your youthful heart overflow to them?'

'Certainly not. I don't like talking about myself.'

'Well, that rather proves my point. However, we'll leave it. Did you enjoy continuity?'

'Yes. I wish I could have done more.'

'I've suggested to Pat that you train as a continuity girl.'

'You're joking.'

'I told him I thought you'd be rather good.'

'That first day—'

'Oh, forget about *that*.'

'Millie wants to do continuity—'

'She's too tender a flower. It's useless if you can't cope with the continual stream of barbed malice that the crews call "good-natured ribbing." Don't you want to do continuity?'

'Well, of course I'd *love* to, but it's still so odd that I'm working at all let alone that I'd get promoted. When the war broke out I was on the point of being presented and I never in my wildest dreams imagined I'd have a job. I thought I was going to marry well. I still intend to do *that*,' she adds with a look that forbids any mention of Tom Berkeley's name.

'I can see it all. You'll have one of those misty photographs at the front of *Country Life* saying you're engaged to Sir So-and-so. Then you'll become one of those women in *Vogue* you see photographed arranging flowers in the drawing-room with a town house with a black and white tiled hall and a country estate where you can wear tweeds and be photographed with Labradors.'

This is indeed alarmingly close to Virginia's fantasies.

'I suppose you think it all sounds very trivial.'

'If that's what you want, you'll undoubtedly get it. But I fear you're destined to be very bored. Bored, but safe. Is that what you want?'

Virginia is beginning to feel cornered.

'You ask a lot of questions.'

'You've said that already. All right, you can ask me something.'

'That *presumes* that I'm sufficiently interested to want to find out.'

'I think we can assume that,' says Alexis with one of his most direct stares.

Disconcerted, Virginia abandons a rather impertinent question as to the state of *l'affaire Holly* and searches round in her mind for a topic of conversation.

'I wondered why you wanted to go into documentary films,' she finds herself saying, much to her own astonishment. It's really only half the story; for it is a matter of continuing debate amongst the more dedicated of Alexis' admirers (female) as to why he gave up a promising career in feature films to come across to the documentary sector, which is big on prestige but minimal on pay and conditions. Alexis shrugs and turns his fish over with his fork.

'Would it offend you if I smoked while I'm eating?'

'It certainly would.'

Alexis sighs but puts his cigarettes away.

'I'll answer that one when I know you a little better. Next question.'

'Oh,' says Virginia, nonplussed. 'Perhaps if you were to give me a list of topics that require a closer acquaintance, then I won't be in danger of treading on your sensibilities.'

'Oh, there aren't many of those, I can assure you.'

'Well, tell me about your mother and Ferdinand's. I can't imagine two more unalike than you and Ferdinand.'

'I suppose we are. But he's so close to me that he's almost like an extension of myself. Yet we don't share a single interest, we think quite differently on almost any subject you care to name. There are times,' goes on Alexis, faint incredulity tingeing his voice, 'when I'm not even sure he likes films very much. Yet whenever we see each other it's – I don't know. There's no one in the world I can speak to so directly. Strange, isn't it?'

'He has that effect on me, too. Though he does irritate me at times with his insistence on the proper form of things.'

'Oh, Ferdy's a great one for preserving appearances – the letter of the law if not the spirit of it. I gather he has you marked down for a glamorous and successful marriage.'

'Oh, we're quite in agreement *there*,' says Virginia briskly. 'But what about Ferdinand himself? I've never dared ask him about his own private life. Does he have one?'

'*Now* may I smoke?'

'Until our dessert comes, certainly.'

Alexis draws heavily on his cigarette, offers her one, then suddenly starts laughing.

'What's so funny?'

'Oh, I was just remembering the only glimpse I've ever had into Ferdinand's personal life. It was the year before the war started – I was in Paris that Easter. Was I on my own? I think I must have been. Anyway, I turned up at the notary's office where he works – awful place, like a setting for a Simenon film where the clerk suddenly goes berserk and makes off with the wages then kills himself – anyway, we were due to have lunch and Ferdy had the afternoon off. There was a gallery I wanted to go to, I think. Ferdy and I met, him looking very respectable, and he said, "I'd like you to meet a friend of mine," so I said, "Fine," and expected to go to a café or something. Instead we went to a block of flats somewhere off the Boulevard Raspail and we were shown into this Victorian flat. It was all desperately respectable. Everything had antimacassars. I don't think there was actually gaslight, but you felt as if there was, and there were these sort of heavy velour cloths with bobbles on all over the table. I remember we had one at home in the nursery. There were blinds and festoons and swags at every window – it was permanently early evening in that flat. And in the middle of it all sat this middle-aged woman, very dignified, very staid, wearing a black satin dress with about a million tiny buttons down the bodice and a little lace collar. I couldn't think what we were doing there. She was introduced to me by Ferdinand, who kissed her hand as if she was an elderly aunt *and* recently widowed at that. I kept thinking he'd said something that I'd failed to hear – you know, that this was a friend of his mother's or an old friend of the family or even his godmother. Anyway, we sat down and had the most excruciating lunch.'

'Was the food terrible or what?'

'The food was fine, though I did notice *en passant* that it was all Ferdinand's favourite dishes. No, it was the conversation. I can't describe it. Madame clearly had a series of set topics and she held forth in a sort of monologue. She started on the politics of the day, then she went to the weather, the chances of a good summer, the scandalous way the British had treated Mrs Simpson – that was a topic of hot debate on the Continent in 1938, though I only gradually realized Madame's peculiar interest in the affair – then the state of Ferdinand's digestion, whether that slight trouble he'd been having in sleeping had passed. I really began to think the whole thing was an elaborate practical joke. Then at two-thirty Ferdinand got up, bowed, formally thanked her and we left. As we were going down in the lift I was about to say, 'Is she a friend of your mother's?' when mercifully Ferdinand got in first. 'She is *formidable, n'est ce pas*? She is all woman,' he said reverently, and I realized in a blinding flash that she must be his mistress. She was in her late forties if she was a day. Probably why she kept the blinds down.'

Virginia has long since laid down her spoon, her sorbet completely forgotten.

'I simply don't believe it,' she marvels. 'What an absolutely wonderful story. Does the affair still go on?'

'It certainly did up to the Germans entering Paris. Ferdinand's been keeping her since he was twenty-one. We finally got drunk that holiday together and he gave me all the gory details. He goes there for lunch most days and comes back at the end of work for his "cinq à sept", then he goes home to his own flat and in the evening he puts on his dancing pumps and squires eligible daughters to dances of hideous formality. I suppose eventually he'll marry one of them and Marie-Hélène will have to find another protector. Or perhaps the arrangement will simply continue but more discreetly than before.'

'It doesn't make me feel terribly optimistic about what Ferdinand had planned for me in terms of respectable marriage.'

'Oh, he thinks women are better-placed in the structure of marriage and anyway that you're the kind of girl who simply reverts to type once your salad days are over.'

'What do you mean?'

'The black and white hall. The Labrador in the front drive. The two children at prep school.'

'Films may be your career,' retorts Virginia. 'I happen to think that marriage is going to be mine. There's nothing wrong in that, is there?'

'Not if that's what you want. Do you want a brandy?'

'Yes, please,' says Virginia recklessly, alarmed to notice for the first time that a bottle of wine has apparently disappeared and that Alexis has barely touched his own glass.

'You still haven't told me about your mothers.'

'You're doing it again, you see.'

'Doing what?'

'Steering the conversation away from yourself. It's all right. I don't mind.
I love talking about myself. Except I don't think I've ever known anybody
show such interest in my life before. Our mothers – well, they really aren't
alike at all; a bit like Ferdy and me – but they were devoted in their own way.
My mother painted and she came over here one summer for a course at the
Slade. She met my father at a gallery-opening in Grafton Street. Dad was an
art dealer in a small way and he edited a poetry magazine. He was abysmally
unsuccessful as a dealer because he could never bear to part with anything
good. If he did make any money, he tended to give it to a poor deserving
artist who promptly drank it.'

'Were they happy?' asked Virginia, riveted by this glimpse of Alexis'
background.

'Oh, extremely most of the time. Except when times got tight financially.
I suppose it sounds a certain recipe for disaster. Dad was exactly twice
Mamma's age when they married – forty-four to her twenty-two. But it
seemed to work. I think Mamma needed a lot of freedom and my father gave
it to her. She got on with her painting, and after I was born I just played in a
corner of the studio. When Tante Honoré and Ferdinand came to stay she
almost had hysterics at the way I was being brought up, but sometimes I
think Ferdy quite envied me. I suppose when you're happy you don't really
notice it, but I can never remember my home as being anything else but
happy. It was always the most interesting place to be.'

'Did you always live in London?'

'Yes. Buying the place in Chelsea was one of the few sensible things Dad
ever did. I don't mean that the way it sounds. It's just that he had a very soft
heart and he was always lending money to people who promptly disappeared
with it.'

'So what happened?'

'Oh, when I was nineteen my mother's health began to fail and they
found she had TB. She died within a year. Sometimes now, even, ten years
later I can't believe she's dead. She was the most alive person I ever knew.
And we always joked about how she'd outlive my father and be a merry
widow. She was only forty-three when she died. Father died ten months
later. His heart hadn't been that good for years, but it wasn't really that. I
think the heart really went out of him when she died. God, what a gloomy
conversation this is.'

'Were they pleased about you going into films?'

'Sort of resigned, more like. Mamma wanted me to go to art school and
paint, but by the time I was thirteen I knew I wanted to make films. They
were very good about it. When I was eighteen she got all the relations to have
a whip-round and I got a camera and projector for my birthday. And all
through Cambridge I made my own appalling films. When I came down I got
an apprenticeship at British Empire Films. That meant I worked in an
editing-room, keeping the trims in order for the first year, then I was allowed
to carry lights for location work for another year. Eventually I graduated to
the person who plugged in the lights and got it all wrong and nearly killed
Billy Gavin the first time I went shooting with him. Have you finished? Our
bill, please.'

320

'Thank you for a lovely meal,' says Virginia, drawing on her black suede gloves.

'I didn't ask you if you wanted coffee because I thought you might like to come back to Chelsea and have some there.'

'Oh,' says Virginia, trying to pull herself together, somehow feeling she's cutting a very poor figure in the seduction stakes, 'that will be nice, thank you.'

Alexis' car is something sporty, though somewhat aged, and fortunately without a fold-back hood. The days when Virginia found an open car with its concomitant pleasures of draughts and leaking rainwater attractive have long since passed.

'Do you know Chelsea?' asks Alexis innocently.

'No,' says Virginia uneasily, peering dubiously at the blacked-out streets as they leave the familiar purlieus of Belgravia and then Knightsbridge behind them.

'You can relax. The natives are perfectly friendly.'

Virginia maintains a dignified silence. Eventually Alexis parks the car at the end of a terrace of three-storey houses which show a ghostly whiteness in the unlit street. A thin sliver of moon slides reluctantly out from behind banks of rainclouds. Virginia is overwhelmingly aware of the presence of the river at the end of the road. There is a wetness in the air and the sense of a vast canyon of wind and rushing tide behind the flood-wall.

'Take my hand or you'll break your neck on the paving stones. It's the moss or something. As you're a first-time guest I'll take you in the front door,' says Alexis briskly.

Gingerly clasping his hand, Virginia clatters through a silent dripping garden up a steep flight of mossy steps flanked by two white peeling pillars. Alexis feels around for keys, then pushes open the front door.

'Leave your coat in there, then come down to the kitchen when you're ready.'

Alone in the drawing-room Virginia simply stands and stares for quite a considerable length of time. Her own tastes in interior design, despite all Stephen's attempts at re-education, have still not advanced much further than a liking for Colefax and Fowler. Her first alarmed impression of the Seligman home is that she has strayed into a junkshop by mistake. The walls are glazed a fierce lacquered red but hardly visible between paintings, sketches, tapestries, wall hangings, screens, and carpets mysteriously hanging on the walls instead of properly placed on the floor. There are almost an indecent number of books contained in scarlet lacquered cabinets with glass fronts. Every item of furniture is painted and gilded in the Italian style. There are two long amber-coloured velvet sofas covered in cushions that look like small tapestries – anything in fact except what a cushion should look like. The overall effect is like a blow on the head, and Virginia, catching sight of herself in the huge gilded mirror over the fireplace, sees she has an extremely startled, not to say alarmed, look on her face. Against this gorgeous background her simple black dress and string of pearls are just an inky stain beneath the sleek pallor of her pageboy waves.

Nothing in this house is what it appears to be. The doors and the paintwork look like marble, there are painted cats striding along the wainscot, windows revealing vistas of summer gardens where no such windows or gardens exist. Even the loo is painted to resemble an arbour of roses. Footsteps sound on the stairs.

'I thought you'd got lost.'

'Oh, I was just – er – looking,' says Virginia hastily and follows Alexis meekly down the wooden stairs into the kitchen. It is unusual enough for a kitchen but conventional in comparison to the extremes above. One wall is patterned with stencils of the profiles of Roman emperors, but there is a perfectly normal cream Aga in the alcove. An old-fashioned wooden dresser, crammed with gaily coloured pottery, postcards, invitations and bunches of artificial flowers and dried grass, runs the length of another wall. In the centre of the room is an enormous scrubbed farmhouse table covered with an untidy heap of sketchpads and loose-leaf sheets. Underneath, Virginia can't help noticing, is a double mattress, two blankets and a pillow. Alexis follows her gaze without embarrassment.

'That's my air-raid shelter. I came to an arrangement with the warden that if he'd leave me alone I'd promise to dive under there when the sirens went. That table would withstand an earthquake. There's an Anderson in the garden next door but it's always a foot deep in water. Hey, you're in luck, I've still got some of the coffee Ferdinand brought.'

As Virginia sits quietly at one end of the table taking in the delicious, almost forgotten aroma of real coffee, her thoughts are chasing themselves through her mind with the merry inconsequentiality of the Flopsy Bunnies playing tag in their burrow. If only she hadn't drunk so much! Why has Alexis asked her here? Could she be *quite wrong* as to why he'd asked her here? Perhaps he was simply intending to show her pictures of himself and Ferdinand in sailor suits. On the other hand, if his intentions *weren't* honourable, didn't this rather remove the initiative from Virginia? It was not at all how she'd envisaged her revenge.

'You're very quiet. Do you like the house?'

'Well, yes, it's quite hard to take in at one go. Is the river really on the other side of the wall?'

'Sure is. We got flooded one spring. I was away at school sadly. It's a hell of a place to keep dusted,' goes on Alexis, absently running his fingers disapprovingly along the dresser, 'especially when your "treasure" suffers from asthma and can only face dusting once a month. It's always the same when I'm making a film—'

'And you're always making a film,' finishes Virginia for him.

'Well, yes, I suppose I am. I used to be the most indolent person in the world, and then – I don't know. I suddenly felt obliged to drag every last possibility from every minute allowed.'

'Why?'

Alexis shrugs, hands her a gaily painted cup and saucer, and sits down at right angles to her at the bottom of the table.

'I don't know,' he says, more to himself than to her. 'At the beginning of the war I had a sudden intimation of how precious life was. Since then I've been living on a continuous double summertime. Milk? Sugar? Damn, there's none left.'

'I think I've got some lumps in my bag.'

'Don't tell me Willy supplies you with lump sugar as well.'

'No,' says Virginia coolly, indicating that tonight she is definitely not going to be caught by such obvious provocation. 'He limits himself to cigarettes and nylons. I make it my duty to hoard them. Here. They're a bit fluffy but they'll taste all right. As a matter of interest, why were you so nasty to me last night?'

'I'm afraid I'm going to have to cadge one of your cigarettes from you. One of Willy's cigarettes.'

Silently Virginia proffers the case, then lights Alexis' cigarette with her own lighter.

'Was I nasty to you? Yes, I suppose I was. I'd had too much to drink. Anyway, I'd bet myself that I could get some response out of you. I've never met anybody who manages to go through life so completely poker-faced.'

'You could have tried being nice to me. The shock of that might have provoked me into a complete personality-change.'

'No, I rejected that plan early on. If I was nice to you, I'd be relegated to one of those frightfully sweet people you know. I know what *that* means. So I reckoned my best bet was to irritate you into betraying your true self.'

Alexis grins at her, and she smiles unwillingly back.

'I wish you'd leave my true self out of things. Anyway, I thought you had spies keeping tabs on my life. Weren't they efficient enough?'

'Extremely helpful.'

'Who were they?'

'I never part with information without a reward.'

'Look, I'm in your house drinking coffee and being nice to you. That's definitely reward enough. There are men who'd faint at the prospect of half the luck you're having.'

'My goodness, what a change from last night. You really are in control now, aren't you? What's brought this about, I wonder.'

'I realized I don't give a damn what other people think of me,' says Virginia, aware that she's by no means as in control as she'd like. 'And, while we're on the subject, let me say that I think it's pretty low of you to keep poking your nose into my private affairs.'

'You appear to care like anything about what Tom's family think of you.'

On the verge of seriously losing her temper Virginia scalds her throat in gulping down the rest of her coffee before replacing the cup in the saucer with a pointed clatter.

'I'll tell you what I told David Berkeley if it matters to you so much. But it'll cost you.'

'What?'

'A kiss.'

'Alexis, how corny. Don't ever make a remark about "B" films in my presence again. All right. If you're that desperate for a kiss, you can have one. But only after you've told me what you said.'

'Is that a promise?'

'Yes.'

323

Alexis grins, deliberately prolonging the suspense for as long as possible.

'All right. I said you were very beautiful, rather spoilt, bright and very shy.'

Virginia is silenced. Somehow it's not what she'd expected.

'My kiss, please.'

Deliberately Virginia leans forward and kisses Alexis chastely on the cheek.

'You bloody cheat. That wasn't what I had in mind at all.' Unhurriedly he draws her towards him and kisses her parted lips with a kind of angry intensity. At the conclusion of that long, startling, open-mouthed kiss, when Virginia opens her eyes it is as if she has travelled forward into a completely new landscape where other vistas, other unlooked-for trembling delights are suddenly within her startled imagination. As they regard each other without smiling, each taken aback by the intensity of that casual embrace, Virginia suddenly feels a painful spasm of desire. Her stomach seems to have turned to water. Suddenly embarrassed, she drags her gaze from Alexis and stares at the table.

'Well?'

'Well?'

'Did you approve of what I said to David?'

'I'm not sure. I'm not sure,' murmurs Virginia, mesmerized by the shape of Alexis' mouth, and leaning towards him gently runs her tongue over the tender indentation of his upper lip.

A long time later, on the pavement above their heads a couple clatter by, laughing and talking. Virginia is acutely aware of the lateness and the silence of the hour.

'Are you going to insist on me going home?'

'Yes, I am,' says Alexis harshly. There is another long silence. Virginia takes Alexis' hand, presses it against her cheek.

'Don't you want me to stay?'

'Of course I do, but —'

Angrily Alexis pushes back his chair and pulls Virginia to her feet.

'Alexis.' Alexis turns back suddenly, with a look of bleak hopelessness on his face. Afterwards it is never clear which one of them moves first, but they are in each other's arms, holding on to each other as if to a lifeline, Alexis' hard body pushing into hers. Virginia is shocked to discover that they are both trembling.

When slowly and reluctantly they part there is no further talk of Virginia going home. As Alexis stops to turn out the lights in the kitchen Virginia moves closer to him, and in the darkness he pushes her back against the wall and kisses her slowly and lingeringly with an intensity that makes her feel faint with desire. But there is no shock, no strangeness in the embrace. It is not like the embrace of strangers. It is like coming home. Reluctantly the kiss ends, and they put their arms around each other in a companionable sort of way and walk slowly up the narrow darkened stairs to Alexis' bedroom.

CHAPTER
TWENTY-SIX

'Is UNCLE CHARLES coming home for Christmas?' asks Toby.

'I don't know. Anyway, it's six weeks off yet. He's . . . very busy, you know. He only got these few hours off today as a special treat.'

'Do you want him to?' demands Ern acutely.

'Ern, what a thing to say.'

'Harry Tonks's Elsie says it's odd he doesn't come home more, him being your husband and that.'

'What business is it of theirs?' says Beattie, outraged.

'Well, I hope he does,' says Toby unexpectedly. 'If it snows, he said he'd show me how the Eskimos fish on the village pond.'

Both boys collapse in paroxysms of giggles, and even Beattie, tense as she is, has to smile.

'I haven't seen too many Eskimos on the village pond.'

'You know what I mean. What are you getting up for again, Aunty Beattie? You're like Beetle when he wants to go out for a walk.'

'I've got the lunch to watch. Charles'll only be here today for a few hours, so I want it to be nice for him,' says Beattie, wondering without much real interest what it is that Charles does in High Wycombe.

'Are you going salvaging this afternoon?'

' 'Spect so.'

'Who's going with you?' Beattie, handing Annie her rattle, tries to keep her tone casual.

'Oh, I don't know. Someone, I expect,' says Ern with maddening vagueness. 'It won't be the vicar. His cold's worse.'

'So who else might it be?'

'Major Jones, or Mrs Musgrave's friend. If he gets back in time.'

There is a long silence. Beattie puts Annie back in her cot and goes to inspect the contents of various saucepans standing by the range. Both boys are bent over ancient copies of the *Magnet*. Beattie stands looking out into the garden, which is showing painful evidence of last night's frost.

'What are we having for puddin'?' asks Ern.

'Apple pie,' says Beattie absently, 'with top of the milk.'

'What time do you think Uncle Charles will be here?'

'He said just before lunch.'

'Do you think he'll take us for a ride in his car?'

'I don't suppose there'll be much time after your salvaging. It's dark now by three o'clock almost.'

'Give over, Toby. I was reading that first.'

'You read it so slowly,' complains Toby.

'Give it here.'

'I will not!'

'Will you two boys stop that!' says Beattie with quite unaccustomed force. 'Go up and make your beds or something. Mother will be back from church in a minute and she'll want to see you've got tidy rooms.'

Left alone in the empty kitchen Beattie opens the range door, bastes the very small leg of lamb and checks again to see the vegetables are all peeled and ready. Restlessly she wanders out into the hall to inspect herself yet again in the hall mirror, tugging at the belt of her new dress and wondering for the hundredth time if that seam under her arm really is crooked. That's the trouble with plain fabric – it always shows hasty workmanship. Still, the colour was so lovely it made up for everything. If only Charles had given her more warning he was coming! Still, she consoles herself, he's only staying for lunch and tea.

Abruptly Beattie remembers the real source of the day's anxieties and almost groans aloud with tension. Regardless of her new dress she sits on the bottom stair and rests her chin on her hands. Brooke is back in England. Back at Gatton. Vividly Beattie recalls the aerodrome, the officers' mess, Brooke's own spartan room with his pictures of the Manor and his parents in silver frames. It is months and months since she has allowed herself the luxury of thinking properly about him. By day she can govern her own thoughts. But at night she dreams of him again and again with anger, with desire, with reproach. Sometimes in her dreams he is kind to her. Sometimes he's cruel, offhand, aloof. Sometimes – and these are the worst dreams of all – she is simply looking for him and Brooke is nowhere to be found. Nobody – *nobody*, not even Louie, remotely realizes the extent to which he still obsesses her. They all think, Mrs Blythe, Louie, Mr Blythe – Charles as well for all she knows – that Brooke in behaving so disgracefully has somehow enabled Beattie to sever him completely from her life. But it is with pain and humiliation that Beattie realizes that, while she may well perceive most of Brooke's acts as being morally wrong, it in no way diminishes her feelings for him. What does it say of her own morality, she asks herself constantly, that she can fully recognize a person's weakness and still crave that person's presence?

Suddenly decisive, Beattie gets up, pulls on her coat and hat, picks up a surprised Annie and, buttoning her up in her outdoor clothes against the November morning, walks the pram firmly up the village street. The church door is still shut; the service must be over shortly. Let Mrs Blythe take care of lunch. If Beattie stays indoors even another second, so she tells herself, she will explode with sheer tension.

Why, *why* had Charles chosen this day of all days to come? Yesterday lunchtime she got a message from the post office saying he had rung and would call back at five o'clock. Making no reference to the last disastrous time he'd tried to contact her by phone, he'd merely said that a friend was coming up to Ipswich for the day and had offered to go halves with him on the petrol. Would it be convenient for him to come in and see her?

Already primed by Mrs Blythe, Beattie managed to inject some enthusiasm into an invitation for lunch and tea. Charles, who had up to then sounded both tentative and unsure, audibly relaxed and said he was looking forward to seeing them all.

By now she is outside the village and her steps slow. Annie sits up in her harness, from time to time clapping her mittened hands together, delighted with this unexpected walk in the misty morning, the sun just a red disc behind the black tracing of the elms. Frost still rims the ruts in the lane, and a pheasant honks crossly at Beattie as it runs across the road. Annie crows for joy. Unwillingly, Beattie smiles at her, then stops to give her a kiss. Whatever problems had been caused by Annie coming into the world, Beattie recognizes now that she needs her as much as Annie needs her mother. Without Annie to bring her out of herself, away from all that endless brooding and introspection, she would have gone mad. For against all the odds, considering the circumstances of her birth as Mrs Blythe is still moved to say, Annie is a blessing. She is an exceptionally happy, good-natured baby, her little world peopled entirely by open arms and warm laps. Annie is all right. Annie is going to be all right in the future. But what about the future for Beattie? Reluctantly Beattie turns the pram round and heads for home. The church clock is striking half-past twelve, a car is heard on the approach to the village and Beattie increases her pace until she is almost running, Annie swaying and blinking in perplexity as the pram bounces up and down on the uneven road. But it is only Major Jones, his car as ever crammed with people, sacks and animals. He salutes Beattie and drives noisily by.

Her throat aching from the icy air, Beattie slows down, trying to calm her agitated heart. There is absolutely no reason to have assumed it would be Mrs Musgrave. After all, if she'd spent the night at Gatton she'd probably have taken Brooke out to dinner. So she'd hardly leave at the crack of dawn the following day.

Mrs Musgrave is with Brooke. She has talked to him, spoken to him. It is now sixteen months since Beattie has even seen him. Surely he will realize how worried, how broken-hearted she had been when he had disappeared. *Surely* he must come and see her. He must want to see her just as much as she longs to see him. When she'd heard he was back in England it had taken all her self-control not to hitch a lift to Ipswich and take the train to Norfolk. Then common sense had intervened. If he wanted to see her, he would write to her. He knew where she was.

That was a week ago. Then, on Thursday, Lily had told her that Mrs Musgrave was off to see Brooke on Saturday and coming back on Sunday. Beattie's immediate reaction was that at last she would have firsthand news of him. Then another thought had occurred, making her almost breathless with excitement. Perhaps Brooke would come back with his mother. Surely he must yearn for home comforts after the deprivations of life on the run? And if he came home – Beattie had frenziedly started to finish the dress that she'd cut out in a perfunctory way in September, then left unsewn at the bottom of her wardrobe.

There is the sound of running footsteps up the lane, and Toby and Ernest tear round the corner, legs pumping, long woolly scarves flapping round their flushed faces.

'Eh! Aunty Beattie! There you are. Uncle Charles is here already. He came in a car with a friend. He's been looking for you.'

'Oh heavens, I thought I'd meet him on the road. He must have come round the other way. Come on, we'd better run.'

'The friend's gone but he's coming back later. Your mum's lit the fire in the parlour. She's mad you weren't there to greet Charles.'

Beattie tightens her lips and says nothing.

All in all it doesn't seem to go too badly. Notwithstanding Beattie's last-minute defection, lunch is a success.

'Beattie did it all herself, you know,' remarks her mother – as if I was a housemaid needing references, thinks Beattie crossly, perfectly aware of the motive behind her mother's words.

'We're off salvaging this afternoon,' Toby tells Charles. 'You can come, too, if you want, except you might dirty your uniform.'

'I'd love to come, but I don't think I've really got the time, old man,' Charles replies courteously. 'Alec said he'd be back at five o'clock prompt. I've only got a short leave, so I feel I've got to make the most of it.'

Ernest then produces his cigarette cards of famous planes, and Charles obligingly identifies the ones he's seen. Beattie, looking at his dark and handsome head bent over the oilcloth tablecloth, feels the usual conflicting set of emotions that Charles always manages to arouse in her. There's no doubt that Charles is welcomed by almost every member of the Blythe household. Mr Blythe has already shown him the blackened frostbitten garden, while Mrs Blythe is positively loquacious. The boys, initially so full of awe of his uniform and his stripes, rapidly move from tongue-tied admiration to demanding his whole attention. Annie favours Charles with her sweetest smiles. Perhaps he can just move in and marry the family, thinks Beattie with a certain sour humour, then with any luck I can slip away to London on my own. Out loud she says: 'What would you like to do this afternoon, Charles?' It is a large offer considering the nature of the options. They can either sit in front of the fire in the parlour with Mr Blythe snoring in the corner as a chaperon or they can go for a walk.

'I think I'd like a spot of exercise after that splendid lunch,' replies Charles equably.

The two boys are getting changed for salvaging.

'Don't forget to put on your wellington boots. You leave those dishes, Beattie. I'll do them later,' says Mrs Blythe.

'Where are you going this afternoon?' Beattie asks Toby.

'Oh, we always try the ponds first. We've done all the ones round the village but we're going a way off today to Heath Wood. That's on the farm where Lucy works. We can only go there with the farmer's permission. There's a big pond in the wood there,' goes on Toby rapidly. 'If we find anything, Lucy'll go up tomorrow with the tractor and the trailer and bring it down on to the village green. It's ever such fun, isn't it, Ern?'

'Spiffing. Sometimes the vicar takes us but today it'll be the Major Jones or Mrs Musgrave's friend. If he's back,' observes Ern innocently as Beattie stiffens and searches frantically for a topic with which to divert him. To her horror she hears Ern go on confidingly: 'Mrs Musgrave's gone with her friend to see her son Mr Brooke. He came home from Holland last week, did you know? He crashed his plane, then had to hide. It was all in the local paper. We cut it out at school. He must be ever so brave. That's why his mum's gone up to see him. I wish he'd come back here.' Ern's tone is wistful. 'I'd get his autograph. It'll be worth a few swaps, that will.'

The atmosphere in the kitchen is very still.

'On your way, you two,' says Mrs Blythe at last. 'Are you taking Annie, Beattie?'

'I might as well. The air will do her good.'

Once at the top of the lane the two boys run off, leaving Beattie and Charles to walk along in silence.

'We could go down to the reed beds if you like. The path's quite dry.'

It is a fine, dry, though frosty, afternoon; but even by half-past two the sun is already beginning to dip towards the horizon. The light is clear and pale with just a tinge of green. From one of the bases on the other side of the village three planes take off into the blindingly clear lemon sunshine, and Charles shields his eyes to watch their progress into the cloud. As they walk down the main road two jeeps pass, full of American air-force men bound for Ipswich and its various pleasures. Notwithstanding Charles's presence they whistle good-naturedly at Beattie, who smiles back in a noncommittal way.

'Do they bother you much?'

'Not really. They know I'm married,' Beattie says without any irony. 'It doesn't suit everybody, though. The older women have complained to the camp, and they drive Lucy mad. I don't think she likes the Americans too much. But Lily's Greg is really nice. His parents come from Italy, and he says he's an American of Italian extraction; it always makes Lily laugh.'

'Oh, I remember. Doesn't he live on the West Coast?'

'That's right. I asked him if it was near Hollywood, and he said it was sort of. Seems so glamorous. He treats Lily very nicely.'

'You sound surprised.'

Beattie colours.

'It's not that I'm surprised about; it's just all so different here now. What was here in the village' – Beattie gestures back the way they have come – 'it's been like that for – well, I don't know how many hundreds of years. Really and truly. I mean we've got things like oil-lamps and bicycles now, but apart from that it's exactly the same world that my gran and my great-gran and her great-gran must have known. People don't travel much around here, you see. Why, half the folk in the village have never even been to Ipswich and they don't want to. They say what's the point. And suddenly we've got a village full of strangers, and not just people from the next village – people from across the other side of the world. You can't imagine how strange that seems. Everything's changed. None of the women here has ever had a job – well, not once they were married. Now there's a bus comes round every morning to take the women to work in Ipswich. There was an absolute uproar when it was announced.' Beattie grins at the memory. 'They had a special meeting of the Mothers' Union and said no decent woman would want to go. But on the very first morning there were fifteen women waiting at the bus-stop. The older women were *furious*. Then by the end of the week they'd started work, too. So a lady from London opened a nursery in the village hall.' Beattie smiles at the memory. It had effectively stopped any complaints from Mrs Blythe. She now looked after Annie all day, and Beattie was able to pay her way in the household. Charles's money she still put in the post office.

At the osier beds Charles takes out a cigarette and they sit down on the pram rug. Annie is tucked up and fast asleep in her pram. As usual they sit with a decent distance between them. Charles stares unseeingly at the pale watery expanse of reeds.

'They use it for thatch,' Beattie ventures at last. 'They've been cutting it over there, you see. Though there can't be many thatchers around at present. . . .'

'Beattie,' says Charles abruptly, 'I wanted to talk to you about us. Well, your intentions, I suppose, to be more precise.'

'What do you mean?'

'I mean things can't go on like this.'

Carefully Charles stubs out his cigarette and turns to face her. Unconsciously Beattie braces herself.

'We just seem caught in some kind of limbo. I don't know what you want. All I can deduce from your letters is that you don't know, either. But it's stopping us moving forward. Either together or separately.'

Beattie is alarmed at the accuracy with which Charles is voicing her own thoughts.

'Well, do you know what you want?' she asks him curiously.

'Yes, I'm quite sure I know what I want. I'd like to take a house near High Wycombe and come down and collect you and Annie for us to go and live there as man and wife. I've been looking at some properties and I think I've found somewhere you'd like. You only need to rent it to start with to see how it works. There's a school nearby; I'm sure you could find some work if you wanted to. I'm tired of this existence. It's not that I want to settle down, but I'd just like to live with you and have a home life with you. And I'll be honest, I think we could be happy together. As it is we aren't committed or free. What do you say? Will you come and live with me and give it a try?'

'*No*,' says Beattie with such force and harshness that she herself is appalled. Beside her Charles tenses.

'I see. I wanted an answer, and you've certainly given me one.' Charles feels in his pocket for another cigarette and lights it with shaking fingers. 'You've used me pretty thoroughly, haven't you, Beattie?'

Beattie turns to him in a fury.

'You offered to marry *me*. *I* didn't ask you. And I certainly didn't hold a gun at your head.'

'That's true enough. Only I really thought there could be the beginning of something between us. I didn't realize that I was just something for you to

330

mark time with, enabling you to put your heart into cold storage until such time as Brooke Musgrave deigned to take up with you again. Has he been in touch with you? *Has he?*'

'Charles, will you let go of my arm? You're hurting me. No, he hasn't.'

'Nor will he, you stupid, stupid girl.'

Charles's face is flushed dark red with anger, yet beyond that Beattie senses he is shocked and deeply hurt.

'You simply aren't being fair. You knew when you married me that I wasn't in love with you—'

'Beattie, that was well over a year ago. A lot has happened since then. We've had an opportunity to get to know each other. I haven't forced the pace, I've tried to let things happen in their own time, but I did think we had enough in common that we could make a home together, that we could have more children.'

Beattie jumps to her feet like a demented woman. 'Stop it! Stop it! Don't talk to me about children. I don't want any more children. I didn't want the one I've got. I don't even want to be *married* and certainly not to *you*. You expect me to be grateful, grateful all the time for the fact that you've condescended to marry me and saved me from my shame. Well, I'll tell you, I wish I'd taken my chances and had Annie and tried to bring her up on my own. You're as bad as my mother. And I can tell you she's only being so nice to you because you've saved her from the shame of having an unmarried mother as a daughter.'

Beattie knows she is going too far but is unable to stop the stream and vituperation of spite that is pouring from her lips. Charles is white with anger.

'In that case let's just go back to your house and I'll pick up my things and go. You can spend the rest of your life hanging around to see if there's any messages for you from Gatton. That's what you're waiting for, isn't it? I kept wondering why you were looking at your watch during lunch. Well, let me tell you, Beattie, you're wasting your time. Only from *now on* you're wasting your own time, not mine.'

Breathing hard, Beattie kicks the brake off the pram and turns it abruptly round. In a subdued silence they walk back to the cottage. To Beattie's vast and eternal relief Lily Kedge and Greg have turned up in her absence, ostensibly to collect some onions for Lily's father but are easily persuaded to stay for tea, thus postponing any further tête-à-tête between herself and Charles. By five o'clock it is as dark as the grave outside the kitchen window. There is a sudden tentative tap on the back door.

'That must be Alec.'

Alec comes in brushing the rain off his greatcoat. 'Sorry if I'm a bit late. I lost my way.'

Alec turns out to be the man who was Charles's best man at the wedding.

'You will stay and have a cuppa, though, won't you?'

'Well, just one. We'd best be on our way; we've got a fair old distance to go tonight. How are you, Beattie, and how's Annie? She's a pretty little thing, isn't she? And she's grown like anything, hasn't she?'

Seeing Beattie's surprised look, he adds: 'Charles has got your picture up on his bureau. I feel I know the pair of you intimately. Come and say hello to your Uncle Alec, sweetheart,' he adds easily and takes Annie off Charles's knee where she has been sitting comfortably in the crook of his arm.

In the end it is Charles who has to remind Alec that they have a long journey ahead of them and reluctantly the pair get up to go.

Beattie puts on her coat and walks to the top of the lane with them. Tactfully Alec makes something of a business of wiping all the windows and leaves them to themselves, presumably for a final fond farewell. In the darkness it is almost impossible for them to see each other's face.

'Thank you for coming down today. I'm sorry it all turned out like this.'

'Thank you for having me,' says Charles with frigid politeness. 'And tell the boys I'm sorry I didn't see them before I went. Here, take this for them.'

There is a chink of coins in the darkness.

'Take care of yourself, Beattie.'

No word about writing or seeing her again, she notices.

'Take care of yourself, Charles,' she answers quietly. 'And have a safe journey home.'

With that the car door slams and the old Rover noses its way cautiously into the night.

At half-past six, well past their suppertime, the two boys appear, muddy, cheerful and ravenous.

'We had a grand day, Aunty Beattie. Two bedsteads and a tyre. Oh! Has Uncle Charles gone already?'

'Yes, he said he was sorry and to give you his love. And he left you half a crown each.'

The two boys caper with delight.

'If you wash your hands, I'll put your supper on the table. Were there many with you?'

'Six of us. Major Jones told us we were real white men to turn out.'

'So it was he who took you.'

'Yes. We saw Mrs Musgrave and her friend coming home as we were setting out. More fool him. He missed an ace day.'

By eight o'clock the dishes are washed, the floor swept, the table laid for breakfast and the boys in bed. Beattie sits marking Form III's composition by the light of the purring oil-lamp. Mr Blythe is brooding over the written plan of his vegetable garden at the Manor. Mrs Blythe is hemming a skirt for someone in the village. There is a concert on the wireless. To all intents and purposes it is a peaceful scene. In reality Beattie can hardly keep her thoughts on the books in front of her. She shouldn't have spoken to Charles like that. She just *shouldn't*. But in the midst of her shamefaced acknowledgement of her anger and malice, she is glad, because it has brought things out into the open and cleared the decks for action. Cleared the decks for Brooke more like, sniggers a small unpleasant voice inside her. Well, what if it has? Beattie sits back and unconsciously pushes her hair from her face in an attempt to see things more clearly. Suddenly she knows with absolute certainty that Brooke will contact her. Knows it in the very marrow of her bones. And she also knows that if he asks her to go to him she will leave without a second's hesitation. She'll take Annie of course, but a way will be found for them all to live together. If he still wants me that much after all this time, then it will

332

work out between us. His experiences as a prisoner of war will have changed him just as her own experience of motherhood has changed her. They are both more mature people now, Beattie is sure of it.

With a new calmness Beattie returns to her task. She has done the right thing in telling Charles it is over. Now it is simply a matter of waiting.

By Tuesday, Beattie is still quietly confident. It is the beginning of December, and she is able to tell a clearly disappointed family that Charles isn't going to be joining them for Christmas. She does not feel obliged to give a reason. On Wednesday, Beattie's spirits are still sanguine as she reminds herself the post is not as good as it might be because of Christmas. Then on Thursday her patience is rewarded. On her way to school in the still dark and frosty village street Lily waves her down to give her not one but two letters. One is clearly from Charles, the other is typewritten. Beattie cycles quickly round the next bend and stops almost at the entrance to the Dower House drive. Not even bothering to take off her woolly gloves, with feverish fingers she tears open the stiff heavy envelope of the typewritten letter and unfolds the thick sheet of paper inside. She stares at the contents in perplexity. At the top of the letter is an address in Lincoln's Inn Fields. The letter is signed by Mr P. R. Thoroughgood of Pleydell, Grimsdyke & Grosvenor (Solicitors). The letter is short and to the point. It informs her that Brooke Musgrave has asked them to contact her with a view to putting some money in trust for his daughter Anne. If Mrs Hammond is agreeable and will contact them with the details of her bank account or the means by which she wishes to receive the money, payment will be made from 1 January 1943.

That is all. That is absolutely all. This is clearly as much as Brooke is prepared to do. Beattie stares at the sheet, leaning on her handlebars, suddenly so weak she is afraid her legs will not support her.

There is a subdued toot of a car horn and the Musgraves' Daimler slides over the gravel beside her. The driver's window is rolled down and Mrs Musgrave, in full maquillage and gaily coloured headscarf worn turban-fashion, leans out.

'I thought it was you, Beattie. Letters from your husband, eh? School going all right? Your father said you were doing awfully well.'

'Yes, I'm fine, thank you,' says Beattie mechanically.

'You must be breaking up soon for Christmas. I'm off to Ipswich for my Christmas perm. Really, you'd never know there was a war on. Christmas is such a social round. One always longs for a quiet family affair, but there's almost a responsibility to try to make things as gay as possible, don't you think? One has a certain duty not to let standards slip in these difficult times, don't you know. Are you spending Christmas at home?'

'Probably.'

'We're off to my brother's at the Towers,' goes on Mrs Musgrave happily. 'I've been trying to persuade Brooke to come and stay with us. After all, it is his last Christmas in England for goodness knows how long. God knows when we'll see him again.'

Mrs Musgrave's painted scarlet mouth pinches itself into a grotesque moue which renders her absurdly like a particularly aged clown. Beattie stares at her, suddenly transfixed.

333

'He's off to Rhodesia, you know, straight after Christmas. We only heard about it yesterday. Apparently he's going to train colonial pilots. Of course, if it was a choice of having him here and still risking his life or having him thousands of miles away in safety I suppose there's really no question of what's best. But it's very hard to know you may not see your only son again for years. My goodness, is that the time? I'll be late. Goodbye, Beattie, and do give my regards to your mother.'

As the Daimler pulls out on to the main road Beattie tries to compose herself and after two abortive attempts manages to get back into the saddle and pedal slowly towards the Ipswich road. Something seems to have gone wrong with her legs, for each down-thrust on the pedal is like pushing down a lead weight. She is going to be late because she simply has not got the strength to pedal fast enough.

It is ten past nine by the time Beattie has reached the gate, let herself in and parked her bicycle. Miss Gold, who teaches arts, crafts and elocution, is lingering agitatedly in the front hall.

'There you are! I've taken your lot in with mine to keep them quiet, but I don't think I – Mrs Hammond, what is wrong? Are you ill?'

'I just feel rather . . . faint,' says Beattie heavily and proceeds to illustrate her words by passing out cold on the parquet flooring, still wearing her coat and hat. When reluctantly she comes to she finds herself propped up against the wall, her head between her knees.

'Give the girl a glass of water,' someone is saying, and Miss Gold thrusts a mug into Beattie's face. 'Just sit still for a moment, Mrs Hammond, and we'll help you into the staffroom.'

Mr Grey (PE and Woodwork), who has clearly been elected to the task because of his muscles, hauls Beattie to her feet and bears her bodily into the empty staffroom.

'I've made you a cup of tea,' says Miss Gold. 'I wish there was something stronger I could put in it.'

Seated on the sagging cretonne sofa Beattie pulls off her hat and unbuttons her coat.

'Are you really better now?'

'Yes,' says Beattie in a firmer voice, aware that Mr Smythe the headmaster has joined them. 'If Miss Gold could just deputize for me for the first period, I can take over from there.'

'That's excellent,' says Mr Smythe. 'You just sit there and get your colour back. Are you warm enough? Shall I open the window?'

'No, I'm fine. If I can just rest up for a minute.'

'I'll leave you in peace, then,' says Mr Smythe, clearly relieved to be rid of his role as nurse and comforter. 'Oh, Mrs Hammond, I hope you won't mind me asking this, but in view of . . . your faint it just had crossed my mind. . . .' He pauses delicately. 'There's nothing you want to tell me, is there?'

'Tell you?' Beattie stares at him.

'You're not planning on leaving us again in the coming months, are you?'

Belatedly the penny drops.

'No, I'm not pregnant, Mr Smythe.'

334

Mr Smythe almost recoils physically from the directness of the word. 'I hope you didn't mind me asking, but we'd be so very sorry to lose you, Mrs Hammond. No, you stay where you are. I'll leave you in peace now.'

Left alone Beattie wills herself to get up, hangs up her coat and hat and straightens her hair in the mirror over the empty fireplace.

'What am I going to do?' she demands quite rhetorically of her reflection. She has the stunned look of someone who has received a powerful blow in the face. Opening her attaché case to find her comb, Charles's letter falls out on the floor. Automatically Beattie opens it and smooths out the two closely written sheets. At first she cannot take in what Charles is saying. Then, furrowing her brow, she goes back to the beginning again.

From the date it was clearly written late on Sunday night.

Dear Beattie, [it begins,]
I've had plenty of time to think things out on the journey home, and I've come to the conclusion that the sooner we take steps to end the marriage the better it'll be for both of us. Perhaps I was unfair in ever hoping there could be a future for us, especially since I knew you weren't going into the marriage heart whole. I think I, too, was perhaps deceived. I thought I was performing a disinterested act of charity, which in itself sounds pretty patronizing. But it wasn't meant to be patronizing. If you are in agreement, I suggest that you take the necessary steps to set our divorce in motion. I'm enclosing the name of our family solicitor in Great James Street, and God knows you've certainly got a choice of grounds. I'm suggesting that you do this because I will be leaving the country before Christmas. Last week I was offered a post to set up a photographic reconnaissance unit somewhere in the Mediterranean. At first I didn't take it seriously but I've just written my letter of acceptance.

I can't say that I don't feel a good deal of bitterness about what has happened. But there's no point in wishing you ill. While you remain set on the course that you've chosen I know you won't find any happiness. That's not a wish, just a fact. But it's your decision.

Maintenance will go on as it has done unless you actively want it to stop. Don't write to me again. There's no point.

Yours,
CHARLES HAMMOND

Beattie folds up the letter and puts it tidily back into its envelope. Dispassionately she thinks back over last Sunday's events. Could things have worked out with Charles? Well, whether they could or not, it is now too late. She has really got her wish now. Her decks are clearly completely stripped. It is her and Annie from now on.

Beattie finds it is a conscious effort to think at all. It is as if her thoughts are bruised. Dully she remembers Mrs Musgrave's face in the early morning, that bright brittle mask mouthing sentiments about responsibilities and standards. Those Musgraves. Those bloody Musgraves, thinks Beattie without any particular emotion. Between them that family's ruined my life.

She is still sitting there staring vacantly into space as the bell rings to announce the end of the first period.

335

CHAPTER
TWENTY-SEVEN

'Y OU'RE LOOKING awfully pleased with yourself,' observes Devora without pleasure. It is half-past eight in the drizzling Bayswater Road.

'You've hardly been in lately. Are you in love?'

Carefully sidestepping the question, Virginia says happily:
'Brooke's back in England, you know. Ma rang me on Monday and told me.'

'Oh. That's good news, I suppose,' says Devora rather grudgingly. 'Is he going back to his old squadron?'

'Well, he's at Gatton at present, but I sincerely hope he won't be flying for the time being,' says Virginia as they get on to the number 88 bus.

'You don't wriggle out of things that easily. Who is it you're seeing on the quiet? And don't tell me you aren't, because I know perfectly well you are. Old Willy can't be very pleased with you. Anyway, I thought your heart was pledged to Tom Berkeley. We hardly see you now. Oh God, this weather. My stockings will be ruined before I even get to work. I'm so fed up.'

Still grumbling Devora steps heavily off the bus at Bond Street, while at Bourne & Hollingsworth Virginia skips off the platform, shakes out her umbrella and begins to walk slowly through to Soho Square. It is a freezing December morning, with the kind of yellowish half-light that will never lighten properly into day. Stepping briskly out, Virginia's response to all this is to think what a lovely fresh day it is and, catching sight of herself in a shop window, she notices with detached amusement that she has the most inane smile on her face. Still, there's plenty to be cheerful about. Brooke is coming to London for the day and is taking her to lunch at the Ritz and, although Alexis hasn't said anything about seeing her that night, there is a very good chance he will turn up. What more could a girl want?

The production offices are empty save for Millie massaging her chilblains. She is hardly speaking to Virginia since it's been agreed that Virginia will train in continuity from January. So incensed was Millie at the news that she had actually gone to Pat Blain himself to complain. Only a rise and a personal assurance from Pat himself that she was essential to the production office had stilled her tongue but had in no way decreased her resentment. Ignoring her, Virginia begins to type a pile of estimates with about a quarter of her mind. It is almost impossible to concentrate when you feel you're coming out of a long dark tunnel of despair. By some miracle Brooke is safe. And, most important, there is Alexis. Though it's hard to know how to categorize what is happening between them.

For the past month she has been spending at least every other night, not to mention two weekends, at his house in Chelsea. After that first fateful night together when he'd said goodbye to her early the next day there had been no suggestion of meeting again. And she had been miserable all day, not to mention half-drunk with lack of sleep and physically exhausted. An early night was imperative until later that evening someone had shouted up the stairs at the hostel that she had a visitor, and she'd gone down to find the heart-stopping sight of Alexis standing in the entrance-hall, critically examining the portrait of Lady Grangemouth.

Immediately tiredness was forgotten. It had been the first of many such impromptu appearances. Alexis had a positive knack for managing to ring her when Millie was out of the office, for long jokey indiscreet conversations. She knew perfectly well that he was riddled with guilt about Holly, who wrote daily. But, telling herself firmly that it couldn't last anyway, Virginia simply hardened her heart, shut her ears and enjoyed what was happening, particularly in bed.

Which was strange considering the disastrous start they had made. When it came down to it Virginia had found herself as nervous as a virgin, remarking, as she'd entered the bedroom, that it was nearly two years since she'd been to bed with anyone.

'Well, you needn't have any anxieties on *that* score,' Alexis had remarked drily. 'The basic techniques haven't altered at all.'

After that they had simply stood and looked at each other for what seemed like a very long time. This is absurd, Virginia had thought. We both want to make love and we're both terrified of taking the first step.

'Can you see the river from this room?' Virginia had asked finally, and for answer Alexis had turned off the lights and pulled back the heavy curtains that also served as a blackout, then gestured her to his side.

In the short time since she had arrived the sky had miraculously cleared and the silver of moon had risen in the empty vault casting fitful beams on the broad silver band of the Thames visible beyond the flood-wall.

'It's beautiful.'

For answer Alexis had put his arm round her waist and tilted up her face so that it caught some of the light from outside.

'You don't have to, you know, if you don't want to.'

'Alexis, I sincerely hope you aren't going to say something as corny as "Why don't we just go to bed and cuddle each other".'

This at least had the useful function of making Alexis laugh outright and dispel some of the tension as he dropped the blackout curtain back into place.

'I wouldn't dream of offering so corny a line to a woman of your beauty and experience.'

'Though you're not above flattery, I see.'

This time they did actually make it to the bed and undress. It was

337

paralysingly cold. Alexis had put a match to the gas-fire, which responded with a series of small explosions then settled down to a contented purr, faintly illuminating the room.

'So how come I got lucky after two years' abstinence?'

Actually in bed with Alexis after so much plotting, Virginia had cudgelled her brain for something amusing, something lighthearted yet sophisticated to say that would, in a single phrase, display her own *savoir-faire* and lack of involvement. But, instead, when her bare flesh finally brushed Alexis they simply held each other with a fierceness that even now, four weeks later, still had the power to make Virginia's face burn with the intensity of the memory.

Being in bed with Alexis turned out to bear no resemblance to any previous sexual encounters. Then, she had simply lain back and let it happen. It was quite nice in a detached sort of way, having her breasts stroked, and even nicer to hear the broken words of gratitude with which grateful young men assailed her when their curiously undignified heavings were done. But the motive that had led Virginia into bed so repeatedly had never had much to do with pleasure; the pleasure came from that delightful sense afterwards of being one up on someone – that someone carefully never specified. The sheer fact that she was doing what she had been told never to do was revenge enough.

But with Alexis, from the first kiss, almost from the very first caress, it had been completely different. For a start, as she was to find out, no matter what time it was, no matter how strange the circumstances, in direct contrast to every other area of his life, Alexis always made love to her as if he had all the time in the world to enjoy her. Furthermore, from the beginning he insisted on what to Virginia were blushmaking and barbaric practices; for example, he apparently wanted to make love to her on *top* of the bed, with the light *on* so he could see her.

'Alexis, I can't, I really can't, I've never—' She was still protesting feebly as he switched on the small bedside light. She was overcome less by the embarrassment of being seen naked herself than by the fact that in spite of her seemingly wide experience she had very rarely seen a man entirely starkers before. But Alexis was governed by no such inhibitions, and in the warmth and glow of the fire she had gradually begun to relax, then was alarmed and disconcerted to discover that under his gentle but insistent hands she began to feel waves of longing and desire which frankly terrified her.

'Relax. Don't fight me,' Alexis kept telling her gently, his lips and hands never ceasing their assured and deliberate arousal of her body until at last every nerve of her flesh seemed to be burning under his delicate and inflammatory touch. It was like heaven, it was like being beyond conscious thought, but even while she groaned or moved in response to the questioning fingers a part of her was still terrified. Her very worst fears were being realized. Slowly but inexorably she was losing control, losing that hard sense of self-armoury that proclaimed 'I am Virginia' which she had always used as her strength and mainstay in life. Part of her longed to surrender, to be drawn down that warm wet path where Alexis was leading her, while another part cried out in panic that if she did she would lose herself so completely that she would be weakened and might never find her way back to her inviolate self again.

'Don't fight me,' Alexis had said again, but now it seemed to be from a long way off and when he finally came into her, hard and insistent, she was past any conscious thought. Instead she found herself moving for the first time to the rhythm of another's making, found herself moved forward within sight of the very brink of that terrifying waterfall which she had evaded so scrupulously up to now. To the very last moment she fought Alexis, her nails raking his back, her head thrashing from side to side. But he would not let her evade him, would accept nothing less than her whole surrender as he made her come with him, physically forcing her over the brink of that waterfall on wave after wave of shuddering pleasure. When she cried out, harsh ugly noise from the very depth of her belly, he held her tighter, reassuring her against that painful sound.

It had been like heaven, it had been like dying, but – what was far worse than both – while Alexis was still on top of and inside her Virginia had suddenly burst into floods of noisy tears.

What would her other lovers have done? Virginia had soberly asked herself later that day. What would Simon or Adam or even Willy have done? Why, leant over the bedside table for a clean hankie from the pile of small change, keys and cigarettes, all the articles that a man feels impelled to remove from his trouser pockets before committing the said garment to the back of the bedside chair. He'd then courteously have handed her the hankie, told her to 'bear up, old girl,' and never referred to the incident again.

Alexis had certainly gone for the clean hankie but he'd used it to wipe away her tears before tucking her into the crook of his arm and demanding to know what was wrong.

'Did I hurt you or what?'

'Oh, no. It's just – I don't know what it is.' Virginia had found herself in the extraordinary position of having continuous water pouring from her eyes apparently without even her own volition.

'What is it, then? Tell me, sweetheart.'

'That's just it, I don't know what it is.'

'Are you feeling awful because we've done it?' demanded Alexis, the gentleness of his fingers as he wipes away her tears belying the bluntness of his question.

'Oh lord, no – that is, I suppose I ought to but I don't. It was heaven. No, I—'

'Is it – is it what happened to you when you were blitzed?'

Virginia was silent, then sobs began to surge out of her lungs in a terrible agony of pain.

'I don't know why I should feel it now,' she said, her voice wobbling with the desperate attempt to stop herself from more crying. 'It's just that every time I wanted to talk about it after it happened everybody kept saying "There, there. Best forgotten about," and I knew it wasn't best forgotten about because I loved Cecily so much and I didn't tell her or show her and she was so concerned for me.'

'Was she the girl trapped with you?'

'Yes. She worked for the WVS, and I used to help her. She had a weak heart, you see, and they couldn't get us out in time. I'm sorry, Alexis, I'm sorry. This is so stupid.'

Virginia was already aware that by tomorrow she would bitterly regret having revealed so much of herself.

'Why does it cause you such pain? What are you feeling so guilty about?'

This actually succeeded in stopping Virginia in mid-sob.

'I didn't realize I did feel guilty, but I suppose I must do. She was a much much better person than I could ever be; it seems so wrong that she should die and I live. And she loved me, and I – I cared about her but I never took the time to show it.'

'Look,' said Alexis, not unsympathetic but briskly practical at the same time. 'There are two points here. There's no reason for you to feel guilty. We've all got a certain span allotted to us, and from what you say she made better use of her life than most people, didn't she? And if she really did care about you she wouldn't want you to grieve about her. She would have wanted you to go on and be happy, wouldn't she?'

'I suppose so.'

'And if she loved you – and if *you* can feel this much about her now – she must known how important she was to you. Even if you never said so.'

'Do you really think so? It feels to me like you're just letting me off the hook.'

'That's because you don't want to be let off the hook. You can't believe anybody likes you. Quite a lot of people do, you know.'

Gravely Virginia studied the dark face lying beside her on the pillow. In that fleeting second the strangeness of this whole encounter suddenly focused itself in a full comprehension of the facts: it was two o'clock in the morning, she had a full working day ahead of her, she was wide awake and she was somehow in bed with Alexis Seligman.

Alexis had stared back at her, smiling faintly as he caught some of the confusion in her face. Then, quite gently but firmly, he had put a finger on her lips.

'No questions. Not yet, anyway.'

Virginia had first kissed the finger then bitten it quite hard.

'Ow! What was that for?'

'I wasn't going to ask you any questions as I'm not at *all* sure I want to hear the answers.'

'Talk about a more neutral subject. Tell me more about Cecily. How long did you know her?'

'Oh, all my life,' said Virginia, aware that she was deliberately being distracted yet as unwilling as Alexis fully to examine the situation that had developed between them. Besides, it was hard to resist the chance to ease the soreness in her heart about Cecily. 'We were some sort of cousins, you see. Though her family are much grander than mine. And I – I always found Cecily rather a bore, to be honest. She was a Girl Guide, she was at a very posh girls' boarding school which she absolutely loved – all the things I despised. I've always hated belonging to anything. And I only agreed to

340

come to London with her because after my season was cancelled I knew unless I did something drastic I'd be stuck in Musgrave for ever. Cecily wanted to come to London because she couldn't join the services on account of her heart and she thought her best bet was working full-time for the WVS. That was – goodness, it must have been spring 1940. It just doesn't make any sense that it's only two and a half years ago. When we came to London we didn't see much of each other. Then suddenly we did. I was – I was fooling around a lot and I suppose pretty fed up despite the fact all the girls thought I was having a wonderful time. But when Brooke disappeared the whole thing started to go wrong and I couldn't pretend any more.'

There had been another long silence while Alexis had stroked Virginia's hair. Then she found herself saying in a rush: 'That night I didn't see you, I didn't really stand you up, you know. Though it must have seemed like that. Perhaps you've forgotten about it anyway.'

'I certainly haven't forgotten,' said Alexis coldly, much to Virginia's dismay, then she smiled sheepishly as she realized that he was teasing her.

'You don't have to explain. Unless you'd like to, of course, to restore my wounded vanity.'

'I should think your vanity is proof against almost anything. Where girls are concerned anyway.'

'It was the first time I'd ever been stood up,' Alexis had admitted with a wry smile, 'But I never seemed to get the kind of attention from you that I was looking for.'

'First I ignore you—'

'Then you stand me up.'

'But not deliberately. That night I really didn't want to go out. I felt frightful; it was the curse, and I'd actually gone to bed when Jim rang and said he was in London and could he see me. There are lots of reasons I can give you why I felt I had to make the effort and be with him. Not least of which that his brother had died a few months before. And in the end I was glad I made the effort. He was so lonely and unhappy. He was leaving for West Africa in a troop-ship the following day, and they were torpedoed about a week later.'

'I didn't realize that. I'm sorry.'

'You really did mind, didn't you, being stood up?'

'Of course I minded. Wouldn't you?'

'It doesn't happen to me,' Virginia told him sweetly. 'Ow! That wasn't fair. Anyway, I told you I *didn't* stand you up. Then I was going to ring up the next day and apologize, but you'd given me such a nasty look I didn't. Anyway, I couldn't think for the life of me why you were asking me out to start with.'

'And I couldn't understand why you agreed to come.'

'I was . . . curious about you.'

'I was pretty curious about you myself.'

'Is your curiosity satisfied now?'

'Not by a long chalk,' Alexis had answered roughly, and soon afterwards conversation had become an irrelevance. . . .

'Here, are you deaf? It's Ira on the phone for you.'

Abruptly Virginia pulls her thoughts back from the pleasant place where they'd been, puts on her poker face and picks up the phone and her shorthand-pad. . . .

For Brooke's sake she has taken a great deal of time and trouble over her appearance, then ruins it all by bursting into floods of tears as soon as she sees him coming to greet her in the entrance-hall.

'Come on, old girl, bear up. Mother drove up to Gatton on Tuesday and I don't think she stopped blubbing the entire time.'

Standing back to feast her eyes on him, she finds that Brooke is just the same, a little thinner perhaps but tanned and cheerful and resolutely refusing to dramatize the events of the last six months.

'But what *happened*?'

'It was just a raid like any other. We were doing some oilfields near Rotterdam. We'd dropped our load, and I was just pulling the old girl round to head out to sea when we got caught in a great burst of searchlight and a barrage of flak. Then one of the other boys radioed there were fighters coming up from behind us and there was the most monumental bang in our tail, and I knew at once that that was it. The rear gunner and the navigator must have been killed at once. Tony and I got out as fast as we could. The really damned odd thing was that after we'd parachuted out I saw the plane still circling round over our heads as we drifted away. I landed in a group of trees on the edge of a sand dune and managed to break both legs as I hit the sand. I lay there for a couple of hours listening to the seagulls and wondering if a coachload of Nazis would appear saying things like 'For you the war is over', but in the end an old chap appeared on a bicycle and saw me from the road. He was such a decent old man. He took his beret off to keep my head warm, then covered me up with his coat and told me to stay where I was. As if I had any option! Then he went down to the village and got the doctor to come back to give me a shot of morphine.'

'That was brave of them,' says Virginia soberly, trying to envisage the scene.

'Don't I know it,' said Brooke with some feeling. 'It was still before dawn, fortunately, and out of nowhere a cart appeared down the road, drawn by this incredibly old horse and an old farmer with what seemed like an idiot boy who picked me up, put me in the back of the cart and covered me with straw then took me to a farm. I was completely out for the count. They carried me up to an attic, and in the evening the doctor came and set my legs. They found Tony later the same day. He'd managed a rather better landing and had only sprained his ankle. So he was able to set out on the homeward journey fairly quickly. God, those people were decent,' Brooke says, pulling nervously on his cigarette. 'It wasn't a question of putting their lives in danger overnight. I had to stay there for nearly three months because of my damned legs. And even then it took me ages to get them working again. I was able to help a bit on the farm with the harvest, then in early September they told me I could move. I was passed from hand to hand, from one safe house to another until they got me to the coast in northern France where I was picked up and brought home. I'll never forget the sound of that plane coming out of the night sky to pick me up.'

'Did you actually see Germans, you know, in the street?'

'Of course.'

'Weren't you terrified?'

Brooke shrugs negligently. 'It never seemed quite real somehow. I never knew anybody's name. Or the places where I'd been. Just in case I was caught. At first I thought it was going to be hell stuck in that farm for months on end while my legs knitted up. But in its own way it was a blessing. For the first month I did nothing but sleep. They couldn't believe how much I could sleep. Then I just waited and hoped. You're just like Mother,' Brooke goes on, gesturing to the waiter. 'She kept on asking me what it was like. It's impossible to say what it was like. At the time you just survive.'

'Are you going home to Musgrave?'

'I doubt it,' says Brooke, crushing his bread roll and not looking at her. 'Now, come on, tell me what you've been up to.'

Knowing the limited nature of Brooke's attention, Virginia obligingly makes her account as brief yet as interesting as possible. When she mentions that it is her film company who actually made *Bomber Command*, Brooke looks almost interested.

'Dashed good film that was. Though I gather all the blokes they filmed bought it. Just as well they didn't choose me. I met the director chap while I was at Mildenhall. He said he knew you.'

'Oh, Alexis,' says Virginia, trying to sound casual. 'Yes, he's one of the directors. He's Ferdinand's cousin, you know.'

Brooke flicks her a lazy glance. 'You're blushing. Is he your boyfriend? One of many?'

Virginia shrugs prettily and gives him a glance as blank as his own.

'Perhaps,' she says, then quickly changes the subject. 'So what are you doing next? Flying missions again?'

'To my great surprise, I find I can't face it,' says Brooke. 'I've been told I'll have a spell training the lads now.'

'At Gatton?'

'Not likely. Rhodesia, to train the colonial boys.'

'Rhodesia! That's in Africa, isn't it? It's *miles* away. How would you get there?'

'There are troop-ships going all the time. I could leave early next year, and it strikes me as being a pretty reasonable place to be for the next few years. It's bloody awful being back in England. You can't buy anything unless you've got contacts or black-market friends, and it's almost impossible to get whisky. As far as I'm concerned that's two good reasons for going. Besides, Rhodesia is full of rich girls. And right now I badly need a rich girl.'

'Have you met Bertie?'

'I suppose so. He was certainly introduced, but I can't say he made a lasting impression.'

'Do you think he's – er – here to stay?'

Brooke impatiently pushes his dessert away uneaten and lights another cigarette. 'Ma's a fool. She should have remarried when Father died and she still had all her looks. Still, she could do far worse than him. You mustn't forget that behind that dull exterior he's stinking rich. His mother was the heiress to the Re-Lax Company, you know.'

'I don't believe it!'

'It's true. Ma told me. She hates trade but loves the money. Besides, I think she's come to conclude, as I have, that trade has rather more of a future than land in this country. I used to have fantasies about riding over the old ancestral acres. But what's the point? I'd never have the dough to put the place to rights. Ma tells me there's a Dr Barnardo's home there now.' Brooke's contempt is immense. 'This war has been the end of everything for people like us.'

Virginia is silent for a moment before finishing her dessert.

'You really have made up your mind about Rhodesia, haven't you? You almost make it sound rather . . . permanent.'

'I'll just have to see how it works out. That's what I've come up to London to do – to see Grimsdyke and get a few affairs sorted out before I go.'

Virginia takes her courage in both hands, hardly knowing why she does so.

'Are you going to see . . . Beattie?'

Brooke surveys Virginia with the ice-blue stare that she herself has used so effectively.

'I hadn't planned to, no. Why?'

'Have you been in touch with her?'

'Why should I be?'

'It is your child.'

Brooke takes out his cigarette-case, selects a cigarette with care and makes a great show of tapping then lighting it.

'You're rather better-informed than I thought. Who else knows? Mother?'

'No. I guessed from something Lucy said. She came to London at the end of last year and mentioned she'd been to Beattie's wedding in the summer.'

'Beattie certainly lost no time in finding herself someone else.'

There is something in her brother's face that Virginia cannot read.

'Come off it, Brooke, presumably you must have refused to marry her, so she didn't have much choice, did she? She's hardly in a position to support a child on her own.'

'I didn't want her to have it,' says Brooke expressionlessly. 'The whole thing was a ghastly mistake. I offered to pay for an abortion, and she refused. I didn't see her after that. Then I heard she'd got married. I gathered from my rigger that she'd had a girl.'

'That's right. Called Anne.'

'I don't know what she expected me to do. And then she went and married someone I detest.'

There is almost a note of injury in Brooke's voice. Virginia stares at her brother in disbelief.

'Do you think she should have married someone you approved of?'

'Well, she didn't have to choose someone I actually disliked.'

Virginia is almost at a loss for words.

'Brooke,' she goes on carefully, 'she must have been terrified out of her wits when she found she was pregnant. It may be just about OK to have an illegitimate child in the anonymity of London, but they still aren't too nice about that kind of thing in the village. Don't you think it would help if you just – I don't know, showed her you were still friends or that you cared about her?' says Virginia rapidly. 'You were together for how long?'

'Two years, give or take a month. It may be a long time, but things end. And this is very unlike you, Virginia. What's brought about this sudden change of heart? The only time you saw us together you were absolutely vile if I remember rightly. You plumbed new depths of disapproval and unpleasantness. Has love succeeded in softening your fibres or what?'

'No, it hasn't,' retorts Virginia crossly. 'And I'm not in love. I just happen to feel that she must have loved you a lot and suffered terribly when you disappeared. It would be a kindness to contact her and make some sort of gesture.'

'When I sent her a cheque for an abortion she sent it back,' says Brooke at last as he stubs out his cigarette. 'Last week I got my solicitor to contact her and offer to settle some money on the child. She sent a letter back by return of post, signed in her married name, saying she didn't want any further contact with me.'

'Oh, that doesn't mean anything,' broods Virginia from the wisdom of her own experience. 'It's the kind of thing I'd do. It just means she's still furious with you. If you wrote again yourself, she'd see you like a shot. Can't you just write and say you're sorry about everything?'

'Sorry?' Brooke stares at his sister in amazement. 'Sorry for what? I couldn't marry her. She knew that. I did what I could.'

'You offered her money. Don't you see how wounding that must have seemed?'

'Virginia, this discussion is pointless and boring. As far as I'm concerned, I made the only gesture I could to Beattie and she rejected it.'

'Don't you even want to see the little girl?'

'Virginia my darling, I've already got at least one other child and probably two. Let's have some coffee and, for God's sake, leave things at that.'

The office is empty when Virginia returns, already dark enough at half-past two to need artificial light. In its dusty disinfectant-smelling privacy Virginia sits for a long time with a cigarette and thinks about her brother. She is aware that some process of disillusionment that started in the gardens of the nursing home is now complete. The fact is that, whatever Brooke says, she feels he has acted badly. But when she examines the statement she is annoyed to find that what she actually means is that she feels that under the same circumstances, Alexis would not have behaved in the same way. But how can she so confidently ascribe caring behaviour to a man who is himself involved in a highly questionable emotional mess? But deep down she knows that it isn't just the not marrying that must have hurt Beattie. It was the fact that Brooke was so anxious to keep his hands clean that he could not afford to

345

give anything of himself at all. Lucy had been right. It didn't really matter about Brooke's or Beattie's class; the fact was that Brooke hadn't behaved like a gentleman. Virginia wrestles with unfamiliar, almost heretical thoughts. What, after all, did behaving like a gentleman really mean? Come on, Vir, says a crisp voice inside Virginia that makes her jerk her head round in astonishment. It is Cecily's voice, speaking with all her old briskness and authority. You know perfectly well what that means. It means Brooke evaded his responsibilities. And don't tell me it would have given your mother a death-blow – she's much too frightened of Brooke to deny him anything. He could have bullied her into good behaviour. Startled, Virginia sits slumped on her typing-chair staring into space. If the whole question of good behaviour is under review, then there is an unpleasant personal application here that she cannot ignore. What about Holly? Could either of them be said to be taking their responsibilities seriously towards her? And what of Tom? Even if there was no formal commitment between them, he was under the impression that she was at least contemplating some kind of future with him. Oh God, what a mess, thinks Virginia before firmly pushing the whole matter to one side and getting on with her work.

At half-past three Pat Blain, Mr Myerberg and Millie appear fresh from the cutting-rooms. Virginia has abandoned her letters to track down £4 10s 4d which is missing from the accounts of one of the food flashes. She is just getting to grips with it when the door opens again and Millie promptly lights up like a Christmas tree, a pre-war one.

'Hello there, Alexis. Gosh, you're a stranger here. You can't have finished editing your film already.'

'On the contrary,' says Alexis gaily, unwinding the long black knitted scarf from inside his tweed coat. 'Owing to my excessive zeal, exceptional brilliance and ability to delegate, I think we're very nearly there. I've actually come up to see about the music.'

'Are you coming to the Christmas party?' asks Millie. 'I've put you down for two tickets. We're having a cabaret this year. Everybody's got to do something. You're down to sing a song. What can Holly do?'

'Oh, you'd better ask her yourself,' says Alexis casually. 'She'll be back in London next week.'

Virginia bends her head to her accounts. Two of the cameramen appear and begin to shout at Millie about a missing light. Virginia grits her teeth and tries to concentrate on the column of figures in front of her. What she wants most to avoid seems inexorably upon her: if Holly is coming back, then Alexis will be forced to make decisions. If only Holly's film had overrun its shooting-time, preferably till Easter.

'Someone on the phone for you, Virginia.'

'Thanks,' says Virginia and goes across to answer it, pointedly turning her back on Alexis. By some miracle it is Tom Berkeley.

'Virginia my dear. I say, what luck to catch you. Are you frightfully busy?'

'Gosh, yes,' says Virginia gaily, 'you know me. Singlehandedly winning the war. This is an awfully good line – are you ringing from Northern Ireland?'

'No. I'm in Liverpool actually. The good news is I'm on my way down to London, and I was ringing you up to book you well in advance. Any chance of dinner tomorrow?'

'I'll stand everything else down,' Virginia assures him, secure in the knowledge of many pairs of flapping ears around her. 'What time will you pick me up?'

'Say seven-thirty. I'll book a table for eight and we'll go dancing afterwards. I can't tell you how much I've missed you.'

'Me, too,' Virginia assures him, warmly. '*A bientôt,* then. Until tomorrow.'

Still ignoring Alexis, Virginia goes pointedly back to her typewriter.

'Are you free tonight?'

Virginia looks up and finds Alexis standing beside her ostensibly studying the estimate.

'I could be.'

'What's wrong?'

'Nothing's wrong,' she snaps and promptly regrets it.

'I've got to go up to St John's Wood about this music. But I should be done about eight. I'll come round to the hostel.'

'We've got tea and cake, Alexis, if you want to stay,' says Millie with a simper.

'Well, perhaps just for a moment. . . .'

'Forgive me if I don't stop,' says Virginia savagely, 'but I do have to finish these estimates by today.'

Alexis calls for her at half-past eight. Virginia is attending an Advanced First Aid lecture in the library and goes up to her room to collect her coat. Alexis is standing in the entrance-hall, muffled up against the cold, but hatless as ever.

'Good evening,' says Virginia, and Alexis wheels round sharply. They eye each other warily, and Virginia feels the usual mixture of desire and annoyance that he always seems to arouse in her.

'I thought we might go somewhere and have something to eat. Unless you've got some other plans.'

'Fine,' says Virginia, and they go to a restaurant in Baker Street.

During the meal Virginia listens attentively enough to what Alexis has to say about the editing but contributes little herself. Finally he says abruptly: 'Shall I oblige you?'

'What do you mean?'

'By saying, "You're not saying much", so you can say "Oh, I didn't realize". Then I can say "What's wrong?" and you can say "Oh, nothing" and sigh. Then I can say, "No come on, I'm sure there's something", then you can say "No, nothing" again, and eventually you'll tell me whatever it is that's making you so sulky. I've blocked in all the early dialogue, so we can dispense with you looking tragic and martyred and get right down to what's wrong.'

Virginia is furious.

'I'm just curious to know what happens when your friend comes back to London.'

'You're curious. I'm curious. I had a letter from her this morning—'

'Just the one?' sneers Virginia.

'Don't be so bitchy and stupid.'

'Don't be such a bloody prig, Alexis,' Virginia snaps, her annoyance finally spilling out.

Alexis is equally angry. In fact it looks remarkably like their first quarrel.

'She said she's coming back as soon as she can. They finished shooting yesterday and apparently it's not gone at all badly. She thinks that with a bit of—' .

'Alexis, you may be naïve but kindly don't be bloody stupid as well. I could not give a twopenny damn about her bloody film, and the last thing, the very last thing in the whole world is to discuss it with you. Oh, come on, let's go.'

In silence, and each in a bad temper, they get back in Alexis' car.

'Shall I drop you off home for an early night for your date tomorrow?'

'Suits me,' says Virginia, whom it does not suit at all, and stares resolutely out of the window.

At the end of Oxford Street Alexis slams on the brakes.

'Is this what you really want?'

'You suggested it, not me,' says Virginia rudely.

He starts up the engine again but instead of going down to Bayswater turns left into Park Lane towards Chelsea.

As ever it is paralysingly cold in Alexis' bedroom. He puts the gas-fire on and they sit with their coats on, looking at it, faces averted.

'Are you staying the night?'

'Jesus,' seethes Virginia, 'what the hell do you think I'm here for? To read the meter?'

'Let's go down to the kitchen while the room warms up. I'll get us some coffee or something.'

Eventually they take their coffee back up to the bedroom and sit rather more companionably in the darkness as the room slowly warms up.

'Music?'

Virginia shakes her head and turns to lean against Alexis. Then she feels the touch of his lips on her hair and raises her face so they can kiss violently, angrily.

'Christ,' says Alexis a moment later, 'I can't find you. This is the first time I've tried to make love to a woman wearing an overcoat and scarf. Are you warm enough to take off your coat if I take off mine?'

They both burst out laughing.

'Come on, it's warmer than it looks in this bed; you should know that by now.'

It is going to be all right, but it very nearly hadn't been. Some time later Virginia stares at the shadows on the wall and says: 'Are we going to go on seeing each other – after next week, I mean?'

Alexis has his head on her bare stomach and stares up at her.

'It's a great pity you never wanted to act. You're marvellously photogenic, particularly with a shot like this from below your breasts.'

'*Alexis.*'

'I don't know. You bloody well know I want to go on seeing you. I just don't know how to do it, though.' Alexis sits up energetically. 'That day at the party, when you had your hair up. Put it up like that again.'

Virginia pushes up the heavy mass of blonde curls on to the crown of her head, aware that her raised arms do splendid things for her bosom.

'You look like Constance Bennett.'

'She looks like me.'

Alexis reaches up and takes one of her hands and guides it without embarrassment to his crotch.

'What, again?'

'What do you mean, again? We missed last night, didn't we?'

He pulls Virginia on top of him. Immediately Virginia begins to relax and as he comes into her abruptly tightens her muscles and begins to move against him. When she finally comes she hears him say her name, then he clings to her for a long time afterwards. She is about to slide off him when he holds her in position.

'You just want me there to keep you warm,' she says teasingly.

'Not just that. You feel nice there.'

Leaning over to put on the light by the bed, Alexis is about to ask Virginia if she knows where his cigarettes are when they hear a sound that makes them both go rigid. The front door slams, then there is a series of light footsteps coming up the stairs. Before either of them can move, the door to the bedroom bursts open and a radiant-faced Holly stands on the threshold, her smile of welcome slowly fading as she takes in the scene before her.

Abruptly Alexis tips Virginia off him and sits up, thus revealing Virginia as being as naked as himself. There is a very long pause during which all three parties take in each other incredulously. Then Holly gives a kind of sob and slams the door shut. There is the sound of footsteps running downstairs, then the slam of the front door followed by the clatter of frantic feet running down the steps to the road. Alexis swears furiously, jumps out of bed and begins to pull on his clothes. Virginia watches in a kind of daze.

'Are you going after her?' she asks stupidly.

'Of course I'm bloody going after her,' he says, giving her a look of such anger that she flinches. In another minute the front door bangs again and the house is completely silent. Virginia looks at her watch. It is past midnight. She won't be able to get back into the Grangemouth now. Pride will not let her stay here a moment longer. Slowly she pulls on her clothes and goes downstairs. In the King's Road she hails a taxi and tells the driver to take her to Willy's flat.

Though in retrospect it seems stupid to have been so upset. Or so Virginia reasons to herself, dancing languidly in Tom's arms the following evening. There is no question surely that Alexis is crazy about her, she tells her reflection in the ladies' loo. True, he hadn't rung her up, but presumably he had to sort things out with Holly before he could proceed with Virginia. Faced with such a choice, there could surely only be one final decision.

Whatever claims Holly might think she had on Alexis – affection, long friendship, duty, whatever – they could be as nothing compared to the intensity of those recent nights. It's a shame that Holly has to suffer, thinks Virginia, briskly putting her compact back into her bag, but in love someone always has to be the loser.

With such thoughts Virginia strives to calm the mounting tension which is knotting her stomach with anxiety. Then anxiety gives way to anger. A full week goes by before Alexis contacts her. And then it is only to make a date for a lunchtime drink.

Virginia is fully apprised of all the nuances of a lunchtime as opposed to the evening encounter. But she will not reveal her feelings, she tells herself firmly. Let Alexis get all worked up. She will turn up at the meeting looking cool, amused and more than a little disinterested. This all works perfectly well until she arrives at the pub and finds that Alexis is late. In the end he is twenty minutes late and has barely sat down with their drinks when she finds herself behaving in a way that makes her scream inwardly whilst externally she is powerless to stop herself.

'Well?' she demands fiercely.

'Well, what?' says Alexis irritably.

'Well, why the hell haven't you rung me for a week?'

'Don't you ever think about anyone except yourself?'

'I suppose you've actually bothered to see me today to tell me you hope we'll always be good friends.'

'I don't see how we can go on seeing one another, no,' says Alexis, his eyes on his glass.

'Is it to be a Christmas engagement, followed by a spring wedding?' jeers Virginia.

'You've always disliked Holly, haven't you?'

'I hate feeble people,' says Virginia in a savage undertone. 'If it had been me coming home and finding you larking around with someone else, I wouldn't have gone running out of the house, sobbing, in the hope that you'd follow me. I'd have stayed where I was and fought out the ground, first with you then with me. *Then* I'd have broken the place up. Then, and only then, I might think of negotiating. Still, her technique seems to have payed off nicely. She's managed to make you feel properly guilty.'

'Perhaps I ought to feel guilty,' says Alexis, his face red with anger. 'I happen to love Holly.'

'I'm sure you do. She must bring out the father in you.'

Having successfully provoked Alexis into saying what she least wants to hear, Virginia, to her eternal humiliation, feels tears spilling down her cheeks on to the collar of her coat.

'Oh, don't cry. Don't cry. Look, take my handkerchief.'

'Have you spent the last week with her?'

'Of course I haven't, silly. I've been at Pinewood with Pat and his wife.'

'Do you really mean it?' asks Virginia pathetically. 'About us not seeing each other.'

Alexis sighs. He looks older and more drawn. Then he says, apparently at random: 'Look, Virginia, quite apart from whatever there is between

Holly and me I can't honestly see there'll ever be any future for us—'

'What do you *mean*—?'

'I mean we want different things. The war has turned everything upside down, and you're finding it amusing to hang around Fitzrovia. But I don't honestly think you'd find my life amusing for very long. I don't make much money, as you know. Though I know I may be a success after the war, there's always a chance that I'll never be earning very much more than this. I couldn't remotely give you the life you want or the life you're used to. And quite apart from that I'm very selfish and I admit it. Whoever I'm with has to live my life. That's partly why things used to work so well with Holly. She didn't mind. After the war I just don't think you'd find my life much fun.'

'Don't talk such absolute bloody tosh, Alexis,' snaps Virginia furiously. 'And let me be the judge of what I can and cannot do without. You sound like something out of *The Student Prince*. For Christ's sake, I'm not asking you to marry me. I just think you're incredibly stupid to let something as good as this fade away. Does it occur to you that if things were really that great between you and Holly you wouldn't be so readily available to the first girl who tried to seduce you?'

'Perhaps you're harder to resist than most girls,' says Alexis with something like one of his old smiles.

'If you were with me, you wouldn't want anybody else. Anyway, I'd make absolutely sure that nobody else got to you.'

It is a quarter to two. Virginia is in despair. She is due back at work at two to hang paper-chains for the office party.

'What are you doing for Christmas?'

'I haven't even thought about it yet. Are you . . .?'

'Yes. It was arranged weeks ago. Do you want another drink?'

Virginia shakes her head. Alexis fetches himself another half-pint, then fixes her with his own direct stare.

'Tell me something. I've been thinking quite a lot this week about what's happened between us. I must confess I'm curious as to what the original trigger was to get us into bed together. I admit I fancied you for years. But I really can't flatter myself that it was likely to be lust for my body in your case. Was it sheer dislike of Holly?'

'Originally it was just to get my own back on Holly. I didn't like the way she patronized me that night. It gave me a motive. The Yanks have this wonderful motto: Don't get mad, get even. I disliked Holly from the moment I clapped eyes on her radiant little face.'

'She's never done anything to you.'

'There are some people, you just don't have to do anything, they simply have to be and they get to you. And she is so bloody pleased with herself.'

'She's as insecure as the next person. And her life hasn't been a bed of roses, I can assure you. Are you going to the party tonight?'

'It's all right,' Virginia says nastily. 'No, I'm not. Willy's taking me to the Christmas thrash at the embassy.' She is delighted to see that the news does not cheer Alexis.

'Where did you go to last week?'

'Oh, you did notice I'd gone, did you? I went round to Willy's of course.'

'Didn't he mind you getting him out of bed?'

'Of course not. He's barmy about me. Anyway, he was up already, playing poker,' says Virginia with a briskness she is far from feeling.

Outside in Museum Street it is snowing heavily.

'So this is goodbye, is it?'

'I've told Holly I won't see you for a couple of months to try to make a go of things with her.'

'In that case,' says Virginia, adjusting her fur hat with care, 'I hope you have a truly fucking awful Christmas and an absolutely disastrous New Year. And forget about the couple of months. Just don't bother to get in touch with me again. Merry Christmas, Alexis.'

Part Five

January 1943–January 1944

CHAPTER
TWENTY-EIGHT

EXTON Castle, Melton Mowbray,
Leicestershire
28 December 1942

My dear Lucy,

We've had a quiet but very agreeable Christmas. I don't know why I've started off in this fatuous style, I'll be writing 'X marks our window' next, or 'Wish you were here'. It's certainly been quiet but OK as Cecily's family are always absolute ducks to me. Sorry to have been so long replying but I've been a bit down. You asked me last time how my love-life was going. When I got your letter I'd have said it was pretty terrific. It isn't now, though, even though I'm still going out with Tom Berkeley. (I spent Boxing Day with his family. Très snob. They still somehow manage to have footmen. One can only assume they were all gassed in the First World War or something.)

I'm sorry not to have been entirely frank about what was happening before Christmas, but most of the time I wasn't sure myself. Quite unexpectedly in the autumn I – what is the word? I don't know. I got involved with someone I've known for a while and didn't even much like. It was Alexis Seligman actually – Ferdinand's cousin. I don't know what I was hoping for from it, but it's all over anyway. He had a long-term girlfriend and she – well, I suppose she won. It ended with the utmost acrimony on my part, I'm ashamed to say. I keep consoling myself with the thought it wouldn't have worked. I can hear Uncle Piers saying 'Is he our kind of person, Virginia?' in that Colonel Blimp way of his. Meaning, is he County? Do we know his people? Does he hunt? And to all those questions I'd have to reply: 'Well, no, not really.' But I still think it might have worked. I'm sorry to drone on but I've never talked about it to anybody else. I don't even know why it all felt so marvellous. Except that Alexis and I just seemed to get on. He seemed to like me. It's so hard to put into words, isn't it, why it works with one person and not with another. I was thinking about this when I went over to Tom's for the day. I really like his people, I think they like me and Tom himself is a regular white man as your father would say. (I got such a nice card from them.) But in Tom's company I always seem to have to watch myself. I don't mean that I'm secretly longing to have a go at the gin-bottle or to shout 'Knickers' during the loyal toast. It isn't anything like that. It's just

355

with some people you feel completely at home and others, I suppose, you feel you're presenting selected bits to – in Tom's case, the best bits.

Having covered three sides about fascinating old me, it seems only polite to ask how you are, to thank you for your present which was absolutely lovely. I was delighted to be able to get you something you wanted and I am bound to say, were it not for my former connection with Marwicks, I doubt very much if I'd have been able to lay my hands on a copy. After all those glowing reviews in the dailies the first edition sold out in a fortnight. Theo, my old boss, is like a dog with two tails – he's been fretting about their fiction list and now suddenly he's got a bestseller on his hands. I hadn't realized that the neurotic "Eleanor" whose job I got was Charles Hammond's old girlfriend. What a dismayingly small world it is. I had a Christmas letter from Theo in which he spent pages pondering as to whether they'd got a real writer on their hands in C.H. or would he turn out to be a one-book wonder. Still, knowing Marwicks, they'll have got him tightly shackled by a three-book contract, so time will tell. I suppose Beattie will have been thrilled by those reviews. Did you go there for Christmas? I gather Ma went to the Towers and Brooke went to the Alberrys'. Daphne's married, incidentally, to that nasty smarmy-haired Michael Something-or-other. She must have finally given up on Brooke, especially since he's off to Rhodesia next week. We're having lunch and I'm seeing him on to the train afterwards. I do wish he wasn't going.

Someone has come in and asked me if I'd like to walk the dogs. I feel it's a question expecting the answer 'yes'. So I'll have to go. Do write and tell me about your Christmas. Any chance of seeing you in the New Year?

Much love,
Virginia

PS. You are probably asking yourself quite justifiably where Tom fitted in in the context of the other affair. Well, I'm afraid he just didn't know. The funny thing was I didn't feel at all bad about it, because it made me so much nicer to him. The trouble is that Tom is an 'ought' and Alexis is a 'want'. I wanted Alexis and feel I ought to want someone like Tom.

Home Farm,
3 January 1943

My Dear Vir,
Thanks for your long and jolly interesting letter. I can't tell you how reassuring it is to hear about a life where people still have love-affairs. There is nothing wrong with the milk quota as a topic of conversation except when it is the only one on offer, save for a purely abstract discussion as to whether the teeth of the chaff-cutter will last another season. To take your points one by one. Glad you had a good Christmas, so did I – we had a lot of snow, which made for some drama when the pigs got out. It's the only time I've ever known them to return voluntarily to their sties! There was a full complement of family at the farm, plus two boys called Donny and Dougall who have just been sent down from Lanarkshire to learn farming. I'm in charge of them and if I take my eyes off them for longer than a minute they're

scrapping on the floor like a pair of puppies. But they do make life easier.

I did go to the Blythes' for Christmas Day and it was jolly nice – we had sixteen round the table including most of the Kedges. I thought *Murder by Rote* was first-rate and told Beattie so – she's saved all her husband's reviews, there doesn't seem to be a bad one amongst them. Beattie seemed very down, I don't know why except that Charles has apparently gone abroad for an indefinite period. I can't tell you where (fifth columnists!) but I can give you a hint in so far as it's near Hugh. Talking of whom I actually got a Christmas card from him wishing me a prosperous 1943. After nearly a year's silence I thought that was pretty cool. Needless to say I didn't send him one – the most I can do is actually refrain from hoping that he and Julia Heap are run over by a camel. I've come to the conclusion that the sun must have driven Hugh barmy – it happens in India, doesn't it? I hope it doesn't happen to Charles.

I'm so sorry things didn't work out with your Alexis. You told it all in such a determinedly cheerful way that it makes me suspect it matters more than you're letting on. Funnily enough, I've been thinking quite a lot about this whole business of 'our kind of people' lately and wondering if it isn't all a load of bosh. Surely if you like someone and share interests in common that's what matters. I mean, ideally one would prefer someone who didn't drink his cocoa with a knife, but beyond that who's worried?

I may indeed be seeing you in the New Year, because I feel I must go up to Harrogate and see the folks. I got the strangest Christmas greeting from them. Ma sent me a two-liner of the kind she normally signs for the Leafy Tree Club (perhaps she's frantically busy, I don't know). Whereas Daddy sent me a ten-page screed in almost *illegible* writing talking entirely about Mother's success and how proud of her he was. It was as if he was trying to convince himself not me. He ended up quite plaintively saying being able to help Mother achieve success had been one of the great sources of pride of his life. Then he added rather oddly: 'I console myself with that.' What *can* he mean? It may be that he's simply not well – apparently his heart isn't good and he has to take a lot of pills. I wrote back and said I'd come up and see them when I could. It's a shame that Dad never comes down to London with Mother any more – she's apparently convinced him that the journey's no good for his health.

If I do come up, I'll let you know. Keep me posted viz. Tom Berkeley and don't dismiss him out of hand.

Lots of love from
LUCY

Langdale Road, Liverpool 8
9 January 1943

My dear Beattie,
I got your letter at lunchtime today and read it during the break and feel I must answer it immediately because it upset me so much. I've been wondering and wondering why I haven't heard from you and I suspected something might be wrong.

Oh, Beattie, you are a chump. If you're angry with me for saying that you'll have to put up with it: you know it's my way and I haven't any other. I rue the day you ever clapped eyes on that Brooke Musgrave who's been nothing but a whatever it is that they use to lure ships on to the rocks with. I've not met Charles, so I can't speak up for him. But I do know he did his best by you and I don't think you've treated him well. If you're absolutely convinced that you don't want him, then the kindest thing is to get a divorce and give him a chance with somebody else. You may very well be consoling yourself at the thought that you stand a better chance yourself as a divorced woman with a child rather than being an unmarried mother, but I personally would feel better about the whole business if I didn't know that you were making your decision based on whether or not Brooke wants *you*. Have you ever really thought what your life with him would be like? Or Annie's, either, come to that?

I'm sorry to go on like this but the alternative is to sit idly by and let you throw away your happiness. For goodness' sake, put Brooke out of your mind once and for all and try to concentrate on a happier future. I can see you sitting back now with tears in your eyes saying 'What right has she to say these awful things'. No right at all except that I can't bear to know you're so unhappy about such a worthless cause. You've got your health and strength, a pretty baby and a job. And I think it's downright decent of Charles to go on supporting you until the divorce comes through. That lad's got some sense of his responsibilities, unlike some I could mention. Well, let's leave that all on one side now.

We had a grand Christmas. I wish you could have been here. Vince had five days' leave and I don't think I've ever had a better Yule-time. We're officially engaged now, though I haven't got the ring yet and I don't expect we'll marry for quite a while. We're both saving hard for a deposit for a home. But I'm definitely coming down to Gatton this summer. Is there any chance of seeing you then? This is assuming we're still talking after this letter! I hope we are. I think of you a lot – especially now that I know you're so down and long for things to get better for you. It's grand news about Charles's book – it's all over the bookshops up here.

Much love from
LOUIE

CHAPTER TWENTY-NINE

'ARE YOU HAPPY WITH THAT? I don't think the light's going to get any better.'

'Not really, but we can't spend any more time on this shot. We'd better call it a wrap. Is everything set up for tomorrow, Virginia?'

'Yes, they're expecting us at the milking-parlour at four-thirty – a.m., that is, not p.m. You've got an hour to set up and we'll be ready to film by five-thirty.'

Deryck's pale face grows visibly paler.

'Will you tell the hourly boys? I don't think I could stand any more abuse.'

'I already have. They'll be there.'

'Virginia, I don't know what I'd do without you.'

'Nor do I,' thinks Virginia drearily. Out loud she says: 'You can buy me a gin later. I feel as if I'll never be warm again. OK, everybody. That's everything.'

'Want a lift back to the hotel?'

'Rather.'

'Trudy and Pat Blain will be down later tonight. You have arranged about showing the rushes, haven't you?'

'Yes, ten o'clock on Thursday morning at the Empire in the High Street. Don't *worry*, Deryck, it'll all be fine.'

Sid the cameraman gives Virginia a hefty wink. Virginia rolls her eyes in frustration.

'Are you going to give us our call-sheets, then?' Sid asks.

'As soon as I've had a hot bath and a drink. Several drinks. Do you think it went all right today?'

'There's only two ways of shooting a cow, and we covered both ends. So I reckon it must be. Hey up. His Lordship's beckoning.'

In the car back to Cirencester, Deryck expands at some length about the peculiar pressures of a director's life. In the warm and blessedly fuggy atmosphere of the car Virginia almost dislocates her jaw trying not to yawn, having early grasped that the secret of being a successful continuity girl is never to be bored by what the director says.

In the reception area of the George, Trudy and Pat Blain are signing the guest-book.

'Blimey! This is the back of beyond and no mistake,' Trudy greets her.

'You should see it on early-closing day. Are you down here long?'

'Long enough, in my opinion. We're reccying something for somebody – I forget exactly who. We're going to look at your rushes. How's it going?'

Deryck is standing hard by.

'Oh, very well,' says Virginia enthusiastically. 'Very well. A couple more days and we'll be there. Hello, Mr Blain.'

'You look well, Virginia. Are you missing London?'

'A bit. Though you certainly sleep more peacefully out here.'

'There was a bomb next door but two to the office on Monday night. 'S put cracks across all our ceilings.'

'Anyone hurt?'

'No, it was just offices.'

'I'm going up to get dry. See you in the bar later.'

As usual Virginia has timed things to a nicety. There is no one in the bathroom, so, hastily hanging the 'engaged' sign on the door, Virginia turns on the water, pulls off her sodden clothes and winds her hair into curlers before stepping into the measly five inches of tepid water which is all the authorities will allow. In the time it has taken to sit down and relax and soak one elbow, footsteps arrive in the corridor outside as the rest of the unit appear and are soon rattling the door and demanding to know if she's going to be all night.

'All right! I can hear you,' shouts Virginia crossly, finishing her soap and leisurely wash before vacating the bathroom and returning to her own cheerless room to change for dinner.

Pat Blain is right. She does look well, Virginia decides staring dismally at herself in the cracked and fly-blown dressing-table mirror. Nine weeks of enforced fresh air, regular meals and early nights have completely restored her health and vigour. Resolutely she puts on her face, gets dressed and joins Trudy in the bar.

'I ordered you a gin,' says Trudy.

'Oh, thank God. Cheers. Is Deryck down yet?'

'No, he's trying to ring his mother.'

'Oh, good, he'll be hours yet.'

Trudy makes herself more comfortable on the bar stool. Her clothes, which, even in London, stand out more for their colour than for their cut and quality, look positively garish in the quiet oak-panelled saloon bar. The two farmers in gaiters and tweeds can hardly take their eyes off Trudy's platform heels and long expanse of nylon stocking.

'Have you brought a pullover with you? You'll freeze in that rig-out tomorrow.'

'I've brought my slacks. What's it been like? How do you get on with Deryck?'

'Oh, fine. We've got a mutual friend called Stephen Seaton. Once I knew *that*, I knew how to handle him.'

Trudy gives Virginia a glance of amused respect. 'Didn't take you long to work that one out, did it? Did Mavis mind you taking over?'

'You bet she did. But she did her best to fill me in; she didn't sabotage me, which she could perfectly well have done.'

'Poor Mavis. Thick as a brick where men are concerned. She keeps inviting Deryck home to meet her mother in Streatham. I tried to wise her up one day, but in the end I just couldn't bring myself to. So what's happening?'

'Not a lot. We've done twelve shorts on how to produce better vegetables from your allotment. Now we're doing three longer films for agricultural colleges. I wish to God cows weren't milked so early. We're doing a sequence about the virtues of a clean milking-parlour, and it's been a four-thirty start three days running.'

'I still quite envy you being out here. You look awfully healthy. Except when you came in I thought you looked a bit down. Another drink?'

'Oh, I'll get them. Two more of the same, please. Oh, I suppose I don't mind the country, but this bloody weather doesn't cheer me up. I always hate after Christmas. And far from finding frail harbingers of spring down here – why, the snow only went three weeks ago. I'll be all right again by April. I suppose I do feel a bit blue,' Virginia admits, crossing her fingers under her bag against the half-lie she is about to utter, 'because my brother left for Rhodesia at the beginning of January. It'll probably be years before I see him again.'

'I saw his picture all over the dailies when he came back. Handsome beast, isn't he?'

'It runs in the family,' says Virginia comfortably. 'They made an awful fuss of him, didn't they? But the RAF wouldn't let him go back to flying missions. He'd been flying for three years non-stop and he was on his third tour of duty. Most pilots don't last a single one.'

'What's he going to do?'

'Oh, train colonials. I suppose he might come home before the end of the war, but goodness knows when *that* will be.'

'Do you think about it much? The end of the war?'

'Yes and no. Things have been like this for so long that it's hard to imagine them being normal again.'

'I suppose you'd never have had a job, would you? If it hadn't been for the war.'

'No,' says Virginia equably. 'I'd have been presented and married by now. Probably to someone in the City with a town house in Belgravia and a Georgian gem somewhere in Wiltshire.'

'Funnily enough, that's exactly what Alexis said,' says Trudy reminiscently. 'When you joined Reel Films we had bets on as to how long you'd last, you know. Alexis gave you three months. He said you were using the war as an excuse to sin a little but once you were married you'd revert to the way you were brought up.'

'What a bloody cheek.' Virginia is furious.

'Well, he must have changed his mind. It was him who got you this job, wasn't it? His recommendation at least. It was a shame you missed the party for his film. It was at Holly's parents' flat in Grosvenor Square. *Unbelievably* posh. And that's just their London *pied-à-terre*.'

'Holly's parents must have fifty times the loot that mine have, and no one suggests *she'll* never work again after the war.'

361

'That's because she comes from a working family. Her ma's a journalist, you know. But your lot don't work usually, do they? They do charitable works, don't they?' Trudy grins maliciously at Virginia, knowing she is riling her. But Virginia, who has by now rightly divined that much of the ribbing she gets from the other girls is motivated by envy, refuses to rise to the bait.

'No, of course we don't work, Trudy,' she says witheringly. 'When I marry I'll probably set up the East Suffolk branch of the Distressed Gundogs Association and give coffee mornings. Will that satisfy you? Tell me what's happening in the production office.'

'Oh, it's all been fairly quiet recently. No parties. Not since Holly and Alexis.'

'Was he pleased about the notices he got for his film?'

'Well, he must have been. Though now you come to mention it he didn't seem quite his normal cheery self at the party. He was drinking a lot, which isn't like him.'

'Have they fixed the day at long last?'

'Not officially, but I gather it's some time in September. Whoops, here's Deryck now with Pat. Skirts down over the knee, girls, and attention, please.'

After dinner (Brown Windsor soup, a white fish under an indeterminate sauce and two veg, rice pudding, and a jam composed almost entirely of pips) Virginia pleads the call of duty and returns to her room and her typewriter. The call-sheets will actually only take half an hour, but Virginia wants an early night. More to the point, she wants time to brood.

When it gradually became clear that Alexis was not going to phone either now or in the future, Virginia had passed from fury to resentment; then, trapped in the frozen waste of Cirencester, into a depression and gloom which she could hardly believe possible. Standing around, clipboard in hand, up to her wellington-tops in slurry, her unhappiness had passed unnoticed in the general despair. But it required a considerable amount of self-control to keep her mind even remotely on the job. Fortunately Deryck's conversation required very little response other than the occasional assent and reassurance.

As Virginia had tramped drearily through puddle-filled furrows it had been relatively simple at first to feel furious with Alexis and the choice he had made. Her *amour-propre* made it inconceivable that anybody could choose *anybody* in preference to herself. These feelings of rage and fury had fed her anger perfectly till the end of January. Then gradually depression had begun to work its insidious spell. The simple fact was that she missed Alexis. She couldn't believe it was possible to miss anyone as much as she missed him. And not just in bed, although that was certainly part of it. It was his company, his presence, the fact that he had no particular illusions about her; perhaps it all boiled down to the fact that he simply liked her very much. There was an immense difference, Virginia had sadly concluded to herself, in spending an evening or a night with someone, both of you nicely dressed and on your best behaviour, and actually wanting to spend all your time with someone, both the good and the bad moods. What she missed most was what she had never known before with anyone; the ordinary sloping round and being in someone's company, whether it was taking a Sunday walk along the Richmond towpath or wandering through the bombed-out wreck of the City. Not that their time together could really be described as ever being that ordinary; Alexis, after all, had a girlfriend elsewhere, and at any moment both of them expected to meet a boggle-eyed Millie or a knowing Trudy. But mysteriously no one had known anything of the affair. It had remained hermetically sealed between them.

As the depression had deepened, so Virginia's confidence in her own desirability had slowly begun to ebb. During the hectic round of the past three years there had been little opportunity for self-appraisal or introspection. Now when she had time to examine her own behaviour she found there was much that she could not approve of. In fact, by this time, cold, bored and thoroughly miserable, it gradually seemed not surprising at all that Alexis had preferred someone other than herself. Perhaps it all boiled down to the fact that Holly was clearly a much nicer, kinder person than herself. Certainly Virginia had not always been kind in the past, she brooded, automatically logging shots about the correct growing of potatoes. Why, there was poor Lucy with her marriage in tatters around her, and Virginia had done nothing but write a few very perfunctory letters.

Fortunately, before Virginia could actually decide to dedicate her life to prayer and enter an enclosed order, common sense did finally reassert itself and she contented herself with writing a series of particularly sympathetic letters which were very gratefully received by Lucy. But the insights gained about herself are not forgotten. And one unlooked-for result is her decision to end things with Tom Berkeley. It is not easy to do, but the affection in his letters suddenly makes her ashamed. He clearly believes they are moving inexorably towards marriage. A year ago, Virginia might have gone along with his assumptions. She did not love him but she could have been the wife he wanted. But now other vistas, the potentiality of a real relationship made her unable to accept that compromise. Perhaps she did Tom an injustice, perhaps he was more capable of a real involvement than she allowed. But the inescapable fact was that she did not love Tom; for that reason alone she owed it to him to be honest and end things with him.

The immediate sensation after writing to him was one of relief. But pain of losing Alexis does not abate. And will not as she now knows that his marriage will actually take place.

Savagely she yanks the sheet out of the typewriter and takes it back to the bar.

When Virginia returns to London in April it is to find she has a new and rather nicer room at the Grangemouth. Furthermore there is a letter from Brooke telling her that he has arrived in one piece and can't think why he didn't decide on life in the colonies years ago. Which does not seem to bode well for his speedy return.

So far as employment is concerned, presumably to temper the delights of Cirencester, Virginia finds she is to work in the main production office while

Millie goes to hospital with her adenoids. She is on tenterhooks lest she meet Alexis. Even the news that he is out of London, actually in south Wales doing a recce for a film about a mining community, does nothing to calm her anxieties. It is bad enough to have been rejected by a man but infinitely worse to have to face him with his fiancée in tow.

The production offices are remarkably the same, but the welcome from Mr Myerberg, Pat Blain and even Millie is surprisingly heart-warming.

'Bet you'll find it dull here, though,' Millie promises. 'There's no one in at present. You'll have a really quiet time.'

'After three months in a cowshed I can do with a quiet time,' Virginia assures her. She has taken care to turn up groomed to band-box smartness, cheered by the prospect of dinner with Willy at the Savoy. She is glad to be back in London. What does it matter about Alexis? She's got over that now. It's in the past.

Which is just as well, for at that precise moment Alexis walks in and stops dead at the sight of Virginia at her desk.

'Hello, Alexis,' says Millie in surprise. 'You're meant to be in Welsh Wales with Billy Gavin.'

'His wife's ill,' says Alexis briefly. 'I said we'd hang on till Wednesday to see if she got any better. Hello, Virginia,' he adds unsmilingly. 'How did you get on at Cirencester?'

'Fine, thank you,' Virginia says dismissively with her face as unwelcoming as his own.

'You're lucky Deryck let you go at all. He's asked for you for his next shoot. He says he can't do without you,' Millie informs her with malicious glee.

Virginia smiles wanly and takes in Ira Myerberg's tea and *petits fours*. When she returns to the outer office Millie is engaged in a furious phone conversation with one of the electricians and Alexis is sitting on the end of Pat Blain's desk apparently threading paper-clips together.

'Pat's down at the cutting-room if you want him.'

'I was waiting to speak to you,' says Alexis in a rapid undertone. 'Is there any chance of a drink at lunchtime?'

'Absolutely none whatsoever,' says Virginia with a venom that takes even her by surprise. For the first time she looks Alexis directly in the face. Alexis says nothing, picks up his raincoat and goes out without a word. The other phone starts ringing, and automatically Virginia goes to answer it. The working day has begun.

At a quarter to one there is commotion on the stairs outside as somebody puts their foot in the fire-bucket.

'That sounds like Billy Gavin,' says Millie, mystified. It *is* Billy Gavin, drunk, amorous and clearly delighted to see Virginia, who cannot resist smiling back at the sight of him, beery, perspiring and wearing a suit of quite extraordinary vulgarity.

'Well! Miss Loveliness herself back from the sticks and the frail embraces of the drooping Deryck.'

'Come off it, Billy, you know my heart is pledged to you. My relationship with Deryck will always be purely platonic.'

'With Deryck I fear it's always destined to be platonic, my chuck. Give me a kiss, Duchess; it's not been the same without your lovely face around the office.'

Millie sniffs.

'I thought your wife was ill.'

'*I* thought my wife was ill. My wife thought she was ill. It turns out to be just another visit by the stork.'

'Billy, that's wonderful. How many does it make?'

'Five that I know of. It's taken me a wee bit by surprise. It's all the fault of Hogmanay,' Billy confides, sitting heavily down on the corner of Virginia's desk. 'Anyway, it sparked the old plugs into action, I can tell you. Seven mouths to feed come September. Has young Seligman been by?'

'Been and gone.'

'I needed to talk to him . . . Did he say where he was going?'

''Fraid not.'

'Well, now.' Billy tips his flat cap back even further and scratches his balding pate. 'Maybe I'll catch up with him later. In the meantime I hope you'll join me in a drink to wet the baby's head. I did a wee bit of celebrating on my own on the way in this morning.'

'Billy, come off it. The baby's not due for months yet—' protests Millie.

'All the more reason to prepare a welcome. When are you going to hospital?'

'Tomorrow.'

'You'll need a drink or two to speed you on your way. No, no excuses.'

Half-amused, half-exasperated, Virginia finds herself swept down the stairs with a far from reluctant Millie towards the Intrepid Fox.

Almost the first people they see on entering are Pat Blain and Alexis, deep in conversation.

'Eh, Duchess, where are you off to? Come back this minute. You can't not celebrate with me. Now, what's it to be? Gin and gin?'

'Thank you,' says Virginia, seething. Millie has automatically bounced over to join Pat and Alexis: there is no option but to follow. Alexis hooks out the chair beside him with one of his long legs. Millie begins to pass on the morning's messages to Pat, while Virginia stares determinedly at the Watney sign and prays that Billy will speedily return. Alas for her hopes, Billy has met a chum from the Army Film Unit and completely forgotten the order.

Alexis says nothing. After five minutes of silence Virginia can stand it no longer, and turns round to glare at him. Immediately Alexis' long mobile mouth twitches into a grin, for he has succeeded in getting a response from her.

Virginia searches round for something rude, stinging – something even remotely unpleasant would do – and instead finds to her eternal shame that her eyes are suddenly full of tears and she knows she is going to break down and cry. Swallowing hard, she gets up and walks quickly out the door. As she makes her way through the crowded street her heel catches on a grating and she almost falls headlong on to the damp pavement. Someone grabs her and steadies her while she disentangles her heel. It is Alexis.

'Let go of my arm, please.'

'If I do, you'll fall flat on your face. Calm down.'

Her arm still rigidly in Alexis' fingers, they look at each other properly for the first time. Then Virginia hastily looks away as unbidden tears start to pour down her cheeks.

'Dear Virginia, what's wrong?'

'*Nothing* is wrong. *Nothing at all.* I've got a cold coming. Just leave me alone, please. I didn't want to see you again.'

'Well, you won't after today. Let me take you back to the office.'

'No, just go away and leave me alone.'

Virginia cannot believe that her own iron façade and carefully prepared defences against Alexis have so completely melted away.

'Look,' says Alexis angrily, pulling her closer to him. 'I just want to see that you're OK. All right? I'll see you back to the office, then leave you. You're in no fit state. Take my arm. Go on, Virginia, take my arm.'

Humiliated beyond words, Virginia mutely takes Alexis' arm and with eyes still blurred with tears allows herself to be led back to the production offices.

Both of them are mercifully empty. Alexis sits Virginia down at her desk and proffers a clean folded hankie.

'Go on, use it. I don't mind the eye make-up.'

With that Alexis puts the kettle on the electric ring and prepares to make her a cup of Millie's sacred tea. Virginia starts to protest, and Alexis, misunderstanding her, interrupts.

'I'm going when I've done this. You could do with something stronger.'

'I was going to say that's Millie's tea. She'll go mad.'

'Let her.'

There is a silence while Virginia wipes her eyes and avoids looking at Alexis. Alexis makes her tea in Mr Myerberg's special cup and puts it firmly down beside the typewriter.

'Look, sweetheart—'

'*Don't call me that,*' hisses Virginia, tears rolling down her face again. Alexis sighs and says apparently at random: 'I made a real cock-up of things, didn't I?'

'Yes,' Virginia tells him harshly. 'You did just that. And I'd like you to go now and stay away from me.'

Almost blinded by tears, Virginia gets up to leave the room, collides with Alexis and finds herself being pushed back hard against the wall, her hands trapped in his, pushed roughly up against her breast. Then, deliberately, Alexis pushes her hands apart and pins them against the wall either side of her head. For a long moment they look at one another. Afterwards Virginia cannot remember who moves first. Perhaps it is a single spontaneous movement. A magnetic force draws them together as they kiss.

Afterwards Alexis holds her so tightly against him he almost crushes her. Then he holds her away from him so he can look at her, his hands painfully gripping her shoulders.

'I didn't know you were going to be here. They told me you weren't going to be back for another week. I'll be away for months. I thought we wouldn't

have to meet. I'm so sorry. So sorry about everything. That was all I wanted
to say to you at lunchtime.'

'Are you really going away tomorrow?'

Alexis nods. Virginia takes one of his hands and, without meaning to,
presses it against her cheek, turning her lips to his palm. Alexis' fingers
tighten convulsively on hers.

'Are you free tonight – for dinner?'

'You're mad,' a voice says clearly in Virginia's head. 'Completely and
utterly mad.'

'Yes,' she says definitely, then more urgently 'Yes' as she hears footsteps
on the stairs outside. 'Yes, I'm free.'

CHAPTER
THIRTY

'*D*O I LOOK ALL RIGHT? *Really* all right?'

'You look absolutely wonderful, Vir. Truly. Is that the material Ferdinand gave you?'

'Yes, it's heaven, isn't it? It's silk georgette. He'd brought me enough for an evening dress, so there was plenty provided I didn't want a train. I do wish he could have been here today. He doesn't even know I'm getting married. *And* in the dress made from his material. Did you get your corsage? You look awfully nice, Lucy.'

'It's such a treat to get dressed up. Have you got everything? Gloves? Bouquet?'

'Yes. Uncle Piers is due in twenty minutes. How are you getting to the Church?'

'Oh, a nice man and his wife said they'd drive me there. They're down in the bar. Called Gavin.'

'Billy? Is his wife hugely pregnant?'

'That's right. They're Scots, aren't they? Are they friends of Alexis or yours?'

'Oh,' says Virginia with a reminiscent smile, 'I suppose you'd say they were mutual friends really. You do *like* Alexis, don't you?'

There is a note of unconscious appeal in Virginia's voice.

'Yes, of course I do, very much,' Lucy assures her. 'And they all liked him at the Dower House. Bertie told me so. Uncle Piers really spoke up for him.'

'Oh lord,' says Virginia, instantly dismayed. 'Did he feel he had to?'

'Oh, Vir, no. I just meant he obviously thought really well of him.'

'He put Alexis through the third degree when he went and asked him for my hand.'

'Did he *really* have to do that?'

'Uncle Piers insisted. In the absence of Brooke he told me he felt the role of male protector fell on him. Can you beat it? He took Alexis out to lunch at his club and positively grilled him about his prospects. Then he insisted on going back and inspecting the house in Chelsea. Thank God the "treasure" had actually been in that day. Uncle Piers did everything but inspect the drains. The funny thing is I thought Alexis would be livid but he didn't seem

368

to mind at all. He said he understood! Actually I think he was rather amused. But he's been an absolute duck, Uncle Piers – and Aunty Grace, too. They booked me into here overnight so I wouldn't have to be married from the Grange. I think Uncle Piers feels responsible because he was the one who brought me back to London.'

Virginia is aware that she is talking too much and that she has a hectic flush on her face. But what does it matter? Today is her wedding day. There will never be another day as happy as this.

'Anyway, you'll meet everybody at the reception. I'm dying for you to meet the girls from the Grange and the people from the production office. I was sorry your parents couldn't make it , but you'll be staying overnight, won't you?'

'Rather! Ma's suite at Claridges. I'm on my way up to see them tomorrow.'

'What's the farm going to do without you in your absence? What about the harvesting?' teases Virginia.

As usual Lucy takes the question literally.

'Well, fortunately we don't start harvesting for another four weeks; it'll be the first week of August, and that's assuming this weather holds. It's heavenly today, isn't it? I've put Dougal in charge of milking. A whole week off! I simply can't believe it. Lord, it's ten to eleven. Let me give you a good-luck kiss without disturbing your make-up. Dearest Vir, I long and long for you to be happy.'

'I know I will be,' answers Virginia humbly. 'Do you remember when we were younger we used to say we'd only ever marry someone we felt we'd really been lucky to get? Well, that's how I feel about Alexis. I hope,' she goes on practically, 'that he feels the same way about me.'

'He'd be mad if he didn't,' the loyal Lucy robustly assures her. 'I'll leave you alone for a minute to compose yourself.'

Virginia wanders over to the window to stare down at the Thames, which is at full tide, sparkling blue in the July sunshine. Overhead the barrage balloons are gilded the purest silver against a cloudless sky. Tentatively she checks her hair and examines her nails. She is completely ready, yet even now it is impossible to believe that she and Alexis are getting married. In just four months since her return from Cirencester, life has been turned upside down.

Not that things had seemed at all propitious on her return. It would be nice if reconciliations in real life even faintly resembled what went on on the silver screen. Far from melting into each other's arms over a candelit dinner that first night, Virginia and Alexis had been so busy shouting at each other that they had never even made it to the table. And after nearly three hours of verbal recrimination Alexis had driven her home to the Grangemouth and that had seemed to be that. It had been another two weeks before she saw him again. Alexis had been to Wales to set up his new film, and this time when they remet they were simply so pleased to see each other they fell into each other's arms and again never made the dinner reservation.

Much later that night, Virginia said: 'I didn't mean it. All those things I said in the car and at Christmas. I was just so angry with you.'

The house was the same. The room and the bed were exactly as she remembered them. It was as if she had never been away. They had looked at each other for a long time.

'I missed you terribly,' Alexis had said at last.

'I missed you all the time,' Virginia had said honestly. Then, gathering her courage, she had muttered: 'But it can't go on like this, Alexis. Not the way it did before. It's just not fair on—it's not fair on anyone.'

'I know that,' Alexis had soberly replied. 'It just seems that everything I decide is wrong. I had plenty of time to think while I was in Wales. The trouble is I love Holly.'

Virginia had lifted her head anxiously from Alexis' bare chest. 'But what about me?'

'I love you, too. I knew when we split up at Christmas that things weren't finished between us. But I felt I was treating Holly so badly. I'd been with her for so long and I do care deeply about her. But for these last few months—'

'What?'

'Things just haven't worked between us. Or perhaps I've changed. I just seem to want something different now. I don't know what, though.'

There was much much more that Virginia had longed to hear from Alexis, but the relationship was too fragile and too precious to take unnecessary risks with. For something as valuable as this, even she would learn patience.

The following weekend Alexis had ended things with Holly. It was a further fortnight before he contacted Virginia again. And it was clear that he was wretched about the unhappiness he was causing. They had met for a drink, but by mutual consent he had returned Virginia early to the Grangemouth. During the next three weeks Virginia was engaged in making food flashes for the Ministry of Food office in Croydon and had sunk to a new low of depression. Alexis did not contact her. By now she was sure he would not again. After all, Holly had been his friend for eight years and his girlfriend for three. What chance did she stand against a relationship of such depth and habit?

Then suddenly Alexis had rung her again and arranged to meet her. And mysteriously it was all all right. No, it was more than all right. It was ecstatic. It was like that first glorious period before Christmas when she had moved everywhere on wings. The only difference now was that the affair was out in the open; they could go anywhere and do anything.

Which had its drawbacks. The news of the affair was round the production offices in no time, and the atmosphere was thick with disapproval, Holly being so sweet, etc., etc. But Virginia found she simply didn't care. She wanted Alexis and she wanted him so badly that she was prepared to grow a hide like a rhino if that was what it took.

Then three weeks after her reunion she saw Holly in Regent Street. Fortunately Holly did not see her. Even Virginia was taken aback by the change in her. It wasn't that Holly looked physically any different. She looked destroyed from within, as if the certainties and securities that had fed her optimistic nature had dried up for ever at the source. Seeing her, Virginia had had a sudden terrifying premonition of how she would look if she ever lost Alexis. In Holly's face she saw real heartbroken unhappiness. Virginia, who had tasted that unhappiness, was chastened by her despair. At that moment she would have done anything to give Holly back her old certainty.

Anything, that was, except give her back Alexis.

Devora, pea-green with envy, questioned her endlessly as to why she was so completely in love. Virginia evaded her gracefully. How could you convey to anybody the simple relief – there was no other word for it – of having someone who knew you through and through who was not taken in by your looks, who knew you at your very worst and who still loved you? What she experienced with Alexis was the relief of recognition and through that recognition the possibility of being saved. He gave her the courage to be able to say she loved him – something that she thought she would never feel, let alone say, for anyone. She had really doubted her own ability to love. But Cecily had given her her first intimation of loving and being loved; and now, it seemed, she was being given a second chance. And this time, she thought staring down at the Thames, she knew the value of what she was being given and intended to appreciate it and cherish it from the very beginning.

'We must be nearly there by now,' says Uncle Piers anxiously as they turn off the King's Road. 'Otherwise we're going to be late.'

Turning, his morning suit creaking ominously, he pats Virginia on the hand.

'Everything all right with you? No butterflies? No regrets?'

'None at all,' Virginia smilingly assures him.

'Powerful smell from that bouquet of yours. What are they?'

'Gardenias. An American friend ordered them for me.'

Uncle Piers surveys his niece with something like tears in his eyes.

'I don't think I've ever seen a prettier bride.' Embarrassed, he runs a finger round his collar trying to ease its unfamiliar stiffness. 'I'm just sorry Cecily isn't here today. She was very fond of you, you know, Virginia.'

'I was very fond of her,' says Virginia soberly. 'She's been on my mind a lot these past few weeks. Her mother and father sent me these as a wedding present.' Virginia touches the heavy triple choker of pearls at her throat with its oval sapphire clasp. 'They said it would have been Cecily's on her marriage and they felt sure she'd have liked me to have it. I was so touched. Oh, here we are.'

The kerb is full of press photographers. There is an audible gasp of admiration as Virginia steps down from the car. Inside the church is full to capacity and every pew contains familiar faces. But Virginia is oblivious. At the top of the aisle she can see Alexis, very tall and upright in his new suit. As if sensing her presence, ignoring all convention, he turns round to greet her, and she knows it is with a positive effort that he prevents himself from stretching out his hand to her. As she joins him at the altar they look at one another and smile. This is it. This is the moment. It is going to be all right.

*   *   *

371

'Are you sure you're reading the map properly?'

'How on earth can I read a map when it's pitch dark outside and there are no road signs?' demands Virginia with some asperity.

'Oh God.' Alexis slams on the brakes of the van. 'Let me have a look and you can drive for a bit.'

'Only yesterday,' Virginia reminds him as she puts the van into gear, 'you promised to love and cherish me, remember?'

'I will,' says Alexis grimly, 'just as soon as we get to this bloody village. Now, try down there.'

Windscreen-wipers jerking convulsively, they inch their way down a steep valley road, and even their dimmed-out headlights are sufficient to reveal rain falling like stair-rods.

'How can it rain like this in mid-summer?' demands Alexis of no one in particular. 'I just hope to God Billy and the others have gone on ahead. It was that mist at Chepstow that did it. Look, there's a cottage or something over there. I'll ask them the way.'

He pulls open the door and disappears into the driving rain. Virginia turns off the engine, lights a cigarette, and for the thousandth time inspects her wedding ring. Then the door is wrenched open again and Alexis falls in, soaked.

'They say the village is about four miles further down the hill and that another van went past about twenty minutes ago. Let's hope to God it's them.'

Now that they are legally married Pat Blain has consented to let Virginia do continuity for Alexis. It is not the honeymoon that Virginia would have chosen, but then, these are not normal times.

'I can see lights further down the road,' says Alexis suddenly. 'With any luck it's the other van.'

Virginia pulls the van over on to the grass verge and turns off the engine. Miraculously the rain seems to have stopped and equally suddenly is replaced by a swirling grey mist. Pulling open the van door, she jumps down and stretches her legs thankfully, then shrieks. The mist is clammy, wet and all-engulfing.

'Alexis, don't leave me for God's sake. I can't see a hand in front of me.'

'Come here, daft. Give me your arm. Oh, thank God, it is them. What the hell—'

Virginia screams and clutches her husband. With a clattering of many hoofs a flock of sheep suddenly run down the lane towards them and begin to mill round the van in an interested sort of way.

'Oh, go away,' beseeches Virginia, pushing and shoving. 'It's like being surrounded by a vast wet pullover.'

A voice hails them from further down the road.

'Hello there! Is it the newlyweds? I'm afraid we're in a ditch.'

'I don't believe it,' says Alexis grimly as he pushes open the van door, helps Virginia inside and climbs into the bucket seat beside Billy Gavin.

'Enjoying your honeymoon?' Billy enquires politely. 'There's no room in this van, I'm afraid. The front wheel's in a ditch. I must have nodded off for a wee while. The little lad's asleep in the back there.'

372

'Bloody hellfire,' says Alexis, whose language has been deteriorating steadily as they have driven further west. 'You'd better wake him up and we'll come back and get this van tomorrow.'

'Sharpen up your wits, Alexis. My camera's in here, and I don't move without it. And there's no room in your van for a kitten. We'd best all stay here until the mist lifts. Then you can try to push me out. Here,' he says, reaching into his armpit and pulling out a bottle of Scotch, 'the real thing. I was saving it up to toast you later tonight, but I reckon this will have to do. I bet you never thought you'd be spending your honeymoon with three men, did you, darling?'

'After the war I promise I'll take you to France for a proper honeymoon,' Alexis assures her as he passes her the whisky-bottle. 'Cheers, darling. No regrets, eh?'

'None,' she assures him firmly and thinks it worth recording that in spite of the fact she is cold, wet, tired and hungry, that she is spending her next-to-bridal night in a van with three men, that she will undoubtedly have a hangover tomorrow, that she will have to work non-stop throughout her honeymoon – in spite of all this she can truly say that she has never been happier in her life.

CHAPTER
THIRTY-ONE

'ANOTHER sherry, Lucy?'

'Gosh. No, thanks, Daddy. I haven't finished this one yet.'

'Do you know, I think I'll just put one out for your mother. I expect she'll want a little drink when she comes in. She was disappointed not to be at the station to meet you, Lucy. She's been talking about you coming all week. It's just that today is the anniversary of one of the Yorkshire headquarters of the "Leafy Tree" Club and she really felt she ought to make a personal appearance. She really is selfless when it comes to her fans, you know, Lucy. She spares no effort to show them how much she appreciates their devotion.'

And the fact that they still buy her books, thinks Lucy, amused.

'It's partly due to her publisher.'

'Eric Buchanan?'

'That's the fellow. Since she signed with him he's taken a tremendous interest in her career, and it's certainly been reflected in her sales. You know, he's actually succeeded in getting her to sever her connections with all other publishers? I was a bit doubtful at first, but there's no question, she's got a much better deal with Buchanans, and of course they treat her like royalty. My word, when Eve visits the editorial offices it's like the Queen paying a call.' Mr Hallett chortles, enthusiastically slapping his knee. 'She tells me all about it, you know. Now that I don't travel so much. I just stay at home and keep an eye on her press cuttings. I've saved you up some frightfully interesting articles from a South African newspaper analysing the appeal of your mother's work. I know they'll interest you. I say, why don't I get them out right now? It would please Mother no end to come in and find you reading them.'

Lucy, reeling from the exhaustion of a fifteen-hour overnight train-journey, protests weakly.

'Daddy, I'd love to look at them tomorrow. Why don't you get Miss Taylor to leave them out for me, and I can sit in the garden with them.'

Mr Hallett is visibly impressed by this idea. 'That's a good wheeze,' he says thoughtfully. 'And at the same time I'll sort you out a couple of the new titles you won't have seen in the shops yet. By Jove! You really *are* in luck! I've just remembered. I'm sure we've still got a proof of *A Chum in Peril*. It only arrived last week, and I think Eve finished correcting it this morning, so you can have a quick squint before it's even popped back to the publishers. You'll be the envy of everybody you meet!'

Only if they're under twelve, thinks Lucy, resigned. Out loud she asks: 'Have things worked out all right with Miss Taylor?'

'Hermione? She's been a godsend. An absolute godsend. I don't know what your mother would have done without her. She can sit with Mother for up to five hours at a stretch, quiet as a mouse, taking down shorthand. I had a go myself trying to help your mother when we first came up here.' Mr Hallett shifts in his chair. The memory is clearly still painful. 'But, as you know, your mother's got a very particular way of working.' Mr Hallett gives a short uncomfortable bark of laughter. 'We decided in the end that I disturbed her concentration. So Hermione really is a blessing.'

'She hasn't been called up, then?' asks Lucy innocently.

'TB hip,' says her father briefly. 'All over now, of course, but incapacitating. Didn't stop her getting into Oxford, though. Plucky girl.'

Lucy wonders how she can dislike so much somebody she hasn't even met.

'Are you warm enough, old girl? I like to have a fire lit for your mother when she comes in – makes it more of a welcome, I always think.'

'I'm fine, Daddy,' says Lucy, who is perspiring freely and wondering if she can furtively open one of the library windows without her father noticing. Though Harrogate is not enjoying the heat of London, it is a warm July evening and the library is like a furnace.

'Virginia looked all right, did she?'

'She looked a dream. And so happy! It was a lovely reception, at the Savoy and full of the oddest people. Mrs Musgrave looked frightfully nice in ice blue. She sent you both her love and said—'

'That's it! I thought I heard it! It's the car!' Mr Hallett springs into life and hurls another hefty log on the fire.

'No, don't worry, Lucy. Gregg will answer the door. And here she is now. Eve, my dear, what kind of day—?'

Mrs Hallett whirls into the library, her high heels clicking loudly on the stone tiles. She is wearing a very pretty lilac costume with matching jabot and hat. In spite of her heels she has to stand on tiptoe to kiss her daughter.

'Lucy dear! How *well* you look!' Then with a complete change of tone: 'George! For goodness' sake open the windows. This place is like a Turkish bath. I've told you before about getting overheated. And after I've just had an hour in a closed car! Really, George, you might have thought'

'I'm sorry, old girl. I just thought . . . . Well, sit down anyway and join us in a sherry. Dinner's ready and—'

'I know dinner's ready. Gregg told me. And sherry's the last thing I want. I'm awash with sherry. In fact I won't bother about a drink at all. I've been thinking about that proof, and I think I need to ring Buchanan's tonight.'

'But the office will be closed now—'

'Oh, I've got Eric's home number. I don't deal with secretaries. You make yourself comfortable, Lucy, and I'll join you for dinner. No, of course I don't need you to come up with me, George. I can make a phone call on my own.'

With a crash the library door closes firmly behind her.

375

'Daddy, I think I might go and unpack and freshen up,' says Lucy, stunned, and anxious to avoid the hurt look in her father's eyes. 'Mother's clearly had one hell of a day. You know the pressures on her. I'm sure she'll be more herself when she's had a chance to unwind.'

Her father is visibly brightening by the end of this string of platitudes.

'You're absolutely right. I'm not sure anybody really realizes the strain that a top-level author like your mother lives under all the time. Not only has she got to produce a constant flood of the highest quality, but there's also a public persona that has to be maintained for her fans—'

Lucy intervenes firmly: 'You're absolutely right, Daddy. Let's give Mother a few minutes to herself, then we can hear about her day at dinner.'

'Good. Good,' says her father rapidly. 'Excellent scheme. You go and get changed.'

The atmosphere at dinner is visibly more relaxed. Mrs Hallett, by now several gins to the better, has changed into something less formal and is looking rather more herself. The food is excellent, and conversation about Virginia's wedding is enough to keep them going until they adjourn to the drawing-room.

'Well, I hope they'll be happy,' says Mrs Hallett, stirring her coffee. 'Virginia was always such a sulky child – one hardly knew what she wanted. Does Mrs Musgrave like her new son-in-law?'

'I think so. She's rather in awe of him. But Beattie Blythe told me – I must stop calling her that – Beattie Hammond told me she always describes him as 'a brilliant young director' in the village post office, so I suppose she must be adjusted to it.'

'Shame Brooke couldn't be there to give her away.'

'It was, rather, wasn't it? But apparently he adores it over there.'

'Hear regularly from Hugh, do you?'

'He's fine,' says Lucy evasively, adding quickly: 'Goodness, doesn't my wedding seem a long time ago now?'

'You were unlucky there.'

'What do you mean?' says Lucy quickly.

'Him going abroad so quickly. We had such a nice card from him at Christmas.'

'*Did* you?' Lucy is so frankly astonished that her parents stare at her in surprise. She colours and says rather feebly: 'The post was absolutely terrible. I'm quite surprised a card got through.'

'He seemed full of the joys.'

'Really,' says Lucy.

'Have you seen any of Alexis' films?'

'Yes, I saw one in Ipswich about lifeboat men. It was frightfully thrilling.'

'I long and long to know what that Canadian director has made of the "Leafy Tree" films,' broods Mrs Hallett. 'Thank goodness for evacuees – at least they'll have got the English accents right. They've released the films in Canada and they've done frightfully well. Remind me to tell Hermione to get you out the reviews, Lucy. Even asked Eric if he could pull strings and have a couple of copies of the films sent over here. I know they'd do wonders for morale. But the authorities have been *so* unhelpful. It'll be something to look forward to after the war, won't it?'

'Goodness, yes,' agrees Lucy.

In the context of the following week that conversation is to have a peculiar significance, for it is the last time Lucy will be asked a single question about herself. She observes this without any particular rancour: Lucy's view of her place in the universe is a modest one. At the same time she is their only child, and it is some years since she has spent any length of time with them. Not that Lucy has any illusions about the intrinsic interest of farming: she finds it absolutely fascinating and, away for only a few days, wonders endlessly what is going on at Home Farm. At the same time she is well aware that the milk quota, the visit of the ratcatcher with his spoons and sinister tins, the problems that will shortly befall the baler will not enthrall others as they enthrall her. But her week's holiday makes her aware for the first time how much farming has become the filter through which she sees the external world: it is impossible even in Harrogate not to get up each morning to search the skies for signs of changes in the weather, impossible even to stay in bed much past half-past six. And the noise of the town! broods Lucy. How do people stand it? Not to mention the hardness of the pavements, the constant pressure of other bodies, the voices that go on and on, the teashops and restaurants where not a single window emits a breath of fresh air. Not that the countryside is really quiet, she reflects, staring at the attractive jumble of Georgian rooftops that house the Halletts' neighbours. On Home Farm at all times there is the incessant bleating of the sheep, the monotonous bellowing of the bull, the barking, screaming and hooting that all the year round issues nightly from Heath Wood. And that's long before you've added the human element, the noise of the tractor, the thunderous rumble of the thresher and the incessant chatter of Dougal and Donny. Perhaps being outside you simply notice it less, concludes Lucy going out into the garden.

This ought to have been a pleasant enough experience were it not for the row of articles, neatly tabulated and weighed down with stones, waiting to be read on the garden table, prepared by the indefatigable Hermione.

The thought of doing nothing for a week had seemed indescribably attractive. But imperceptibly with the third day Lucy feels depression beginning to seep through her. It is not that the Hallett household revolves entirely around the affairs of Eve Hallett. This is nothing new. What is new is that Lucy, away so long, has begun to view it with a more critical eye. Is it *really* necessary to have a display of her mother's current titles in every one of the downstairs rooms? Must there always be a room in every one of the Halletts' households dedicated to nothing but Eve's titles, published in almost every language in the world? Do all citations for medals and awards actually have to be framed and on display, even in the downstairs lavatory? And those photographs of Mother and Father taken with everyone from Mrs Simpson to the little princesses – shouldn't they be in her mother's study or, even better still, in her bedroom? Is it really necessary for a world-famous author, as Mrs Hallett occasionally refers to herself, to be still mounting all her reviews in cuttings-books (five shelves of them now) and still underlining the best bits in red ink for her long-suffering daughter to read?

Fair dos, Lucy's sense of justice firmly tries to tell her from time to time. If it gives Mother pleasure, I really shouldn't complain. But none the less her sense of unease continues. It is as if Mother's ego, so long barely contained, has now burst out from all its restraining bands. What Mother wants she must have, instantly. Simply because she is so talented and so celebrated. And what Mother no longer wants frankly irritates her.

It is thus with real pain and growing anger that Lucy observes how her mother treats her father. From being the prop, the support, the confidant, the business adviser, Mr Hallett has somehow been relegated to the role of old retainer – sometimes even the elderly relative. There is only ten years' difference between them, but Mrs Hallett, charged with a sense of her own importance and lubricated by the steady drip of flattery from her publisher, her public and now the odious Hermione, seems years younger. From being a couple who were always happiest in each other's company, they have become two strangers eyeing each other uneasily, one desperate to hang on, the other frankly irritated by everything the other says or does.

Even Lucy, prepared by letter against her father's declining health, had been shocked at the sight of him. He looked decades older than his sixty-odd years, and the mobility and spring seemed to have left his step for ever. But the change is deeper than that. It is painful beyond belief to hear Mr Hallett constantly steering the conversation back to Mother and her achievements, secure in the knowledge that this has always been the way to keep their relationship alive and vigorous. But what Daddy hasn't understood, observes Lucy wretchedly, is that that was the old dispensation. There are other people who flatter Mother better now.

Fearing lest her father be left completely out of things, Lucy feels obliged to talk to him as much as possible. But, whatever the starting-point of the conversation, the progress of it is like a nightmare fairy-story from *Grimm's*. Whichever way you tried to go, all paths seemed to lead back to the witch's cottage, that is, Eve Baldwin's books. At the end of three days Lucy finally makes a stand and actually declines to read a file of graphs prepared by the conscientious Hermione, showing her mother's sales figures from 1931 to 1943. If nobody minds, Lucy says firmly, she'd rather read a detective story.

'I tell you what, why don't you and Hermione take an afternoon off and go round the bookshops, and you can have tea afterwards in the Kardomah. I wouldn't mind knowing what stocks they have anyway. And Hermione can ring London if they seem particularly low. . . .'

'Honestly, Mother, I don't think I should risk taking Hermione away from you for so long,' says Lucy with the nearest thing to sarcasm in her nature. 'If your new book's flowing, you really oughtn't to stop. I'll take Daddy with me instead.'

'Splendid girl, Hermione,' says Mr Hallett as they climb into the Daimler.

'Um,' says Lucy, turning on the engine and driving away from the house with a sense of relief. The worst thing that could be said of Hermione, in Lucy's opinion, is that she's exactly like someone out of Mother's books. At twenty-five Hermione is still sporting khaki aertex short-sleeved shirts and divided serge skirts like a gym mistress. She has calf muscles like fists and thick ankles which flush scarlet above her ankle-socks in cold weather. A shapeless yet beefy figure is barely contained in a badly fitting brassière. Her hair, light brown and curly, is cut ruthlessly short to the head, her round gold-rimmed glasses glittering coldly on her unmade-up face. A long-time member of the 'Leafy Tree' club, she regards her work as secretary to Mrs Hallett as something not far short of a vestal tending the votive fire. Good luck to her, thinks Lucy sourly, accelerating out of the gate wondering if it's Hermione's deafening BO or the fact that she has so successfully driven a wedge between her parents which makes her dislike her so much. Not only is Hermione her mother's real confidante now, it is Hermione who constantly urges Mother to go to London to keep in touch with her publishers. Thus to Lucy's secret dismay at the end of her week's holiday she finds herself travelling down to London with her mother, who has decided that the post is too unreliable to be trusted with the only proof of *A Chum in Peril*. Admittedly it means that Lucy can travel first class, but as Hermione has reserved a whole compartment for them it means a fairly lengthy conversation with Mother, undoubtedly about some aspect of her work.

As it turns out, the conversation is by no means what either of them expects. Ten minutes after 7 a.m. London Express pulls out of Harrogate station, Mrs Hallett begins to cross-question Lucy as to how she thinks her father is looking. Barely has Lucy ventured a couple of cautious opinions before Mrs Hallett takes hold of the conversation and in the most caring way imaginable launches into a long string of complaints about the problems of being married to an elderly man. So far as Lucy can judge, the complaints relate almost entirely to the fact that he is actually alive at all. Her mother has just advanced a tentative opening statement – with a quick sidelong glance at Lucy – as to the difficulties of people not developing at the same rate when before Lucy can explode into loyal fury two stout Yorkshiremen blunder into their carriage and take possession of two of the vacant seats. In vain does Mrs Hallett expostulate, point to the 'reserved' signs and cite her international reputation as a writer. 'I have reserved the whole compartment,' she tells them furiously.

'Then, you ought to be ashamed of yourself,' she is roundly told. 'Don't you know there's a war on and people standing ten deep in the corridor down the way?'

Puce-faced with indignation, Mrs Hallett lapses into a silent fury. Unperturbed, the two men start a loud confident conversation about wool prices which in any case is far more to Lucy's liking. It is a fitting end to Lucy's holiday.

Once in London, Lucy and her mother exchange relieved goodbyes. Mrs Hallett's temper is apparently fully restored by the sight of a tall handsome middle-aged man in a vicuña coat waiting for her beyond the barrier.

'This is Eric. How nice of you to come and meet me.'

'Can I get Lucy a taxi? I've got a car for you, Eve.'

'That really would be awfully decent of you. I'm going straight to Liverpool Street; there should be a train for Ipswich in about an hour. Goodbye, Mother. I hope you have a successful trip. Give my love to Father and say I'll write soon.'

With a sense of laying down a great load Lucy clambers into the train and manages to doze the entire journey back.

At Ipswich the platform is thronged with people waiting to take the same train back to London. Lucy fights her way out, hanging on to her case with one hand and her hat with the other. Once through the barrier and out into the mid-afternoon sunshine of the station yard, she sees a dark-haired girl wearing a straw hat and a white dress printed with cornflowers and poppies. The girl halts, irresolute, and Lucy, catching up with her exclaims: 'Beattie! I thought it was you!'

Beattie's face lights up with pleasure.

'How extraordinary seeing *you*! Mrs McFee told me you were going on holiday – did you have a lovely time?'

'Well, crowded with incident,' says Lucy, falling into step with her. 'I went up originally for Virginia's wedding, then I went on to see my parents in Harrogate. I've travelled down first thing this morning. Gosh, it's good to be back.'

'Have you got a lift to Musgrave?'

'No, I was hoping to get a bus. What about you?'

'There's a WVS car going back to the memorial at half-past four, and there's plenty of room.'

'Oh, what heaven,' says Lucy in heartfelt tones. 'I was resigned to hanging round for the six o'clock bus. And I'm absolutely dying for a cup of tea, aren't you? Oh lor! I said I'd ring Dad when I arrived just to let him know I was safe. Do you mind holding on a second? If I've got enough change, I'll do it straight away from the booking-hall. Then I can loll about at the tea-table with a free conscience.'

Beattie sits down to wait on one of the green-painted seats in the station forecourt. But after a minute or two she has to get up, restlessly, ostensibly to study a poster on the wall about holidays in Cleethorpes. Half a minute later she is back on the seat staring at her feet. It is impossible to be comfortable. Or, rather, as Beattie acknowledges privately with some dismay, right now it is impossible for her to be comfortable with herself.

Louie's visit, so long awaited, seemed at first to be set fair to be the high spot of the summer. Annie who is now toddling and babbling words, had any number of amusing tricks to display to their latest guest. Louie had been her usual larky self, delighted to have seen Ken, delighted to see Beattie, a favourite visitor with everyone in the Blythe household. And there'd been so many people around and so much to do and say that they'd hardly had time for a private conversation on their own for the whole week. It had finally been only yesterday, the day before Louie was due to leave, that they'd had the house and garden to themselves. At last there was an opportunity for a gossip about the topics of most interest to themselves, the chief of which had been a letter from Barbra 'Ann, received that very morning, containing details of her marriage the previous Saturday. Barbra 'Ann has married a man called Bernard, who is in his thirties and has a moustache like Clark Gable's. Apparently he is the son of two of her parents' best friends. Bernard's family are in the clothing trade, and he himself has mysteriously evaded call-up, presumably on the grounds of undertaking essential war work bringing utility fashions to the women of the north-east. Five pages written, both sides, are barely enough to do justice to the splendour of Barbra 'Ann's marriage, according to the bride. After the service, two hundred guests had sat down to a ham and salad lunch in a marquee in her parents' garden. Barbra 'Ann had enclosed a newspaper cutting, not of herself and her husband, but of herself arriving with her father at the church. The most interesting fact to emerge from this had been that Barbra 'Ann's father was at least six inches shorter than his strapping youngest child but, not withstanding that, there had been no doubting his pride and pleasure at handing his glamorous daughter out of the Daimler. And as for Barbra 'Ann's wedding – well, as Mrs Blythe had remarked, scrutinizing the cutting with her spectacles on her nose, it would have caused a sensation in peacetime. As it is, Barbra 'Ann's tiara and wedding gown (twenty-five yards of cream slipper satin with train), not to mention the three dozen pink roses liberally interspersed with tulle, must have stopped the traffic.

'But she does look lovely,' Louie had nobly acknowledged, the struggle not to be envious almost visible in her face. It would be a while yet before Louie and Ken could afford to marry, and even when they did Louie would not be wearing cream slipper satin with a tiara.

'Yes, doesn't she?' Beattie had agreed firmly, determined to be as generous herself. 'And she said they had a grand honeymoon even if it was only a couple of days. They went down to London for the weekend and stayed at the Ritz and saw *Gone with the Wind and* went to a nightclub. And it's jolly decent of her to send us this great hunk of wedding cake. Look at it! There must be four slices here at least, and it's got proper eggs and butter in it; I can smell them. I tell you what, let's have it now with our afternoon tea. I'll propose the toast. I'm glad that things – I'm glad that things came right for her.'

'Well, here's to her, then,' Louie had laconically acknowledged, raising her cup. 'Here's to Barbra 'Ann. A happy marriage. Lots of children. But what about you, young Beattie? There's not been a moment to ask you properly about your marriage. Are things showing any sign of coming right for you?'

Louie's words had suddenly taken the pleasure out of the sunny garden. And even Barbra 'Ann's cake, after two mouthfuls, had suddenly seemed too rich. Her marriage had been the last thing that Beattie had wanted to talk about, yet once she had started, to her consternation and dismay, she couldn't stop the furious, shrill, angry tirade of bile that had tumbled from her lips. She was so angry with Charles she could hardly speak. He had told her he had wanted a divorce, then disappeared without a trace and left it all to her. She and Annie could have been dead ten times over from a bomb and Charles would apparently have neither known nor cared. What did he think she had told her parents and the boys as to why there were suddenly no more letters for her? Hadn't he given any thought as to the terrible spot he'd left her in? He hadn't given her any thought at all. If he had, he wouldn't have left her in this terrible predicament. She was neither properly married nor free to accept the invitations she was offered from other men. As far as she was concerned, her marriage had been a washout and she'd gained no benefit from it at all—

'Oh, you've stopped drawing his money, then, have you?' Louie had enquired in so mild and innocent a tone that Beattie had totally missed the set of her friend's shoulders and the ominous darkening of her brow.

'Of course not. Why on earth should I? It was his idea, his whole idea from the very beginning,' Beattie had gone on, vexed and full of self-pity. 'I just wish to goodness I'd had the sense to say no to him when he proposed the whole potty scheme. I'd have been far better off unmarried and taking my chances with Annie—'

'Beattie Blythe, shut up, shut up, I can't bear to hear you going on like this any more.' Louie had actually pushed herself back on her heels, her whole frame rigid with indignation. 'I've read your letters week after week complaining complaining complaining – there are times, Beattie, when I don't think you know you're alive. Better off on your own! Taking your chances with Annie! What book did that come out of? *Tess of the d'Urbervilles*? Are you bloody mad or something? Have you forgotten that two years ago to this very month of August you were sitting round the house petrified to the core because you were pregnant and alone and didn't even dare tell your parents?'

'No, I haven't forgotten,' Beattie had shouted, cut to the quick by Louie's criticism. 'I just regret the foolishness of making short-term decisions out of sheer fright when I could have coped on my own and been a free woman now—'

'Beattie, there are times when I could shake you. You're living in Cloud-cuckoo-land.' Beattie had never seen Louie so angry. 'Have you ever known anyone who's got in the family way with no man to stand by her?'

'There was a girl in the next village—'

'I mean really known someone. Because I did – and do. I never said all this to you when you were in trouble because I thought it would only make things worse. What on earth are you talking about, thinking you could just have had the baby and got on with your own life? Have some *sense*. Unless you'd had Annie adopted, you'd have had no life to get on with. You'd never ever have got a job teaching as an unmarried mother. In fact I can't think what job you could have got anywhere with an illegitimate child in tow. Do you think you could pass yourself off as a widow? You couldn't even have supported yourself. And it's quite clear you wouldn't have been welcome at home with a baby and no marriage lines.'

'I could have gone into a home – there are homes where you can have your baby and they find you a job afterwards—'

Louie had rolled her eyes and raked her curls in exasperation.

'I know all about homes. And I'll bet you've never been within a hundred yards of one. There were two girls in my form who got caught, and I was friendly with one of them – Kay. She went to our church. She was sixteen when she found she was pregnant, and her parents took on just like yours. So Kay had to leave them and go and live in a home when she was five months gone so that the neighbours wouldn't know she was having a baby. I went to see her just before the baby was born. It was awful, terrible.'

Louie's face had been full of anguish at the memory.

'You just don't know what things like that are like, Beattie. It was like a house of correction. The girls were treated like convicts, as if they had to be punished for being pregnant. Just in case they'd had a bit of pleasure at the making of the baby and they had to be punished for it. Kay hardly spoke to me. The girls all hated each other and they had to have their meals in silence. And they had to work at the home to earn their keep right up to when they had the baby. Kay had been cleaning out the warden's room the day I saw her, and she was so exhausted she fell asleep while she was talking to me. They took the baby away from her when it was ten days old. It was a little boy. She wasn't allowed to know any details of where it had gone or what the new parents were like.'

Unconsciously Beattie's glance had gone to where Annie was sleeping contentedly in her pushchair under the apple tree, her sun-bonnet tipped rakishly over her rosy contented face.

'And that was a home with a good reputation – one of the better ones in Liverpool, or so I was told. It was awful. I don't think Kay's ever got over it. Afterwards she went to live with an aunt in Bootle. That happened the year before I went to Hillsleigh. I hadn't seen Kay since, then last week I ran into an old schoolfriend who told me Kay was home visiting her parents. I went round to see her.'

'Did she say how she feels about the adoption? Now, I mean.'

'Oh, she's convinced herself it was all for the best. Well, she'd have to say that, wouldn't she? And who's to say she isn't right? Except that I asked her if it had been difficult at first, and she started to say "no", then she said quite casually that she'd dreamt about the baby every night for the first two years. Always the same dream. That she'd put him down somewhere and she couldn't find him. Presumably in the end the dreams had stopped. You people living out here in the country, you think people are more tolerant in big cities, especially when everything's different as it is now because of the war. But it's no different in towns. It's little communities, little groups, the people you know in your street and at church. I don't see things are much different now where unmarried mothers are concerned. It still seems a crime to have a baby without a father – as if the women had somehow managed to do it all on their own. You'd never know men were involved, would you? But you. . . .' Louie's tone is sharp again. 'You. You were lucky. Yes, you were, Beattie, but you're too blind with self pity to see it. And how you have the *gall* to complain about him not showing an interest in you and Annie when you snapped off his head if he as much as asked you the time of day I do not know. And if that's your mother in the kitchen I'll tell her to come out and join us.'

With that, Louie, two spots of red still burning in her cheeks, had stomped off indoors leaving Beattie on the verge of spontaneous combustion through sheer fury. That Louie, Louie of all people, loyal Louie, should turn on her like everybody else and accuse her of self-pity and unfairness to Charles – why, how could she! When it must be clear to the whole world that Beattie is a woman greatly wronged. Perhaps fortunately, they had been joined in the garden in a matter of minutes by Mrs Blythe, the boys, Lily and Mrs Leary from the post office who dropped in to borrow a knitting pattern. Thus further contentious conversation had been avoided.

In the evening they'd gone for a drink with Lily and Greg, and on her way to bed Louie had kissed her goodnight with all her usual friendliness. But she hadn't offered to apologize for saying all those terrible untrue and hurtful things. Beattie had gone to bed simmering with a sense of injustice. But, try as she might to keep the fires of her indignation burning bright, as the church clock sounded the small hours Beattie had found herself invaded by a new and extremely unwelcome sensation, a slowly seeping sense of guilt.

They had not referred to the conversation again, and to all intents and purposes have parted only fifteen minutes before as good friends as ever. In a sense it isn't necessary to 'make things up' – Beattie knows Louie well enough to know that it is concern for Beattie that has prompted that unwelcome burst of truth-telling: even in the depths of her discomforture she is able to acknowledge that it must have taken Louie some courage to dare to speak out to Beattie in her present disgruntled state.

But Louie couldn't know what a residue of churned-up feelings she was leaving behind as the train had slid off back to London. As Beattie sits, staring vacantly at two sparrows tussling over a dead beetle, to her own consternation she finds herself reviewing her actions over the past two years – in relation to Charles at least – in a rather unwelcome light. For, however Beattie tries to deny it, she knows Charles has behaved well – no, better than 'well' – with generosity, with imagination, with true kindness. And he has not done it to trap her, to manipulate her. He has done it because he has accurately fore-seen the pain and trouble she would face and has tried to spare her some of it. It had been an act of imaginative generosity that few men would have had the courage to make. Perhaps it could be said he had done it as a gesture of acknowledgement and understanding to his own mother. But none the less it was with Beattie that he wanted to share his life. He was not a man in love with an idea, or his own past – she knew from his glance that he admired her, was deeply attracted to her and wanted to know her intimately in every sense; longed, in his diffident way, for her to care about him, craved the strength and security of a loving relationship, yearned for her to demonstrate to him just a fraction of the blind love that she had lavished on Brooke. Brooke. He could never have conceived of an act that put someone else's needs above his own: with a kind of awe Beattie saw clearly for the first time that Charles had done just that: and for her. She felt ashamed.

'Beattie, I'm so *sorry*.' Lucy's voice breaks noisily into her ruminations. 'You'll never believe it, but there was a Polish woman in front of me trying to phone Huddersfield and I don't think she'd ever used a phone before. I had to help her, and then she ran out of money. But I did get through to Dad. He was delighted I'd met you and said to be sure and give you his love. Phew, I'm ready for that tea, I can tell you.'

With an effort Beattie pulls herself together and follows Lucy out of the station yard.

The High Street is so literally thronged with people that it is almost impossible to walk on the pavement.

'It must be half-day,' says Lucy, trying vainly not to hit people with her suitcase. The thoroughfare is full of single girls in brightly patterned summer frocks and cork-heeled sandals sauntering along on the arms of American servicemen. There seemed to be Americans everywhere, leaning against the walls, or just sitting unconcernedly in shop doorways. Tommies in khaki with noticeably fewer girls on their arms eye their American counterparts balefully.

'Say, a pretty girl like you shouldn't be toting a heavy case like that,' says a friendly Texan to Lucy, to be greeted with a look of such fury that he hastily backs away.

'Why don't you two girls come and join us for tea?'

'Not today, thanks all the same,' says Beattie with a courteous smile to the young man who tried to block her path.

Inside the Copper Kettle Lucy gives vent to her feelings.

'The cheek of those bloody Yanks! The sheer cheek, just trying to pick you up in the street without any kind of introduction and expecting you to be grateful.'

'Well, I suppose they judge English girls on the response they've been having,' murmurs Beattie, amused, averting her eyes from the next table where an American serviceman and his girlfriend are engaged in a very public embrace over scones and raspberry jam.

'Most of the time I wonder if they aren't just homesick,' says Beattie. 'And they aren't all like that. Lily's Greg treats her very respectfully.'

'Do you ever go out with her and Greg?'

'I did go to a couple of socials in the village hall with one of Greg's friends just to be friendly, but I haven't been since.'

'Why not?'

Beattie shrugs and catches the eye of the waitress.

'It never works, does it? Whatever's been agreed, they always seem to have to try it on – and in the end I got that fed up I didn't go again. Tea for two, please,' orders Beattie, perfectly composed. 'And sandwiches, too, if you've got them.'

'Tomato? Spam? Cucumber?'

'Cucumber.'

'Oh, it's so good to be back here,' sighs Lucy, stretching. 'Not that it wasn't great fun at old Vir's wedding – she looked ravishing.'

'I know. The local paper had a picture on the front page of her leaving the church with her husband.'

'Did it really?' Lucy is impressed. 'Fancy sending a photographer all the way to London just for that. Unless it was the picture that was in the *Evening News* the same night. And there were a couple of pictures in the nationals the next day. I suppose Alexis is really quite famous. What did the Ipswich paper say?'

' "Landowner's daughter marries famous film director". Mrs Musgrave ordered twelve copies at the village shop, and Mother's cut the picture out and put it in her bible.' Beattie sniffs. 'Was there a proper reception?'

'Oh, very proper. At the Savoy. Lots of champagne and flowers and caviare. It was all rather wonderful.'

'And did they go for a proper honeymoon?'

'Nothing like it. They were setting off almost immediately for Wales to make a film.'

'Oh.' Beattie seems rather cheered by this.

'They'll have a proper honeymoon once Alexis has finished filming. But

Virginia didn't seem to mind. She's very much a working girl now. Ah, food. Thank goodness. Tell me, what are you doing in Ipswich? Of course, you must have broken up by now.'

'Yes, I've been on holiday for two weeks. And I've had Louie to stay again.'

'Oh, I'm sorry I missed her. We had quite a lark last year, didn't we? Have you just been seeing her off? Did you have a lovely time?'

Beattie stares down at the tablecloth and clearly has to struggle to look unconcerned. 'Well, not really,' she says at last. 'We had a bit of a barney. She's cross with me at present about Ch—' Too late Beattie realizes what she is about to say and blushes. Lucy looks uncomfortable.

'I'm sorry, I didn't mean to pry.'

'Oh, it's not your fault. It's just that things are such a mess at present, and Louie's not one for keeping her feelings to herself. . . .'

To her dismay Lucy sees that Beattie's eyes are full of tears.

'I haven't mentioned it to anybody except her, you see.'

'Mentioned what?' prompts Lucy gently.

'About Charles and me getting divorced,' Beattie mutters.

'But, Beattie, you've hardly got married,' says Lucy, aghast.

Beattie wipes her eyes with the back of her hand and looks directly at Lucy for the first time. Lucy has a sudden memory of the shy and unsophisticated girl that day at the garden-party. Beattie is suddenly older, more sophisticated, more beautiful – and sadder.

'Well, now we're getting divorced. It didn't work. You know why we got married, don't you?' she goes on levelly.

'I – well, yes.'

'I was that grateful. But I never – you see, I hardly knew Charles before we married. I remembered you saying about how you hardly knew your Hugh before you married – well, I don't think I had more than four conversations with Charles before I married him.'

Lucy is stunned into silence.

'It's not to say I wasn't grateful. Folks aren't too kind in the village about bastards.'

Lucy flinches from the word.

'I thought it was just going to be a business arrangement until such time as we could decently separate. But I think Charles hoped all along it might turn out to be a proper marriage. In the end he got tired of waiting. He told me at Christmas that he wanted a divorce. Louie' – Beattie's voice begins to wobble – 'Louie . . . gave me a terrible talking to yesterday. She thinks I've treated him badly, and I . . . I began to think she's right. He's been very good to me and had nothing for his pains except my being furious he isn't Brooke. . . .' Beattie's anguished voice trails away.

'Did you love Brooke?'

The shock of hearing his name spoken out loud silences both girls.

'I don't know,' says Beattie at last. 'I was obsessed with him. It was like an illness you couldn't throw off. I saw myself doing things I didn't approve of and I just didn't seem able to stop myself. Have you ever felt like that about anyone?'

'No,' says Lucy sadly. 'Never.' There is silence for a moment.

'But, Beattie, you see Charles so little, are you sure this is really what you want? A divorce is so final.'

'It certainly is what *he* wants,' retorts Beattie harshly. 'I wrote to his old posting in January enclosing a letter saying I was his wife and asking if they could forward the letter on. A month later I got the letter back with a note saying Charles had specifically asked not to have any mail forwarded. That was pretty final, wasn't it?'

Lucy has to admit it is. She is also amazed to find how closely Beattie's situation parallels her own.

'Do your parents know?' she says at last.

'Do they heck! Mother's only just got over the shock of nearly having had an unmarried mother in the family. Goodness knows what she'll do when she finds her daughter's about to become a divorcee.'

'Will it matter that much?'

'Yes. People like you and Miss Virginia, you travel around, you don't stay in one place, you don't know what it's like always to be with people who've known you all your life. Mother's obsessed with having a good name. And yet it's a terrible thing to say,' goes on Beattie in a rush, 'but I still think part of her was furious when Charles decided to marry me. She'd have liked to see me punished. She didn't want to see me get away with it. Funny, isn't it?'

'Mothers are odd coves,' agrees Lucy gloomily. 'But surely your parents must have noticed that you aren't getting any letters from Charles?'

'I told them after Christmas that Charles had been sent on a secret posting – that's true enough – and couldn't write. Toby and Ern were that disappointed; they adore him, you know. Everybody likes him except me. Well, that's not true,' amends Beattie honestly. 'It was never that I didn't like him. He's jolly nice. And kind and considerate. It's just that I never seemed to have enough time for him. And when he was with me I couldn't focus on him properly. My thoughts always seemed to be elsewhere.'

Lucy does not need to ask where Beattie's thoughts had been.

'Do you miss Charles?'

Beattie looks at her, startled.

'It's funny, but I suppose I do,' she says slowly, half to herself. 'I was that used to getting regular letters from him, but I never valued them at the time. And he was always so interested in everything I was doing; he'd done some teaching, too, you see. Oh dear. I wasn't awfully kind to him. Louie says the best thing I can do is give him his freedom, and I suppose she's right. I'm sorry, Lucy, to go on and on about myself. When you've just come back from a holiday the last thing you want to hear is someone else's gloom. You won't tell anyone, will you? I haven't even told Lily; you see, she never knew about . . . Annie. And she's so wrapped up in Greg. Let's talk about something else. Tell me about yourself. Have you heard from Hugh?'

'Not for about eighteen months,' says Lucy briskly, signalling to the waitress for more hot water. 'Nor will I be, I suspect. He met someone else in Cairo. An American nurse called Julia Heap. He wrote a year ago and told me he wanted a divorce. *I* haven't told anyone else, either. Except Virginia.'

Beattie is momentarily speechless.

'You haven't told anybody all that time – not even your *parents*?'

'Certainly not them. I'll tell them when divorce proceedings start.'

'But what about the McFees—?'

'Oh, I fob them off with something from time to time.'

'But, Lucy, how dreadful. And here's me going on about my own problems. You must have been so unhappy.'

'I was at first. And then I felt outraged. He wrote me some silly letters telling me how wonderful Julia was. I ask you. It was hardly tactful, was it?'

Both girls are silent for a moment, then Beattie's mouth starts to twitch and unwillingly they both start laughing.

'Not terribly, under the circumstances. Well, it at least explains why you dislike Americans so much. But they can't all be related to her, can they?'

'That's what I keep telling myself,' says Lucy with a certain grim humour. 'Perhaps one day I'll actually believe it.'

CHAPTER
THIRTY-TWO

*T*O SAY THAT LUCY is warmly welcomed back at Home Farm would be a dramatic understatement: Mr McFee actually raises himself on his two sticks to come and shake her hand, Donny is waiting by the gate, and even the dogs have hysterics. The heat of the day is giving way to a cool fragrant evening as they sit down for supper. Everything to Lucy's contented eyes looks exactly the same – the blue and white china, the home-made bread sliced and ready on the board. Mrs McFee produces an enormous steak and kidney pudding from the range. It is really too warm for such a heavy supper, but it is Lucy's favourite and some pains have been taken to make her feel welcome. Janet, the relief land-girl from Ipswich, is to stay throughout August to help with the harvest, and the first of the threshing gangs will arrive on Monday.

'How long have we got the machine for?'

'Six days,' says Mr McFee. 'So we'll all have to pray for six days' sunshine.' He then launches into a fairly technical conversation about dipping the sheep, and the problems of getting enough of the correct dip. Then courteously Mrs McFee asks after Lucy's parents and Virginia's marriage: the description of the reception at the Savoy has Janet looking envious and Donny's mouth open, unfortunately usually while he's eating.

Lucy finishes her day with a deep sense of contentment. She knows where she is with the McFees. She's never found the Scots as reserved and taciturn as they are alleged to be; she likes the correctness and their courtesy, the fact that they ask the right questions but don't press her for more information than she wants to give.

At nine o'clock it is still light enough to walk round the farm with Mr McFee. Finally Lucy and Donny go to take an apple to Sam.

'Do you think he's missed me?'

'Bad-tempered old brute. Catch me talking to him,' says Donny.

'He should be in a better mood than usual. He's had a week's holiday. It's a pity he's so unreliable else I'm sure we could use him somehow at harvesting. Hey! Sam! Where are you? This isn't like him. Where is he?'

'He must be down at the other end of the field. He's more usually up this end with his head over the fence complaining.'

Donny cups his hands round his mouth and bellows a stentorian '*S-a-m.*' At this, slowly and very reluctantly, a dark shape detaches itself from the gloom at the other end of the paddock and Sam comes towards them in what can only be described as a lacklustre trot.

'There he is, the lazy old devil. I was afraid he'd got out.'

Donny guffaws.

'He's too lazy, that one.'

'Don't you believe it. I caught him the other day trying to lift the latch on the gate. Though I don't know what he'd have done if he'd succeeded.'

Sam condescendingly accepts the two apples, shows no sign at all of recognizing Lucy and bares his teeth at Donny, who backs away.

'Can't understand why you bother with him. He's an evil-minded old brute.'

'He is a bit unpredictable,' admits Lucy, tentatively rubbing his nose. 'But I do love riding. And I've never had an opportunity before. Here! I say, come here a minute, Donny.'

Donny approaches cautiously.

'I don't understand it. Sam's sweating, isn't he? Look, he is, and quite hard, too.'

Sam steps back, affronted.

'He's not ill, is he?'

'Doesn't look it to me. Perhaps he's been galloping round on his own.'

'I've never known Sam to move any faster than a slow trot under his own steam,' says Lucy, puzzled. 'I wonder if I should bring him in?'

'He looks OK to me. Perhaps he's just been thinking about the lasses.'

'Shouldn't think he can remember,' says Lucy drily. 'He's a gelding, you know. I doubt if he thinks about anything except his stomach. All right, old boy, we'll come and have a look at you again tomorrow morning.'

On the following morning Sam is his completely normal disagreeable disgruntled self. Lucy, quickly caught up in the activities of harvesting, forgets all about the incident.

It should have been an easier harvest since there are more hands helping bring it in. But this summer, at the Ministry's instigation, they have five more fields under the plough, so the work is still as fraught as it ever was. Miraculously, however, the weather holds and Janet proves to be a capable worker, though prone to abandon her tasks every time a plane takes off from one of the neighbouring American airbases.

'Janet's got a boyfriend,' confides Donny as side-by-side they pitch the heavy sheaves into the cart.

'Really,' says Lucy, praying it will soon be lunchtime. The sun that has bleached these sheaves into wonderful shades of cream and gold is now directly overhead, and there is no shelter in the middle of the field.

'Two more at your end, Donny. Try to fork them up a bit higher. Hold on.' Nimbly Lucy pulls herself up over the edge of the cart in her dungarees and straw hat and arranges the sheaves more neatly. 'There, there's room for lots more now. Heave those other ones up. What does Janet's boyfriend do?'

'He works on the planes,' says Donny vaguely. 'They fly fighters now, you know.'

'As opposed to what?'

'As opposed to bombers, daft. They moved all the bombers out to near Norwich. You must have noticed.'

'All I notice is that there are still a lot of planes taking off and frightening the cows.'

'Well, the big planes have gone. The ones that fly now are just fighters. They're the ones that go and meet the bombers coming back,' says Donny somewhat picturesquely.

'Really,' says Lucy. 'Like Spitfires, I suppose. Oh, thank goodness, there's Mrs McFee. I'll drive this lot to the yard and we'll call it a morning. I'm parched.'

It is a perfect August. Hot still blue days, and at night the sky is still light enough to enable Lucy to go on working almost until midnight. The throb of the tractor sounds oddly through the moonlight-washed fields of pale stubble. Life at the farm, notwithstanding the constant roar of planes taking off on either side, remains its usual secure oasis.

Towards the end of the month Beattie asks her down for Sunday supper at the cottage. It is Lucy's first evening off in nearly four weeks, and Mr McFee insists she goes. Greg and Lily will be there *en route* for a drink at Dereham Market. Lucy has to decline the drink but is pleased to be able to ride down for supper, leaving Sam tethered in the Blythes' orchard.

It is a pleasant evening. Beattie is getting ready to go back to school, Annie has temporarily stopped teething and is considerably better-tempered as a result, and Greg and Lily are quietly jubilant, having decided to get engaged at Christmas, subject to Mr Kedge ever being sober enough to be asked for Lily's hand in marriage. When Lucy finally leaves at ten o'clock the sky is still glowing and a heavy dew is falling, bringing with it the fragrance of damp roses. Sam is clearly sulking since he declines absolutely to respond to Lucy's call. Or so Lucy thinks, until she finds the gate is unhooked and Sam nowhere to be seen. Sam has developed quite a way with gates and is clearly enjoying himself elsewhere. Thanking God that he isn't in Mr Blythe's vegetable garden, Lucy sets off at some speed up the darkened lane to the main street, with visions of him impaled on the front of a marauding jeep at the very least. But the village street is empty. Which way would he have gone? Would any kind of instinct have driven him towards his home? Somehow Lucy doubts it. By now seriously alarmed, she sets off in the opposite direction along the lane leading to the air force camp. The way is pitch dark beneath the arches of many ancient elms, and Lucy curses herself for not having brought her torch. Then – oh, blessed noise! – from round the corner comes the sound of hoofs on tarmac, and the next moment Lucy sees Sam's disgruntled features in the gloom. He is being led up the road by a very tall young man in a uniform. An American air force uniform.

'What on earth are you doing with my horse?' snaps Lucy ungratefully.

'I found him wandering half a mile away. Thought you'd like him back.'

'Oh,' says Lucy frostily. 'Thank you.' Then: 'How did you know he was mine?'

'Saw you coming down earlier. I've seen you often up at the farm.'

Lucy is disconcerted because she cannot place his accent. He sounds

391

neither like a cowbody nor like Clark Gable. In fact he sounds almost British. Yet he is quite clearly a Yank.

'Thank you for returning him. I must go now.'

'Not on this old fellow. He's lame.'

And before Lucy can stop him he's run a practised hand down Sam's rear leg.

'You mustn't do that,' says Lucy, quite pale with shock. 'He has a beastly temper. I'm surprised he didn't bite you.'

'I guess he knows me. I've ridden him round his field a few times,' admits the young man with no proper sense of shame.

'Then, you'd no right to,' snaps Lucy, gingerly examining Sam's hock. 'Oh, bother! He must have banged himself on something. And I'm back at the farm in half an hour.'

'Supposing you leave Sam in Mrs Hammond's garden,' suggests the infuriating young man most surprisingly. 'But this time I'd tie up the gate.'

Annoyingly Lucy can see almost nothing of this imperturbable person who is telling her what to do. All she can gauge is that he is very much taller than she is.

'Perhaps I can offer you a lift. I'm due back at camp myself in half an hour, and Charlie's picking me up in the truck. He won't mind dropping you off. This horse isn't going anywhere with you on it tonight.'

It seems the best solution, but with surprisingly bad grace Lucy goes back to the Blythes' cottage where Beattie has no objection to any overnight visitor in the orchard. Having secured the gate, Lucy puts Sam's tack in the garden shed and, feeling slightly ashamed of her bad humour, begins to walk up the darkened road with the young man. It isn't his fault he's a Yank and, as Beattie had rightly pointed out, not everybody in America can be related to Julia Heap.

'You appear to know something about horses,' she says at last gruffly.

'Should do. My uncle breeds racehorses in Kentucky.'

'Is that where you come from?'

'No, ma'am,' he says courteously. 'I come from Boston.'

'What do you do at the base?' asks Lucy, having a very imprecise idea of where Kentucky is. Or Boston for that matter.

'I'm a pilot. I've been here a month. We're right across the valley from Home Farm. We moved in after the bomber boys moved out. We fly on our own and they fly in crews. So they call us the "little friends" and we call them the "big friends". When we arrived they told us all about the trouble they'd had with the mud. But I haven't seen weather as good as this since I left Kentucky. Perhaps I should introduce myself. My name's Will Shaughnessy.'

Will has the loose easy stride of a countryman and he seems quite unperturbed by Lucy's lack of response.

'You're Lucy Jennings, aren't you? Mrs Lucy Jennings,' he adds politely. 'I've got a cousin at home called Lucille, but I think Lucy is kind of cute.'

Lucy is just about to enquire how he knows her name when there is a roar of exhaust from further back down the road.

392

'I reckon that's Charlie now,' says the young man, his head cocked to one side. To Lucy's consternation he then steps straight out into the path of the truck's muted headlights and waves it down. Charlie draws up with much ostentatious screeching of brakes and says it will be no trouble at all to take Lucy back to Home Farm. Lucy scrambles through the canvas flap over the tailgate and feels cautiously for the wooden seats against the wall. The truck is pitch black and reeks of petrol. When the young man bounds in beside her they leap forward, Lucy clinging desperately to the side of her seat. They tear up the four miles of narrow Suffolk lanes as if responding to some national emergency. Then Charlie slams on his brakes, nearly throwing Lucy across the truck.

'Here y'are,' roars Charlie. 'Home Farm it is.'

Lucy jumps down on to the road aware that her legs are trembling like jelly. She is about to wish the young man a restrained goodnight when she finds he has jumped down beside her and told Charlie to wait.

'Look, I'm perfectly well able to make my way from here,' she begins crossly.

'I can't let a lady walk home on her own. Young Toby has told us about the wolves in the woods. I'm not so sure we didn't believe him at first. They're nice kids – him and Ern. I see them in the village. I know your friend Lily, you see,' he says and turns to grin at her. 'I asked her all about you.'

As it is nearly three years since any male has addressed a more intimate remark to Lucy than what her current views are on cures for foot rot Lucy finds herself tongue-tied, disconcerted and annoyed. She is glad when they reach the yard gate.

'Look, it's very kind of you to see me home Mr – er – Shaughnessy—'

'The name's Will. Can I call you Lucy?'

'I must dash,' says Lucy feebly.

'I expect you don't get much free time,' persists Will undeterred. 'I don't think I've ever seen a girl work as hard as you do. But I was wondering if you'd care to accompany me to the concert the children are putting on at the village hall on Saturday. I promised young Toby I'd look in. I think he's doing some conjuring tricks, and there's a film afterwards.'

Exasperated beyond measure, Lucy turns round to confront this persistent young man and almost crashes into him. The moon makes a belated appearance from behind the clouds, and for the first time she is able to see him properly. He does not present a particularly alarming picture, being tall, fair-haired and blue-eyed. He also has a very nice smile.

'I don't think you understand,' says Lucy coldly. 'I'm married. I don't go out with other men.'

'But you must like a little company some time. I'm not trying to date you, Lucy. I just thought you might like some company.'

'Whatever you agree on, it always turns into the same thing.' Beattie's words come back to her clearly. But the fact of the matter is she's *not* a married woman any more anyway. Somehow having told Beattie the truth about the situation has made it real. Lucy stares at the ground. Will waits patiently.

'Well, perhaps I could. Providing,' she goes on severely, 'the situation's clearly understood.'

'Pick you up at seven sharp,' says Will and smiles down at her. For the first time Lucy looks him properly in the face and unwillingly finds herself smiling back.

At the appointed time, with pleasing promptness, Will turns up and behaves impeccably throughout the evening, but with absolute firmness Lucy declines a further date. Unperturbed, he takes to turning up to help with the milking, and Lucy's exasperated and increasingly pointed comments have no effect at all. She understands that his squadron has currently been 'stood down', which explains the amount of time he seems to have at his disposal for simply being at Home Farm and helping. But Mr and Mrs McFee are beginning to look slightly askance at Lucy, married woman, having followers, and Dougal and Donny's giggles and innuendoes are becoming more than she can bear. The problem is that whenever she steels herself to give Will his marching orders something mechanical always goes wrong which Will is more than anxious to put right. After which it hardly seems courteous to tell him to be on his way. Lucy has no personal knowledge of Will's talents as a pilot, but she does know that he understands the tortuous logic of the milk-cooler machine better than she does herself. For this alone Mrs McFee is prepared to relax her moral strictures and provide Will with afternoon tea and fruitcake. On one such afternoon, after a long wrestle with the tractor Will joins Lucy companionably on a bale of hay against the sunny wall of the barn. Mrs McFee has brought them out their tea, and Lucy, conscious that things have now gone far enough, takes her courage in her hands to speak.

'Look, Will, I feel I have to say this because I feel I'm in a false position. Oh, goodness, I'm no good at all at this. I'm just trying to say that I'd rather you didn't come up here any more.'

Will stirs his tea and grins at Lucy. The sun striking warmly on his hair turns it the same ashy gold as the stubble in the surrounding fields. Will's eyes are blue, mild and peaceful in his sunburnt face. Lily privately describes Will as a dreamboat. Lucy is less concerned with this than with the fact that he is the most easygoing person she has ever met. He rarely responds with excessive emotion, and now he carefully puts down his mug on the window-sill behind him before answering Lucy.

The directness of his response takes her by surprise.

'Have I tried to come on to you?'

'Well, no—'

'Poison your mind against your husband?'

'Will, *really*—'

'Seduce you with oranges from the PX?'

'You know that's rubbish.'

'So why should I stop seeing you?'

'Because, whatever you say, you're looking for a girlfriend, and I – I'm not free. And don't tell me we can be just good friends because that one's got whiskers on it.'

'I wasn't aiming for us to be good friends,' says Will gently. And as the meaning of his words sinks in Lucy blushes furiously.

'Then, you've no right to assume that. I told you from the beginning I was married—'

'Lily Kedge told me you hadn't had a letter from your husband in nearly two years or else I'd never dare—'

Shaking with anger, Lucy is on her feet.

'How dare she tell you that! She has absolutely no right to do so, and how dare you pry into my private affairs—'

'She told me because I pestered her, and I pestered her because I told her I'd seen you for nearly a month and didn't see any way of getting to talk to you at all,' says Will calmly and matter-of-factly. 'Sit down again, Lucy, and listen to me. I'm not going to jump you. If you really want me to, I'll go. You won't have to put up with so much of me anyway,' he adds suddenly with a grin that reveals his white and perfect teeth. 'We'll be flying again soon. But I'm not trying to mislead you. I'd like to see more of you. A hell of a lot more. I'd like you to be my girl. Look. Can't we just go on seeing each other and it be no big deal? We could see how things go—'

'You don't understand. Everybody knows I'm a married woman. If I suddenly started seeing other men, I'd have to explain—'

'Explain what?'

'About my husband. He met somebody else.'

'Well, it happens.'

'I know it happens,' snaps Lucy, quite rudely for her, 'or else presumably we wouldn't see it so much in films. But it's very different when it happens to you personally.'

'Are you still in love with him?'

Lucy sighs deeply, drinks the last of her tea and furrows her brow trying to be honest.

'I don't know that I ever was,' she says, surprising even herself.

'Well, then, what's the problem?'

'I was very fond of him,' Lucy says reprovingly. 'And it's more than that. It's not just something you undo lightly. We undertook vows to each other – that's important. I said for better for worse in a church.'

'Did you have much time together after your marriage?'

'No, he left the following day.'

'Well, it seems to me that you've had a hell of a lot of worse and precious little better. And he made vows to you, didn't he? And broke them. How long are you going to keep that light burning in the window?'

'For as long as seems appropriate,' Lucy says angrily.

'Strikes me that what really bothers you is having to tell other people that it's over.'

Furious, Lucy opens her mouth to deny the fact, then realizes what he's saying is true.

'Look, do you mind leaving me alone? I've told you how things stand and I—'

'Would you come to the pictures with me at Dereham Market on Saturday?'

'Will, do you never give up?'

'*Never*. No,' says Will with simple candour. 'Not when I'm sure of what I want.'

Furious, Lucy stacks the mugs and plates and prepares to go back to the house. Unperturbed, Will catches her hand and pulls her round to face him.

'Saturday, then? I'll pick you up here at six o'clock.'

In a passable imitation of James Cagney he adds slyly: 'You sure look pretty when you're mad.'

Lucy pulls her hand free, exasperated and trying not to smile. 'I'll *see*.'

In retrospect it all seems to happen so quickly that Lucy wonders if she had dreamt the whole thing. One minute she is living a solitary life dedicated to the care of her dairy herd; the next, she is still equally dedicated but is out either dancing or in the pub with Will three or four times a week and finding herself studying the sky as intently as Donny has ever done to identify planes. She even takes to borrowing Lily Kedge's magazines and reading the beauty tips. But it is a long time before she dares categorize the alien sensation she is feeling as happiness. It is all so simple with Will. Lucy still does not know what she wants and finds herself caught on a personal pendulum swinging between elation and guilt. But from Will's certainty, his delight in her company, she draws a certain assurance. When she tells Mrs McFee the actual circumstances about her marriage no more is said about Will coming to collect her from Home Farm and eventually he is formally invited to tea.

Lucy finds his mixture of foreignness and familiarity intriguing. Tentatively she asks him about himself. As he reveals more about his background she begins to understand why he is drawn to her. Will's family, the Shaughnessys from Wexford, are, he tells her, fourth-generation Irish immigrants who have split themselves into two distinct groups. Will's side of the family have conscientiously made money in Boston via the law. The other half of the family have moved out to Kentucky to breed racehorses. On long walks through the frosty twilight of October and November, Will tells Lucy about the summers spent on his uncle's stud farm near Goshen, the breathless humidity of those long hot summer days when neither man nor beast has the energy to stir, the paddocks with their brilliant green grass and the sight of the thoroughbred mares and foals grazing under old oaks. He also tells her about the pleasures of flying, how his Uncle Sean had bought a monoplane when Will was still only in his early teens and had unbeknownst to his father taught him to fly solo before he was sixteen.

'You'd love it in Kentucky, Lucy,' he says nostalgically, unselfconsciously holding her woollen-gloved hand in one of his own. 'In the evening when it gets cooler you can ride for hours and hours and never see another soul. My uncle's got two good stallions and twenty mares. He can make more money, I think, but he's a sentimental man. He and my Aunty Ellen never had any children, so I guess that's why they always treated me like their own son.'

Will's grandfather is the head of the family legal practice in Boston. In time Will's father will succeed him.

'And then you?'

Will shrugs and falls silent. He is already in his father's bad books for pulling out of his law studies at Harvard after just one year to join the Air

Force. After eighteen months in California as a flying instructor, Musgrave is his first posting.

'I just take things one by one,' he says finally. 'The war gave me a chance, and I took it. You do things for your parents – that's right when you're a child. But since I've been away – why, even when I was in California I began to think about things differently. You can please people so far. If I do decide to go back to Law School, it'll be because I want to. Did you have to please your parents? I wondered if that was why you married so young.'

'Oh, no, I don't think it had anything to do with it. Or did it? I suppose I felt they'd be pleased if I got married. But to Hugh – well, Hugh seemed quite suitable.' Lucy sighs. 'I think probably what's more to the point is that Mummy always made me feel rather a dumb bunny in the brains department. I can see now they never thought I'd succeed at anything. I fully expected to marry at the end of my season and just be a housewife. It's so extraordinary – if it weren't for the war I'd never have found myself near the land.'

Unused to talking about herself, and not given to self-analysis, Lucy finds it a novel sensation to be thought interesting. Hugh had never shown any real understanding about her life as a land-girl – but why should he, town bred? But with Will, as interested in running the farm as she is herself, there is always something to talk about. There is also the fact that Will appreciates her skills, admires her and frequently says so. After the relentless self-preoccupation of Hugh it is balm to Lucy's bruised soul.

About his life at the base, Will says very little. One Sunday he takes her over to show her his plane and she meets his flying colleagues in the Goat and Compasses. Even though they are her own age, they all seem absurdly young. But even the weather seems to be on Lucy's side. The heavy clouds and endless mists of East Anglia mean that throughout October and November for every one raid Will is able to make there are six other occasions when they are stood down, left to kick their heels in the sea of mud which is Musgrave in the winter. Will's job, so he tells her, is to escort those lumbering 'flying fortresses', the B-17s, which she used to see taking off over Musgrave and which now fly from ten miles away nearer to Norwich. Sometimes they go with them on the outward journey. Sometimes Will and his friends go to the German coast to protect them in their battered and damaged state for the journey home. If they do go out on a raid, Will usually rings Lucy later that evening to tell her he is safe.

'Are you in love with him?' asks Beattie. Lucy has called in at the cottage one evening in early December courteously to decline her standard invitation to Christmas lunch. It is an ideal evening for confidences as Mr and Mrs Blythe are both out at a parish council meeting and the two boys are in bed. Annie sleeps peacefully by the range under the watchful eye of Beetle.

'I don't know,' says Lucy candidly. 'It just seems so marvellously right being with him. It's strange, isn't it?'

Lucy is still more than a touch embarrassed at her apparent volte-face on the whole subject of Americans.

'Do your parents know? About – well, I mean Hugh and things.'

'No, not yet. But I'm going to tell them at Christmas. I thought it was better to tell them face to face. And once I've done that I can start divorce proceedings in January and introduce Will to them. I wish I could take Will up there for Christmas, but I think it really would be too much of a shock when they don't even know that I'm getting divorced. Also Daddy doesn't sound at all well. It's the winter damp – his chest was never good even before his heart went wonky.'

Lucy stretches out her hands to the open fire. She is transformed, thinks Beattie. Never has she seen her look so pretty, so confident. As if reading her thoughts, Lucy blushes.

'I just hope people don't think I'm cheap behaving like this. It's not just fun. Will is really special, and I know he feels the same way about me.'

'I don't think it's anybody's business but your own,' says Beattie warmly. 'I reckon you gave Hugh every chance. More than every chance, Does . . . does Will talk about the future?' she asks delicately.

'Not really. He's superstitious like that. He never talks about anything more distant than next Saturday.' By the way, is there any news of – er – er – Charles.'

'No,' say Beattie firmly. 'Nothing.'

'So what are you going to do?'

'The same as you, I suspect. In the New Year I'm going up to London to see their solicitors and start proceedings.'

'But do you actually have grounds?'

'Yes,' says Beattie, not looking at Lucy.

'Oh,' says Lucy.

When Lucy has disappeared off into the night Beattie stokes the fire up and damps it down, then lays the table for breakfast. Finally she puts out the teapot and tray against Mr and Mrs Blythe's return. She has just seated herself in the rocker in front of the range when the door to the hall opens cautiously. Resigned, Beattie looks up.

'Oh, it's you.'

'I heard Lucy go. It woke me up.'

Rubbing his eyes, his hair sticking up in a tuft from his crown, Ern hitches up his dressing-grown which is trailing along the floor behind him. He comes over to the rocking chair and without embarrassment climbs on to Beattie's knee and settles himself comfortably.

'Oh, I see, we want a cuddle, do we?'

'Yes, we do,' says Ern, wriggling unselfconsciously to make himself more comfortable. 'That's nice.'

'You should be asleep.'

'You look tired out,' says the cunning Ern. 'Is it Annie?'

'No. She's a bit of a handful at present, but it's the weather keeping her in that doesn't help. You'll have to go back to bed in a minute now, Ern. Mother and Father will be back and if they find you up there'll be ructions.'

'I'll go up when I hear the gate go,' says Ern unabashed. 'It's much nicer sitting here on your knee, Aunty Bee. When I came in were you thinking about Charles?'

Beattie is startled.

'I thought you were,' says Ern with quiet satisfaction. 'You looked all sad.'

'Oh, come off it, Ern. I was just thinking, that was all.'

'Has he really gone to Africa?'

'Ern, what do you mean? Of course he's gone there. Where on earth do you think he is? He's somewhere near Lucy's Hugh, I expect.'

'Lucy's got Will now, so she won't need Hugh any more, will she?'

Beattie is silent. Mrs Blythe would intervene firmly at this point, making a remark about little pitchers, the devil finding work and this being none of Ern's business. Beattie is less sure of her ground. Avoiding Ern's wise little eyes, she says: 'I don't know, Ern. But it's a private matter, and I think Lucy would be upset if she thought folks were gossiping about her.'

Ern is silent for a moment but is clearly not put out.

'What does Charles do in Africa, then?'

'Well, I'm not exactly sure. But I think it has something to do with making maps. You know planes carry cameras so they can see where they've dropped their bombs? They send more planes with cameras afterwards to see what damage they've done. Well, Uncle Charles used to interpret those photographs. I think he probably went to Africa to make maps in case they landed there. He did geography at college, you see.'

Ern twists round to look at her, searching her face.

'Is that really true or are you fibbin' me?'

'Ern, what a thing to say.' Beattie is genuinely shocked. 'Why on earth should I tell you fibs about Charles?'

'You had cross words with him when he came home last time, didn't you? It was that day we went out salvaging. Me and Toby knew soon as we got in. And then you said he was going away. So we thought perhaps you'd had a quarrel and you weren't going to be married any more. Like our dad,' he adds matter-of-factly.

Beattie stares at Ern in perplexity.

'You've never said that before. You always said you didn't remember anything about your dad. That he'd been sent abroad.'

'Oh, he was sent abroad all right. But he'd left home long before that. Toby said I wasn't to say that to anyone, so I didn't.'

'Didn't they get on, your mum and dad?'

'I don't remember. Toby says they didn't. I was only little then. So Uncle Charles won't be home for Christmas?'

'I don't think so, Ern. But we've got lots of nice things to do. We've got tickets for the pantomine in Ipswich, and if it freezes over hard you're probably big enough to wear my old skates on the Manor lake. Hey! That's Mum and Dad. You'd better scoot upstairs. Give us a kiss and off you go.'

Little pitchers, thinks Beattie, leaning over her daughter's cot and tucking a wandering hand under the sheet. Annie sleeps comfortably, cheeks flushed, bright fair curls shining in the glow of the range. How will she tell Annie about her father? Come to that, how will she explain about Charles Hammond who has come and gone so mysteriously in Annie's young life?

I must get all that sorted out, thinks Beattie firmly. I must. I can't let things go dragging on. After Christmas when I go up to buy those books for the school library I'll go and see the solicitors Charles told me about. And in a year or two, when things are settled and Annie's old enough, perhaps I can get a job where she can be taken care of and we can start again.

The prospect, usually a cheering one, for once doesn't seem to have the power to raise Beattie's spirits. She has a sudden image of what it will be like to be 'back on the market', remembering without pleasure how vulnerable and exposed she had felt at those village socials. Well, that's just something that will have to be dealt with. Unconsciously Beattie fiddles with her wedding ring. Say what you might, it afforded some protection. Even if it was based on a lie.

Three days before Christmas, along with a parcel from Louie and three cards written in loopy handwriting from members of Form IIIB, Beattie receives a businesslike-looking letter in a handwriting that makes her stomach turn over. Inside, without present, card or greeting, is a short letter from Charles. It is dated 20 December.

Dear Beattie,
I have just arrived home and was surprised to receive no communication from the solicitors. I rang them this morning and they told me you haven't contacted them. I was expecting things to have moved rather further on than this. If it is a matter of providing grounds, I will be happy to provide you with the necessary dates, etc. I will be in London until the middle of next month and suggest we meet. Can you write back and suggest when would be convenient? A suitable place might be the RAF Club in Pall Mall.
It is signed simply 'Charles Hammond'.

Beattie is so furious that she crumples up the letter and hurls it straight into the range. A moment later she is desperately trying to stir it out with a poker as she remembers she does not even know the address to reply to. Smoothing out the charred sheet, Beattie sets her jaw. If Charles is so anxious for a divorce, he can jolly well have one. Going instantly to her writing-case, she dashes off a note every bit as curt as his own. She is indeed coming to London on 3 January. She can give Charles an hour. She suggests 3 p.m. With that she slams the letter into an envelope, bangs a stamp on it and goes immediately to the postbox at the end of the lane to get it out of her possession.

'This is it, is it?'
'You wanted the RAF Club, didn't you?'
The cabbie, disgruntled by the snow on the roads and unmoved by Beattie's prettiness, gestures crossly at the building and does not even bother to open the door. Beattie pays him, furious that she is over-tipping him but too nervous to ask for anything back from her half-crown. A commissionaire comes forward with an umbrella against the sleet.
'Thank you,' says Beattie, aware that she's cold, numb and nearly in tears. Her anger at Charles has long ago evaporated in the horrors of the long

train journey, the almost Stygian darkness (even at midday) of the London streets, and the absolute indifference of everyone around her to the fact that she has lost her way and can't find the Charing Cross Road. When she finally finds it, and with it Foyles, it takes all her lunch hour to order the books and arrange for them to be delivered. It is now ten past three, and she is late. Furthermore she has had nothing to eat, not even a cup of tea, since she left Musgrave at 6.15 this morning in the pitch dark. If only she can get to the ladies' before she sees Charles – but no. The vestibule is full of men in Air Force uniform, and even as she looks tentatively round she sees Charles standing by the reception desk with two smart-looking WAAF officers. The sight of him causes her a shock that she had not expected. He is thinner, older, and deeply tanned.

'Oh, Beattie, there you are,' he says coolly as if they had parted only minutes previously. He makes no move to kiss her. 'Let me introduce you to Diana Carrington-Smythe and Fay Beddows. This is my wife, Beatrice.'

For a split-second pause before hands are extended and features composed Beattie knows that this is the first indication that Charles has ever given that he is married.

'Delighted to meet you,' says Beattie clearly. 'You look well, Charles,' she adds in a tone every bit as disinterested as his own. 'Desert life must suit you.' Well, might as well give them their money's worth. It'll give them something to chat about in the plotting-room at High Wycombe during the long winter evenings. 'Are we having tea? I'm starving. But I need the powder room first.'

Leaving a disconcerted Charles, Beattie follows the signs to the ladies' room and prepares to take her time. Since she clearly no longer even exists in Charles's life he can jolly well wait for her. She repins her curls, powders her nose, straightens up her costume and blouse, and tries vainly to sponge some of the splashes of mud off the back of her legs.

'I must be the only woman in London not wearing nylons,' she thinks, vexed, trying to straighten the seams on her lisle stockings. The perfume-dispenser is, alas, not working or she would have indulged herself in sixpennyworth of 'Miss Dior'. But feeling considerably more in command of the situation she climbs the steps back to reception and is taken by a uniformed page to where Charles is sitting comfortably in a large leather armchair. A table is drawn up at his elbow on which a white-coated man has just placed a tray full of gleaming white china and plates of sandwiches. Courteously Charles get up and draws another chair up for Beattie. There is a large coal-fire at one end of the room, and the curtains are already drawn against the dark streets outside. Beattie thinks about the long train journey back to Ipswich in an unheated train and shivers.

'Shall I pour?' she asks.

'As you wish.'

Beattie spins out the business of pouring milk in and sugaring the tea, adds hot water to the pot, passes plates and then offers Charles a sandwich. Finally she says without looking at him: 'How are you?'

'I'm all right,' says Charles equably. 'And yourself?'

'I'm fine. Did you have a good Christmas?'

'Very good. I went to stay with some of my mother's relations in Cheadle.'

So he hadn't even thought of coming to Musgrave.

'How's the family?'

'Fine,' says Beattie again. 'Annie's well. Running around like anything. She's got a lovely head of hair now.'

'I suppose you didn't bring any photographs of her, did you?'

'No,' says Beattie dismayed. 'I didn't think you'd—'

'Oh, it doesn't matter,' says Charles squashingly. 'I was only curious.'

There is a pause. Charles is clearly annoyed at himself for having shown an interest in Annie. Beattie is equally annoyed with herself for not having brought some photographs.

'What time is your train home?'

'There's one at six and one at eight.'

Silence again as Beattie tentatively reaches for another dried-egg sandwich. 'Look, I—'

'I want to—'

Both stop and then apologize.

'Do go on, Beattie.'

'I was only going to say that I did bring you . . . your reviews. Just in case you missed any of them once you'd gone away.'

Charles is about to say that the cuttings agency employed by his publishers probably hasn't missed anything, then, seeing Beattie's downcast eyes, he says instead: 'That was kind of you. Thank you.'

He puts the envelope unopened into his pocket.

'You must have been awfully pleased when it came out.'

'Yes, I was,' says Charles expressionlessly.

'Your parents would have been so proud of you.'

'Yes,' says Charles. 'I think they would.'

'Did you have any time to do any writing out there?'

'Time was the only thing we had an awful lot of. So I did manage some writing,' says Charles, warming to the subject in spite of himself. 'But I didn't get anything finished. I kept trying different ideas. This is all very agreeable, Beattie, but I think we ought to get down to business.'

The abrupt change of subject startles her.

'If you like.'

'Why haven't you started divorce proceedings? You seemed keen enough on the idea a year ago.'

'Just a minute,' says Beattie, suddenly furious. 'It was you who mentioned divorce, not me. It was you who wanted a fresh start. It was you who seemed to have somebody else in mind—'

Charles's anger, which from the beginning of the conversation has barely been contained below the surface, suddenly furiously erupts.

'Beattie, don't talk such absolute tosh,' he says in a furious undertone. 'I want a divorce for one reason, and one reason only. Because if we stayed together we would be toting Brooke Musgrave around with us in spirit for the rest of our marriage. You're still in love with him, that's perfectly obvious. And it's equally obvious that there is nothing I can do to make you even aware of me. You don't want to consummate the marriage, you don't want to live with me; you want the shelter of my name and financial support for Annie, that's all. Well, you'll have to find someone else from now on or get Brooke to start paying for his pleasures. His marriage should mean he'll be well able to afford better maintenance now. Oh God,' he adds dismayed, 'I thought you knew.'

Seeing her stricken face, he adds more gently: 'I thought you and the Musgraves were as thick as thieves.'

'I can't stand the family,' says Beattie almost inaudibly. 'And they haven't said anything about it to anyone. How do you know he's married?'

'I was here just before Christmas and the first intake Brooke's trained arrived the same night. He isn't actually married. Just engaged. Perhaps his mother hasn't had the letter yet.'

Beattie automatically puts her cup, saucer and plate back tidily on the tray.

'Who's he marrying?'

'Who do you expect?' jeers Charles. 'Someone rich. She's older than him.'

'Well,' says Beattie, quietly gathering up her gloves, 'I haven't wasted your day, have I, Charles? It must have made up for a lot, being able to tell me that.'

With this Beattie picks up her bag and walks out of the lounge. It is pitch dark by now and a whirling snowstorm has begun to recoat the road and pavements. But Beattie's luck is in. A couple are getting out of a taxi at the kerb's edge. Beattie taps on the window. 'Liverpool Street Station, please.'

'No,' says a voice behind her authoritatively. 'New Cavendish Street, please.'

'Blimey, make up your mind.'

'This is my taxi. Clear off,' hisses Beattie.

'I'll take you to Liverpool Street for the eight o'clock train.'

'I'm going to Liverpool Street *now*.'

'Look, are you taking this taxi or not?'

'Hey, Cabbie! Want a fare?'

'*Get in*,' says Charles furiously. 'Take us to New Cavendish Street.'

'When the cab has dropped *you*,' says Beattie, sitting as far away from Charles as the seat permits, 'I'm going to Liverpool Street. *You* want a divorce? *You* see the solicitors. Give them the dates and all the occasions and I'll just sign the necessary forms. I didn't want to come and see you today. And I don't want to see you ever again.'

The whirling snow reduces their progress up Regent Street to a snail's pace. Past Oxford Circus. Past All Souls, Langham Place. Eventually the taxi turns right and pulls up outside a block of modern flats.

' 'Ere some of you are,' says the cabbie ironically.

'Beattie, come in, just for a minute. I promise I'll take you to Liverpool Street for the eight o'clock train. I promise. But don't let's end things like this. Please, I don't want to feel you're on that bloody train all on your own, hating me.'

'What's here?' says Beattie distrustfully.

'It's my parents' London flat. You've never been here, have you? It's been let since the beginning of the war. All right, Cabbie, we're leaving. *Please*, Beattie.'

Unwillingly Beattie gets out and waits while Charles pays the driver.

'Take my arm or else we'll both break a leg on this pavement,' orders Charles. They go into the lobby and Charles presses the button for the lift.

'It's only a little flat; my parents used it for shopping trips when Dad had meetings of the Law Society. It was let to a doctor and his wife; he's got rooms in Harley Street. But they've just bought a place of their own in Chiltern Court.'

The lift stops on the top floor, and Charles slips a Yale key into the door facing them.

'The heating is still on, thank goodness. I've been camping here for a few days before I go back to High Wycombe. Give me your coat.'

Beattie hardly hears him, so entranced is she by her first experience of modern living. In the drawing-room there is a radiogram in the corner, and on the other side of the room, Beattie feels almost sure, is a cocktail-cabinet.

'Have a look round if you want to.'

There are two bedrooms, one double and one single, and a maid's room. The bathroom has white tiles everywhere and a white-enamelled bath with clawed feet. The kitchen is like something out of a Hollywood film. It is all done in yellow shiny stuff, and all the cupboard doors match. It is so light and airy and easily cleaned that Beattie feels quite faint with envy. Without thinking she asks: 'Do you have hot water here all the time?'

'All the time!'

Beattie catches the amusement in Charles's tone and colours. The ludicrousness of her enquiry about the plumbing arrangements at what was a moment of high drama between them strikes Beattie forcibly, and defensively she adds: 'You wouldn't find it so funny if you had to light the copper for every drop of hot water you get. I'll bet you'll never have to boil twelve nappies a day by hand.'

'No,' say Charles drily, 'I'm absolutely sure I won't. I wasn't laughing at you, Beattie. Go back to the sitting-room and I'll build up the fire.'

With the red velvet curtains drawn against the sound of swishing tyres on the snowy road it is very cosy in the warm, dimly lit room.

'Is it time for a sherry?' Charles wonders out loud. 'Yes, why not? It's five o'clock. What time did you say that train of yours was?'

'Eight. And it's the last one that connects with a bus for Musgrave.'

'Well, I'll have to make sure you're on it.' Charles goes to the cocktail-cabinet and pours them both a glass of Amontillado.

'Here's to Peace 1944, cheers.'

'Cheers,' says Beattie, dubiously trying her sherry and deciding she quite likes it.

'Look,' says Charles briskly, dropping his long frame into the sofa opposite. 'Let's just have a truce for a moment, shall we? It won't take more than a couple of sentences to work out what you say to the solicitors. I just needed to see you because when you *do* want to go ahead we won't be able to see each other before the hearing or they'll think we're colluding and they won't give us a divorce.'

'Charles, please don't keep saying that I want to go ahead. It was you who brought the matter up and you who keeps pressing things. Is there someone you want to marry?'

Charles looks at her in astonishment.

'Whatever made you think that?'

'You seem so desperate to be free.'

'No – I – I – no.'

'What about Eleanor?'

Charles stares at her. 'Eleanor? I spent the weekend with her, actually,' says Charles matter-of-factly. 'It was a disaster. Her marriage had broken down and she thought – things were pretty bad between you and me at that stage.'

'Why was it a disaster?'

'Married in haste and repented at leisure,' says Charles apparently without malice. 'The strange thing was that, after having been so close, when we met again things just didn't work. It used to be important to me that I was the only one she'd lean on. Halfway through our weekend I realized quite cynically that she'd always find someone else to take on her problems. She's an emotional vacuum. People just get sucked in.'

'But, Charles, you were in love with her.'

'I still care for her a lot. If she was in trouble, I'd always help. But actually living with someone is something different, isn't it? By the end of that weekend I just wanted complete silence and to sleep for about a thousand years. She could see it hadn't worked and she went back to her husband. She left him a few months later. I haven't heard from her since. She's working in the MI so far as I know. Oh God, don't let's talk about her or me. Tell me about yourself. Tell me about your school. And the boys. And Annie.'

'Do you really find us that interesting?'

'Of course I do. It's a story I can't hear enough of.'

'If you wanted to hear that much, why didn't you write to me?'

Charles shrugs and pour himself and then her another sherry.

'Hurt pride, dear girl. I wasn't going to have my letters read later in the day or not at all depending on whether you have any news of Brooke Musgrave.'

Beattie blushes a fiery scarlet.

'Charles, that's not fair.'

'Isn't it? Beattie, you're such a silly girl. Such a beautiful silly girl. Come and sit beside me. It's all right, I'm not going to take advantage of you; I was just going to put a friendly arm round you. You look so forlorn.'

Unwillingly Beattie gets up and goes and sits on the sofa next to Charles, who in a brotherly way slips an arm round her shoulder and hugs her.

'That's better.'

They sit for a while in a companionable silence. 'Was that true what you said – about Brooke marrying?'

Charles nods. 'Did you really not know?'

'No. Mrs Musgrave would have told everybody.' To Beattie's horror she finds tears starting in her eyes.

405

'Do you still miss him that much? Hey, come on, don't cry. I know there's no point whatsoever in telling you he's not worth it. Are you still in love with him?'

'It's not that,' says Beattie, slowly wiping her eyes and turning her face unconsciously into Charles's shoulder. 'It's so hard to explain. It's just the sadness of it all. The grief I feel for Annie because her father acted so badly. I – I – still can't get over Brooke behaving as he did. I know it just shows that I'm not sophisticated. But we'd known each other, been lovers for so long. And if he could treat me like that it can't ever have meant the same for him as it did for me.'

Charles pulls her more firmly into his arms, his cheek resting against her forehead.

'Listen. Don't keep blaming yourself and thinking the worst of him. The last thing I want to do, the *very* last thing, is to defend Brooke. But you mustn't feel because he acted the way he did that he didn't feel anything for you. I've seen Brooke behave badly before, and I know that if he was with you for that long he must have cared a lot about you.'

'Then, why—?'

'Oh, lots of reasons. Most likely he felt he couldn't cope with the responsibility. As I say, I don't want to defend him. But I do know that most of those guys – the tensions those pilots fly under, Brooke probably couldn't put two coherent thoughts together when you told him, and his impulse was just to smash his way out of the situation as quickly as possible. That's not to say that I approve of his behaviour. I had cause enough to think badly of him before I—'

'Before you what?' asks Beattie curiously.

'Before I began to find his girlfriend so attractive. Though I'll give you your due,' says Charles drily, tilting up Beattie's chin so he can look at her properly, 'you never led me on. I didn't get a civil word out of you for the first two years.'

'That's because you always looked as if you despised me.'

'I never felt that. I felt sorry for you if you want to know the truth. The girl who's able to cope with Brooke will have to be as spoilt as he is and as tough as nails. You clearly didn't come into either of those two categories.'

'What category did I come under, then?'

Charles grins. 'Fishing for compliments, are we? Well, let's say "obstinate, wilful, romantic and very vulnerable".'

'Thanks,' says Beattie with some asperity.

'I could add "beautiful, sexy and mysterious" if you wanted.'

Charles tilts Beattie's chin gently again, then pulls her to him and kisses her with such gentleness and passion that Beattie feels her strength actually draining away. The kiss goes on for a long long time until a lump of coal falls in the fire sending up a shower of sparks. When Charles finally and reluctantly releases her he says: 'Do you really have to go back tonight? I've got another day's leave. You could stay here. We could go and do a show and have dinner.'

'I'm expected home. And there's Annie.'

'Couldn't your mother take care of her for just one night? You could ring someone and let your parents know. If it goes on snowing like this, you'd have been lucky to get a train anyway. Please, Beattie. Please,' says Charles softly, coaxingly, and kisses her again. This time he parts her lips with his tongue, and her quick gasp of pleasure makes him grip her even tighter. Beattie feels her nipples harden with desire and longing, feelings so long ignored and repressed that she feels dizzy.

'I don't know who to ring,' she murmurs against Charles's lips.

'You can ring the post office. It isn't six yet. And I've got the number,' says Charles innocently.

Beattie gives Charles a level look.

'You've got it all worked out, haven't you?'

'No, Beattie. I thought this would probably be the last day we'd see each other. For all I know, it still will be. But I don't see why we can't enjoy each other's company even if this is going to be goodbye. It needn't change anything between us if that's what you're afraid of.'

'It's not what I'm afraid of,' says Beattie, flushing. 'Do you have that number?'

For answer Charles feels around in his jacket pocket for his diary, goes to the phone and dials the operator.

'She says she'll call you back when she's made the connection. What would you like to do tonight? It may be a bit late to book for a show, but we could still make a film if you wanted.'

'Oh, yes, please,' says Beattie. 'I suppose it would be too much to hope for *Gone with the Wind*.'

'I think so. You usually have to book, so I'm told. But there's a lunchtime performance. We can always book for tomorrow afternoon if you want.'

'Really? That would be wonderful.'

The phone rings. 'Your long-distance call to Musgrave,' sings the operator.

'Hello? Hello, this is Beatrice Hammond. Is that you, Mrs—? Yes, it is a good line, isn't it? I can hear you quite clearly. Yes, I'm in London still and it looks as though I'm going to have to stay overnight. . . .'

Beattie is still searching lamely for an excuse which is never needed. Mrs Leary interrupts volubly to say it has snowed all day in the village and no one has been in or out.

'They're going to get the Yanks from the camps to clear the roads tomorrow, but until then you can't walk more than a yard. The Ipswich bus hasn't been able to get through all day. You want me to tell your parents, Beattie?'

'Yes, please. If you can tell them I'm staying overnight with Charles and I'll hope to be home by tomorrow night.'

Slowly Beattie replaces the phone.

'The village is completely blocked with snow.'

'So they weren't expecting you?'

'No.'

'Good,' says Charles briskly. 'Then, we might as well make a move. We can get an evening paper on the corner and see what's on.'

It is still snowing softly when they leave the flat, but later that evening by the time they leave the cinema in Tottenham Court Road the night is absolutely still, London's scarred and bombed landscape softened by a deep covering of virgin snow. Beattie is taken aback at the extent of the bomb damage; buildings sway perilously together over huge craters, and everywhere torn and exposed walls show fireplaces and stairways exposed to the night wind.

'It gives you a shock when you haven't seen it for a while,' says Charles. 'When I came back just before Christmas I couldn't get over it. Now I'm used to it again already. Is there much bombing in Ipswich?'

They end the evening at a restaurant in Charlotte Street. The meal is surprisingly relaxed. Charles listens with every sign of attention to her account of her life at Ormond Lodge, to news of Annie's first step and stories of Toby and Ern. In return he tells her a little of his life in Africa.

'Do you ever think of what you'll do after the war?'

'Now and then. I suppose it depends on what happens to my next book. If there is a next book. Marwicks have taken to sending me polite but increasingly pointed letters about the spring list. I'm still not convinced you can make a living out of writing thrillers.'

'Agatha Christie does.'

'Yes, but she's mass-market. I don't know whether I'll be that.'

'What would you have done if there hadn't been a war?'

'Oh, eventually I'd have gone back to college and done a Master's. And I'd probably have ended up a geography don. I could still do that now if I wanted, but too much has happened. I was thinking the other day when I was trying to write a scene about an inquest that it would have been jolly useful if I'd had a legal training. Strange, because it's what Dad always wanted for me. I suppose it's not too late for me to do it even now. What about you? Will you go on teaching?'

'Oh, *yes*,' says Beattie fervently. 'I know I complain about the hours and having to stay late to rehearse plays and all that marking, but really I love it. Mother can't understand it.'

'Does she look after Annie?'

'Yes, but she makes it clear it ought to be me. I sometimes wonder why she thinks I bothered to get a teaching diploma. She thinks I only want to go out to work because I don't love Annie. But I do love her; you couldn't not. It's got nothing to do with that. And it's only six hours out of Annie's day, and quite a lot of that she's asleep.'

'You worry too much about your mother, you know.'

'When you're living with someone twenty-four hours a day you can't not be aware of their approval or disapproval.'

'Do you ever think of getting a place on your own?'

'All the time,' says Beattie dispiritedly. 'But it's not easy when you're on your own. And I had to call Dr Body in before Christmas for Mother because she had another of her turns, and he said afterwards she wasn't nearly as well or as strong as she pretended. So I can't see me moving away from the village for the time being. Anyway, I'd never find anywhere to rent *there*. You wouldn't believe how short of accommodation everywhere is.'

They walk back up Mortimer Street arm-in-arm, the air so sharp and frosty that it hurts to breathe.

'No raids tonight, touch wood,' says Charles as he lets them into the flat. 'Though there's a shelter directly below us, which is lucky. Would you like a bath or something?'

'That would be marvellous,' says Beattie composedly. Her delight at the prospect of total as opposed to partial immersion in lukewarm water in front of the range is temporarily marred by the fact that no arrangements have yet been posited as to where she is to sleep. For the time being the joys of hot water and warm towels are enough. Eventually, however, other problems present themselves. Cautiously Beattie puts her head round the bathroom door and clears her throat.

'Er, Charles. . . .'

Charles appears from the sitting-room where he has been listening to the wireless.

'Oh God, you'll want something to wear, won't you? I'm afraid there isn't anything in the flat. Look, I tell you what. You can have the top of my pyjamas. They'll come down to your knees quite easily. I've put a hot-water bottle in the bed—'

'Which bed?'

'The double bed,' says Charles levelly. 'Which one did you think?'

There is a long silence, then tentatively Charles comes towards her. Beattie, who is perfectly decently wrapped up in a towel, steps back instinctively.

Gently Charles pushes the heavy waves of hair back from her cheek.

'You really don't need that towel, you know,' he says, and before she realizes what he is doing he has untwisted the towel and let it fall damply on to the bathroom floor.

'Charles, don't—' is Beattie's last agonized remark before he begins to kiss her, his hands delicately exploring her warm flesh.

'I want to look at you.'

In spite of her protests Charles takes her hands and steps back, and she suddenly sees herself through his eyes. The dark hair, clinging damply to her shoulder, her breasts even fuller and heavier now, the nipples dark and pronounced from nursing Annie, the narrow waist and the curve of her belly ending in the soft mass of shadowy hair guarding the secret parts of her.

'I hated you so much,' Charles says quietly, almost conversationally. 'I wanted to put you out of my mind altogether. But I seemed to dream about you every night when I was away, and every morning I'd wake up and feel bitter. That's why I was angry when I met you. You look a thousand times more beautiful than even I remembered, and I thought: I'll never be able to make love to her now, I'll never know what it's like to touch her and feel her mouth open for me.'

They kiss again. For Beattie it is as if fire is consuming her between her legs. She can actually feel the most intimate parts of her begin to moisten and swell in the heat of her desire. Later, much later, she wants him to kiss and caress every part of her. But now, immediately, all she wants is for Charles to push into that hot moist wetness. Half kissing, half carrying her, Charles takes her into the dimly lit bedroom and, as if divining her own need, immediately enters her, hard and insistent; and as Beattie cries out in pleasure and astonishment waves of sensation begin to spill out from the hot core where she and Charles are joined.

'Beattie. Beattie!' says Charles urgently. 'Look at me. Look at me.'

Dazed, Beattie opens her eyes, her pupils so dilated that her irises seem almost black. For a long moment she and Charles look at each other.

'What is it?'

Charles smiles at her grimly, tenderly.

'I just want you to know that it's me you're making love to. No one else. And it's my cock inside you.'

Beattie feels a spasm of desire that she's never known begin to contract her muscles, pulls Charles hungrily to her, and as Charles pushes deeper and deeper she begins to find her own rhythm and thrusts against the hard insistence of his hips. The climax is like nothing she has ever felt before, so pleasurable that it is close to pain. For a long long time afterwards they lie in silence bathed in sweat, Charles's lips in Beattie's hair, her arms still round him. Outside an ambulance roars by, its bell going furiously. From the east of the city come muted thuds of bombs falling.

CHAPTER
THIRTY-THREE

RED Gate Stud, Newmarket
26 December 1943

Dearest Lucy,
A very very Happy Christmas: I sure wish we could have spent it together.
You'd love it here. As soon as I arrived it felt familiar – it's just like being in
Kentucky except here there's no heating, no showers and no sun. Other than
that it's just the same! There are fires in the kitchen and drawing-room, but
that's it. I expect the British rely on body heat – there are six adults and seven
children and five dogs, and that's just in the house. Everybody talks about
horses all the time. You wouldn't know there's a war on.

The Jamesons don't have much in their stables right now on account of
there's so little racing. But there's nothing wrong with the quality of what
they've got. Yesterday we went riding on the Gallops in the early morning.
I'd forgotten how great it can be. It was still dark when we rode out but it had
cleared by the time we got up on the Heath. There was frost on the grass and
the sun was coming up like a red disc on one side while the moon was still in
the sky. The air was so cold it hurt to breathe. I wish you could have been
here to ride with us. I miss you so much. I think about all the good things we
could be doing together. I keep wanting to tell you things about home. Then
even as I say that I realize that I don't really mean Boston. I want to tell you
more about Goshen. Last night I sat up late with George Jameson waiting for
one of the mares to foal. It was a good evening.

I hope you find your family well and that when I get to meet them we can
tell them about us and the future. I want there to be a future for us but I still
don't feel sure about what you want. I'm more sorry than I can say about us
having words just before you went. It was all my fault. I guess I was just sore
at you going off when I wanted to be with you. It always makes me feel better
just knowing you are around. Even if I can't actually see you. Most of the
time I can hold what's happening to me and the other boys at arm's length.
You've got no choice, have you? But sometimes I get pretty low. Particularly
when one of the boys in the hut doesn't come back. The only way I've found
to hold it all away is to think about after the war, and I think a lot about
whether there'll be a future for us, and whether you'd be prepared to start
life with me in America. Though even I begin to wonder what I'd be offering

411

you. I can't see either of us being too happy in a Boston suburb with me practising law. Still, all that's a long way off. And I don't want to put pressure on you.

Right now I have to go as I'm taking part in some kind of paperchase. Apparently I'm the hare. Take care of yourself. It's strange, when I came to England I never thought I'd be going to meet the girl I'd want to marry.

With fondest love from
WILL

PS. The Jamesons have asked you up to stay as soon as you've got a weekend free. Did you know your English Derby is held at Newmarket for the duration of the war? Wouldn't it be great to come up to see it?

Stone House, Harrogate, Yorkshire
28 December

Dearest Will,

I can't tell you how pleased I was to get your letter – I've been carrying it round in my pocket all day. Things here are perfectly frightful. My mother left my father on Christmas Eve and poor Father is devastated. I am taking care of him and wishing I was with you. Your description of life at Red Gate has made me feel faint with envy. Here it's like the House of Usher. In a sense I'm glad I didn't bring you – it would have been a terrible time for you. I hope you're getting plenty of sleep and fresh air. You looked so exhausted the last time I saw you. I'd even forgotten we'd had words. It just seems such a long time since I've seen you, yet my diary tells me it's only eight days ago. It seems much more.

I felt bad because you were asking me reasonable questions about what I wanted for the future and I know how exasperating my answers must have been. The truth is I don't know what to do. Or at least what to do for the best. The sight of Father so completely devastated by Mother's departure absolutely haunts me – he's like a child whose mother has turned him out of doors. Hermione (that's Mother's secretary) told me that Mother has been having an affair with her publisher for some time. I can hardly bear to think about it. I'm going to be here for a few days longer than I planned because I can't leave Daddy until he's a bit better. On top of everything else he's got flu now.

I can see your family are going to have the utmost difficulty in getting you back to your law studies after the war! But I have the same thoughts. You can't just go on with life as if these years haven't happened. I wish I knew what the future held.

If I don't get a chance to speak to you on the phone, a very happy New Year for 1944. I love you, dearest Will, and I wish we were together.

Love from
LUCY

Home Farm, Musgrave
24 February 1944

Dear Virginia,

I feel quite awful about how long it has taken me to reply to your Christmas letter. As you probably deduced from my silence, things have not been going well here. I don't think it would be an exaggeration to say they've never been worse. I couldn't bring myself to write it all down before but now I'm at the stage of thinking: Well, what's the point of pretending?

You know I went home for Christmas. I duly arrived in Harrogate laden with presents and Christmas cheer on Christmas Eve intending to work my way round to the subject of Hugh and my divorce. As it turned out the house was in uproar. To cut a long story short Mother has left Father, though he hasn't exactly faced that fact yet. What makes it worse is that she must have left about half an hour before I arrived – she probably took my train back to London. I'm still hoping that it wasn't the thought of my imminent arrival that convinced her her marriage was over. I arrived to find Father weeping in the library, two golfing friends of Father's due within the hour to spend the festive season with us, and ten people expected for Christmas lunch. The golfing friends turned out to be surprisingly decent and helped me keep things together on Christmas Day – if they hadn't been there I don't know what I'd have done. Dad was so completely sozzled by 11.30 that I told him to go back to bed and he didn't wake up until the early evening so we struggled through the lunch on our own. Talk about *Hamlet* without the Prince. Not to mention the Queen. It was a most bizarre situation – I simply said that Mother had been called unexpectedly to London and Father had flu. As it turned out, by some grotesque coincidence I was right – Father did have flu and didn't get up again until well into the New Year.

It was perfectly frightful, and worse still I was left closeted with the appalling Hermione who unfortunately had been left enough work by my mother to take her well into mid-summer. As you can imagine I was absolutely determined not to ask *her* about why things had gone so suddenly and drastically wrong, but I could see from the smirk on her face that she was dying to be asked. Do you remember that perfectly frightful girl at school called Phoebe Something-or-other? The one who spent her time listening at keyholes and then trying to tantalize people with secrets which it always turned out everybody knew anyway? Hermione is just like that. All I got out of Daddy by January 1st was that Mother had said she needed time on her own, she felt they'd grown apart and she wanted time to think. I really can't see 4 p.m. on Christmas Eve as being the most appropriate moment for delivering a bombshell like that. Furthermore no one seemed to know where she was, and it wasn't until some mail arrived for her after Christmas and Hermione said, quite casually, 'Oh, I'll send it on to her, shall I?' that I realized that Mother must have confided everything to her. It made me quite sick with rage. But I was absolutely determined not to give her the satisfaction of knowing how angry I was. So I just said casually, 'Where is Mother?' and she said quite calmly, 'Oh, at Claridges, I suppose, with Eric now that his divorce has gone through.' I sat there absolutely stunned, then I said feebly: 'Eric? You mean her publisher?' When she nodded it suddenly all fell into place – that suite at Claridges, those endless trips to London. I began to feel quite ill. Then to my utmost astonishment Hermione said in a ghastly cosy girls-together way, 'But you must have seen it coming,' and I knew that if I'd have let her she'd have launched into a defence of Mother's genius and how lucky Daddy had been to share her life. So I just cut her short by saying as rudely as I could: 'Hermione, I think you're being paid to be the typist not to discuss your employer's affairs.' She went a really horrible colour, like the stain beetroot makes on a tablecloth, and said with a sort of sneer, 'Well, it's easy to see whose side you're on,' and flounced back to her typewriter.

I spent the rest of the holiday sitting with Daddy, watching icicles form on the conservatory roof. It was perfectly dreadful. He cries all the time. The doctor says he's depressed after his flu; I know it's more than that. It's as if he's just given up hope. And he won't hear a word against Mother, not a word, and keeps saying he could see it coming and how he didn't want to hold her back. It's quite plain he doesn't know a thing about Eric.

I felt frightful leaving him – I'd only had permission to be away a week and I'd already asked for one extension and I felt I couldn't leave the McFees to struggle on indefinitely – Mrs McFee had already written and told me everybody was ill. In the end I told Father that if he and Mother did split up he could always come down to Suffolk to live and I'd be able to see him more often. He just stared and said oh no, that Mother would be back, that she'd just had too much on her plate having to care for an elderly husband. I didn't know what to say to that but left it that I'd write as often as possible.

All this time Will had been writing and telephoning – he had the most frightful January and it looks like an even worse February – they seem to be stepping up those long-distance raids into Germany, so Will's been flying almost every day regardless of the weather. He sounded absolutely exhausted, and I was longing to be with him. Anyway, I got back to Ipswich finally only to find dear Will waiting for me at the station half-dead with cold. He'd been there for three hours. I don't think I've ever been so glad to see anyone in my life. We fell into each other's arms and just clung. There was only time for a quick meal in Ipswich and I went back in one of the farm lorries. Home Farm certainly isn't lacking its own dramas – Donny and Dougal have both got mumps and aren't allowed anywhere near the animals. But the very worst thing of all was the sight of a pile of letters waiting for me in my room. And *five* of them were from Hugh! (There were two letters from Ma – a long string of justifications. Haven't bothered to reply to them yet.) Hugh's letters – I can hardly bring myself to talk about them. It'll come as no surprise to you to learn that Julia Heap has married someone else. She didn't even tell Hugh she was thinking of it – just wrote and told him after the event and said she hoped they'd always be friends! Can you beat it? as Will would say. So Hugh immediately wrote off to me because he felt so badly treated and for some reason was absolutely sure I'd be sympathetic.

I am sorry this letter is so entirely about me and so long into the bargain but I just felt I had to get it all off my chest. I'm so glad everything is going well with you. Do give Alexis my love. Once we've finished lambing I really will make an effort to drag Will up to London to meet you both. You'll never guess, he saw *Bomber Command* in New York! Isn't life extraordinary! I'll have to fly if this letter is to get to the post today.

Much love from
LUCY

Reel Films, W1
26 February 1944

My dear Lucy,
Your letter sent me reeling, and I am snatching half an hour at lunchbreak to dash off a reply at once. It's almost hard to know what to talk about first – your own affairs or your parents' – except that I feel far more personal indignation about Hugh's volte-face. I just think he's got the most colossal cheek even writing, let alone expecting you to sympathize with him. The next thing is he'll be expecting you to wait for him. I'm going to have to be very stern with you, because I know your soft heart and I did feel I detected a faint note of sympathy in your attitude towards him. Dearest Lucy, if Will is what you really want, then don't weaken. Hugh has behaved appallingly, and I don't see why you should give one second thought to his happiness – he certainly never considered yours. But I really am sorry about your parents, and stunned, too. That business about Eric is a bit of a facer – I owe Theo Beavers a letter, perhaps he can fill me in about the state of Eric's private life.

All is indeed well here. Or it will be when I see my husband again. Alexis is currently putting the music to the Welsh epic and we seem to pass on the stairs last thing at night and first thing in the morning. The good news is that only eight months after our marriage we are finally going to have a honeymoon. It's only three days at a hotel in Dorset but it's a good hotel with plenty of log-fires and (I hope) good food. One of the two most chastening revelations about marriage is that if you want good food you are for some reason expected to prepare it. The second revelation is discovering that Alexis cooks rather better than I do. Apparently his mother refused point-blank to cook anything, so he had a lot of practice early in life. She sounds a splendid woman; I'm more sorry than ever that we never met. I'll have to fly now because I'll be wanted shortly. Much love and keep me posted,

Love,
VIRGINIA

Home Farm, Musgrave
15 March

Dear Virginia,
I have been reduced to removing some of the back pages from the Milk Accounts Book as I am completely out of notepaper but long to write. Thank you very much for your cheery and speedy reply. I'm afraid your predictions are all too accurate – I have now had four further letters from Hugh telling me how unhappy he is, how the scales have fallen from his eyes and how he sees clearly for the first time where his duty lies. I am very fearful that he imagines that duty will somehow involve me, and he will be very shortly suggesting that we try to 'make a go' of things. He seems to be deducing far too much from the fact I never got divorce proceedings going. He imagines that I've been waiting for him to come to his senses. The truth is that I was just in such a torpor I couldn't be bothered to. The awful thing is that even while his letters make me simmer with rage the sheer unhappiness of them

undoes me every time and instead of writing back a stiff note saying 'Are you kidding?' I find myself writing consoling little epistles full of platitudes about 'better to know now' and things like that. He really is such a child – he obviously does think I've kept myself in cold storage until he came to an appreciation of my true worth. Well, enough of that. It depresses me.

Poor Father is no better physically, and Mother has resolutely declined to come home. She still hasn't said anything to me directly about this Eric – her excuse for leaving is that being with Father was affecting her writing. I ask you! But she's never seen anybody's point of view except her own. I just hope she comes to her senses before Father gets any worse. He went back to bed at the beginning of March with another bout of flu; I think the doctor really is worried about him. We have just started lambing, so I am up all hours. I am afraid I'm going to have to draw this letter to a rather speedier close than I wanted because Donny (minus his mumps) has just come and told me that there is some suspicious action in the lambing-pen. If only sheep could be persuaded to have their lambs in daylight hours! I'll be in touch again soon.

Much love,
LUCY

Reel Film Productions, 28 Soho Square, W1
20 March 1944

Dearest L,

By happy chance I've got this lunchtime free so I'm able to reply to your letter immediately. My only anxiety is that an hour won't be sufficient time fully to express my outrage at Hugh's perfidy. I long and long to have a proper chat with you – please don't forget the standing invitation to come up for the weekend and occupy our rather damp spare bedroom. (I saw my husband this morning, and when he recognized your writing he told me to give you his love when I replied to your letter. If I sound surprised at actually seeing my husband, that's because he's been at Denham editing for the last two weeks, and he hasn't been able to get home owing to the new bombing. It's a tremendous bore having to go down to the shelter on my own. We had the most appalling row about it as I know perfectly well that when *he's* here on his own all he does is crawl under the kitchen table and sleep through everything. Though things do seem to be getting rather nasty. I don't think I've had a wink of sleep these last three nights – they've got some new kind of anti-aircraft gun in Hyde Park and it makes almost more noise than the bombs falling.)

I've been pondering deeply about Hugh all morning. My advice would be don't take any hasty action, however importunate his letters may be. I think he's just beginning to realize that the war won't last for ever and he's panicking about what he'll do afterwards. Do people talk much about after the war in Musgrave? It seems to be the favourite topic on buses. I suppose it's all to do with the Second Front that everybody talks about but no one's supposed to mention. There seems to be a sense of expectancy in the air – I had dinner with Willy (my US journalist friend) last week and he'd just come

416

back from a tour of the docks. He says there are all kinds of landing-craft there for the Second Front when it happens. So even I am beginning to think it can't be long now. Alexis longs and longs to hear Allied troops are in France. I suppose I do, too; it's the only way I'll get a proper honeymoon.

Write to me soon, Lucy, and let me know how you are. If things get too frightful, don't forget you can always come here for the weekend, and forget your troubles with us.

Much love from
VIRGINIA

Cairo
24 February

My dear Lucy,

Delighted to get your letter – do write regularly, won't you? It makes all the difference to a chap's morale to have post from home. Sorry you're having such a frightful time – I can't get over how badly your mother's behaving. If I were your father, I wouldn't take her back after what she's done. Still, I suppose at their age companionship counts for a lot.

We've been stood by for something special at present – very hush hush, you understand, so we're meant to be on the q.v. the whole time. Chaps have even started to talk about after the war – it is certainly going to seem strange after four years in uniform. Everybody wonders what they'll go back to – I suppose I'm lucky the bank is keeping my job open for me. What I thought might be nice would be to get a cottage in somewhere like Wimbledon. I expect you've got used to the outdoor life and there's plenty of good walks across the Common. And I'm sure you could find some kind of hobby in breeding dogs. I must say it's dashed lonely here without you, Lucy – I look at our wedding photographs sometimes and wonder if things could have been different if I hadn't been posted abroad. It would have been nice to have a couple of kids to come home to after the hostilities cease. Still, that's hardly your fault! Anyway, must go now. You'll be glad to hear my head-aches seem to have almost gone though the knee continues to play up a bit. I suppose it's just the perils of being a fighting man!

Take care of yourself.

Love from
HUGH

Stone House, Harrogate
1 March 1944

Dear Mrs Jennings,

I tried to ring you last night but couldn't get through to the farm. Mrs Hallett wrote to your father last week requesting a divorce. I only know because she wrote and told me at the same time. Your father hasn't mentioned it but I think the letter has affected him badly and I am concerned about his health. I expect he hasn't written to you for fear of upsetting you. But I think he is really unwell and he will not see the doctor. Can you ring, or better still come up and see him for a few days?

Yours sincerely,
HERMIONE TAYLOR

Musgrave Post Office
2 March 1944

Dearest Will,
I am asking Toby to leave this note for you in case the post doesn't reach you on time. I won't be able to meet you on Saturday, I'm afraid, as I've had to go to Harrogate as Father is ill again and won't see a doctor. Mr McFee has very kindly offered to drive me to Ipswich. I'm dreading the train journey as I gather most of the trains have been mysteriously withdrawn to move troops for the Second Front. I will try to phone you from Harrogate but, failing that, will write. I am sorry there's no time to say more but Toby is waiting.

Love from
LUCY

Stone House, Harrogate
5 March 1944

FATHER DIED YESTERDAY STOP AM STAYING FOR FUNERAL ON TUESDAY STOP WILL WRITE LOVE LUCY

CHAPTER
THIRTY-FOUR

OUTSIDE THE BLOSSOM on the apple trees is whirling like snow from flailing branches. Ragged white clouds race briskly across a wet-looking bright-blue sky. Beattie sits by the kitchen window, her forehead pressed against the glass. Annie, temporarily worn out by her struggle to avoid eating lunch, dozes companionably on her knee. There is a sudden bang and a grating rattle from overhead as the April wind wrenches another tile loose from the roof. It is time for Annie's rest; if she puts her down now, it'll be a clear hour before the boys come in from school and Mrs Blythe requires her tea. But as she starts to gather the little girl more firmly into her arms the garden gate clicks and Beattie recognizes a tall figure in a brown felt hat. It is Lucy. With alacrity Beattie opens the kitchen door.

'Lucy, what luck you coming round now; it seems ages since I've seen you. Do come in. I'm all on my own. The boys don't break up until tomorrow, and Mother's having a day in bed.'

But there is no immediate response of welcome from Lucy.

'Oh, Beattie, hello,' she says feebly. 'I didn't think there would be anybody in. I was just going to leave this joint for your mother. I can't stop, I'm afraid.'

'Oh,' says Beattie nonplussed. There is no doubt about it – Lucy is avoiding her eyes. 'So you don't even have time for tea?'

'I'm afraid not. Are you having a special do that you want the joint?'

'Charles is coming to stay for a week,' says Beattie, already wondering if she had been forward in inviting Lucy in. 'I just wanted to say how sorry I was to hear about your father, Lucy. He was always that nice to everyone.'

'Yes – it – it was all a great shock,' agrees Lucy almost absently, and her finger and thumb massage the bridge of her nose, her tall figure slumping suddenly with sheer weariness. Beattie suddenly sees lines of tension and fatigue in Lucy's face. Still with Annie tucked sleepily in the crook of her arm Beattie instinctively reaches out and touches Lucy's hand.

'Lucy, you look done in, you really do. Come in for just a minute and rest your legs. Annie's just off to have her sleep. Come in, do,' she coaxes. Silently Lucy follows her in, the fight suddenly gone out of her. When Beattie returns to the kitchen Lucy has unbuttoned her greatcoat and is warming her hands against the range.

'Make yourself comfortable,' says Beattie briskly, pulling out the rocking chair and putting the kettle on to boil. In a rush she adds: 'I was beginning to wonder if I'd done something to offend you.'

Lucy stares.

'Offend me? Of course not. What on earth made you think that?'

'I haven't seen you for so long, I thought perhaps you were avoiding me. Even the boys said they hadn't seen you. They're that fed up with the airbases being moved anyway,' says Beattie, aware that she is talking too much but dreading silence more. 'I saw Lily this morning. She says she's writing every day to Greg but so far she hasn't had a single line back. Have you heard from Will?'

Lucy makes a noise somewhere between a gulp and a sob and feels blindly in her breeches pocket. Having found an oily-looking khaki hankie she bursts into a fit of uncontrollable sobbing.

'Oh, Lucy, I'm sorry, I shouldn't have said all that,' says Beattie, aghast. 'I just thought you were looking so sad because you must be missing Will.'

'I suppose I am. Nothing very much is going to change about that. I've broken things off with him. After I came back from Harrogate. That was five weeks ago now.'

'Lucy, you *can't* have. . . . Why, he was so nice and crazy about you. Why did you do it?'

'It seemed the right thing to do at the time, but there are other times when I think I did it for no reason at all. Except that he wanted me to make choices and decisions and I just couldn't do it. I was so . . . aghast at Father's death. I got there too late, you see. The telegram must have arrived a couple of hours after I left Home Farm. He'd been so ill, but I'm sure the final stroke was caused by Mother leaving. I really think the loss of her killed him. It sounds melodramatic but it's true.'

'But . . . if your mother wasn't happy with him any more, Lucy . . . .'

'Oh, I know. I've turned it over in my mind again and again. It's just that I still feel Mother could have been kinder. I just don't think she behaved well. She came up to the funeral, of course. And we had a bit of a barney afterwards. Basically she wanted me to say that I thought she'd done the right thing.'

'And what did you say?'

'I told her it had been her own decision and that was that. She got a bit red-faced at that point and said I'd had no idea of what she'd had to put up with during the past few years. And I said that was probably quite true – all I could remember was Father giving up his career to manage and support her and how happy they had been. That didn't go down at all well. But it's almost impossible to talk to Mother. It's as if she's changed gear in her head and she sees everything from a different point of view. She seems to think because of her talent she's always got the right to put herself first. Whereas I think we're all ordinary and if you make promises they should be binding.'

During the long silence that follows, Lucy inspects the mud on her boots and the clock in the hall announces discreetly that it is three o'clock.

'Is that why you broke things off with Will?'

Lucy nods.

420

'I had a week to think about things once the funeral was over. I put the house on the market and sorted through his affairs. It was a revelation. Father had kept almost every photograph ever taken of me, all carefully inscribed on the back with the date and the circumstances. It touched me because I know he'd really have preferred a son. But that didn't stop him liking me. I liked him. He was a decent person, and I feel he deserved better treatment from Mother. After all, you marry people for better and for worse, don't you? And all the time I was up there I kept getting letters sent on from Hugh. Then Will phoned wanting to know what I was going to do about the future, and I got so confused. The two situations seemed to be muddled up in my head. I don't think Hugh has behaved well, either. Yet there's something so sad in his letters . . . . So when I came back to the farm I told Will I couldn't see him any more.'

'But you always seemed so happy together; he was so obviously fond of you.'

'I know . . . I know.' Lucy's distress is obvious and unfeigned. 'But I just felt so confused. I don't feel free to commit myself to Will when I've already taken vows to someone else. Even if that person hasn't been too scrupulous about his vows to me. But I just couldn't make Will see that. And poor Will was always in such a state of tension and insecurity. It's his flying. It never seemed possible for us to be normal and ordinary together.'

Beattie is silent, remembering.

'To cap it all, the orders to move must have come through the next day. From what people are saying, I suppose they'll be providing air support for the Second Front. Poor Will was confined to camp. The day before they moved he actually broke out and came up to the farm to try to change my mind. It was about eleven o'clock at night, and we had the most awful, awful row.' Tears are now pouring unchecked down Lucy's cheeks. 'He accused me of having led him on and never having had any intention of being serious. But that wasn't true. Even though it was Will pursuing *me* to start with, I always felt I'd made a choice about him. I liked him. I liked being with him more than with anyone else in the world. Even when we were working together it was always fun. We . . . we make a good team. Whereas I sometimes think the only reason I married Hugh was because he asked me. You see, I never expected to be asked by anyone,' goes on Lucy, more to herself than to Beattie, 'not with Virginia being so pretty.'

Beattie is startled and intrigued by these confidences.

'Did Will ever talk about marriage to you?'

'Oh, yes,' says Lucy matter-of-factly. 'Lots of times. He wanted me to go back to America with him. He'd already decided that if he lasted through the war he wasn't going back to college. His heart's really in breeding horses in Kentucky on his uncle's farm.'

'Whereas Hugh—'

'Hugh wants us to live in Wimbledon so he can travel to the bank each day. He says if I've really got a taste for the outdoor life we can go for walks on the Common and breed Scotties.'

'Oh,' says Beattie noncommittally as she refills Lucy's cup. 'Have you heard from Will since?'

'Not a word. We parted on such bad terms. I still can't believe it even now. And I can't forgive myself. I should have handled things better. I was just so unhappy. The awful thing is I can feel Will's unhappiness. Even though we haven't been in contact for over a month I know how miserable he is. But I just can't do anything to help him. Hugh writes twice a week.' There is an unconscious note of bitterness in Lucy's voice. 'And he gets quite cross if I don't reply quickly enough. There isn't really enough news to fill my letters. But I suppose Hugh must be feeling pretty unhappy himself.'

'I'm sorry you're having such a wretched time,' says Beattie lamely, feeling she isn't asking Lucy the right questions, but not being at all sure if Lucy wants the right questions asked.

'Well, there it is. I'm sorry to bang on about myself so much. Are you well? You look blooming. Did your end-of-term go all right?'

'Oh, fine,' says Beattie on the verge of a confidence, then catching sight of the weariness on Lucy's face says no more. Instead she adds: 'I'm glad Charles is able to stay for a week. He's been working to death since Christmas on some new project. I haven't seen a hair of him since then.'

When Lucy has gone, promising to come round again soon, Beattie tidies up the kitchen and tries to sort the afternoon's tasks into some order of priorities. There are a lot of clothes to be ironed. There is a further load of washing out on the line waiting to be brought in. The boys will be in shortly demanding their tea. Supper will have to be put on and a cup of tea taken up to Mrs Blythe who is having a bad day. Between these tasks Annie will have to be woken up, bathed, played with, read a story and tucked into bed. At least the bedroom is ready. Toby and Ern had helped her to move their double bed into hers and in return had collected the small camp-bed for Ern from the vicar. It will be the first time that Charles has stayed properly at the cottage.

Waiting for the kettle to boil, Beattie studies herself anxiously in the mirror. The dark red jersey with the glass buttons on the shoulder looks OK as Lily's Greg would say, but already to Beattie's critical eye it is too tight across the bust. In spite of a series of deep breaths Beattie feels a familiar sense of panic rising in her. It is two years since she has felt that panic. Keep calm just until Charles comes, she tells her reflection firmly.

Then the kitchen gate crashes open again as Toby and Ern hurtle up the garden path.

'When did you find out?'

'As soon as I missed. But I thought I'd better wait until the doctor confirmed it. I went to see him yesterday.'

Charles is silent.

'So it's due when – in September?'

'That's right.'

'Are you pleased?'

'I'm not sure,' says Beattie honestly. 'I suppose so. It's a bit of a shock.'

'You don't *seem* very pleased.'

'Well – I am – it's just that – oh, I don't know.'

Absently Beattie rolls down the car window and stares out into the dark countryside. They have been to Ipswich to see a film and stopped on the outskirts of Musgrave to talk. When Charles speaks again his voice has hardened.

'So what is it? Is it you don't want a baby or my baby or what?'

'I don't want my whole life to end,' says Beattie with a sudden intensity that takes even her by surprise. 'You don't know how hard it was after Annie. You men don't understand. I don't want to be home all the time. Mother feels I ought to be. She didn't even approve of me going back part-time after having Annie. If I try to go back to teaching again after two babies, goodness knows what she'll say.'

'What does it matter what she thinks?'

'I live with her. And I need her support.'

'I don't understand you, Beattie. I want to but I just don't. What is it you want? What's so important about teaching?'

'It isn't just the teaching.' Beattie feels for words that will remotely convey the volcanic surge of emotions she feels inside herself. 'It's having a life that just isn't babies and knowing everything is over by the time you're twenty. All my life I've wanted something different from the other girls in the village. I like them but I don't want to be like them. Their minds were closed to everything by the time they were fifteen except who they thought they were going to marry. Then you get married and have your first baby by nineteen and at twenty start looking like your mother. And after that you're nothing but seeing your family and his family and swopping recipes and not even wearing lipstick any more because your husband doesn't like you to attract other men—'

'Beattie – I—'

'And Mother, she's the worst of all. She wanted me to be a teacher and she encouraged me to go on with my studies and not be like all the others. But she never really cared about the skills I was learning. The fact that I had a profession and I'm good at it. All she wanted was for me to get a better class of husband and when I'd done *that* to put all that learning on one side.'

'So I'm a better class of husband, am I?' Charles enquires ironically.

Beattie stops to draw breath, ashamed.

'I'm sorry. I don't mean to go on. It's just it seems that I have to fight everything every step of the way. And if I don't stop fighting at any moment I'll find myself trapped for ever and I'll never get away.'

'Come on, don't cry. I bet you haven't got a hankie, either.'

'I did have but I gave it to Toby to bandage up his finger.'

'Come here.'

Charles puts his arm round Beattie's shoulders, pulling her round until her cheek rests thankfully against his neck. He smells of cigarettes, Pears soap and his own special skin smell.

'Look. Let's take this bit by bit. Are you going to have the baby?'

'Yes, of course.' Beattie is horrified by the very suggestion.

'Right. That's September, isn't it? How long would you want to stay at home with it?'

Beattie is silent.

423

'If I could breast-feed, I suppose I'd stay home until the baby was six months old. Then, if the school still wanted me, I'd go back to teaching in the mornings. And that's provided Mother would look after the children.'

'The answer is not to be so dependent on your mother.'

'She's there on the premises.'

'So move out.'

Beattie is startled. 'Where to?'

'Either rent or buy a house in the village. At least until after the war.'

'A house of our *own*?'

'Why not? It makes sense. If you don't feel you can move away while your mother's still not well, you can at least be near by and get someone else in to look after the children.'

Beattie's breath is completely taken away by the audacity of this plan.

'But wouldn't you mind? Living in the country, I mean?'

'I'd like it. It doesn't have to be for ever, does it? After the war we can decide if we want to stay here or move nearer London.'

'Would you do all that?' Beattie asks slowly. 'Would you really do all that for me?'

'If it would make you happier. I'm on your side, Beattie. Do you think you're *ever* going to believe that?'

CHAPTER
THIRTY-FIVE

*L*UCY HAD BEEN AWAKENED by the sound of rain falling with heavy persistence on the pantiled roof above her attic. It is absurdly dark for a June morning, and the heavy bank of clouds behind the elms seems to indicate that the weather has set in for the whole day if not for the whole summer. The cows are cross because of the driving rain, and milking takes twice as long because of the mud and rivulets of water coursing through the milking-parlour. By 8.30 the cows are milked and turned out, and the milk-lorry has collected the churns. The rain continues to pour ceaselessly out of the leaden sky, but the smell of breakfast is beginning to drift across the yard from the kitchen.

'Lucy, bring that trailer round to the barn and you can take the tractor straight down to the forty-acre field after breakfast. How's the wheat looking?'

'Blown about. Bits are already completely flattened at the top of the field.'

'Damn and blast this weather,' observes Mr McFee, normally the mildest of men. 'What kind of summer is this for ripening grain, I'd like to know?'

There is clearly no answer to this, and Lucy strides off to bring the tractor back up to the barn. She is just deciding whether there is time to hitch up the trailer before breakfast when Donny's piping voice calls her across the yard.

'Lucy! Lucy! You must come away in now, Aunty Agnes says. Your porridge is on the table and they said on the wireless that there's going to be a special news announcement at nine o'clock. Uncle Fergus says it'll be the Second Front. Come on, don't miss it.'

Pulling her hat more firmly over her eyes and clutching a sack around her shoulders, Lucy sprints across the sodden yard to the kitchen. Water fills the cart-ruts, and Mrs McFee's herbaceous border has a broken and defeated air.

Most unusually for that time of the morning, the kitchen is full. Jubal and Len are seated rather awkwardly by the range, clearly invited in to hear the wireless. Barely has Lucy started her porridge when the chimes of Big Ben ring out.

'This is the BBC Home Service, and here is a special bulletin read by John Snagge. D-Day has come. Early this morning the Allied troops began their assault on the north-west face of Hitler's European fortress. The first official news came from the Supreme Headquarters of the Allied Expeditionary Force, usually called SHAEF from its initials. In its first communiqué it said: "Under the command of General Eisenhower, Allied naval forces supported by strong air forces began landing Allied armies this morning on the coast of northern France." It was announced later that General Montgomery is in command of the army forces carrying out the assault. This command includes British, Canadian and American forces. . . .'

'Imagine having to jump out into the sea and wade ashore on a day like this,' ponders Donny more to himself than to anyone else. 'You'd have wet breeks all day.'

Automatically Lucy bends to her fast-solidifying porridge. Is Will there? she wonders. Will he be frightened? Is he still alive? A terrible sadness like a stone sits heavily on her heart. The news is greeted quietly. No cheers or exclamations. Just some deeply felt sighs and then a grave silence.

'That's history,' says Mr McFee half to himself. 'That's history we heard today.'

'Where will they go now? To Paris?'

'I suppose so. Drink your tea now, Donny.'

'There's not much I can really do with the garden until the autumn. Especially with the lawn being so wet. You've got some fine fruit trees and a good kitchen garden. I remember Miss Piggott ordering those trees from Colchester. They'll just need a bit of pruning.'

'Thanks ever so much, Dad. Can you stay and have some tea?'

'No, your mother will have supper on the table by now. You won't stop dropping in, will you, Beattie, now you've got a home of your own? I know your mother's still got the boys, but she misses you much more than she'll say. And Annie of course.'

'Oh, Dad, of course I won't. Annie misses her gran terribly. And you as well. And I want Mother to come round here and put her feet up when she feels like it. After all, I'm only five minutes away. Say goodnight to Grandad, Annie.'

Having drawn the curtains and switched on the kitchen light (would she ever get used to such luxury?), Beattie fills an enamel bowl with hot water for Annie's bath and spends ten patient minutes coaxing off her little woollen garments. The long damp spring and wet early summer have meant Annie being grumpy with a cold almost since Easter. But once in the warm water with her rubber duck the little girl relaxes and kicks her legs ruminatively while Beattie listens to the six o'clock news.

The events are startling enough, but a sharp edge of drama, so apparent to the silent listeners at Home Farm, is lost on Beattie, who is already well into her pregnancy, her mind torpid and filled with the glory of her new home.

With his usual energy Charles had no sooner conceived his plan of buying a house than gone out the next day and actually found one. Miss

Piggott, a brewer's daughter from Ipswich who had retired to Musgrave, had died the previous winter, and her house, a pretty Queen Anne cottage, the scene of Lily Kedge's second period of service, had been empty for the last two months.

'It's awfully big,' Beattie had protested weakly when, the following morning, Charles had driven triumphantly back from Dereham Market with the keys.

'Nonsense,' Charles had told her briskly. 'Four bedrooms? That just means one for each of the children and you and me and a study. It's a perfect size.'

Fortunately Miss Piggott's desire for country life *au naturel* had not in any way lessened her need for creature comforts, and the house was as neat and snug as her father's money could make it. The empty white-panelled rooms were pretty and inviting, the deeply inset windows cut almost to the ground revealing a walled garden and orchard at the back. For the rest of Charles's leave he had busied himself with solicitors and contracts, and before he had left again for High Wycombe it was arranged that the house would be theirs for occupation by the last week of May. On top of that Charles had somehow managed to wangle two weeks of leave to enable him to help Beattie move and buy furniture. It had somehow been like being on extended holiday – Charles had whistled as he had tacked down carpets, moved furniture and bid busily for more furniture at the auction rooms in Ipswich. The first night in their new bedroom, the house in order, the chimney swept and a fire burning in their bedroom grate, Beattie had felt the beginnings of that sense of peace that had so long evaded her. Charles was happy, he sang as he chopped wood for the fires and talked about his plans to redecorate the sitting-room when the weather improved. With Mrs Blythe's help he had seen to it that a reliable woman was engaged to come in and clean three times a week. Mrs Blythe, having been presented simultaneously with the news that she was to be a grandmother again and that Beattie would be returning to her job in due course next Easter, had meekly accepted the news, protesting only at the idea of the children going anywhere other than to her while Beattie was at school. The proper place for Annie and the new baby, she told her daughter roundly, was with their grandmother at the cottage. Beattie had thanked her mother and made no other comment.

With Annie warm, powdered, in her nightie and finally in bed Beattie returns to the kitchen marvelling yet again at the fitted cupboards, the gleaming pale Aga, the taps which guarantee a constant supply of scalding water. Shamefacedly she tells herself that she will listen to the momentous news at nine o'clock with rather more attention. After all, there is a greater world outside Musgrave. By now, thousands of men are landing in Normandy. She tries to imagine Lily's Greg leaping from a boat, wading ashore with his gun held high above his head. But as Greg works in catering supplies it's never been clear if he even handles weapons. And all those boys who had arrived tongue-tied for tea at the cottage all those months ago, Will amongst them, were now concentrating their energies and perhaps their lives in liberating Europe.

Settling herself back comfortably into the wicker chair by the Aga,

Beattie opens her writing-case to finish her letter to Louie. Louie's wedding date has finally been fixed: she and Vince are to be married in November. Beattie has already written to congratulate them and ask them to stay in the spare bedroom on their honeymoon. There had been a time when she had been amused by Louie's fixed determination not to marry until they could afford the down-payment on a place of their own. Now, looking round at her own home, she understands for the first time why Louie had held out so firmly for her own bricks and mortar.

It had nothing to do with the owning of property; it went far deeper than that. It had more to do with having a place recognized and acknowledged in the world. Brooke had never wanted to provide that place for her and Annie. He had never made any provision in his life for somewhere for him and Beattie to be together, to state publicly their intention to live together. It was as if their relationship was something always on the fringes of his life. He had fought or ignored her deep hunger for public acknowledgement of what was between them. It wasn't the lack of a bottom drawer that had constantly dismayed her – it was his lack of commitment. Charles, in providing a home, had demonstrated his caring and understanding of her needs. He was proud to acknowledge her publicly. And she took comfort from this. And Charles had proved himself to be as domestic an animal as any wife could wish. The two weeks they had spent together in their house had been two of the happiest in their whole acquaintance. And Charles had promised he would try to get more leave, even if possible to be there when the baby was born. The writing-pad slips unnoticed from Beattie's fingers as she sleeps contentedly in the wicker chair by the Aga.

'Of course we're going out tonight. Jack rang up and asked us especially. Marie-Hélène is insisting on the most enormous thrash. They've even been up to Hampstead and got all the stuff out of Jack's father's cellar. It'll be a fantastic do. There ought to be a party in every home in England tonight. Come on, put on something pretty and I'll mix us a g. and t. If this isn't a special night, I'd like to know what is.'

With that there are a series of splashes as Alexis lowers himself, yodelling cheerfully, into the bath.

'Did you hear the six o'clock news?'

'Bits of it,' shouts Virginia from the bedroom where she is ruminating over her wardrobe. 'I was queuing up for fish at the time, and the shop next door had it on. Wonderful, isn't it?'

'It certainly is. Do I have a clean shirt?'

'I expect so,' says Virginia, resigned, temporarily abandoning the scrutiny of her own wardrobe to go down to the kitchen and plug in the electric iron. Waiting for it to heat up, she tears off the sheet on the day-to-day calendar. In three weeks it will be their second wedding anniversary. Where on earth has the time gone? Is it almost a condition of happiness that time passes so quickly that you have no time even to register that this *is* happiness?

What did she imagine being married would be like? Pitched somewhere

428

between the cheerful unreality of domestic film comedies and the reality of the bickering and ennui of Ma and Pa's marriage, I suppose, reflects Virginia, testing the surface of the iron. In the event marriage had been like neither. The essential ingredients that both those images of domestic felicity lacked was that she had discovered that marriage could be fun. There certainly were boring bits like the shock of realizing there would be no more clean clothes or hot food for either of you unless you personally organized them. But even these, so far as Virginia is concerned, are merely symbols of what she perceived early on to be a greater truth. That if this marriage was to work – and she certainly wanted it to – it would be down to her efforts. There were already quite enough people taking bets as to how long the marriage would last, not to mention the reasons for what everybody assumed would be its inevitable break-up – their different backgrounds and attitudes, Alexis' political beliefs, and the very large number of people who counted Alexis as a close friend and wanted substantial parts of his attention and his life.

But the fact remained that in spite of disagreements, spats and downright rows there is absolutely no question of either of them wanting anyone else. It isn't just that sex is so good – that there are still nights, even if they tend now to be Friday and Saturday rather than in the middle of the week, when they make love and talk all night. It is more than that. It is things like knowing that when she is to meet Alexis he will always be there, patiently scanning the crowds, longing to see her, his face lighting up when he catches sight of her. The fact that, though he can be irritated with her, he likes as well as loves her and is proud of her beauty and her intelligence. The fact that their happiest times together are still spent simply out walking, arms round each other, completely absorbed in each other's company. The fact that Alexis is some-how touched with grace, that he has a generosity of spirit that makes her able to be generous in return. It is always Alexis who makes the first move to end an argument or heal a row, not because he is afraid of her ill humour but because he genuinely thinks that life is too short to squander it on such trivial matters as sulking. Virginia's legendary sulks and bad tempers, only ever half-heartedly invoked, have been met with such obvious indifference that they have simply ceased to happen. Alexis isn't in the slightest bit frightened of *her*, but Virginia is very frightened indeed at the thought of losing *him*. Hardly a position of strength, comments Virginia drily to herself as she carefully unplugs the iron and hangs her own dress and Alexis' shirt.

With a shout Alexis comes thundering down the wooden stairs to the kitchen.

'Come on, give us a kiss, lovely,' he says, nuzzling into her neck and shoving a warm and unselfconscious hand into her brassière. 'Are you ready? I want to be there early to do credit to the booze and hear the King's broadcast. My God, I wish I knew where old Ferdy was. I know how he'll feel tonight. He'll be completely blotto.'

Jack and Helen live off the Holland Park Road. It is barely possible to open the front door of their little Regency house, so jammed full are the hall and drawing-room. Inside the atmosphere is like one of the afternoon drinking-clubs that Virginia used to frequent off Windmill Street, where servicemen on twenty-four-hour passes drank and danced in an atmosphere of permanent New Year's Eve revelry. A gramophone is playing unheeded in the background, the air is thick with cigarette smoke, and everywhere there are familiar faces. Stephen Seaton waves drunkenly from across the crowded room. Devora is sitting on the knee of an English major, forced back into the arms of the native soldiery by the virtual withdrawal of Yanks from the London scene. Pat Blain and his wife are squashed together on a sofa. Trudy is mixing the fruit punch on the sideboard.

'What's the time?'

'Three minutes to nine.'

'All right, everybody shut up and sit down,' roars Jack in stentorian tones. And the radio suddenly booms out into the expectant silence. There is instant total attention, and Virginia finds Alexis tightly gripping her arm.

The King's voice, halting, stumbling, booms through the room with shocking suddenness.

'Four years ago our nation and empire stood alone against an overwhelming enemy, our backs to the wall, tested as never before in our history. In God's providence we survived that test. . . .'

At the end of the broadcast Virginia turns to Alexis and finds his face wet with tears.

'I can't believe it,' he says, shamefacedly wiping his eyes. 'I really thought I'd never get to see my grandfather's home again.'

'Well, you will,' Virginia assures him. 'I haven't forgotten about our honeymoon even if you have. It's wonderful news, darling, the very best in the whole war. Yes, of course we'll have another drink, Jack.'

430

CHAPTER
THIRTY-SIX

*B*Y SEPTEMBER there is subdued street-lighting in Dereham Market. The news on the wireless continues to be cautiously optimistic. Nature promptly retaliates with the coldest winter for fifty years. It starts to snow early, and by Christmas drifts six feet deep guard the approaches to Musgrave. The village shop has bravely taken down its blackout, and a set of pre-war Christmas lights twinkle enticingly in the window. But so far as goods are concerned there are still as many shortages as ever.

On the Saturday before Christmas, Beattie and the boys are waiting to be served, ration-books in hand, by the sweet-counter. Beattie has brought Annie and the new baby well wrapped up against the piercing cold. Though it is only half-past two, the sun is already disappearing behind the elms by the church as dusk begins to cast long blue shadows over the white landscape of the village.

'Well, what'll it be?'

'Fruit Gums.'

'You know you haven't got enough points, Ern.'

'I would if you gave me some. Please, Aunty Bee. You know I give you all the black ones.'

'That's only because you don't like them. Oh, all right. I hope Annie doesn't grow up with a sweet tooth like yours.'

'Which one's my sweet tooth?'

'Never *mind*. Is Annie all right?'

'Yes, she's fine. She's eating a conker.'

'Then, take it away from her,' says Beattie, exasperated.

'I saw Lucy down the road while you were talking to the verger. She said to give you her love and she'll see you on Christmas Day.'

'Oh, goody,' says Ern.

'It'll be our first Christmas lunch at your house, Aunty Bee, won't it?' Toby states.

'It certainly will. Oh, stop that, Annie. Come on, you'll have to hurry up or she'll wake up Tom.'

'I still wish you'd called him Winston,' Toby says.

'Everybody in the village is called Winston. Or Dwight,' protests Ern.

'Not the girls, I hope,' says Beattie drily. 'Buck up, you two. I promised Annie we'd have a walk round the green before it got dark to feed the ducks.'

431

'But the water's all frozen,' Toby points out.

'I know that, daft. But the ducks are still there.'

Once off the village street the path to the duck-pond is almost impassable under the snow.

'Are you sure you want to go, Annie?' groans Beattie.

'Yes, see the ducks. You said so,' says Annie, beginning to cry bitterly on her seat on the top of the pram.

'Oh, Annie, I don't even know if the ducks are still there. They may have got cold and had to go home. Wouldn't you rather we went and saw Granny instead?'

'Saw Granny this morning. Want to see the ducks.'

'She'll start Tom off if you don't,' says Toby wisely. 'Come on, Annie. I'll push the pram. Look, Annie,' he adds encouragingly. 'Look at Beetle rolling in the snow.'

'Silly,' says Annie disdainfully, pulling her woolly hat more firmly down over her brow.

'Who's that on the other side of the green, Aunty Bee?'

'I can't see properly in this light. Let's get a move on.'

They have almost reached where the pond presumably still is when the other walker draws abreast. With a shock Beattie realizes that it is Virginia Musgrave. Or whatever her married name is. In a single glance Beattie takes in the sharp edge of the other girl's glamour, the marvellously cut, bright scarlet swagger coat and fur hat, the perfect make-up. Should she say hello? The matter is taken out of her hands when Virginia recognizes her and actually comes towards her with a warily friendly look on her face.

'Hello, Beattie. How are you? It's ages since I've seen you.'

'I'm very well. Are you here for Christmas?'

'Yes, I got down on Thursday. My husband's driving down tonight and we're staying at the Dower House. I can't get over all this snow. I saw Lucy, and she told me you'd just had another baby.'

'That's right. This is Tom.' says Beattie, aware that Virginia's glance is more keenly directed towards Annie who is sitting quietly on the top of the pram, her thick blonde curls slipping out from under her beret.

'This is Annie. Say hello.'

'Hello,' says Annie obediently.

'This is Toby and this is Ernest.'

'My goodness, I remember you,' says Virginia in her clipped drawling voice. 'I can remember the day you came to Musgrave.'

'I was five then. I'm ten now,' says Ern.

'I was seven then. And now I'm twelve,' Toby adds.

Both boys are clearly dazzled by Virginia's glamorous good looks.

'Ducks,' says Annie, clearly tired of the conversation.

'Are there any?' Virginia enquires.

'We're hoping so,' says Beattie firmly, manoeuvring the pram back into the track leading down to the frozen water's edge. To her astonishment Virginia walks along beside her, her hands thrust deeply into her pockets.

'I'm meant to be walking two miles a day according to the doctor. I'm sure he'd think twice about it if he could see this snow. I'm expecting a baby.'

432

'Oh, congratulations,' says Beattie lamely. 'I didn't realize . . . I haven't seen Lucy for weeks. When is it due?'

'The end of March, I think. I blame it all on the liberation of France,' says Virginia vaguely. 'I've hardly mentioned it, because I thought I'd go on working for as long as possible. Funny thing is I was quite prepared to take to my bed but I feel fine.'

Their erratic progress through the snow is rewarded by frenzied quacks as the ducks shake themselves free of the reeds and flop across the ice to meet them.

'Ducks,' says Annie, this time in tones of the deepest satisfaction, and soberly throws her pieces of bread across the ice.

Beattie is aware that Virginia is studying Annie intently, clearly looking for a resemblance to her brother. For a moment she is about to make some remark when she clearly changes her mind and instead says: 'It's so quiet. I'd forgotten how silent the countryside can be. Do you get doodlebugs?'

'I think they've had them in Ipswich and quite a few in Norwich, but so far none here.'

'Alexis, my husband, wants me to stay here until the baby's born. But I don't. I'm still working at the production offices and it'd be dreadful knowing Alexis was in more danger than I was. I suppose you aren't teaching at present, are you?'

'No, but I'm starting again after Easter,' says Beattie with all the firmness she can muster, pushing to the back of her mind the memory of Tom's voracious appetite and the long string of sleepless nights it involved. 'I suppose you'll be staying at home once the baby's born.'

'Certainly not,' says Virginia much to Beattie's surprise. 'Oh, I'll take some time off. But I'd have to do something after that. I simply can't imagine not working now. Mother thinks I'm mad. But, then, she never had a job. I sometimes wonder how on earth she fills her day.'

They turn to walk back.

'You heard Brooke got married?'

'Yes,' says Beattie calmly. 'Lucy told me. Does he still fly?'

'Oh, yes. Though they bought a huge farm. But Brooke's still in the RAF.'

By this time they are only a hundred yards from the main street. Suddenly Virginia turns and stares intently at the darkening Ipswich road.

'Do you hear a car?'

Beattie is about to say no when beyond the bend in the road there is the faint glow of dimmed-out headlights and a small two-seater inches its way cautiously along the snow-packed road. With an exclamation of delight Virginia begins to wave madly and, slipping and sliding, runs to the roadside. There is a screeching of brakes and the car draws up beside her. An immensely tall man in a grey-and-white-tweed overcoat levers himself out and hugs Virginia, then kisses her full on the mouth there and then in the street. Acutely embarrassed, Beattie quickens her pace to hurry by when Virginia's voice stops her.

'Oh, Beattie, wait a minute. Do come and say hello to Alexis. Alexis, this is Beatrice – I'm afraid I don't know your married name, Beattie.'

'Hammond,' says Beattie briefly, none the less accepting Alexis' courteous hand.

'Good lord, are these all your children?'

'Just the two babies.'

'I'm Toby and this is Ernest. We're evacuees,' Toby tells Alexis, even more impressed by his car than by his wife.

'I'm afraid we must go or the children will catch a chill. A happy Christmas, Miss Virginia.'

Toby, Ern and Beetle disappear down Church Lane to the grandparents' cottage, leaving Beattie to manoeuvre the pram back to her own home. Charles will be down on Christmas Eve. There is a lot to be thankful for, or so Beattie tells herself.

The jogging of the pram on the snow-packed ruts disturbs both children, and by the time Beattie has let herself into her own kitchen Tom is roaring and Annie is grizzling because she wanted to spend longer at the pond. Though Beattie is dying either for a cup of tea or to go to the lavatory, Tom's terrifying cries of hunger as usual take precedence and crossly she pulls open her cardigan and shoves the nipple into Tom's roaring mouth, shouting at Annie to stop making all that noise. She is being unfair and knows it; and Annie, unused to raised voices, dissolves into real tears, and Tom, distressed by all the commotion around him, actually refuses to feed and begins to cry himself.

Immediately contrite, Beattie says: 'Oh, Annie, come here, darling. I'm sorry. Come on, you get on my other knee beside Tom and have a cuddle. Come on, sweetheart. I'll tell you what, we'll go and see the ducks again tomorrow morning in the daylight.'

It is some time before either Tom or Annie will consent to be pacified, and the prospect of either tea or the lavatory recedes further and further into the distance. Resigned, Beattie puts her feet up and lets Annie doze in one arm while Tom lies comfortably in the crook of the other, contentedly feeding. There will be a problem when Tom wants to change breasts, but Beattie will deal with that when it happens.

Guiltily she kisses both of them, upbraiding herself mentally the while. Why is it that every time I come in contact with the Musgraves I let them unsettle me? This morning I was pleased about the house and the children and the fact that Charles was able to get Christmas leave. Now I just feel bad-tempered and resentful. Why, oh, why is it that some people seem to have everything? The man they really want, the house in London, a glamorous job, and a life full of excitement, not to mention glorious clothes and some-one to take the baby off your hands? As usual Virginia seemed to have got everything. She and her brother, they were a right pair. They walked through life taking what they wanted and never paying the price of what they took. Beattie finds her mouth is tight with anger, then suddenly sees Annie's eyes are open and that she is watching her mother intently. Resolutely Beattie relaxes her features and smiles at the little girl. Uneasily Annie smiles back.

'Mummy cross with Annie.'

'No, darling. Mummy's just cross with herself for being silly. Come on. You swop over knees and I'll tell you a story.'

'Cindrella,' says Annie instantly.

'If you like. Then I'll get us some tea. Daddy's coming home on Monday. That'll be nice, won't it?'

'Yes,' says Annie politely. 'Cindrella.'

At seven o'clock Annie and Tom go sweetly to their slumbers. It is snowing hard again when Beattie finally retires to her bed, determined to make an effort to keep her moods under better control. But the image of the girl in the red coat and the fur hat, redolent with an aura of love and happiness, stays in her mind and haunts her troubled dreams.

The cold Christmas of 1944 gives way to the equally cold spring of 1945. The initial exultation at the string of military successes rapidly becomes buried under the surge of resentment at the paralysing cold and the lack of fuel to do anything about it. Virginia, finally forced to acknowledge she is pregnant, rapidly comes to the conclusion that bed is the warmest place to be for most of the day.

Still, it could be worse, she concludes to herself, lying cosily in the big brass double bed with the Home Service switched on while she smocks tiny garments in black-market cream Clydella. The 'treasure' comes in at lunchtime most days and lights the sitting-room fire, so after a leisurely bath and a snooze Virginia transfers herself to the sofa to have tea with whoever drops by. The blackout has been ceremoniously removed from the windows, and through the leafless front garden, lit by fitful gleams of pale sunshine, she can see the Thames ebbing and flowing towards Chelsea Bridge.

Towards the end of February Lucy comes to stay. It is a curiously peaceful and restful time. Beyond venturing up to Peter Jones for elevenses and going twice to the cinema, most of the time is spent in the warm drawing-room, gossiping. Lucy seems happy enough to be in London, but Virginia senses that there is a deeper core of unhappiness there. She would like to draw her out about the situation with Hugh. But a curious torpor seems to have overcome her. Only once does the subject come up and then obliquely. Lucy mentions casually one day that Hugh has already written to his bank and has his old position.

'So it's the pleasures of Wimbledon and suburban life.'

'I expect so.'

'Where will your mother and Eric live?'

'Oh, somewhere in Berkshire. Sunningdale, I think. Mother did tell me, but I've forgotten.'

Mrs Hallett had quietly remarried at Christmas. She had written and told Lucy after the service and, though initially upset, Lucy had decided that in the event she was more relieved than indignant at not being asked. They had driven down to Musgrave to see her one Sunday and afterwards had had lunch at the Dower House. Mrs Hallett had been transformed, radiant. Eric had mysteriously taken on the role her father had so successfully fulfilled as the protector of the gallant little woman and her creative flame. Both men had been properly taken in, in Lucy's private opinion, but none the less she wished the couple well.

'How do you feel about all that – the idea of seeing Hugh and making a home?'

435

'Blowed if I know,' says Lucy honestly. 'I just can't imagine it happening. You know, at Christmas when we heard about the new German offensive I was appalled to find myself feeling faintly relieved and thinking: That means the war won't end for a bit yet anyway. Isn't that frightful? I suppose I'm just putting off normal life for as long as possible.'

'But don't you ever get bored working on the farm?'

'Not really. I know it all seems routine, but it isn't. You're always learning. The only thing is I sometimes wish that I was running my own place, because I've read quite a bit of the bumf from the Min of Ag and there's lots of things the McFees could be experimenting with. Though Angus is a jolly good farmer, he's too set in his ways.' Lucy's face, which had grown quite animated, falls slightly at the prospect of trying to find an outlet for these skills in Wimbledon.

'Do you know what happened to Will?'

'No. Lily asked Greg if he'd seen him, but apparently the squadron split up after they left Musgrave.'

'You never even feel you want to write?'

'I don't even know if he's still alive. Anyway, what would be the point? He'll have found someone else by now, and I made my decision.'

There is a silence while both girls contemplate their lot. The baby directs a well-aimed kick at Virginia's ribs.

'Are you happy?' asks Lucy suddenly. 'Are you really happy? You know, the way we hoped we'd be when we used to talk about getting married? Everything's turned out so differently from what we expected, hasn't it?'

'I suppose it has,' says Virginia slowly. 'I certainly couldn't imagine anything beyond being presented and having a season. Neither of us ever imagined having a job, did we, let along *liking* it. I just wonder what the baby's life is going to be like, whether she'll want to be presented at Court.'

'You're sure it's a girl, are you?'

'Alexis is. He was from the word go. And he had a name ready and everything. He wants to call her Catherine after his mother. So we're going to look pretty silly if it's a boy, aren't we? But, yes, going back to what you were saying, I supose I am happy. What I mean is I suspect you never know when you're really happy until you look back on it afterwards and recognize it. Certainly I'm very content. I hope the baby isn't going to make too much of a difference. But I don't think it will. It's extraordinary the way you gallop towards marriage and you haven't got a clue about what really goes on beyond the altar. I can say it's quite different from what I expected. I started off with a great many notions of "well, I'm certainly *never* going to put up with *that*", then quite often you find you're painlessly accepting all the things you'd never put up with. And it doesn't matter. Perhaps you'll find it's like that with Hugh.'

'Perhaps,' says Lucy, unconvinced.

'Do you see much of Beattie?'

'Quite a lot. Now that she's got a place of her own it's easier to drop in.'

'Is *she* happy?'

'In her marriage, you mean? I don't know. Beattie's a very private person. You'd think there was nothing you couldn't say to her – yet there are some questions that you'd never ask. She's very fond of Charles, and he's obviously devoted to her. And she's very good with her children. But, as I say, there are some things you just never ask, aren't there?'

As the last days of February slip away Virginia ponders deeply on her conversation with Lucy. How do you ever convey the sense of a happy marriage? she wonders. All the ups and downs, the moments when you feel murderous, the things you find yourself doing that you swore you'd never do, even the quiet acceptance of the complete dislocation of your own life to fit in with your husband's career. But that was just how things were. So long as Alexis proposed to make his career in films, it was down to Virginia to fit in. And this meant accepting that a good deal of their married life – sex, conversation and general togetherness – had to take place before seven o'clock in the morning. It was better when Alexis was editing and didn't need to leave much before eight but less good if the editing was at Denham. The sensible thing, or so various directors' wives have told Virginia, was to go and live near Denham. Virginia listens politely but keeps her own counsel. So far as she's concerned, being out of London would be the end of her marriage. Whilst she's in central London she is fully involved in Alexis' life. The moment she moves out she becomes the wife and mother he comes home to. And though that might have suited Alexis (or would it? To give him his due, he'd always wanted to include her in every aspect of his life) it certainly wouldn't have suited Virginia. Particularly since the film industry was far too full of girls exactly like herself and equally unscrupulous. She doesn't believe in trying a man's strength beyond himself. No, London is the place where she's going to stay, and once the baby is weaned and content with her nanny, Virginia will pitch herself back into work.

Though what Alexis' future would be remains to be seen. Reel Films will presumably only last for the duration of the war. And already Virginia knows that Alexis' thoughts are moving away from straightforward documentary to other kinds of film, particularly full-length features. On this particular morning the subject of Alexis' career is uppermost in their minds.

'If you could come along tonight, it would be terrific.' It is 6.30, and outside the window branches lash the glass with driving rain. Inside the gas-fire is on, Alexis has brought up an early cup of tea and they have already, albeit sleepily, made love.

'Well, I suppose I could if it was in good cause.'

'It's the best cause I know – my career, in other words. I had a phone call yesterday from old Harry Ray. He told me that someone wanted to set up a new production company at Ealing once the war's over.'

'So who's putting up the money?'

'Oh, some Northern industrialist who fancies having his name on the front of films. Apparently they've already approached some pretty starry directors, but I'm the first person they actually want to meet. Harry's being very cagey about the names involved but he told me the man is in London and staying at Claridges and wants to meet me tonight. I was going to suggest seeing him at lunchtime but I hadn't reckoned on having to do these extra shots. But we'll be done by four, and we can be at Claridges by eight. If you had a sleep this afternoon, you could manage that, couldn't you?'

'Gosh, yes,' says Virginia, instantly interested. 'You're being very *piano* about the whole thing. It sounds rather wonderful.'

'Well, it could be if it all happened. I've got loads of ideas for films and I've read several scripts lately that I couldn't place anywhere.'

'Will you be sorry to leave Reel Films?'

'Yes, in so far as they've enabled me to find my feet.'

'*And* you met me.'

'*And* I met you. But it's part of growing up, isn't it? You have to move on.'

'Is your suit clean or do you think it'll be black-tie?'

'I'll check with Harry and give you a ring at lunchtime. My God, is that the time? I must run. We're meant to be setting up for an early-morning shot.'

'Alexis, you are *not* going out in that filthy old sport's coat. Not when I've virtually had to sell my body to buy you a new one.'

'Oh, come here and I'll swap it. I *like* that other jacket; it's comfortable, I'm used to it.'

'It makes you look like a tramp. Give me a kiss. I'll wait to hear from you later.'

Promptly at one o'clock the phone rings. It is Trudy relaying Alexis' apologies and the news that it is black-tie and the table is booked for eight.

'How are you feeling?'

'Huge. Like Moby Dick's sister. I'm beginning to long for labour day.'

'When's that?'

'The thirtieth of March, I think. Almost a month. I just don't know how I'm going to stand the boredom. Do come round and have a gossip some time.'

'I'll do that,' says Trudy, surprisingly friendly. 'We'll have finished here by this afternoon and there should be a bit of a lull before I'm needed again. Take care of yourself, won't you? See you soon.'

After brushing and pressing Alexis' rather motheaten evening suit and her own black evening dress, carefully let out to conceal the impending event, Virginia turns on the Home Service, listens to a talk on 'Preserving Fruit' and decides to her own surprise that she'll have to go back to bed. It must be all that bending over the ironing-board which has given her backache, she concludes, hauling herself up the stairs to the third floor with her hot-water bottle tucked warmly under her smock. The baby is clearly equally tired, making only a series of half-hearted kicks as Virginia slides comfortably under the satin eiderdown. The 'treasure' won't be in today, so there's no reason, sirens permitting, why she shouldn't have at least a couple of hours of undisturbed slumber before four o'clock. Plenty of time, then, to set her hair and do her nails.

When Virginia finally wakes up it is mysteriously as if it has become early morning again. It is pitch dark, the rain and wind beating furiously against the uncurtained window.

My God, thinks Virginia, desperately trying to surface from what seems to be the very seabed of sleep itself. It must be early evening and – oh lord –

that's Alexis at the front door. He must have left his keys in his other jacket.

Still groggy with sleep Virginia pulls on her dressing-gown and slippers and lurches tiredly down to the deserted hall. The clock in the drawing-room chimes as she goes to draw back the bolts: it really is six o'clock! And my hair not even set, groans Virginia as she pulls open the front door.

Outside it is pitch dark and rain is falling like stair-rods. On the steps is Pat Blain. For a second all Virginia feels is relief.

'*Pat*. I thought it was Alexis. I must have overslept. Do come in.'

Then, as he steps forward into the light of the hall, Virginia catches sight of his face and knows instantly that something is dreadfully wrong. She catches his arm.

'It's Alexis, isn't it? Has he had an accident? What is it? Do tell me.'

It is as if she is still asleep, caught in some unendurable and unending nightmare. Dimly she is aware that Pat Blain has his arm around her, supporting her and half-carrying her into the unheated drawing-room. She can hear his voice, but it seems to be too far away, and the movement of his lips seems to be out of sync with what he is saying. She does not want to listen, she does not want to hear the words he is trying to say to her. And when he tells her as gently as he can that Alexis is dead Virginia's whole being locks rigid, her mind a blank screen of horror, her body jerking spasmodically as she starts to scream. Then someone is trying to lift her up and put her on the sofa as Virginia thrashes and fights with a demented strength, aware that someone in the room is making a terrible noise like an animal caught in a trap and that a great gush of water is pouring from between her legs and staining the sofa cushions.

How long this goes on for she cannot tell, because the pain inside her has suddenly become a real pain, great waves of it coursing at regular intervals through her womb. It is her worst fears made manifest; the pain is taking over, she is completely out of control, and the one person who could have made her steady and lent her his strengh has gone, and gone for good.

The drawing-room is suddenly full of people. The doctor and ambulance men are asking if she's packed her case, and in the middle of it all Virginia is screaming and screaming for Alexis and then for Cecily and then for Alexis again.

The labour is long and painful, and it is nearly noon the following day before Virginia's baby is born. In Virginia's mind Alexis' death and the baby's birth have somehow become fused into one unendurable lump of pain.

'It's a little girl,' the nurse says, proffering the tiny squalling purple-faced infant to her mother.

But Virginia simple turns away, desperate for oblivion, sleep, preferably death. Sleeping-draughts carry her through the first few days, but each time she wakes it is as if there is a weight of masonry lying on top of her that she physically has to push away before she can find her way back to a consciousness she does not want. The baby is beside her in its cot, constantly squalling in a thin mournful cry. There is no question of Virginia feeding her – she has no milk. And at her own request she receives no visitors. Lying in her private room, her face turned away from the baby, she withdraws from the present and makes her plans.

439

For three weeks she is alone in the nursing home, her only permitted visitor Pat Blain, and then only for one visit so he can tell her how Alexis died. They had been doing the final location shots in Paddington, in a street Virginia had walked down a hundred times on her way to the Tube. That streets was now completely gone. A rocket, what the newspapers called a V-2, forty-five feet long and fourteen tons of explosive, had fallen on the street just as the remains of the unit were packing to go home. Most of them had already left, but Alexis, Billy Gavin and little Dennis, the messenger boy who longed to be a cameraman, were still there. No trace of any of them was found. The rockets had travelled so fast, and so silently, that there was not time even for the sirens' warning.

Virginia thanks Pat Blain and courteously declines an invitation to go and stay with him and his wife at Denham when she leaves the nursing home.

'Do think about it,' he coaxes. 'The country air would do you good.'

What he actually means, as Virginia well knows, is that she should try to put off going to the little house in Chelsea for as long as possible.

'It's really sweet of you to ask me, Pat, and do thank Marigold, but I expect I'll go back down to my mother's home. And I don't want to be too far away from the doctor while the baby's got jaundice.'

'Have you decided on a name?'

'Yes, I'm going to call her Alexia. Don't worry about me, Pat; I've made all the necessary plans.'

The following Tuesday, waved off by two extremely worried-looking nurses, Virginia makes her way home by taxi with the yellow-faced squalling baby wrapped in the shawl that Billy Gavin's wife had knitted. A nanny is booked to arrive the following day. Virginia has agreed passively to everything. It makes no difference. By tomorrow morning, she and Alexia will be far beyond the reach of anybody's interfering help.

Opening the front door, actually being in the hall, is a bad moment, even though the treasure has been in and lit a fire in the drawing-room. Because she has been away for several weeks she is able to see the house the way she saw it that first night she came home with Alexis. It is impossible to believe that he isn't waiting for her upstairs in the bedroom, gone ahead to put on the gas-fire and warm the room. Impelled by she knows not what madness, Virginia finds herself sprinting up the stairs and throwing open the door to the bedroom at the front of the house. But it is all silent, tidy, empty. Alexis is indeed not there. On the hook behind the door hangs his old sports-jacket. Virginia buries her face in the tweed, the smell of him as familiar to her as her own body. On the back of the chair is one of his polo-neck jerseys. Virginia slips it on over her own blouse, then pulls on the jacket, rolling back the sleeves. Alexia's wail travels reproachfully up the stairs. She will give her one more feed. The other plans can wait.

Alexia takes nearly two hours to manage her bottle and afterwards shows no signs of having enjoyed it. Finally she falls into a restless slumber, leaving

440

Virginia to root out the old newspapers and position herself comfortably in the bedroom. Not long now, she tells herself with a curious lightening of the heart. Very soon all this will be behind me. . . .

Except that, of course, it doesn't work out like that. It feels downright silly, not to mention melodramatic, to be rolling up newspapers and fitting them into the cracks under the door and into the keyhole. It recalls one of those awful 'B' pictures that Alexis had always poked such derisive fun at, prior to actually guessing the correct resolution of the plot. And the gas, far from bringing instant oblivion, has made not only her but also Alexia extremely sick. In the end, exasperated beyond measure, she switches off the fire, opens the window, checks that Alexia is comfortable and still breathing, and goes down to make supper. When she comes back up to the bedroom she turns on the fire and sits down to think.

Alone, listening to the swish of tyres on the nearby King's Road, Virginia sits staring into the fire, almost till dawn. She feels extraordinarily light-headed, almost as if she'd been drinking. As the light changes from grey to white and the cold wet March morning finally dawns it becomes clear that there are two alternatives, two ways that she can deal with the pain of Alexis' death.

The first is to acknowledge it, to live through it, to carry it round like a weight that will bend her almost double, in the hope that one day, one distant and unimaginable day, the pain of his loss will grow less.

The other is to ignore the pain, simply to pretend that Alexis and the three happy years she has spent with him have never existed. Everything she has learnt from Alexis tells her that this is utterly wrong. But her whole being cries out in revolt at the prospect of the full acknowledgement of all that agony. The pain feels like some vast cancer at the very heart of herself which, if allowed to spread unchecked, will simply destroy her whole being. The panic engendered by these thoughts makes her breath come faster. She must survive at all costs.

Either way the price is terrible. But survival is now the only thing that counts. And not allowing herself to feel anything, actually denying the reality of the pain, is the most familiar way and the way that beckons most enticingly. It will mean ignoring her loss, cutting her ties absolutely with the old world, even making other arrangements for Alexia. But at least she can be sure that she, Virginia, will survive.

At times that night it is almost as if Alexis is in the room with her, pleading with her. She knows to the very depths of her being what he would want her to do. And if he had been there, supporting her with his love, she could have done it, could have taken any risk, would have been able to give love in the secure knowledge that she was so deeply loved in return. But like a terrible tidal wave that sucks the harbour dry, leaving only barren sand, Alexis' love had been completely withdrawn from her life and Virginia knows she does not have it within her to remain the person she had become through Alexis.

Alexia wakes three times, and each time Virginia feeds and changes her. Afterwards she holds her in her arms while she sleeps. A month ago, a little month, this child was loved and wanted. But there is no place for her in the new life of the Virginia who is to survive. Perhaps when she is stronger she

441

will be able to include Alexia in her plans. But not yet. Right now a place must be found for her.

At seven o'clock Virginia goes down to the kitchen to make herself a cup of tea and, waiting for the kettle to boil, looks around with pain and regret. She loves this house for the happiness she has known here. But for that very reason she cannot stay. It takes half an hour to put all the baby's clothes in a case. She knows where she can buy black-market petrol. At eight o'clock the postman pushes a handful of letters through the letter-box. Virginia puts them unopened with the rest of the enormous pile of letters of condolence on the hall table. She will deal with them later. Much later.

By nine o'clock she and Alexia are in the car and on the road for Suffolk.

Mrs Musgrave's response to her first grandchild is, to say the least, lacklustre. Only when the agency at Ipswich has actually rung back to confirm that a nanny will arrive tomorrow will she finally consent to let Alexia stay.

'I suppose she'd better sleep in your room with you. That way we'll save on fuel,' is her not very gracious conclusion.

'Oh, I'm not staying,' says Virginia briskly. 'I've just brought her down to be here. Once I've unpacked her things I'll be on my way. It's much too dangerous to have a baby in London. You must see that, Mother. And she's sickly, too; she needs the country air. Dr Body will be able to keep an eye on her, and I'll be down when I can.'

Completely deaf to her mother's expostulations, Virginia hands Alexia's suitcase to Jenks, the parlourmaid who has been deputized to care for the baby until the nanny comes. The last thing Virginia hears as she gets into her car is the distant despairing cry of her daughter.

In the village street she pauses for a moment, aware that she is drenched with sweat, and tells herself that the best thing is instantly to find the Ipswich road and drive back to London. But instead she takes the road into the village, then heads out towards Home Farm. It is already dark as she drives into the farmyard. Distastefully she picks her way up the track and hails a small boy (or so Donny seems) who is driving in the cows.

'I say, is Lucy around?'

'She's away in the barn, mending harness.'

At this moment Lucy herself appears and without self-consciousness strides through the mud to Virginia and holds her for a long time.

'I'm so glad you've come,' she says at last, still holding on to her. 'I've written, but I don't expect you've got round to opening your letters yet. Look, Mrs McFee's down in the village, so the kitchen's empty. Come in and have a cup of something. You're half-frozen.'

Virginia sinks gratefully into the Windsor chair beside the range. For a time neither of the girls says anything. Then: 'Have you brought the baby with you?'

'Oh, yes, she's at the Dower House.'

'Is she well? Your mother said she was quite tiny when she was born.'

'Not really, I'm afraid. She was nearly a month premature and she got jaundice. She doesn't seem to be gaining much weight.'

'Perhaps you'll both do better here.'

Lucy cannot bring herself to mention Alexis.

'Oh, I'm not staying.'

'Not *staying*.' Lucy is visibly appalled. 'Oh, Virginia, don't do that. Don't be like this.' Lucy's long acquaintance with Virginia makes her instantly aware of the implications of what she has said.

'I can't stay, Lucy. I know I should but I can't. It's beyond me. There's a nanny coming tomorrow. Perhaps later on. . . .' Virginia's voice trails away.

'But it's *Alexis' child*. . . .'

'Yes, you see, but he's not here.' Virginia's fingers close convulsively on the comfort of the blue-and-white-striped mug.

'So what'll you do?'

'Go back to town. Move. Get a new job. Get on with my life.'

'Couldn't you stay down here with us? I've got loads more free time than I used to have, and I could take you into Ipswich, or Dereham, and we could go to the pictures . . . .' It is now Lucy's voice that trails away. Virginia looks at her friend with more affection than she has ever shown.

'You're a dear girl, Lucy. But it wouldn't work. Thanks all the same. I'll write when things get a bit more settled.'

Lucy stands at the farm gate, waving until the lights of Virginia's car have disappeared into the dusk. Donny appears inquisitively at her elbow.

'Is that your posh friend from London?'

'That's right,' says Lucy absently.

'She's a stunner, isn't she? Looked like Constance Bennett.'

'Mm.'

'Is it all right if I go down to the village later?'

'What will you do about supper?'

'Oh, Aunty Agnes will keep something in the oven.'

'Well, if the cows have settled, then it's all right by me.'

Back in the barn Lucy sinks down on to the bale of straw, but the broken harness lies forgotten in her lap as she stares out into the sodden darkness of the East Anglian landscape. For a long long time she stares out unseeingly, then stiff, cold but resolute walks back to the house. Donny is Brylcreeming his hair in the mirror over the kitchen sink.

'Can you wait ten minutes and post a letter for me, Donny?'

'So long as it's only ten minutes. My cycle-lamp's not that good.'

'You can borrow mine. I'll be down in a tick.'

In her attic bedroom, ignoring the piercing cold, Lucy lights the oil-lamp and gets out her pad of airmail paper and an envelope. Next to her bed is a bundle of airmail letters. Lucy contemplates them briefly and turns back to face her task.

Home Farm
28 March 1945

Dear Hugh,

I have given a great deal of thought to what you have said in your letters

443

about our chances for future happiness. Reluctantly I have come to the conclusion that though we may have meant a great deal to each other in the past, we have grown too far apart in the intervening five years to start again. Our lives have diverged too sharply, and I feel I cannot be the kind of wife you want, nor could I be happy living the kind of life that you envisage. I know this will cause you pain, but am sure that I am acting correctly for both of us. . . .

'Hello, you two.' Beattie stoops to kiss Toby and Ern, who crowd expectantly into the house, string bags in hand.

'Have you brought everything with you? Pyjamas, toothbrushes, the lot?'

'Checked them myself. What's for supper, then?' asks Toby.

'Treats.'

'Sausages?' Ern's tone is full of hope.

'Not quite. But cheese on toast. And I made you an apple pie, and there's half a tin of evap.'

Toby and Ern are quietly jubilant.

'How's Annie, then?' asks Toby, unselfconsciously taking the little girl on his knee and ruffling her curls.

'She's well – aren't you, poppet?'

'And Tom?'

'Oh, Tom's always well,' says Beattie with a rueful look at her son who is propped up against cushions in the kitchen chair. With his mop of unruly dark curls and his rosy cheeks he is a picture of rude health.

'Does he mind the bottle?'

'I don't think so. I let him have a bit of a suck before he goes to sleep, but I think he prefers the other now – he gets more to eat.'

'It said on the news at lunchtime that General Montgomery had crossed the Rhine. Think of that! That means the war will soon be over, won't it, Aunty Bee?'

'But there's no sign of the Germans surrendering.'

'What'll happen to Herr Hitler when they do?'

'Do you know, I was thinking of that today. I suppose they'll put him in prison.'

'Charles will be coming home then, won't he?'

'Yes. For good. It'll be strange to see all the men in the village back from the war. Do you want to give Tom his bottle, Ern? I'll be dishing up in twenty minutes.'

'Right-e-o, then,' says Ern, obligingly taking the eager Tom on his knee. 'Coo, he hasn't half got a powerful suck.'

'Mrs Musgrave's nanny's given in her notice,' says Toby, who always knows the village gossip.

'How on earth do you know that?'

'Lily told me. Jenks told her. The nanny doesn't like the country, but Jenks thinks it's because she doesn't like the baby. It's not putting on any weight, and Mrs Musgrave keeps blaming the nanny.'

'That doesn't seem fair. She's only been here a fortnight. What are they going to do?'

'Get another nanny, Lily says.'

'Why isn't the baby putting on weight?' asks Ern.

'She can't want her feed,' replies Beattie, laying the table. 'She had jaundice before she was born. I saw her in the shop with Mrs Musgrave the other day, and the poor thing looked like a little wizened monkey. If Tom's finished, you can put him back in his chair, Ern. Come and have your food while it's hot. Do you want the wireless on?'

Mr and Mrs Blythe are at a beetle drive in the village hall, and the boys are staying over with Beattie. Tom and Annie adore them. What will it be like when their family comes to claim them? wonders Beattie, and not for the first time. It never seems to bother either boy that they must have real family somewhere. Yet there must be many like them faced with the prospect of peace and wondering for the first time who they really are.

'Oh, I nearly forgot,' says Toby suddenly. 'Lily cut that piece out of the *News Chronicle* about Virginia Musgrave's husband. I've got it here for you in my pocket.'

Curious, Beattie smooths out a tattered piece of newsprint. There is a picture of Alexis bending over a camera and two columns describing him as a brilliant young director whose career had been tragically cut short before he could fulfil his great promise. Beattie sighs and puts the cutting carefully away. Virginia's husband means nothing to her, but the double tragedy of his death and his daughter's premature birth have weighed her down with a sadness she cannot explain. It is impossible not to be involved in that family's tragedies. Twice Mrs Musgrave has actually stopped her in the street to lament poor little Alexia's lack of health, father and (more recently) mother.

'If only Nanny Holwill was here!' Mrs Musgrave had lamented, actually wringing her hands in the street. Little Alexia cried night and day, she could not keep her bottle down and Nanny was threatening hourly to find a more attractive charge.

In spite of herself, moved by this tale of woe, Beattie had actually consented to go back to the Dower House to see if she could persuade the little girl to take her bottle. (It was Nanny's afternoon off, and she had bolted hotfoot for Ipswich.) Beattie had actually succeeded at first in feeding the little girl, then Alexia had bought up the entire contents of her stomach over Mrs Musgrave's coat. It certainly made it hard for anybody to love her, concluded Beattie ruefully, staring at the yellow-faced angry-looking little girl on her knee. In addition to her unappealing appearance, despite daily baths and copious flourings with talc, Alexia smelt mysteriously unpleasant. Even Dr Body is at his wit's end about her.

Toby is inquisitively inspecting the kitchen.

'I say! Are these yours, Aunty Bee?'

'Yes, Charles sent them. They're marvellous, aren't they? I sent him that photograph I had taken in Ipswich of me and Annie and Tom, and he sent them back to me by return post. They're for when I start teaching after Easter.'

'I've never seen a fountain pen as fine as this.' Toby's tone is frankly envious. 'And these things, these folders, are they for you to put your papers in? Aren't they a lovely colour? Charles must have really liked that photograph. We've got the other one on the mantelpiece in the parlour, did you know?'

'I'm glad Mum and Dad liked it. I'd better take the two little ones upstairs. You make yourselves comfortable. I'll be down shortly.'

When Beattie returns to the kitchen Toby and Ern are peaceably playing Ludo.

'When are you going to take your blackout down, Aunty Bee?'

'I haven't thought about it. I suppose I'm still a bit superstitious. Why, do you want to?'

'I wouldn't mind. I could do with some tacks.'

'Well, do it carefully. It's probably full of dust and dead flies. Here, you'd better wait until I've got a duster—'

There is a sudden tentative knock at the back door.

'Are you expecting anybody,' asks Ern inquisitively.

'Not that I know of,' says Beattie and goes to open the door. To her astonishment, outside in the darkness stands Bertie, Mrs Musgrave's friend.

'Mrs Hammond?' he says courteously, yet urgently. 'I'm sorry to bother you at such a late hour. Could we possibly come in?'

To her further astonishment, Beattie sees that he is not alone. Mrs Musgrave is standing behind him, dressed in her old fur coat with her hair tied up in a turban. She is carrying something in a shawl. It has to be Alexia. Beattie silently lets them in, wondering if they should be taken into the drawing-room, then reflects that there hasn't been a fire in it for over a month. Instead she offers them a seat at the kitchen table. Toby and Ern politely stand up. As Mrs Musgrave sits down the shawl gives a heave of indignation and a long-drawn-out rasping cry comes from its folds.

'There, there,' says Mrs Musgrave ineffectually, and Beattie wonders how she could ever have found her a frightening person. Why, she's just a foolish old woman with over-plucked eyebrows and over-bleached hair, and lipstick caught in the lines round her mouth. She looks up at Beattie in frank appeal.

'Beattie, we've come to ask you a favour because I'm at the end of my tether. Could Alexia stay here for a day or so to give us a breather? I don't think we've had a night's sleep since she arrived. I've just had a telegram from the nanny I've booked saying she can't get away until Friday. We'll pay you for your time and trouble naturally. But I thought of you first because your children always look so bonny. . . .' There is a note of despair in Mrs Musgrave's voice. 'I told Virginia that the baby was too young to be left, but she would go back to London and *we've* been left,' she laughs unhappily, 'holding the baby.'

Beattie is interested to note that her immediate response to this request is one of complete fury, How bloody typical of the Musgraves' cheek to imagine once a servant, always a servant. Then Beattie looks at the baby and pity stirs. There is no doubt about it – even in the two days since she has seen her, Alexia has gone downhill. What she wants to say is that under no circumstances can she take in any more of the Musgraves' waifs and strays. What

446

she actually finds herself saying is: 'Well, it can only be for a day or so. My hands are already full with my own.'

'The agency *assures* me that the nanny will be here on Friday,' says Mrs Musgrave, hope taking ten years off her face. 'We'll be round to see her tomorrow.' With that they escape thankfully into the darkness. As the door shuts behind them Toby observes: 'You are a daft soft thing, Aunty Bee. You've got more than enough with Tom and Annie, haven't you? And she doesn't half pong.'

'She probably needs changing. Take her for a minute, will you, Toby?'

Gingerly Toby takes the pitifully small bundle, while Beattie undoes the suitcase that Mrs Musgrave has left on the table. In it is a layette which would not have disgraced a royal baby. There are endless piles of tiny hand-smocked garments. There are matinée jackets and piles of bootees. There is a stack of unused terry squares. There is also talcum powder and zinc ointment and baby lotion in pre-war abundance. There are also bottles, tins of powdered milk, a pink rabbit and a teddy bear. Beattie puts the milk on to heat and begins to mix up some feed.

'Is that what Tom has?' asks Toby.

'Yes. Let's hope she likes it as much as he does.'

Tom's appetite is a legend in the family. Apprehensively Beattie tests the milk's heat, fills the bottle and, taking the little girl back from Toby, tries to feed her. Alexia sucks thoughtfully for a moment or two, then turns her head away with a yell of rage and indignation.

'No wonder she's always so cross; she must be absolutely starving.'

'Whatever are you going to do?'

Twice more Alexia is offered the bottle and twice more she refuses. By this time she is purple in the face and yelling at the pitch of her tiny lungs. The boys are beginning to look rather scared.

'How about some Jersey milk from Mrs Munn's house cow?'

'She's too little. It'd be too rich,' says Beattie, worried, and puts the baby on her shoulder to try to calm her. Already she's bitterly regretting her impulses to take the baby in. Alexia burrows her face crossly into Beattie's neck and makes a half-hearted grab for the buttons on her dress. Without thinking Beattie automatically goes to undo them, then she stops and more slowly undoes the bodice of her dress.

Getting the breast into her sights Alexia instantly clamps her tiny gums over the nipple with the terrifying ferocity of a terrier seizing its prey. She begins to suck urgently. There is a sudden deafening silence and the tiny purple fists relax.

'So that's what she wanted,' says Toby.

'Make us a cup of tea, Toby. She's going to be a while yet.'

Again at ten and then at one Alexia wakes up, and without preamble Beattie puts her back to the breast, praying that Tom will not take it into his head to wake up and demand a cuddle. By this time the boys are tucked up in bed, and when finally at four o'clock Alexia wakes her yet again for another feed she takes the baby down to the kitchen to sit in the warmth of the range. In the space of a few hours there is almost a physical change in the baby. Her colour is better and her movements are less jerky and frenzied. But even when she's finished feeding she simply will not let the nipple go. Fearing never to see it again, she cries piteously every time Beattie tries to dislodge her. In the end she leaves her where she is, staring into the little girl's face who regards her intently back.

Cupping the dark head in her hand, Beattie rocks the little girl, softly talking nonsense to her the while. There is something about this baby that touches a deep chord in her. It is not just imagination that makes her sense a real despair in Alexia, a despair that there will never be enough love or feeding or care. For what else has been her experience? Beattie intuitively responds to her, knowing quite literally that if she does not care for this baby, then she will die because no one cares enough.

Yet even as part of her recognizes this, the familiar surge of resentment is triggered as the familiar trap snaps shut. It's not fair, she tells herself furiously, not fair when I've got things so nicely sorted out. In three weeks I'll be back at school and, God willing, that'll be the end of babies for ever.

But already the bond growing between herself and Alexia renders those thoughts flimsy, ephemeral, unworthy. Who will speak up for this helpless person if Beattie will not? It's not my responsibility, she tries to tell herself. I've already got one Musgrave cast-off – why choose to have another? The brutality of her own words serves only to shock herself into memory. How lightly she had had Annie. How little thought she had given to the fact that she was bringing another human being into the world. Now the bond between herself and her children is so fierce that Beattie knows she would kill anyone who showed them serious harm. But who will fight like that for Alexia, who was parentless, alone and undefended?

And besides—

And besides, says another voice in Beattie's heart, she's Brooke's niece. His flesh. His blood. Beattie sighs and begins to walk Alexia up and down the darkened kitchen.

Perhaps just for a week. Well, just for a month at the very most. Until Alexia is able to be weaned. Or at least able to cope.

Through the window from which Toby has half taken down the blackout Beattie can see the darkened village street gleaming with moisture in the first light of day. And what will Charles say?

Charles will do anything you ask him, a voice says sardonically inside her. It is Charles's strength that he will concede anything she asks him for, and it is her weakness that she has come to rely on it. And with equal certainty Beattie knows that Virginia had known all along that it would be Beattie who would end up caring for Alexia. Knows it as surely as the fact that the moon is pale in the sky over Musgrave church. Alexia lies contentedly asleep in her arms, her lips even in slumber delicately pursing themselves as she remembers the nipple. Beattie puts her into Tom's old cradle and goes back to bed for what remains of the night's sleep.

CHAPTER
THIRTY-SEVEN

'ARE YOU READY, BEATTIE I've got some more change now if you need it. You've done well. My word! New books! Where do you get these from?'

Mrs Leary, freed from the counter of the post office, sniffs the new volumes appreciatively, her thumbs caressing the shiny new covers.

'Charles was sent them by his publisher, and he didn't want them so he said I could have them for the jumble sale.'

Mrs Leary is reading a title short-sightedly.

'*The Flora of Northern Umbali* – well, I'm not one for travel books, but it almost seems worth buying just for the smell of it, don't you think? Yes, put it on one side for me, Beattie, and I'll pay you after the raffle. Are you going to help Mummy, Annie?'

Annie nods importantly, an empty Oxo tin held firmly on her knee.

'She's keeping the money for me, aren't you, sweetheart? Mother's got the babies, so we're having a day out on our own, aren't we?'

'You'll do all right with books. It's still what people want. Have you any magazines?'

'A few *Home Chat*, and a whole bundle of *People's Friend*.' There had been some old copies of *Vogue* and *Tatler* donated by Mrs Musgrave, but these had been stealthily purloined by Mrs Blythe.

'It all helps. Though I doubt if we'll make five pounds on this lot today.'

Mrs Leary casts an experienced eye over the jumble-tables in the rectory drawing-room and sighs for more commercial times.

'A year ago we'd have had twice the goods and a queue twice round the rectory. We'd have been trampled to death in the rush. But with the Yanks and the evacuees gone . . . and people don't seem to want to put up with old things any more. You wouldn't believe the war had only ended six months ago! The complaints I get in my shop! They seem to expect a full pre-war stock the day after VE-Day. And now I can't even tell them there's a war on.' Mrs Leary's tone is full of regret. From outside in the hall comes a muffled shouting.

'That's it! It must be two o'clock.'

The door to the drawing-room is ceremonially opened to admit a dozen or so hatted and muffled figures who make as one woman to the clothing-table. Annie sits up straighter on her stool, poised and expectant, her tin clasped firmly. After a minute or two has passed she turns to Beattie in consternation.

'Why don't they come here? Don't they like our books?'

'Oh, yes,' Beattie assures her hastily, 'you just wait and see, Annie. As soon as they've done looking at the clothes they'll be over here. I tell you what, why don't you go and get an orangeade and by the time you come back I'm sure there'll be something to put in your box.'

Relieved, Annie clumps down and goes to join the queue by the tea-urn. She is wearing a blue-and-white-check gingham dress, her curls subdued by a hair-slide and a dark blue ribbon. The dress is still slightly too large, the collar standing away from the vulnerable nape of her neck where her fair hair curls into the downy softness. As if she feels her mother's gaze Annie suddenly turns round and smiles at her, her habitually grave face suddenly transformed. Beattie smiles back and blows her a kiss, wondering for the thousandth time what it is about Annie that always causes her such pain. It is absurd: Annie is a happy and healthy child, as much the centre of her grandparents' life as Beattie had once been. And when Charles had been home a month ago Annie had silently attached herself to him and followed him wherever he went. She would now beg to scramble on to his knee with the same alacrity with which she had once sought her mother. She was his pet. It has certainly made it easier to cope with the babies, thought Beattie, wondering how Tom and Alexia were faring at Church Cottage. Perhaps they'd—

'Beat! Can I have a sit-down for a mo? My shoes are killing me. How do I look?'

'Lovely. Are those your new shoes?'

'Yes, worse luck. Mind you, I knew they were too small when I bought them, but they were the only ones that would go.'

Lily, resplendent in her new costume over a pink satin blouse, stares discontentedly down at her feet which resemble pig's trotters jammed into two small black court shoes.

'And I've got my only pair of nylons on,' she continues. 'I must be daft. After all, it's only a picture of my head and shoulders. But I felt that depressed I thought it would do me good to get dressed up.'

'How are you getting to Ipswich?'

'Major Jones is picking me up at half-past two. Thank goodness. It's not as easy as it used to be to get a lift. I thought I'd go to a matinée afterwards at the Regal. Have you got anything worth reading? Something soppy will do.'

'There's some romances here somewhere – have you read any of these?'

Lily selects *Folly's Flame* and *Tomorrow's Heartache*, declining *The Man for Monica* on the grounds that her handbag won't take any more. Annie reverentially places her six pennies in her tin.

'If you wanted any more, I could put them by and you could pick them up from the cottage some time.'

'In that case I'll have the lot.'

Annie, open-mouthed, accepts a shilling piece, and Lily stuffs all six remaining volumes into Beattie's shopping-bag.

'Give them to your mum. I'll be round tomorrow with a rabbit for her. I think romance is becoming my secret vice. I read them all the time, one after another. Anything to stop our mother going on and on about me going to America. *If I ever go.*'

Lily's tone is savage as she eases a foot out of its shoe and tries to massage some circulation back into her toes. 'It's like a madhouse. There's Mother moaning on because she thinks I'm going, and me moaning all the time because I'm sure I'll never go. But Mother's the limit. I just don't know why she didn't say all these things when we got engaged. I actually asked her that last night, and she had the cheek to say she never thought the engagement would come to anything. Then she backtracked as usual and said she thought that if we married we'd both go on living with her and Dad and the little 'uns in the cottage. Can you beat it? With Greg helping Dad out with his traps, I shouldn't wonder.'

Beattie sells two slim volumes on bee-keeping to the vicar of the neighbouring village.

'And, if that weren't enough, I get letters from Greg asking me if I've fixed up my passage yet. He doesn't know how hard it is unless you've got the money to travel privately. And we certainly haven't. They say there's going to be a ship to take us all over, but nobody seems to know when. So it doesn't look as if I'm even going to see him until next year, with him in Berlin with all those German girls who'll do anything for a cigarette, or so our dad says—'

'Now, how on earth would he know? The annuals are threepence each, Mrs Thomas.'

'Says it's common knowledge,' goes on Lily *sotto voce*, her eyes fixed on the doorway for the missing Major Jones. 'You know I never had a moment's doubt about Greg when he was here, for all that those Ipswich girls kept on plaguing him, but it's been seventeen months since I've seen him. I expect he's forgotten me,' she adds suddenly quite pathetically. 'That's why he wants my photo.'

'Oh, Lily, come on, cheer up, do. You know his letters couldn't be fonder. He's always talking about the future and how much he hopes you'll like Santa Monica. He thinks the world of you. And his parents have written and everything, haven't they? There must be loads of Suffolk girls like you, waiting to go and not knowing when.'

Lily sighs, resolutely blows her nose and shuts her handbag with a decisive click.

'I know it doesn't do to give way. But you don't know how lucky you are to have a husband already home. He's a treasure, your Charles. How is Alexia, by the way?'

'She's never sick now, never,' puts in Annie suddenly.

'Keeps all her food down now, does she? Must be odd having two so close like that. Tom's – what, six months old now, isn't he? It must be like having twins.'

'Tom on his own is like having twins,' says his mother with feeling. 'Alexia is as good as gold compared to him.'

'Does Mrs Musgrave still come to see her?'

'Oh, yes, or else I take the chldren up there. It's strange, I think she's quite fond of Alexia really. But she just doesn't know what to do with her. She holds her in a funny way. I can't explain.'

'Well, she always had nannies for her lot, didn't she? A lot of good it seems to have done them.'

Lily is about to make pointed remarks about the absent Virginia when she catches sight of Annie's intent face and refrains from further comment.

'Where's Charles?'

'He had to go up to London today to see his publisher.'

Annie wanders off to talk to Mrs Leary. Lily looks after her fondly.

'Little dote, looks just like you. What's your Charles really think about his large family?'

'Well . . . he wasn't very happy at first, but I think he's more used to it now.'

'It beats me how a mother can abandon her own child like that, and her with her husband just dead.'

'Men leave their children, too.'

'Yes, but we don't think the better of them for it, do we? Not all men are like that. Take your Charles. . . .'

Beattie glances quickly at Lily.

'Lots of men would refuse point-blank to have the little one to stay.'

'Oh, yes,' says Beattie, relieved. 'He's been very good about Alexia. By the way, have you seen Lucy? She wasn't at church on Sunday. I wondered if she was coming along today.'

'I saw her in Dereham Market Saturday. She said she'd come along if she could because she's got a ticket for the raffle.'

'Does she know what she's going to do next?'

'Doesn't seem to. The McFees would like her to stay for ever. But she could afford to buy her own farm, couldn't she? At last! There's the Major. Ta ta, Beat. Tell your ma I'll be round tomorrow.'

There is a lull now until the village school comes out at half-past three. Beattie does some brisk trade with the magazines while Annie sits quietly under the table with an Enid Blyton holiday annual, leaving Beattie free to think her own thoughts. There is no doubt, simply to be away from the babies for a couple of hours is a relief. But Lily doesn't know the half of it, thinks Beattie, rearranging her wares.

Charles's initial response to the news that he was now – temporarily at least – father of three had been far from encouraging. Beattie had written a defensive and apologetic letter, explaining the circumstances, and had received by return an extremely frosty missive suggesting that it might have been more tactful to ask Charles what he thought of the idea before rather than after the event. To which Beattie had replied truthfully but rather hopelessly that it had hardly been possible: the idea was simply for Alexia to stay until she was a little stronger. And surely Virginia would have her back.

This was greeted by an ominous silence; then, out of the blue, one Friday night in April, Charles had simply turned up, having got a weekend's special leave. He had opened the back door expecting, presumably, a hero's welcome, looking forward, no doubt, to enjoying more of the peaceful orderly home he had left. Instead he found a scene of such noise and chaotic disorder that he'd physically recoiled.

'Oh, it's you,' had been Beattie's far from gracious welcome, barely audible above three lots of crying. 'Are you stopping? Take Tom, will you? *All right*, Annie. I'm going to get you your tea now. And get out of that basket – those clothes aren't even ironed yet.'

Charles had made his way across the disordered kitchen, trying to avoid painful slaps from the line of dripping nappies hung above the Aga. He had been furious.

'What on earth is going on? Why is Tom crying? There, there, old chap.'

Tom, overcome by the sight of Charles's uniform and the sound of a male voice, had been shocked into silence. Annie actually climbed out of the laundry-basket and hung on to his knee. Alexia, propped up in the kitchen chair and furious because of a very wet nappy, had cried on regardless.

'What on earth is going on?' Charles had repeated, stunned by his hollow-eyed and demented-looking wife, the teetering piles of unwashed crockery, the clothes on every chair and floor, the smell of the nappies soaking in a pail by the door.

'It's called teatime,' Beattie had retorted angrily.

'But hasn't Mrs What's-her-name been in? And why are the children all shrieking?'

Beattie had looked at Charles with the pitying smile reserved by those who live with children for those who do not.

'The children are shouting,' she had said tersely, 'because Tom is teething, Alexia wants a feed and is sopping wet and I've got no time to feed her because Annie needs her tea not to mention a lullaby, a bath and a story, none of which she's likely to get before midnight at this rate. Mrs Hobbs hasn't been in for a week because she's got flu. Mother's got flu as well, or else I could have asked her in to help. I have been up nearly all night for the past six days with either teething or feeding problems. I haven't bothered to tidy up because, while the children won't die in an untidy home, they will die if I don't feed them.'

'Then, what in God's name are you doing taking on more responsibilities when you can't even cope with the ones you've got.'

'I can cope,' Beattie had shouted, beside herself with rage. 'You're just looking for an excuse to get rid of Alexia. She's the very least of my problems.'

The sight of the normally calm Beattie screaming then suddenly bursting into tears was the final straw: all three children had started to roar in unison.

Charles had cast a despairing eye over the trio, juggled Tom up and down and put his other arm around Beattie to hug her.

'Come on, love, it's all right,' he had said awkwardly, kissing her hot tear-stained cheek. Tom had bawled on regardless, while Annie had sobbed bitterly into the material of Charles's trousers.

'Look, you sit down – and feed – er – what's-her-name – Alexia,' he had said finally, trying to get his bearings. 'I'll make us a cup of tea. What about Tom?'

'There's a bottle cooling on the window-sill,' Beattie had muttered, lightheaded with emotion and lack of sleep.

In ten minutes the kitchen had been quiet if not orderly. Beattie had had her tea and fed Alexia and was sitting, too poleaxed to move, with the baby at her breast. Tom was taking his feed, his eyes riveted on his father, and Annie was sitting comfortably on Charles's other knee, hunger forgotten, as she told him about the garden that Mr Blythe had promised to make for her.

Finally all three children had fallen asleep where they were, mouths open and cheeks flushed with the heat from the Aga.

'I'm sorry I shouted at you when I came in,' Charles had said *sotto voce*.

'It isn't always like this,' Beattie had said tiredly, following his eyes around the room. 'It's just a combination of things and Tom's teething. Are you able to stay? Or,' she went on suddenly smiling in spite of herself, 'do you want to?'

Charles had looked at her, startled, then he had laughed with her.

'I handled the Luftwaffe all right, so I suppose I shouldn't be worried by three small children, should I? Let me have a look at the little girl.'

Beattie had got up heavily and held Alexia so that Charles could see her. She had slept on, her dark lashes fanning out over her plump peach-like cheeks.

'Pretty little thing, isn't she?' he had said finally.

'She is now she's feeding properly. I really thought she was going to die,' Beattie had said soberly. 'Look, I know it's a cheek expecting you just to fit in with whatever I suggest, but really there wasn't anything else I could do. She wouldn't feed, you see.' Inexplicably tears begin to pour down Beattie's cheeks again. 'Nobody wanted her. They'd have let her die, I know they would. Old Mrs Musgrave doesn't mind seeing her now, for an hour or so, because she looks so pretty. When she was ill and seedy and ailing no one wanted her.'

'What about her bloody awful mother?'

'She writes regularly to ask how she is—'

'She *writes*?' Charles could hardly believe his ears. The emotion in his voice had made Beattie pull away from him.

'I know it's awful of her,' she had hurried on, driven to defend where Charles had attacked, 'but I do think she must be in a terrible state to do it – and it's only for a little while, Charles.'

'Then what? Don't kid yourself, Beattie. If she doesn't want her now when she's got most need of her mother, she isn't going to want her later. Don't you see that in providing an alternative you're taking away any chance of Virginia bothering to make an effort? You're helping her to avoid her responsibilities.'

'Look,' Beattie had snapped, suddenly furious. 'Perhaps you're right. Perhaps I *am* colluding with the Musgraves to let them off the hook *yet again*. But I do think that it would be a pretty dangerous experiment to give Alexia back to Virginia in the hope that it might shock her into some kind of proper behaviour. Alexia might just die as a result. I didn't mean to have her here. I wanted things to go on the way they were, orderly and calm, with me starting back at school next week. But there's no help for it, is there?'

Charles had been silenced. Later, when the children were in their respective baskets, cots and beds, they'd had supper together and talked about rather less emotive topics. Then, leaving everything as it was, they'd gone to bed and had the best night together they'd known since Tom was conceived. The following day Charles had got up early and helped her tidy up the house and offered to take them out for the day. It had been the most relaxed weekend for months. After that Alexia's future had simply never been discussed. When Charles had come home for good in September he had not only fitted in as if he'd never been away, he had managed to lighten Beattie's load considerably. His energy rapidly became a legend in the Blythe household. This morning, when Beattie had come down to the kitchen after feeding Alexia, she'd found the table laid, Charles giving Annie her breakfast with Tom on his knee while he glanced through the galley proofs of his new novel. What she would do when Charles got a full-time job did not bear thinking about.

'Hello, Aunty Bee, are you doing a roaring trade?'

'Oh, hello, Ern. I didn't see you. Is school finished?'

'Yes. Miss Baxter brought in a cake.'

Ern is normally a stickler for preserving the decencies in public, which means no sloppiness or kissing. But today, of his own accord, he sits down beside Beattie and puts his face up for a kiss. Afterwards he doesn't make even a pretence of grimacing and wiping the kiss away.

'Did you say all your goodbyes?'

'I suppose so.'

'I've saved you a couple of books; I thought you'd need them for the journey on the boat. Oh, that's sixpence for those *Home Chat*. Here, Annie. Look, there's one about aeroplanes which is quite new – and there are two film annuals somewhere.'

'Ta ever so,' says Ern politely, putting them into his satchel with hardly a glance. 'I shall miss you, Auntie Bee.'

'Oh, goodness, Ern, I'll miss you both terribly.'

'Will you really?'

'I'll say. And as for Mum and Dad – I just don't know what they'll do without you.'

Ern's head is drooping, and his eyes are suspiciously bright. Hastily she goes on: 'But we keep cheering ourselves up by thinking what a good time you'll be having in Australia with your dad. All that swimming and all that lovely food.'

Ern gives a watery sniff but allows himself to be comforted.

'I'll expect we'll go in a speedboat. If I write, will you write back?'

'Of course I will. You know I love getting letters. Look, if you've got all the books you want, why don't you go back to the cottage? Mother's getting ready your special tea, and Charles and I'll be along just as soon as we've finished here. You could take Annie with you; I think she's getting a bit bored. Oh, there's Charles now. We're over here.'

Charles kisses Beattie fondly. Unembarrassed, she slips an arm round his waist. 'What's this, drooping behind the shop counter of life, Miss Blythe? Waiting for Prince Charming to come along and sweep you away? Will I do instead? These little hands weren't made for selling books.'

'You are funny, Uncle Charles,' comments Ern.

'With Tom teething, there's no other option open than madness. Are you all packed, Ern?'

'Yes.'

'He's just off home now for tea,' says Beattie. 'We'll have to pack up smartish after the raffle because I said we'd be there, too.'

When Ern and Annie have disappeared into the October dusk Beattie says suddenly: 'Do you think they'll be all right?'

'Toby and Ern? I think so. Your parents liked their father, didn't they?'

'I know, but it's just all so sudden. One minute they're orphans, next moment their father turns up out of the blue to claim them. They don't say much, but I know they hate leaving. Though they seemed pretty pleased to know they had a father.'

'I'm sure they will be. They need a family of their own.'

'Well, I shall miss them. I just don't know what Mum and Dad are going to do without them, I really don't.'

'With any luck they'll offer to adopt all three of ours and we can take Beetle and go and live in London.'

Beattie smiles in spite of herself.

'I don't think he'd take kindly to being a London dog.'

'I don't think I'd like to be a London dog after today. It was so full of people. And there's something about the sweetness of the air as soon as you get off the train at Ipswich. I love it.'

'It's the smell of silage, probably,' says Beattie drily.

'Probably. But I think I'd find it difficult to write in London.'

'How did you get on?'

'Oh, pretty well. Theo Beavers took me up to lunch at the Savoy Grill. That's the power of good reviews, I suppose.'

'Lucky you,' says Beattie enviously. 'What did you have to eat?'

'Oysters, a sole, a lot of jolly good wine.'

'Well, the good news is it's shepherd's pie for supper. Not that we'll probably want any after Mother's goodbye tea.'

'Sorry to hear it. I like shepherd's pie.'

'I'd love to try oysters.' Beattie's tone is wistful.

'Next time we're in town we'll go to a good fish restaurant. Which reminds me – I had a letter from Guy's parents this morning. They're expecting him home next month. They want to know if we'll come up for the weekend. If I know Guy, he'll want to do as many shows as he can in as short a space of time and get roaring drunk.'

'I'd adore to go away for the weekend,' says Beattie fervently. 'but what about—?'

'I've already asked your ma. She thought it would be a good idea for us to go away on our own.'

'She said yes?'

'Of course. Why not? Anyway, as I said, she won't know what to do with all her spare time, so she can spend it quite usefully on Tom's teething troubles.'

'Did you tell Mr Beavers about your plans?'

'Yes.'

'What did he say?'

'Well, he looked a bit glum, to be honest. But he knows as well as I do that, even with good reviews, it'll be years before we can live off my books.

So I'll have to find something else to do. And, if I do study law, at least I'll get the detail right for the books.'

Charles had made overtures to a firm of solicitors in Ipswich and from January will be taking articles with them.

'Anyway,' goes on Charles cheerfully, 'if I don't like it there's always another job somewhere.'

Beattie is silent. Charles moves optimistically through the world, secure in the belief of always being needed. She has begun to hope that in time his inexhaustible confidence will eventually brush off on to her.

'Is the raffle due? Will anybody mind me having a look round the house? It's absolutely magnificent, don't you think?'

'It's just the rectory,' says Beattie, surprised. 'I suppose it's quite nice; it's all so shabby somehow. And who'd want eight bedrooms nowadays?'

'But the proportion of the rooms! And those mouldings! Did you see that lovely cedar in the garden?'

'It's got a terrible old-fashioned kitchen. Nothing modern in it at all, not even a refrigerator. And all the water comes from their own well.'

'Really?' Charles is entranced. 'Perhaps I'll just slip down and have a look. Oh, there's Lucy. Lucy! Hey!'

The draw for the raffle has taken place at the other end of the room, and on consulting her tickets, Beattie is delighted to find that Toby has won a box of biscuits and that by switching her own ticket with Ern's he will have won a bar of chocolate. Lucy fights her way through the throng.

'Oh, dash it all. Have I missed everything?'

'I'm afraid you have.'

'Drat. I wanted to get off afternoon milking, but Donny's had to go to the dentist.'

Lucy slumps down uninvited on to Annie's vacated stool.

'My goodness, it says something about your social life when you're furious at having missed a jumble sale.'

'You look done in, Lucy.'

'I am a bit weary. I was up all Sunday night with a sick cow, but it's not just that. I feel a bit exhausted generally.'

'I thought you were going to see your mother this weekend.'

'So did I, but she rang up last night to postpone it. Hermione, her old secretary, has come to London for the weekend, and Ma wants to see her. I'll go another time, I suppose.'

Lucy's tone is listless. Beattie is indignant on her friend's behalf.

'Oh, that's rotten – after you'd had your hair done specially.'

'I know. I was a bit peeved myself to start with. On the other hand, though it might have been a change, I don't know if it would actually have been a rest. Ma's been sent the ten "Leafy Tree" films that they made in Canada during the war and she was proposing a special showing for me. Can you imagine? *Ten* half-hours of Mimsy and Tonks! And there's never any question of ducking out or falling asleep – Ma always quizzes me like anything where her writing's concerned. And anyway', adds Lucy soberly. 'I don't think she's forgiven me yet about Hugh. About going ahead with the divorce. Crikey, she only met him a few times and yet she's been going on at me about trying to make the marriage work as if I've suggested casting off her only son.'

'But that's ridiculous. Didn't you tell her about the American woman?'

'I tried to, but Ma sort of pooh-poohed it all. I think it's the old double standard for men and women,' said Lucy rather surprisingly. 'You know, men always have to be forgiven because they're so weak without a woman to keep them on the straight and narrow. Hugh had *two* women to keep *him* on the straight and narrow,' Lucy concludes with a glimmer of her old gruff humour. 'And it still didn't succeed in keeping him on the path of righteousness. I'd say there's no hope for him.'

'So you're still determined to go ahead.'

'Oh, absolutely. Funnily enough, I think Ma could understand it better if she thought I was in love with someone else. She could at least draw on her own experience.' Lucy's tone is disdainful.

'You never told her about . . . Will?'

'No. What was the point? It's all in the past now. And I can't stand the way Ma always wants to meddle. She'd have been on the phone to the American Chief of Staff in twenty minutes trying to find out what had happened to Will.'

'Would that be a bad thing?'

'I think so. I feel I've treated Will very badly. I'm quite sure that if he's alive he wouldn't want to see me. For all I know, he's probably married by now.'

'Lucy, this isn't like you. You're so – so . . .'

'Fatalistic? I feel a it like that at present. It's as if my engine's run down. I thought coming out would cheer me up. Is Lily about?'

'She's gone to Ipswich to have her photo done lest Greg forget her. She seemed a bit out of sorts, too.'

'I thought so when I talked to her. Mind you, her mother would drive you batty. She even asked me if I would have a word with Lily to try to persuade her not to go. I ask you! And there's poor old Lily worried to death she won't be asked to go anyway. Did you notice that she'd stopped wearing her ring?'

'Well, she had it on today for the photograph at least. There, that's everything now.'

The drawing-room is emptying fast as the trestle-tables are folded up and taken out to be stacked in the vestry.

'What are you going to do now?'

'Oh, go back up to the farm, I suppose.'

'Have you brought Sam down?'

'No, I cycled.'

'Well, why not come back to tea at Church Cottage? It's a special spread for Ern and Toby – we'd have asked you except I was sure you were going to your mother's this weekend. Come on, do. It'll be fun. Charles is here, and all the children are going.'

'Are you sure it's not just a family do?' says Lucy gruffly.

'Well, you're practically family, aren't you?'

Lucy colours.

'That's really nice of you to say that. I really do feel a bit gloomy at present, so it would be a lovely treat. Here, let me carry these things for you.'

'No, you just sit there and relax.'

Without any further bidding Lucy slumps back on her stool. The truth is that even if she'd wanted to help she doubted if she'd be able to: a curious inertia hangs so heavily on her limbs that there are times when she can hardly find the strength to get up in the morning. It is ridiculous; she is not ill, feverish or suffering from her period. What is wrong with me? thinks Lucy drearily and with very little interest. It is somehow as if life had just stopped. Ended. Run down. Leaving Lucy to go through her tasks mechanically like a wound-up toy. Perhaps it is just the events of the last two years finally catching up with her. Even now there are areas of pain in her mind connected with Will, her father and Virginia that have her frantically directing her thoughts elsewhere. As for Hugh – well the pain there has long since died, leaving only anger. If she had still hoped for a belated flowering of maturity in her absent husband, Hugh's reaction to her request for a divorce quietly dispelled those hopes for ever. He had written back a furious tirade saying that it was inconceivable that she could think she had the right to let him down like this. This has been followed by a positive avalanche of letters employing a variety of different tones and tactics to try to make her change her mind. There was heavy paternalism ('I know about stress and strain, old girl, and what it can do. Don't forget that, whilst you've been sitting it out in England, us soldiers have been fighting a war! I think it's probably all got a bit on top of you – and I bet that farmer's been giving you a bad time, eh? But a few early nights should put it all straight. Have you thought about going to the doctor for a tonic?') True, he hadn't actually suggested she went out and bought a new hat, but Lucy suspected that even this was only a matter of time. There had been thinly veiled threats ('I'm not at all sure I can go on living with all hope of happiness so ruthlessly snatched away'). This had been followed by a series of tender injunctions urging Lucy to think very carefully before putting herself back on the marriage market at her age and with, no doubt, a complexion ruined beyond repair by five years' farming. It was mildly interesting that in over a dozen letters it never even seemed to cross Hugh's mind that she might have met anyone else. Clearly Hugh saw himself as a kind of Ancient Mariner of the heart; one glance from his glittering eye and women were transfixed for ever. Finally, getting no reaction from her, Hugh had hit upon the ploy of simply ignoring the matter altogether and had started urging Lucy to send him estate agents' lists for properties currently available in Wimbledon and Merton. At this point Lucy gave up the correspondence altogether and wrote to her father's solicitors in Southampton Row, citing Julia Heap and asking them to set the divorce in train. Since then, she had heard nothing from Hugh, who instead had taken to writing to Mrs Hallett to complain about her daughter. The end of Lucy's marriage, in her own opinion, seemed destined to be as farcical as its beginning.

As for Will. What was there to say? Except that she still dreams about him every night and wonders incessantly whether he is alive, uninjured or happy. But already he seems part of the last two years' violent unhappiness. I should put it all behind me now, Lucy keeps telling herself. There is, after all, much to be thankful for. Her divorce is going through. The war is at an end.

It should be a time for rejoicing and fresh hope, new plans, a sudden surge of energy. As it is, Lucy dreads the start of every day when the rush of consciousness makes her aware of her unhappy state. What is she going to do? Grow old in the service of the McFees? (Lucy is twenty-four). Buy a farm and run it with another farm girl? Stick with the McFees for the time being? Leave the McFees (her mother's suggestion) and take a long holiday? Lucy wants to groan aloud. It is not that she dislikes what she's doing; on the contrary, on a good day she still loves it. But with the ending of the war it is as if the tension that had held her together and saved her from thinking painful thoughts has finally been removed. Now, with time on her hands on the farm, she dreads being alone. Where she had once dreamt of having time to relax she now dreads her own company and the companionable silences of the McFees' kitchen. It is a relief to be anywhere other than the farm. So it is doubly gratifying for her appearance to be greeted with shouts of acclaim by Annie and the two boys and the quieter but none the less warm greetings of Mrs Blythe and Charles, who has finally been persuaded away from the rectory's plumbing arrangements.

Beattie is conscious that this is the very last of these celebration teas at Church Cottage. The pattern of six years is about to be broken, and in a sudden flash of memory she recalls coming home for tea after the Manor garden-party. They had sat down, just the three of them, in the quiet, orderly and empty kitchen to talk about Miss Lucy. Now Lucy is seated at the same table, Toby and Ern are about to leave, and she has mysteriously acquired three children and a husband.

'What are you thinking about, Aunty Bee?' asks Toby.

'That I'll miss you.'

'You will write?'

'Of course I will. And you must send me pictures of where you live.'

'When I'm properly grown up I'll come back to England on my holidays and I'll come to see you, Aunty.'

'Well, your old room will be ready for you,' says Mrs Blythe, trying to simulate some of her old briskness. 'Any more tea for you, Charles?'

When the meal has been cleared and the six o'clock news given its due attention, at Toby's insistence they all play charades. It isn't until nearly nine o'clock before the party ends and Beattie and Charles prepare to go home.

'Let Annie sleep over here,' says Mrs Blythe fondly. 'It seems a pity to wake her up. You can put her in your old room, Beattie.'

Fond and emotional goodbyes are exchanged between Lucy and the two boys.

'Do you know, I really will miss those two little tykes,' she says to Beattie as they walk up the lane to the main street. Charles has already taken the two babies on in the car. It is a cold clear night without a breath of wind: great clusters of stars are visible in the cloudless night sky. The girls' breath makes white clouds on the frosty air.

'Why don't you come back and have a cup of tea with us? The babies will be asleep for a good few hours yet.'

'No, really,' says Lucy awkwardly. 'It's been the most marvellous evening – really. Such a treat. And so unexpected. Look, isn't that Charles come back to meet you?'

460

It is indeed Charles, whose footsteps ring out confidently as he walks back the couple of hundred yards to escort Beattie home. There is a gaiety and a cheerfulness in his stride that betoken a contented man. Lucy says good night and turns to watch them go, quite unselfconsciously moving together to put their arms around each other, suddenly breaking into a laughing uneven run to get home more quickly. The street is dimly lit with light from the cottages. She does not begrudge Beattie her happiness – goodness knows, Beattie had seen enough heartache earlier in the war to deserve the present joy. Things have come to a pretty pass, she tells herself sternly, when the sight of other people's happiness makes you feel miserable. Shame on you, Lucy Jennings Hallett. Resolutely she turns to walk back to the rectory to pick up her bike, and begins the journey up to Home Farm. She could very well cycle but is in no hurry to get back. Instead, warmed by the unexpected pleasures of the evening and Mrs Blythe's spectacular special tea, she slowly pushes her bicycle up the lane. Once beyond the houses she turns left at the clump of stunted willows which mark the path of the village stream and follows the road as it climbs slowly away from the village. On impulse she stops at the top of the rise to take one last look back. After six years of blackout it is still a minor pleasure to see even the subdued lights of the village: standing there, breathing in the damp clean night air, Lucy is suddenly sharply reminded of another occasion when she had stood like this, listening to the immense silences of the country-side. When had that been? Lucy asks herself idly, leaning dreamily on her handlebars, staring up at the Plough which tonight seems almost close enough to touch. It must have been before the American airbases had arrived to split the silences every evening with night flights. Then the memory come sharply into focus. It had been that night when she had returned from her honey-moon, when the snow had been so thick the car had skidded coming back from Ipswich and she'd told the chauffeur to go on home without her. She had been on the other side of the village, and when she'd been alone she had stood in the snowy road in her gong-away outfit and gum-boots, apprecia-tively breathing the country air. At that moment she had decided once and for all that the open-air life was the only one for her, and accordingly had set her course to work on the land. Remembering that night, remembering the storm of disapproval that had greeted her decision – from her mother at least – Lucy suddenly breathes deeply down to the bottom of her lungs and feels surprisingly better. She had made her choice, she had stood her ground. And she had done the right thing. Whatever else had subsequently gone wrong, this was one part of her life that she could feel proud about. Nothing can touch it. Though at present her daily lot seems mechanical and dreary, she still loves life on the farm and would not trade it for any other. And this is valuable precious knowledge.

An owl swoops silently over the road: two rabbits, lulled into security by her immobility, scamper out of the ditch almost at her feet. The rest of life will right itself, she thinks suddenly, obscurely comforted. Things will come right in the end. I don't have to go on mourning for Dad for ever – he wouldn't want it, that's for sure. He'd tell me to put my shoulder to the wheel . . . no, he'd find some sporting metaphor about the game not being over until the last ball was bowled. The thought makes her smile affectionately in the darkness. As for Hugh – and as for Will – perhaps it is just time to admit that that part of her life is over and gently let it go. Hugh will find someone else. Will undoubtedly already has. It costs her a strange pang to wish him well in her thoughts, but she manages it and now calmer, if not happier, is about to turn to push her bike on up the remaining four miles to the farm when an extraordinary sight stops her dead in her tracks. It is a pair of headlights stabbing the darkness of the Ipswich road. Intrigued, Lucy watches as a car crawls slowly round the twisting road, then drops down into the village. Who on earth had petrol to be out at this time of night? Dr Boddy on a mission of mercy? Not the vet; it had been a car, not a land-rover. Perhaps it is Lily, thinks Lucy, screwing up her eyes. Lily had long been threatening to go on a bender at the Station Arms in Ipswich to forget her troubles and perhaps even now was returning maudlin and much the worse for wear in the station taxi. Perhaps she'd blown all the money she'd been saving for her bottom drawer. Well, she'll see Lily first thing tomorrow morning with the post, so she'll soon find out if that's the case. Whistling cheerfully, Lucy sets off on her way, wondering if Mrs McFee has left out any cocoa for her.

At the very gate of their cottage Beattie and Charles have also seen the headlights and, equally curious, have stopped to see who is arriving so late in the village. Like Lucy, Beattie believes it may be Lily, returning in shame from Ipswich. But Charles, screwing up his eyes, announces that it is a man getting out of the car.

'It is the station taxi,' he confirms, 'But I don't recognize who it is. He's very tall, whoever he is.'

A door slams, the taxi reverses, turns round and drives back the way it has come. A man at the end of the street stands irresolutely outside the dimly lit public house.

'I can't think who it is,' says Beattie at last, intrigued. 'But I'm sure – yes! He's got a uniform on, I'm sure of it.'

'What sort of uniform?' says Charles, so sharply that Beattie turns and looks at him in surprise.

'I don't know. A great coat and cap I think. Oh, this is ridiculous, stealthily peering at him through the branches. Let's go and see— Charles! Where are you going—?'

But Charles is already halfway down the village street. Beattie, torn between an overwhelming curiosity and the fear that if she moves even a foot away from the cottage it will immediately spontaneously combust, immolating the children within, stands hopping from foot to foot in impatience. Then to her astonishment she sees Charles walking back deep in conversation with the stranger. As they draw nearer Beattie sees the other man's face for the first time and actually cries out with pleasure and surprise.

'Will! Will Shaugnessy! Is it really you?'

Will opens his arms and embraces Beattie.

'Yes, it's really me.'

Beattie looks up at him and hugs him again.

'What a wonderful surprise. We wondered and wondered where you'd gone. Lily's Greg said your squadron had split up—'

'I've been in Berlin this last year,' says Will, still clasping Beattie's hands, unaffectedly pleased to see her. 'I flew in this afternoon.'

'Are you here on holiday?'

'Hadn't we better go into the warm?' says Charles half-amused, half-exasperated.

'Well . . . well . . . I was hoping to kinda, hoping to go straight on up to Home Farm if it's not too late.'

'Oh, you've just missed Lucy. She left about ten minutes ago.'

'Really? Well, if I move fast, maybe I'll catch her up—'

'I'll drive you up if you want.'

'No, I – I'd like to walk up. I've thought about that road often enough. And it's a fine night. Gee, it's good to be here and see you all again. Can I leave my kit here and I'll pick it up tomorrow? I've only got a forty-eight-hour pass—'

'Well, be sure and come down for lunch tomorrow,' says Beattie. 'Tob and Ern are leaving in the afternoon – they're off to Australia – they'd love to see you. But don't let us keep you. See you tomorrow.'

Inside the warmth of their own kitchen Beattie hugs a surprised Charles.

'Isn't that *wonderful*! He's come back for Lucy, I'm sure of it. Unless. . . . Oh Lord,' Beattie's face falls. 'Unless he's got married. But he'd hardly come back to Musgrave to tell her, would he?'

'Beattie, calm down, for goodness' sake. I'm sure he isn't married.'

'I can't believe it. I just can't believe it.'

Beattie sits down on the kitchen chair, her face glowing. 'I asked Lily to ask Greg if he knew where Will had gone, but he couldn't trace him. Oh, it's so wonderful. I suppose he just turned up on the off-chance to see her.'

'Off-chance nothing,' says Charles, filling the kettle, rightly divining that if he wants a cup of tea it will be he and not his euphoric wife who will make it. 'I wrote to him.'

Beattie stares at her husband in the purest disbelief.

'*What?* But you've never even met him—'

'I felt I had after all those conversations between you and Lily,' says Charles drily.

For a moment Beattie is actually silenced. Then she says; 'But how did you – and why?'

'I've got a lot of contacts in the United States Air Force. I just got one of them to find out where Will was posted. At first I thought I'd just find out where he was and if he was alive. And when I found he was alive and flying in Berlin I wrote to him.'

'What did you say in your letter?'

'Just that Lucy's circumstances had changed and that it was your opinion – I hope you didn't mind me quoting you, but after hearing you and Lily chewing the cud I felt I was on pretty safe ground – that she was still missing Will a lot. That was last week. He must have got my letter yesterday or the day before.'

Beattie looks at her husband open-mouthed, speechless with admiration.

'Charles! You are *wonderful*. Truly wonderful. But why did you do it? Why? I know you like Lucy, but she's just a friend to you—'

'I do like Lucy – very much. And I know what a soft-hearted, sentimental, romantic old thing you are. Anything to make you smile. I knew it would make you happy if it all worked out. No, sit there, *I'll* make *you* a cup of tea.'

Still whistling but now slightly breathless, Lucy has almost reached the Home Farm boundary when she rounds a corner and lets out a shriek of consternation. Spread liberally across the road and into the ditch is the entire dairy herd seemingly awaiting her return.

'What are you *doing* here?' she demands furiously of the nearest cow, who looks away, apparently embarrassed.

The cause of the breakout is clear enough: there is a hole next to the gate which Donny had sworn he had blocked up which is now large enough to allow the passage of a small family car. There is no possibility of mending it tonight, so Lucy has no option but to take the cows up to the yard and leave them there until milking-time. Consoling herself with the thought that, if she hadn't come by tonight, the cows could well have been down in the village by daybreak, Lucy parks her bicycle in the empty field and begins to move the cows briskly along to the farm. Progress is slow, owing mainly to the fact that the cows, disorientated by the time of night and the certain conviction that it is not yet milking-time can only be persuaded to walk backwards. None the less the yard is in sight when Lucy hears a noise further down the lane behind her and turns to listen. Above the clatter of hoof and the heavy breathing of the cows it is almost impossible to hear what's going on – and she turns back to the herd, thinking she must have imagined it. But, no, there it is again. Someone is actually calling her name from further down the darkened track.

Puzzled, Lucy leaves the cows to their own devices and strains her eyes in the darkness. The moon suddenly disappears behind a bank of clouds, leaving Lucy between the high hedges in almost total darkness. Then there is the sound of running footsteps flying up the road towards her. Perhaps it is one of the boys out looking for the herd—

'Lu – *cee. Lucy.*' Lucy stands rigid, disbelieving, electrified. Every cell of her body is tense with shock. It can't be. She is hallucinating. It just can't be. Then a figure appears out of the gloom and almost crashes into her, grabbing hold of her by the arms.

'Lucy! Here, Lucy! It's me. It's Will.'

Breathless, laughing, Will envelopes Lucy in a bear-hug. Lucy is so stunned she stands there unresisting, unable even to embrace him.

'I ran all the way from the village in my greatcoat. I must be fitter than I knew. You out walking the cows? Huh?'

Lucy can't decide whether to laugh or cry or even speak. Instead she clutches Will's lapels with shaking fingers.

'Why are you here? Where have you been? Oh, Will, I thought you might be dead or married or—' It is all too much for Lucy, who bursts into tears.

Still keeping his arms tight round her, Will feels in his pocket for a hanky.

'You take this. We'll rest here on the stile for a minute. The cows aren't going anywhere on their own. Now, just you relax a bit.'

'I just don't understand why you're here,' sniffs Lucy, clutching at the material of Will's sleeve lest he dematerialize before her very eyes.

'I never thought I'd be here again,' says Will, looking around at the silent countryside with every sign of satisfaction. 'I thought of you so often and the airfield and the farm. Oh, Lucy, I missed you so much. I never stopped thinking about you. Never since I left here.'

'I never stopped thinking about you,' says Lucy softly. 'But I'd thought I'd done the right thing even though it didn't always feel like it. And I never, never thought I'd see you again.'

'I've been imagining you planning the future with Hugh, and for a long while I hated you so much because I knew you loved me and yet you chose someone you didn't care about.'

Then Will turns so that Lucy can see his face properly in the light.

'But finally I got to thinking. And some sense finally got through to me. When I thought back over how we'd parted I felt pretty ashamed. You had all that trouble and sadness with your parents, with your father dying. And I know now I just made things worse, didn't I, by pestering you. I should have let you have time to make up your own mind. Instead I was just so frightened of losing you that I made your problems much worse by behaving like a child.'

'Oh, Will, you were unhappy, too—?'

'Yeah, but it didn't make me think too much about your unhappiness, did it? It was just – I knew you loved me. I knew we'd be a great team. Yet you seemed to be wilfully trying to destroy the good things between us. But, even so, I should have respected your decision – after all, Hugh was your husband. Instead I said all those terrible things to you—'

'Oh, Will. Don't blame yourself. I didn't hold all that against you. I knew you were saying them because you were unhappy. It was an awful, awful time for both of us. I just couldn't think straight. And I couldn't bear you to think I'd deliberately led you on.' Tentatively Lucy touches Will's cold cheek. 'You see, I couldn't decide what was right—'

'Have you decided now?'

'Oh, yes,' says Lucy in heartfelt tones.

'Do you still care about me?' says Will at last. His face is vulnerable and unsure.

'Yes,' says Lucy simply. 'I've never loved anyone the way I loved you, Will. And it took your going away to make me realize it. Just hold me, please, dearest Will.'

Will is silent, content, his arms tightly around Lucy, his cheek pressed against hers.

'It's a miracle we met,' he says at last.

'Two miracles,' Lucy reminds him. 'A miracle that we met and a miracle that we remet. Will you help me drive the cows?'

Will starts to laugh, and with their arms tight round each other they urge the cows up to the yard.

EPILOGUE
June 1948

*I*T STARTED OFF like any other Sunday. They had been to church in the hot hazy early morning. After breakfast the children went out to play with Beetle, who had wandered round from Church Cottage. At ten past twelve Beattie is dreamily peeling potatoes whilst listening to Frank Sinatra on 'Forces Favourites'. The kitchen is full of the Sunday smell of roasting meat, mingled with the heady green fragrance of new-cut lawn. With the virtuousness of a man who has performed his duties Charles has retired with the Sunday papers into the dining-room. Faintly, Beattie can hear shouts of laughter from the garden. Mr and Mrs Blythe are due for lunch at one o'clock sharp. A gooseberry pie stands waiting to be put into the oven. It is the kind of day when afterwards, much later, you realize that you were happy.

Annie, six years old and tall for her age, tugs at Beattie's skirt.

'I'm hungry. Is it dinner soon?'

'Lunch. An hour.'

'I'm hungry. Can I have a biscuit?'

'No, it's too near.'

Annie pouts. 'What's for pudding?'

Beattie indicates the pie.

'With cream?'

'Custard.'

Annie frowns and regroups her forces. 'Can I go round and see Granny?'

'She won't let you have a biscuit, either.'

'She will,' says her daughter calmly. 'She's afraid I'm going to outgrow my strength.'

'Really,' says her mother, amused. 'Where are Tom and Lexy?'

'Dressing up Beetle. Oh, please. I'm starving.'

'Oh, give me an apple and you can have one half and give the other—

In the hall the telephone rings. Beattie and Annie look at each other, transfixed. The phone rarely rings in the Hammond household, and no one rings at the weekend – not even Charles's publisher.

Beattie frowns and runs through the possibilities. Most likely it is one of Charles's many friends 'finding themselves' in the area. Mentally Beattie measures the size of the joint. They certainly can't come for lunch, that's for sure. Perhaps tea. She'd still have time to make a cake—

Charles pushes open the kitchen door and looks enquiringly at his wife.

467

'It's for you, Beattie. It's a Frenchman. He says he's Alexia's uncle. He says he wants to see her.'

'*What?* Are you serious?'

'Absolutely. Buck up, it's a trunk call from London.'

Perplexed, Beattie wipes her hands on her apron, goes into the hall and picks up the phone.

'Hello,' she says uncertainly. 'This is Mrs Hammond.'

'Mrs Hammond, many many apologies for phoning you without an introduction, but I arrived in London only last night and proposed to see Virginia today so I could see Alexia. But I have discovered she is away tonight and that Alexia is with you. I am most anxious to see my niece as soon as possible. Would it be a great imposition to visit you this afternoon?'

So the cake would be needed after all.

'Well, no, do come, by all means,' says Beattie slowly. 'I'm sure Alexia will be delighted . . . er, Mr—'

'Aumont. Ferdinand Aumont. Virginia's husband was my cousin. You are most kind. I have your address. At what hour should I call?'

'Well, any time after three.'

After another exchange of pleasantries Beattie replaces the receiver with a vague but unmistakable sense of unease.

'Do you know him?'

'I don't think so. Unless. . . . There was a Frenchman staying at the Dower House just before the war. I wonder if that was him. . . .'

'Did he say how he was coming?'

'He's being driven.'

'Good heavens. Where on earth did he get the petrol? What's wrong?'

'I don't know,' answers Beattie slowly, going back to the kitchen to put the potatoes on to boil. 'It just seems so strange somehow, not having heard of him before, then he turns up out of the blue and must see his niece immediately. . . .'

'He told me he'd been in Egypt since the end of the war and this was his first opportunity to come to London. Come on, it's rather good news. Poor Lexy is hardly flush with family, is she?'

'Mm. You'd better go and tell her. I'll get the rest of the lunch on.'

There is absolutely no reason for Beattie to feel anxious, yet throughout the noisy family lunch the feeling grows. Mrs Blythe is as intrigued about the news as Charles but, unlike her daughter, sees nothing sinister in the visit.

'It'll be the best thing in the world for the little girl, to know she's got other kith and kin,' she says decidedly, vigorously scrubbing out the pie-dish after the meal. 'You put this too high in the oven, Beattie. You want to treat pies in a kindly way else you end up with a crust like a biscuit. And since her grandmother's in Africa,' she goes on without a check, 'She could do with a few more aunts and uncles. And cousins for that matter. *He* must have had a family. So where are they, I'd like to know.'

'In France, presumably,' frowns Beattie, poring abstractedly over her cookery-book.

'Give that mixture here. You haven't beaten it half hard enough. Go on, you finish this washing-up and I'll put your cake in the oven. The vicar said he'd had a letter from Mrs Musgrave, did I tell you?'

'Really?' Beattie tips out the sudsy water. 'Does she like Kenya?'

'Oh, yes. She says you never have to wear a cardigan.'

It is hard to imagine what the vicar has made of this particular remark, harder still to envisage the context in which it must have been proffered. Charles would enjoy it anyway.

'I'd better go and change the children.'

At three-thirty precisely a rather grand car with a diplomatic crest moves almost noiselessly up the village street and insinuates itself into the Hammonds' drive. The uniformed chauffeur gets out and opens the door. Beattie recognizes the yellow-faced man in the light-coloured suit from the garden-party – goodness, nine years ago.

'You'd better go out and greet him,' Charles tells her briskly. 'Go on, he looks quite harmless.'

Shaking Ferdinand's hand, Beattie dimly perceives in this rather stooping man the person she had seen on the Manor lawns just before the war. Ferdinand is courtesy itself.

'You are very kind to let me come, as you say, out of the blue.'

'We're delighted. Do come through. The children are in the back garden.'

As they step out through the french windows of the drawing-room into the sunlit back garden the children, hearing voices, turn and run towards them. For a brief, almost hallucinatory instant the moment freezes for Beattie: as the children stream towards them it is as if she is watching a film, what the GIs would call a 'home movie'. Annie's bare brown legs flash across the lawn, hotly pursued by a panting sturdy Tom pulling Alexia along firmly by the hand. What makes this ordinary domestic image suddenly so frightening is Beattie's sense that she is looking at something that is already in the past – that she is looking back from some standpoint in the future at a particularly vivid and poignant memory. Then, just as inexplicably, the moment passes. The scene dissolves into the present and the familiar sight of her three dishevelled children.

'This is Annie. This is Tom. And this is Alexia. Say hello, Alexia darling.'

'Hello,' murmurs Alexia obediently, staring doggedly at the lawn.

'Hello, Alexia. I'm your Uncle Ferdinand.'

'You do talk in a funny way,' observes Tom, tipping back his head to examine the visitor more closely.

'Tom, really. That's not at all polite.'

'I come from across the sea. There they all talk like me. Would you like some sweets? Let me open my bag and see what there is here.'

With all three children now cutting capers, Ferdinand undoes his bulky attaché case and solemnly produces a positive cornucopia of bars of French chocolate. There is a moment's consternation: chocolate, as far as the children are concerned, comes either clad in the purple wrapper of Cadbury's or else has a picture of Fry's five boys on the front. Ferdinand, correctly divining the cause of their hesitation, quickly unwraps a bar and breaks a bit off.

'See – it is chocolate just like yours. You try it.'

Very soon the children are all agreeing that it is indeed chocolate just like theirs.

'I'll put the rest away for them,' says Beattie firmly. 'It's awfully kind of you, Mr Aumont – we're still rationed for sweets, as you probably know. Oh, Charles, this is Mr Aumont. This is my husband, Charles. If you'll get the deck-chairs out, Charles, I'll bring the tray of tea out on to the lawn.'

They have their tea in the shadow of the big oak tree. Tom and Annie are engaged in a boisterous game of pushing Beetle around in the wheelbarrow. Alexia joins in, then comes back to the adults and, without looking at him, sits on the grass near Ferdinand. He is discussing the Nuremberg Trials with Charles which have been reported extensively that day in the *Observer*, but Ferdinand's glance, fond, sad, captivated, never strays far from the little girl sitting peaceably near him. At her own wish Alexia is wearing her best dress: blue flowered Tana Lawn smocked with a darker blue. Her thick glossy dark hair hangs in neat plaits on either side of her gently earnest little face. Notwithstanding her robust good health and equable temperament, there is something about the little girl that makes everyone who comes within her radius, even Tom and Annie, automatically want to take care of her.

'She seems to get on well with your children.'

'Oh, very well. I'm astounded really – they hardly ever quarrel, and if one of them has a barney with the village children they all gang up together.'

'How old is Annie?' asks Ferdinand noncommittally, but even as he enquires Beattie is suddenly sure that he knows the full story of Annie's parentage.

'Nearly six and a half,' she says, composedly enough, 'and Tom's just six months older than Alexia.'

'They are a true family for Alexia,' says Ferdinand with some feeling. 'Myself and Alexis, we were only children. We always had each other. But – who's to say? – perhaps now Alexia will have brothers and sisters of her own.'

There is a long perplexed silence. Ferdinand, rummaging through his pockets for something to amuse his niece, seems unaware of the bombshell he has dropped. Finally Beattie says: 'I'm sorry, but I don't quite understand what you mean.'

'There—' Beaming triumphantly, Ferdinand produces a little silver rabbit. 'I carry this for luck. It is yours now.'

Alexia rushes off excitedly to show her prize to Tom and Annie. 'I mean presumably Virginia will want to start another family now.' For the first time he registers Charles and Beattie's perplexity. He looks quickly from one to the other. 'You do know she is to remarry?'

Beattie is so startled she spills her tea.

'Remarry? Virginia? But when? To whom? She's said nothing to us at all, and I had a letter only last week—'

'This is very strange. Didn't you realize that that is what I was in London for—?'

'You mean she's actually getting married—'

'This week. On Friday.'

Charles vigorously stirs his tea, a sardonic look on his face. His opinion of Virginia is already so low that very little could surprise him.

'You mean you know nothing of this?' Ferdinand's tone is sharp.

'Absolutely nothing,' says Beattie firmly, trying to stifle a feeling of hurt and anger that Virginia had apparently not even thought it worth mentioning to them. 'Who is she marrying?'

'A man called Geoffrey Desborough. He is a businessman. Very wealthy, from what I understand. They have taken a lease on a house near Eaton Square where they are holding the reception.' Ferdinand is silent, biting his lip. 'Has she said nothing of this?'

'Not a word.'

'But surely Alexia must have mentioned it – or at least said something about meeting her new papa. Does she like him by the way?'

Confusion upon confusion. Beattie and Charles look first at each other and then at Ferdinand.

'Why should she? She's never met him.'

'Never met him?' It is Ferdinand's turn to look mystified. 'Virginia's leaving things rather late, isn't she?'

Beattie is still reeling from the news of Virginia's remarriage. 'Well, only if she's planning to have Alexia to live with her when she's married.'

'But where else would she live?'

'Look,' says Charles, moving firmly and authoritatively into the breach. 'We all seem to be walking around in a fog. You do realize that Alexia lives here with us and always has done since she was a month old?'

There is another silence, but this time it is a silence of sudden blinding comprehension on Ferdinand's part. For a moment he is unable to frame a sentence. Then he says hoarsely: 'You mean she isn't down here with you for a summer holiday?'

'Some holiday,' says Charles.

'You mean she's never lived with Virginia? *Never?*'

'As I said, not since she was a month old. Virginia brought her down to her mother. She couldn't cope. So Beattie took her in.'

Ferdinand actually takes out his handkerchief and wipes his brow.

'But Virginia visits often, sees her, spends time with her?' There is almost a note of pleading in his voice.

'Well—' says Beattie wretchedly.

'Virginia's never been back since that day,' cuts in Charles brutally. With a sinking heart Beattie realizes that Charles's resentment of Virginia, so long kept decently under wraps in Alexia's presence at least, is now forcing its way out into the open.

'She writes to Beattie and sends clothes for her child and pays in a monthly allowance at the bank for her. But she's never shown any interest in actually seeing her. She brought her down to the Dower House as soon as she came out of hospital. But when Alexia didn't thrive Mrs Musgrave asked Beattie to care for her. And Virginia's never been back since the day she brought her to the Dower House.'

Ferdinand's face slowly turns crimson.

'She told me she was staying with you for a holiday. I don't understand her. I don't understand her at all. And she's said nothing of her marriage – of having Alexia with her?'

471

'No,' says Beattie hurriedly. 'But, Mr Aumont, if I'm honest, I'm glad she hasn't. We love Alexia so much we'd be devastated—'

'I can see how you love her. What I cannot forgive is the way that Virginia summarily' – Ferdinand masters the word with a tremendous rolling of the *r* – 'abandons her only child then lies to me about her actions. I have asked her again and again for a photograph, but each time there is always some reason, some reason. I cannot believe that she can behave like this to her own child. Do not misunderstand me, Mrs Hammond. I can see that she could not be better loved and cared for. *Except by her mother*. You have amazed me. And now you must forgive me if I leave. It is a long drive. Tonight I must see Virginia. She has been in the country with her fiancé, and there are many things we have to discuss.' Ferdinand's tone is grim.

'You won't have another cup of tea?'

'No. A thousand thanks.'

Galvanized with a certain furious energy, Ferdinand goes over to Alexia, kisses her, bids her goodbye and promises to come and see her again soon, pausing only to thank Charles and Beattie and press a bottle of brandy into their hands. He is soon on his way back to London.

'I reckon Virginia will be more in need of this than we will tonight,' Charles observes, studying the bottle with satisfaction.

'I wish—'

'You wish what?'

'I wish it hadn't had to be us to tell him, that's all.'

Charles stares at his wife.

'What on earth do you mean?'

'You enjoyed it too much,' says Beattie flatly.

'What the hell are you talking about?'

'Telling Ferdinand what she's done. I know she's behaved badly.'

'Oh, really. Well, all I can say is you'd never know it. I've never heard you say a single word against that self-centred bitch.'

Charles was clearly stunned by Beattie's remark.

'I'm perfectly aware of how awful she's been—'

'Then, why do you always defend her every time her name comes up in conversation?'

'Because you're always so quick to condemn her,' yells Beattie, furious. 'I just think she must have been absolutely broken-hearted when her husband died.'

'So broken-hearted that within a month she's disposed of his child? Have some sense, Beattie, do. What kind of logic is there in that? I've never seen any evidence of her caring for anyone. She's never even as much as asked for a photograph – and I notice that while you're good enough to foster her daughter, you don't seem to be quite good enough to be invited to her remarriage.'

Beattie stands silent, her face averted.

'It's time I took the children up.'

When all three children are in bed, if not asleep, Beattie prolongs her usual tidying-up in the children's rooms, folding up towels, gathering discarded clothes for the linen-bag. Alexia is already asleep, her hair brushed and in its night plait, Peter Rabbit tucked in against her cheek. Tom drowsily plays with his Dinky toy. Only Annie is still fully awake.

'Will he come here again? That man with the glasses.'

'I don't know.' Beattie tucks in her sheets. 'Perhaps.'

'Will he take Lexy with him? Over the sea?'

Beattie stares at Annie.

'No, of course not. Why should he?'

'I don't know,' yawns Annie. 'I just wondered.'

Downstairs Charles is studying the documents in a complicated right-of-way suit. But he has set the table for supper and made an elaborate salad, which is his way of showing, Beattie knows, that he is sorry about what he said.

'It just doesn't make sense, any of it,' Beattie says finally in bed later that night. 'I mean, she must have known – she must have known it would all come out eventually. What do you think she'll do about Lexy?'

'Don't know. It depends on whether the new man wants a ready-made family or not. She'll have to make her intentions public now, though. I don't envy her.'

'Envy her what?'

'Having to face Monsieur Aumont.'

Monday is a normal school day for Beattie: Mrs Blythe comes round to see Annie off to school and collect Tom and Alexia, leaving Beattie free to pedal off to school. She is so certain that someone will ring and put her anxious mind at rest that she can hardly believe it when, on her return, at four o'clock, her mother tells her the phone hasn't gone all day.

Then, it'll be this evening, Beattie tells herself firmly, wondering why she is consumed with a sense of mounting apprehension.

But no one rings. Charles is due at the Assize Court the following day and is immersed in his papers. Beattie has Form 3's end-of-term composition papers to mark. On Tuesday morning Charles leaves at seven for Bury St Edmunds. Beattie is pondering what to do with Form 3, who have a free day now their exams are over, when at half-past seven the phone rings. She sprints to answer it. The operator tells her it is a trunk call from London. It is Ferdinand.

'Mrs Hammond, each time I speak to you I start with an apology. I'm sorry to call you so early, but it was essential to let you know as soon as possible of Virginia's decision.'

'What? What has she decided?'

'Alexia is to come back to France with me. Virginia has appointed me her guardian. She will return to France with me on Friday after the wedding. Mrs Hammond, I know how sorry you'll be to let her go, but I truly believe that it's for the best that she grows up with her family, and Virginia agrees with me. Had I known the true facts from the beginning' – Ferdinand's tone is grim – 'I would have arranged to provide Alexia with a home long ago.'

'But you can't do that,' says Beattie stupidly. 'She'll be broken-hearted about it—'

'She ought to be with her own family. And, Mrs Hammond, believe me, I would not suggest this if Virginia were not completely in favour.' Then suddenly, explosively, Ferdinand blurts out: 'I cannot understand her at all. She has avoided me. Last night, late, I went and saw her in her flat. She told me she never intended that Alexia would come to live with her when she remarried. And it is wrong, wrong, *wrong* that a child is brought up one hundred miles from her mother and has no contact with her. What can the child think or feel?'

'Then, how . . . when?' says Beattie numbly.

'Virginia suggests that you bring Alexia with you when you come to the wedding. I gather there is an invitation for you both in the post.'

'You want us to bring her?'

'If you would be so kind. I would not stay for the wedding but for the fact that I have appointments with your government which I cannot neglect.'

I don't believe this, Beattie tells herself as she replaces the receiver. I simply do not believe it. It's a nightmare, and I'll wake up soon. . . . Friday! To take her away to people she's never even met – it's too cruel, even for Virginia. Oh, Charles, why aren't you here when I need you?

The children are out playing in the garden. Distractedly Beattie presses her forehead against the kitchen window.

She can't do this. She just can't. I won't let her. She'll listen to me, surely. She just hasn't thought things through. She probably doesn't even know how much we love her. Probably Ferdinand suggested the French idea. She doesn't really want it, but she doesn't want to offend him, either.

Lexy tears past the window in hot pursuit of a butterfly. In half an hour Annie will have to be got ready for school.

What shall I do? I must do something, thinks Beattie in despair. I'll speak to Virginia. That's it. I'll write – no, better still I'll phone her. I'll do it tonight. No, I'll do it lunchtime. No, I'll do it right now.

Suddenly galvanized, Beattie goes to the bureau for Virginia's last letter with its address and phone number embossed at the top of the blue sheet. With any luck she won't have left for work yet, thinks Beattie, suddenly purposeful, and asks the telephone operator to get her a London number. It takes some time for the connection to be made, and by the time the call is put through Beattie's courage is beginning to ebb away. To her initial relief the phone rings ten times unanswered. She is just about to replace the receiver shamefacedly when suddenly Virginia's phone is abruptly answered by a peremptory voice – Virginia's – giving the exchange and number.

'Hello?' says Beattie feebly. 'Is that Virginia? It's Beattie – Beattie Hammond.'

Even across the crackling phone line there is an audible intake of breath.

'Yes?' says Virginia, not politely. 'What do you want?'

No greeting, no 'How are you', no 'How's my child'. In the space of one second Beattie's feelings turn turtle from fear to fury.

'What do you think I want?' says Beattie in a manner quite unlike her own. 'I have just had the most extraordinary phone conversation with Alexia's uncle. He *says* you want him to take Alexia back to France. Naturally I didn't believe him.'

There is a long silence. Then Virginia speaks again in a quite different voice.

'Beattie, you've been quite wonderful about . . . Alexia, but you must have realized that eventually—'

'Eventually we thought you might take your responsibilities more seriously,' says Beattie in a voice of dangerous calm. 'Since you clearly still continue to find yourself unable to do so, then the sensible thing would surely be to leave Alexia with the people who are able to love her. You may have forgotten, but she is only three years old; you can't just transport her at a moment's notice like this. She doesn't even know her uncle. For goodness' sake, Virginia, do think again, please.'

'Beattie, you seem to have forgotten that I am her mother.'

'I haven't forgotten,' says Beattie angrily. 'I thought *you* had.'

Virginia is clearly fighting to keep her temper. 'Look,' she says tersely, 'I'm getting married in three days' time. This is my last day at work for nearly two months and I've got a desk full of things to settle before I go. I simply don't have time for this conversation. Ferdinand says he'll make the necessary arrangements and *I have made up my mind*. If he's spoken to you, then that's all there is to say. I'm much too busy for conversations like this and I'm already late for work. I'm very grateful, Beattie, for all you've done, but now other arrangements have been made for Alexia. Goodbye.'

Dumbfounded, Beattie stares for a long time at the purring receiver. Virginia has rung off. She has actually had the effrontery, the rudeness, the brass neck to put the phone down on Beattie. Furthermore she has spoken to Beattie as if she were a servant who had failed to understand the new conditions of employment. Except that it isn't a question of terms of employment: a child's future happiness is at stake. For the very last time Virginia has evoked the Musgrave manner to try to bully her into subservience, relied on the deeply ingrained conditioning of Beattie's youth to put her in her place. Beattie finds she is shaking from head to foot. Then, very slowly, she gets up and goes to the kitchen door.

'Annie. Come inside to get tidy for school. Tom, Lexy, you can come in as well and get yourself ready for Granny.'

She stares round without seeing the kitchen. There is a pile of ironing waiting to be done, most of it Alexia's. She'll need all that to take with her, says a small unwelcome voice inside her, and Beattie rubs her forehead in disbelief. It is *inconceivable*, impossible, that Alexia should leave like this. And it is Virginia's doing: though Ferdinand clearly longs to care for his niece, if Virginia had vetoed the idea Alexia would be staying in Musgrave. Beattie feels a wave of anger building up inside her, of such heat and strength that at this moment she could tear telephone directories in half, halt express trains with an upraised hand and force back the waters of the Red Sea with a single contemptuous glance. The world proposed, but it was still the Musgraves who disposed.

'But not this time,' says Beattie out loud to the kitchen clock. 'Not this time. It strikes me it's high time that somebody fought back.'

It takes only a few minutes to ring the school and to arrange for her class to be supervised by someone else for the day. Then Mrs Blythe appears to collect the two youngest children.

'Mother, I've had a change of plan,' Beattie starts without preamble. 'I'm going to London. Can you take Annie into school and pick her up if I'm not home in time?'

'I suppose so. But have you asked Charles? And what about your teaching?'

'I don't have to ask Charles. I couldn't get hold of him anyway; he's in court all day. And they'll just have to do without me at school.'

'But what's taking you to London at a moment's notice?'

'I'll tell you tonight. Can you take the children quickly, because I want to get the nine-thirty bus from the Cross and I've still got to change. 'Bye 'bye, darlings. See you this afternoon. I don't know when I'll be back exactly, but it'll be long before your bedtime.'

Naturally, Tom chooses today to make a scene. It is twenty minutes before he can be prevailed on to go to Church Cottage and even then only with the promised bribe of a present from London on Beattie's return. Beattie sees all hope of changing into her best costume rapidly fading – she barely has time to find her everyday hat and, thanking heaven that she still has the money for the milk bill, has to run to catch the bus by the Cross.

There is a train waiting at Ipswich, and by a quarter past ten Beattie is on her way to London, wondering for the first time what Charles will say about her impulsive action. And what could she possibly hope to achieve in confronting Virginia face to face? Other than the satisfaction of another slanging match? Yet the thought of doing nothing, of letting Alexia go unchallenged, unfought for, fills her with an anguish which she can hardly bear to contemplate.

As the train bucks and roars its ways through Essex, Beattie's mind veers from the present to the past and back again. There are so many images of Virginia – the cold-faced malevolent harpy at the Grosvenor Hotel dance, the fashion plate who had outstared Beattie with such impudence and indifference across the church – truly a thousand million reasons for disliking her, for never speaking to her again. So why should she ever think of defending her to Charles? Perhaps it was that Charles had never bothered to read Virginia's letters; if he had, perhaps he would have been less swift to make a judgement. There is something about the way Virginia painstakingly enquires after every new stage in Alexia's development – every cough, cold, new tooth or new word achieved – that touches Beattie's heart. At first she had replied briefly, then in more detail, then finally even talked about the two other children, and somehow a curious cautious friendship had sprung up between them.

Beattie had been under no illusions as to why Virginia had suddenly decided to confide in her: by this time it was the beginning of 1946 and Lucy was completely and happily preoccupied with preparations to go to America. *Faute de mieux* it was thus to Beattie that Virginia began to reveal more about her life, the most astonishing fact being that she had taken a job as a fashion assistant on *Modes* magazine. When Beattie expressed an immediate interest in the world of fashion journalism Virginia was only too willing to oblige with details of her new life. Apparently there were four fashion assistants all working for an assistant fashion editor under the fashion editor herself, both of whom were tyrants of unsurpassed proportions. Life spent in the service of making women miserable about the way they looked was in itself curiously rigorous: the editorial staff of *Modes* were apparently required at all times to look as if they had recently stepped out of the Royal Enclosure at Ascot. Even Virginia, preoccupied as she was with her appearance, found herself com-

476

plaining about the time and preparation it took to get her ready even to go into work. And this all had to be done on a minimal income. Virginia had remarked quite casually how, at her first interview for the job, she had been asked in all seriousness if she had a private income as she would never be able to live on the salary available. How true, Virginia commented bitterly, adding that you couldn't keep yourself in lead pencils on what *Modes* was prepared to pay you. To Beattie it seems an extraordinary and often terrifying world. There is an enormous divide, according to Virginia, between the editorial and the secretarial staff, the badge of distinction between the two being that at all times of the day and night the editorial staff have to wear a hat. The atmosphere is one of bitchery and in-fighting, with everybody fighting for their lives, or at least a by-line. In addition, there is the grandeur of the photographers to come to terms with, the learning how to deal with models, all of whom insist on putting the dresses on back to front, and the general sense that at any moment everyone is hoping you'll fall flat on your face. But Beattie notices that, complain as she does, Virginia never shows any sign of wanting to leave *Modes*. In fact, according to her, she'd even notched up some kind of promotion: this spring the senior fashion department had travelled *en bloc* to Paris as usual for the collections, and this time Virginia had been the fashion assistant chosen to minister to the photographers. Thus, Virginia had actually been there at the moment when Christian Dior revealed his New Look, echoes of which are even being felt in Ipswich. And it was to Beattie that she'd written exultantly to tell her the good news, assuming that Beattie would be as pleased as herself about the promotion and the trip to Paris.

By now they are almost at Liverpool Street. Beattie stares anxiously at herself in the mirror. If only she'd had time to change into her best suit and hat. And her hair could do with another perm. . . . A sudden realization of what she's intending to do sweeps over Beattie and leaves her feeling quite faint with horror. There is actually perspiration on her brow. Supposing she can't find the place? Supposing they won't let her in? Supposing Virginia isn't there or simply refuses to see her?

Nonsense, Beattie tells herself firmly with considerably more confidence than she's actually feeling. Desperate situations require desperate remedies. Her own feelings of doubt or inadequacy shouldn't come into it. Alexia's happiness is at stake, and she owes it to the little girl to try to do her very best for her.

The taxi from Liverpool Street seems to travel an immense distance, finally turning into Golden Square. In one corner there is a modern office-block with the name of the publisher engraved on the glass door. Inside, in reception, there is a board containing the names of five magazine publications, one on each floor. Beattie asks the liftman for *Modes* on the fifth floor.

As she pushes open the heavy doors into the reception area Beattie discovers, to her consternation, that reception is full of people and that inexplicably they are all waiting for her. For as soon as she appears they move as one woman towards her, and it is only when Beattie is about to make a panic-stricken bolt back the way she's come that she discovers that her way is barred by a tall imposing man in a grey three-piece suit with two red-faced young men trailing doggedly behind him. The tall man ignores them all, and it is only when he sets off at a brisk pace down the corridor and reception empties behind him that she realizes that all these people have been waiting for him: his appearance and disappearance is the cue for all the girls carrying hats and bags and gloves, the two girls pushing the shrouded rails of dresses, other girls with shorthand notebooks and finally three long-legged, nervous and pretty young girls to trail after him. He is clearly the photographer. In a matter of seconds the room is empty, leaving nothing but a wisp of expensive perfume and a gimlet-eyed receptionist dressed, made up, hatted and coiffed like a goddess. Her function seems to be to answer the phone and announce the *Modes* telephone number in accents so refined as to render the numbers almost unintelligible. When Beattie announces, somewhat uncertainly, that she wants to see Virginia Musgrave, the goddess takes a full thirty seconds to inspect Beattie's shoes, stockings, bag, gloves and suit before announcing that they have no one there of that name.

'Seligman, then. Mrs Seligman.'

Another thirty seconds pass, time for a leisured survey of Beattie's hair, face and make-up. In spite of herself Beattie grows hot under the scrutiny.

'Mrs Seligman does not see anyone without an appointment,' says the goddess rapidly in a sing-song voice, as if reading the words off a prompt-board. 'If it's secretarial work you're enquiring for, I suggest you write in to the main address of the magazine and your letter will be acknowledged. Members of *Modes* magazine do not see people without an appointment ever. Thank you. May I help you?'

This to a man standing behind Beattie. She turns away, her face burning. What a fool she'd been to think she could just drop in and see Virginia like this. Charles would have known better. Charles would have told her to ring first or perhaps not even to have come. Oh, *why* had she come?

Almost ready to weep with vexation and disappointment, Beattie turns to go. Then abruptly, mutinously she sets her jaw. This can't go on, she tells herself crossly, this constantly feeling inferior, feeble, weak, passive. It's just an excuse to explain away failures and ineptitude. There is no need to feel so inadequate simply because she is the only woman in the building not wearing the New Look. She is after all a married woman with a life of her own, a job and a husband who has been written up by this very magazine as a young writer of exceptional promise. What is the difference between her and that awful condescending woman at the desk? Simply access to expensive clothes. Alexia's future happiness shouldn't be set on one side simply because Beattie hasn't got her best suit on. Virginia is clearly here somewhere, and it is up to Beattie to find her. Resolutely she turns back to reception. This time she is cunning. The goddess is directing guests to the photographic studio, and a cheerful young man folding sheets of coloured paper is making his way through to the offices beyond the desk.

'Excuse me! I'm here to see Mrs Seligman and I've forgotten where her office is.'

'Right then, go down to the end of the corridor and sharp left' is the prompt reply. Beattie moves off equally promptly, anxious to get away from those unpleasant eyes as quickly as possible. So agitated is she that the instructions go straight out of her head, and in the rabbit warren of offices beyond the grandeur of the reception area she is soon hopelessly lost. Striving to look relaxed yet purposeful, which is not easy when you know you are dressed wrongly, are here uninvited and furthermore are completely lost, Beattie strolls on apparently unconcerned, looking for someone else to ask the way. But there is no one about, and it occurs to her for the first time that this is probably lunchtime and by now Virginia may very well be quaffing champagne cocktails with her intended. Then with relief Beattie hears footsteps coming the other way.

It announces the arrival of a most singular figure – a dark short stumpy-looking woman with a beaky nose who walks bent forward like a slug drawn irresistibly to the scent of new seedlings. She is making her way down the corridor with her gaze fixed, her handbag carried on an arm folded rigidly across her chest. Her clothes and hat are quietly splendid, but so unprepossessing are the face and deportment that you hardly notice them.

'Excuse me,' says Beattie boldly, wondering whether it will seem rude to bend down in an attempt to engage this bowed creature in eye contact. 'But I'm actually lost.'

The woman straightens up and slows down, focusing a mild but all-seeing glance at Beattie. The glance, like the receptionist's, is all-embracing, but here the scrutiny is merely interested, not offensive.

'Are you one of Edward's models? He's arrived and they're already in the studio, I believe.' The woman's voice is deep and cultured and not unfriendly.

'Er, no. I'm here to see Mrs Seligman.'

'Ah, Virginia. You'll find her with the other girls in the room at the end on the right.'

With a queenly nod the dark-haired woman glides on her way.

The door to Virginia's office is pushed to but not actually shut, and when Beattie pulls it silently open it is to discover Virginia on the other side of the room, seated at her desk, pen in hand, staring into space. So deep is her reverie that Beattie is able to stare quickly round the room and take in Virginia herself while Virginia apparently stays lost in thought. There are four desks in the room almost buried under piles of shoes and hats. There are two rails of clothes covered in muslin sheets, and hanging on the wall an immense linen bag which seems to contain an evening dress. Virginia herself is wearing a small dashing dark-brown velvet side-beret and a full-skirted pleated dress with a velvet collar. She looks poised, elegant, defended. As Beattie steps forward she looks up and slowly focuses. Then she starts with disbelief and jumps to her feet, her face crimson. Without preamble or greeting she says tersely: 'What the hell are you doing here?'

'I want to talk to you,' says Beattie quietly. 'You wouldn't talk on the phone, and I'm sure you'll find a thousand excuses to avoid speaking to me before your wedding—'

'Get out of here at once. How dare you come barging in—'

'If you'd had the courtesy to speak to me this morning,' says Beattie coolly, shutting the door behind her, 'or even the guts to tell me that you're getting married, it could all have been settled ages ago.'

'I'll ring you tonight, I promise.' Beattie notices to her satisfaction that in the midst of her fury Virginia is very frightened indeed.

'Look, if you think I've made a trip to London, stood down my job, been patronized by you and condescended to by your receptionist and all for the *promise* of a phone call from you tonight, you must think I'm very stupid indeed. I want to talk to you about your daughter now. And, if you won't, I'll stay here and cause a great deal of embarrassment until you do. No, I am *not going*,' she repeats as Virginia tries forcibly to take her arm and pull her towards the door. Side-stepping, Beattie pushes her briskly away, removes two pairs of shoes from a chair and sits down.

'Beattie, *please*. . . .'

Beattie stays where she is and studies her gloves. Abruptly the fight goes out of Virginia, who opens her bag and makes a considerable play of lighting a cigarette. Beattie is pleased to observe that Virginia's hands are shaking quite badly.

'You've got no right to turn up like this.'

'You've got no right to blight your daughter's life and cause her such pain and suffering.' Beattie's voice is passionate. 'Isn't it enough that you've cast her off and rejected her when she could have died from lack of love and caring? She's happy now, no thanks to you at all—'

'I wanted her to go to you—'

'Then, you should have had the guts to say so instead of leaving it to chance. Look, Virginia, you won't believe this, but I didn't come to have a quarrel. I just came to say that we love Alexia and she loves us. We all love her. Can't you see the suffering you're going to cause to her and to all of us if you uproot her now? She's only three years old.'

'Ferdinand wants her – he insists on having her.'

'Don't give me *that*!' Beattie suddenly shouts, so angry she feels she is going to suffocate in this smoke-filled, Miss Dior scented atmosphere. 'She's your child. You know perfectly well it's your decision whether she stays with us or goes. You've only got to say the word and she can stay with us until she's grown up.'

Virginia gets up and walks over to the window, drawing deeply on her cigarette. Beattie actually gets up and walks after her, talking to the averted profile in a low angry voice.

'Virginia, what you did in abandoning Alexia was awful and terrible and unforgivable. And no one dares tell you that, not even your mother.'

Virginia is white-faced, silent.

'But, believe you me, what you're proposing to do now is far, far worse. I don't care how much Mr Aumont feels for her. The fact remains that we are people she knows and loves. And if you take her away now, however kind people are, she's going to cry her little heart out for months to come. In the end she'll stop crying and just write us off as other people who didn't care enough about her and let her go just as her mother had done.'

'Beattie, don't say these terrible things to me, please.' Virginia is crying now, her immaculate make-up streaked with rivulets of mascara.

'I've got to say them to you. There's no one else who'll dare to, is there? I can't understand what you're doing. Was your marriage so unhappy that you have to bury every trace of it?'

'No,' whispers Virginia in a kind of anguish. 'No. It wasn't like that at all.

480

I loved Alexis so much I can't bear to think of him now, or her. . . .'

'I've got a photograph of Lexy we took at Easter. Look—'

'*I don't want to see it.*'

Abruptly Virginia turns away and walks back to her desk. After a minute she turns back to Beattie. With her red eyes and dirty face she is almost unrecognizable. The habitual mask of disdain has gone, and in its place is a girl with haunted swollen eyes.

'Look. I really wanted to. . . . There were times, lots of times when I actually had my hand on the phone to call you to ask you if I could come down and see Alexia, but I couldn't do it. Not again. I can't go back again to all that pain. You don't know what it's like.'

Virginia buries her face in her hands, wrecked by inner visions, old memories.

'Look, Virginia,' says Beattie gently. 'I'm not asking you to take her back. I can see that's quite beyond you. All I'm saying is let Alexia stay with us. Not for ever, perhaps. But just until she's a little older, until she can cope with the separation better. When she's older she'll probably love to go to France for her holidays. I can see, too, that it's going to be good for her to have some other family. But you don't know her. She's such a tender little girl. The other two always try to protect her, to take care of her; they love her. . . .'

Virginia is now looking for her handkerchief. Blowing her nose briskly, she turns back to Beattie.

'You're angry because I didn't invite you to the wedding.'

Beattie stares at Virginia, hardly able to believe her ears.

'Have you been listening to a word I've said?'

'I heard every word.'

'And?'

'I've told Ferdinand he can take her to France. And that's that.'

Virginia will not meet Beattie's eyes.

'Then, damn you, Virginia – or, rather, if there's any justice I truly hope you will be damned.' Beattie tries desperately to keep her shaking voice under control. 'There's no heart in you, no love, nothing.'

'Well, I'm sure you feel a lot better for having got that off your chest,' drawls Virginia in a poor attempt at her old *hauteur*. 'Perhaps you feel these things more than me – you've got so much experience with children, haven't you, Beattie? And how is Brooke's baby by the way? Doing well, is she?'

'She's doing very well, thank you, Virginia, no thanks to your brother. I never realized how alike you two are: in fact you're exactly the same. Neither of you wants to accept your responsibilities. You cause unhappiness and suffering everywhere you go. I could have written off Annie the way you've written off your daughter. But I can see that she's got rights as well. The right to be cared for by the person who brought her into the world. And I'll tell you something else, Virginia,' Beattie says quite menacingly, causing Virginia to look up in alarm. 'This' – Beattie's contemptuous glance takes in the glamorous confusion of the office – 'this doesn't amount to anything. Caring for Lexy would have been the making of you.'

'Really,' says Virginia in a bored tone, blocking in her lipstick and closing her compact with a decisive click. 'Well, we'll have to disagree on that one, won't we, Beattie? I don't think I've ever heard such eloquence. You must try some of your theories out on Brooke. He's over for the wedding, didn't you know?'

Virginia is delighted to see from the stricken look on Beatties's face, quickly suppressed, that she did indeed not know.

'It's immaterial to me where he is,' she says at last, picking up her gloves and unable to meet Virginia's glance.

'As we seem to have concluded our little talk, would you mind scooting off now? I take it Ferdinand's been in touch and made all the arrangements. So far as I know I'm up-to-date on the account, but if you're worried that I owe you money I suggest you get in touch after the wedding. There's no need for you to concern yourself any more with Alexia. She isn't your concern now.'

'She'll always be my concern,' says Beattie briefly, deliberately avoiding Virginia's jibes. 'Someone's got to care about her, and it's clearly not going to be you. I don't care that you've thrown your own life away, but I do care about your daughter, because she's got a loving heart. If she grows up hating you, then you'll have brought it on yourself. If she doesn't hate you, it's because, thank God, there's more of her father than her mother in her.'

Without bothering to say goodbye Beattie turns and makes for the door. Her last sight of Virginia is of her bending ostentatiously over her papers.

'Then what?' asks Charles, agog.

'I took the train home.' They are sitting in the kitchen over a scratch supper of cold meat and boiled potatoes later that night.

'But what was it like? I can't picture you going in there somehow.'

'I'm not surprised. It wasn't me at all,' says Beattie honestly. 'It was very rich, very sumptuous. It smelt expensive. And everybody looked as if they were on show. I couldn't survive in an atmosphere like that, but I could see Virginia would thrive on it.'

'Were the people horrible?'

'The ones I spoke to were. Oh, except the woman who showed me the way. The funny thing was that on the way out I saw her picture on the wall. She's got a name like Hamilton-Stringbag. Mrs Hamilton-Stringbag. Apparently she's the editor. Oh, it was all a waste of time, a waste of time. I didn't do any good at all.'

'Well, we can't be sure of that.' Charles looks with new eyes at his wife. Beattie catches his gaze and flushes.

'I suppose you think I shouldn't have gone. That I wasted my time. That I didn't bother to think things through properly.'

'Well, if we always thought to think things through we'd never do anything, would we? I suppose in terms of actual results you could say that nothing's changed. But you never know – things grinding slowly but exceeding small. There are still three days to go, and your words may have the water-dropping-on-a-stone effect and may yet change Virginia's granite heart.'

'What made me so angry was that she just wouldn't admit that it was all her decision.'

'Well, she couldn't face up to it, could she? Though, if anyone can make her do it, you will. It must have been a wonderful moment when she looked up and saw you framed in the doorway like Nemesis.'

'But I haven't changed anything.' Beattie's eyes suddenly fill. 'Darling Lexy is still going. I'll have to tell her tomorrow. And what am I going to tell her – that she's going on holiday and she'll be back soon? It's all lies, and I know it's wrong to tell a child lies. And I'll have to get all her clothes ready. I can't bear it, Charles. I just can't bear it. There must be something we can do to prevent it. Can Virginia legally do this? Couldn't we go to court or something?'

Charles puts his arms round Beattie and pushes a wave of her hair back from her wet cheek. 'I'm afraid the law is completely on her side. She is her mother.'

'But supposing we just didn't deliver her? Supposing we took her away a bit until things have calmed down—?'

'Sweetheart, if there was any way round this, I'd find it for you. But eventually they'd come and get her and that might be much worse for poor Lexy. Virginia could make things very unpleasant indeed if she had a mind to.'

'I've never felt so completely powerless in my life. It's not right, it's not fair, and I can't seem to do a thing about it.'

Charles keeps his arm round his wife.

'Will you take her up to town on Friday?'

'I don't know,' says Beattie dully. 'Part of me says Ferdinand should jolly well come down and pick Alexia up himself. Then I think: Well, if I go, I'll at least have a few hours longer with her. But I don't want to go to the wedding. Mr Aumont seems to assume we'd want to stay, but I can't think of anything I'd like less. Will you come?'

'Hadn't thought really. I'll go to give you moral support, but beyond that – I don't know Virginia and I doubt if there'd be anyone I know at the wedding.'

Beattie is silent, ostensibly studying her nails. She actually feels Charles grow tense beside her.

'Is Brooke going to be there?' he says, in a quite different, sharper voice.

'Yes,' says Beattie reluctantly. 'So Virginia says.'

'Did you ask her if he was going?'

'Of course I didn't! She just wanted to lead me off the subject of Alexia. She suddenly announced he was coming. Quite honestly she'd have told me that the building was burning down if she'd thought it would have distracted me from getting at her.'

The intimacy of the moment is suddenly abruptly gone. Charles gets up.

'I'll lock up. I'm going to bed.'

'Charles, I—'

But he has gone.

Beattie sits alone at the kitchen table for some time. Perhaps Virginia will have second thoughts. From Virginia's other news she tries resolutely to avert her thoughts. But that night, she dreams the old dream of Brooke's body rolling over and over in the cold North Sea and wakes up exhausted and drenched with perspiration. It is as if Virginia's casual words have somehow undone the catch on a box that had been carefully locked and bolted. It's too much, it's all too much, thinks Beattie drearily watching the light grow pale at the edge of the curtains, listening to the birds starting their harsh and discordant chorus. What do I do first? Do I tell Alexia? What do I tell Alexia? What do I say to the other two children? And what clothes of Alexia's need mending? Oh, it's all too much.

But, as the next two days are to show, indisputably the worst fact of all is that Charles, the prop, the support, the one who might have carried her through, has suddenly withdrawn and resolutely refuses to respond to her unhappiness. It is like a nightmare, like the split seconds of calm when a car has gone into a skid and is about to crash. Somewhere up ahead there are screams of anguish, tears and blood. Now there is just a sense of suspended pain and unreality before the inevitable collision.

Every time the phone rings Beattie races to answer it, certain it will be Virginia with a changed heart. But Wednesday and Thursday pass by with no reprieve. Alexia receives the news that she is to go on holiday with her uncle without comment. The other two children, older, more experienced in the ways of adults, look warily from one parent to the other but say nothing. It has been arranged that Beattie will deliver Alexia to her uncle before the wedding. Then, wholly unexpectedly, by the last post on Thursday, comes an invitation to the wedding addressed to Charles and Beattie.

'You will come, won't you?' Beattie appeals to her husband later that night.

'I told you I didn't want to go and I don't intend to,' Charles replies tersely.

'Charles, it's not fair. It's not just for me, it's for Lexy. I don't want to go to the silly wedding. But if you'd just come up with us.'

'I said no.'

When Charles's voice takes on a certain note there are no grounds for further negotiation. Beattie goes to bed that night praying that he will change his mind. But the following morning, having loaded up Alexia's little suitcases, still wearing his work-suit, he drives them to Ipswich. The goodbyes to the other children and Mr and Mrs Blythe have all taken place the night before. Charles drives Beattie and Alexia through fields that are still white with early-morning mist. It is a fine June morning with a promise of heat later in the day. Beattie cannot remember ever feeling so helpless and wretched. At the station Charles goes to buy Beattie's ticket while Beattie and Alexia walk on to the platform.

'See Tom and Annie again soon?' asks Alexia, her small face suddenly full of anxiety.

'Very soon,' Beattie assures her, hating herself. Conscious of her new coat and matching velvet beret, Alexia soberly walks over to the porter's trolley to examine the boxes. Charles reappears and silently hands Beattie her ticket. Then, wheeling round to watch Alexia, engrossed in trying to climb on to the trolley, he says in a furious undertone: 'This is all wrong. Have you told her she's isn't coming back to us?'

'No, I just can't bring myself to. I think it's better she realizes it gradually. I don't think she could face the fact if she was told it now.' Beattie is almost incoherent with distress. 'I just can't believe that today is happening.'

Face averted, ostensibly keeping an eye on Alexia, Charles stands with his clenched fists thrust deeply in his pockets, his whole stance rigid. Beattie furtively wipes her eyes and tries to steer the conversation to less emotive channels.

'I'll ring you from London to let you know what train I'm coming back on. It should be early this afternoon. But if you aren't free I can always get the bus home. With any luck I might be able to get the one o'clock train—'

Abruptly Charles turns back, his even dark features so distorted and strained by anger and suppressed emotion that Beattie involuntarily takes a step back.

'Oh, shut *up*, Beattie, for Christ's sake,' he says savagely. 'Stop kidding yourself. You're going to find some reason for having to stay on for the wedding to see Brooke. Why bother to pretend?'

His own fury is enough to ignite an explosion of anger between them.

'How dare you speak to me like this?' hisses Beattie in a furious undertone. 'I've told you I'm not going to the wedding – I don't want to go to the wedding. Aren't things bad enough with Lexy going today without you making them so much worse? You know the only reason I'm going to London is to deliver the little girl to her uncle—'

'Oh, that's why you're wearing your best suit, is it? And why you bothered to have your hair done yesterday?'

Beattie goes very red.

'And I notice you've taken Annie's picture with you – that's for Lexy's benefit, too, is it?'

'I thought – I thought I could leave it with Virginia,' says Beattie, unable to meet her husband's eyes. 'I thought he might just want to see what she looks like.'

'Well, better late than never, eh?'

There is a sudden silence.

'I'm sorry,' says Charles at last. 'I shouldn't have said that.'

'That's all right,' says Beattie almost inaudibly.

'It's just those bloody Musgraves. Bloody awful brother and sister. Whenever they come back into our lives everything starts going wrong. They spread unhappiness and destruction everywhere they go. A father who won't acknowledge his daughter and a mother who runs out on her child. What a bloody pair.' Then Alexia is tugging the edge of Charles's jacket.

'Are you cross, Uncle Charles?'

'No, of course not,' Charles assures her, and with a truly heroic effort of self-control rearranges his features into a look of genuine affection and welcome. 'Where's my best girl? Come on, let me pick you up and we can have a look down the line and see when the engine's coming. Then we're going to find you a nice seat by the window so you can see what's going on outside—'

'The engine. I see it.'

With a feeling of dread and impotence Beattie watches as the train for Liverpool Street slides noisily past them. She finds them an empty compartment where Charles, still carrying Alexia, puts the suitcase on the rack. Then he hands Alexia over and gets out. Beattie can see from the look of dawning apprehension on Alexia's face that she has only now grasped that Charles isn't coming with them. Imploringly the little girl tries to clutch his arm through the open window.

'Uncle Charles, why aren't you coming with us?'

'He's got to go to work, sweetheart. But you say goodbye now and give him one of your very best kisses.'

But instead Alexia lets out a heartrending wail while trying desperately to hang on to Charles through the open window.

'Don't cry, darling,' says Charles, now visibly distressed. 'You'll have a lovely holiday. Look, there's the man waving his flag. 'Bye now, darling.'

'Charles—' says Beattie, suddenly so full of panic she can hardly breathe. But already they are moving out of the station, and he has not kissed her goodbye. It feels very bad, like going to sleep without making up a quarrel. But it is too late. Beattie leans out and waves frantically instead, but her last view, as the train rounds the corner, is of Charles standing bare-headed and unsmiling at the edge of the platform. Hopelessly she turns back to Alexia and sees her own apprehension mirrored in the little girl's face. Hastily she says: 'Why don't you sit on my knee, Lexy? We'll get Peter Rabbit out, and he can sit and talk to you.'

Alexia hauls herself up on to Beattie's lap with a little sigh, undoes the stiff new buttons of her coat to install Peter Rabbit next to her heart, then promptly falls asleep. Beattie finds she is gripping Alexia so tightly that her arms are aching. Telling herself to relax, she loosens her hold and strokes the glossy dark pigtails and then the smooth curve of the little girl's cheek. However will she bear losing her? However will she ever be able to bear any of the things that will happen today? Her thoughts veer round like an animal frantically trying to escape from a maze. It has got to the stage that her head almost aches from averting her conscious mind from painful topics. Whatever subjects her thoughts veer towards – the heartbreak of Alexia's departure, the humiliation of her encounter with Virginia, the unwelcome and totally unexpected presence of Brooke in England – it is like colliding with a brick wall. There have been times in the past two days when, in the middle of ironing Lexy's clothes or going to find her sewing-basket to do some mending, she has found herself standing stock still, staring into space. It is impossible that a week ago, a little week, she had been teaching Form IIIB and wondering if the butcher would have beef this weekend and, if he did, whether she'd have enough points for a joint. Five days later, Charles is distraught and the tranquillity of the Hammond household seems to have gone for ever.

And in spite of all efforts Lexy is leaving them. In the very marrow of her bones Beattie knows that this is a wrong move for the little girl, and she can do nothing to stop it. And, far from persuading Virginia to change her mind, she now believes she actually hardened her in her resolution. With an inward groan Beattie recalls Tuesday's débâcle at the *Modes* office. It was kind of Charles to say she'd been brave to go. (She wasn't sure if that was what he'd be saying this morning.) But in retrospect all that seems to have come out of it is humiliation and defeat.

Sighing, Beattie eases Alexia down on to the seat beside her, still keeping her arm around her, and bleakly ponders the coming day's events. She is to take Alexia to Virginia's new home off Eaton Square where the wedding reception will be held that afternoon. Ferdinand and Alexia are to leave for France in the early evening while her mother, presumably, sets out on her second honeymoon. Beattie feels such a wave of anger building up inside her that she has to remind herself that after today she need never contact Virginia again. Charles can hardly bring himself to speak Virginia's name, and Beattie has ceased to have any desire to defend her. Virginia is clearly beyond any decent human feeling. She is not even worth thinking about.

Then, why does the very thought of that scene on Tuesday still fill her with strange private pain? Hurt pride, Beattie tells herself sardonically, staring out at the bright countryside hurtling past the window. She had really thought that Virginia had begun to look on her as a friend. Oh, come on, jeers a small unpleasant voice inside her. You must really fancy yourself to think that. You were useful to her, that's all. You were no more than the daily who Virginia probably describes as a 'treasure' or her secretary at that magazine who's an 'absolute poppet' until she has an off day or has the cheek to get ill. Once people have outlived their usefulness or start questioning the status quo of the Musgrave patronage, any idea of true friendship abruptly evaporates, leaving the true position exposed, of employer and employee. So why does it upset you? asks another equally angry voice. Why do you want the friendship of someone so utterly loathsome and cold? I don't, Beattie shouts inwardly to all those voices. There are things that Virginia has done that Beattie can never, ever forgive her for. The only way she can express this complete disapproval is to sever all connection with Virginia for ever. And that she intends to do.

And as for Brooke. . . . Abruptly Beattie finds she is grinding her teeth with tension. Brooke is back in England. In London. She may even see him when she delivers Lexy. Oh God, it is terrible, wicked to be thinking about him at all when the only real true cause for concern today is Lexy's happiness. But the fact is that the news of Brooke's presence in England had shaken her profoundly – she had not realized until now how much her peace of mind depended on the idea of him being safely contained a great distance from her. For, though nowadays she rarely thinks of him, it is never without an immense and conscious effort on her part. Through controlling her thoughts, through denying herself even idle speculation as to how Brooke's marriage has turned out and whether he's happy, she has achieved a kind of peace of mind. There are now layers of happy memories and shared pleasures with Charles which should have extinguished for ever any torch she was carrying for Brooke. But all it had taken was a single sentence, a goading remark from Virginia, to trigger off a series of memories that she had thought erased for ever. Since Tuesday a film had been running continuously in her mind as odd disconnected scenes come back to her. At one moment she is standing in the frozen snowy woods at Chillington waiting for the beam of Brooke's headlights in the night before he drives her to the mess dance. The next moment she can almost smell the trodden grass and the hot perfume of the herbaceous border in the tea-garden on the day she told Brooke she was pregnant. In a series of gut-wrenching memories she has been put in touch with the painful intensity of her love for Brooke – a love so absorbing and obsessive that it sometimes seems inconceivable that she could ever have accepted parting from him. Then the memory of the way he had treated her – the hurt, the humiliation that she had felt – engulfs her in a wave of such hatred that she finds herself longing to see him dead. Then she remembers the pressure Brooke had been under, remembers that gaunt hollow-eyed exhaustion on Brooke's face, the slump of his shoulders, the bone weariness during that last fatal tour of duty. Had she judged him too harshly? Had she tried him beyond his strength? Rubbish, she tells herself briskly, wryly aware of how easy it is even now for her to blame herself for everything that had gone wrong. But it is impossible to deny the fact that the very thought of Brooke still has the power to throw her entire life into turmoil. Even now – by a freakish quirk of fate almost seven years to the day since she last saw him – he has the power to undo her calm and happy life.

Cautiously, so as not to wake Alexia, Beattie slides open her handbag and studies the picture of Annie taken on her sixth birthday. In a Liberty print dress lovingly smocked by her grandmother, Annie has her mother's features and the creamy blonde colouring of the Musgraves. If there has been speculation in the village as to how two dark-haired parents could have produced a child like Annie, then none of it has reached Beattie. She is proud of the little girl, proud of her prettiness and quick-witted intelligence even though Tom, for all his rages, is the easier child to live with. But perhaps some of Beattie's own ambivalent feelings have been picked up by the little girl. It is with pain that Beattie sometimes catches Annie regarding her mother intently, and when asked what's wrong Annie always silently shakes her head and looks away. Perhaps it is fortunate that between Annie and Charles there has grown a deep unspoken bond. For, while Annie is not always perfectly at ease with her mother, she will sit for hours quietly getting on with her colouring, while Charles tries out ideas for stories on the other side of the table. So far as Annie is concerned, Charles is her father. Though presumably at some point she will have to be told the truth. But not yet.

Beattie sighs deeply.

This won't *do*, Beattie tells herself forcibly. Precisely to forestall this kind of pointless brooding she has brought her writing-case with her in a forlorn attempt to catch up with her correspondence, and there is certainly no lack of letters which need replying to. For a start there's Lucy in Kentucky. Every month an affectionate letter arrives with news of stallions purchased, foals born and (more recently) news of Lucy's own health: she is expecting a baby at Christmas. Well, for once Beattie will have some real news for her. Unscrewing her fountain pen, Beattie goes to open her writing-pad, then abruptly stops. Will Lucy know of Virginia's marriage? Will Virginia want to tell her herself? Anyway, the thought of having to explain Alexia's fate due to her mother's unforgivable behaviour is more than Beattie is capable of today. Perhaps she'll write to Lucy next week. It would be simpler to write to Lily in Santa Monica. She writes almost weekly to her mother or Beattie, enclosing photographs of little Bert and Greg and herself and of their diner, demanding to know why she receives so few photographs of Beattie's children. But today Beattie has nothing to say to Lily. Perhaps Louie is the person to whom she can unburden herself, and she certainly owes her a letter. But, then, Louie, happily married in Liverpool and also expecting a baby later in the year, is waiting for a parcel of baby clothes that Beattie has promised to send her. Surely it would be better to wait and put the letter in when she sends the parcel next week. So there's no point in writing to Louie straight away. And as for Ern and Toby in Sydney – there was no point in writing to them, because she couldn't post it in London as her mother and father always wanted to add a postscript. Far better to wait and write to them on Sunday.

With a feeling of guilty relief Beattie puts pen and writing-case back into her handbag and stares out of the window. They are already on the outskirts of London. Hardly worth making a start now. For by the time Alexia has been gently woken up and taken to the ladies' they are pulling into Liverpool Street Station. Charles has given Beattie the money for a taxi, and at her instigation they drive past Buckingham Palace so that Alexia can see where the King and Queen live. The little girl is her usual gravely cheerful self: it is hard to know how much she understands of what is going on or grasps that she is to see the mother she has never met. The taxi turns into a quiet cul-de-sac off Eaton Square full of houses with wedding-cake façades. In spite of the peeling stucco, it is still grander than anything Beattie could have imagined. Three Harrods vans are drawn up outside the open door of number 9, and a butler in a green baize apron is directing the flow of traffic up and down the stairs. Two girls in blue overalls run past Beattie, carrying elaborate flower arrangements. She halts uncertainly at the foot of the stairs. Then she sees Ferdinand at the front door, and in a minute he is shaking Beattie courteously by the hand and hugging his niece.

'Ah,' he says, 'the little lady herself.' He looks down at Alexia with beaming affection. 'And what a grown-up little girl she looks today.'

Alexia tries to smile but clearly finds the crowds of strangers too much for her.

'Come inside and we'll try to find something to drink,' says Ferdinand, leading the way. 'We're all at sevens and sixes this morning,' he explains, leading them into the magnificent black and white tiled hall. There is a vast curving marble staircase lit by a crystal rainbow of a chandelier. In the two reception rooms maids in uniform are laying out trays of champagne-glasses. There are bowls of flowers everywhere, and more maids are bringing up china and crockery from the kitchen. Ferdinand leads them through to the back of the house to a small conservatory overlooking the garden. After an enquiring look at Beattie, Alexia wanders down the steps into the garden. Beattie sits down and gratefully accepts a cup of coffee.

'Is Virginia here?'

'No, but she'll be here to inspect the arrangements before they go to the register office. They haven't moved in yet. Her fiancé spent last night at his club.' This clearly satisfies Ferdinand's sense of propriety. 'I've booked a place on the midday plane for Alexia and myself. A car will take us to Croydon in twenty minutes.'

Beattie stares at him. 'You aren't even waiting for the wedding?'

'No.' Ferdinand is quite firm.

'Oh,' says Beattie.

'Alexia,' Ferdinand calls, 'come, there's some chocolate here for you.'

'You'll have to tell her you mean cocoa or she won't understand.'

Alexia comes back up the stairs into the conservatory, smiling uncertainly at her uncle.

'Hey, chérie,' he says, smiling, and reties the ribbon on one of her plaits. Here is your cocoa. Is the coffee to your taste, Beattie?'

'It's simply wonderful. You must have brought it from France. I can't remember the last time I had proper coffee.'

'On Sunday I had no time to ask you about your career. Virginia says you are a teacher.'

'That's right,' says Beattie, trying to wrench her thoughts away from Alexia. 'I teach at a school that was evacuated to the next village. Unfortunately the lease has run out there and they are going back to London at the end of the year. So I'll have to look for another job.' Then abruptly she abandons all attempts at social chit-chat and lets out: 'I'm so concerned about Alexia. We'll miss her dreadfully. I can't bear to think of her being unhappy.' Abruptly Beattie bursts into noisy tears.

'My dear Mrs Hammond – my dear Beattie, if I may call you that. Look, here's my handkerchief. Now, I know how much you love Alexia and I honour you for it. And I suspect you must be angry with me because I've – well, it is I who have insisted that Alexia should be with her own family. But, believe me, I feel this passionately from the heart. And I know it is what her father would have wanted.'

Ferdinand's yellowy features briefly suffuse with red, but he goes on in a calmer voice: 'Her father would have wished Virginia to have loved the little girl. But since Virginia will not allow herself to do that I feel the responsibility is even more mine. Her father Alexis was not like a brother to me; to me he *was* a brother. And believe me, Beattie, it will be my aim in life to see that his child is truly happy in France.'

'Oh, I want to believe that,' says Beattie shakily. 'I want happiness for her as passionately as I long for it for my own children.'

'Beattie, you *can* believe that she will be happy. I think I know what you are feeling and I promise you that she will be happy.'

There is a sudden commotion in the hall.

'Perhaps that is our taxi already,' says Ferdinand, hastily swallowing the last of his coffee. 'I have left my suitcase outside with the butler—'

At that moment Virginia's voice is heard in the reception rooms.

'I specifically said I wanted the champagne on the other side of the room. And why aren't there any flowers in the passageway? There is a garden after all. Some of our guests may want to use the conservatory— oh.'

Virginia stops dead in the doorway, and it is instantly apparent that she had imagined Alexia and Ferdinand would have been long gone by this time.

'Hello, Virginia,' says Beattie boldly.

'Why, hello, Beattie. And . . . hello, Alexia,' says Virginia in a too loud voice. 'There's a taxi in the road, Ferdinand. Is it for you?'

Alexia takes a step forward. It is painfully evident from the excited look on her little face that she knows who this gorgeous stranger is.

Virginia's response is actually to take a step away from her.

'I think you'd better be on your way, Ferdinand. You'll miss your plane otherwise. Have a safe journey.' With that she turns and almost runs out of the room. Beattie and Alexia stand open-mouthed. Abruptly Alexia's lower lip begins to tremble, and automatically Beattie bends down, picks her up and holds her tightly, so angry that she cannot even bring herself to speak. Then fury at Alexia's hurt bursts through her habitual reserve.

'How could she! How could she! She knows you're both going off now. She doesn't even bother to say goodbye to— Oh, little girl, little girl.' Distraught, she rocks Alexia in her arms.

Ferdinand is struggling to keep his composure, but below the surface Beattie can see the presence of a terrible anger. Nevertheless he says quietly: 'It is her loss. I think we should leave now. Mrs Hammond, never, never will I forget your kindness to Alexia. Never. I will write to you and tell you how she is, and I hope that you in turn will keep in touch with her. Come, *chérie*. Say goodbye to Virginia for me, please.'

Slowly, reluctantly Beattie puts Alexia down, and uncertainly the little girl puts her hand into her uncle's and with him walks through the hall into the street. Outside Beattie stoops and hugs the little girl repeatedly.

'You'll have a lovely time, darling. 'Bye 'bye now.'

The taxi is ready at the kerb. With a dubious look Alexia climbs aboard with her uncle then turns and sees Beattie through the window. For the very first time, it is clear, she has fully grasped what is happening, that she is leaving Beattie behind. Abruptly she starts to scream, and Beattie's last sight of her as the taxi draws away is of Alexia's anguished face pressed beseechingly against the window.

For a moment Beattie feels so ill and faint she has to lean against a neighbouring car for support. She will never ever speak to Virginia again. Never, never, never. It is impossible that anyone could be so cruel, so uncaring.

This simply can't be happening, she tells herself, hanging on to the mud-guard next to her, her eyes shut and her face wet with perspiration. She will wake up in a minute to find the three children in the kitchen clamouring for their breakfast. But this nightmare does not end. When she opens her eyes she is still in the bright London sunshine with the world going unconcernedly about its business, as indifferent as Virginia to Alexia's pain.

'Here, I've just polished that car. Now, what are you doing? No, go on, I'm only teasing. Feeling the heat, are you?' A chauffeur in a smart dark-green uniform offers Beattie a strong arm and helps her on to the pavement.

'I just felt a bit faint for a moment,' says Beattie heavily. 'Can you tell me the time?'

'Eleven o'clock. We'll be off to the register office in a minute. You are with the wedding party, aren't you?'

'No,' says Beattie, with quite unnecessary firmness. 'I'm just a passer-by.' She is about to set off there and then for Liverpool Street Station when she discovers that she's left her handbag in the conservatory. If it wasn't for the fact that her return ticket was in it, she would cheerfully have abandoned the bag and gone home anyway. As it is, setting her jaw, she walks back into the house where the preparations have reached a peak of confusion. The hall is full of people, and a severe-looking woman in a maid's uniform tries to pin a corsage on Beattie's suit which she angrily refuses. She has just found her bag and is turning to go when the butler suddenly appears in the conservatory doorway.

'Mrs Hammond? Mrs Seligman told me to tell you there's a space reserved in one of the cars for you.'

'Could you tell Mrs Seligman that it was kind of her to think of me but I'm not staying for the wedding,' says Beattie levelly.

'Mrs Seligman's expecting you to stay.'

'Then, you'll have to tell her that I had to change my plans,' says Beattie and is halfway across the black and white hall when she hears Virginia calling her name. She turns round but does not walk back to where Virginia is standing by the door of one of the reception rooms. In the end Virginia has to come to her.

'Beattie, what's this? Davidson says you aren't staying.'

'That's right. I'm not. Goodbye, Virginia.'

'Beattie, *please*—'

'Mrs Seligman, your bouquet has arrived.'

'Then, look after it for me,' snaps Virginia to the housekeeper. Then, turning to Beattie, she says urgently: 'Beattie, please, just give me a moment.'

Unwillingly Beattie allows herself to be dragged to a small study on the other side of the passage.

'Beattie, please stay. I was counting on you being here.'

'Are you mad?' shouts Beattie, almost beside herself with fury. Then, abruptly recollecting where she is, she lowers her voice, but even so the anger breaks through. 'Look, Virginia, after today I don't want to see or speak to you again. And as for going to your wedding – well, as I understand it, you go to weddings to wish people well. After what you've done, after what you just *did*, I don't wish you anything except misery and unhappiness.'

Abruptly Virginia sits down, oblivious of her full crisp uncreased skirt.

'Nevertheless, Beattie, I'd still like you to stay. Please.'

'Why? You know how I feel about what you've done. Do you want to enjoy the sight of me being upset by Brooke and his wife?'

'*No*. I hadn't even thought of that. Believe it or not.' Virginia speaks tiredly. 'Anyway, when you meet Brooke and his wife you'll see that things aren't all that. . . . But that's not at all why I want you to stay. It's just that virtually all the guests are Geoffrey's business friends. I hardly know a soul on this list.'

'But what about your own friends?'

'I don't have many now,' says Virginia without self-pity. 'There was a girl I was very fond of but she died and . . . and Lucy's in America. So there didn't seem to be anyone else I really wanted to ask. I wanted to invite you from the beginning but I – I was afraid to tell you I was getting married. I was so desperate I even invited a girl I used to be in a hostel with whom I actually can't stand. But Devora's married and living in Scotland now, so she couldn't come, either. . . . It would be really nice just to see one friendly face in the congregation. Do stay, Beattie, please. I know how much you don't want to, so it would be a real kindness if you would stop. Mother's over from Kenya, did you know? She was asking after you. Please do stay if you can.'

Davidson appears. 'I think it's your car at the door, Mrs Seligman.'

'Tell Uncle Piers that I'll be there immediately.' To Beattie she adds: 'Perhaps I'll see you later, then, Beattie. Thank you for all your— Thank you anyway.'

When the noise and commotion of Virginia's departure have died away

Beattie resolutely picks up her handbag. You must go home straight away, says an angry voice in her head. You know what she's done to poor Lexy, and one pretty speech – probably not even sincere – doesn't change anything. And, if you do stay, you'll be confirming all Charles's worst fears and apprehensions about Brooke. Try telling Charles that you felt sorry for Virginia! Come on. There's no need to hang about. Get going.

It is clearly the best course of action, and resolutely Beattie straightens her jacket and turns to go. And she is reinforced in her resolution as suddenly, unbidden, an image of Alexia as she had been that morning on the train, sleeping so trustingly on Beattie's knee, flashes through her mind, causing her eyes to fill with tears. She cannot forgive Virginia for what she has done. She must leave the house now. But as she stands, worn out with sadness, pressing her forehead wearily against the window which looks down into the passage at the side of the house, another thought strikes her, causing her momentarily to straighten up. Was it still really too late? Could Virginia's heart be touched even at this late hour? Though it would be pitching it too far to describe Virginia as experiencing some remorse for what she'd done, in that last conversation she had revealed a vulnerable side of her that Beattie had never seen before. She had as good as admitted (in so many words) to Beattie that her marriage was a grand sham. So wasn't it still possible that her feelings could be worked upon to make her show a more proper regard for Alexia's future? Was it really too late even now to persuade Virginia to bring Alexia home at the end of the summer, home either to Beattie or to her mother?

'Mrs Hammond, the car is waiting for you outside. You'll be wanting this, won't you?' Davidson is in the room behind her holding out an orchid and a delicate spray of fern. 'Let me pin it on for you. There. It's five to eleven, you know. You'll have to leave fairly quickly if you're going to be at the register office in time.'

'Thank you,' says Beattie wearily. 'Which car will it be?'

'One of the maids will show you the way.'

Beattie walks soberly out to the sunny street again, her shoulders squared. The battle isn't over yet by any means. Virginia can still be won round. Alexia's happiness may still be retrievable. She will go to the wedding and afterwards she will corner Virginia and try to force her into good behaviour. After all, she stayed on for the wedding at Virginia's special request, so in a sense Virginia owes her a favour. And besides. . . .

And besides. She will see Brooke again. And as his name forms in her mind she feels a quiet explosion of pain and pleasure in her heart.

Virginia and Uncle Piers travel slowly in the hired Rolls-Royce to the register office. So anxious is their chauffeur to make sure they arrive on time that they end up being much in advance of themselves, and in order to fill in the requisite ten minutes, to her consternation, Virginia finds herself cruising slowly along the Embankment, through the Royal Hospital Gardens and into the King's Road – an area she has steadfastly avoided for the past three years. She shuts her eyes and to her horror finds herself staring at Alexia's hopeful little face.

The scene in the conservatory is indelibly printed on her memory. It is like an electric shock, a bad omen, a pain in the very centre of her heart that today of all days she has seen Alexis' face in his daughter. Not with an angry look, not even a reproachful glance, just an expression curiously lost and sad. *Oh God*, something screams inside her. It's not too late even now. You can jump out and get a taxi or tell the chauffeur to take you to Croydon. . . .

Then she remembers Geoffrey and the crowds of people waiting for her at Caxton Hall, the hundreds who will join them after the ceremony, the Cabinet minister, even the very minor member of royalty.

'Did you say something, Virginia?' asks Uncle Piers suddenly.

'No,' says Virginia dully and slumps back in the seat. They are at the top of the King's Road now, just before the turning into Sloane Square, actually passing the entrance to Sloane Street Mews. In a sudden unnerving flash of memory Virginia recalls the dark damp March night when she'd driven back from Musgrave and made straight for the Mews. Without preamble she had banged on Stephen Seaton's door and demanded entrance. Stephen had been furious; then, when he had seen her face, curiously kind. He had ended offering her a room and then actually made her cocoa and run a bath for her. She had stayed there for a week.

It had taken only three phone calls to sever all ties with her old life. Pickfords collected the furniture from the Chelsea house and put it into store: the house was let to an agency, she herself had taken a flat off Baker Street, sight unseen, a dull characterless place in a modern block. From there she had written a letter of resignation to Reel Films. With Stephen's help she'd found a job on *Modes* magazine. He had abandoned the BBC and literature for the more lucrative byways of journalism. He was now particularly known for his gossipy interviews with the stars of light musical comedy which somehow always made them seem just like you and me. But he also edited, with tremendous venom, the arts page of *Modes* magazine where his animosity towards young poets and novelists made him one of the most detested reviewers in Fleet Street. He is enormously successful. At his insistence the fashion editor of *Modes* had been persuaded to take Virginia on as a fashion assistant. And in a remarkably short space of time Virginia had revealed a real flair for fashion journalism. She had found she could 'read' a fashion look almost in a single glance. With a mind unseduced by the new, the meretricious or the purely ephemeral she could pinpoint at a glance what would percolate downwards into next season's mass market in terms of hemlines, colour and shape. In those early frightful days she had forced herself to put all her energies into the job. And it had paid off. Some day, she knew, she would edit *Modes*.

It was earlier this year, after her trip to Paris, that she had decided the time had come to remarry. At twenty-six the charms of a bachelor girl's flat had long since faded. What she wanted was an establishment and a man with money. She had met Geoffrey at a cocktail-party in Belgrave Square, instantly noting him down as the kind of man who would 'do' if she ever contemplated remarriage. He was incredibly, embarrassingly rich from the family firm, and did something mysterious in the Foreign Office. She could tell almost immediately what he wanted in a wife. Primarily a hostess, someone who could run a couple of large establishments in London and Scotland and would eventually

494

produce the boys to send to Eton. He didn't mind about her career provided she always put it second to him. As a matter of fact he thought it rather a good thing for a woman to have a hobby. Furthermore he thoroughly approved of having a wife exquisitely turned out at wholesale prices. When he had proposed, at a house-party in Sussex, Virginia had made only a token demur and had accepted him later that week. It was all right in bed, which meant he didn't want it too often. Yes, Geoffrey would do for her new life.

'Here we are,' Uncle Piers says suddenly. 'Hat on straight? That's the ticket. Where's my stick? All right, I'm ready if you are.'

As Virginia steps out of the car smiling for the benefit of the photographers, she pushes the memory of the bewildered face of her daughter from her mind and tries to quieten the trembling of her hands round her bouquet.

The pavement outside Caxton Hall is thronging with guests and photographers, and two policemen are holding back a crowd of curious onlookers. Almost as the chauffeur slams the door behind her, Beattie sees the Musgraves standing slightly apart from the rest of the guests. Brooke, who has been scanning the arriving cars intently, meets her eyes in a long unsmiling glance. Then as she turns to walk into the register office he is suddenly at her side.

'Hello, Beattie,' he says as coolly as if they had parted only an hour before. 'You've just made it in time. You look well.'

'So do you,' says Beattie feebly, but it is no less than the truth. Brooke's eyes are the old vivid blue in his suntanned face, he is elegantly and expensively dressed and his hair is bleached pure gold by the hot African sun. Against the drab austerity of the London streets he has a positve aura of Hollywood about him.

'Are you on your own?'

'Yes—'

'Good. I'll see you at the reception.'

With that he is gone, leaving Beattie wondering furiously how it could be that within thirty seconds of meeting Brooke again she is as angry and discomforted by him as she's ever been. Reminding herself sharply that she is here on Alexia's behalf not her own, she resolutely resists the temptation to stare at Brooke's wife and instead follows the rest of the guests up the steps into the register office.

The service is brief and impersonal. Afterwards there are photographs and confetti on the steps. Beattie stands with the crowd, trying not to bite her lip, conscious that Brooke is looking at her and fighting off the mounting sensation that she wished she'd gone home after all. Virginia is surrounded by well-wishers – any plan to talk to her seems to be receding further and further into Beattie's fantasies. And that's even before they go back to the house where another 200 guests have arrived for the reception. Beattie looks at the vast line of people waiting to be received by Mr and Mrs Desborough and suddenly feels angry and defeated at herself for being so completely taken in by Virginia's entreaties. If Virginia even noticed her in the rugby scrum, it would be a miracle, let alone give Beattie the opportunity to make one last desperate appeal on Alexia's behalf. None the less she accepts a glass of champagne from Davidson and awaits her turn to be received by the bride and groom. As she draws nearer the magic couple it gives her the opportunity to observe Virginia in action in her new role, remembering everybody's name, deferring to the great, gently patronizing the lesser. Being, in fact, the perfect hostess. Her behaviour is the exact counterpart of her perfectly finished exterior. It is almost as if Virginia has become inanimate or coated in shellac: she has made her choice and put on her armour, as it were, for life. Beattie is expecting her normal blank blue-eyed stare and a limp pressure of the glove; instead, when she stiffly congratulates the couple, Virginia actually clasps her husband by the arm to get his full attention and, shaking Beattie warmly by the hand, says: 'Geoffrey, you must meet Beatrice Hammond. She's an old friend from Musgrave.'

'Ah! Good of you to come,' says Geoffrey loudly. 'Good to see old friends, eh? Make sure you've got plenty of champagne for the toast. Why, Monty, you old sinner. You made it after all.'

With that he turns away, leaving Virginia and Beattie looking uncertainly at each other.

'I *am* glad you stayed,' says Virginia rapidly in a low voice. 'Look, before you go make sure you come and see me, won't you? I know it's going to be like a bear-garden in here, but stay for a little, won't you?'

As Beattie turns away she hears Virginia exclaim as if she hadn't a care in the world: 'Darling Coral, darling Pip, how lovely to see you and how sweet of you to come.'

A phalanx of maids are waiting with more champagne and trays of canapés: eating something she suspects may be caviare, Beattie quietly ascends the main staircase to explore the rest of the house. She discovers the whole of the first floor is taken up with a vast L-shaped drawing-room. Cautiously she pushes open one of the heavy double doors and tiptoes in, her heels tapping hollowly on the polished wooden floor. Even after the spacious rooms of the Manor this room is awe-inspiringly huge. What can two people do in a room like this? wonders Beattie. Presumably fill it up with guests and strangers: anyone rather than face being on your own with the person you allegedly love. The blinds are half-drawn against the hot June sun in deference to the Turkish carpets; the room is cool, dim and curiously impersonal. There are much gilded and emblazoned mirrors on every wall and over the vast marble fireplace a huge triple mirror surmounted by a golden eagle. The many heavy portraits may be Geoffrey's ancestors; on the other hand they may just as well have come as a job lot with the house. What furniture there is comprises blue and silver Regency couches, anchored on little islands of Turkish carpet. The spaces between the sofas are immense: it is probably just as well that Geoffrey has such a loud voice, reflects Beattie, or else he'll never be heard if he wants another log put on the fire. There is a strange funereal feeling about the room, compounded by the half-drawn blinds, a distinct feeling of life going on outside rather than inside the room. Its style reminds Beattie of some film she'd once seen about life in an ambassadorial residence: she must remember all the details of how things looked for Charles since it is exactly the kind of setting he loves to hear about to file away for possible use for a—

Charles! For goodness' sake! She had completely forgotten to ring him, and now the time was already— The clock on the mantelpiece obligingly informs her that it is now two o'clock. Oh Lord, thinks Beattie in a panic and,

496

closing the door behind her, almost sprints back down the stairs where the helpful Davidson is dispensing champagne. There is a telephone apparently in the pantry on the floor below and, making her way through the guests, Beattie thankfully finds the relevant room, shuts the door and dials the operator.

It takes five minutes to get through to Ipswich, and when Beattie is finally connected to Charles's office it is to discover that he had left work at one o'clock and was not coming back for the day. He must have gone home, thinks Beattie guiltily and hastily asks the operator for her own number. There is no reply. Perhaps he's gone to Church Cottage to meet the children from school. If she rings Mrs Leary at the post office. . . . But what's the point? He certainly won't want to go back to Ipswich to meet her now. And whatever she says she knows he'll be angry with her for staying on when she had sworn that she wouldn't. Slowly Beattie replaces the receiver. By now Alexia is probably in France. Perhaps already in Paris. The thought sobers Beattie considerably. It is for Alexia's sake that she has stayed: the moment of confrontation with Virginia can be put off no longer.

Downstairs in the reception rooms the party is still in full swing. Through the thickly peopled hall Beattie catches sight of Virginia issuing animated fare-wells to the departing Cabinet minister and his wife. They will apparently be seeing each other in Scotland in August, or so a politician's stentorian tones inform everybody within a twenty-yard radius, yet none the less fond embraces and tender words seem necessary to make their immediate parting bearable. It is ten minutes before they can finally tear themselves away and Virginia turns back to the rest of her guests. She sees Beattie talking to Mrs Musgrave – or, rather, listening to an account of Mrs Musgrave's new home in Kenya – and briskly intervenes.

'There you are, Beattie. Ma, will you excuse us for a moment? I need to freshen my make-up and I'm quite sure Beattie wants to wash her hands, don't you, Beattie?'

Without waiting for a reply she leads the way confidently upstairs to the third floor to what is presumably the nuptial bedroom. It runs the full length of the back of the house looking into the leafy square gardens. It is decorated entirely in shades of white with vases of apricot roses on every flat surface. Beattie notes that there are two large single beds with white satin coverlets.

'Make yourself comfortable,' calls Virginia from the adjacent dressing-room. When she comes back, her make-up flawless, she is swinging a bottle of champagne by the neck. 'I hid this up here earlier in the day in case I needed Dutch courage later on. Be a sport and have a drink with me. Toast my marriage.'

'I don't want a drink and I'm damned if I'll toast your wedding,' says Beattie, furious. 'I just want to have one last try to make you do the right thing by Alexia. You could have all this – she gestures to the palatial room around her – and still allow Alexia her little bit of happiness with us. You couldn't resist the thought of having her out of the way altogether, could you? It was nothing to do with Ferdinand. You just want to forget that part of your life ever existed, don't you?'

What on earth am I attacking her for? thinks Beattie confusedly. I should be trying to cajole her into good behaviour. Strangely enough, Virginia does not respond with anger. Instead she seems to be considering what Beattie had said.

'I didn't actually plan for her to go to France, but I suppose if I'm honest – it didn't seem like a bad idea. You think I've behaved pretty badly, don't you?'

'I don't think you have, I *know* you have. Oh, Virginia,' says Beattie despairingly.

Virginia looks up, startled by the appeal in the other girl's voice, then looks away.

'It's not too late, even now. She could come back in a month's time. It could just be a holiday for her, and she could come back to us. You're not talking about an adult you can reason with. She's a little girl, and sending her away is going to cause her the most dreadful unhappiness. She's a serious little girl; things go deep with her. I know she'll think she's been sent to France because we didn't want her. And I know that, however much Ferdinand tries to make things up to her, in time she'll know she had a mother who didn't care about her and that even the people she was a baby with simply passed her on. What do you think she's going to feel when she realizes that? I just don't understand you,' goes on Beattie rapidly. 'It's not as if you don't care about her. You couldn't have written all those letters, asked all those questions if deep down she didn't matter to you. And yet you seem afraid to show you love her. What is it you're afraid of? It doesn't harm you, loving someone.'

'Really?' says Virginia bleakly. 'Where did all your loving Brooke get you?'

There is a stunned silence as the two girls look at each other properly for the first time.

'You can't – you can't add things up like that,' says Beattie at last, fumbling for words, knowing that at last she truly has Virginia's attention and fearing the clinching arguments she needs will evade her. 'You can't say "If I love you then I must get something back – or be loved in return". It's the act of loving, of being able to love – of taking that risk – that's important. It shows you're alive. It shows you're human. You can't always be looking ahead, weighing the pros and cons, being cautious, measuring out your feelings with a spoon. I don't – I don't regret what happened with Brooke.' Beattie falters for a moment, biting her lip, then goes on bravely: 'Perhaps it was a mistake. But it was my own choice. And, yes, I don't regret it. I got Annie. I love her. I wouldn't wish the affair undone.'

'Oh, come on, come on, Beattie, that's all hearts-and-flowers isn't it? The difference between you and me is that I'm a realist.'

There is a sudden silence, and Beattie looks dispassionately at Virginia, perhaps for the first time in her life. 'The only difference between you and me, Virginia,' she says coldly, picking up her gloves, 'is that you've got no guts.'

Virginia actually flinches and bows her head. Then she looks up at Beattie. 'Yes,' she says quietly, 'I'm afraid you may be right.'

'I have to go now,' says Beattie coldly. 'I can see I'm wasting my time here.'

Silently Virginia gets up and goes to follow Beattie out of the room. Then with her hand on the doorhandle she turns to look at her, feeling for words.

'Odd, isn't it, how things change? Six years ago, if I'd wanted to say something nice I suppose I'd have said "Brooke should have married you". As it is now, the nicest thing I can say is, "I'm glad you didn't marry him. You'd be as unhappy as my sister-in-law".'

Beattie does not reply.

Walking down the final curve of the staircase into the hall, they are met by the roar of conversation from the reception rooms. Virginia is already nodding and waving at friends who still haven't got to congratulate her. Beattie is about to disappear into the crowd when Virginia touches her arm and Beattie turns.

'Well?' Virginia looks at her oddly, clearly debating something in her head. Then finally she says: 'Be careful of Brooke, won't you?'

Beattie stares at her, blushing in spite of herself.

'Be careful? Careful of what? What do you mean?'

'I'm not quite sure, but I know my darling brother. Just be careful.'

At this point there is a halloo from the other end of the hall as Geoffrey Desborough comes to claim his bride. Beattie turns and abruptly plunges off in the other direction, colliding heavily with someone coming the other way. It is Brooke, cigarette in hand, white carnation hanging drunkenly out of his lapel. He catches Beattie's arm and looks hard at her.

'I've been looking for you everywhere. I want to talk. Not avoiding me, are you?'

'Why should I be?'

'I thought you might – oh, what the hell. It's water under the bridge now anyway. Where's the "husband"?'

He stresses the word lightly and ironically.

'Charles had to work,' says Beattie, angry in spite of herself. 'Where's the "wife"?'

'Oh, Paddy's in there somewhere. Why, would you like to meet her.'

'I already have done, thank you.' She looks quickly at her watch.

'Going somewhere?'

'Yes, home shortly, I hope.'

'Oh, you mustn't do that. I counted on you staying over for the dinner.'

'I have to get back to the children,' says Beattie, looking Brooke straight in the eye. This time it is Brooke who cannot meet her gaze.

'I want a breath of air. Do you fancy a quick spin in Hyde Park?'

'No, I've got to go—'

'Tell you what. I'll drive you to Liverpool Street afterwards if you want. Please, Beattie. I really do want to talk. And we're going home the day after tomorrow.'

'You aren't even coming down to see the Manor?'

'There's no point, is there? The Dower House is let, isn't it? What's there to see?'

Beattie hesitates, aware that she ought to go, yet compelled in spite of herself by a craven need to prolong the conversation.

'Very well,' she says finally, reluctantly, immediately aware of the look of triumph in Brooke's eyes. 'But only for a little bit.'

Outside the pavements are warm with late-afternoon sunshine. Once in Eaton Square, Brooke negligently unlocks a new dark-blue two-seater Bentley Continental.

'Picked it up yesterday. We're taking it back to Rhodesia by boat.'

The interior smells almost overpoweringly of new leather. Brooke starts the car with a nonchalance that does not remotely conceal his deep-felt satisfaction at being the owner of such a sleek and costly beast. Once in Hyde Park he manoeuvres the car into a space by the Serpentine Bridge.

'Let's walk a bit.'

The sheet of water is dazzling in the late-afternoon sun. Brooke shields his eyes and inspects the shabby façades of the houses overlooking the park.

'Is it nice to be back?' asks Beattie at last.

'Christ, no. I hate England now. It's all so dirty and shabby. And there are too many people. The wrong kind of people. I suppose I've just got used to open spaces.'

'Virginia says you have a farm.'

Brooke looks at her, amused, calculating, assessing.

'Not quite a farm, Beattie. About 125,000 acres. I've got a small plane for inspecting it. We bought it when I got married.'

'Oh, Paddy flies, does she?'

Brooke grins, 'She bought it for *me*.'

'Oh.' Well, that was one wedding present Brooke would never have received from Beattie.

It is true that she'd been introduced to Brooke's wife but it had been in a crowd of half a dozen other people and there'd been no look of dawning consciousness on Paddy's face as she'd shaken Beattie's hand. Though Beattie had looked at her attentively enough. Her first response, she'd noticed wryly afterwards, was relief when she saw how much older than Brooke his wife was. Yet in the same moment she'd felt a sudden feeling of sympathy for the other woman. In spite of her breezy goodwill Beattie knew intuitively that Paddy felt no more at home in this milieu than Beattie did herself. But she was gallantly prepared to try to make a go of things, determined not to be a wet blanket, to keep her end up – Beattie could almost see the phrases forming in Paddy's mind. But there was something defeated in the way her eyes followed Brooke everywhere, a look of unconscious appeal whenever his glance met hers. They have come to London, via Paris and, in Paddy's case, via the salon of Christian Dior, but the results are not happy: the full skirts and narrow waists that make Virginia look like a particularly exquisite shepherdess look wrong on Paddy's stocky figure. It is as if she is wearing fancy dress. She looks awkward, ill at ease. Her life is jumping down briskly from horses and throwing her reins at the African groom or sitting on the veranda rail in tan shirt and slacks, urging people to come on up and have a drink.

Brooke and Beattie sit down on one of the stone seats overlooking the Serpentine.

'I don't know how you do it, but you're prettier even than I remembered,' says Brooke, running his eye over her in impertinent approval. 'Do stay on. We could have dinner together. Virginia will put you up afterwards. We can skip the formal do at Quags and go somewhere quiet.'

'With your wife?'

'Don't be stupid. She wants to see some frightful friends in St John's Wood. That doesn't suit *me*. What do you say?'

'It's impossible, I'm afraid.'

'Oh, come on. Don't be such a wet. I know you want to. Go on, admit it.'

Brooke's voice has slipped automatically into his old lazy, charming, bullying tone.

'Brooke, I said no.'

'I know what you *said*,' he says imperturbably.

'Then, you should know what I mean,' she retorts furiously.

'OK, OK,' says Brooke peaceably, clearly thinking it politic to change the subject. 'Did you know I've decided to sell the Manor?'

Beattie's mouth drops open in silent disbelief.

'What? You're going to do *what*?'

'Sell the Manor, I've been to see the agents this morning. It'll be advertised next month. I've been thinking about it for a long time. I needed to talk to Ma, but she doesn't seem to have any special feelings either way. Frankly I think she'll be quite glad of the capital. Virginia will probably keep the Dower House.'

'Brooke, how can you even think of it? It's your home, it's been in your family for two hundred years. Doesn't that mean anything?'

'It's never been my home,' says Brooke with the beginnings of an edge in his voice. 'My uncle saw to that. When I finally made the decision to sell the only thing I felt was relief.'

'But you don't understand. Virtually every family in the village works on the estate—'

'Oh, you mean your father. He'll be all right. . . .'

'I'm not *talking* about my father,' says Beattie angrily. 'He's in his fifties, he's got no dependants, it doesn't concern him overmuch. But there are few enough jobs around the village anyway, and what will happen to the young men? Their families have been employed by yours for four generations—'

'Then, we don't owe them anything, do we? High time they stood on their own feet. They've had their money's worth out of us.'

Beattie thinks of her father's twelve-hour day, six-and-a-half-day week and is almost too angry to speak.

'Anyway,' goes on Brooke casually, clearly completely unaware of what's going on in Beattie's mind, 'whoever buys the estate will still need people to run it. There'll still be work there.'

Brooke's complete incomprehension – no, his complete indifference to the possible consequences of his actions leaves Beattie breathless.

'Is that what you wanted to tell me about? Selling the Manor? I thought you might want to talk about Annie.' The edge in her voice would have been apparent to almost anyone: as it is, it passes completely unnoticed by Brooke who, comfortably self-absorbed in his plans for the future, merely says: 'Well, yes, sort of. It's everything really. Paddy and I have decided to split up.'

Beattie is aware that five years ago this news would have had her on her feet with excitement. Now, remembering the older woman's defeated look, she says quietly: 'I'm sorry.'

'Oh, come on, there's no need to be. She'll be all right. They get married a lot out there,' he adds indifferently, then pulls out a heavy gold case, offers Beattie a cigarette and lights his own with a matching lighter. Everything about Brooke shouts luxury. As he slips the lighter back into the pocket of his jacket, there is a glint of gold from the cufflinks in the heavy silk of his shirt-cuffs. His hands are suntanned and beautifully manicured. He has all the arrogant confidence of the Brooke she'd met at the garden-party before the war. The lines of tension and strain have been wiped by good living and a sense of a secure bank balance.

'Will you stay on in Rhodesia or come home when you're divorced?'

'Rhodesia's home now. I did think about trying Kenya, but it's a sight too close to Ma. England has had it as far as I'm concerned. They don't know how to live here any more. You see, that's what I really wanted to talk to you about. I want you to come to Rhodesia with me.'

Beattie's mind is reeling.

'Brooke, is this a joke?'

'No, it's bloody well not a joke,' snaps Brooke, nettled. 'I mean it. Once things started to go wrong with Paddy I thought a lot about you. I realized I should never have let you go. But my hands were tied. It was money. But I'm all right now. Financially, that is. With my share of the estate and the money Paddy settled on me when we got married, we'll be well set up. If you wanted, you could bring Annie with you. I don't mind. Otherwise there's plenty of time to have another child.'

Beattie does not know whether she wants to laugh or cry or simply make rude noises at the top of her voice.

'You must be mad. I've got a husband now and two children—'

'Oh, come on. You only married him because I wouldn't come across. It's all right, I don't hold it against you. Perhaps things seemed pretty desperate – I don't know. As I've said, it's all different now. And in Rhodesia – well, it's a much freer place than England.'

'You mean my social origins will go unnoticed because it's the Colonies?'

'Something like that,' says Brooke, unruffled. 'You wouldn't have any embarrassment on that score. Anyway, you'd be with me. So what do you think?'

'I think you're bloody mad, Brooke Musgrave,' snaps Beattie. 'Do you think I've been keeping myself for you for six years? You deserted me when I was desperate. You behaved like a cad.'

Brooke goes red, then white.

'It's Charles Hammond, isn't it? You don't have to give him a second thought. He only married you because you were pregnant.'

'Yes,' snaps Beattie, 'and with someone else's child, if you remember; and, yes, I was grateful, but that's a thing of the past.'

'Oh, you fell in love, did you?' sneers Brooke.

'That's right,' says Beattie, acknowledging the fact for the first time. 'As a matter of fact we did. I don't *understand* you. You haven't said a word or a syllable about Annie – how she is, even what she looks like. You don't even want to see a photograph of her.'

'Why? Have you brought one with you? I'll look at it if you want,' says Brooke.

'I want *you* to want to see it, not just to do it to humour me,' shrieks Beattie.

'Oh, come on, Beattie.' The caressing note is back in Brooke's voice. 'This is all so stupid. I've been longing to see you and I know you've been thinking about me. We can start again. You were in love with me—'

'Yes,' says Beattie sadly. 'I was. But that was a long time ago. I've got another life. It wouldn't work. We're different people now.'

Something changes in Brooke's face. The good humour abruptly fades, leaving a very angry man.

'You're the one that's mad, not me. Oh, Beattie, for goodness' sake, you can't let me down like this, you can't let me down again—'

Beattie can hardly believe her ears.

'Let you down? Let you down *again*? How did I let you down the first time, pray? Do you think I got pregnant all on my own? And, as for letting you down *now*, how you have the nerve—'

'Beattie, stop it.' Abruptly Brooke pulls Beattie to him and tries to kiss her. The smell of his skin and hair is sickeningly familiar.

Angrily Beattie pulls away. 'Will you *please* let go of me?'

'Look, Beattie, listen to me.' Brooke's voice is urgent. 'When I was on that farm in Holland I had a lot of time for thinking. And I kept wondering why my luck had run out. Then one day I realized that you had been my luck. When we bust up it all ended. But I – when I came back to England I was too frightened to see you. I was frightened of how angry you'd be with me. But I didn't want to go back on another tour of duty because I knew I wasn't lucky any more. I need you, Beattie. We need each other.'

'Oh, Brooke. It's no use, it's all too late. If you'd have come and seen me then, I'd have dropped everything and gone with you.'

'Well, then. . . .' Brooke's tone is triumphant.

'But it wouldn't have been any good. It wouldn't have worked.'

'I don't see why,' retorts Brooke, nettled. 'We seemed to get on well enough before, didn't we?'

Beattie is silent, then reluctantly she says quietly: 'Because I didn't see you, Brooke. I loved you but I didn't see you. Now I *see* you.'

The full impact of this remark slowly sinks in, and Brooke's mouth tightens into an angry line.

'Well, clearly I got the whole situation quite wrong, didn't I? Shall we go now?'

In silence they walk back to the car. A part of Beattie is screaming: tell him you'll go with him. Go on, take your chance. You've earned it. But the larger part of her, the sadder, older, wiser part, compels her to silence. When they get to the car Beattie says: 'I've got a little time in hand. I think I'll walk back and take the Tube.'

'Suit yourself,' says Brooke, offhand. 'I'll see you back at the house.'

It is cooler now, and a breeze has sprung up off the lake. Beattie walks on, blind to the bright green leaves of early summer and the distant prospect of Park Lane, so stunned by Brooke's proposal that she can think of nothing else. Yet even more extraordinary than his proposal are the strength and force of her rejection of it. She had not known until now that that period of her life was so conclusively over.

As she walks slowly on, unconsciously she throws back her shoulders and straightens her back. It is as if someone has removed a great burden from

503

her – a load of delusions, fantasies, romantic notions. Never mind who'd put them there to start with, Beattie had faithfully toted them round with her for all her adult life. All this time she has been pigheadedly facing the wrong way. She has been preoccupied with the search for the great love which will transform her life into something heroic, a love that will fill every nook and cranny of her consciousness and make everything meaningful. All *that* had achieved was a destructive preoccupation with a man who even on this afternoon's evidence alone is self-centred to the point of certifiable barminess. And how feeble and passive she had been in waiting for someone else to transform her life instead of seeking to do so by her own efforts. And, perhaps most destructive of all, preoccupied with her own immature fantasies she had completely failed to grasp the reality of the love that surrounded her, love of a real kind. For Charles must love her deeply or else why would he have come back to her to wait around while she worked her discontents out of her system?

Those Musgraves. Those bloody Musgraves, as Charles would quite rightly say. Was there anything, after all, to choose between brother and sister? Both went on their way, indifferent, uncaring; selecting and discarding without a qualm. But even as she frames the thought Beattie knows that this is not true of Virginia – that she has the capacity to feel, to comprehend what she's done. Perhaps that makes her crimes worse. Yet while Beattie can now dismiss Brooke she cannot dismiss Virginia. There will come a time, Beattie suddenly knows, when Virginia will have to pay for what she's done to Alexia. A time when she will have to acknowledge her. A time when only Alexia will be able to give her mother the forgiveness she craves. And Beattie will see Alexia again. There will be a time in the future when she can make up for the horrors of today and the sadnesses of that child's life. She knows it.

Across the park lights are coming on, and Beattie is belatedly aware that she is attracting some very unwelcome attention. Abruptly she turns round and makes her way back to Knightsbridge Tube station. It is six o'clock, and the pavements are crowded with stenographers and clerks hurrying home. It is getting dark, and she hasn't spoken to Charles since this morning. Across the road a sea of faces waits for the lights to change. Then suddenly, on the pavement behind them, Beattie catches sight of Charles, standing irresolute outside the entrance to Knightsbridge Tube station, scanning the hurrying crowds. Frustrated, Beattie stares at her husband, seeing him objectively perhaps for the first time since their marriage. She sees a tall, good-looking man with an anxious unhappy face – he desperately needs to find her. Two girls waiting to cross the road beside him eye him speculatively with obvious approval. But Charles is oblivious to anyone around him who isn't his wife.

Drawing a deep breath, Beattie goes to shout his name, but all that comes out of her mouth is a feeble embarrassed croak. How deeply it goes against the grain of her nature, her natural caution, her deep pessimistic lack of trust in the world to find the courage actually to shout out her needs. But for Charles's sake she must assert herself, knowing he has more than earned the right to feel secure, chosen, wanted – all the things he has showered unstintingly on her while demanding nothing in return.

Drawing another breath, Beattie shouts again. And this time she produces a decisive noise, much to the disapproval of the people standing around her.

But Charles, far away across three lines of traffic, is oblivious. For a third and then a fourth time, desperately Beattie shouts and waves, knowing she can't be heard but knowing she must act, however fruitlessly, to try to reach Charles. But in the end her luck changes. Though her shouting goes for nothing, her frantic waving and gesturing at least attract the attention of two youths beside Charles, who obligingly follow the line of her gaze and point Charles in the direction of the mad woman jumping and waving on the other side of the Knightsbridge Road. She see Charles turn and stare, perplexed, before his face lights up and he waves madly in return. At long last the traffic stops, and Beattie is borne across on a tide of commuters. Charles comes halfway to meet her then steers her safely back to the pavement.

'Oh, thank God,' says Beattie, hanging on to him. 'Thank God. I saw you across the road and I shouted, but you couldn't see or hear me.'

'Where the hell have you been?' Love and anger struggle in Charles's face. 'I rang the house at midday and left a message that I was coming up to drive you home. I've been there since five. That butler fellow said you'd gone off to Hyde Park with Brooke. Did you get my message?'

'No, or else I wouldn't have gone out. I rang your office and they said you'd left, and then I tried home and you weren't there, either. I've been walking around Hyde Park and I just forgot the time.'

'On your own?'

Beattie faces her husband directly. 'With Brooke. But we didn't seem to have anything to say to each other in the end. So he left.'

'He had no right to leave you in Hyde Park at this time. You might have been accosted.'

Beattie starts to laugh and puts her arm through his.

'What did he want? Well, knowing Brooke I don't have to ask what he wanted.'

'His marriage is over. He wanted me to go to Rhodesia with him.'

Charles stops dead in the street, his face pale with anger.

'Oh, that's it, is it? So you're off, are you?'

Beattie squeezes his arm.

'Come on, see the humour of it. *I* can. It's so wide of the mark, it's funny.'

'Did you say no?'

Beattie bursts out laughing. 'Of course I said no. Oh, Charles, I do wish you'd come today.'

'Did Alexia – was she all right?'

'No. It was terrible. I can't tell you how awful it was. Ferdinand – Mr Aumont does care for her, I can see that, but it's not right. I know it's not right. I stayed on hoping I could persuade Virginia, but she's too frightened – I don't know what of.'

'I think it's appalling.'

'So do I,' says Beattie slowly. 'But in the end it'll be all right. It'll come right eventually, I'm sure of it. This has been a frightful day, but it's made me more hopeful in a funny kind of way. It's made me see things properly for the first time. I just wished you'd been here.'

'I should have come.'

Charles turns so abruptly she almost bumps into him.

505

'Are you still in love with him?' he blurts out shamefacedly.

'No,' says Beattie, surprised. 'In fact I don't think I ever really was. Not in love like the way I love you. Loving means knowing someone, doesn't it? I never knew Brooke.'

For answer Charles kisses her there and then in the street.

'You've been very patient,' says Beattie at last.

'I love you, that's why.'

'You never said it before.'

'I didn't feel you wanted to hear it. Let's get your things and go.'

'It's going to be all right now, isn't it?'

'Yes,' says Charles with absolute certainty as he takes her hand. 'Things are going to be all right now.'